The Place In Flowers Where Pollen Rests

The Place In Flowers

Where Pollen Rests

PAUL WEST

Doubleday
New York   London   Toronto   Sydney   Auckland

Published by Doubleday, a division of Bantam Doubleday Dell Publishing Group, Inc., 666 Fifth Avenue, New York, New York 10103

Doubleday and the portrayal of an anchor with a dolphin are trademarks of Doubleday, a division of Bantam Doubleday Dell Publishing Group, Inc.

Portions of this novel have appeared in considerably different form in the following: *Chelsea, Conjunctions, Crosscurrents, Kenyon Review,* the New York *Times, Parnassus, The Pennsylvania Review,* and *Sites.* One of the sections printed in *Conjunctions* was reprinted in *The Pushcart Prizes, 1987.*

Library of Congress Cataloging-in-Publication Data

West, Paul
    The place in flowers where pollen rests / Paul West. —1st ed.
        p.   cm.
    1. Hopi Indians—Fiction.   2. Indians of North America—Arizona—Fiction.
I. Title.
PR6073.E766P55 1988   88-9412
813'.54—dc19   CIP

    ISBN 0-385-24565-3

"What giants?" said Sancho Panza.

CERVANTES, *The Ingenious Gentleman, Don Quixote, De La Mancha,* I.8

Then the infinite one created the finite. First he created Sotuqnangu, saying to him, "I have made you, the first power and instrument, as a person, to carry out my plans for life in endless space. I am your Uncle. You are my Nephew. Go now and lay out these worlds in proper order, so they may thrive in harmony together, as I intend."

Hopi myth

First World

Sotuqnangu

Her eyes in the final spasm had this far-beyond-it-all and happy look: well, if not exactly happy, then at least resigned, as if she was glad it was over and done with for this lifetime anyway, all because of a fluke. Yes, the eyes, blue and calm like those of someone who had just had a wonderful sleep, woke and saw twinkling just beyond the half-open slats of the shutters that soft bomb, the indestructible uncaring sea. Fancy waking up to that every day of your life, like music played without instruments. No creases spoiled her looks, and her blond hair sat naturally in place like a crop growing in some field. Oswald looked for the corn next to the tassels; he always had. Her mouth, open of course, but not beseeching or twisted, looked as if she had just been saying the word *home* at great length and had run out of breath. That she did not inhale again, ever, was somebody's fault and always would be, but let that pass. She looked as if she had seen a familiar ghost and was just on the point of greeting it, her eyes wide with gentle surprise and her mouth ready to switch from *home* to *who*, the latter being a little higher up in her mouth and farther back than the other. She looked every inch in contact with her life, see, much more so than some of the self-righteously vital who were still running around with egg, blood, or dog-do on their faces, in Palookaville. *Wake up*, he said, but it was no use, she was far beyond that kind of talk. Odd, he thought, when you come to think of it: the dead, Trudy included, should look suddenly different, like charred bark or exploded frog spawn, lest you should touch them. But they don't. At this point, death and life look much the same, so it must be mother nature's way of getting you used to things. We could have held a wake and she would still have been the best-looking person present, although a bit stuck in one place. Even while Stu and Clu were telling him it was his hands that did it—"You're the one, you"—he was blowing at her eyes to close them or fluff the lashes. He was puffing into her mouth to get her going again, get her started up after the shock of it all. He blew in her ear, not to get her worked up, but to make her jump and giggle back to life. "Sorry," he said. "I always was heavy-handed. I never did handle anything lightly. I was the same up on the mesa. I blundered a lot." Not a sign did he see, not a move. It was weird to see a human being as still as a felled tree, but there she was, and she still smelled warm and alive, what with the talc and such, one last whiff or two of her underarm spray. For a last time he inhaled it deep, preparing to give her a little hug as if she had just had a sudden disappointment, a bad letter or a lousy phone call. Never mind, he wanted to say, you'll get a better one tomorrow. The phone will ring and you'll be saying, "Can you believe this?" That sort of thing. "That's enough, Trudy. You can come out of it now. You scared us all." Nothing but that first faint reek of baby napkin, coming from below where the muscles had begun to relent a little. She was only being normal. Her body, where she had recently been, was behaving like a body. There was no time for tender formalities, none of the usual polite and grave motions people made in the presence of the departed. None of that lingering, none of that teary-eyed trying to will them back to life so that everybody could pick up where they had left off. He could see how she had begun to sag, all slack and quite rested-looking. Not heavy, he thought, or heavily built, but neat and nifty, with sharp tips in her shape. She worked out, he could tell that, but she wasn't muscle-bound at all. She was naked, of course, but nobody had thought of covering her up. She worked naked and naked she had died. It was as if her breasts and thatch were all of a sudden invisible, which was what happened when he looked at those ghastly pictures from the death camps. There was nothing to get prudish about, although he personally had a stronger need to cover the dead than the living, although not when confronted with them in bulk, which he had so far been lucky enough not to have been. It was so quiet, though he could hear some gurgling from deep inside her. The vital processes were still going on. Eggs and bacon. He knew her habits. It was only midmorning. She was always hungry. It was amazing how regular her teeth were, capped flawless, small and shiny and as clean as limestone cliffs. That was why he had always found her breath so mellow. He knew, having been close to her like that on many occasions. Not a speck of mascara in her eyes. No conjunctivitis. Not a shred of food between her front teeth. Nothing crusted in her nose. Her skin clear like certain stretches of untested sand only a few inches under pastel-blue water. She had been just about perfect, though with a twisted mind. Where had her mind gone now the body untwisted itself like a cat stretching out after a good feed? "You're still lovely," he told her in a drab voice. "Come off it now. Be reasonable. Don't give us a tough time. Lighten up. I didn't mean to. *We* didn't mean to. Let us off and we'll be good in future." Not a word came from her. Not a sign. Okay, he was on a jetty looking out at Santa Catalina through the fog. It could have been the coast of Africa for all he cared. If he looked away, he went away. Now, where had he heard that? The planet was so final, in spite of all the religion and the science fiction. Nobody ever came back. "Give her at least," he told them, "a last kiss." They hung back. He himself kissed her on the forehead, gently but firmly enough to feel the bone in it. Pat her thigh too. Stroke her on the booby. Wipe the blood from the place right underneath her nose. "*You* do it," Stu said. "This is all your doing. You too heavy-handed to be around." He did, then stowed the tissue under the pillow, but Stu fast as light fished it out and took it all the way to the bathroom. It was going to be in the ocean within the hour, ripped up. Then Oswald got his marching orders. There was a flurry of newspapers and plastic bags, ropes and sticky tape, as if Stu and Clu had been ready for this all along, and all he could think to do was dress and go wash his hands over and over. He never saw her again. At the bacon and egg that morning she had not the faintest idea that she would never be eating lunch. Ever again. Never need to visit the bathroom for any purpose whatever. Things had gotten that severe today. And she was not alone. In that same instant, several thousand others from Spokane to Nantucket had died along with her, not even called up by name to do the bravest deed of their lives, enough of them to make her seem less isolated on that bed, a little hulk of seeps and stains she would never need to be self-conscious about. No more pardons begged. Past etiquette and into the waste bin, her last second had been preserved on film, although none of them had meant to do it that way. Now Stu could kill Clu while Clu was killing Stu. It was as if a comic strip had suddenly included the sight of God with an erection, lips poised in the crouch. Oswald could see now that there was no limit to what any of them might do if they got careless enough. He wanted to sit in the sun and read the newspapers for fifty years. He wanted to eat a meal that never ended. He wanted to fall into the Grand Canyon and smash the surface shine of the blue Colorado River. He did not want to be in Los Angeles anymore. An Indian belonged at home on the mesa, not at this game of lust during which he had never, never, shouted with carnal joy. It had been a stint of work: no more, as far from Uncle George The Place In Flowers Where Pollen Rests as spit was from ivory. He had found out an odd thing. If you killed somebody without meaning to, as maybe Uncle George had the day they said he'd drowned his wife, those who knew you didn't kill you on the spot in retribution. They kept you fresh to keep them off the hook. You became a kind of trophy, a souvenir, to keep their eyes on. You could could always be found so long as you were alive. As long as you went on living, you left a shower of clues behind you, big as old-style alleluias. When they wanted him they could come and get him anytime; just one of them, Stu or Clu, could do it, with an ice cream cone in one hand and a kazoo in the mouth. When they came to get him, Stu or Clu or the two of them, they would find all the fight gone out of him, his throat arched in soft welcome to the razor, her image on fire in his vacant eyes.

Face to the lamp in the motel room, he pretended he was asleep in the sun, with its big orange bulge close to his face. He would never be able to do that on the mesa. The main thing was to go to sleep as if he really was going to wake up again in a motel with monthly rates, sharing a kitchen with the Morales sisters and Menelaus the gimp cameraman. Better the bedroom than the bathroom, where the twin overhead neons were too harsh, too searching, turning his face the ghastliest color, all grays and rotten buffs. It was like being x-rayed. He saw all the pores in his skin, all the hollowness of his hair, the lines under his eyes. Light was supposed to cheer you up, to wash warmly over you, making you feel it as something soft and healthful as if you had just had a swift vacation in the islands, not make you feel like a dummy in a police line-up, hit with searchlights or an extra flash just to make you look like a convict. Light's long velvet tongue was not the enemy, he reminded himself; it was supposed to make you feel as if all the insides of all the mouse nests in the world and all the fleece from all the best lambs had become a fluid available to you alone. He flinched at the very sight of himself in the mirror flecked with shrapnel from flossing. Who is this, he said. Who am I? I am death warmed up. Where did I read about those lovers who leaned toward each other until their eyelashes touched and then snagged each other, not that they couldn't pull loose when they wanted to, but it was some kind of trap, a lovely one to be sure, especially if they caught sight of themselves tangled up like that. A sideways glance in any mirror would reveal it. Fifty strokes of the lash. What a punishment. We should have made home movies, he told himself, like that. Close-ups with every lash in glowing Technicolor. They would fidget, I suppose, if they held the pose for too long, with the crust falling off the lash roots into the eyes and all those little animals that inhabit the roots getting into a panic. If the lovers held still, though, they might last for days, hardly daring to blink, almost holding their breaths, tangled tinily together, oh what a coiled-up furry feeling that would be. Even if they did it only on Sundays. There was too much commotion in the rest of the week. Right. He knew they could never go to cafeterias together with their eyelashes linked, the two of them entering sideways together, or one backing in while the other walked in face first. Millions of the envious would shove them apart, he knew that. But these two he had read about, or heard about, they had had their eyelashes linked up like two dogs. How long, he wondered, would it take to get into position. You wouldn't want too much bumping or fluttering, and heaven forbid one of those twitchy eye muscles that makes you wink at someone you don't want to wink at at all, least of all the person who, so close to you already that your lashes are mating or at least beginning foreplay, doesn't need to be winked at or even egged on. You are so close that a baby's breath would pull you apart. He wondered if eyes that close to each other could see the other eye's color, or if the eyeballs, in some little canting maneuver, could actually rub against each other in the most lubricated contact of all, just a little tear of joy to each. Or pain. It all helped when people were as close as that. Had there ever been an eyeball touch? The whites could do it, not so apt to flinch as the colored parts, which had too many nerves. A smudge could easily turn into a scratch. Such delicacy of touch. Thousands, forbidden to cheer, would look on, marveling at the tender precision. Who would ever want to land on a moon when you could roll your eye over the eye of a loved one? Or even one you had never met. Glide and slither with lovely how-de-do's, eye curtsys, and eye bows, eye fawning on each other until the first tactless blink, and then the parting, only to be renewed as the lashes like heavenly barbed wire got to grips again and the two partners moved, one left right, the other right left, gently brushing each other's lashes like a couple of soft combs doing a waltz. It would not even matter, he said, if the lashes were false, provided there was no rough stuff; you'd still feel it, the tenderness, through the glue. He always wanted the orgies over fast, even when he had nothing better to do in the whole of Palookaville, and he could bear them only if he was able to think of something aloof and delicate such as the eyelashes. Up on the mesa, he knew, such pastimes could never happen: it was too windy anyway. There was no chance of swooning through life. Anyone who got soppy or exquisite up there would turn into a pillar of cottonwood for his gifted uncle to carve into dolls. He woke, a choking unborn baby with the lampcord around his neck, waiting in the doctor's waiting room in Keams Canyon while Uncle George went inside. Oswald's hands were cold, his testicles having already fled up into the body cavity in sheer fright. One day, he just knew, Stu and Clu would come and kill him *(Hold your breath then let it flow, son, like sliding down a greased slope)* and then shoot each other like the Chinamen standing opposite one another in that old Dietrich movie. They all fired at the same time. All fell. Stu Constanduros. Clu Epaminondas. Two Greeks. Three with Menelaus the gimp. Why did he have to be surrounded by Greeks? Who had told him about the Greeks? Why, once upon a time, Mitits Judson and Mitits Holmes at school, women with catherine wheels over their ears: hair spun into disks of like tiny plaited horse dollops. He wondered if Trudy Blue too had been Greek, her real name Gertrude what? Gertrude Abanol. Trudy Blue had been her stage name as his had been Roy Rivers. It would be wonderful if only Trudy had gone down the tubes and Gertrude was alive, but both Oswald and Roy, in either order, in either world, knew how true that was, and cried because of it.

They let him check into another motel all right. Old Dlöng (Chopstick) at the desk had been the ambassador to Peru or somewhere wild. He had lived through weirder things himself, he said, and Oswald thought how difficult it must have been to switch from the language of the diplomat to that of a deaf and dumb witness to an auto accident in thick rain. From Mandarin to sign language, back and forth he went until Oswald signed the card and went up one flight to the cheapest room of all with its trenchlike suntrap with high sides for privacy. Oswald, given one year of community college, was far from being the mesa idiot, just the black sheep, squatting on the bed and wondering if there was really any evidence at all except in people's memories. Down he went to Mr. Dlöng, lonely, asking this and that, but Möt Dlöng saw clean through him, mentally wearing the silk hat and the fancy striped pants of his office. "You still got your old Orient serenity," Oswald told him half genially. "We got no old Oriental nothing," said Mr. Dlöng. Out Oswald went to buy some flowers for himself, just to show he didn't care. "I'm out of here," he said to the open air, cackling discordant like a parakeet, as ever rolling a bit of paper into a perfect small ball he then rolled on to a counter top. They told him it was Valentine's Day, and all of a sudden he wanted to join the human race in its joy. Out he went, six roses in hand, his tuneless whistle frying between his teeth, as crude and dry and awful a whistle as he could make: the whistle of somebody rebuilding an old clock, utterly absorbed in horology. All he could do was count the money in his safety deposit box, try to live as long as possible on it, then shoot himself. He heard it now, the whisper like a big wave rolled in from the central Pacific: At first he would live it good, on about a hundred bucks a day, but after three months he would be down to fifty, and soon after that he would be sleeping outdoors with only a hundred left between him and the trigger. To begin with, a Sheraton: pool and golf. Then the Wesleyan Motor Lodge with prayers at breakfast. Then the Tijuana Inn (fifteen dollars), Ike's Ramp (ten), followed by the Salvation Army. There was always the shelter known as Ossa Negra. In fact, if he lowered his expectations, finding just the right cardboard box for a human Indian, he could count on being happily alive for months and months. In the end he squandered fifty on a hooker, couldn't make it, got half back, gave her the roses, squandered the refund on a fancy dinner of squab and braised celery, got the runs, did not bother to check his bank box, and headed back for Mr. Dlöng's lobby. Some doctor, Dlöng told him, had been injecting sperm into the elderly, somewhere up Santa Barbara way. *Maybe you should call him and offer your services?* No, Oswald wanted to go home to his mother, and Uncle George, his father, not go gallivanting with a needle in dark hallways plus a gurney and a stopwatch. He no longer cared if Uncle George had shoved his Bessie in and down or not and held her until she became as quiet as a kachina doll. He liked quiet things, that was all. So did his nephew. Times had been when Uncle George had set his hands on Oswald's throat and would have cut it with that knife of his: wood knife, carving knife, whittling knife. Any knife. And he would have said something like this: "Nephew, never mind that thready, tingly feel of it. It's only the cut sinking home deeper than you'll ever know until you can't even fetch up a cough for it. It is just like a goat nibbling your thumb, son." He must have been a great drowner too, Oswald thought. There was nothing up here, in the world of men, worth swimming back to, anyway. Grainy, gnarled, that's how Uncle was. He knew roses long before roses had thorns. If only his Bessie had been popular, like Natalie Wood, say, he wouldn't have gotten away with it. People would have asked. But she wasn't, she was too busy, too much of a bossy boots. Too brisk. He was kind of mothballing her, Oswald decided, for safekeeping in Mormon Lake. Except they had fished her out for decent burial. An accidental death. It was everywhere these days. Uncle George treated her like wood, he told himself, and worked his will upon her form. Bessie and Trudy were goners, in their palpable, fragrant prime. Uncle George cleared his decks and Oswald sang his swansong without knowing it, one half of his mind telling the other: Make it up with Mother, then. Did we ever fall out? Up on the mesa the air blows free. The only smog is that from corn smut. Maybe Uncle George would carve the living Oswald, just to make a sideshow, trimming his ears and lips before getting to larger orders. Oswald grinned. One sunny morning, he thought, a really clever carver could sit down and, by dusk, have cut himself into a fair likeness of a wolflike doll, only the teeth and eyes remaining untouched, still there in a carefully deployed scarecrow. First the lashes, then the lids. Much likelier that Oswald would gather wood for his uncle, as when he was a little boy. Anything to keep the hands busy, the legs tired. People, he was certain, judged you by what they saw you doing day after day, not by what they had

never seen you do. A man who carved a hundred dolls a year was a
man who carved a hundred dolls a year. "Folks," he would say, "I
have entered the big league of the damned. I went over the line." But
all they would say was "tough tiddy," or whatever that became in
mesa language. He'd take his mother some *Architectural Digests* stolen
from waiting rooms, hoping they would not drive her crazy to get off
the mesa. She'd love the peacock tile from another planet, the pools,
the arbors, the trellises, the roofs, the decks, the patios, the doors, the
roofs, the walls, the sinks, the baths, the stairs, the rugs, the commodes, the stained glass windows, the beams, the French windows,
the walks, the driveways, the phones, the tables, the wastebaskets, the
cats, the bidets, the very paper it was printed on.

He found it hard to sleep, with every sound hearing the step of
somebody coming to get him. To mash his head in with a baseball bat.
Tuning his radio to a part of the AM band where there was nothing
but static, he found a kind of white noise, but it turned to a shriek in
the small hours and woke him up. He found another spot, just as
noisy, but when the sun came up he started hearing the noise of
sunspots. What he needed was one of those sound-of-the-sea machines, but he didn't dare go look for one, and no store would deliver.
Which was the more likely? That they would come for him in the
dead of night and slice his throat, as if in some scene from a snuff
movie, or that the police would pick him up when he was having a
milk shake around the corner? He should have left the business
sooner, he told himself, and let his figure go to pot like some of the
others. As soon as they quit making movies, they became fat as
eunuchs. He stayed home, listening to his blood and the erratic purr
of the refrigerator. Come and get me, Uncle, he thought, on your
magic carpet of eagle feathers. Your nephew went too far. He got
implicated. He dared not make a move. How get home to the mesa
without crossing the space in between? Oswald yearned to be home,
where a man had to work hard to get into trouble. Uncle George was
a carver of dolls and his wife had been a jock, a swimmer. Somehow
they had never overlapped, he and she. Then she drowned, mysteri-
ously, and he adapted very fast, he never pursued it with the police.
Oswald went out and bought a paper with trembling hands and stood
there on the sidewalk waiting for them to spring. No shot. No pair of
thugs strong-arming him into a car with blinds. It wouldn't be like

that anyway, he said. It would be by night with a pillow and chloro-
form, and he would end up floating down a sewer to the sea. There
would be no blood, just a friendly encounter that all of a sudden went
sour. It might happen even during the filming of a movie if he ever
went and worked again. On the night he decided to go home to the
mesa, his radio functioned perfectly as a white-noise machine, and his
brain began to work again. But the phone rang even as he was lying
there, staring at his packed bag. "Remember, Oz," Stu said, "even if
they get us, there will always be somebody around to nail your scrotum to the floor and set you afire. Think about it up there among the
chickens, and keep your mouth shut." All Oswald could hear after
that was the voice of his Uncle George saying, "Lean back from the
mountain, son, lean away from it, or you will slip. Get your weight at
right angles to the face. It's slick and that makes it worse. You mustn't
put your weight forward. You have to lean back." He talked with the
authority of rain falling. Then Oswald knew he was not going to
make the first blue movie to be made on the mesa. Need there might
have been, but whatever was blue had been grafted into the ceremonial dances. Whatever was murderous up there had already bled into
the dry soil and been trodden down. He was never going to return to
what he called Palookaville. Once again, his mother would look at
him with that crumbling gaze and say nothing of what scorched her
mind. She no more believed in the wholesome, ordinary movies he
was supposed to be making, and to have made, than she believed
Uncle George had ever sunk so low as to cause the death of his wife.
Oswald was going to find a local girl, one of those who hung around
Keams Canyon maybe, or who worked as far away as Tucson and
came back for the ceremonies and then went back to sexy dancing
and stiletto heels.

Then the voices came, other people's voices out of his own head, and
he wanted to wear earplugs on the inside of it. That Roy Rivers, they
said, he was always chicken, he never saw a chick snuff it before. *He
been around too long.* Who would believe him anyway? There was no
corpus delicti. His hormones had died, what Stu and Clu called
mones. He was always Clu's, Stu said. Always Stu's, said Clu. Truth
told, he was neither's. Back to bow and arrow land, Buster, they told
him. *We get some real stags in here, you was never no cocksman, not for real.*
He certainly, though, they said, had the hands for a windpipe, once

he lost his temper. All the girls complained, saying they would draw the line at making it with guys in wheelchairs whereas Stu, all he'd ever wanted to do really was make movies of the royal couple, the Duke and Duchess who, said the Duke, could do things with her mouth that other women couldn't dream of with their gashes and he wasn't going to give all that up for some shitlicking crown. Oswald got tired of being told how passé he was, how he talked like he had a full scumbag in his trap, how all he had was this good Indian skin of his. *Kalimera, genius,* they would say to him, *you got your oiled satin ready to go?* Stu, he liked to dress up as Hitler and have this Indian dump on his face. Clu, he liked to dress up as Hitler and dump on this Indian's face. It was never monotonous. Then Clu told Stu they had better get some circums into it. The audience liked the meat unskinned and that kind of let the Indians out. *We better look in Frisco,* one of them said, and Oswald chimed in, told them they had better steer clear of that because the San Francisco Mountains were a holy place. *Get Hiawatha,* they said. *Scumshuck him.* It was he, they yelled, who had made it with cigar tubes, corncobs, dildos, bottles, bananas, cucumbers, airpumps, dogs, mules, baseball bats. *You suck on that, you Ethiopian asshole,* they told him. *Nobody asked you.* Then Oswald stalked out, his clothes around his neck like some big untidy scarf and walked bone naked past the pool, peed into it, then jumped in while they were all getting out in a hurry. Then he was out on the boulevard still naked, and this patrol car grabbed him, did not arrest him, but brought him home and threw him back into the pool with a warning. Those cops, Clu said, they had their holes crammed with those little antiseptic tucks you get for piles. How could they ever tell how Oswald held on to her throat until she was turning blue and long after? The sooner, they both said, in their vehement earthenware way, he went back to his cottonpicking ancestors, or whatever his ancestors did, the better. In the big sky of the palaver he would be the only redskin ever scalped in the ass. What he wanted, demanded, insisted on, as a sinner beginning to mend his ways was a soothing sound, a mama's lullaby like one of those big orchestral washes at the Hollywood Bowl. All over him, it could be Sousa, he wouldn't care so long as it washed the nasty out of him, made him feel part of the chiming universe once again so that they might be saying of him: Having at last recognized the error of his ways . . . Or: having at last realized the poor quality of his days . . . And then it was all downhill easy, except, he knew, there were debts and dues. You were never entirely paid up. You couldn't be. Life cost more than a man ever earned. That was why they called ads "messages" to make you think you were not being dunned. He was going to be one of those low-profile people, a snake made of jellyfish stuff, with the light going right through him. And Roy Rivers would be long gone, south of the border, his laundry burned, his phone bills shredded, his receipts flushed down the toilet. All of him would have been sent packing in a dozen different directions, with only Mister Chopstick Dlöng to blab. It might work. He was going to miss the neat little handles on the laundry boxes when his shirts came back and the more-or-less clean sheets the motel put on his bed once a week, the bed ready-made for him to slink into, the bath and washbasin wiped clean. Up on the mesa he would be roughing it, but at least with his money buried where men and eagles could not help themselves. It would still be there, if he wanted, after his escape by Concorde to Saudi Arabia where, after all, among the harems, he would soon be dealing in oil. If only Uncle George The Place In Flowers Where Pollen Rests could see him then, Oswald Beautiful Badger Going Over The Hill, George The Place In Flowers Where Pollen Rests might be impressed with Oswald Beautiful Badger Going Over The Hill. Or not. No, he would more likely be an apprentice to his uncle's chisel, yelled at and incompetent, the sorcerer's apprentice with no skills. There, he said, that should bring him down from eagle territory. *Come and get me, Uncle, I am yours. One day I'll flower again, like the sun pinking the mesa clouds. Delicate, Regular. Shy.* Such fierce friends he'd had in Palookaville, called Palookaville because he'd heard Marlon Brando make that speech in the car in *On the Waterfront.* He could never forget the day when Clu or Stu, merged into one trivial monster, told him something had just come in by fourteenth-class dogmail and they peeled the corner back, whispering about the heft of it, telling him to lay his hand on that, old buddy. It still had the hairs on it like a carrot and even some kind of white scum around the rim. Oh, they told him, it would kill a buffalo. Imagine having that between your legs. "How do you walk, hey?" They did not always use a knife, sometimes a cheese wire with two wooden toggles. It was the same with a neck as with a schlong. It bit right through the Adam's apple, see. As for Trudy, she would be sleeping with the fishes or hardening up under concrete. Never you mind, honeyshuck, which was what they called him when at their most dangerous. That or honeysuck. He felt safer when being called you Ethiopian asshole or something hostile. When they got winsome they were maneuvering. And when they said only fronts or backs of words: *circum, nost, mone,* words like that, often multiplied into *circums, nosts,* and *mones.* Once upon a time, Clu had had a trained blow-fly attached to his thumb by a little thread; it buzzed and he petted it. Stu, not to be outdone, had attached a bluebottle to a similar thread and anchored it to a gold earring set in his nose. No decent place allowed them in. Then they laughed like madmen because Oswald had taken the mail order shank for the real thing when it was only rubber, something to scare the girls with, Trudy included. *Her,* they said, gobbling like turkeys, "she be like somewhere new, like under the foundation of the Northstate Federal Savings and Loan. All that white rubble on her and then the big clock tower. No, not really there, but somewhere like it." Not a bad place to put some lousy Indian either, they told him. He had better watch his mouth. And he knew they were already moving on, using girls imported from the Caribbean, putting their faces in rubber headsets, then shoving them into white plastic raincoats, bashing in their faces and cutting their throats from in front while the camera whirred. It was their job. *We got miles of snuff-snuff in the can, honey boy. Down Mehico way.* What a beneficial climate that would be, Oswald thought, for both the living and the dead. Sun and oranges. The surf. The wind coming in off the ocean, stinking of all the dead laundry out there, the rotting bodies the crabs and fish are using for a motel, and the dead washing about, to and fro, like rouletteers looking for a wheel.

He phoned the phone company and handed back the shiny set. Now he had no number in his life. Was he going to miss the nightly click of the economy switch as it shut down the juice to the water heater? The two single beds wrapped together in king-size sheets? How could a grown man get attached to an apricot shower curtain, the fluff on new towels, the faint scrape of the washcloth? He always enjoyed throwing out the used soaps, the empty tissue boxes, the tubes from the toilet rolls. Gravity from beneath, light from above, were the powers that had guided him where life was loud and sly. To soothe himself he thought of how Uncle George, before he got himself declared legally blind, used to start guiding people with his hands, on his face that shifty naughty-boy look, shoving them forward or aside, steering them as if he owned them and had a license to drive them. He would talk quietly for a while, to almost anybody that came along to watch him carve, and then he'd wump his hands down hard on something handy and there would be a long wait after the thump. A demon lived in the top of Uncle George's voice, his throat. Nobody argued. They always waited for what he was going to say next. Then came his opening yell: *"Maybe, for once, maybe, some of you people will let somebody get on with—his life's work."* It was terrifying but grand. The can he thumped on would go gong gong and his tools would fly upward from it. He never once yelled before he had banged his fist down, so he never took anybody by surprise, not out in the open anyway. But Oswald, as boy, had seen oysters, beetles, butterflies, wasps, nuts, roots, pebbles and birds' eggs come flying up from where his uncle's fist slammed down, as if he had ruptured a chunk of the universe, with the busted bits flying off to Winslow and Keams Canyon, Phoenix and Tucson, Flag and Mormon Lake. Uncle George had the power to make people do what he wanted, not like the leader of a tribe, say, but more like a kachina, which was to say a human being dressed up like a kachina doll. Everybody knew there was an Uncle George The Place In Flowers Where Pollen Rests under the tribal trappings, behind the weird noises he made, but you had to have your wits about you to remember it. "Why," he'd say when it was all over, "there's one tribe, they call themselves The Human Beings. That's their name. What do you make of that? Isn't that highhanded?" He shuttled back and forth between uncle and apparition. More than human always, and then, toward his blindness, more like a cloud with a voice, a mesa in his own right, no longer bellowing or thumping his fist, but whispering as if he had come a long journey on no food, all the way from the San Francisco Mountains or a hotel so smart they cut your tongue out on arrival in case you said something wrong. Some folk, Oswald told himself, were big-league from the very outset, and the rest were hangers-on: groupies and fans, nephews and godsons. All he could say for himself was that he had, as a nephew, staying power. That was what he'd had in the porno trade. Ass was never sore. Dong never bled. Jaw never ached. But what was he going to do when they, whoever they would be, came for him and said the usual thing: "Come with us or we'll disembowel your mother in front of you"? Would he have his old staying power then? Hadn't he best head right now for Cairo or Leningrad? The upheaval of being killed was maybe not as bad as that of having to leave forever. He had burned out on a succession of smelly mattresses. Instead of taking his battered grip, with just dollars and a passport, and heading

for the Palookaville airport like all the other petty criminals, he was
going to hang on. He had seen too many clean breasts, in his time, to
make a clean breast of anything to anyone. So fill the truck with gas
and aim mesaward, to the east. What was so hard about that? Take 10
to 15, then get off 15 at Barstow and take 40 all the way to Flag. God
had mapped it for him. The world was too pretty to resist. Out he
went, taking his portable hot-water pot to where it would not be
needed, the land of the old enamel kettle, his mind already rehearsing
the first exchanges, Uncle to Nephew, unmediated voices dredging
their hearts. There was only Uncle to tell, only Uncle George The
Place In Flowers Where Pollen Rests to hear Oswald Beautiful Badger Going Over The Hill. The Place was the Badger's even now.

What a blessing it must be, he thought, never to remember, as I think
Uncle George, my uncle-father, does not remember either my making or my being born, or the weird truth about his Bessie's drowning
at the hands of more than water. Two dummies had done it. That's
what Oswald had heard. Up on the mesa, when he was only eight or
nine years old, he had found on a dump an old bicycle, chainless,
seatless, tireless, and covered with rust old enough to have gone shiny
here and there, like spilled glue. It went, though. It would go downhill, with a tearing, grating sound as the crumbled axles ground in
their nests. He humped his rear end up above the crossbar and tightened his teeth against bumps as the two hard-rust wheels unwound
slowly over the rocky ground, and then he was gathering speed toward the canyon, into which he would have gone had the bicycle not
run out of speed. It lacked oil, it had no bearings. It was a Croak, that
was all, but it was all he had and how he loved it, shoving it around as
they all laughed and offered advice on how to use it. The whole thing
was so denatured it would burn, no longer a metal frame but a skeleton. Ruddy colored. Oswald sometimes also called it Engine or Injun.
It was another Indian, a first Indian friend. Mostly, though, it was
Croak to him, in memory of some bird he could not quite recall. After
that, there were Croaking days, most of all, and Croak-cleaning days,
on which (never with help) he tapped the biggest bits of rust away
and tried to sand down what was left, all the way to the metal surface,
which was never there. All he ever found was layer after layer of
fully matured rust that reddened his hands. With all these cleanings,
Croak actually became thinner and spindlier. But Oswald's own, for

always. He was a child playing with a relic already halfway back to natural decomposition. It might have been some ancient man he was riding, his little rear end on the shoulders, his legs astride the groin. He wanted to say *Whoa* and *Giddy-up*, but he knew you did not talk to Indian engines, even those alive and not so much kicking as wheeling. Oil was no use. It just smeared and befouled everything without easing the wheels. His feet he flung out sideways for balance, but also to provide forward shove, which meant he advanced, always on a gentle slope downward, in a series of jerks. Then they bought him a new secondhand bike, but it never had the same primitive appeal as Croak the wreck, and Uncle George, although he never said much, motioned him on from where he sat. When Uncle George did speak, he'd say "Go for it" or "Look to your front, son," and that was enough to propel him at unthinkable speed to whatever he bumped into next. The steering wheel of the second bike had jammed by then. Croak ended up in the canyon, flung down by a group of the envious who knew what was really close to Oswald's heart. He let them ride the new one, while it lasted. When a heart got broken, toys were not much help. It was still there, he guessed, fluttery as leaves, rotted into a blueprint of its former self, like those shadows of dead people cut by searing light into the stone of Hiroshima. Hardly as grand, as awful, he thought. Croak and I covered several miles all told. Had I been given the chance, I'd have given it a decent burial, down in the canyon, up among the wind, where all life ended or began.

Second World

George

So the nephew is coming home from whatever it was he went away to. I am going to lose two hours a day to him while he tells me all about it. The chisel will slip, the hand will bleed. Maybe he could be bribed to go back. He wants to learn the trade. Whoever told him he could be a carver? I am more likely see him with kits bought in stores. How to do it. Instructions nicely printed. Why is he so eager, they say he changed his mind altogether and all of a sudden, like some big thing bit him in a dream and he knew, he just knew, that his life was going to change from that point on, back from the lap of luxury to the stone age where every tenant hangs himself in the landlord's doorway. How was it when I saw him last? Was there weather? It must have been one of those rare days of random rain. It was not hot, it was a lukewarm day. His hands were cool. From holding a cold can of something to drink. He shoved them into his pockets to warm them up, also a good way of keeping them dry. I could see the fists bunched up inside the cloth. Were there bats in the daytime? Mistaking light for dark? Lies, all of it, I was blinder than they. It was their nagging squeaks I heard. His hands were cool, then warm from the pocket

lining, then wet from the rain, then wet-warm from the pockets, then
cool from the can again. It was all his hands. What was he doing with
them? Was he fussing me? They must have been his, his alone, they
got so personal. They zipped me up, as ever. They put things to my
lips, maybe a plateful of the right words. "Chew on these, Uncle, then
spit them out." I would have too. Crawl to my door. I did that. Then
sallied forth like a sheep to the slaughter. Humming. Sucking my
teeth. Asking for a pill to take. Any pill's better than none. "What is
that warmth on you," I said. "Blood," he said. "I have cut myself
carving." "You are carving," I said, aghast. No, he wasn't, but he had
been. Imagine. Him. Carving. Better to gnaw on your thumb tips. I
used to put my head down and weep on to her groin, wetting that
curly coarse hair she had. Mostly for getting things wrong. Then I'd
cheer and laugh. I mean I'd cheer up and laugh out loud. No veil
covered her down there, she was as naked as a sheep, never had un-
derclothing, it chafed her and made her walk funny. Her groin was
strong as a workbench. Never buckled or gave way. Strong smell of
sausages like she was cooking. She smelled cooked. It was not that she
was not fragrant, as they say, she was; she gave off an uncanny body
heat down there as if awaiting a river to flow toward her and cool her
down. I was that river. Muttering, mumbling: Show me where it
chafes. A little spit works wonders. It has a thing in it that stops a
hurt. I sniff my finger from it. But how can you sniff your nose when
you've used your nose? I don't want your nose, she'd say, I want your
thing. You want me to blow my nose, I said, and she knew I didn't
mean that other thing. She ran across entire deserts for fun and
plunged into whatever lick of water happened to be there. Scamper-
splash. That was her. She will be twirling in the wet now, I suppose,
due south of almost any hunk of sandstone. Then the Sunday paper,
so heavy you'd think they would fit wheels to it. We'd open it out,
spread it beneath us, and roll about on other people's faces and words.
Sunday picnic, we said. So as not to mess the floor. No, for the novelty of it. The floor was a mess to begin with. They could always tell
what we had been doing. We were black-fingered with ink. It crackled
under us like thin white pine needles. All the way from where was it?
That place. Keams. No. It came from Flagstaff. It was Flagstaff's flag.
Then over us it went, a tent, a tent of sliding squares or oblongs,
propped up by a knee or a toe. It all shuffled over us and slid away
like some skin an animal had shed. It rustled. It was leaves. It was
sheets. Wet, it would cling to any part of us and keep that shape. Dry,

it kept you warm. Ten sheets worth any blanket. But it mussed you up good, getting its own back, whispering Now who can read me now? You have shuffled me apart. It was its very being coming apart right between your hands, and you could never find the numbers that put the pages back together again in the right order for someone else to read. We didn't read it anyway, we used it like a hotel or one of those little Japanese houses that is having an earthquake under it and, instead of timber and cinderblock crashing down on to your lovemaking, it is only like a paperhanger going crazy. Sheets and slices covering you with a gentle patter rainlike. No bones broken. Least said, soonest mended. I used to imagine whole newspapers, and not just Sunday ones, made of bricks and rock. Then the earth would quake and all under would be mangled. Were we mice under there? It was not a mouselike game. We were pumas. We were wolverines. We were goats. Everybody knew. "Have you read your Sunday newspaper?" They knew what was going on underneath. It was always amazing to have a long piece of you stuck right up to the hilt in somebody else. What a relief to pull it loose and know it was my own again. Imagine all the people there have ever been being connected just like that, a sort of daisy chain across the ages. As long as you had more men than women, it would work, because, at a pinch, men could push into men if they weren't too particular, though not even our own gods would ask that of us. What a procession, all pokers and lips. That's the human figurine for you. Once she set it on fire, the Sunday paper, and we lay there feeling the flame come around us to where we lay and then we had to flap and stamp like two clowns. She liked that smell of smoke, that whiff of danger. You could thrust a hand and an arm right through it, giggling, or you could kick it to bits, lofting it up on one foot then smashing it with the other before it floated down. Those who peeped, and there were some grown-ups among them, must have wondered why we never read it, but I for one knew it was made from wood, and my Bessie found it a way of telling the world she didn't care. If you let the sheets lie flat, and took care to make the layers overlap a bit, so that there were never gaps, after a month of Sundays you had a gentle rug of paper underfoot. We walked on the world. We walked on the air in other people's lungs. We were the way the Anglo dogs are, made to stand and lie on sheets of it, mainly for doing their business on, but also when their paws have mud. We were like two dogs having a spring frolic. Don't fret, I'd say, newspapers are meant to come apart, they aren't fastened together. Look what a wind will do to them. Your newspaper is the least lasting of all Anglo things. They must be ashamed of felling a tree to make them. A coin will buy one. A bucket of water will lose its shape for it in seconds. Yet I have seen them on windy days blowing about all over the place as if born to fly, never tearing, never quite snagging on anything, just going along with the gusts, touching things here and there like a priest's hand up on the high mesa or the San Francisco peaks. Like a sail with no boat under it, it should have been part of our bedspread too, but that was much later. It was too late. She was gone by then. She had dissolved. We should have set fire to ourselves one windy Sunday and let the paper burn us up for fun. It would have made a headline in our hearts. Then sometimes during our Sunday morning romp on the news, at different times we felt we both had to go, and like dogs we went on the newspaper, my own dark coil ending up on her much lighter one, over there in the corner. Two snakes curling out of us for the ceremony. I wrapped them up in a neat package with sharp corners, which I set to one side to be carried away later, and we got on with our loving. An hour or so later, when we laughed and looked over that way, the package had gone, and all we could see was a grinning dog sniffing at the opened newspaper. There must have been a lesson in that, even for us, simple children of nature. I often wondered at it. There was no difference. With the coils of it inside us, outside us, we doted on each other without a thought. Dogs will eat anything and humans will go on loving despite all. Fat hug with a bite in it. Fat murmur with groans. Around and around entwined we went at it as if making a meal of each other, she able to laugh during it more than I ever was, but I more able to think about something else, carving or weather, while doing it. Everything would go black for a moment, and we would hold each other close as if going off the edge of some canyon, though I think her blacks came more often than mine. How we nibbled and licked, squirmed and stretched. It was like being born full-sized, the newspapers our one and only mother, into whom, hand in hand, we climbed back, gasping, glad to please.

Oswald

He is supposed to be dying, so how does he manage to work up so
much energy during it. Yak-yak. Not to be disrespectful. He talks
more, dying, than he ever did alive. Maybe it's the thought of that big
satchel full of silver dollars going to waste, hidden away behind the
chest that kept inching forward over the years the more the satchel
bulged. The hook he made stronger. He wants the money to die and
take him with it, not the other way around. Imagine. It's not the
dolls, it's the dough. He could have paid his medical bills with those,
and then some. I'm still the audience, he can't do without me, but he
no longer seems to need me to talk. I do declare, the thought of death
has woken him up. He is bristling with life. Not even Abbott and
Thomas, those two watchful ferret brothers of mine, dare come too
near him now. They no longer offer. He's telling Sotuqnangu off.
When you're old and far gone, choose any god and let him have it
right between the eyes. They let you off, they know you don't know
any better. The python swallowing the rat head first doesn't worry
much if the rat grumbles or wobbles about; the meal's assured. That's
right, Uncle George: get it off your chest while you can. Death scares
the relatives more than it does the one doing the dying.

George

Picking my way along a wash not far from home mesa, I had in mind a certain length and girth of the water-seeking cottonwood root, but nothing even of the wrongest kind came to hand, for which I blamed Oswald Beautiful Badger Going Over The Hill, who distracted me, as a boy will, by finding hunks of aspen that no carver would want to handle, say just prizing or weighing it in his hands like something someone newborn. Along the Little Colorado we trudged, heading west. At Grand Falls, where once I always used to find windrows of scoured roots heaped up by floods, there was nothing left. Too many carvers had been there already, moving from the east to the west, taking more than they needed, competing with scavengers who arrived in ancient pickup trucks. Gone the woodpiles left to bleach and dry for years. Gone the occasional tree swept downriver in the spate. It was as if, I told myself, trees no longer grew. If they did, they never ended up in the river, but were removed wholesale before they were ready. The whole world must be carving. They would not be burning it, would they? Such a sacrilege was unthinkable, even then. I half decided to settle for a cottonwood limb, heavy and a brute to carve, but I was not that desperate then. Now I was sending Big Oswald on an urgent mission some thirty miles away to where the real thing had become available for a price ranging between a dollar or two for half a foot, a long time ago, and fifty or sixty now. "Be a hundred by the time I get there," he said, but he went anyway. He does. How I loathe this turning of the almost ocher, sun-dried raw material, a gift from Sotuqnangu the giver and provider, into folding money. To pay for wood in coins, in brass or nickel, is one thing; a man might carry a dollar or two in coin, but thirty times as much weighs heavier than stone and loses the carver his dignity. How can I go on, I wondered. Even when you are resolved to carve until your very heart gives out, how do you go on when there is nothing left to cut? Or has the right wood been hidden from me, and me alone, as if to confirm my blindness, to give me the message once and for all? Not even Sotuqnangu is that bleak a god, he who peopled the empty mesas. If only we could carve stupidity; if only it were dry, light, and reasonably soft. Carving nephews could be quite a sport. Carving new nephews out of old with minimum waste of blood. How many times have I sent Oswald Beautiful Badger Going Over The Hill over the hill? Some carvers do not even have a nephew to send or to grumble about. Years ago, wellwishers used to bring me wood, knowing I was ailing, sometimes unloading a root at my door overnight, simply to firm up my belief in magic or providence. I knew the day would come when, because all the wood had already been turned into dolls, I and my like would have to switch to jewelry and rugs, or fetishes cut from coral and turquoise. Unless we turned to carving new dolls from old (as with grown-up nephews), the final cannibalism, rasping all the old paint away, deforming with an angry chisel limbs made final by earlier hands, my own or others'. The prospect numbed me. Most prospects did. They still do. I saw ever-smaller dolls coming out of dolls made scores of years ago, all the way back to the Spanish invasions, and even earlier, even to the spit-and-dirt twins which Spider Woman rolled into being between her palms to get a little population started. And a comfort came. At least *my* dolls were always plumper than those of others, so there would always be a thinner doll within my dolls, and within those thinner ones dolls even thinner, and so on, until all that remained was your true starvation doll. Like the leastfed Jesuses on the postcards that found their way to us, not through the mails, but passed from hand to hand in the village, banned and quaintly upsetting, as if Zuni carvers, the neighbor tribe who always carved thin dolls, had gone headfirst into the love of death, nailing a bony ghost to a length of two by four. So I, George The Place In Flowers Where Pollen Rests, wondered at the lack of gladness in things, happier always to deal in paunches, humps, chubby cheeks, well-fed upper arms, and stout rear ends. My mind strayed back to the cottonwood root, its scarcity and the way my natural style had its start in a plentiful supply. Of all carvers I wasted least, hoping (if that was not too strict a view of what simply felt right) to save in the doll, visible beneath even the most beautiful trimmings, the bulk of the original tree's heart, its basis in growth. A dead root is a dead root, I knew that all right, but there was honor to dead wood, wasn't there, even when it turned, squirming, to coal? Charcoal, anyway. In this sense I was not the complete artist, neither copying things nor letting the grain of the wood decide me. And heathen too, if it is that to remind the doll's recipient just as much of a found root as of the adult kachina who performs the dance. All is Sotuqnangu's anyway, and he is most of all welcome to the nephews. Never mind. I knew I needed to fashion this god again, maybe my fortieth attempt to carve him, with that catlike face mask, his body painted bluish gray with mud from the bottom of a waterhole. Hat shaped like a star. Hair hanging down his back. Bull roarer and lightning frame in his hands. Feathers about his face. In moccasins if masked, otherwise barefoot. I always liked to carve a god, not just a spirit. There was no original, I always told them, to test your work against, whereas, if your doll copies a grown-up dancer, a mere human, and never mind how holy, you have to toe the line, with your thumbs anyway. Had I gone crazy? Gone I had, and come back again, sane as an empty bottle. Then, even as I settled on such a thought, my finicky Oswald Beautiful Badger Going Over The Hill plucked a crust from one of my eyes, no, from one of the eyelids. Seal it up instead, I told him, it is a cement from the gods to keep me quiet. I said nothing else, deciding to do a Sotuqnangu, letting my mind lead me. Those of us close to the edge, the brink, have bite. If so, then it is high time to bite back. What was it they always said before they became too polite? You are inventive beyond the call of duty; you do not vanish into your work. You shine forth from it like a dancing bear who has lost all modesty. To which I could only ever answer So long as you shine at all. The living are forever on the point of vanishing into something else. It takes so little to blow them out. So I am against going into hiding before I have to. Gods hide, but men show off, show up. At last, as always when I began, I laid the cottonwood root on the shawl, knelt on one leg, and held the saw level. My other hand gripped the wood while Oswald Beautiful Badger Going Over The Hill lowered the sawteeth to the mark I'd had him make. Now, with three unhurried backstrokes, I made a groove for the saw to move in, then quickly cut the root in two, making the usual apology as I did so. The lopped end clonked on the stone paving, retrieved by Oswald Beautiful Badger Going Over The Hill. It was just like sawing up a piece of cloud. At this point the carver should sit and study the wood he is going to work, gauging various sizes and imagining the doll roughed out with saw and chisel. Instead, bitten by some demon leaping across the ages, I rolled the wood between my hands, patted it again and again as if to knock something loose, and then seized it with real severity, squeezing shape into or out of it as best I could. I had to plumb it to the core, make it obey and relax. It may sound odd, but these dramatics were usual with me. I knew now that the wood was not going to split, wobble, or sway. Half a dozen cuts, most of them made with the shawled wall underneath, created the space between the legs (less holy on a god than on a human), as well as the bottom of the kilt, the one forward arm, the other low and dangling, and then the neck, followed by the two chunks, either side of the head, that would be the ears. Now, free-handedly, with Oswald Beautiful Badger Going Over The Hill aghast and expecting to see a finger drop away, I trimmed the cuts, using the saw as a rasp. As other blind men read faces by touch, I read the wood, evolving and abandoning contours at a speed that made my nephew dizzy and almost persuaded me that I could actually see again. Then I shaped the head, not so much like an egg as like one of those spinning tops I used to whip when I was a boy. Almost a cylinder with rounded rims. The ears I could have made separately and glued them into slots in the head, but such ears sometimes come off, and it is a matter of pride to carve a doll—a god after all—in one piece, as even my apprentice nephew does, except when he carves behind my back, which these days means in front of my face. The wood smelled of flour and peanut butter, I had no idea why, and it felt shaggier than usual, almost as if the bark were still in place. Somewhat nervously I pressed the crude form to my forehead, either to show it who was boss or to try and read its mind. I then handed it to Oswald Beautiful Badger Going Over The Hill, asking him to check for flaws: vees not deep enough or, worse, too much cut away from the shoulders to form the neck. He knew the ruff would hide the

gap, but he was still a perfectionist, which is to say that, as a perfec-
tionist-in-the-making, he did not yet know which things in a perfect
perfection did not need to be flawless. A complete memory of the god
floated in his mind and gave him pain. Was that it? Had I, like him,
made love with men in Hollywood, slept under the blanket called
electric, or pumped images across the TV screen with a hand-held
tapper that sent no Morse? No, I had not wandered far in all my
years, and had done only the same few things again and again. I had
not *been around*, and I never would be, but my notion of the god was
roomier than his. My god was plump and broke wind from too much
medicine taken to calm and firm up the rhythm of his heart. "No,
Oswald Beautiful Badger Going Over The Hill," I told him, "I am a
handler; I don't just touch things, or touch them up. I like to feel I'm
molding things. Like shaping a dog from ground-up beef." His only
answer was something muttered about perfection. "No slip," he told
me; "nothing to fix, Uncle George The Place In Flowers Where Pollen Rests." I resumed, shaking my head at such nephew-tact, whittling with my penknife, from time to time applying the wood to my
lips to seal something within it, to wet it, to somehow feel sorry for
what I was doing to it. You had to care or the wood might fight you.
Cool, it shivered. Wet, it could probably catch a human cold. A recess
for the spine's ridge appeared. The big rear plume, dangling from the
kilt's top, emerged as a long fat flap of wood, as is the wedding sash
that flanked the kilt on the right-hand side. I whittled belt and feet,
the two bulges on Sotuqnangu's upper chest, then cut away at the
head until on either side I had an ear shaped like a spatula's tip. To
carve the hands I made five grooves, for in between the fingers, with
an old steak knife, its handle wadded with insulation tape to give me a
better grip. No fingernails, no nose. No beak, no snout. No mouth to
cut, not for this god, but now I had to make the belt stand out above
the kilt at least an eighth of an inch, and this I did with a rasp I next
applied to the whole figure, blending arm and torso, leg and foot. By
far the most difficult space to carve was that beneath the kilt, between
the back of the legs and the inside of the low-slung plume. Yet I got
the bottom of the kilt even and smoothed the thighs up into it, thinking, Why, this is like feeling the skin on my elbow, it was on the
surface of the Earth before I was born, there is something unthink-
ably old about it. I felt my way by fingertip pressure, first a grazing
touch, a tap held firm, then a push that rammed the finger cushion
hard against the bone. If a surface felt flat, I always left it rough,

already attuned to the uneven air as it clung to every twist and nick. I
sometimes felt as if I were carving the doll only to shape fresh air
itself. The rasp I used as I once also used a towel, with a sawing
motion to and fro, and with the doll-to-be locked hard between my
thighs. Over the shoulder blades I'd go, inside the arms, over the
dome of the head, then, with Sotuqnangu upended, this one time I am
recalling, over the tops of the feet, the inner flank of his plume, and
the backs of his knees, which I rasp to a sharper angle as if the good
old god of the sky (and who knew what else) were flexing his leg
muscles: exactly what creaky elders cannot do when they imperson-
ate him during ceremonies. As if he had overheard my mind, Oswald
Beautiful Badger Going Over The Hill breathed out in admiration, a
noise he often makes, although not always in admiration, wishing he
too could have such a peaked hat as this god, sign of the towering
thunderheads he lords it over. Oh, to be as moody as he, never needing—that's it: never needing. Never needing to look where to hurl
some lightning bolt, or to check where it has landed. George The
Place In Flowers Where Pollen Rests longs to be that indifferent, to
become a being whose only chore is to throw his weight about for
ever. "You're bleeding, Uncle," my nephew told me. "You rasped
yourself some." I dabbed the scratch with spit, for whatever there is
in spit to make you well. Never mind how slight the scratch, I feel it
more nowadays. I look forward to when the saw, the rasp, get warm
from being worked so hard. I learn the teeth one by one. There even
seems to be more to feel at in sandpaper and sandstone. Feathers are
friendlier somehow, too, yet a loop of wool seems harsher to the
touch, I have no idea why. I asked my nephew, but Oswald Beautiful
Badger Going Over The Hill had no such knowledge at his command; he never had. It was like asking him, "Oswald Beautiful Badger Going Over The Hill, is it true that, in the white man's language,
the past tense is the one for narrative, the present the one for description? I have heard it said, but we are tenseless and timeless." The
causes of things have never appealed to my nephew, who only notes
and reports that, since one miserably bitter winter, I have dropped
things more and work in fits or starts. I am less dependable than I
was. It is, he says, as if my ancestors have nudged me from a long way
off: my caustic father, my easygoing mother, not to mention the
grandfather who carved dolls and signed them with a zigzag mark,
and the other grandfather who incessantly rolled a length of rope
beneath his foot to tighten up the weave. Someone, if not they, had

begun tugging at my nerves, urging me to rest, not to rush things, not to push my luck too far, not with a talkative gifted nephew at my elbow, offering me the coffee I ought to have given up years ago, brewed in that old yellow margarine container. I thanked him for the coffee, if coffee it was, he being capable of having fooled me with some substitute made from acorns and beets. If you held your breath over the steam, declining to inhale the ghost, somebody began to seem very close, not someone dead but someone near death, not quite at death's door, but certainly on death's porch. If you let your breath out all in one go, you could make them disappear forever, not dead but just wafted sideways from life. Even back then, my hands were weary, always colder than the coffee. Trying to do yet another Sotuqnangu (hobnobbing with the gods again), I wanted to leave him raw, unsanded even. Who polished gods anyway? The tremor in my hands was my punishment for aiming too high. Of course. All very well for the carver to pretend he scoured the Little Colorado for cottonwood root, and to enjoy saying, When I can't walk to some place nowadays, what with my eyes and all, I just *go* to it instead. That, I tell Oswald Beautiful Badger Going Over The Hill, was when *go* meant to get there without going anywhere at all. The throb in my arms, the nerve endlessly flickering in what used to be the fleshy part of my better arm, the stab-ache behind my watchband, these were not the fruits of being stiff, but the faint, faraway laughter of Sotuqnangu saying, "You will none of you get to where I am, carvers and blasphemers. Drink your coffee. Now we have taken care of the eyes, what shall we attend to next? Liver? Bladder? Memory? Taste? Smell? We have made a start. The Furies had you, but they let you go this once. Now carve some personage more within your scope, you smelly, farting, hesitant, self-satisfied old man. I am not the free toy in a box of white man's Cheerios. Dolls are the outpatients of a mind unhinged. One day you will stink like a marsh." Superstitious as I, George The Place In Flowers Where Pollen Rests, am, I could hardly believe the god had already entered the unfinished doll. But when you had hewn three or four tons of wood with a little knife the very forests began to fight back. I half decided to move on to bronze or rock. I saw dolls planted in fresh flowerbeds, or heated in a kiln made from tin lids and fueled with dung. Used by midwives in their gruesome probings. Dipped in a mixture of cement, quicklime, and broken glass, then dumped into the canyons in the west. Or split down the middle for kindling. Such was the fate of all my dolls. At least until I heard Nephew telling me I was dawdling. I was. And far away: I had never been so far away, he said. At which point I said no thank you to his bandage and told him I was bled out. The tearing up of my eyes was beside the point since the tears made little enough difference, in a way multiplying my ration of light. The ray bounced through saltwater helped me along. Being looked after, I told him, was one of the most burdensome boons a man can have. Someone was pounding my eyes to mash, in the dream anyway, but it did not hurt, not as much as not having seen for countless hours the roundish, mellow face of Oswald Beautiful Badger Going Over The Hill, who had been to high school, had once let drop the worth-learning-by-heart phrase *andante cantabile*, which I knew was not Navajo but might be the Spanish of Coronado, who called my people Tusayan or, more insultingly, Moqui. No, it meant, Oswald Beautiful Badger Going Over The Hill said, a slow thing you could sing. He himself had sung such, in the class in school. At that I told him a tree was a slow thing you can carve. What a small world it was. The world was full of slow things you can do something to. Not even the plastics move away. There they sit and do not rot. They wait for whatever you are going to do to them. Then Oswald Beautiful Badger Going Over The Hill told me, in his usual hurry, that once you have begun to carve a tree, it is not a growing thing any longer. It is not whole, where the sung song remains untouched by those who use it. Who on earth, I asked, would carve a living tree? The idea had no appeal. If you cut a yawn into a tree, the yawn would widen as the tree grew. Then my nephew told me about the custom of cutting your initials into the living flesh of a cactus, not for ownership, but out of loneliness and the desire to live forever, at least as long as a cactus. Yet no one ever came back to look at his initials. Then, I told him, what they carve into the cactus is a form of goodbye. They have my sympathy. After that blurred morsel of talk, I set to work again, this time with a hunk of sandstone, removing the worst rough edges, although a smooth finish had never meant that much to me. Wood was wood, not ivory. All the same, driven by some scruple not mine until that particular Sotuqnangu, I took the sheet of fine-grade sandpaper from Oswald Beautiful Badger Going Over The Hill, who emptied the last drops of coffee into his mouth with a wet sigh, and began to pass it over the main contours, at first slowly. When I doubled it over upon itself to get a better grip, I speeded up, feeling my hands coat over with a white dust I had always loved to inhale, and never mind the lungs. Warmth grows in the doubled sandpaper, hardly a welcome from the god, or the wood, but an adequate sign to me of my own busy presence, lifted by coffee. But soon the paper had frayed into holes and tatters, nothing but an untidy rag. So I polished with both sides of it, having energy to burn. Oswald Beautiful Badger Going Over The Hill was already mixing what was to come next, kaolin from a thin cup, but I still had to fashion from a flat strip of wood the zigzag lightning bolt for Sotuqnangu's right hand, and then the round rattle-gourd for his left. Both would plug into holes bored into the clenched hands, but I was not going to glue them in place until the main doll had its final coat of paint. Both the lightning bolt and the rattle-gourd I would paint beforehand, although many carvers both then and now glue the extra parts in place before painting. Or they attach them with tiny dowels not much bigger than toothpicks. No, there is and was only one way. Have a free hand with the glue, especially if it happens to be the white kind that dries invisible, leaving only a shine, a touch of ice. Now, that shine, or sheen, calls up the aether through which the true kachinas move when they come down from the San Francisco mountains. Then I slept four or five hours, afterward feeling light and frail as a husk, and wryly remembering having dreamed. I sat outside on the low wall (had I ever left it?) with a piece of cornbread in my hand, spread with lumps of margarine, which I knew the sun would not melt. In my dream I was not blind, and a young man who was myself when sixteen or seventeen was looking at me hard with tears in his eyes. As if to say, you have let it come to *this?* Where had the margarine come from? Only in winter did it keep. Only in summer would it spread. No one bought it. If it came into the village, it came as a gift, as did powdered milk, powdered potato. Powdered human? Powdered anything, to be mixed with rain or urine. The sun was going to spread it for me, I told Nephew, who was accustomed to Uncle's vagaries before getting started on a doll: whole days of dither, and mental rambling, while I collected myself and rediscovered what my hands could do. "White folk like their food slimy," I told Oswald Beautiful Badger Going Over The Hill. "Perhaps they have too little spit. So they spread grease all over their bread. They oil themselves like machines. Imagine the dry mouths everywhere." My nephew is twenty-some years old, but I think of him as a boy, able to respond to boys' jokes. "Imagine," I told him, "what would have become of us if Spider Woman had had a dry mouth when Sotuqnangu commanded her to put life on the barren earth. *We see no joyful motion,* said the god. *We hear no joyful sound.* What did the Spider Woman answer?" To let it all sink in, I paused, chewing dry corn bread with my few remaining teeth (lamb and hominy stew are quite beyond me unless almost a slop). "Is it even known?" he asked. There was no question, I told him. "Oh," he said all of a sudden, "she picked up a handful of dirt and mixed it with her saliva, of which as Spider Woman she had more than her fair share." "Out of the paste," he said, but I interrupted him, eager to get to the fashioning of two beings, the twins, whom she then covered with a white cape which was creative wisdom itself, the mantle from the mind. Like snow. "Just think," I told Oswald Beautiful Badger Going Over The Hill, "about an object disappearing when over flowers. As if the flowers have sucked it in and down." "Or suet," he said, his mind on things white and filmy, I suppose, as far away as the white man's angels to those little thistle hairs that fall from a nostril, embedded in a little blob of strawberry that isn't strawberry at all. If George The Place In Flowers Where Pollen Rests, whose name only in English is long, whose name in our own language is short but resounding, cannot teach Oswald Beautiful Badger Going Over The Hill better than that, then they should both choke themselves on any doll within reach. I talk to him only to fend off his talking overmuch to me. I have no desire to teach him my so-called trade. I would rather it died with me. I have created a monotony all of my own, which was certainly unknown on the mesas before I began to carve. I begin all my utterances with an image of myself. The world has fallen away from me and become a trimming only. The kachinas come down from the mountains only because we will not go up to them, who, the higher they go, become taller and bigger. Homely smells I smell of: hens and turpentine. As if I painted eggs with tar the whole year long. But what do *I* know of years? My sense of its ever having been this year or that, a Nineteen-Something-Something, is poor, and, although I can tell early from late on the scale of months or days, I do not know how to part one clump of years from another. My life has been a nonstop carving out of wood. Out of doors as well. I like the joke. I have not really carved my dolls out of doors manhandled off their hinges. I have been, I still am, an outdoor carver, free as a buzzard while the air billowed all around me. I have gone through, truly gone into, several tons of cottonwood root, gallons upon gallons of paint and glue, thousands of fallen feathers, dozens of knives and a score of saws, so as to model for my tribe upward of three thousand

gaudy dolls which, quaint or moody, fierce or lofty, have taught the
children of several generations the names and forms of the beings the
dancers mimic in their dance. Given over to holy carving, I have
weathered the arrivals of collectors, tourists, professors, soldiers, po-
licemen, tax collectors, missionaries, and smart interviewers, and
have hardly ever nicked my thumb. "My name is George The Place
In Flowers Where Pollen Rests." I say it aloud. It takes a long breath
from an old man. Not the most ordinary of names, but, compared to
some, it's curt. To whom am I saying this? *I* am the strangest stranger
to be found? There is no need to tell, but to be heard, or overheard, oh
yes. I talk, and they nudge my elbow to show they have heard me. I
talk in my head, and their warm breath lands on my face, saying they
have tuned in to my mind. Now I feel it: those watching me begin to
move in closer (it is natural), hoping for another glimpse of what
they've seen hundreds of times already. Here I am, in the faded flesh,
yet not really here at all. I am the ghost of my own smell, the martyr
of my own silliness. Had I been wiser, I'd be wiser now. Aloof from
ticking time, I live in a skewed rainbow, vaguely aware that, in the
days when my eyes were good, the east was pink, the west crimson or
violet, whereas the compass rose of my people shows the east as *white*,
the west *blue-green*. Always say the color words heavily. Their north is
yellow, their south is *red*. But did north and south ever look that way?
Not to these eyes. I have often worried about the gaps in this won-
drous color wheel, saying: Should southeast be *pink*, then? Where
does gray belong if black, as it always was, is down? What about *blue*
in its own right? When it is unspliced with *green?* If those coming
from a certain point of the compass bear upon them that point's
color, are they not wrongly lit as they heave into view? Always this
has bothered me: seeing the world as it is, then finding the folklore
says something else. Nowadays I like to think according to the half-
day of the sun, whether or not I steer myself any longer by its blaze.
It is one way of staying in touch with something new. Yet how glad I
am that the color wheel of all of us spins the full twenty-four hours,
whereas those who go by the sun doom themselves to half a day each
day of blank. Blank is the native hue of downward unless you can
persuade me otherwise, listeners, eavesdroppers, readers of the mind.
In two minds about the whole thing, I wonder why the core of the
Earth must be black to a tribe skilled at seeing one color where another is. Why are we so literal? Why are we so willing to imagine? I of
all men quibble about colors, having lost them now: either, on bad

days, in a pale and snotlike mist, or, on better days, in a solider mist
with clots of unripe fruit looming up where sheep or people stand.
From the sheeplike silence in front of me just now, I conclude that I
am surrounded by people. Their silence is a kind of raving fit. Eyes
going, going, I chant, to make myself uneasy, and then I shut tight to
wring from them a frantic display of brilliants, a visual pins and
needles, a big cornstalk of inward sparks. Yet I see all this no longer
against what I used to get: a pinkish film of squeezed-up blood in the
outmost bulge of the eyeball shoved against the smooth glove of the
lid. Sparks in the void is what I see. Like, if my comparisons hold
good nowadays, someone reading who tears each page out of the book
as he finishes it, until only the covers remain. George The Place In
Flowers Where Pollen Rests reads nothing anymore. Not now. Do
you see them kneeling, leaning, toward me? Not altogether lacking
the aromas of sheep, they wait to be led, and all I do is murmur or
gesture at something beyond them all, with what must seem an ill-
bred carelessness. Now legally blind, which sounds like something
awful made an object of desire, I should surely be a natural to flout
the evidence of my senses and see what I want to see, what no one
else has ever seen, not even my farsighted tribe, who change their
verbs to reflect the done-to rather than the doer. With all my dolls
scattered among three mesas, as proof that I once indeed did see, I
should be free to feed the mind's eye on things unseen. Instead, I try
to arrange all those dolls in my head, from my first attempts (with
many a slip of the knife and too much cut away from under the chin
and armpit), through my long maturity (when I developed *this* portly
imposingness of build), to the almost abstract figures of recent years,
cut from darkness, with the paint barely covering the kaolin primer
(or so they say), and the features more and more slapdash—dolls cut
blindly yet with thick and savage style. They all go back into the
wood, away from me. The paint flakes off and away and again becomes a chemical waiting for use. Some of those huddling around me
begin to inch away, snubbed by my haughtiness. Seeing themselves
unseen, they take the huff. And seeing themselves, as they think, unheard as well, they go to make a noise elsewhere. My life was always
full of the sounds of people sneaking away to watch something else.
They somehow lost faith even in themselves as hangers-on. Who *was*
this George anyway? Who is he now? I no longer choose to find out.
A striped shawl, as always, hides the doorway as my big hands cut the
cottonwood root into semihuman shape. I mean that is true of always,

and not only of just now. All I know, rapt in the seasoned act, is that my nimble fists have bronzed amid a presence so thick it kept the sunrise white and the sunset blue-green. Strong magic. Even now, I ride a private whirligig, jostled by spirits who inhabit the steam from cooking, the prickly pear cactus and its jelly in the tourist jars, even the storm of sleet that freezes the peach blossom. Crammed with ghosts, my world makes sense. The ghosts have names and faces. For half the year, they come down from the San Francisco mountains, and then men in masks dance the roles of ghosts whose likenesses I make in wooden dolls. Thus our children learn who is who among those who have come to scare and chase them, although too many kids (boys being boys, girls being girls) go swap their dolls for candy, soda pop, or gum at the trading posts, dumping even the kindliest of kachina dolls on the altar of tooth decay. Let them, I say. I had my fun. I have made my fuss. Those who by now have not trudged away, wondering why I cease to carve for as long as an hour at a time, have begun to mouth the words they think I am going to utter when I utter again. But this time, I am pausing longer than anyone should before uttering one single word, as if going through all the sweet agony of inventing it from scratch. *"Helmet,"* I say at last. One of my favorite words. "Helmet," I whisper, beginning to recite the blueprint for something I have made over and over again, and quite forgetting the god I am supposed to be carving. It's one way of ducking out from a god. It's one way of not having to live up to obligations a bit beyond you. It's like a weekday of the mind, nothing to get dressed up for. Sotuqnangu, do not strike me dead: I am coming back to you. Please, for the time being, allow this mention of another doll. Helmet mask painted black, yes, with white marks for bird tracks. A good start. Feathers from just about any bird. Ruff of Douglas fir. White coat, white pants. Or buckskin would do. The moccasins red. One rattle only. Now, what else? I calm down, but old age and waned sight calm me more than anything magical I whisper. He who sat out in the sun, and always went indoors when it got cloudy, now sits out in the light, getting as much light as he can. And it is all a bilish green wherever he aims his face, or holds up his hands big as mallets but more or less unscarred. The left hand is the feebler, the dreamer, but to me neither hand is just a hand. It is made of wood and shavings, kaolin and paint and corn smut, part of all it has ever handled—those things and fry bread, breasts, the chin of my dead father where the pocks of pox were worst—but also part of what has always been out of reach: cloud, sun, the wheel that steers an airplane. Not that these hands ever fall quite still. Empty, they mold or carve at rest on my thighs, alert to the contours of whatever I am going to carve next. Cumulus Cloud-Maiden. For purity. Guts in the Snow. What a story is there! You can hear me sighing at it. A whole village was starving. There were no sheep. This certain kachina hunted down a cow and slaughtered it right there on the snow. Soon only the guts remained. Like sudden flowers. Blood clots quivering in the winter wind. And after that? Cold-Bringing Woman, who combs your hair upward and whips you with twigs. They all come unbidden. My head is their playground. My head teems with people made from trees. It has been said my dolls are not anonymous enough. Merchants have checked them against the patterns in the reference books and have complained, wanting to give the pearl back to the oyster. Bless them for noticing, say I. It is like having a thousand nephews. They can have their money back. I had my fun, I made my fuss. Nothing is ever wasted. I am only a man. I am not The One Who Sucks Belly, otherwise called the Dog Star. I am not The Cliff That Runs In Two Directions. Or The Short Rainbow. I am not, although I sometimes wish I were, The Perfect Rounded Feather, or even The West Water That Keeps Rolling, far beyond the San Francisco Mountains. I am George The Place In Flowers Where Pollen Rests. George to none. Those still observing me say not a word in answer to what of this I said aloud. Maybe only the one word: *helmet*. They are as legally silent as I am legally blind. They are thinking my thoughts for me, to save me some time, to free my hands from their trance. When I am not carving, I am sometimes an old bugger of a bore. They all say it. I try to live up to it. I cannot help it. Were I a gifted talker, I would have gone to Hollywood, before the talking pictures came in. I tell the truth as if no one had ever bothered to tell it to me. Crouched thus, or seated, over my low rock wall draped with the brown and white rug, I have become a fixture, in red bandanna, shirt and jeans almost the same pale blue although of different material, buckskin boots, watch with expanding bracelet on my left wrist, a Zuni chain on the other. Hammer. Saw. Woodrasp. Penknife. Sandstone. Paint. Some tin cups. Almost the perfect image of the workman, I have made two dolls a week for life, almost like somebody sentenced to life for murder. Chubby, muscular, big-handed, small-footed, they resemble no one else's dolls. When I saw the work of others, I just shrugged and noted the presence of something official and routine, a doll carved by too many heads, or too few. My own dolls are sometimes off-balance until glued to a plinth of whatever wood comes to hand, boxwood or balsa. I am not, I always used to shout, a factory but an imaginer. I am one who invents. Every version of the same doll has a different face, at least for me: a simper, a fierce grin, a look of paralyzed astonishment. My effects came as much from looking away as from looking at the work in hand. I always came back to those lovely silent memorized directions in my mind, as if to hymns. Helmet mask without ears. Fox skin ruff. Or: sack mask black with spots red and yellow, blue and white. Gourd on top. You have to have that. No diagonal lines on cheeks. That would never do. Frogs, maybe, painted on the back of the mask. A grass ruff. It has never been laid down what each doll's expression must be. Such is the nine-inch playground in which I have combined ears, feet, teeth, horns, kilts, rattles, whips, bells, breech clouts, leggings, bows, garters, red tongues, snout mouths, tube mouths, pop eyes, and feathers, feathers, feathers, always feathers, some of them from what came to be known as the endangered species. I have endangered them myself at times, wandering loose with a net and a slingshot, as no one else among my people ever did. But what thrills me most of all are the kachina dolls forgotten, no longer prized, or those unworthy, stunted, or stolen from other tribes. I once upon a time heard about a man, a white, who made himself a book. He made a book up. He made his book by listing everyone he had ever met in seventy years. "Generous with his bicycle," he wrote about one. "Operator 55, Las Cruces," was another. Another was the one of whom he wrote, "Died in barn fire." These were lives. Well, George The Place In Flowers Where Pollen Rests will not be making any such book of meetings. Time has a way of wasting memory, and that is like time's reading and forgetting of the book within your mind. If any of my hearers are still there, I would tell them this, but I would never reveal how my ruined slum of a mind mounts a procession I cannot live without, fixing me on several dozen favorite dolls, one of whom is the blind kachina who carries the paralyzed kachina on his back. One of your less-known Rural Free Deliveries, it is perhaps how uncles carry nephews, the first thing being to get the nephew paralyzed in the first place, seeing that Uncle is already blind. We are halfway there already. I make that old familiar irritable motion downward with my right hand, clutching as if to retrieve a fallen hammer. Did they see? Surely, by now, those remaining around me have developed a marble quality as they patiently watch me doing nothing, to do which is a foretaste of every death. They take the hint, ignore their lives, and seem to have begun imagining me as I was when a little boy, then a rambunctious youth, and later a man beginning to quieten, having fathered children plentiful as a flock of birds, all of them pigeon-toed like me, their armpits full like mine of dangling pale moles. Where are they now? Which death did they have?

Oswald

For once I manage to get a word in. *"Butt in,"* he always says, but I am too awestruck for that, I keep my peace. I bite my lip. I am not as bold as he thinks I am. He does not so much hear me out as imagine what I might have said if he'd given me the chance. To him I am a ghost, a reflection, a mirage from Palookaville, which for him has now come to mean the whole of Southern California. He doesn't so much think as pour out like a volcano, as either himself or as him imagined by me, a rabid ghost on the horizon. All ghosts, really, in this ghastly business of his being half dead, almost dead, then hearty and hale (to vary that silly double). All I can tell him is what he thinks I'm going to say, so there's no point in telling him anything. Of course he's not just a carver, some kind of village idiot artisan, he's an artist through and through, which is why I tend to fix on him, always did, I wanting to be an artist too, although I went in a different direction. All my life I have gone to him, asked his opinion; he has mothered and fathered me, which more or less leaves uncle-ing out in the cold. Two misfits, that's us. He's the burly social presence, the mesa notable, whereas I am the black sheep who turned his back. *He* did not so much turn his back as turn his mind. He just blundered right through life like an elephant blundering through painted scenery.

George

It soothes me deep down, to hear about things, now as much as yesterday, to think of someone who knew war and its airplanes and who, stopping by, told me stealthily, They do not, George The Place In Flowers Where Pollen Rests, fly their airplanes by hand. Not all the time. They have what is known as an autopilot, a machine does it for them while they rest. And their name for this is *George*. I, too, am an autopilot, I told myself on that occasion, and I have reminded myself of it ever since. I am the machine that flies my tribe while their consciences rest. Their imaginations too. I am the kachina-machina. Had I not carved dolls, I might have been a hero instead. Am I dreaming or is my audience, none of them young, thrilled at the look on my face? My nephew coaxes me into it, with coos and whispers, nudges and grunts, like someone—how do they say it?—restoring an old master by the light of a hurricane lamp. "But," I asked the wartime visitor, "tell me about it all over again, this autopilot, who guides without hands and steers without feet and thinks without a head." Anything that automatic has to be just about divine. Could it be this autopilot's nature to be blind as well? Even if his hands do not smell of turpentine and hens? Nephew, who was a mere toddler at that time, tiptoes away, motioning to them to stay put. I know his moves, he who has learned both to carve and to listen. I call him back. "Oswald Beautiful Badger Going Over The Hill?" But he steals away from the sound of his name. You cannot call him up by it, you cannot trap him in it. He walks away to where, perhaps, he has no name at all. Our names are excuses for keeping still and never asking who your neighbor is. They mention a whole thing going on, a process, a regular even in nature. Yet already a new botany has sprung up among us, with seeds from earlier worlds. New stars are seeding the heavens. New names are needed. All we have to do is create the dolls so that these new kachinas can come among us without shyness. So why go on carving likenesses of old gods? Practice, practice. In my day, with rather solemn modesty, I have told the tribe how, before new beings reveal themselves, they selectively test certain humans with this or that affliction, or indeed with almost intolerable joy, on one level racking the body's joints, bloating the marrow in the bone, stuffing the head with spiky mucus, yet on another level—this to pain as the shining front of a dime store mirror is to the dark nitrate on its back making the heart ripple with pleasure, the nerves glow with the white heat of visitation, the mind folds in upon itself like oiled silk. "You end up numb," I tell them, "just like after tramping miles through snow or rain to the trading post so as to use the one and only telephone, shoving that least handsome of the white man's coins into the slot, and hearing an operator's voice from Holbrook, a hundred miles away, as you stand there, outside, in the weather, facing the kachina of the Bell System." Some of them giggle at this, but most of them frown. I can hear the air tightening around them as they do it. It is like being hemmed in by walnuts. Why has my nephew gone? Does he know his uncle's reveries by heart? Does he urgently need alcohol? One thing about George The Place In Flowers Where Pollen Rests: you can depend on him to vary things enough to keep you coming back. That is what they used to say. Well, maybe I am not varying it enough. How does a carver become a soothsayer without a few centuries' preparation? Some days, my heart flickers within me like a snake's tongue. Others, it bounces in its cage like a skinned rabbit tossed live on embers. Today, however, the image has gotten away from me, but I give thanks for having grown up as I have, taught how to cope with the white man's gadgets without actually having any, without sending a wire ever, or answering a phone, or having a socket

into which to screw a light bulb. I offer them my pinched, gnarled
smile in the lamplight of frosty January (I *know* when lamps go on),
perched on the rug atop the low wall, both of my hands on the lamp
to warm them. I know the lamp is warm before I let my hands feel for
it. "You have to put up with almost anything if you want to be old.
Anyone who complains about having to trek to Keams Canyon, just
to buy a hamburger, has no sense of pilgrimage." As I tell them this,
they answer, "We know, we know." I wonder how to carve such a
thing as a vertical cup that has no top. It goes up and up, so high that
no one can get high enough above it to pour anything into it. I almost
fall asleep, rigid in the cold, arguing with myself that, nonetheless,
this cold is the cold of the light, and it is therefore bound to have
some warmth in it, whereas the cold of night, that is the cold of
subtraction, just like nine minus nine is zero. Once in a while, tales of
a world elsewhere fill my head and will not go away, like premoni-
tions of nostalgia, none of them quite so disturbing as that of a college
town in the mellow weather south of Phoenix, where as you stroll of
an evening to the drive-in liquor store, along streets lit by yellow
globes, dozens of college girls, freshly bathed and perfuming the air
around them, clatter by in carefully carved heels and dresses made of
fog, eager to be plucked. It is the cleanliness of this vision I like most,
or so I pretend. Nothing lustful, though I have in my time carved
kachinas with cunts full of teeth and painted buttocks red. Then they
say, "If you're so pure about it, George The Place In Flowers Where
Pollen Rests, why don't you talk about the boys? Is this a town of
girls only?" God I have carved a thousand penises in my day, I think,
and glued feathers to them like the drugstore ticklers the white men
buy. But they have plumbed me for the dastardly old lecher that I
would like to be, licking the dew from one slit after another. Only a
dirty story will keep my listeners awake. Look, I work with wood,
not words. I think, but I do not talk. No, they have come to look at a
silent mouth, except that Nephew is back, silent as a log, but with the
smell of Bourbon ahead of him, and telling them about Hollywood,
where he has been an extra in Westerns. When an uncle runs dry, a
nephew has to talk. When a nephew has to talk, an uncle should doze.
Nephew knows too much. Ever since a tourist with a strange, bottled-
sounding accent came by and spoke of blind men in other lands, my
nephew has troubled me with untestable allusions, with each recital
adorning them with touches filched from Hollywood. Nephew is a
kind man, whom I think of as a youth, whereas of course he is already

twenty-odd years old. He, not I, studied at school in Tempe, studying the sexual habits of frogs and the bowels of comets, or the bowels of frogs and the sexual habits of comets. I am confused. Someone should right this muddle. There is always somebody everywhere, doing something, whereas in the realm of myth, as natural to me as mortar to a bricklayer, there are lots of empty spaces for new myths to flower in, or where things just withered. Whoever this visitor was, he was a windbag, full of wind and facts. It seems, then, we have had two visitors: one who spoke of the autopilot, and one who told about the blind. Were they one and the same? "Is the autopilot the only way a blind man has of piloting a plane? Do these autopilots turn you blind from lack of looking where you are going?" "Yes, George The Place In Flowers Where Pollen Rests, tell us that part. Tell us," they say. They want the blind old sot with ulcers who made a poem about the great western ocean that keeps rolling, in the depths of which roams Sotuqnangu himself, sucking the belly of the Dog Star and whispering, "Homer, Homer, Homer," the name of that old poet as well as the new word for lost ball. Now they want the name of that ancient wanderer about whom Homer wrote his poem. "Him who sailed," they tell me, touching my elbows as if to unlock them. "Oh," I josh them, "him who sailed and sailed. He was obliged to do his military service and ended up with the young pacifists who had to build a road up Mount Lemon. We do not need *him*, any more than that other, Jim, who made this other man's poem into a chant which melted all the words together. Some of those words would take a year to say aloud. That was his way, this Jim. And who needs that other chant either, made by the blind woman hater who sat at a pipe organ all day, fouling his pants from visions of an ogre kachina called Satan who flew and crashed into one of Sotuqnangu's mesas. His autopilot could not save him." Some of them, no doubt egged on by my nephew, start to laugh and ask me to say the other heroes' names. Starting with the one who sailed nonstop. They do not know it, but I am beginning to wander like Oh-dis-ee-ous himself. I am getting blurred. The only one who ever appealed to me, at least in this bunch, was the tiny chicken farmer George Borhez, deep in the jungles of all the Americas below us, who made up riddles about knives and executions. George The Maze In Jungles Where Anacondas Rest. Borhez rhymes with Cortez. He walks with a white cane among the anacondas and the man-eating pupfish of his native land, calming himself amid his green mist with parables about exploding gardens, bamboo canes wedged in sacred mud, and the constant need for upset. Where he lives, they write on the wings of butterflies—just *I love you* or *Your breath stinks.* The freshwater dolphins there actually father human children, and the birth records list the fish under *padre.* It is too easy there to be a dreamer. This George Borhez had a phoenix too, but not our own one, and an abiding lust for having his dreams dreamed for him by another who was nothing like a god, oh no, or for having his actual life become another's dream. *Mañana,* they call it, this laziness about doing your own dream homework. Sullen and mad, he of all the sightless ones mentioned by this visitor (who was not the visitor from the autopilot) might have carved for Sotuqnangu. If the legends are true, the forests down there are thick with balsawood, which we spurn except for soft plinths that will not scratch the sideboards of the rich, who insist that their kachinas stand. A blind man could carve balsa with his fingernail, or with a pointed wart. Easy, then, to make what this blind George of the Mazes says the master carver has to make. Four things. The doll within the doll. The doll who is another doll's double. Well, almost. The doll who journeys through time like an empty Greyhound bus, even as far as the three stars in a line in the white man's Orion. And the interference of one doll's life with another doll's dream. Is there nothing better to do in those forests? Turds there turn into wood. Piss turns into lovely Zuni silverwork. Eighty generals lick his boots these days and pluck the tear crust from his eyes, whereas when he was younger the same generals *as sergeants* tortured him with molten tin until he began to carve legally and become much less of an autopilot. Well, they did not obliterate him. The most we have seen up here on the mesas is a colonel, as unskilled with eyes as a rabbit at turtle catching. Blind sages: the world overflows with them. They speak to everyone but me, sucking their caramel, inhaling ocean salt, paddling their syrupy seed between their fingers until it sets up a whorehouse between their hands. *Let* them lead one another. Let them lead Oswald Beautiful Badger Going Over The Hill over the hill, who only the other day put on a blindfold in order to carve as I do. And drew blood in the first moment of active carpentry. The Jesus they nailed to a star sign was better than that, though they blindfolded his loins instead. Trying to carve a ruff with a butcher knife, your average nephew will behead himself without even trying. This seems to satisfy the listeners who remain. They huddle, confer, compare, as if I were no longer present. What you cannot see you cannot hear. I could have done better, but today I did it with gusto and the right amount of refusal. One day I will say it with more color, and perhaps more frequent pauses. I do tend to gallop away once into my stride. And next time, I must omit all references to Nephew, it is undignified. "George The Place In Flowers Where Pollen Rests," they say to me now, "you gab." Little do they know that words are fleece, and listeners merely weather. I want to dream of wood and flying blades. If I look back. Well, dare I? Only in a hurry. Diabetes, bursitis, sciatica, spurs on the spine, and a minor stroke briefly numbing my mouth and my left hand have slowed me down, but I was never that fast, Nephew. Now, when I wake, and it is always very gradual, I feel I have come from a state far more dead than that of sleep. Less human, less friendly, and less restoring. The names of the things wrong with me sound like those of long-lost deities, for whom someone if not I should make masks and costumes. Then carve the Diabetes Doll from a block of sugar, the Bursitis Doll from human bone. I more or less understand how close I am to some edge, but also how little any so-called edge matters, any more than the Battle of Gettysburg, wherever that was. I have never sat on a toilet in my life, looked through a porthole at the land receding or nearing, or checked a bag. Yet every day on the plaza where everyone meets, I bow my head to touch the place where my parents were cremated after the smallpox outbreak, and then I know I am somehow ascending, perhaps because any hard push against the ground will lift you up, with scablike moles on my brow and dirty fingernails tapping them. The harder I push down, the faster I rise. Each day piles up on top of all the others like the latest in a tower of empty chairs, ascending to the blue star Saqua Sohuh whose name evokes blue kilts, blue flutes, and the extinct Ladder Dance, in which the ladder is as long as you have courage to climb high. I glimpse a blue amid which nothing lives or dies, and I know how blueness, forever inventing itself out of nothing, shoves against no other color. George The Place In Flowers Where Pollen Rests is going to carve again, joining materials never before combined. I am ready. The blue star awaits its autopilot. And no recital of grocery prices, the uses of aspirin, or economy bus fares to Phoenix is going to hold me back. "Was this star ever born," they are asking me. "And therefore of a certain age, like a harvest mouse? Tell us," they plead, "about this blue not of earth, the blue before there was blue. Is there a blue space where blue was going to be? What was there? What color is emptiness?" They ask, but I cannot say. Their myth has to stop their minds before they become lost like children transported to a different mesa. "I will, I will." I tell them yes, but before I can lie, as they really want me to, I have to know the truth, which I continually invent in the back part of my head. One day, even out of doors, or sheds, or ancient roof beams, I will carve the doll that makes all telling obsolete. The wooden doll will exert so powerful a spell that all of life not devoted to awe must halt and end. "You simply look," I am going to have to say, "and hold on to the whirlwind in its mind." "Yes, yes," they will say, "but what makes this doll so different?" Same wood, same knives. Same paint, same feathers. The difference, I will have to say, is somewhere between the notion I have of the doll and the doll itself, then somewhere between that point and the doll and then the notion of the doll going toward him that Sotuqnangu would have if Sotuqnangu were in the least way aware of the doll. There: that should stop them for an hour or two. The tighter the fix you get into, the more you have to be only too glad to carve an Arizona-sized portrait of a human pore. It is no use saying, Get on with it, George The Place In Flowers Where Pollen Rests, when George The Place In Flowers Where Pollen Rests can only do what George The Place In Flowers Where Pollen Rests says. They scowl as if they have dung up their noses. They want instant results, whereas I, I try to do what I am not utterly disqualified for. One hint of bungling, and I hold back, which has kept me from thousands of useful things, carved or said, shot home into the womb or mashed against the nose of an opponent. I used to wrestle and punch, but all that exercise was bad for my carving muscles, just as, they say, those who write or paint or play piano just cannot go out and hew wood, it unstrings the muscle tension, it yields many a botched endeavor. I wonder how many children I have had by sheep, I who have squirted free in any hole that came along. Certain ancient lambs once bore my face, my mannerisms of limb, my slightly pigeon-toed way of walking. The main thing in a life is to shoot all that stuff out of your system until you are left with only the tubings it goes through. Not hollow, quite, but certainly blown clear. Then you begin, having nothing to lose, as out of place as a lighthouse with a limp, bang in the middle of the continent, with bison and puma all around you, and crying, "Ahoy, there! Are you a ship?" It is hard to know, for a landlubber to know, exactly how to address a ship that passes. By. You. By. Day. You falter thus, handier with sheep, corncobs, and beautiful badgers going over the hill. When, as now, a bunch of folks is gathered around you, almost as if to keep you from sliding over the face of the planet and off, into thinness near to vacuum, you have to feel a scrap grateful. Every move you make, a wall of faces shoves you back. Even a wrong look bounces off their gaze. It is as if a dozen of them have been told to hem you in, all day, all night, and to pretend to be listening or otherwise attending, when really they are there to keep you on the reservation. No floating off and up. No blowing away on an unruly wind. No little jaunt disguised as Oswald Beautiful Badger Going Over The Hill. You feel obliged to talk, to carve. No one feeds them. Where they are is where they are all day: Just make sure the old duffer doesn't wander off and fall into a ravine or go finding his own kin by (as usual) sniffing in between the legs of the women, cackling No, damn it, our women reeked more of sulfur, it was touched with scallion in there. I could run at the cordon and bust through, of course, or wheedle my way past. Point an arm skyward to the autopilot and get them looking there. Then off, fast, to the nearest hole in the ground to hide. "The white," says Oswald Beautiful Badger Going Over The Hill, "not the white stuff in your eyes, Uncle, I mean the kaolin primer. Let us put it on the doll and let it dry." He sighs that sigh of permanent reprieve, but his uncle fidgets and complains. "It will not bind to the wood, Oswald Beautiful Badger Going Over The Hill, it will peel, and much of the paint along with it, so we shall soon have a shabby god on our hands, not worth giving away. I would rather use the white stuff from my eyes. A week's worth ought to do. Let us use the most local clay of all." His shudder is vocal, and you can tell at once, even if you know nothing about him, that his sense of humor is far from graveyard. "How about an acrylic finish," he asks. "It would be brighter." But I ask him why bother to be brighter. "Time past," I tell him, "I would spray the colors with hairspray to fix them. To keep them perky. But not anymore. I am willing to have my dolls, even my gods, peel and fade, just to remind me of who I am, who I can never be." My shirt sleeve has come unbuttoned, and for a moment I am unsure if I am telling him that, in so many words, or just noting the fact to myself. Let it flap, I tell him at last. "It will keep the flies away." "What flies, Uncle?" "The flies," I answer, "that flit across the surface of my eyes. You have never seen them. Like swifts in the void they scoot and soar." The basic torso is done, I tell him, and then there is a flurry of action. "Hatchet," he says, and I say no. "Mallet," he says, and I again say no. "What you must do, Oswald Beautiful Badger Going Over The Hill, what you must do now is find me a chunk of white clay and then soak it until the grit sinks to the bottom of the bucket. Then we will daub and not until. No gesso, no acrylic. If I had my way, it would be a yucca brush too, and none of your sables, and mineral paints from oxides of iron and copper. Colorful clays and vegetable dyes. I have nothing, as a has-been, against tempera or poster paint, but I ask you, where do we find the legendary blue-green you could only get with copper carbonate? There is no other way for that, just as you cannot create geese wheeling in the sky out of a handful of pen nibs. If I must use acrylic, I must; at least it will stay moist longer and won't easily rub off. You don't want a god who makes no lasting impression." Away goes Nephew with the unprimed doll, to coat it and dry it. He has learned how not to make a ruff from shiny plastic such as they sell to children whose tiny trains need hedges to run past or forests to chug through. Nephew was a purist until he realized how a ruff of real spruce goes brown and falls away, and it was I who taught him about the dyed seaweed you can buy in hobby shops, culled from a place known as the English Channel, where no doubt they farm it. Or there is green yarn, sometimes larded with white glue to stiffen it. Shells from the Indian Ocean and the South Pacific. "Why, Nephew, our dolls have become international." They deserve a tall building in New York City all of their own. Will you ever find real mouse or squirrel skin these days? Seal, more likely, and bits of fur from cast-off coats. Down of eagles was clouds. Buckskin has become suede. And carpet tacks abound. If it matters much of what a god be made, then our gods are cut-rate, like the cookies in the big round cans in the drugstores. I lapse into telling them about the crude old days, when you could always make an effect with feathers from the scarlet tail of the military macaw, or the red-tailed hawk. Eagle plumes were black as charcoal and just as hard. There were mountain blue birds and green warblers. Many's the time, after one of the ceremonies, I've scrounged around on the trampled soil for some leftover feathers, getting my hands trodden on in the process, and squeezing many a lump of dung by mistake. Now we will have nephews find our feathers. Hard, when neither the dancers nor the carvers have real feathers, and it is a lucky day when you can plunder such birds as sparrows or starlings, not to mention clucking hens, whose feathers you have to tint. "All this," I tell him, "is a world you will not have. Never again will anyone be able to make the old kinds of dolls, the real thing. Am I then supposed to teach you how to make imitation

ones? Better to leave you untouched, so that you will never form
longings for what you cannot have. You would be better off building
balsawood kachinas from the kits sold in hobby shops for grown-up
idiots to make. The makings have gone. There is not even wood to
begin with. So what you need, Oswald Beautiful Badger Going Over
The Hill, is one of those desert islands, where the springs run fresh,
and there you will find roots of all shapes and textures. Start anew,
and wonder why, back here, the gods have become so well established
they no longer make certain that enough of the right trees grow, or
that the white man, in his craze for protecting birds, does not come
around and trim certain feathers off certain dolls. You should never
have left Hollywood. At least it never runs out of celluloid. Who
nowadays hangs dolls from rafters or hangs them on walls? Remember, too, that nowadays is the time of the jumping doll whose limbs
are jointed and move about when you pull the strings. What non-
sense. Now they make giant dolls too, and dolls only half an inch
high. Clowns, clowns, clowns is all they want. I do not do clowns.
Not for people wanting clowns. I do the clown who wants to come to
life, not otherwise. Once upon a time things were better, when several of us would go off together to gather salt or capture eagles. It was
permitted, then, to think hard about what you went out after, because
according to our tribe's beliefs, the more you think about something
the stronger it becomes. Harder to conquer, perhaps, but also more
worth the struggle. The salt is harder to dislodge from the ground,
the eagles are warier than ever. It is almost like praying to the object
of your quest." One day, Oswald Beautiful Badger Going Over The
Hill and I came upon a fox with its leg in a trap, and I told him to
watch me as I removed its foot from the clamp, stroked its entire
body gently for a while until it stopped shuddering, and then just as
gently pushed its nose into the loose dirt to smother it. "Why didn't it
try to bite you," he asked. "It wasn't scared," I told him. "It was all
right. It knew how to behave." Soon after that he went off to Hollywood and stayed away at least two seasons, sending money home of
course, but out of tune with our ways. "You took undue advantage of
the fox," he said at the time. "It thought you were going to let it go."
"It did not know anything," I told him. I did not even sprinkle it with
a bit of sacred meal, as if it had been a plant, a bean, or a melon. Then
you offer a prayer to the plant family it belongs to. With animals it is
different, they are more individual. As it was with the turtles, when
we went out to collect rattles with a few cans of tomatoes, a big ripe

watermelon, and a bag of wheat flour, all in a big cardboard box. We
also had a ball of tough cord and a thin, sharp knife, a coffeepot, stew
pan, fry pan, some cups, and a coil of rather new rope. In Flagstaff we
paused to buy an extra loaf of store bread. If the truck went slowly
enough we might end up eating more often than we had planned over
five hundred miles or so. Down to the Colorado we rattled, hoping to
find the right kind of backwater without mosquitoes. First we cut a
few willows an inch or so across and sharpened either end of each to a
point. At the riverbank we stripped down and both swam out into a
depth of four feet, then dived to the bottom with our pointed sticks,
on the ends of which there were lumps of dough, mixed the night
before. "Bait," I told him, "the dough is bait for turtles." Each time
we started deep and worked our way back toward the bank of the
river. Oswald Beautiful Badger Going Over The Hill was the first to
catch a turtle, which he correctly grabbed within his arm, and then
shoved into the cardboard box, whose lid he weighted down with a
log. When we had five, which was steady going for two men, we went
back to where we had parked the truck and began the cleaning of the
shells. With two slipknots we trapped the first turtle by two of its feet
and him on the ground upside down. Then we tugged at the ropes to
bring his feet into the open, after which came his head and neck,
ready for my knife. Down into the body I thrust the blade, and soon
we were cutting the body from inside the shell, not an easy job with
the muscles hard as leather and the joint with the shell a place firm as
teeth. It was clear the turtle had not been designed to make carving it
up easy for any tribe of men. And you had to be careful not to scratch
or gouge inside or outside. It was almost dark before we finished, and
my nephew was complaining about being stiff, his having used muscles he otherwise never used, and the stink of the turtle meat as this
was summer. We shared a cigarette and spent the next day scraping
the inside of our shells for the least fragment of turtle meat. "I can see
them fastened to the knees already," I told him, "held in place with a
buckskin thong, the flat underside against the calf, and within, to
rattle during the ceremonies as the dancers pound their heels against
the ground, a few dried hooves, antelope or deer, culled from another
hunt in which we had no part." It is a much lower tone than that of
the skittish rattles. Down goes the dancer's foot and the turtle shell
makes its doleful clanking sound. After that little teaching expedition, two men alone with nothing but a few sticks and loaves and
ropes, it was time to get back to carving, and I told Nephew that I

sometimes wished my dolls were hollow and might thus be rattled about instead of being what my dolls always have been: dumb, dead, and farther from the tree than the shell is from the living turtle. "No," he answered, "you do this better, you should catch twice as many turtles as you did." "With proper help," I retorted, "I would, I have to have help that swims better than a dead horse. Tarzan the Apeman would be a useful man to have along, not that I have ever seen him, but his name is one I think about. He who can wrestle a crocodile would make easy meat of turtles." "And of turtle catchers, too," he said. "Hollywood is not all yellow-bellies, Uncle George The Place In Flowers Where Pollen Rests." "We were always four," I told him. "You have forgotten. My nephew the moviestar has forgotten the spirit companion who goes everywhere with us, lending a hand in inscrutable ways, keeping you from botching the turtle shell, from impaling yourself on the pointed sticks in the deepest water, especially when the balls of dough fall off the points, and making sure that you do not run into any of the Navajo on the way out or the way home, from whom your possessions are never safe." Some Navajo worked with him in Hollywood, he said, and these were not all thieves, and I thanked Sotuqnangu, lord of the unblemished turtle shell that no such Navajo, who were not all thieves, had come along with us on our expedition to the Colorado, by way of Flagstaff and Kingman. Then he gave me his old-fashioned look, which, since his face is wide and chubby, seems blunter than it really is. His eyes are brown. I still see them although I no longer see them. Could not the blind be allowed to see at least the *eyes* of others? Into their kennels they go when I ask him why, for a man forbidden all coffee and tobacco, I go on enjoying both. It was the same with the pills. One day, my mouth went numb, my tongue and neck along with it, and then my left hand, the dreaming one caught in the act. After a month of pills, I felt better. "You should have kept on with them," he said. "One was to thin out your blood, Uncle George The Place In Flowers Where Pollen Rests. It is used elsewhere as a rat poison." I snorted at him. "Then there are the others, to make your heart beat more firmly and less often, oh yes, they can do that with tiny pellets no bigger or heavier than birdlime. Where are they now? Moldering away in a jar?" I had no idea, I told him. You take these bits and bobs until you feel better, and then you set them aside with a holy thank-you to the spirit of the pill. He has tried this argument with me before. "And," he says, "there is the one, from across the eastern ocean, that plugs the locks in your brain, so that a certain key will no longer fit and speed up the action of your heart. It is called adrenaline, and now, although you make this thing in a big gland, it now has almost nowhere to go. It just swills around and goes to waste." "Then surely," I told him, "this adrenaline will never forgive me, having no future, not allowed to do me the good that was intended, like the fleece for the sheep, the feathers for the bird, the money in the bank. How wretched I am that no longer use it well." For a while back then, it was nothing but fuss. George The Place In Flowers Where Pollen Rests was trying to tell them he couldn't talk properly, which they could tell anyway from the dreadful muddle of the sounds he was making while the spit rolled down his chin. They knew, all right. Off we went to Keams Canyon, where a doctor told me to take my pills without fail, and they attached all kinds of wires to my chest just as if I was going to the electric chair. "You have to mend your ways," the doctor said. "How do I mend them up on the mesa," I asked him. "You would have to change the landscape first to make many changes in folks's lives." He could tell what I said because the slur had gone from my speech and my face muscles worked again, it did not feel as if a sack of wet corn was hung on my jaw. Instead of writing something out longhand, which I was aching to see him do, he handed over a lot of little samples, pills sealed in noisy paper and slippery plastic, some in twos, some in sixes, and I was to take this pink one when I woke, and a white one with it, which had a clockface on one side stuck at half past ten. "Pink and white," I said, "is useless to the blind. This is the half-past-ten pill." I asked him, but he shook his head and said not to be so fucking smart, do as I say or you will soon be in hospital. "You got hypertension," he said, but I was not nervous at all. "And you threw a clot," he said, which I was not in the least aware of doing. So he tells Oswald Beautiful Badger Going Over The Hill. He could speak our language some, at least half as well as turtles do. "Oswald Beautiful Badger Going Over The Hill," he said, "you will have to watch him, he is not going to take his medication when he should. He is going to goof off like nobody's business and I got sick folk enough without having to tell him everything twice." "Okay, Uncle George The Place In Flowers Where Pollen Rests," he tells me on the drive home in that same truck as once took us turtle catching, "once a day you take the blood thinner, and four times a day the one you can feel ten-thirty on the back of, and once a day the little pill made from foxgloves, and four times a day the little knobbly one that

lowers the pressure of your blood." "No, I will never get the hang of
it," I told him. "Let me take them all now on the way home and that
will be that." "We will bury you tonight, under a place where the
deer jump, if you do." He had this barking sound in his voice. "Then
I will shove them all up my rear end," I told him, "just to keep both
hands free." "No," he said. Then he explained about the rat poison
that made rats bleed to death and how what killed rats would keep me
lively. The foxglove one I kind of liked already, what with its feeling
natural and so forth, right from the ground. The one with the clock
on its back, he said, was made from a bark that grew down in South
America where blind George Borhez lived, and was probably the
same thing as he took for blindness. I was not quite so blind as I am
now when all this happened. I couldn't have been. I think I saw the
clock on the back of the pill. And here I still am. "This other pill," he
was telling me, "this is what you take for nervousness if you are going
to play the violin in front of a whole bunch of folks. It is for stage
fright or butterflies." "If I am going to play the violin," I said. "If *I*
am going to play the violin? I am all for butterflies, Oswald Beautiful
Badger Going Over The Hill," I told him, "you can write stuff on
their wings like messages and insults. It only takes a couple of eyes to
see it well." "It makes you mighty smooth," he said, "and you will
sometimes feel serener than any eagle." "In that case," I said, "I will
take only the rat poison, the foxglove, the pill from South America,
and the one for butterflies. I will never cheat by taking any other kind
of pill. Trust me. They will suit me fine once I get used to them."
"You will have the runs from them," he warned me, "and your
dreams may be longer and more colorful." This had a blissful sound
to me, whose dreams had always been poor. "Your skin might itch a
lot," he went on, "and you will feel dizzy when you stand up all of a
sudden. You will get gas too, the doctor says, and in the night your
hands will go numb and you will have pins and needles when you
wake. Apart from that you are going to feel wonderful and you will
not ever again have your arm go useless or your mouth unable to
speak. I will fetch you your pills from Keams Canyon." And he did.
The trouble was, I forgot to take them, and I lost count, and then I
took too many all at once, which made me feel mighty strange as if I
had been swung at with a lump of granite. I had even, when I remembered, gotten to the stage of being able to tell the pills apart even in
my blindness: the half past ten, as good as Braille, was the one I
always began with as I shuffled them around in my pocket, and then

the rat poison which had a curly snake shape on one side. The one for butterflies had a big fat bridge on of its sides too, so I knew the one that was left was the one from foxgloves, and I wondered what do they have against the foxglove that it has no sign upon its side. You would know a flower from just feeling at it. It was too small for anything to be written on it, I told myself. It was a baby among pills even if, in cahoots with these others, it sets you shitting in your sleep with pins and needles and an itch, makes you dizzy when you stand, and gives you nightmares even after you have gone to sleep. The good these do is mighty invisible compared with the other things they do. Surely, pills that give you no trouble do no good at all. It was not long before Oswald Beautiful Badger Going Over The Hill began chiding me about not taking my pills. "I feel good," I kept telling him. "Soon as I feel low, I will get them down deep into me." "Every day on time," he said, "or you will never speak again or walk or talk, Uncle. It is a matter of life and death." "No," I told him, "it is a matter of feeling poor and feeling not so bad. It is enough to have to go without coffee, tobacco, an occasional beer." "You do nothing of the kind," he told me, "you drink and smoke as much as you always did. You coffee up too. I guess there is no holding you on that front. I just want you to remember your pills. What is the point of driving to Keams Canyon if you stick them in a corner and go for weeks, if you're lucky, without any of the stuff that's going to save you?" "I am saving them," I told him, "for a rainy day. You know how we enjoy a rainy day up on the mesa. I'll save them for when you have gone back to Hollywood and there is no one to bring me pills from Keams Canyon. I can't go there myself. I will take an aspirin or two when the need comes on. And a couple of those little minty pills for indigestion. I swear." What he said next was like thunder. "It will kill you," he shouted, "mixing aspirin with rat poison, you will bleed to death." "Then," I said stiff as I could, "I will do without the rat poison, Nephew. Maybe the aspirin will save me. Maybe I am right." "Maybe it will after all," he said, and with that we began to talk of carving once again. Those who do not do it like to talk about it. That was the crisis, before I got quite so blind. I wonder if they will one day invent a pill to bring back sight, never mind the taste. I'd wolf it down if there were. I might as well eat wood. When the night is deep I sometimes reach for the coffee tin of pills hidden behind the stove and rattle it, not so loud or so carrying a noise as they make with knee rattles made from turtle shells, but loud enough for me, alone in the night, hearing the snake and the fox, maybe a hundred of them tapping and rattling about in the can, which amounts to just over a week's supply, best taken with lamb stew salted with salt from the dried-up lake, or the tea made from juniper and the sand sagebrush, which is very good for indigestion. I wondered if I were to make a little fire of dry corncobs and cook the can over it until the pills had all mixed up with one another: what would happen? Surely that would be a potent medicine to drink in a cup of sage tea. Wait for the next crisis, I told myself. "Do as you are told, Uncle George The Place In Flowers Where Pollen Rests," my nephew said. "I am very fond of my pills," I told him. "They talk to me." "Take them," he said rudely. "We need to know your blood pressure on a daily basis and I am going to bring you a little sleeve to wrap around your arm, and a rubber bulb to pump up so that the whole thing will work. It isn't the cost I mind but the thought that whatever we do you will please yourself." Then I told him I did not want to be any trouble, but all he said with a twist of his puffy mouth was "Oh, oh."

Oswald

When I tell him that I wish I were as good a carver as he is, he thinks I think I have some gift at carving, but all I mean is that I would like to be as good an actor, a player of bit parts, as he is a carver of dolls. If I were going to be a carver, I would like to be like *him:* he does original, stylish, rather Picasso-like work, and those who collect him prize those qualities in his dolls. One is a storeowner in Tucson; Apperknowle is a professor in Phoenix; one is a guy from Pennsylvania who flies in once a year to see what he can pick up. You would never guess his life from his dolls, but you might guess at his hands, which rather than big and lumpish are pliantly long, and always on the go, whether they are holding a lump of wood or not. Anyone less an uncle I have never seen. He belongs in some poster against nuclear war, huddled there against his wall like a hag from out of melodrama with that old army blanket wrapped around him and the number stenciled black still visible when the light is good. He's always telling me to keep the crowd back as they jostle to get nearer to him, but there is never a crowd, maybe a couple of sensation seekers. Up on the mesa they leave him to himself. They no more think of keeping an eye on him than they do of urging the sun to do its daily stint. *"Back off,"* he tells them, but as often as not he is talking to himself and me, and maybe some runt of an unwanted dog. They have seen him all they need to see. Not one of them has not been at one of his famous deathbed sequences, as he goes into a swoon with his limbs flailing, his mouth wide open to receive rain; they know that, a few hours or days later, he will be supping hot soup and biting into lumpy marga-rine not so much smeared as arranged on a hunk of Anglo bread. He is an ace recoverer, not out of spite, but because to him it is an art form, a little ballet of trial and error. He dawdles. He carves his performance with much greater delicacy than he carves his wood, but he is very definite with both, and, truth told, is really rehearsing his death. But he has rehearsed it so often he has it down pat. When he dies, unless some truck knocks him over, which is unlikely up on the mesa by his wall, he will know exactly what to do and how, unless his memory goes altogether by then. So, in a sense, his most recent re-hearsals are just exercise for the sake of something to do: heavenly aerobics. I'm used to them by now. He needs no audience; I have heard him go through the same routine when he thought I'd gone away. "If I go crazy, shoot me," he says. "There isn't a gun on the whole mesa. Shoot you with what?" "An arrow will do," he says. "The same goes for arrows. How about a knife?" Thunderstruck, he knows what knives are for, telling me he will take care not to go mad, knowing he'll get no help. "On a windy day," he says, "take me right to the edge. It might blow me down into the canyon." "You might be lying down," I tell him. "Then you could roll me over the lip," he says as if he has thought it all out. "I wouldn't linger," he adds. "Even if the fall did not kill me, the loneliness down on the canyon floor would. The heat. The snakes. The lack of water. No pills." What he says is part jest, part not; but how much is either? I sometimes think he has become mighty serious about it, begging for the nudge, the tweak, that would save him the pain of waking up blind. Why me, though? He seems to think I have had something to do with death already, whereas only on one occasion, about which I knew little enough beforehand. Life is a closed book. "No, no, Uncle," I an-nounce, "I don't have the right. Nor do you. We must keep each other company as best we can, without making trouble for each other." Somewhere, somehow, a day, a time, has been set for each of us, and that is the pattern of our lives. The climax. I promise not to go away as much as I did. I'll hang in here, like a leech. What does it take to put your clock back? Do you do it with your mind? When was it that BertandAnna used to come around with a small churn of goat's milk, clanking their tin cup against it to tell us they were coming? Whichever of them did it did it from a height liking to see the milk flow through the air even with the light coming through it more than it ever did with cow's milk. The milk was like a ribbon, a cord, a rope. Then it hit the bottom of the jug you were going to take it away in, and then it curled around real fast and evened out, not so interesting as it was when in midair. You had to keep the pair of them from lifting their fingers into the pour, they liked it so much, they kind of cuddled the pressure of it coming down. When they finished, and always with some milk on their hands, their clothes, their faces even, they would face each other and she would set her feet on his feet, her shoes on his, and they would trudge around like that whatever the weather, face to face, humming something nobody could ever figure out, but it sounded like a military march, real slow, maybe a funeral march from another country. Left, right, they went, slower than ice melting in the shade. They peered into each other's faces as if they were doing it in no place at all, but in the air like the milk, a couple of simple folks doing the light fantastic for themselves after making sure there was goats' milk for everybody. Actually, nobody needed goats' milk as they did in Uncle George's time; there was always milk in waxed cartons from Keams Canyon. But BertandAnna liked to do it, it was one of their things, and it made them laugh, at the splashy sound, the clonk-clank of the metal, the feel of it against their hands when they managed to feel at it before you could stop them. Funny milk they called it, but we never saw the goat. They kept it in some secret place not worth walking to, not if BertandAnna were willing to fetch the milk. We took the milk to be polite, if we used it at all, and I do believe it gave us all the runs, but what could you do, mix it with blackboard chalk? In the dead of winter, when the flu was everywhere, you'd see BertandAnna trying to pour the frozen milk and, every now and then, trying to wipe their noses on the same handkerchief, except it often wasn't a handkerchief at all but like one of those roses made from tissue paper, all dried up and rough to the touch, not so much a nose wipe as something to cut your nose open on. Once it was a hankie all right, but between them they had loaded it with wet and then it had dried and been re-used, you could see them un-crinkling it with a noise like that of tearing paper. Some laughed at them, but most everybody was nice to them because they meant well and acted out the kind of goodwill we all often wished we had more of. If only I'd been able to be as foolish and wise as them, fitting in where I belonged instead of all that Palookaville. OswaldandAnna: something like that. But I couldn't even get as close to them as Uncle George, who sometimes dipped a finished but unpainted kachina doll into their milk, floating it around and stirring with it, which made them laugh until they cried. Then he had to wash and dry it or the milk would have curdled the paint. I only took them to the dentist's once, but it was enough. They howled while the dentist, who was also the doctor, sweet-talked them into it. Or tried to. They never smelled too good, something like burned paper and mothballs, but it wasn't that. Folks thought they would catch a disease from them, and some wouldn't even go near them, not even to shake hands. Many days they ended up with milk they couldn't even give away, so they stood face to face on each other's feet, but mostly her on his, and drank from the little gill measure until it was gone. Then they'd be wetting themselves an hour later as they tromped around, saying hi to every-body, being themselves as if they weren't human beings but some kind of a climate, a season. They were so simple they puzzled me. Very old, they don't serve milk anymore, and they don't walk on each other's shoes or boots, but they still hi you when you catch their eye. They sometimes hi you a dozen times and maybe for five minutes after if you so much as answer them. They have staying power. "You get some grand young men in movies these days." This they must have said to me a thousand times. It was one of their things to say. They hope to mean what they always end up saying. Then, some-times, this: "Nice and clean young men. You'd like to pat their heads to see how it felt." We all smile. "With open faces you could trust." No secrets, nothing hidden. That's what they mean. They ought to know how bad folks can be, but they don't and they won't ever. I am nothing but lies and fraud and if Uncle George ever finds out he will strangle me, I think, and then I'll never again hear BertandAnna going on about me in the movies, I the leper with the hand of gold. To them, anyway. BertandAnna should have been in the movies, not me. In the real movies, I mean, like *Birth of a Nation*, something as serious and good as that, with Bert and Anna made separate, to stand

for different American types, different Indians—Engines, as they like
to say of themselves. Where on earth did they get the idea of calling
themselves Engines? From the dentist-doctor in Keams Canyon, Doctor High and Mighty Mouthful racist Matlock. "What does a hurt
Enjun suffer from? A enjury." It was BertandAnna who somehow got
their hands on one of those jars of bath powder, that makes a blue
foam in the tub, but they spread it all over themselves with their
clothes on, and they looked like a couple of pale blue bears, reeling
about and laughing. If they had fallen into water, they would have
died in the foam, which would have covered the whole mesa, I think.
For weeks after, there was a soapy smell to the goats' milk and I
knew, I just knew, it had been Matlock who'd given them the bath
powder, just to see what kind of a balls-up they'd make with it. Indian
giver, him. What I always wanted to do with him was strap him in
the chair and set him on fire. Yank out his teeth and make him swallow them, but the most I ever did was sneer. Open my mouth and, for
fun, he'd have poisoned Uncle George. Maybe he did. You never
know what's in those free samples they hand out with a big royal
smile as if they have just dug them up from the bowels of the earth.
Them simples, he used to call BertandAnna. "Those goddamned simples. Boy, would I like to plant them." Instead, though, he drilled
them with maximum force and took out teeth he needn't have
touched. His come-on was real cute until you realized he was laughing about it to himself, dotting their faces with blood until he had
some kind of polka pattern that made him laugh wide as a garbage
can. Then he'd do the other one, red-spotting the same way, and then
he told them he couldn't go on until they had cleaned up their faces.
"Seems like every pimple's a-poppin today," he'd say to them, and
hand them a towel. If ever there was an Engine, it was him. "Seems
like every simple's poppin today." Next he showed them, tried to
show them, how to make a baby, but he lost patience with them and
just kept saying something about Bert peeing up Anna's ass every
Friday for a whole year, and then he left it at that, having as it were
blown his nose on the nation. Even in Palookaville life's a breeze
compared with that. Or it was, until. Anybody could have told him
they would wet his black and silver chair, the only thing missing that
day being Uncle George, who would as surely have bust something
loose in the toilet or the waiting room, just to prove he was an Engine. But they were the happy days, warm as home, and I'd surely

bust a gut getting back to them if only I knew where they were. Wrapped in brown paper on somebody's dresser, and even my mother won't remember half so well as she did. It has all gone away from us, Uncle, somehow without ever having been lived through.

George

And I resented that, feeling that if nature had put me wrong it was up to nature to put me right. Trouble was the last thing I had in mind. A whole lifetime of never doing what you're told, mainly because that is not how you see the living of a life, not doing what others want, but sitting still, going out, coming in, according to some private hunger. Anyone who lives otherwise is living some other's life within his own body. No, I didn't want to make trouble, but I didn't want to lose touch with myself. I didn't feel too bad, a bit dizzy now and then, and that pounding in my eardrums or the old familiar ping and squeak, all signs as the doctor in Keams Canyon said, but what *isn't* a sign? Sometimes they use the word *symptom*, and the two words are different, but everything is a sign to me. Since the one bad time when my lips went dead, and my throat, my tongue, I have had only the odd sense that my lips are permanently thicker and obey me a little less than before. Not that I stammer, but I hear the stammer in my head even when others do not, and I speak very little anyway. It doesn't amount to much. There seems less room inside my mouth, so the extra thickness must be all on the inside, what with my tongue also being larger than it was. No one has measured me, of course, and how would you begin to measure a tongue or the inside of a mouth? I should have given up the coffee, but I did not, I have not dropped dead on the wall here, and there is no doubt that my lips and tongue feel better after coffee, as if they have come back to complete life, and to hell with what they tell me about being a walking time bomb. *"Uncle George The Place In Flowers Where Pollen Rests,"* my nephew begins yet another of his polite barrages, *"it is only a matter of time,* what you had was a warning, and next time will be more severe." He goes on for hours, and sooner or later he persuades me to try a pill or two, which he then tells me is just as bad as taking none at all. "Once you have started with them, you must not let go or you will be worse than before. You start and then you taper off." "Well, how do you taper off from one pill to a crumb of it? Maybe that is how to start, Nephew. A bit now and then is worse than none," but he insists, hoping that I will go on taking them, scared by what will happen to me if I don't, but I don't have that much sense of future. Or, if I do, it is the future of others I have a sense of, not the future of me, which to be obvious about it does not have much future in it. Maybe they should donate me to a hospital right now, so that they could study the process of decay from the beginning, cramming me with pills and then tapering me off until I am no more than skin and bones. I ask him about this, but he wants me to go on carving, even when I can't see what I am doing, now like the sexual act of old, done in the dark for shame, for stealth, for the sake of sheer excitement. Yet an intimacy that close is as nothing likened to what happened after the attack, the seizure, the thing that happened, when after all the fuss had died down I finally got back to dreaming and sleeping, and who should walk into the dream but that spit image of me at age seventeen or so, his face fixed in horror, but his eyes full of I-can't-believe-it sympathy, oh yes, as if he had come along to say, no not say, to mime his opinion of all this, and the way he came into the room was delicate, forbearing, as if to whisper, *You should never have let it come to this,* at which he came right over to me, slowly as if I might explode, and leaned his face against my shoulder, nuzzling like a colt, son of myself, and I recognized him at once, hugged him close as if to suck the very youngness from him and so force it back into my ailing hulk. Is it really *you?* How can it be *you* if this is still me, heading for sixty years and beyond? How could the

young me and the ancient one be alive at the same time? All I knew
was that, somehow, he had freed himself from me during the moments of paralysis, knowing he didn't want to talk as I talked in those
moments, or to have his heart flutter and his hand go numb. I did not
know that you can feel such crushing tenderness for yourself as you
were, about whom you had not thought in many years, yet he somehow hung in there, waiting for you to make a bad move, buried inside
you but still his own man. I saw this youth looking at me as I looked
at him and at his looking at my looking. Then his face quailed. It
shuddered as it saw how his quailing affected my own gaze. We were
both in tears, oh not very constructive ones, the one set asking how I
could have become so careless lately, the other asking how could the
youth in my past have given me so little guidance? Young George The
Place In Flowers Where Pollen Rests asks his ancient incarnation,
How could you have come to this, who once were me? "Slack living, boy," I
nearly answered, but thought better of it, arguing with myself that, if
this he who once was me was me still, then he knew my thoughts in
any case, being essentially unsevered, still trapped in me but allowed
an occasional roam in his elder's vicinity, just to keep a bit of cheer in
the mess, as if nephews did not exist, for all their book-learning wisdom and their Hollywood certainties. How long we lingered thus,
the young on the old, the old on the young, I do not know, but it was
surely the bud blaming the bloom and not the other way around. You
could tell from his face that what he wanted least was to have to
spend the rest of his life inside me, and vanish with me as I died,
allowed no other manhood but mine, though clearly mindful of other
manhoods he might have had if little he had not grown up into unruly I. Funny to see him thus because I had never seen him at any
other age, in a groping memory, yes, but never in a dream. As a baby,
a boy, a mature man, he had never called on me before, gently shoving others aside in his delicate march to my side, not insisting on his
right to look me in the eye, yet knowing he could take such a liberty
because, in the truest sense, he started from within and would go
back to there, the doll back into the wood. Then I saw what had
happened, and I felt a little more at home. He was the kachina of me,
the spirit who inhabited my bulk, whom I could please or anger with
my every move. It was he who sat by, tucked into the inmost
branches of my being, fully aware that, if I were good and took my
pills, this was the pill that both slowed and strengthened my heart

whereas this other was the pill that made the beat more regular. Armed with such knowledge, he had no control, had no right of interruption. He had to ride me while I rode myself, wishing hotly that I were the child and he the veteran. And yet, he being me, and I him, perhaps no change would come about except that I would do my foolishness early on, and he would do his late. That kind of swap. Wet-eyed, we leaned on each other, knowing it was almost too late even to have a talk, never mind mend our ways, and it might have gone on forever if the dream had not ceased of its own accord, a phantom soaring on chemicals not even mine, neither to be pleaded with nor banished. He has never come again, so perhaps I should take my pills as told, the right dose at the right time. There must be only one combination that is right, the one that brings him forth to chide, to hold my hand, while whatever it is that flutters in my chest whips my blood to cream, making it pool and thicken, dawdling into lumpiness. Were he small enough, pixie or goblin, he might flail around in it and somehow unthicken things, throwing out the solids, having a fine old swim in the thin gruel left. But he is no such size, and he is spread throughout my being, which means he is equally damaged everywhere. I keep waiting for him, always in the wrong dream, of course, so I hope that he will appear in some other corner of my being, as when I get up suddenly, not so much to stand as even to sit, and all the blood drains away into my trunk, leaving only a skull full of air. Dizzy then, I hope to catch a glimpse of him, cautioning me to do things slowly, to get up in stages, but never a sign of him, never a tweak from his lodger's mind. When my lips quiver as they never did, or my tongue feels thick as a hammer handle, as it never did either, I yearn for it to be him moving about among me, amid me, but not even fierce believing makes it so. You have to have the right order of pills, in the right strength, week after week, to ferret him out. I struck on it once, when in the days of good behavior, I just wanted to feel well again and would have heeded even a tribal doctor, with his Mormon tea, his piñon gum, his coyote sunflowers. Or I would even have gone to Phoenix, a town reputed to bring life from the ashes of the dead. Since then, however, George The Place In Flowers Where Pollen Rests has gone back to his slovenly old ways, hoarding his pills for when he really feels at death's door and not just on death's porch. No more little George The Place In Flowers Where Pollen Rests: they only come to you once in a lifetime, and it is possible that they do not even show up at your death, having once put in their plea and been sent away empty-handed. Instead, all you get is a nephew saying *"Eat plenty of bananas,"* as if bananas grew up here on the mesas, and drink plenty of milk, as if even BertandAnna milk were plentiful. I try to see a Little George in Oswald Beautiful Badger Going Over The Hill, but the lad's almost callow sensitivity is missing. He would no more say Eat this or Drink that, in order to make the heart muscle squeeze or rest than Oswald Beautiful Badger Going Over The Hill would hunt in his own interior for the superior ghost of himself. Yet I have no one else to work with, unless it be some child my nephew can bribe to come and dally with me, out here on the wall, warming my hands against the lamp or her brow. Boys I would deny myself, not having the boy I myself was, the youth who was my ancestor and hides away in dreams I do not have by night or day. When was it that Oswald Beautiful Badger Going Over The Hill made me look at some long streamers of paper, right there in the doctor's office in Keams Canyon, and told me these were pictures of my heart? In my seeing days, it must have been then, but I do not remember much more except what looked like a flat landscape, pretty much like they say it is up in Canada, with again and again a sharp little pylon with a small hump of land just next to it, then a stretch of flat land followed by a smaller, sharper hump of land and then another pylon. It looked okay to me, and he said, yes, that was a picture of my heart behaving well. Then with a rather sour smile he said he was glad *his* heart wasn't in this mess too, and he showed me a picture of my heart behaving badly, with all that flat-land area turned into a squiggly line with three or more humps or what looked like angry jagged scribble of the kind you do if you want to scratch something out. "Don't it make you sick, Uncle, to have all that coming out of you, without you doing the least thing about it to make it happen?" "No," I said, "I don't get sick that easy—I mean throw up. If that is how my heart wants to sign itself, then that's fine by me. I must say, I kind of prefer the excited scribble to the other, it seems to have a more interesting exertion in it." *"Never,"* he said, "that is the bad stuff, when your heart is beating all over the place and the little muscle strands are not working together." He shut up then, maybe because his Hollywood script writer had given him no lines to say. He sometimes had lines, but most often was another dumb dead Indian who had lost his scalp collection to an Anglo with pale blue eyes. Anyway, this was way back when, and now all those *time strips*, which is for some reason what they called the paper streamers, are sitting unlooked at in a dusty office, yellow and faded. Not our yellow, which is good, but Anglo yellow, no good at all. It was his eagerness that pleased me: not so much his eagerness to have me well, what with taking my pills and all, as his eagerness to talk me to death about it. He had learned it all by heart and had been waiting half his life to say it. Up to then, I had not taken him for a well-informed man, a man of our world, so it gave him some kind of a thrill to show me up through my heart prints, so to speak, ready to blame me before I even opened my mouth. I was always one to let the world go its way. Well, if not always, then mostly. I liked to make something that took me so far out of myself I wasn't home half the time, to be sick or hungry or sore. I lived by overlooking myself. Then the heart began its ways and the eyes called it a day. First the heart, bumping like a little blacksmith, then the eyes; the eyes hardly got a look in, as Oswald Beautiful Badger Going Over The Hill said with a sort of stammering smile. It was one of his jokes, told in ripest Anglo. Having been frail so long, from this or that going wrong with me, I had gotten used to things going wrong. It was as if they happened to somebody else close by, whose name I had forgotten. First the eyes, then the blood, then the heart. At least we have always had these names for them. It is not something going wrong with things we have not even named. I fixed on images of various gods, just for something to hold on to, not to bow to, but to keep me steady. It was like the game we played as children when, to keep your balance on one leg, you looked at a tree or a rock, something still enough to keep you still while you stared at it and tried not to blink. Well, not to blink for too long. So Sotuqnangu, to keep you still whether you blink or not. But gods are not there to give, not unless you put something into them. Heaven is made of homely sausages. It was not the gods, after all, who gave me even more pills, these to make me empty all the water from my body, bucketful after bucketful, night and day until I gave up. If we are that full of water, then a man can wash himself away. Then my nephew said, "If you lose that much you lose potassium, so you take another pill to make up the potassium, but this pill flushes you clean of something else good, so you have to take another pill whose only drawback—" "Put your pills," I told him then, "where umbrellas do not open. I will go on having my coffee, Nephew, and go to white man's hell. Do you think they would let me in? Do they need dolls down there? Is the wood too hot to carve? Do you have to carve dolls from red-hot charcoal in some kind of sacred torture?" He gave up on me then, muttering something I could not catch. Or, rather, in that worked-up way he has, he almost quit. There was a flutter in his face, and sand in his talk, when he told me how close he was to giving up, although he had not given up yet. If I would agree to take my pills as told, he said, he Oswald Beautiful Badger Going Over The Hill would draw money from his savings account in Keams Canyon, or Los Angeles, even if it cost him a penalty, and take me for a flight in an airplane right through Grand Canyon. My heart would go up in a puff of smoke, I told him. "Did you say through?" "Through," he said. "They not only fly over it, very high, they also go down below the rim and fly about halfway along it, and you can go from Las Vegas or Scottsdale, it doesn't matter where you start from." Bribed, I said yes, but my yesses were always meltable things. It was just like me to take the airplane ride and lie about the pills. "*Yes,*" he said, as if I had spoken out loud, "if you take the airplane ride without the pills, you will end up gasping for breath, Uncle. You do not breathe so well. Up there you will be looking for heaven to breathe in, any kind of air to keep you awake." Well, I took the ride, without the pills, gasping for breath, my ears plugged with wads of squeezy yellow foam, and carving a lump of cottonwood root in my lap as the airplane edged down into the Canyon. Afraid to look out, I felt better when all I could see alongside of us was the rock face itself, dangerously close. But what bothered me was this: I could not breathe, and what he had said about heaven was coming true. All along I pretended to have taken the pills. And I pretended to screw up my face with delight while I was choking for air. Yawn-yawn, I went, trying to find it. Where had it gone? I had not even enough breath in me to grunt as I carved, and the ride was bumpy, an old pickup on a mountain road. This made carving a danger to me and to the others too. Try hard, I told myself, this is something that Oswald Beautiful Badger Going Over The Hill is anxious to have me do, for which he has slaved many hours in Hollywood. One day, he will have gone back to the movie studios, and it will be as if I never had this ride. Or at least it will be if I do not enjoy it now. I forced myself to like every second of it, yawning as small as I could, and looking sideways in delight, when I would have given a lifetime's kachinas to be back on the ground. So as to remember something well, you try so hard that you cannot put the bad part of it behind you. With us, the gods come down, we do not go up to them. For all his grandness of gesture, Oswald Beautiful Badger Going Over The Hill had not set us up with an airplane all to ourselves. There were others on board, not Indians at all, who seemed nervous about an ancient Indian carving a lump of wood in his lap instead of looking out at the natural wonders. In fact, for looking over at me and maybe wondering what I was going to do next with the knife, some of them missed the Grand Canyon they had paid to fly into. Just another dumb Indian, the kind they like to put in charge to make the tribes behave. Smart Indians, like my nephew, are never the ones they put in charge. Anglos are best at dealing with the dumb ones, they want the smart ones to go to Hollywood, where they really know how to deal with a smart Indian. "It would have been cheaper," I told my nephew, "if they had stowed me in the nose with the bags," but there were no bags on this flight anyway. It was as if we knew there was no coming back. No stop on the way. All the passengers were supposed to look out, and not think about what was going on. Feeling at those windows made me nervous, big deep windows all the way down to my knees. My head was buzzing, maybe with blood, and my eyes seemed to have fresh-dug pits behind them, and I wondered where the wet eye-soil had gone. My belly heaved and sometimes seemed to float. This was my first flight, of course, and I wondered that this was the prize a nephew gave to a sick uncle in order to make him take his pills. It was not I but someone else who threw up on to the worn-feeling rug. Nephew says they lost the little paper bag whose top you fold over tight as soon as you have finished. George The Place In Flowers Where Pollen Rests would sooner have made himself nauseous by chewing and chomping his pills, never mind how bitter the quinine or dreary the rat poison. "Feel it," my nephew kept telling me, "we are going lower," but I could feel whatever was in my stomach turning to a purple-colored gas thick enough to be carved, and the cottonwood between my hands was getting colder than metal. If this was a pleasure flight, and paid for, then I would have been better off hunting turtles along the Little Colorado or, in the big city, as a stranger belittling strangers. Then we landed at the Grand Canyon airport, which was like setting down upon a sawn-off cloud. During the bus tour I fell asleep, and then we flew back, but my forehead felt full of pins and needles all the way. Then we sloped downward again, as if to crash, and all my head began to burn and sting as if I were on fire in there. It was all so long ago, before blindness, and because I survived the breathlessness I decided against the pills. They would do for a nastier time, I thought, when there was just no hope of getting through without them. I'd even eat the green mold that had begun to grow on some of them, or the pale brown mottle that had come to the surface of others.

Oswald

What do you do with somebody when you know this is the last time they are going to see something? For him, first and last. Not even Trudy Blue had readied me for this. Neither she nor I nor Stu nor Clu had any idea it was going to be her last—well, her last anything, whereas Uncle George had been going blind a long time, from before I went away the first time, and he got worse while I was away, and I had managed to get him to the Canyon only just in time. Should you push their faces harder against the windows? Should you tell them everything the pilot doesn't, if you even can? You have to know.

George

At that point, not the actual return to earth so much as my return to the village, I decided to try to instruct Oswald Beautiful Badger Going Over The Hill in chiselcraft, whether the tool he wielded was chisel, knife, or ax. Crouched near that wall, as always, with surrounding us the usual motley group of idlers and time killers, I held the knife close to his face and told him to shut his eyes. "You have to be able to tell the difference," I told him, "between too close and too far." What I meant, really, was that you have to be able to sense the blade's shadow on the wood, so that your best work is done almost blindly, and the virtue of the carving is in the hands, not the eyes. Starting with the most severe, I pressed the knife against his chin, which you can do with great force without ever making a cut, but you must not slide the blade. He felt that and did not like it. Next I eased the pressure, but not so much that he no longer felt the edge against him; it was just a keen touch. The third stage, which I forced upon him even while his nerves were still quivering from the blade held against him both hard and soft, was what mixed him up. Steady-handed as always, I held the edge as close as I could without making contact, but he felt it touch him all the same because his nerves were living in the past whereas the blade was living in the present. You did this, I explained to him, to sense the outline of a doll in the root you have chosen, not touching the wood but tracing an outline, somewhat like a water diviner, that lies only a skin's depth beneath the surface. Or it is deeper than that, in which case divining the outline is even more difficult, and (this is the remarkable part) you have to hold the blade even farther away, not nearer, as someone unaccustomed to carving might think. I was not going to recarve the chin that nature had given him, though he still had his eyes closed, and I could sense the outline it should have had, but nature does not so much carve as throw things forth fully fashioned. To the wrong observer, of course, it must have looked bad, what with the uncle holding the knife to his nephew's chin and throat. Something deadly, or at least heroically disagreeable, was afoot, but all I wanted him to do was to sense the closeness of metal to his blood vessels, to the places he shaved without a thought, to the underlying bone. I too have sensed the face I should have had, thinner here, bulkier there, but beyond carpentry or carving, just like the little chamber in my heart which, over the years, quietly enlarged itself as if preparing for something important that never came along. It must have wearied of the workday in there, chugging away behind my ribs, and haunted by the career it might have had. A year or two later, it must have been a year or two but it might have been longer, I repeated the lesson without being able to see, and clearly it was a much more delicate performance because the actual instruction depended on the principle being taught. I mean: in order to teach him sensing I had to sense him with almighty gentleness, whereas the first time, in some attempt to thank him for the Grand Canyon and all he had found out about my pills and my heart, I had kept a close eye on him throughout, in a way cheapening the lesson, making it as some thought easier, whereas of course I had only made it cruder. He flinched all the while, quite unable to tell when I had the blade upon his skin and when it was a petal's thickness away, in a sense proving my point, although I doubted at the time if he could put such awareness to practical use. Could he send his soul journeying through the upper layers of a cottonwood root? Would he know the difference between skimming the underside of the surface with his mind and, like some mining prospector, delving down into the pith, where he was not wanted? I have been accused of making carving more difficult than it needs to be, of making oversensitive an act that is both coarse and physical, and it may be true. A man can tell of his own ways only, underline or say that loudly. It is no use speaking for someone else, instructing your only interested nephew in how someone else would set about carving a doll. "Would you," I asked Oswald Beautiful Badger Going Over The Hill, "be able to tell the difference between the actual cutting of your throat and someone merely scoring a line across it, enough to draw blood, of course, but not going through the muscles and the vessels?" At that he did a big shrug and pulled his head away, and I knew it, I just knew, he had had his eyes open all the time, trusting little to a blind man with a knife practicing on a patient himself unable to see. "Yet what could you see," I asked him, "at that range? What could you see of what the knife was doing to your throat? At best a guess. You would have done better trusting to your other senses. When someone asks George The Place In Flowers Where Pollen Rests if he will instruct Oswald Beautiful Badger Going Over The Hill in the art of carving, then George The Place In Flowers Where Pollen Rests brings into play an almost unheard-of range of fine attunements, none of which amounts to cutting the throat you are trying to teach. Understand me: there are uncountable degrees of closeness, far more interesting than degrees of farness away: not a matter of distance, Nephew, but of well-developed touch. We do not have a sense that reliably informs us if our traveling kinsman is five thousand or five thousand five hundred miles away from home, but there are ways of telling, without actual feel, if the razor is one, two, or three petals' thickness from our throat. Not razor, that was a slip, I mean knife or chisel. So too with the wood. If you want to become a serious carver, you have to school yourself in the depths of thinness, and I most of all, because I sometimes have to find out if in fact a root is too thin for what I want, and that means sensing the space the doll would occupy in air if the root were bulkier than it is. It is one thing to think inward to the pith, it is quite another to think outward from the surface, getting a solid notion of where there is no wood at all." All this time, he kept trying to answer, to make a useful comment, but the knife at his throat kept him quiet, almost obedient in his way. It was not that he wanted to become a master carver, or even a good one, it was that some hunger for novelty drove him to find out what I would do next, as if I were not aware of how voluntary his interest was. "Ask more of your senses," I told him, both after the Grand Canyon when I saw, and afterward during my blindness, and they will provide. "No need to be blind, just don't be dense, Nephew. A sharper knife than this would have nicked you already, and you would know you were bleeding not because of a wet trickle but because blood smells dusty." Perhaps I have said this to him every day I have had him with me, but the more recently I have said it the less he has understood me, no doubt from the faint slur in my speech ever since my heart began to flutter and drift. Is it true that, the less you can see the face of the one you are speaking with, the less clearly you say things? Not to mention the slur in speech, the undue chubbiness in the way my lips feel. With a specially sharp penknife, I tell him, you might shave away at the lips and tongue until enough raw nerve is exposed to bring the old snappy feeling back, and the same goes for the left arm, from which you have only to peel back, petal by petal thinness, layers of skin and flesh until the same thing happens and your system comes back to life. I hate this feeling, I have gotten into the habit of telling him, of being dulled down. It makes a man want to bark, to yelp, to come out with bird cries. "Take your pills, Uncle," he always tells me, "be sensible. People are *made* of chemicals." "No," I tell him, "dolls are made of wood, people of flesh, and gods of human intentions." If a doctor *came by*, just to check on me, I told him once, but he snapped the answer back at me fast as thought. "Doctors do not *come by*, Uncle. Doctors do not even stop by to see other doctors. That is the way in Hollywood too. They do not like to leave their machines." "Nor I *my* tools," I told him. "Don't these doctors have dolls they can send out instead of themselves? What has happened to the ancient and honorable idea of the messenger? Will we hear?" At that moment I found myself amazed that our language had a word for this last idea: the messenger, but it does, like someone you send out to talk with the untalkable-to Navajo with their uranium mines and their wells of oil. "Am I pale with the pallor of death," I asked him. "When these hands go numb, as they seem to like to do for causes unknown to me, do they tremble with a shake I cannot feel, or for that matter see? Am I stammering?" "*Negatorio*, Uncle." He says this silly word of his. Then he said I should take my pills, just to make sure. "You were going to carve a Sotuqnangu," he said, "then you stopped. Isn't it time to get back to work? I painted on the undercoat and it is dry." "It is likely," I told him then, "that you may have to paint the rest of it too. Study the pictures in the books, do as I say, and a fairly accurate god will see the light of day. I surely am not fit to paint a god again. Red hematite, yellow limonite: that is about the limit of my skills. I can still tell one

color from another by smell, but all poster colors smell alike and the
only colors I can really tell apart are those the dancers paint their
bodies with. No poster colors on *them*. But a carver cannot go around
sniffing at people just to prove his point. Gods are entitled not to be
botched."

Oswald

You would think I had outgrown it, but I am still Oswald Beautiful Badger Going Over The Hill, not so much a name as an expedition. It sings to you about yourself and those who went before. Unhandy names, these, but they bring something to life on the mesa: a touch of color, which is the obvious thing to say, but also, to the very act of naming, something narrative, as if all of nature had been in motion at the moment of your birth. It was. They are names for when there is lots of time, not so much to kill as to tread down, reverent as can be. When he talks Mesa to me, I think it into English, but answer him back in Mesa, thus making both his name and mine and all the other names mentioned shrink and expand at a touch. Trust us to have one word for something the Anglos blunder around in half a dozen. Uncle George is *Silena* and I am *Kuwányamtiwa*, so he seems to have gotten the better of that trade-off; I am almost as long in Mesa as in English. Away from here they call me Oz anyway, so I am getting my birthright back after all. You have to go to Palookaville to get your just deserts, your name shortened or your ox gored. They will do to you anything you ask except hire you for life. I marvel I ever got credit cards. They must have been looking the other way when I applied. I dote on my uncle because my Aunt Bessie loved him, little knowing that she was going to drown while doing one of the things she was best at. He still does not accept it; to him, she swims on and on across Mormon Lake without ever getting cramp. She can no more drown in his world than he can uncarve the dolls he's carved. Then, he had this untreated VD, whatever it was when it blazed through him, coarsening him somewhat, and I do believe he did it deliberately, looking for the most sulfuric slit to shove himself into in the dumbstruck rage of his grief, wanting to burn off the part of him that lusted still. Which whore it was, we will never know, nor does he care. It did not kill enough of him. No wonder he excels at what I call his passing game, when he drifts off into death's preliminaries without warning, malingers there awhile, then comes back all the stronger for having faced it. Head-on. He is good at living on the edge. He looks over. He recoils. Now he looks again, leaning over a bit farther. Recoils again. Then he will lean even farther out, daring the void to suck him down before he puts his mind to it and actually jumps. *"Catch me,* Nephew," he cries when he's fading. I do not have to move at all, it is taking place in his mind, before, during, after. Then I pretend to let him go as he hauls himself back only to get ready for another look. *"Strong,"* he tells me. "You could lift an ox." "When," I usually ask him, "did you last see an ox, Uncle? What ox? Where? If ever." It's as unreal here as ivory. An ox is. He finds me too squeamish, I think, too gentle, even too womanly, but he is just picking up the side of me that reads, dives into galleries and museums. Nothing sexual at all. He would understand, I think, that I relish all human bodies regardless of sex, indeed approximating sexually what he does with wood. Is it any wonder? For so long a stud, he became a whoremaster (I like these ancient words instead of cocksman and hose beast), then became quite neuter while I, his substitute son, plied both sides of the street, stopping only at dogs. It doesn't matter with whom you do what, so long as you have this other stratum to your life. I was going to say layer, but that is asking too much of one simple pun. No, I think you have to have the other thing, the tenor whose vehicle is sex. He likes to call me a man of the world, but I am only a youth of it, street-wise as I am. I have not grown up in the world, among its ways; I have only passed muster, falling in with this or that overture mainly for lack of anything else to do, or for lack of conviction. I am too pliable, too plastic, not that he knows it. I am, perhaps, the ideal nephew for such a tyrant, never bugging him to take his pills, check his pressure, but instead plying him with toys in what seem his last days. The only trouble is that each series of his last days seems to fortify him for another lease of life. Almost dying builds him up for the next unsuccessful death rattle. Then I thought again. If a god is a god, then what does it matter if the god's image is botched? Gods are not bound by half-baked images of themselves. All-powerful, they please themselves, so there is no such thing as a caricature of any god, surely. If you are legally blind, then it does not matter how you image the god you have in mind, so long as you intend homage and respect, you would hardly be making a doll of someone you despise. That thought of mine disturbed me since it seemed to leave everything wide open. It was humans who insisted on this or that way of representing gods, whereas gods were probably indifferent, and all those wonderful-sounding qualities such as awe, reverence, and yes, homage and respect, were something for humans to warm their hands at. It may not sound like much of a discovery, but it shook me, making me realize I had tried too hard all along, yearning for skill and convincingness and individual stamp when, for the whole of my career, I could have gone ahead and carved as I chose, obligated to nothing at all since (and this was the nub of the whole thing) gods are only too willing to accept all versions of themselves. Their power consists, in part, anyway, in their being willing to swallow all ideas their being alive brings into being. Hatred, envy, contempt, slander, mockery, all these are grist to the mill of any self-respecting god. Your god is not there to be *liked*, sucked-up to, made great through human attention. "Your god, Oswald Beautiful Badger Going Over The Hill," I had begun to tell him in a loud voice reminiscent of my father, who always set the dogs barking, "is not a flirt or a weakling, oh no, he devours his reputation with unpicky relish." We are the fusspots, preferring this to that, whereas your god is willing to let anything happen because, well, say this even louder: It is the nature of gods to be in the vicinity of whatever is going on, not involved or responsible, but aloof in a kind of half-asleep vague musing endless delay in which, having neither to eat nor drink, they chew on ideas like someone nibbling on a flower stalk or those gifted loungers who (you can watch them do it) so relax and blur their eyes when they look at you that they both see and don't see you in front of them, a few colors, maybe, a rough shape, but no more than that, and that is all the

attention they will give you. Shall we say that they can no more bear
to attend than they can bear to look away. They notice everything,
but they remember nothing (say this quietly, whisper it into the ear
of a tree only). With the gods you can always start again, so it is no
use worrying about what sort of figure you cut in front of them, but
merely being yourself, which means you have enormous scope beyond blame or accuracy. "Of course you do, Nephew, and all these
do's and don'ts from within the tribe are as so much unleavened
cloud. Like a blindness diminishing it is becoming clear to me now
that, because of the limited converse with gods permitted us, the converse held with yourself is all there is, even if it amounts to no more
than walking barefoot in a yard of broken glass. It is your one and
only thing, subject to no laws and no norms, a private muddled mut-
ter in a hairy ear as big as Arizona. So: if I wished, I might as well go
ahead and paint my Sotuqnangu all wrong, making of it as big a mess
as possible because, truth told, there would be no one alive anywhere
who made that exact mess of it." And I did, I made the mess: instead
of painting with a steady hand the curly white lines on the pale blue
of the chest, the sawteeth in black on the white of the kilt, the twin
pyramids of black dots that make the eyebrows, the complicated diamonds and brackets on the sash, the white welts on the brown moccasins, the orange and green slant markings on the belt, instead of all
this I free-handedly daubed and lined, making such a mess as made
Oswald Beautiful Badger Going Over The Hill whistle in astonishment, urging me to stop, at least to let it dry, and then he would
sandpaper the whole thing and we would start again, my hand guided
by his as if I were a blundering stallion's penis. Then I laid down the
brush and began to mold or knead the god, sometimes with a twisting
motion, sometimes drawing the doll with one hand through the loop
made by the other's fingers curled, sometimes beginning at the middle (the sash) and drawing either hand away until the doll actually fell
into the dirt and sand, coming up gritty and with, to a legally blind
man, dark textures against my thumb. "Give this a chance to dry and
set," I told him, "and I will have a wonderful grip of my doll, it will
never slide free again, I will be able to grip it while adding the one
hundredth coat of paint until it is too fat with pigment to go through
my hand anymore. Only when," I told him, "your doll is too big to be
handled at all, is it godlike enough. Which means," I said, "applying
enough paint to make it more than man-sized, easily a lifetime's
chore." They found me interesting, a *character*, when I went off like

this, excited by my new idea, I who had not had an idea in ten years, and this abrupt rustle of clothes, this cluck of giggles and ah's, was something I could soon get used to, indeed something I might need in the worst way of the addict. I had no idea what my doll was like. It would be finished only when I tired of it since, and keep this down to a whisper, it no longer corresponded to anything known. It stood for itself, and only in a distant sense for me, who with no doubt ugly hands would have to hold it to the feeble sun until it dried or froze. Oh me! He keeps talking past me, as it were, to other ears. Who is he talking to? Sometimes he addresses me direct, sometimes he seems to be humming to himself, or humming at me, it is hard to tell, yet I do believe, if I listen carefully enough, I can begin to figure out what his humming says, and when he switches from humming at me to humming for himself, but there is always the chance that in thinking I am picking up his thoughts I am only inventing thoughts of my own. As always, caught between fawning on him and giving him spunky devotion, I end up caring not so much what he thinks as how he came to think it. How he comes to. I was a lover once. I bungled it. I was a lover beginning to come on strong, which is like saying I said my prayers amid the steam and suet of the abattoir. Oh yes. I had begun to feel something like desireless affection in the heart of all that slime. And she liked me, maybe more than just a little. Yet we went on with it. Why not? We had something they couldn't touch, although in the other sense they could. It was, for me, like keeping my mind on something impossibly far away, in Orion or the Pleiades, and none of them cared about it or knew. As for her, I never said a thing outright, but she could tell from my expression. If only we had stopped in time, but somebody had wound us up and we had to run down.

George

You can tell I am not a pill-taking man, although to say that isn't much use as a description of how I am. There are so many things I am not anymore. No, but those I was, whereas I never took pills. You do not so much come into this world as this world comes into you. You stay yourself pretty much. I would never have gone to Hollywood either. Imagine, taking an airplane ride to a place in which you pretend to be someone else while someone else takes pictures of you doing it. It doesn't add up. You could lose who you are, and the one who pretended would be different from the one who spent the money they paid out. Once, trying to start to get to sleep, I felt a sharpness at my side, and I said oh another bit of rock stuck there, how did that get in? When I felt, it was prickly and crisp, and when I looked it was a bee. It felt very different from me, not part of me. I didn't want any bee sleeping alongside me. It didn't sting, though. It was just having bad luck that I was not a hive or a flower. "Suck me, bee, you get a mouthful of dry dust." No bees go to Hollywood, of course, but they could. Who would they be then? I sometimes think there are two worlds, one pretend and the other not. And those in the pretend world are there because they do not like the other. Well, those in the other do not like the pretend. "Do they tell you what to say," I asked my nephew. "George The Place In Flowers Where Pollen Rests," he said, "you know very well they give me lines. Otherwise they'd have no control. You don't say whatever comes into your head. If you did, no one else would know what to say. They plan these things." "They could make it up as they went along," I said. "It would be more natural. Who cares, anyway, what folk say? What matters is how they look after their crops, how they carve their wood, if they observe the rituals. Abide by them, I mean. If being alive makes you tremble, that's enough, Nephew, surely. You do not have to say any bigger thank-you than that. When dead, you do not tremble. It is a difference worth many books." But he was not listening, he was always ahead of my talk, knowing what I'd say and so scampering ahead like a puppy. Even now, he is always answering, if he answers, to what he thinks I might have said. It makes our conversations over the wood, the paint, not a very good fit. I say chicken, and he thinks I said beef, so he answers beef, and then I have to deal with what I didn't say, but I can only do this by mentioning beef, and this convinces him I began with beef in the first place. We are never up to date on each other. Or it would be more true to say he is up to date on my sickness, but he can watch that like a cloud coming over, it doesn't take much willingness to listen. Pills, airplane, stuff like that is what he thinks I need. Then, one day, he comes with a rustling paper bag. He has been to the drugstore in Phoenix. "Uncle," he sighs, "there is more than one drugstore in Phoenix. It doesn't matter, *truly.*" I feel at the thing he's brought, it might have cost him a year's pay. You never know when he tells you something like that, you have nothing to test it against. Something cold and hard is all I feel. "*Plastic,*" he says. "And that is a liquid," I tell him, "that sets hard like paint or primer." "A bit," he says. "This is called a blood pressure machine. You switch it on, wait awhile, and then it reads your pulse and your blood pressure. After a while, out comes a little ticket that says what the numbers are." I ask him what numbers, but he says that is for doctors to worry about. All I have to do is slip the cuff over my arm and flip the switch. Then it goes peep. Then it reads what is going on in your arm and your insides. It goes fast or slow, peep   peep, or peeppeeppeep, but sometimes it says peep   peeppeeppeep   peep   peep. Nothing steady in there. Like it has a broken leg, whatever it is. "What *is* this blood pressure," I ask him. "How does it press? What does it press against?

Is every person different?" "Depending on how worked up you are,"
he tells me. "This thing measures it real fast." "Then, Oswald Beautiful Badger Going Over The Hill, it always says the same. I could put
the cuff on once a year." "No, Uncle, it changes all the time." "Then
what," I ask him, "is the use of reading it?" He ignores that, and
explains how when you flip the switch it pumps up the cuff with air,
like you had a balloon around your arm. Tight. So we try it. I switch
on. It goes peep peep peep, like it was speaking to you: Hi, George
The Place In Flowers Where Pollen Rests, how's your blood today? I
am going to answer but the little engine inside starts chugging away
to blow up the cuff with air. And it is tight. I like the smooth rubber
tube the air comes through. I hope no one ever cuts the tube. Then
the chugging stops and I can hear some sort of whirring. "It is slowly
letting the air out so it can read your pressure," he says. I hear him
and wonder, but what use is it to say *how* when he knows so much
about it all? "Listen to the peeps of your heart," he says. "It sure
sounds all over over the place," I tell him. "I am scared. This cuff is
kind of rough." "Velcro," he says. "It catches against itself. No fasten-
ers, no buttons. You do not need to alter it. It stays the same for your
arm once you've adjusted it." "How come," I ask him, "it reads my
pressure in silence but does the other thing, the heartbeat, with so
much noise? How come?" He is not in the mood for that kind of
thing. *"When,"* he says, "it is quiet it is relaxing, the air is going out of
it. When you hear it, it is playing your heartbeat back to you for a
minute." "Sure," I tell him. "It starts with a peep-peep-peep and it
ends with one. That has nothing to do with me?" *"No,"* he says, *"and
it will switch itself off if you forget to, and I know you're going to."* I tell
him that, if the machine is so clever, why doesn't it carve a kachina
doll or two to save me the trouble? No answer. Oswald Beautiful
Badger Going Over The Hill doesn't mess with what doesn't count.
"You do this, Uncle, several times a day, and I will collect the little
tickets and take them to Keams Canyon." He sounds annoyed, not so
much with me as it. Maybe it comes from having to deal with all
those folk in Hollywood pretending to be who they are not. He
thinks the machine is a bit like him, maybe. How would you feel, I
say to him, if you could only hear it, like me? It is like having a bird in
your lap. Only the same one song. It will die. "It will not," he says,
"it has batteries. Every month I will replace them." "You can pay for
all this," I ask him. He can. He is going to be in some musical. "Does
that mean," I begin to say, "they don't always have music? How can

you have dances without music?" "They don't always have dances, anyway," he says, "and it is not the kind of music you are thinking about." "Jazz?" I ask him this, feeling I am doing all right, knowing the exact kind of music they might have, but he sighs and says jazz went out before he was born. "You are a musical Indian, then," I tell him. "This here thing is a musical box. How hard and cool it feels, and you don't need to wind it up like those little boxes at the trading post. I never thought I would see kachinas that wound up to play music, but they had them way back when I could see." This is not one of my nephew's best days, I can tell that from his voice, all hoarse and bottled up. "Keep it by you," he says. "Don't let it fall, it will break. And don't mess with the back. Here, feel it? Or the batteries will fall out and it won't be any use." "You sometimes," I tell him, "sound like an old gringo. I know about batteries and things. All I do is start it up. It will switch itself off. It reads itself. I don't need to talk to it. It reads me deep down. Nephew, what a wonder you have brought me." "One hundred and sixty over one hundred," he says, "you haven't been taking your pills. And your heart is doing a fairly fast fib." "My heart is lying," I murmur. "How?" "It doesn't mean that," he says, "it means the beat is untidy, and too fast. Why don't you take your pills?" "I see," I tell him, "this thing is like some detective from Keams Canyon to check up on me. Have you also brought a machine to check on me to see if I am using the first machine?" "It is to help you," he says. "It is to help the doctor. We need to know, Uncle, what is going on in your insides. They aren't private anymore. We need to know. You are famous. Folk ask how you are. We want you to live forever." He says a lot more of the same kind of thing, but I don't listen. Nothing is sillier than trying to preserve a near goner whose time has almost come. It isn't natural. I guess I could spend the next twenty years with this thing alongside me in bed, and it could sing me to sleep. I could play it without using it. I must have said this aloud because he comes back at me fast, almost shouting. "No you won't, it won't play if it isn't on your arm. It has to have a heart to listen to." "My heart," I tell him, "I can hear it anyway, most of all when I put my head down at night. I don't need your machine for that. It goes boom all night, it almost shakes me out of bed. It wakes me up." "Well," he says, "it is either this, Uncle, or the monitor, that they put around your waist for twenty-four hours, and there is a heavy tape recorder attached to it." "I know," I tell him, "it makes a movie of whatever you do, and then they take it off. They glue those pads to your chest, and you sit there all wired up. I'll be just fine with this," I tell him in a hurry. "I don't want that other thing again. Will it pick up the ringing in my ears?" "Of course not," he says. "Uncle, you don't seem to know the difference between a tape recorder and a movie camera, or between them and a blood pressure machine. Machines are different, they are not all the one machine. If there was one machine that would do for everything, we'd use it. Somebody would have invented it by now." "Yes, they call it a woman," I tell him, but he just does not hear half of what I say to him. I can tell, he is getting ready to leave me alone with the peep-peep. When he is ready to go, his feet shuffle in his voice. It is like yellow lights going out in Tucson town. He is going away to be a musical Indian with lines made up for him and one of those fancy Hollywood women to collect the tickets from his blood pressure machine. "Tell you something," I say at my most troublesome, "if my heart goes too fast, this machine will give it a speeding ticket." "Or too slow, Uncle," he says. "Your heart will always get a ticket. A little roll will form. Leave it alone. Don't tear it off. I will see to them when I come through. We need them in the right order." He sure has my life planned for me. He will work me to death to save me. I have a patient, careful way of talking, but he rushes past that. I say things as gently as I can, but he has no time to pause and enjoy the waterfall of a worn-out voice. He wants me well so he can forget about me, and not have to pay for me. Then he will go and make movies out in the Pacific somewhere. As if, well, I forget. He didn't even say goodbye, and I can hear his pickup truck starting to go. He does not, like the few who have them, rev up the engine for half an hour, as if they were boasting about what they have. He does not say I am going to go now. He just goes. I myself was never good at going. Are *you?* If you are good at parting, then it means you are good at going away. No one ever wrote the words that would get me away from someone near and dear. They have to come from someone else. But I never went away that much. You are born to stay where you belong, watching the sun and the ground. Either one is a big enough chore for a kachina carver. I do not like being made to look away. Or that was how I felt when I could see. Now I do not like having to think away from what I have on my mind. I am somehow faithful to what's expected of me. I play the machine to see how it sounds in his absence. Three peeps. It is waiting for me to put my arm into the cuff. Not a sound. I do not move my arm, but I switch on anyway, and the cuff on my hands plumps up like one of those chubby hens you used to find squatting by the Little Colorado River. You couldn't get an arm into this cuff if you tried. It's all tight. Now it slackens and goes down. I did it wrong. If I keep on doing it wrong, maybe the machine will bite or sting. I will get one of those electric shocks they say are bad for the heart. I used to think that about the telephone, but it never did me any harm. So, to make a pleasant sound, I slip my arm into the cuff. Plenty of room now, like a bridle. Off we go. I hear myself, the little tune I make deep inside me. There is only an echo of this in my wrist. Now I have to restart the thing, it quit on me. Here we go again, peep-peep, nothing steady about it. It must have been the excitement. Now, if using the machine gets you all fired up, what good is the machine except to tell you are excited when you are? You know before you begin and can save the batteries from trying too hard. What did he call it? "Long fancy word," he said, "you do not ever need to know it, but it is what is printed on the front, not far from that little grille. The air comes out. *Fig*," is all I heard him say, and *fig* will do. I can sit up here in the wind and play my fig. And, when I carve, I can put it down right by my foot. The cuff could even go around my ankle. It's the same blood after all, the same heart. Count me up from head to toe, but I don't like the idea of it reading me and shooting out the little tickets I can never read. "Nephew," I say to him who is no longer here, "isn't there a model for the blind, with the print raised up in those little dots like that other test I took, when they pricked my arm and three days later the little bumps came up? Three of them. You filled out the card and mailed it and I didn't have TB. If only this machine had tickets like that card. You felt them all and marked your choice. Then I would know. It would be more private. If I was dead, the machine would not peep-peep at all. There is not a dead man it would pick up. You have to have the heartbeat going on within you, or it will not do its job. It can tell who is alive and who is not. It is almost worth taking the pills to hear the different noises it will make. One tune is not enough, which is why I could never stand music boxes." I speak thus from memory and other kinds of distances. When he comes back, the batteries will be dead and the roll of paper that makes the tickets will have come all the way out. Wind blowing it this way and that. I can feel it now, floppy and easy to tear. It says something about me they don't want me to know. Yet why have a toy and not play with it? I put it around my arm and carve. Peep peep. Everything goes fast when I carve, or even think of carving. What you live for works you up. So

does what you die for too. Fig it is. I'll try it. Did he really say his
name, out there, was Roy Rivers? Or was that someone else, another
musical Indian, with, I guess, no old kachina carver to fuss about. It is
hard to tell if he really went away when he went or for how long.
Maybe all he did was move away a yard or two, just to watch, or he
put somebody else in his place to keep the air from taking over the
space he was in, so's I'd feel that pressure from not far off. He said he
went away to make the movies, but all that could be just in his head.
When he'd been gone only a few minutes, he could come back and tell
me all about a movie he'd made months ago, and I'd be none the
wiser. I have acquired a distaste for time, so anything could be true.
The sleepy are given to making excuses, and the old don't exactly
write everything down copperplate in a little book, which is what
they made us do when they took us away to the Anglo school and
forced us to learn their language. That was the first time we saw
electricity. The streets were all lit up when we arrived that night. So
I ask him, on this or that visit, and he says that funny Hollywood-
type word, *Negatorio,* instead of simply saying No. He was away for a
week, in which time I did not carve an inch. I don't have to. Time
will cure us like old leather. When a water pot has done its time, you
knock the bottom out and use it as a chimney pot. After that, I don't
know, it must have a further use, maybe out in the fields to keep the
sun and wind off a crop. I think he, on the other hand, wrote things
down much of the time, egging me on to say this or that so he could
tell his smart friends in California. Or other members of the tribe.
"Folk always want information," he tells me. "They want to know
how things work, the whole damn universe. They don't want to
know how other folk feel about it. You get on the Ameche and they
ask how you are, but they really want you to tell them how to make a
pile of dough." Oswald does this, from time to time, using an out-of-
town word (as he calls it) to say something quite simple, although if I
used the telephone as much as he does I too would have a pet name
for it. "George The Place In Flowers Where Pollen Rests," he says,
"there was an actor called Don Ameche, who played the inventor of
the telephone in a movie, and that is how the telephone got that
name." He seems to know, but I never heard that name before except
from him. He is always willing to explain what he explained only
yesterday, so I guess he is mighty patient. "I could have been a star,"
he tells me, "if only I had gone to Hollywood earlier, and not had to
keep on coming back here, I'd have been able to put you in a fancy

home in Beverly Hills, with a pool and lots of guys to look after you, even one of those recliner beds that vibrate, but it's too late now. All I ever had was a one-way ticket to Palookaville. Bit parts. Hand-to-mouth stuff. Go when they wanted me. Long layoffs in between."
"All you are, you're telling me," I say, "is a musical Indian. That is something. It isn't nothing. It's kind of an honor, isn't it?" He seems to disagree, so I tell him, to make him feel better, about the bad old days when you started at the south side of your field and worked your way north, or from west to east. I recollect someone having begun north to south, or east to west, but he was stopped and made to start again. You had to do things right. You dug with a greasewood stick and carried seeds in a bag. There was hardly any water except from rainfall, so you had to shield your plants as much as you could from the sun, with windbreaks made from rabbit brush, dried out and arranged on the sand to keep it from drifting away. Now they use plastic, tin cans, and that funny tile you can't hear through. Just about the only job I had then was to stand in the field and throw rocks at the crows. I was a carver even then, not much use for planting crops. In those days we had sheep as well. We even used the sheeps' brains to cure the *piiki* stones we cooked the bread with. We wasted nothing. Nowadays, if you want a hunk of mutton, you have to trade with a Navajo. "Cheer up, Oswald Beautiful Badger Going Over The Hill," I tell him, "I too could have been a star farmer, with the best crops of corn and beans, chili and coxcomb, onions, sunflowers, but I became what I am going to die as. I would sooner have bottled bear farts than worked in the fields. I had to have both hands free, you see. It was no use even doing a simple job like watching the burro while it grazed. You curbed it with a hobble. I needed my hands free, you understand. So I guess I was something of an outcast, in my useful way. Many's the time your Mama has been up on the roof putting peaches and apricots to dry, and she's looked down at me carving right there in front of the door. 'Some folks are born lucky,' she'd call. 'All you do is sit and whittle. It would help if now and then you would put some white clay on the outside of the house instead of daubing wooden dolls with it.' 'But,' I told her, 'these are *kachinas*, there is nothing holier.' There I sat among the bunches of string beans that hung in the sun, the watermelons buried in the ground for storage, and the little coxcomb plants we dye things red with, and I knew, I knew in my bones, that this was the only thing worth doing lifelong. In a useful way, I was carving kachina dolls for little girls to

play with. It wasn't all religion, it was fun as well. There was magic in the cottonwood root. Out of the earth it came and I put another shape into it, in which it stayed. It's the kachinas who give the girls the dolls. A carver carves them, but the gift comes from those who live up in the San Francisco Mountains." None of this cheered him up much, he is far too broody I can tell. He is thinking about Palookaville and all the things he could have had. He has me, and the fact annoys him. I am not much of a catch. I am like a stack of blue corn that somebody has to turn over every few days so it will dry out all the way through. He comes and turns me over to dry me out. I am not going to resist. I am not going to climb up a pole ladder to get away from him. No, I am going to hold my hands out to him, through that green and snotlike mist, to reach for him even if he is a mile off and still coming toward me over the rocks, in his pickup or on his feet, kicking aside tin buckets, and brooms, and washboards, enamel basins and old cooking pots, just to get at me, not to throttle me, not yet, but to ask me what my favorite words are. You can't ask the dead, so he asks me now, calm as if he is grinding corn or making *piiki* bread from ashes and cornmeal batter. "My favorite word is the wail," I tell him. "The cry. The gasp. The death rattle." But he wants something else, so I keep him at bay by saying *Ahaliya*, uncle of the kachinas, and *ahselviki*, glue, and *chunta*, adultery. Any word I say is my favorite. When you are as dim as I am, any word you still have the strength to say aloud is an object of overpowering love. "I love them all," I tell him, "not just a few. It's all or nothing." I think he hears my cackle, my laugh with its broken back, but he gives no sign. He is going to ask again when I am not so tricky. I ought to set up as a professional listener, with a clock and a comfy chair. Like that nurse in Keams Canyon, fitting me out for the blood-in-the-bowels test. "You can take it off the paper, you don't have to go digging around." She gave me three little sticks. "I'll feel my way," I said, "now I know what to do. The blind have strong senses." Not that he was eager, my nephew offered to help, but I got a kid to go and rub them on a dog's droppings. Then I smeared it all over the inside of the little cardboard folder. It was not me, but maybe the dog they rushed off into hospital and cut him wide open to see what ailed him. I didn't want to spend the rest of my days with an unseen man's finger up my ass and my head over the latrine trench, trying to locate the right size of speci-men. Well, he listened good, and he said nothing back. They do. They write everything down, and you get that feeling that you are a criminal and the next thing you will get jail. For not taking your pills. For monkeying around with your fig or whatever the real name of it is. For faking your specimens. What a life. They look hard at your droppings and go home to a T-bone steak. We might have been filthy in the old days, before running water, when you had to collect up from puddles with a frypan, but we were never like that. But I do hear there is a pretty pattern in everything provided you stain it right and have a big enough magnifying glass. It has to be thin enough for the light to shine through it. *"Negatorio,"* he says, "it is more complicated than that." Poor nephew. I did not even know I was speaking to him, so he seems to have read my mind and answered it. Maybe, if you spend enough time in Hollywood, or on the Ameche, you can. "Uncle," he says, *"it isn't Hollywood anymore, it's Beverly Hills."* "Hollywood to me," I say. "What's it matter? I am not exactly going to mail them an application." It goes like this day after day, month after month, whether there is blue sky or not. And I can't fathom why the weather has nothing to do with it. We are not a crop, I guess. We do not grow like that. Now he is telling me that death must be bad because heaven and paradise are supposed to be so nice. I have no idea what he is talking about. We don't go to these Anglo places. "It's," I say, using his words, "more complicated than that, Nephew. We are already part of where we are going to go. We have no priests, we have no sabbath. If you have been really bad, you go on into the body of a coyote, but who believes that anymore? You just go on to new chores elsewhere. Only a child's soul can inhabit a dead body. Its own, I mean. To die is to wake up. Heaven and paradise are at Keams Canyon these days. Or Hollywood. Soft drinks and Sunday school. I have never understood why the Anglos divide things up so much. We live among kachinas all the time. That's enough. I guess there are pill givers and pulse takers in the spirit world too, otherwise how are the kachinas to stay healthy? All that is here is there." He doesn't say Negatorio, but I can see he believes in nothing at all, not even in this heaven or paradise of the Anglos. He believes in the next movie, and the captive eagle on his roof, a sign of how he will one day vanish in his pickup and have the life he should have had. When that happens, who will care for an old kachina carver? Maybe I won't be here at all. By then we'll all spend our days like the Anglos, watching movies of people driving cars. "Nephew," I tell him, "something has come to me. When these people in the other world watch people driving cars on TV, they don't seem to know the difference between what is on the screen and what their lives are like. Maybe they are astounded to see their kinds of lives on TV. Now, that is very like how we see things. There is no difference between life here and life in the spirit world. So, in that sense, we have TV. We have that principle." "Uncle," he says, "we have TV anyway, and your spirit world has nothing to do with it." "No," I persist, "the TV frame is an illusion. It seems to divide things off, but they are truly one and the same." He doesn't want to hear it, he wants to think there is a better place elsewhere, and he doesn't want this one and that to overlap. We are getting nowhere. I talk, I do not carve. A blind man, I can see too far, and that is what bothers him. "Nephew," I tell him, to win him back, "a doll covered with chisel scars is not more beautiful than the universe, of course not; but it is cut to our size, like the television." No, he is not buying that either, he wants me to say the one thing that will change his life forever, switch him from Palookaville to paradise, with a little wand in his hand, at the top of it a spinning celluloid propeller.

Oswald

Going his own way, as usual, he is full of salt and margarine. Doctors
are as meaningful to him as stockbrokers. A purist is what he is. He
wants the body to be an affable host to its deadly diseases. He wants
them to have a welcome, a space to move around in and show their
stuff. For some reason he believes in not getting in the way of things.
He doesn't wish to be a wall. He lives for the day, thinking along
some such lines as these: to get from day to day without even trying is
better than a week won by grand effort. Even his ailments he regards
as gifts given, trophies singled out to gift him with, and he takes a
certain pride in owning them, in their ownership of him. Parasite in
his way, he remains a host to them, fostering them through neglect.
There are phases in an uncle-nephew bond. When you have a thirty-
year difference, thanks to a child born late, you have the sweet impulsive time that is close to a father-son bond; I mean one of the good
variety. Twenty-five years later it has changed, neither wishing to be
the age he is. The nephew feels the term somehow makes an infant of
him still. The uncle wonders how ancient he has become if he has a
nephew already fully grown. It is a less happy thing than it was. You

say such things to him as: Being headstrong is okay, Uncle, so long as
the body holds together. He has this mummified look, not that he is
going to sleep for long, only half an hour at most. Doze well, I half
say, wondering what his dreams are, if any. He comes and goes
among us, and his especial place in the landscape is going to look
brutally empty one of these days. Imagine: in that spot, no one else
has dared to sit or to doze for half a century. He has worn the wall
away with leaning against it. Lolling, rubbing one shoulder like a
horse against a tree. The ground beneath him caves in a little, like an
outsize hiphole such as campers make. He has sat the world into
shape, squirming and bracing, and he would rather doze here than
sleep inside. He cannot stand to be hemmed in, so at least his shavings
and wood chips have never irked a house-proud woman, such as his
Bessie never was anyway. She too was happier in her own element,
water rather than air, so neither of them spent much time indoors,
whatever the weather, finding walls got in between them and the
outdoors. Now Uncle comes to, murmurs a little, then sinks away
again. He dozes with tiny fits and starts, of course, almost doglike.
His hands are more active than when he's awake. The feet do not
move, encased in fleece. They say he has, at times, called out something close to "Sotuqnangu," but I have never heard this, nor do I
believe it. They are thinking wishfully. To him, the god is the god,
maybe to be thought of by name, but hardly even referred to in talk
except as the god, as if the god were some hated rival, a carver better
known. Uncle is one of those people, maybe many, whose information comes out of their own heads. Hence his notion of Palookaville,
but not, I am sad to say, his notion of my career in movies. How was
he ever to know exactly what kinds of movies I was making? A
raunchy side he may have, but nothing like the trash I played in the
last four or five years making low-budget stag to begin with, then
during my own version of an economic crash a stint with inflatables,
followed by action with humans again, all kinds, until now. I con-
sider myself retired, with no more checks to come. Up here you can
live on next to nothing, so long as you live according to nature, planting when the others do and reaping too. When I told him I'd like to
begin a career as a carver, I vaguely thought I'd be able to cut rough
dolls and endow them with novelty sexual organs; but this would
finish me on the mesa, I would have to emigrate to Phoenix or Tucson. But I wanted, still want, the mesa as a bolt hole, a place to heal
and come into my own again. Because I have posed, I tell myself, he

has had the pills he will not take, the doctors in Keams Canyon, the time strips, the EKGs, the warnings, the blood pressure kit, and the shortwave radio. A poor showing for so many years suffocating in my own scumbag, but better than being broke in Hollywood. After a while you get used to it. Far too strong a personality to be dealt with in the usual way, he snores while talking, blinks incessantly whether sleeping or not, and has the rumblingest stomach in Arizona. When he lectures me in that splintery, bullying fashion of his, what he means is that art is a ceremony interested in results. I once told him the story of a man whose job it was to guard a very valuable machine which he must never touch; so they put a dog there to keep him off the machine. "Now," I asked him, "who guards the dog?" Something wild in him missed the point of the story. He preferred, when he could see, to go to the little supermarket in Keams Canyon and set a cart off rolling downhill, crashing into the cars. That was him all over. I have seen him cuff a moth as if it had insulted him, murmuring, "Give me a hand until I'm dead. After that, you're free." Gone tomorrow, he used to say, without ever uttering its partner piece: Here today. He splits the world up and then never again brings the pieces together. Just because you suffer doesn't mean you're serious: that's the kind of thing he said at his best, but, as often as not, he'd brandish a wooden doll at me and tell me to sand it or apply the primer, he didn't care how I did it; he just wanted me very busy, a captive audience for his harangues.

George

My nephew's mind has been wandering, like someone heading southwest from the Three Mesas toward the Dinnebito Trading Post with only the Painted Desert between him and the San Francisco Mountains. I am what they call a whizz at geography, not that I have ever needed it. Maybe he is looking for Mormon Lake, which his aunt once swam across, stark naked, just to prove she could. She stood there in the shallows, braced her ripe young body in the sun, flung her mane of hair backward into a big bush, and stepped in. Eight hundred feet if it's an inch. And then she swam it back. Was there anyone's pickup she didn't borrow for the hundred-mile drive, as far as Flagstaff, and beyond? She had the strength, the staying power. If *she* had gone to Hollywood, she would have been running it within the year. What I do not tell him is that, although she was all muscle, it curved like fat, and her crease was always wet. She was always leaking sap, which was why all those fish came after her to lap it up while she swam across Mormon Lake. Strong enough to snap my neck, she was always ready. *Bait*, I used to call her. I could never resist. I never tried to. What else were we for, in those days at least. Her name was

Object Disappearing Over Flowers, and she was Bessie to my George. Oh, how her Bessie Bessied my George! More than, somehow, her Object Disappearing Over Flowers did for my Place In Flowers Where Pollen Rests. You can't have what the bees have. In short, she was *Syámtiwa* to my *Silena*, but, as I have learned from the Anglos, it is warming and nourishing to spread a name out and pluck out the heart of it. Spell it out in full. "Nothing makes my heart beat more than realizing, Nephew, how much the very name that sets you off from nature, and from others, is really the means of becoming everything around you. All you have to do is say your name, or hers, or yours I suppose, and at once you have a landscape, a whole array of lovely things to gladden the eye. She is all those things disappearing over flowers. I am the place in those selfsame flowers where pollen rests. And you, for all your Hollywood Palookaville, *are* a beautiful badger going over the hill, much better, isn't it, than a movie camera operating on the same principle as a trash bin? Sometimes, when I am most alone, I think I can see my pollen vanishing over her flower, *above* it, even as she swims that lake. Separate beings in the same fold of nature, differently named, but unsevered from what they live among, from glue to bear farts, from yellow rabbits to hot weather birds. Like some fabrics, Nephew, we are porous. Everything there is and has ever been pours through us and over us into our eyes and out of our mouths and into our ears and out of our pores. You tingle with it. There is nothing else, because everything is already included in what we are. It is like the jar with several openings, so you don't know which is the way in and which the way out. All ways are both ways. You asked about my favorite words. If I told you, they would add up to a poem, never mind how much you rearranged them. Each word, each name, happens to be a poem. One favorite I haven't told you about is *kuskuska*. See, you don't even know the word. It's old-fashioned, out of date. It means *lost*. Isn't that wonderful? We no longer need that word for lost." He grips my arm, squeezes my hand, muttering something about finders keepers, and I try him with something else, asking if he gets to kiss the stars in the movies he makes. "Do they let you? Do they ask you to, Nephew?" Now I have really gotten his goat. He gets to kiss nobody, he says, only—sometimes—to shoot an arrow through somebody, and that's faked of course. He rides, he scalps, he spies, he scouts, he drops from trees, he tortures, he smokes the pipe of peace, and he sometimes meets a squaw by a stream. Yet for this he makes a fortune, at least by the standards of his tribe, enough to keep me in pills and machines, tests and trips. I make my fig whirr and chug at him, but without the cuff on my arm, and he chides me for acting the fool. *"I'm sure glad,"* he says, *"I didn't bring no set of drums."* Then he seems to go, having put in a long day. His belly rumbles. You can tell that doing good for others isn't enough for him. He wants to be beautiful, like an object disappearing over flowers, and he never will. Hard as you try, you can't photograph a name. One thing is getting clearer, though. What he wants is to put a shape to his life, while I, I just want to get from this day to the next. Tomorrow is another year. He would like to put a little shape into my life too, I guess, well-meaning busybody that he is, except it's already got all the shape it's going to have. Time was when I worked hard at making my days add up to something, but even that was hardly a shape. It was just going about my business of carving dolls, more a way of making each hour meaningful than anything overall. That's the difference. If you make things like dolls, you kind of limp along from hour to hour, with not much else in mind, and after a while you get used to that rhythm. You're like the corn rattling in the mesa wind. You don't so much intend to change the world by pushing your own shape at it as you alter it with your thoughts and prayers. Nobody could tell the difference, but things around you change all the time, depending on how you think of them inside you. I have always been much the same as little girls playing with dolls cut from bone, a kind of useful fidget, but even children have more intent in them than I ever did. Nowadays they have the TV to play with, recliner chairs, and that funny colorful puzzle cube you have to rearrange. Just as long as my last breath turns into a cloud, and so into a kachina, I don't much care. Now, you would hardly call that an ambition, but it will do me, one who has just about outstayed his welcome. It figures. When I was born, they kept me in the dark for twenty days with a pinch of corn in my mouth. It was aunts who did that. Then they gave me a name at dawn as they held my face up to the rising sun. So you don't have to worry about the direction you'll take. The direction has already been decided. I was given to the sun to nourish and it has done its job. More or less, I've done mine too, not counting a few curses here, a little meddling with women on the side. "Nephew," I keep trying to tell him, "there is no need to run off to Hollywood, Palookaville, or any other place. There are cycles inside cycles. There have been three worlds before this. This is only the fourth. Ease up. Tune in with nature. Don't try to force things." But he wants to

make a name for himself, and, if he ever does, he will not be Oswald
Beautiful Badger Going Over The Hill, but, so he tells me, Walt
Badge, or something ever worse. They have no patience out there
with long names. Everybody is Joe or Al, they have no Josephs, no
Alberts. Oz or Walt he is allowed to be, but even those are a bit out of
the way. Two syllables you get, and then you have to hurry by.
Maybe it's just as well. Insisting on a name is kind of nervous. The
ground knows who you are, and how you feel about putting your foot
down. Either you walk on it heedlessly, or you don't, and if you don't
you are glad it is there to hold you up. You could go right through.
You never asked it to do anything for you, and it goes on holding you
up as long as you last. To walk, and then to lie down. Oswald, now,
something haunts him, you can hardly tell what, but it burns away
inside of him, making him want stuff, whole crates of it shipped in
from the California coast, maybe to prove to himself that he exists.
Maybe he doesn't. It is not given to everyone to exist, but only to be
a shadow without an object casting it. A something. He knows a man
who travels everywhere collecting bits of famous buildings. He chips
a bit off each and labels it. I am surprised they let him do it, he might
bring it crashing down. If he were pious it would be different. He'd
be saying a short prayer to the building as if it were some animal, and
then the building might let him chip it some. If your heart is right, a
snake will not harm you when you handle it. Plants are different, but
even a plant you have to sprinkle with a bit of sacred meal before you
cut it off or dig it up. Maybe the famous building man would sprinkle
a little mortar dust on the bit he's going to chip. You should never
behave with the world as if you aren't in it. Nephew said they were
going to put him in a new movie soon, about an Indian, but not an
American Indian, no sir. This is a queen or a princess who for years
has been living at the railroad station. Then she moves to a run-down
house in the jungle, with hyenas and bats all around it, and her children too. It was an old hunting lodge, with lots of wide verandas. So
there are peacocks and sometimes riders from what they call a polo
club, which happens to be close. They chase a ball with mallets while
sitting on horses. There is no water or electricity, so I kind of like this
movie already. The princess's servants have to ride their bicycles to
where the water is, half a mile or so, and Oswald Beautiful Badger
Going Over The Hill is one of them. One kind of Indian dressed up
as another. Maybe it is a musical. No, that is unlikely because this
princess has a dozen savage dogs that bark all day. So they have broke-

down tables with fancy crystal on them, which she has saved from
better days. She gives what they call audience, on a raised platform.
Her guests take their shoes off and sit on an old expensive carpet. The
princess never talks to anyone direct, she always talks through one of
her children. They call this, Oswald says, the royal refrain, though I
thought that was some kind of song. She says the government had
promised to fix up the house in the forest before she moved in, but
they forgot, so she moved in anyway, she was tired of living in the
railroad station after eleven years. What happens then, I have no idea,
but my nephew says a handsome explorer, a polo player, arrives one
day and helps her to fix things up, and then they get elephants and
start an ice factory. His part in this movie is going to be small, it will
mainly be riding his bicycle and unloading water. He will have to
bow a lot too. But he will get the price of many washing machines for
so little work. "Could they," I once asked him, "make a movie about a
layabout carver of kachina dolls? Who lives in a run-down house on
top of a mesa?" He said he would tell them, but I think he lied. He has
no say where he plays the part of a servant. He did not understand
me when I told him someone would have to stay and keep my place
for me. "You always have your place," he said. "No," I told him, "I
mean someone who will sit where I sit, stopping the air from filling
up my room. Who will keep the air out of my piece of space? I don't
think that is a very holy way of going on, but I don't care. Whether or
not you have shrunk a bit, or begun to stoop, you more or less always
push air out of the way of you for as long as you live. Even a corpse
does that. If you never existed, air would have that much more room
to move about in." When I said room, he thought I meant a room in
my house, but I meant my place in the air. You need somebody to sit
still for you in just the same way you sit still, until you come back.
That would be some kind of place saver. When he comes back I am
going to tell him the old story about the Jimson weed girls and how
they all had teeth where they shouldn't have, and what the young
men did. If he can tell me about a jungle princess, I can tell him that
dirty story about the Jimson girls, and now I would alter it just a bit
to suit my taste. They would never be allowed to make a movie of
something as crude as that, but if they did my nephew could play the
part of a boy and so get himself Jimsonized. Most of the movies I hear
about have to do with killing and sex, so that would be all right. They
would still shrink from the crudest parts, though. It could never be
on TV. It would have to be shown in some football arena with armed

guards. Or a drive-in like the one I saw in Tucson. They sit in their cars. They eat in their cars. They fuck in their cars. They listen to the radio in their cars. They have themselves buried in their cars, some do. It is easier, I guess, than being buried in your house, which would need a much bigger hole and be awkward for those left behind. I myself could be quite a spectacle. A blind man takes his own blood pressure. A blind man carves a cottonwood root. A blind man takes his pills, telling one from the other by feel. A man going blind flies weeping through the Grand Canyon. My life is full of things to photograph, I am surprised they haven't gotten to me already. I would not act, I would just be me. See me carve and cut my hand right off. Telling the Jimsonweed story, which always gives you that old feeling of importance. They listen while they look away and pretend to be figuring out the price of mutton. It is awful when your hands lose their busyness. They were not meant to lie in a lap, not their owner's lap anyway. But lie they do, like weary burros. I have not carved, or painted, since I don't know when. It was to be a Sotuqnangu, god of gods, the master of all ceremonies, but I let him get away from me. Rummage around. Where can he have rushed off to in his godlike way? He was wet and we had to let him dry. I had mussed up his paint. I was going to do him again with no guidance whatever from nephews. Here he is, at my feet, drying on his end. Dry. Sandpaper in my pocket. I rub him smooth again and ready to repaint. Odd, he doesn't feel like he did, so maybe Oswald Beautiful Badger Going Over The Hill has done him a favor or two with chisel and rasp, learning the trade while ruining his uncle's handiwork. The dust makes me sneeze. But the wood warms from the rubbing. By now the paint must be fading, this is a coarse sandpaper in my hand. Get the cracks. Feel for those bits you're bound to miss. Feel for the thicker parts where the paint has pooled. Get those. Smooth them out. Even out the ridge. Check for blebs. First rough, then gentler. I have spent most of my life doing this, not blind, oh no, but doing something until it feels perfect. When you can't just look, you feel a dozen times more than you need to, with your eyes prickling from the pointless effort to see. They always try. They wear themselves out trying to do a dead job. They are not so much mine anymore as Sotuqnangu's, so he will forgive me. I'm still attending to him, and as if he were a fox or a head of corn he will know it. George The Place In Flowers Where Pollen Rests, he'll tell himself, is still trying to do his chores, helpless as a newborn foal. Well, he always had more skill than he needed, so all his being blind has done is to cut him down to the level of everybody else. Paint me, George, make me half human. Skip the primer, go to the blackslot eyes, the triangular gash that is my mouth. Paint my ears red. Paint my torso pale sky blue and then the wavy white lines I have to have to show clouds on the sky of my chest. At such a time as this, I George know Sotuqnangu creeps into my heart and whispers. As if telling a dirty story that no one else can bear to hear. And the story might kill you, it is so savage and dreadful, it has no start and no end and no stop, in other words a roundabout story with no subject and no human touch. "Paint me, with the last shake of your hand, George," he whispers. "I am watching you. Any moment I can snatch you off. Paint it well. You have made a mess of the sandpaper work. Now botch the colors. Be as human as ever. Soon we will plug your nose and mouth, your ears and anus, and then we will paint you in the colors you deserve, first of all, though, sanding you rough until the skin has gone, and then we will apply paint to the raw flesh of you. It soaks in fast and has to be done again and again. You will always be being painted, to make you presentable. If your heart had been as pure as pollen, and your life as sweet as honey, you would be better off than you are. You remember how a man challenges the kachinas to short races, not so much to win as to go fast? Then you remember what followed. If you lost, the kachinas could whip you with yucca, daub your face with ashes, cut off your hair, and in general make you look silly. For years your work has been crude and thick, the painting smudged, and now you dare to make a Sotuqnangu. Why, even when planting sweet corn in April, you left a shallow pit above the seeds to catch the sun's rays. Then you fitted small leaves of grass and twig windbreaks around each plant, or tin cans open at either end, and the cans worked better at keeping mice and worms away. Even that called for skill and care, and it was hardly the carving of a god." On he goes, but it is only George The Place In Flowers Where Pollen Rests talking to himself. You can imagine gods, but they do not show up like aunts and talk to you. Not when you want them to, not even when you do not want them to. You carve them into being and you watch your mouth. We came into this world through a hole found by a shrike. It might have been different. It was before cowboy boots and pickle jars. Or the mail-order catalog. Oh, George, why aren't you as good as you used to be? I hear these things, but all I do is rub spit into the newly sanded wood. I dare not paint it, with no nephew at hand. I could not even lay linoleum on a dirt floor or get into a pushing match with children. Before glass windows, there were selenite ones. Before George the helpless, there was George the capable, even when he was little, squatting on a sheet laid on the ground at the Sunday school picnic, with tin cups and tin plates, bread and corn to eat. I am in a dress with my hand against my mouth, palm outward, giggling or trying not to speak, backhanding the words. The Anglos gave us plows and cultivators then, but we had no horses. For bringing me to school, my father received lamps, axes, and hammers. They would give you almost anything to get you to do what they wanted. But that is not Sotuqnangu's way. For what he wants us to do, he gives nothing at all, not so much as a camp kettle or foolproof vision. You could not even run to the Zuni tribe to hide, who always took us in when there was fuss. So there is no way. The voice that is the god's voice but is really my own has nothing to sweeten the pills with. I am an honest fake. Even when lying to myself, I stick to the rules. It never occurs to me that, because the gods give us nothing, unlike the Anglos, the gods are not there. The rules do not allow them not to be there. It occurs to me now, just like that, as if Navajos have raided us or the smallpox has come back. The gods are our way of saying we do not know. *Negatorio*, as Oswald says, you can't even reach them on the Ameche. There, I've said it. I am still alive, more or less. It was not hard. It was too easy. Any fool can commit sacrilege, it's living up to it for the next fifty years that costs you. So, George, carve for the sake of carving. Paint to paint. Breathe to breathe. There's a charm in just going on from breath to breath. Maybe Palookaville isn't such a bad place after all. Would they leave an old blind man out in the weather for hours on end? They would run their cars over him if he took the trouble to lie down in the road. So George stays put, but willing to talk about moving on. It happens just like that. You are tasting a peach until the first misgiving dawns. Not once has a real living god come down from the mountains and removed a human from his kachina outfit. You'd think that, every half century or so, one of them would feel moved to come on down and interrupt the dances, just to show us we are on the right lines. To take some of the strain away. It never happens. It's all faith. I'm running out of faith, not in the universe but in the ghosts that run it. It's like a big lunch counter. You serve yourself all the time, and leave your money. The money piles up and no one removes it. We keep on pro- viding bread and frankfurters, which we then sell to ourselves. And nothing ever happens. The place never closes, the money stays put, the owner never shows. Is it kind or cruel that I only get to think this now? Having put him down, to cool me off rather than him, I feel for him again, to rub across my mouth or to pat against the palm of my hand, but he isn't there, and instead my hand finds another hand, a warm and well-fed one, which can only be the hand of Sotuqnangu come to get me. I am to be throttled one-handed by a god. The hand moves upon mine, then holds it, lifts it up, settles it in my lap as I hear more than usual bird sound, and the wind fluffs my eyelashes like there was snow beginning to come. Into my hand comes the bare wooden doll, ready to explode or plunge through my belly on its way back to the San Francisco Mountains. Then I smell the aftershave. Only a musical Indian would use one he calls Canoe. "It's you," I say with a trembling catch in my voice. "You never went away. You've been here all along. No, you *must* have been away. How quietly you do both. You must have had a lot of practice in Hollywood. Who the hell put me to bed, fed me, saw that I kept myself clean?" "All of them," he says. "You don't remember. They do it so often, so quietly, that you sleep through the whole business of putting you to bed. And you wake so slowly that they have walked you out here before you know the sun is up and asking for you. Nuncle," he says, although I ask him not to say that word, it sounds so un-American, "do you recall the movie about the princess in the jungle in that weird old bat-infested house?" "The one that has no running water and no electricity," I say, "and all those crazy wild dogs and the old crystal on the rickety tables, with hyenas all night and the polo club nearby." "Yes, polo," he says, "in the acacia forest and the Persian rug and her name is the begum. Like raygun. It is near New Delhi, a long way from the railroad station. I asked them if I could make a few suggestions, such as letting me be one of the polo players too, and one of these guys, who really doesn't like Indians of any kind, shoves a polo mallet into my face and says, *Suck on that, you Ethiopian asshole*, and fires me as an extra. Then he hires me back, but just to ride bicycle and carry water. What do you make of that, bang in the middle of the twentieth century? They treat me like dirt just like that Gandhi I told you about." He pauses for breath. I do not recall this Gandhi much, but he must be starring in the movie. I tell him so. "Oswald Beautiful Badger Going Over The Hill, I remember the princess, the begum, but not this Gandhi. Now, who said this thing to you, and what is—" "Ee-thee-op-eyan," he says through his teeth, "which is to say that this asshole thinks I am black, the same as black." "I cannot see you," I tell my nephew, "have you changed color? And where is the kachina? I sanded it down and I am going to repaint it." "In your hand, Uncle," I hear, and then he says that long word again. "That's what he called me." "Well, suck on *what?*" I ask him. "Suck on nothing," he says, as if grieving, "it is an expression they have for musical Indians. It is an insult," he says. "They save it up. Hell, Uncle, here we are, you in your prime and me fast approaching grown-upness, and we can't get a respectful time of day from the Anglos." "Speak for yourself, Nephew," I tell him, "I'm not doing so bad. But I have news for you, nothing to do with respect. It came to me just now, though it could have been yesterday, that the gods have never really been there. There is no Sotuqnangu anymore. There never was." "Tell me news," he says. "I dropped that crap in grade school, Uncle. The real gods are over in California, and even if you pray to them, they serve you up on a platter, they call you asshole to your face and pretend to fire you." "Well, *be* fired," I tell him. Such rubbish to be fired from. But he has hopes, he tells me. He wants to be a polo player, in real life too. "What," I shout. "You want to mallet a ball from on horseback up here on the mesas?" I ask him about the doll in my hands. "It it ready to paint?" "It is ready to burn," he says. "It is just a lump of wood, Uncle. You would be better off without it. Here." He snatches what I then snatch back. He leaves it be. I tell him Sotuqnangu is watching him. *"He's back, huh?"* "Gods come and go," I tell him, according to the whims of the big-league kachina carvers. It is going to be a quarrel. He needs to get all that bad energy out of him. "Ethiopian," I begin, "Hollywood, negatorio, Palookaville, your world is crazy as that jungle movie. Why don't you plant yourself some corn, old style, then find a new eagle for your roof?" He just looks at me. "Who needs eagles?"

Oswald

How childlike sex is. Huffing and puffing so that your house won't fall down. Dangling it, wobbling it, thrusting it, wiping it off, oiling and powdering it while making myself available from behind. After a while, once the modesty has worn off, shredded and spat out, you end up doing it all by reflex, living in the spasm or even the fake spasm, perhaps even soldiering through by thinking about George The Place In Flowers Where Pollen Rests, and his infirmities, while barking, grimacing, quivering, assuming the face of outright distorted lust. I almost became its monk, paddling about in the mud while thinking about Mont Blanc. An acquired distaste has carried me this far, from bloodletting bondage and fist fucking to boot enslavement and toe sucking. Uncle George would have a fit, of one kind or another: disgust or envious delight, I am not sure which. I am not even sure that one of the last things I did, a drool saga called *The Wild Young*, in which sex-crazed girls attack the very bedposts, would not speak to the raunchy side of him: just so long as *he* didn't have to do it. As it is, I led a life full of rammed-out tongues, widespread cheeks, and coy combinations. When I look back on it, the several years, I see a tangle of snakes from old myths. Golden showers and enema sex with rubber clothes have been my bread and butter for just long enough to give me some kind of martyr complex, and I now have no sex drive at all, not in the personal way. I save it, or used to save it, for professional use. I used to imagine what the mesa would be like if they all got this stuff on their screens at night, with me identified, Oswald Beautiful Badger Going Over The Hill becoming Oswald Hideous Badger Going Over The Edge, and not even a badger anymore, but a billy goat. Would they stone me or forgive me? What would Uncle George do if he ever got more of this than the whiff he's already intercepted? Maybe he knows already, through sheer force of imagination, being not exactly a Pollyanna in these things. Educate a youth and drive out the decency. Maybe not: he is after all the local version of what used to be called a Bohemian. He's been around, he's gone down for the count, and he's come up for air. He's licked more than stamps if he's ever licked a stamp. I kept trim by working out in the sleaziest gyms in Los Angeles, and not only did I fake sexual ecstasy with the best of them, I stayed thin and muscular, although my lower joints ache as they never did and the muscles get more and more crystalline every day. I was a loin artist, in no way comparable to Uncle George, but an artist all the same, even if of the lowest stamp. He and I are different from the others, from the customers: we apply our energies to this or that, and then the product leaves us. Thank heaven it leaves us. Has he ever heard of Winnetou Seothoudt, Ulo Ying, or Viktor Molloch, Jr.? The D. W. Griffithses of our game. Will he ever actually see, and throw up at or be aroused by, *Harry Brown's Birds, Too Long To Be Human, Subway Sluts, The Ass Portfolio,* or *Death Orgy?* To my credit, I guess, I never knowingly got into porno snuff. I drew the line at murder, which sounds oddly old-fashioned when you have sunk as low as I. No, I am not hung like a posthole digger, but I have only bored people to death, I have never done it for real. There was just that one mistake, since when everything seems tame and ordinary, from bear snouts shoved into young girls to *vérité-* style nonmedical acupuncture, but the line I had drawn. No killing, Uncle, I'd say. I had never taken that godforsaken liberty. He would only ask if I meant Sotuqnangu by that, and pass on to his next reverie. The depravities going on in what he likes to sum up as Palookaville have no bearing in his fond dream of cottonwood root. Obscenity is not something he can carve; it is merely a noise off, to be attended to, if at all, after death itself. He has saved up all the irrelevances of living for some time in the afterlife, a sunny August afternoon when his hands are warm and his retired flesh develops an old quiver, to be close, to be stroked, to be tickled into a frenzy. It will be such a time when he wants his human envelope licked, and he will say to himself: Oswald Beautiful Badger Going Over The Hill was quite a beautiful badger after all, thinking his blind old uncle never noticed or favored him, whereas all along George The Place In Flowers Where Pollen Rests understood all the wildness that drives a man, including the wildness that comes from having no jingle in your pocket, no bulge in your billfold, and the only bulge you can spend is the one in your fly. Never, for the makers of porn, will there ever be enough holes or plugs. There will always be a permutation barrier akin to the speed of light, past which nothing can be done. After enough of it, the screen goes blank, and eroticism begins to repeat itself in a dappled bedlam amid which even the lubrications give out and the staghorn epic becomes a grinding chore. I can never tell Uncle these things, but I hope he imagines them. The distance between his blind vigil on the mesa and the semisordid motel room with the overused mattress minus its stain cape is something hardly graspable. That the two could be on the same planet, spawned by the same race, makes even my own eyes open wide. How could it be? Wasn't there some power prohibiting such violent contrasts? My uncle would answer no: whatever is possible is allowed. So why do I go to such lengths never to shock him, then? It must be because I want to fudge up an image of him purer than he can ever be. He is my lighthouse and I want him farther from the ocean than ever. I want him perfect, so as gladly to die for him. During the worst excesses of the sperm letting, I thought of him, and how what I was doing would see him through to the next week. All I have ever been, if I believe myself, is a goody-two-shoes in hell. Yet at first it was a novelty to find flesh laid out in front of me as familiar, as commonplace, as lettuce in a salad. Holes, puckers, prods, nozzles, globes, moons, blebs, globes, pears, boloneys, figs, and hair, hair, hair. Or stubble, stubble, stubble. Then there were the buzzing and shuddering "snakes," like slivers of crocodile hide, and so-called Reamer-Creamers, that looked like the center of some miniature jet engine. Two horny girls stall their car in order to be found by Big Jim and his black buddy. Mighty Meat invades a bubble bath and its occupant. The so-called plots melt together. The home-come sailor finds his wife and her playpet making it together in the sauna on a houseboat moored near a penitentiary, from which three lusty convicts escape, only to end up in a cowshed with milkmaids, who finally take them along to the sauna. It all takes organization, as I used to quip. Eventually you go dry, you get more kick from fondling a typewriter ribbon. Never have you seen such boredom as on the faces above the bright silk neckerchiefs, between the touch-of-finesse earrings. Girls with their mouths utterly bunged appear to be thinking about all the trains they've missed, while the men look on calmly like immigration inspectors. Only those over thirty appear to feel any enthusiasm for the poses, the contortions, the dragged-back flaps and the jissom trapped in cling film filched from a bakery. Hand Uncle George these penises and he would carve into them at once, hammering the crammed scrotum flat for a base, rounding out the peepee hole into a kachina's mouth. Never was brazenness so dull. But it was regular, and we joked among ourselves like office staff concerned all day with computer printouts, letters dictated, and conference calls about the installation of new plant. You would not think we dealt in sex at all. We dealt in sham, after the delighted licentiousness of the first week on the job wore off. It is amazing to have come out of it without scars or tattoos, old enough now to prize the contrast porno makes with these gentle-minded people living on a windy mesa. Back from the scuffling and the squirting to the life that sees beyond itself, its faces, its crops, its dolls, I am beginning to realize for the first time what our word *koyaanisqatsi*, or life out of kilter, really means. Out on the extreme edge of everything, George The Place In Flowers Where Pollen Rests is more in harmony with nature than any carver, or porn performer, who gives the public what it wants. One day, with luck, I will become as old and as aloof as he, spurning my pills and their boon. And anyone strangled or throttled by accident, not by me although I was part of the scene, will have blown away from my life like so much lamb's wool on the breeze rolling in from the Pacific full of wet.

George

I can tell night from day because night is colder, even in summer. Otherwise I might have no sense of when to sleep, except of course people come to fetch me and steer me toward whatever it is I ought to be doing. When you are blind, your mind limps even if your legs are good. You cannot go by the cooking smells because some meals take days to prepare, but when I hear laughter, the clatter of an oil drum lid, and the rattle-thud of corn as they shovel it into the baking pit, I know what is going on. They bake with herbs, and when the corn is ready someone will come, maybe at dawn with a flashlight in his mouth, to dig them out piping hot. There are other ways to burn your lip, but this is one of the best. What they bring me they have cooled by blowing on it, and I gnaw away without the usual exclamations of pain. Bread and margarine apart, I do not recall eating much, day to day, but surely they force a bit more into me than that. It is like being a child again, in sombrero and double-breasted suit, going to the Anglo school to learn from Mrs. Judson and Mrs. Holmes. In those days they fed you as if you were a slot. You ate without chewing. If they had somehow been able to cook the food into the shape of books, they would have rammed those into our mouths just like that. Eat and learn. We might have been foxes or moose. Somewhere in that jolly throng, my nephew is being himself, no longer bound to hear out a groaner like me. He has his life, he has his lives, and what he does for me is almost like a muscle twitch, he does not think too much about it. I guess he wouldn't sleep nights if he left me alone for days on end, both full of flour and sleepy, but I know how his mind travels while he sits with me. It is just possible that he needs me as much as I need him. He needs to get things off his chest once in a while. He is a salmon swimming across stream, so as neither to breed nor return to the sea. Every now and then in human history, someone has to do just that, not just avoiding the customary way, but avoiding them all, and trying to carve a new kind of kachina, at any rate old kachinas with new style to them. To us he is not so much an actor as a man of the world, at home in banks and doctors' offices and the eating places of the rich. Libraries, rest rooms, bus stations, post offices where you take a number and go sit down to read. You can take the man from the mesa all right, but can you get the mesa out of the man? No doubt not, but Oswald is brave enough to try. They will no doubt kill him with worry, but he will have a more exciting life than he would up here in the wind, a good place to carve if you want to carve, but we do not make many movies here, we just listen to ourselves in the act of existing. It is quite a skill. Even in the desert, it is not quiet enough for that. You have to tune out the desert sounds in order to hear yourself. You have to blot out the droning of the wind, the calm birds and the frisky ones, the whine and twitter of insects, those tiny scatters in the sand which tell you some creature is on the move. It is not just listening to yourself, there isn't that much to hear. It's more like using the wrong senses on things, almost hearing what you see, almost seeing what you feel. Not dividing up into sight and touch, hearing and smell. Some things you become aware of only if you have gone without sleep for days. Others come to you only if you have slept too much. Maybe only in the desert can you truly enjoy a fish. Only in the middle of the westward water that keeps on rolling can you truly enjoy the prairie dog. To love life as you should, you have to be dead. Maybe this is why Oswald went to Hollywood, so as to prize his home village all the more. Nothing can exist without being next to something else, so he who lives successfully will have a certain next-door-mindedness that, far from leading him on wild-goose chases, endears everything more and more to him. There is always an adorable thing beyond the one you're looking at. That is nature's way. Unpeelable. Always another layer. Over the horizon, forever something else ignoring you or coming toward you as itself. He comes home tired from carrying water and riding a bicycle too small for him. What a strange punishment to force on one so willing. He has poor luck with bicycles. He could tell that he just had the job because no one else would take it. "Fix your mind," I say, "on the eagles banking over us, not the ones on the roofs. Think of a canoe crossing a lake surface that no human hand has touched in a hundred years. Think of that wake, of the bow gliding through." "The movie's over and done with," he says sheepishly. "For me anyway. They shoot your part all in one go, see. Then cut it up and spread it out all through the movie." "That's bad medicine. It must feel like being taken to pieces," I tell him. "You never see the finished kachina." *"Ethiopian assholes never do,"* he says with a sad twist in his voice. "It is all bits and pieces, but it is still a better living than . . . well, it's a living." "Than carving dolls, you mean?" "No," he answers, "I was thinking about farming, planting. Carving okay but not farming, planting, not sheltering them." "What you need, Nephew, is a dose of the Jimsonweed girls, told as they told it in the old days, before Sunday schools. Could they ever make a movie of that? I asked that once before, didn't I? Then, next time you to go Palookaville, you will know something they don't, something even our people are beginning to forget. What is a tribe without its dirty stories?" He might be smiling at this. Certainly there is a leaven of cheer in his voice. An old kachina carver can soothe him even now. "Well," I begin, "it all happened longer ago than anyone can say, but not an eternity ago, as you can tell by the up-to-date references you have to make in telling it. *Aliksa'i.* I forgot," I tell him. "You say that as you are about to begin. The Jimson weed has large, trumpet-shaped white flowers, as I'm sure you know. It doesn't smell too good, and some say that you only have to touch it and it begins to take over your mind. Once upon a time they were living in Oraibi, never mind who they were. A story such as this needs a *they* to begin with. It was long ago when this youth, whose name has not come down to us, heard that a herb gathering would soon take place. Should I go, he asked his parents. Please yourself, they told him. You might enjoy it, as a young single fellow might. There is nothing to tie you down. That is what his parents told him, and he was in the habit of hearing them tell him a lot. You might call such a young man mother-bound, or housebound. Early

the next day, the girls and young men set off without him, but he ran
after them. Unfortunately, when he arrived at the southern edge of
the mesa, no one was there, and he almost turned back. He wanted to
watch his mother making pottery. As it was, he started downhill after
the herb gatherers and soon saw someone ahead of him, although no
one he knew. It turned out to be a beautiful girl, who also had
thought of not going but had changed her mind and was trying to
catch up with the others. So we're both late, he said, and she sug-
gested that they walk along together, which they did until they found
the main group, sorting through their finds, and getting ready to have
lunch, after which everyone started for home again, but the two of
them lagged behind, picking herbs and edible greens. Then they
raced to catch up and found the others already at the foot of the mesa.
Notice now what the girl says. She has to be watched at this point."
"Why," asks Oswald Beautiful Badger Going Over The Hill, "why
watch her now?" "Because," I tell him, "man is at best only wicked,
whereas woman is base. A true man wants two things mainly, danger
and play. In a woman he finds them both in the form of a dangerous
plaything. No, Nephew, wait. The time for interruptions comes
later. The two of them decide to take a rest while the others walk
upward to the top of the mesa. After their rest, they too begin the
long climb to the Oraibi plateau, but the girl says, Come this way
instead. I live here. Now they came to a terrace, at the foot of which
there was a big overhang with, inside the base, a plentiful crop of
Jimsonweed. Made to feel at home, he saw that all the people in that
dwelling were girls, and very attractive too. They fed him and argued
over him while he ate, each wanting to be the first to go to bed with
him. Now the story becomes very coarse. Would you tell those people
who are pushing forward to sit down, they are making too much
noise? The finer points, if there are any, will be lost. There followed
one of those sudden exchanges that can ruin a lifetime, even if the
words said amount to precious little: words like *I'm first, then*, and
First for what, and *What do you mean*, and *I just wanted a meal*, and *It is
too dark for you to leave now*, and *You will have to stay the night with us*. Do
not forget that this youth was something of a mama's boy and needed
some schooling in worldly ways. Such schooling he was soon to get,
little realizing that, if a story depends on you for its finish, you have
to remain within the story, there is no honorable way out. Some
people have no life outside the stories they become famous in. So it
was with this youth, who tried to leave but could not find the door,

any door. Now the girls made the beds, with a big show of patting and smoothing, they wanted everything to look inviting and just like home. After they had tucked him in, with well-behaved kisses for good night, he fell asleep, he was worn out. He slept soundly until he felt another body in the bed, and it was the girl who had brought him here, whispering the famous words you never hear in the Anglo Sunday schools: *Um as nuy tsopni,* Please fuck me. Not a move did he make, he had never heard anything like it, not even between his mother and father, but the girl climbed on top of him, she being wet and agile and full of good edible greens. Then she left him, but another took her place, urging him and trying to tease his manhood until he could think of doing nothing else. Woman is base, remember, and should be curbed. So, this time he was on top, like an eagle on a roof, on almost any nephew's roof, where I suppose it has to play with itself all day long. One after another they all came and fucked him until he hardly remembered who he was. He had heard about this thing, and it was supposed to hurt the woman only, but all these girls had teeth between their lower lips, and, as they raked him about, he began to stream with blood, although the raking set him on his mettle, made him fiercer and stronger for all the pain, for as we know pain is a great love potion. I'm going to faint, he told them, I have fucked you in the teeth until I have no manhood left. Let me go home. Only if you do me again first, said one. *Home,* he pleaded. Only afterward, said this nibbling hussy, I really need it once more, life in here is boring, we don't often get visitors so well hung. So he did it again with her, in extreme pain. Now they showed him how to find the door, in the eastern base of the wall, and he walked out into the dawn. Who are you, he said from a safe distance, and they told him they were the Jimsonweed girls. Somebody should explain at this point, I will do it, I seem to have enjoyed the hot corn from the baking pit, that because all this took place in the dark it was possible that the girls, not out of spite so much as out of a desire for novelty, had wriggled around and put their mouths where he thought their loins were. Had he known, he would have gone about things more carefully, you can do such things only with the oldest hag, who of course always has one fang in the way, so best go equipped with a small hammer to trim her before the Jimsonweed game begins. This story is bad enough, and I hope there are no children listening. You people steal up on me like ants. How can I watch my mouth when my eyes are dead? We are now at the moment when the youth explains that he spent the night elsewhere because it was dark and he was too tired. Is that the only reason you didn't show up last night? They do not trust him, they want very much to deflower him themselves, but the moment has not arrived and it never will. We are now at the point—well, he tells the other youths that they had better start to carve some penises for themselves, cottonwood root of course, and this is to say that, although they recognized this only dimly, they needed some armless kachinas to go and get their own back with. Or his own back with their help. The chisels and knives flew and a whole array of different sizes began to see the light, long and thin, short and fat, piglike ones and floppy ones. Use your wooden penises first, he told them, and then you can fuck them in the usual way later. This sounded like good double value to the youths, who were already feeling more than ready. One was trying to carry a log that was too heavy for him, so he left it behind to split. That night they went to the Jimsonweed girls and ground away on them with their wooden penises. There was soon nothing but sawdust in the beds, and the girls' teeth were ground down to stumps, which meant it was all right for them to use their own penises, which they did, after which they resorted to the cottonwood again because the girls preferred it, although by now it was making them bleed. Big clots of blood were hitting the walls, and in some of the girls the cottonwood cocks had bored holes that were never there before and never meant to be. You can see how the moral of the story builds up gradually. One by one, the girls died of their excesses. How is yours, asks one. I think she's dead, says another. These bitches would rather die than go without it. Now, when all the girls were dead of having such a good time, the youths went home, rattling their wooden penises together as they walked, and wondering what to do with them next. Did you kill them all off, the first youth asked. Yes, we did, they said, and they will never need to be fucked again. Now we have to put these penises away somewhere. You never know when they might be needed again. What they did with them I cannot tell you, it is not part of this story, but don't think for a moment they have gone to waste. Painted, they look even more attractive, and they come with little legs and arms in some of the better trading posts. It is all a matter of personal preference, really. It is said that the first young man did not survive, having had his penis bitten off by the last girl to possess him, and she wolfed it down as if the place with the teeth were really a mouth after all. In that story, the youths come looking for him and find his body, so they go outside and find the cottonwood root in the forest nearby, then things go on as before. And some of the cottonwood penises are filled with sumac seeds, I am not certain how. They must have hollowed them out, paused to bend down and open a little trapdoor, and then blown hard through the hollow cottonwood penis to get the seeds home among the teeth. Sometimes these women without their teeth turn to stone overnight as well. If you can grow teeth where no teeth are, you can turn to stone as well." I am surrounded by a hum, a wail, a chant, a buzz that burns up into a roar. Of rage or joy? I cannot tell, but I am being jostled, hit on the back, patted on my knees, tapped on top of my head. They want me to tell it again. It is better than "The Love Boat" they sometimes watch in black and white. What this "Love Boat" is, I have no idea, not even having overheard it, but it cannot have aboard it enough cottonwood penises to go around. Sometimes a narrator just cannot oblige. All I want to do is sleep. "Yes," I say, "I'll tell it soon. Take me in to bed." That small one-room house again, not much in here save acid memories. They should lock me up in here. "You really told it that time," my nephew says, "you could go on the talk shows." But my own mood is different from his. Not excited, lifted up, but down in the deep trough. "You know what to do," I ask him, "with a dead man? You know about the silent name?" Without a pause he goes into it, tells me how they will wash my hair with yucca suds to ready me for my journey. "Usually," he says with faltering voice, "a man's father's sister will do this. An aunt." "Go on," I say. "Then," says he, "they rub his face with white cornmeal, so that it will look like a spirit face, and then they put the mask of white cotton over his features, this being a cloud, Uncle, which is the soul." "Well done, Oswald Beautiful Badger Going Over The Hill. And then what?" "We fasten around his forehead a string with feathers stuck to it, which hang over his face. Four of them." "Then," I tell him, to take the strain out of his voice, "you or someone will have to stand in front of my body and speak to me, telling me that I have finished with this life and am going to a new home. I will need a new name. So then somebody says, 'Your new name will be—,' but no one ever says it, the name. No one ever says the silent name, but the dead man knows it. Good. I wish they would take me out of the village and away from my big earthen water jar, away from the little stove and the few kachinas I keep by me, to the far end of the mesa where there's a small hollow a man can sit in. From there, huddled in that hollow, you watch the sun come up. I like the idea of having my own niche. Once I was in place, in the correct sitting-up position of course, and facing the east as I should, I might be all right forever, provided nobody else wanted to view the sun from there. In which case, a quick shove and George The Place In Flowers Where Pollen Rests goes over the edge, a huddle of old rags and rotting bone. He was a dirty old man with lots of dirty stories to upset people with. He had filthy habits. His medicine gave him wind. No wonder the ones who look after the burial have to purify themselves with smoke. What you ought to do, Nephew, is to burn some piñon gum, four times. I remember my father building a wall that would make a new room for the house, but he died when it was higher than the child I was. *Grow, my boy,* he'd say, *and then I can make it higher. But I will have to wait until you are a young man before I can put the roof on.* He kept a few silver and turquoise treasures in a knotted handkerchief he kept by him as he mixed the mortar and trimmed the stones. It sat by him as if it were a small radio and he heard it playing to him. At some point, I think, he built the little bundle into a cache in the wall. I never knew, but one day it was gone and it would have been rude to ask. We never got the roof on, and the wall has crumbled. When he was building his wall, he'd sit like he sat to eat, one leg doubled up underneath him, the other with the knee upward and the foot planted hard on the floor, so that he could get up fast and defend the wall, or his son. My mother, though, she sat square on, with both legs drawn up under her, and no chance of leaping to her feet. She had no need, because my father was in that watchful position all the time, but it broke his back to build a wall in that way. Other men squatted or even lay down to it. Not he, he was wary. With his mouth close to my ear, he whispered our things to me, and he showed me how the drippings of mortar had to remain within the walls until next day, when he could sweep them out, by which time they were little hard balls and sometimes hard to dislodge from the ground. *Never throw things, always carry.* He was always saying things like that, but I forgot them, and I was always carving, so there was always a mess around me and no one dared to grab the shavings and toss them outside. No, a holy law made us live with them a night and part of a day. You became fond of what you'd shaved away. If it is bread, though, it is all right to toss it around, and I saw bits of bread and even melon thrown to kids sitting on the roofs of their houses. You never throw, my father taught me, to women and girls. You offer. That is why they remain at the windows and the doors. When, each night, he walked outside to pray under the stars, with his nose looking sharper every year, he would arrange my shawl, the boy's thing of broad brown and white bars, around his shoulders, and he never missed going out, last thing, to do it. You could not hear him, his prayer was like the silent name. A strong boy, he'd always say, must wear heavy clothing in midsummer and be stripped down to moccasins and loincloth in winter. Once, when I was playing outside with a can in each hand, clopping along on all fours as if I were a burro, with another boy on my back riding me, he came out and told us about the time he got lost in the desert when chasing after a horse that had broken loose. All he could think of is where there might be an empty can. Navajos paused there to rest their horses, and sometimes they threw an empty can away, a tomato can usually. He went there, found such a can, and dug with it deep into the sand until it began to fill with water. *So*, he said, waving his trowel at me, *never waste a can, it might save your life. Always think where you might be able to find an empty one to use.* It was sad, and to me awful, that having saved himself so well in the desert he did not live for long after it, as if he had used himself up. *Do not trust rainbows*, he also said. *A rainbow keeps the rain away from you, it is all stuck fast on the other side.* I often wondered what would happen to you if you mistrusted a rainbow and the rainbow got to know. Would it rain icicles upon you and cut your face? The more I heard him, the more I knew that the things I lived among were not the real world at all, but things put there instead of it. There was always something behind what was there. Nothing was quite itself. Downy feathers are breath. If you pray for rain, use the feathers of a duck. If you want good peaches, use the breast feathers of an owl or a yellowbird because they are the good companions of good weather. And a little breast feather fastened to a bit of cotton string is the breath of life. It was always like that. So you always looked for what was behind what you saw, and you also looked behind what was behind what you saw, and so on forever. There was no telling how much you missed from passing by too fast. Most of all I liked to go with him into the storeroom, with ears of corn all stacked neatly by color, shelled beans in bags, dry mutton hung up on wires, and all manner of dangling things from pods to string beans all ready for the famine or just next winter. It was a whole siege of smells, that place, and, if you didn't watch where you walked, you would walk into long dried-out spirals of squash that hung from nails. It was a dry, tidy, sunlit place, and you could sit in there and dream, with all the wealth of the earth tightening and shrinking around you, and I always mixed it up with the little shrine in which there were four thin sticks, each curved over at the end, and these were four old people. From each curve there hung a cotton string with a nice soft feather at its end, rather like the one we used as a pretend whip when playing burro with the cans. The largest of these sticks was the youngest of the old people, and the smallest was the oldest."

Oswald

When he gropes his hand for mine I can feel the weight of the ages within it, not that he's anything like ancient. He is older than his years, that's all; lately he has aged heavily, eager to get old as fast as he can, and if old he has to be, then as old as possible. "Get it over with," he mutters, "let's have done with the going downhill. Soon. Then I can take stock, Nephew." I feel older than he does: who thinks of a nephew as anyone grown up? A nephew is always a tiro, isn't he, not someone almost halfway to thirty? Just past it for porno movies. I sometimes think he keeps me by him in order to feel older than ever, but surely the logic of that is to keep a teenager alongside you to make sure of that almost-had-it feeling. By the same token, I ought to feel younger while around him, seeing how fast he wanes, and maybe I would if only I had something worthwhile to do, apart from cheering him up. Neither a jolly nor a morose man, Uncle George is a droning misfit, needing neither love nor friendship nor worship, but only a witness who will not preach at him. It is as if he is trying to remember the whole of his life and then throw it away, which he cannot do until it has all come back to him in a molten shower full of his Bessie and the days when he thought knives and forks were jewelry, he was so poor. Lucid, blithe, detached, as he can be at his best, he likes to gather up my own life in order to toss it aside. "How many women have you done it with?" he says. "How many men? Men are tighter," he says, as if he knew, but most of his sexual expertise comes from hearsay and tall tales. He is the perfect type of the faithful spouse, having long ago committed the desirous part of him to carving. Wood, as I keep thinking, was his true flesh. For him, there was lust, love, and artistic passion, and they all three overlapped, but the last one sapped the other two lifelong. As they say around here, he is not BertandAnna Chasing One Another On A Green Field. He is not easygoing like those two, who have come to embody a certain approach to life. Well, they say (not BertandAnna themselves), you are not BertandAnna today, are you now? You should take things easier. Well, he is never BertandAnna. Too tense for that, about his standing, his name, his vanishing skills, he sits for hours uttering a mesa child's primitive attempt, no doubt like his in Keams Canyon school, to say the word *Missus*, which he never found easy. In the old days, addressing or answering his teachers, he used to stammer Mitits Judson and Mitits Holmes, knowing better but unable to skew his mouth right. "*Mitits,*" he murmurs now, perhaps reliving those early fumbles, wishing Mrs. Judson and Mrs. Holmes could see how famous he's become, with his eyes wide open, his hands forever feeling the grain of the cottonwood root. It is a long time since some doctor told him to avoid salt, so Bessie would wash the canned potatoes and carrots for him in a colander, but then she would add a tablespoon of it to each panful, to improve the taste, and he didn't find this outrageous at all. Salt from Bessie's hand was a blessing, a tenderness dealt out, whereas salt from the can was a taboo. "Learn the best Anglo," he kept telling me. "Nobody talks our talk anywhere else. If you don't you'll be like someone deaf and dumb." But of course, I had no choice, he had forgotten how the schools insist, how they insisted that he too learn the other language, but not, as he always said, much of a language for the fleeting apparitions that make us rejoice when we have time to ponder things. Where else, he liked to say, would you find *one word* for the muscle pulling the back of the knee? He had not thought of doctors' Latin, which surely has a word for every human part; but what he really meant as he sat clasping one thumb tight in his other fist was those little pictures that impress us so much that we make them easy to sum up: animals running on green pasture and corn covering itself with a green cape and Something Disappearing Over Flowers (this our Bessie's other name). "Who else," he liked to ask in his total disregard of other languages save English, "who else has one word for a butterfly sitting on a flower? *Políkwaptiwa*. Who else cares about the butterfly bearing pollen on its wings? *Talásveni-uma*. Who else would join the shortest ear of corn to the length of a newborn rabbit?" *Sowiwa*. He babbled my heritage at me as if I had never spoken my own language or heard a word of English, or knew that far from the mesas there were Latin and Spanish and, even farther away, the Inuit with all their words for different kinds of snow, and the shepherds of the high Andes who have more than half a hundred words for the brown coats of their sheep. "No, they don't," he used to snap. "That is *our* way. We must never credit it to others, who are no more than imitators." He is still like that, but he doesn't insist any longer. He is willing to let the outside world be its bright, puzzling self, like some gorgeous bird he doesn't want to pet. Never again will he fly, or see, or carve, have an erection, a steady heartbeat, a good appetite, an unbroken night's sleep. I think I would have given up the Presidency of the United States to come here and be with him, whereas all I gave up was what really had no further use for me, and might come after me to do me in, close my mouth forever. Where could I be safe? "Where would you like to go," I ask him. "What would you like to smell? Would you like to hear the sounds of the hot desert? Is there anything we can make captive to please you? A caged bird? The eagle from my roof?" "You are getting old," he said. "Your eagle has gone. They cut it loose." "Oh, I am just talking, Uncle," I told him. "I know you don't want to be bothered. We are not short of anything we've got, as we used to say in the old days." I have not yet dared to tell him that, some time ago, I had a zigzag part cut into my hair, a bit like Sotuqnangu's lightning wand, but not for religious reasons. It was something for them to film, it made me different, and all you need is an old-fashioned razor to keep it clear. So, instead of having my hair split in two by a normal part, I have it split this way and that, against the grain. And then, sometimes, the hair was pink. Who cared? In Los Angeles they took it in their stride, but when the mesa first saw it they assembled the women and the girls to laugh me into shame. *"Mana,"* they giggled, meaning man got up as a woman, although to me there was nothing essentially feminine or female in a zigzag pink or blue. "Feel, Uncle," I told him; he was already losing his close-up vision. He liked it, but all he could tell was that I'd had my hair cut, and he thought I was asking for his approval. For being a good boy. He cannot abide long hair, saying the tip is too far from the heart that nourishes. "Cropped," he said. "Good boy. Good boy. Your head feels smaller, less like a mesa." "Do you see what color it is?" He said no and at once turned away, into the distance, where the place I needed to escape to really was: nameless, addressless, quite unmapped. He never knew about the part although his fingertips had grazed it. I was back among the only rare and serious people, as he called them—sweat of the sun, tears of the moon—and that was enough. He asked if the movies I was in would appear on the half-dozen TV screens in the settlement, and I told him no, there were problems, they were for export only. Nowadays he talks darkly of plans, not to carve or to go foraging for wood, of course, but one day to bring all his dolls back to the mesa, heaven alone knows how, and put them all in one place for everyone to look at. *Hundreds* of them," he sighs. "Just imagine them all together, Oswald." I do, and I suddenly realize that there has never been a family reunion. Those that left his hands left his hands forever, replaced only by other dolls that also went away from him. He has been a serial. At the end of a vanishing line. He's heard about Picasso and Matisse, about one-man shows, and he's getting ideas. He doesn't want a museum show in Phoenix or Flagstaff, but he wants some kind of career tribute, unless, as he sometimes promises, he carves a brand-new piece with some hundred dolls all milling around in frozen animation: an effigy of all his kachinas come home, embracing and dancing together in total disregard of their traditional roles. No, it will be Bessie as a storyteller doll, overrun by kachinas as if she were their Spider Woman creator. Yet he has done nothing about it. It's a carving for his lovesick mind's eye only, a last enormous fidget from those tensed-up mighty hands. He wants. He yearns. He bathes his want and his yearning in secret memories, of a life that went right, as his did not, of a tribe that became prosperous, as ours did not, of a new world order that never came to be, in which the eyes' delicate tribute was recognition enough for the forces of nature, whose hands are rough and hard.

George

In that little shrine of the storeroom, as a dreaming child, I never asked for anything, but I asked it for my parents. Any trick to get them a few years extra. It was not as if there were some limited supply of years to be handed around. Everybody could have more than their fair share and there would still be enough years for emergencies. My father was an emergency, but they gave him no last-minute supply of time, they let him dwindle without lifting a hand. A more devout man there never was, with such a fine delicate feeling for everything, but it did him no good. He paid his respects as often as a fishbird dives into water, and they cut him down. Then there is me. Now there is me. A less devout man there never was, wondering all the time about things forbidden. I toed the line, as I say, with my thumb, and I kept my mind on how to make things that were beautiful. My hands were busy, my brain fidgeted. There was nothing beyond me, if I had skill enough. In one sense Oswald Beautiful Badger Going Over The Hill is a chip off that old block. He too goes his own way, damning the formulas, taking after his uncle in making up his life as he goes along. Neither he nor I take too easily to being members of anything. What's the good of being inventive if you can't invent your own life? When someone leaves you when you're young, you never lose his presence, you live it tenfold for him, and he becomes a very personable ghost alongside you, with whom you argue and joke, talking to yourself of course, but in a frank and gentle way with whoever isn't there. You lose yourself by leaning over toward him, talking about this or that kachina, this or that change in the weather, the latest foolishness in the Anglo world. I have always supposed that, if you get into the habit of talking to the gone, you end up talking to everyone gone. They are all available, unable to say so, but you can feel their hum in the air, that upset of their minds left behind, like the air was magnetic where they sat down most, or mostly leaned to watch the movement of the sun. If a man can talk to his kachinas, he can talk to his dead. After all, the kachinas are away half the year, or there would not be half as much fuss as there is when they return at the winter solstice. When a man has made a wall, you can go talk to that, or at least go stand beside it and think your thoughts into his absence. The same with linoleum, a brush-and-earth roof, a rose-colored wall made from clay. Maybe I am practicing talking to the dead me, who will surely be as quiet as any other corpse. I no sooner say something aloud, or in the storage chamber of my head, than my mind seems to circle around behind me and take up another position, not so much to answer, but to listen, and then I somehow know what the George whose name is silent thinks of what I've said. Or done. No doubt this shapes the way I carry on. I do or say something in order to let my guess at the dead-and-gone me sample me beforehand. It is as silly as that, but when you can't see you have to make up something else to make up for it. When you have spent your life carving and coloring, and then can no longer see anything of what you do, you have to fill the gap. Now that is like death, it too filling the gap. A bit of me died, so the other bits have to work twice as hard. I wonder if my nephew would believe this even if I told him, shuttling as he did between a dead him in Palookaville and a dead him here in this village on a mesa. Neither is alive to him when he's in the other place. But he can see, and he can see me, whereas when your world is voices you tend to sound off. You tell a dirty story, you have nothing to lose. You address the dead, who have already lost. You insult the gods, who were never there anyway, save as wish figures no more huggable than wind-drifted smoke. In the world he sometimes went to, where they have flush toilets enough for an army, he noticed something strange, he says. The women flush the toilet, but always leave behind them a big ball of rolled-up tissue on top of the fresh water. They wipe themselves dry, he says, after they have finished, and they leave it there to sink. I wonder how he knows, it must be from staying in someone's home or flying out of Flagstaff. I know, because the men do not flush where the women flush. It is all separate. As soon as something is familiar, people think no more about it. They must be like animals, leaving their droppings to mark their ground, except that they leave something not so crude. So they both flush and mark, they have it both ways. They were there, but their shit isn't there to say so. I do not want to die so long as there are such wonders to hear about. I once asked if the gods move their bowels, but no one would hear me out. George The Place In Flowers Where Pollen Rests is moving his mouth again, he should stick to carving and show more respect. That's what they always said whenever I thought something up and came out with it. Nowadays I ask if the gods take their pulses, their pills, if they put the cuff on their arms and let the little peep-peep machine count their blood pressure. They press against us, or so it's told, but does their blood press harshly against them? This is not good wondering. You have to be stone-souled to say any such thing. You have to be so close to death as not to care. But the gods can still get you for disrespect, if anyone really is minding the store up there. I doubt it. Gods do not pay house calls, they do not come by. You go to them and, even as they try to figure out who you are by reading your file fast in front of you, they are thinking about lunch, the next kachina doll they are going to buy, the way they will sit in that hollow at the end of the mesa to watch the sun come up. They are interested in our diseases, not in us. A fast cancer gets their attention more than an Engine with a really fastidious sense of the universe. So you have to keep your weather-eye out for them, whether you are in Palookaville or Hollywood or up on the mesa, off in Keams Canyon, or going to swim in Mormon Lake. These gods accept a lot of hospitality, but they never return it. They just let you drop off the edge as if you were a pine cone, a cloud of tansy mustard, a broken loom. They never fix you, they let you fall apart. Sotuqnangu is no god at all, but a toy of mine, whom I can bring into being with my knife and a hunk of cottonwood root. I can burn him in the fire whenever I want, or hand him over to the Jimsonweed girls to use as a penis on their too-sharp teeth. "How are you, Uncle?" my nephew asks, as he does dozens of times each day.

Fair to middling, I tell him. He does not want a long answer, full of this or that special thing, he wants that murmur, that blank, he wants to know if I am in a fit enough condition to make a noise to him. We live by overlooking, by overhearing. It is no more definite than that. You can stay alive an awful long time without even trying to. If you are gifted that way, you can tell a far-off stray sheep, gray against the sandy desert, without even forcing your eyes, and, at night, as you walk home, you can pick out a cactus from the desert floor on which it lies in wait. If folk went wrong every five minutes, there would not be time enough to invent all these tales about the gods and their Palookavilles. A human is one who complains until he dies. A god is one who does not accept complaints. There is always another bureau down the hall. So I am very close to Oswald Beautiful Badger Going Over The Hill. He disobeys by going away, and I disobey by sitting still, an anthill of curses and complaints. My eyes feel full of hot sand, especially after a whole night of trying to see, but I have learned that there are limits to the human blink, it will not solve everything. Something flutters in my chest when I lie down to sleep, but it is quiet during the day, when I cannot sleep at all. That will be the way of it for another week, another month, who ever knows his portion? Then it will be done with and no one else will feel it. I go on to carving a higher breed of kachina doll. In fact I rather liked the sound of it when the doctor spoke the word *cataract*, as if saying I had a waterfall in either eye. Of tears, yes, but he meant something as grand as Niagara, which I have never seen, though my nephew has, and he half wished he was going over the edge of it, it looked so final and complete. Yet who can trust him? He goes around saying condone when he means condemn. He picked it up in Hollywood, I guess, and thought it was a politer version of the same word. If he had gone to school with Mitits Judson, Mitits Holmes, he would have gotten it right, and he would have carried around within him that little nut of satisfaction you get from knowing you know another language, more or less, and do not get your paws caught in its traps. Bless him for trying, though. At least he talks. To him a word is a mouthful, worth chewing on. He likes the act of saying. He likes it when I chirp up with my latest lump of grown man's filth. One day he brought me, sweet thought, a motor car made of soap, when I could see, and it was cream-colored with soap windows and soap wheels, and, until you tried a bite, you thought it was white chocolate, and here it is even now in my big brown jar of pills, ready for use in the next world.

Imagine ever having enough water on hand to make it melt away,
wheels and windows and all. After a week of watching me handle the
soap and pretend to begin carving it with my knife, he said this thing.
"It's really in the news, Uncle." He meant it had really caught my
attention, taken my fancy. A month later, after I had put it aside, not
out of anything near dislike, but to get on with my work, he said,
"For a while there it was really in the news." Well, what is really in
the news these days is blindness. It is the big new idea on the mesa. I
am surprised that more don't hanker after it. It isn't infectious, it
doesn't kill you, and you don't need to take pills for it. So it is better
than liquor, smoking, and sex. No wonder it has been around so long.
If only more of us were blind, we'd have more faith. Or should it be
the other way around. Faith is blind, they say, but so is wondering.
It's when the outside world no longer has a hope of taking you in, I
mean conning you, that your mind really begins to bite home into it.
Who's there behind this dark, you ask, and the answer is Knock,
knock, who's there? *You* are. Amazing what you can talk yourself into
with enough drums pounding, enough turtle shell rattles in your
ears, enough chanting to blur your mind. We paint our faces and our
bodies, but the one thing you never paint is the eyeball, isn't that
right, George? Or the tongue. It wouldn't hold. It wouldn't take.
Daub, daub, what daubers we are, what purloiners of feathers and
furs. We dress up as if going to a celebration, but the only thing to
celebrate is our own lack of being in the news, as Oswald would say.
We are never in the news, whereas the gods are. How clever of us to
concoct them all. There are no limits. You could have gods of soap
with fudged-up names like those my nephew used to use. Lacombe
Bailey. Ritchie Burns. Laser Andrews. Lester Coronado. Who can
Roy Rivers be now, I wonder. Has Oswald Beautiful Badger Going
Over The Hill really become Walt Badge at last? Or is he more or less
a nameless, but musical Indian, a water bearer here, a bicycle rider
there? A class of human, not a person at all. If so, I should be calling
myself already by my silent name, which only the dead and the gods
know, which means that only the dead know it. Cottonwood, I am
willing to die being called Cottonwood. It doesn't matter. It's cheap
at the price. Nameless people die all the time. It is not good to be
singled out and called this or that. We never belong to ourselves anyway, so it would be better if we were all named for what we belong
to. We are all Sotuqnangu's then, with pale blue chests and red teapot
ears, with a lightning zigzag in our right hand. All that vastness

wasted now. A snail of birdshit on the face is much more real. The gods are an acquired distaste. Out with it now. Cottonwood I am, cottonwood I will evermore become. Chop me up and cut me true. There they are again, on the fringe of my doom, whispering, whispering. Mitits Judson, Mitits Holmes. Those getting angry or lustful. Bessie and Fermina. Impatient and angry. Emory and Matlock. Those who do not intend to come and listen at all to George The Place In Flowers Where Pollen Rests. Apperknowle and the other men of money. Those who come and sleep through what little I say, these not excluding Thomas and Abbot. What draws even the most unwilling of them is a grown man showing off. No, I am dreaming, they have come to see what he does when he dies. They have come to watch that long slither into nothingness. Will he moan or do a little pinched smile, or maybe just fold over sideways as if going to sleep? At the end they talk filth, don't they? They are not responsible. *His face grows black as thunderheads, he is straining to remain alive.* They go through things with you, but only to a certain point, then they let you sink. Even those who have smoothed your pillow, washed your face, found your tools for you, and placed them in your hand. I should know their names, but I have forgotten their faces, and that wipes their names from memory. I feel small, chubby fingers upon me, breath that smells of bright fizzy water or hominy stew. Life is going to go on without me. You always think they will stop everything out of respect and grief, but they don't. A life is a life and a death is ungraspable. After a birth, there is a baby to hold, but after a death what you would like to hold has gone. Would it be possible to hold your breath while dying, and then keep it in forever? Then you turn into a drum, to be beaten on special occasions. Keep him dry, bang an ancient tomahawk on his rib cage. Hear the boom. No, bang on him with a big thick kachina doll until the paint comes off, it will not hurt him, he is immortal now. They say that, upon dying, he held his breath and death froze him in the act of holding it, so there was never a death rattle. Deep inside him is a small chamber of air. A souvenir in case he should wish to come back to life and carve again. He smells of lime. His eyes are sealed in a golden crust almost like pastry. His nose looks ready to breathe, every day a little sharper. His mouth is going to talk to us through his teeth. He will always be like that. He won't, he comes to, comes back, and asks for his nephew. No, his nephew is away making a movie. Does he need water, has he slept well, what would he like to eat? There is no need to fast, Grandfather.

Now, which of these lambs milling about said that? It is soon going to be pointless. Each waking-up gets in between him and his destination, that velvety wormhole through which the soul must grope its way. Who needs alms, a talisman? Better a fistful of feathers, the better to fly with. "Calm, George," I say to myself, "keep calm. I know what a death rattle is. You hold it in your left hand and it is a gourd full of seeds. You shake it hard and you survive to eat bread and margarine again." The talking goes on, but is it talking at all? Rather, a headlong murmur in the head. Are there voices even? As alike as eggs, theirs, yours, mine, voices freed from mouths. It is all very slight. Something, you begin to believe, might get said on behalf of someone who no longer talks. A baby gurgle would do. There is nothing exact needing to be told. Where are their ears? My choked breathing is the only sound, you could pick it up in any tin cup held to the ear. *He is nowhere, he is cruising high above us all.* When he is dead they will still have him to look at. He will not return their gaze or they might be able to read the mysteries behind his eyes. Help him now to the next plateau of it. Hoist him higher into that final faint. Lower him to his last exhausted stretch. Tell him to gasp, he is keeping the children up past their bedtime. He learned lingering in a good school. He gives nothing away. His heart is hard as leather. His face has begun to shine like polished corn. His toes do a little scamper as if running away. His hands, too big for any human, have locked into fists. When he becomes this calm, he is very close. It is like the solstice when the sun stands still and you hope the world is not going to end. He is between all places. It could not be said what his exact position is. He is just prone in the middle of nowhere. Floating without water. They are afraid to touch him in his death-bound cramp. He dribbles. He moans. He asks. It is a miracle. He is asking for a piece of *piiki* bread. Next it will be his chisels. He has been far away and chose the mesa instead. It is no use smiling a welcome at him, he does not see it, and it seems almost a breach of the peace to call to him. Mop his brow. Wipe his lips. Unlock his hands. Turn him over so that the air can feel him. Coax him to sit up. *He looks so big, but he weighs nothing. Surely his bones are large and airy.* Fetch his pills. But nobody knows what he has to take. They find a motor car made of soap. The pills have a soapy smell. Some are white, some pink, some yellow, and some sky-of-midwinter blue. Find his machine and ask it how he is. Nobody knows how to read it, though. It might do him a mischief. Call him names, then. Of course there is no one present to call him son or whom, in full view, he can call just that. He is not very related, except to his nephew, who has been an everybody to him. Then give him some wood to hold. A root of cottonwood. He will just feel at it and know where he is. Am I underground, beneath a tree? Am I buried? Now he knows where he is. The root has two ends. Take him out into the sun, it will not warm him, but he will feel its touch. He smells like an old rug that has been left out in the rain. See how he plays with the cottonwood root. He has not lost everything. That much gladdens him. Oh to be with him when he soars away. Anyone living this long must have forgotten many memories. He is tuning up in order to speak. He chokes, he blurts. If that is language, we are gods. What can he mean? He points, but there is nothing in front of his finger. He is pointing toward California, he wants his nephew. As soon as the finger comes down, into his lap, he begins to talk sensibly. He has been through something, neither asleep nor awake. What could it have been? He felt numb, he wanted to run, there was a wind blowing from under his lip. He thinks it was the beginning of becoming an eagle. He has no feathers yet. What does he say? He wants us to set free the eagle on his nephew's roof. We already have, ages ago. The nephew has a temper. "Free it," he says, "I would have gone with it had it been loose." He will not be *said*. Just pretend to go and release it. He cannot see it from here. And take your time. Now he wants us to lift him up to his nephew's roof. Does he wish to be tethered as well? He is safer on the ground. Ply him with water. He seems more peevish than usual. He soon forgets what he wants, but he doesn't want anything new in its place. He wants to want things. He cannot think of many, though you see, there, his lips form to receive a sweet cookie. Then go hold him over the trench, he needs to *go*. He never goes. He goes where he sits. No, he *goes* only when his nephew is around.

Oswald

As I watch him, he comes out of a sleep, although his way of going into one is oddly similar. The corners of his mouth pull themselves back as if invisible fingers were at work, and he crosses his arms, folds them, with a palm against each shoulder. Almost as Adolf Hitler used to do in those old newsreels, thrilled to death with himself at his latest mouthful. You half expect George The Place to vanish into the wall, to pass through a secret door into a chamber of horrors, much as others have entered mirrors or the backs of refrigerators. But he remains, while Thomas and Abbott as usual attuned to his every motion go inside and fish out something for which I know no name: a big velvet double boot, double slipper, that keeps the two feet together warm. Where this came from I have no idea. Not old or shabby, it has the distinct look of a nursing home gift. You could hardly walk in it, meant as it is for the chairbound, to keep the cold out. None of my doing, it must have been left or shipped by a well-wisher from during the last five years, maybe one of his customers, Byrd or Apperknowle, wondering why he sat outside most of the time, resolved to carve in the fresh air. A thorough well-wisher might

have given him a muff to keep his hands warm too, during intervals of
thinking, but the George of now would have been unable to release
his hands to help his feet or, less handy, the other way around. So:
now his feet are just as strong. Fat lot of good that does. Sometimes, to
make me mad, he'll call me Mitits, or Mitits Oswald, mocking the
female side in me. Then why put up with him? The simple answer
would be that he's continuity, but it's deeper than that. He's art as
well. He's added something to the world that was never there. Far
from replicating or duplicating what hundreds of others can do, he
has carved his own way, leaving behind him a thumbprint all his
own. No one would wish to match it. This is the thing that draws me
to him, the thing he can never explain, the thing the others can't
copy. Like his ailments, it was a given, which is no doubt why he
treats them equally, the gift and the ills, to be taken on trust and
given a free hand. It is not a view of life I fancy, but I can see what
drives him: rough and smooth, turning him into some kind of a doll
too. He's been shaped like a riverbed, by natural force. *You.* Now he is
calling me. I saunter over to him, marveling at the coldness of his
hands, convinced they must be numb. I ask. He ignores me. "A little
stew, he whispers." "It could be with bread and margarine." So he
woke up peckish. He felt a bit more alive. "Slop stew," he murmurs,
"I can't take the hard stuff in it. Plenty of water, Nephew." I almost
get him to let me take his pressure, but at the last moment he resists,
willing only to let the Velcro cuff inflate, except that without an arm
in its grip it won't inflate at all. The used-up portion of the numbers
roll is half an inch thick. Supposed to go as high as 170, the numbers
in the window go to 3, then fall back, as if you had a dead man here,
barely any pressure at all. He cannot see this. He hears the whirring
pump only. Now he feels the cuff, which as if by magic at his touch
inflates, all the way to 160, then collapses with a sigh, a live trapped
animal. He likes this effect and has me repeat it half a dozen times,
wearing the machine out, running its batteries down. It swells like a
penis into the rough shape of a breast, and then E for Error shows in
the tiny window, the numbers dwindle to zero. With nothing to measure, the machine switches itself off, as designed. "No peeps," he says,
"to wake me up." "No pressure, no peeps," I tell him. "Put your arm
in, Uncle." I ask him to try. Not on his life. He never likes to do it,
not right after waking up. Or just before going to sleep. Or right after
eating, or just before it. Or during a meal. Or when it is dark. Or
light. When he is well, of course not. When he feels rotten, of course

not. When, then? He has no answer, but promises me the time will come. "Not often," he says, "but now and then." Then he draws back, saying not before or after a bowel movement, a headache, a cold, a bout of rheumatism, or when it is close, dry, windy, or cold. "In hot weather," I ask, clutching at anything. "Most of all not then," he answers, half sly. I put the cuff and its pump away in their plastic pouch, knowing I have lost. There was never anyone who could win. He's nature's, he's his own. When you have looked at someone as much as I have looked at him, you find he has been the focus of so much looking that you take no further notice of him. He's worn his chance out. This doesn't mean, though, that he doesn't go on reviewing and reminiscing, talking or brooding; it just means you have lost the capacity to listen to so much life lived. He did this, he did that. He seems not to have had a moment's rest, but he must have spent most of it simply carving wood. Is that why his mind has developed this trick of floating free? All he has to do is carve, and his memory comes loose like a glider. There is no holding it. Every memory reminds him of something else. It is all stitched together. What he tells is the smallest part of it, too. If only he'd come out with all of it. No, I've heard enough already. I am going to have to guess. They revere him up here because he stuck to his carving, but there must be more to him than that: what they know about, what he's never told, what they must have caught him out in, red-handed, red-tongued, in the days when he moved around and interfered with others' lives. Was he always that dedicated? Or did he wander? Well, never to Palookaville anyway. He never got that far, but surely all the key moments of his life he hasn't spent with me. That would have been like a successful mystic having his life depend on a local telephone call. That really shows me up. If I were more local than I am, I'd never be wondering such things. Up here, they leave you to it. There's a holiness of doing. What matters is so far inward that nobody knows. They just assume a lot of you is inward, according to tribal tradition. Walking miles to fetch water, they respect the act of fetching it, but they leave out of reckoning what the mind does with itself while making the walk. Did he ever fetch water? He fetched wood. So the same applies to that. While fetching, did he list or dream? Was his mind a blank? Did he think of birds, food, seasons, his wife, his mother, his nephew? Or what? It's gone. It's nothing. Sad that, although you often know what somebody thought lifelong, you never find out how he thought it up. How did he think, then? In long arcs? In fits and starts? His mind hopping about? He's unknown, unknowable. Asked, he would lie so as not to let you down. So it's fair to ask if, while thinking, he often lied to himself. As I. As all of them. Give the mind an acre and it will invent to fill the space.

George

Imagine something different. Those who can no longer talk in their own right will have their tale told by what they have worked with, the butcher's by meat, the hunter's by his prey, the farmer by his crop. And, in my case, the carver by his dolls. Oh what a story they'd unfold. We always shrank from his big bluff hands, he always split us in some place, he squeezed our necks harder than is needed to keep us still. He muttered all the time under his breath. His spittle wet us, in the eyes as often as not. You always knew you were in good hands, but you sometimes missed a friendly stroke, the way some carvers pick you up and gently slide you along the length of their jaw. And when he stuck you in his crotch to hold you firm, although never for cutting, his body smell was strong, that of wet dogs. He smudged us, roughed us up, cut us squishy, sometimes used his sandpapers in the wrong order, moving from smooth to rough, and leaving you far from sleek. All the same, you know he cared, or he cared too much, he never wanted to let us go out into the world, not even as far as a little girl's arms. In the end, he sent us packing, of course, for simple lack of money, but he clung, he always added an extra scratch or two before finally parting with us, as if he wanted to spoil us before letting go and, in so doing, make us less worth having. If only my nephew could hear them talk. Now, if it was the wood doing the telling, it would complain about my favoring one or two dolls over others. The wood wanted to go into all the shapes there were, never to bog down with a favorite few. And the wood never much liked the way I'd dump it in the corner until I needed it, letting it dust up, letting spiders go wandering along its length. Wood, I have found, is very tricky stuff, it has tender spots we humans know nothing about. Knots, cross-grained hunks fit only for the fire. It shrinks and fattens out as well, it is always on the move. It gobbles paint and will always, always, show the scuff mark you have been trying to hide. It likes to make a chisel skid, a rasp bounce into his groin. Yet, the wood chirps in its broken-voiced fashion, if you are going to get manhandled, then let him do it. You always know who's boss, he works so hard his knife and chisel never cool down. He works so fast, once he knows where he's headed, you have to get used in a hurry to what you're going to be. Here I was, a slab, and I'm fast turning into *Guts in the Snow* after several hundred cuts, all of them certain as the sun coming up. He never spilled coffee on us or, once he'd begun, left us out in the cold. His wood was always part of him, at any rate once he'd begun to take an interest in you, your quirks and your funny side. No nose picker here, as some of us know who've been begun by one carver and then dropped, fobbed off on another pair of hands. None of that nose daubing from him, even if they only plant snot on a piece they're going to cut away seconds later. It's the thought that counts. And none of those deep, thrusting cuts to the core of us, just to see what lies beneath, how much strength there is. No, he carved from the outside in, he never got ahead of himself. With blood, though, he's different. It doesn't happen often, anyway it didn't, but if he cut himself he at once rubbed blood into the grain as if to stake some kind of claim, and, if he took long enough on the carving, you got used to the tang and feel of it. Kind of treacly, not much of a flow to it. Minty, with a hint of sage. As for sweat, he did not sweat much, but it always seemed to fall away from him and never forward. The hands were always warm and tight, you never slipped between his palms, and every now and then he'd wipe the dust away, hold the grain up for the best light, and eye his wood hard. You'd have sworn he was carving bone from his leg, he took such care with it and sometimes hummed cool and gentle. But, when he wasn't too well, and he held

his work against his chest to calm his heart, you'd hear such a battering and a thumping in there as if a wolf were trying to get out,
cubs and all. He hurt when that happened, you could tell. He was
wishing he was wood too. He'd bang root or kachina against his chest
to make it stop, but it never worked. On his heart thumped, he could
hardly get his breath, and the sweat poured off him then as it never
did when he carved. How many times has he thumped a kachina's
head against the front of his ribs? He never cried out, but he mumbled, asking it to stop, and all that was before he went blind. A long
time before. Sometimes he seemed on the point of throwing up. He
heaved and throbbed, but nothing moved from where it was, trou-
bling him and pleasing itself. He wept some, not from pain, but because he didn't know what to do next. The pills he sometimes took
did nothing for him. He was supposed to be taking them all along,
but he never much bothered to. And he spoke to his heart, calling it
bell, friend, block, rabbit, ball, fist, puppy, wolf, and doll, but nothing
happened. Maybe he was calling it by the wrong names, and lamb,
lemon, egg, bottle, or strawberry would have worked better. He had
to wait it out, and so did we, clasped against him, so long that we got
to know the beat of his heart better than we knew the motion of his
carving hand. Did we, dolls or wood, beat with him, throbbing along
our dead length while he prayed to get over it and begin to carve
again? He gnawed on us, he pressed us against the bridge of his nose.
No use. Then it would be gone and he'd rush to get on with the work.
He couldn't cut rightly when his heart was tumbling, he'd do it care-
lessly, or not quite take off the depth he had in mind. And, once he'd
done it wrong, he had to work with the mistake he'd made, making
the doll thinner in that place. Well, no wood likes to be shoved around
like that, even by someone grown old in the trade. He just could not
paint, either, when the spell came on him, he ended up dabbing and
dotting all over the place, which of course, as he got blinder, he left
alone for someone else to put right. It was untidy, it got worse, and he
seemed to see right through things. You can't paint what you don't
see, and you can't carve it either, so he was just as likely to find his leg
on the other end of the knife. He wasn't looking, he was trying to
swallow down what had climbed up too high in his chest. Then he
seemed to think it was a doll, all joints, doing jumps and vaults right
there inside him, to get its own back for all the other dolls. Damned
dancing doll, my heart, he'd say to no one, he talked whether or not
someone heard him. You could see he wanted to shove a doll down his

throat and tell whatever was bouncing around in there to quit and leave him be, it had gone on for ten minutes, sometimes an hour or two, he would be glad to faint right out, to pass his heart out in his stool at the latrine trench. Strange how a man can call himself not I but he. Pushes himself off into the distance like that, knowing all the time it isn't true. An I stays an I until it can't be anything at all, not anymore. So it's just a game, really, pretending you aren't who you are, just to be different. You can never be as different as that, not to yourself anyway. You just get sick of saying *I* in front of everything. *He's* a change. That's all. None of those little words—I, he, we, and so on—are better than a fox's cough, and never half so certain. We say them only to peg our bodies to what we say, so as not to lose it when it goes wafting away from us into the fresh air. What I said just now, to myself, floating away, there it goes, it was only just in my head, like the breath I breathed out was only just now in my chest. Look how you do it. I say, "He squeezes snow between his hands." My nephew says, "Oh, he squeezes snow between his hands all right." You say it of just about anyone: There he is, squeezing snow between his hands. But a he is nobody. A he could be anybody at all. We talk of the dying and the dead as if they are still he's. Even the she's. The they's. That's it. We say *he* meaning when he *was* a he. It might be better to say a *hewas* for one dead, joining words up like BertandAnna as more trustworthy. Not as if you have forgotten them. Oh no. It is more honest, though, and it shows you are attending to them. What kind of attention is it to go on calling a dead him a *he* even after he's died? As if you haven't even noticed he's gone. I would like to say, *Is squeezing snow.* Never mind the who. *When carving, sometimes also squeezes snow. When squeezing snow, sometimes also carves.* As a people, our people think more about what is being done, and to what or to who. Never mind the doer. So, when someone says *carving,* all those who carved and carve no more are in the word, and all those carving now, and all those who will come to carve in future times. Just so long as the thing itself goes on. We are all the same. And when I say *you,* I don't mean the looking-into-my-eyes you, I mean Anybody around who happens to be doing such and such, my point being that if you're vague enough you never die because you're not very definite to begin with. These are not the tricks of an ailing man. This man is an ailing man, a man so ailing he has no right to what the uppity Mititses back in the old days called the pronoun. Not many use that word these days, most of them never knew it anyway. Now, Mrs. Judson and Mrs. Holmes, they were worth an I, and sometimes a *we* when they stood together, as one, the one with a hooked nose, the other with a turned-up nose, but both with their noses lifted up high above the smell of us all. Teachers or no, the living man has to talk of life and death as they both were his, not just the one. That is how we do things, cramming it all into a lifetime because there seems no other way to do it. You live your death as best you can, which is why it is always best not to talk about it, it sounds so silly. The living take great liberties with things they know nothing about. "Wake up, Uncle," Oswald is saying, as if part of me has fallen asleep. I am not asleep, but I have been somewhere without colors, somewhere that will not remember I was there. "You looked asleep. I have brought you something." "Oh," I say, becoming myself briefly again, even if only to please him a bit, am I entitled to anything more? I long since expected nothing more. "What is it this time?" He says nothing, but I hear a tiny click, and then a great big babble, a sort of frying noise, maybe a grizzly seething his breath hard in the frost. No smell comes with this frying, though, no smell of grizzly or anything else. Into my hands he slides something like a tile, but not quite so cold. A book made of Bakelite, as they used to call it. It quivers. He guides my hands along a hard smooth rod that gets thinner toward its end. Crash, crackle, hiss, it is voices coming on top of one another, some singing, some reading the news, I guess, and some doing a more casual kind of talk. My thumb finds the rough knob that turns it on and off, and also makes it louder. "Short wave, Uncle," he says. "Havana, Cuba; Moscow, Russia; London, England, all of them coming in just for you." I am not that far gone, I tell him, that I can't tell a radio when I hear one. "It comes from all over the world," he tells me. "Move your thumb and the whole world comes in. Just tune it fine." "Then," I say, "it should bring in the past and the future too. Can you fine-tune *them?*" That stops him. "Uncle, there is no wave band for them," he says. "It is all going on now, they are all competing for your attention, on the air." He laughs a bit. "I can shut them all up too," I say. "Have you brought me a machine that makes me feel powerful because I can make it shut up tight with just a motion of my thumb? That's a real gift. What I would really like is a machine that would shut me up for keeps. Tune my head out once and for all. This Havana, I don't need it. Or the noise of strangers. They must all be Indians, they are not speaking Anglo." "No," he says, "they are of all kinds, with many languages." "It all sounds to me," I tell him, "like something coming down a long tunnel. It is the sound of Engines getting mad with themselves." *"That,"* he says, *"is the atmospherics."* I put it down and it is as if I have flipped the switch to Off. I can hear nothing. "It is broken, Nephew, it didn't live long, did it?" "No, Uncle George The Place In Flowers Where Pollen Rests, you hear it better if you hold it. It makes you part of its antenna then. The signal comes through you. It is picking you up." "So," I chide him, "this machine needs a man to help it. Why don't they design machines smart enough to help themselves? You must have gotten me a cheap one. Thank you, anyhow, Oswald Beautiful Badger Going Over The Hill, but you should have spent the money on yourself." He mutters something I can't make out, but he knows what I am fumbling about for, what I am trying to find, and I can hear the few who come to watch me, shuffling nearer, getting fidgety: Now, what is the old guy up to this time? He does not want to die, he always has something left to tend to. His life is one long unfinished business. I grip the radio, turn it up loud, so all those overlapping voices fry themselves real good while the crash-clank comes in behind them from the atmosphere, as he says, and then I start the pump on my blood pressure machine, which whirrs and winds, then begins its peep-peep sound while the rumba music from Havana, Cuba, ebbs and flows. It is like the tide coming in, only it is not proper waves, just a sort of ripple in the noise. This part I like. I tell him, "I like the way it goes peep-peep, then does a sort of peep-peep wail when it signs off, but the radio keeps coming and going, from a lot farther away, Oswald Beautiful Badger Going Over The Hill. I don't suppose they can hear me and my machine in Havana, Cuba. It would only be fair." "Not a fair world, Uncle," he says. "It does not transmit. It does not send." "Oh." I show how disappointed I am, and tap him on the arm with it, but I have hit him in the face, his face was low. I hit him with the blood pressure machine, I thought it was the radio, but he was on the other side. I am working the pressure machine right-handed, the radio with my left. "Nine bands," he tells me. "It has FM as well. And Medium Wave." "What wave am I," I ask him, hardly expecting an answer, but he never quits, he always comes back at you with some notion or other. *"Tidal,"* he says, in his smart-ass way. Then I hear a word, *ombray*, and something like a string fiddle out of tune, then a man saying *marking* before his voice fades out, without my thumb moving the tuner wheel at all. They fade out more than they come in. "Why have you brought me a radio?" He says nothing. "How many more machines must I have before I am ready to die? How many more pills?" "*No* more anything, Uncle, I wanted to bring the world to you, from as far away as possible. You can hear the Russians even. Moscow. They talk Anglo too. Even from Havana, Cuba, they talk English sometimes. It is for our consumption. Aimed at us. They do not talk English among themselves." Then I say it: "Can we get Palookaville? Hollywood?" He says nothing, but I am sure my thumb touched Palookaville a moment before it faded out into the grinding-frying noise. If that is how Palookaville sounds, then I do not blame him for coming home to stay. I say so. "*Negatorio,*" he is telling me. "Palookaville does not broadcast, it doesn't need to. People go to it, not it to them, Uncle." He seems to be shuddering, or just clearing his throat a lot. "It isn't every place that comes in. Just a few. Some stations," he says, "are more powerful than others and blast clear across all wave bands. You have to tune them out." "I like the idea of wave bands," I say, "like bands you wave at or bands that wave at you while playing. Stations too. Toot-toot." "Such stations," he says, "do not have trains and they are not the so-called stations of the Anglos' Christian cross, as in the Jesus of all schoolbooks. No, Uncle, they are stationed on the bands, one place or another. They do not move. Well, they move about a bit, but that is the effect of electricity in the atmosphere." "So," I ask him, for the first time getting interested in my new toy, "what we hear is the sound of them moving about as the lightning strikes them one after another?" He doesn't think much of that, I can tell. But he doesn't explain either, instead taking the radio as if borrowing a book and turning the volume up loud, then tuning in some fifty stations fast as if wiping them out one after another like a bombardier in World War Two. The noise of all the voices and the music is harsh, and those hovering around me flinch backward. I can feel the air changing as they move. Surely there is some music I would like to hear and not tune out. Somebody talking in friendly fashion for half an hour, just to get a man from one hour to the next, if get he is going to do. You could walk around the village with these two machines, peep-peeping and crackling, and scare half of your friends to death. Like a medicine man. Or a kachina with whips. Was there ever a radio kachina? I would like to have carved one, with an antenna sprouting from the head, and the blood pressure cuff around his waist like a kilt or a deep belt. Yes. And this kachina would play music, would have a little wheel in its side for you to move with your thumb. Come and get me, it would say, and I'll get you instead. "*Uncle, be calm.*" "No, Nephew, I felt a flash of life just then, something that came back inside of me. Maybe the juice in the radio." "It is not that powerful, Uncle. It does not pick up anything much for very long, except the loudest and most painful stations. I'll take it away if you like." My Beautiful Badger Going Over The Hill has taken the huff. Uncles can be so tactless, especially when showing more affection than they can explain. "No," I tell him, "leave it, please: I can train myself to use it. Just wait until I know exactly where things are. I like those stations that talk foreign. They all are more soothing, Nephew. You needn't listen too hard. Where would I be without you?" "In a hospital in Keams Canyon," he says fast as a shot. "Or worse. Where you should be now. I keep getting in my own way, Uncle. If I weren't so fond of you where you belong, I'd have shipped you out ages ago, to where nurses and doctors can get to know you really well. Doing what you want is the worst thing for you, and I ought to know better. They would make you take your pills. *They* would pinch your nose and flush them down your throat."

Oswald

"One day," he tells me, "one day soon those nonstop Anglos will come and doze these hills." "Doze them how? And why? The tops are flat already." He says that one day they, meaning the government, will demolish the settlements here and remove the people to zoos, museums, slums, and peepshows. "We don't belong," he says. "We're freaks." He may be right, but what bulldozes them, us, is the propaganda about the need to be both poor and prosperous at the same time: poor, so as to cost the government nothing, but prosperous to fit into some asshole's vision of the American dream. This is the renegade seer in him talking, with whom I have some sympathy. He knows he is the last of his kind, carving offbeat dolls for offbeat customers, defying the templates of his tribe so as to express himself. He calms down only when, on that radio of his, he hears classical music, of whatever kind, whereas he mostly hears rock, and this puts him into a fret and a lather, he can make nothing of the noise, the words, the beat. His foot has tapped only to kachina dances. He likes to tell me that music on tape, which he's heard, is different from music on the radio: it isn't vulnerable to the weather, he says. The weather cannot get into the cassette player. Such distinctions please him more than they would if he were not beginning to fade out, harping on what I told him about Verdi dying, when they laid turf on the Via Manzoni to muffle the noise of passing carriages. "Poor crittur," he said, using a word he'd picked up from somebody passing through. "Up here they'd just flip off their radios until the death rattle was past, and then they'd turn them up again." He may be right. He wants respect, but he doesn't want it to make him respectable. He has only ever seen one movie, and that was a Western that bored him and got him shouting at the marshal on the screen. If he'd had a gun he'd have fired it, he got so riled at the marshal for being so polite with the rustlers and outlaws. Nothing much interested him. He is so special- ized. He does one thing and that is that, and he happens to have done it exceedingly well for forty years. To know him well, you have to loosen him up about his mother and father, about Bessie, and the children they thought they'd have together. I once told him how cut dandelions looked like worms, and he finally bought it after about a year's pondering. In return for which bit of observation he gave me this. "When your body has laid in the ground a year or two, the head has not changed except it doesn't ever move, otherwise it is close to what it always was. It reminds you of how folk look when they've been shut up. The dead face might still wake up and interrupt you, so close to life it looks." Suffering, joy, grief, love. He turns them into contours of the wood, turning his entire world into cottonwood root, where others turn it into conversation, fast driving, lost sleep, food uneaten. I guess what gets me about him is what seems his superb ability to swallow something down and bury it in what he's already doing. Assimilate, that's what. He feels like hell, but he files that hell away in a twist of his knife. Was that it? How did it feel to be him? I can ask the wood only, all those kachinas. Who have nothing to say. The best you can get is a general response from the swollen quality of his carving. *That* is what life's ups and downs drove him to. It's the only sign. It hardly makes sense. All his living reduced to that. Sim- plified. Winnowed. Channeled away from him. As if the carving were some kind of lightning conductor. So, in that sense, his life passed through him as if he were a pipe, a tube, and left no obvious trace. His face aged, his heart began to misbehave, his hands became slightly weaker, but that was it. His eyes failed. Thanks to the stroke. Two things, then. I am at dead ends, two of them. First, he left no trace except in the wood. Second, he no longer carves, so there is no trace of what he feels like now. You have to make goodwill guesses and he lets you dangle, forever wondering. His mind is mainly, I would guess, fixed on the unspoken rivalry between himself and Sotuqnangu, if gods exist at all. "A god exists," he once told me, "only as a dying man exists. These creatures almost don't exist, Nephew. They hover and falter. They are always on the brink. Don't make the mistake of thinking that makes them care at all about the likes of us. They don't like to be almost human in that way. They don't want that much in common with us. So you might say there is no such thing as a god in even average health. They are never well. All they do is done out of irritation. They hate the dying most because that's when we're most like them. So they kill us off. Swat us. It would be nice if the gods were young, some of them anyway, in the first flush of fucking, but they never are. They are like generals: old and bloodthirsty. Never tell you if you're right or wrong about them. So you carve and carve, if you are lucky, and that shuts out much of the wondering, like husbands when they hear their wives howl in childbirth and they laugh, they say it's all right, they like to suffer. They dote on pain." In that, I thought I'd found some clue to him. I guessed at him while he guessed at them. It sounded neat, but it came to nothing. How could it? Like a god, he would never let on, not enough anyway for you to form a clear idea of the person behind the talk. Once I asked him outright. "How does it feel to be you, Uncle George?" "Nothing special," he said. "I am not very much myself. I am no one really. Just a pair of hands on the mesa, twiddling bits of wood. It's hardly worth being born for. All that fuss. I'd have been a poor soldier, though, a poor maker of pots, no raiser of crops. No cook, no Anglo middleman. My so-called carving was the best way of hiding how little I am fit for. Take that away and I'm a flop. There's nothing left. Like a man whose only knack is the stacking up of bottles. Or the arranging of feathers on a floor or a stick. It's enough. It doesn't look like much, but it feels like making mesas." After a while I stopped asking him. He wasn't lying. It was just that the truth about his genius, I call it that, wasn't very interesting, whereas I, well there's more color to my own life, five minutes of it, I suppose, than to his fifty-odd years. The difference is that I'm not worth wondering about, any more than yesterday's fried chicken wrapper. Uncle is. I hang on. I haunt him. Hoping something will rub off. Not the baffling stuff, but what makes him somebody who matters, as distinct from what entitles me to Palookaville and all stops downward. "Uncle, how be big? How make yourself count?" He says, "Never talk too much." "Uncle, how does somebody become great?" "Work in your sleep," he answers. "Uncle, how can somebody do things that live on after he's gone?" He tells me, "Never—be too much anyone at all. Be anonymous," he says. "Be like a fluid. Don't ask. Don't do as you are told. Don't not do as you are told. Let yourself happen. Happiness is an accidental thing like a feather falling from a bird in flight. Fly, be a bird, and the feathers will fall. They will take care of themselves." That was when. That was when and how I learned to stop trying. At least a part of me learned it. There is the part that's willing to quit, but there is also the part that hungers for him. If I don't find it out from him now, I'll never know. It's the part that says that. I am down in the desert, among the shrikes and the flycatchers, and he is up on the mesa, where the eagles cruise. I want to move. I don't need to make a living. I can bum my way for a year or two. I need. That's it. I need. I need so much I don't really know what I need first. I need him. As an anchor. As a monument. As an uncle. Something pulls me. His being a success, even though he's tough to get on with, tough to talk to, tough to be with, tough to get through to. I've tried. He is willing to let the world have its way with him. He seems not to mind. He doesn't resist. He never wavers. Fear he does not know. He behaves like a bird, a rattler, a deer. He is close to all the things I'm far from. How did he get there? Is he intact? In a shredded way, yes. Is he dying? In a hearty, devil-may-care way, yes. Has he any idea how different he is? No. Perhaps if I shocked him? Told him the truth about my life? Did something awful he could hear or feel? Would he then come across with something he didn't know he was going to say? Has he ever slapped me? Has he ever yelled hard and long? Why ask. I'd as well talk to the mesa as bother him. He is too weathered to respond. Half a lifetime ago, was it really he who winched me hundreds of feet down into Canyon Diablo to collect an eagle? I bumped against red rock until I dangled out of sight. Then I roped the claws. The others were on top of the canyon, but I was the smallest, the easiest to lower and raise. We took the eagle back to the village wrapped in an old shirt to keep the sun off it. Swinging into its nest, wondering if the mother would rip my belly or my eyes out, I felt like a seed, blowing about there in the canyon on my steel umbilical. I had learned that, if you want an eagle, you do not order it from Winslow or the mail-order catalog, you go in there and tussle for it. I clambered past one ledge sticking out only to run into another sticking out even farther. Then the whole canyon wall went backward and I was plumbline over space, obliged to swing to keep contact with the rock. I never thought I would be so glad to touch rock, sharp and hard. We needed the eagle because, having never hunted, it was pure. It was young enough for that. It cried as if it had a claw stuck in its throat, making its whistle higher pitched than I would have thought possible. All I had was two gloves, the cable, and an ability to bounce into and out of nests. I was one of the carefully selected nephews allowed to do this thing, but even if you are among the select you rarely get to keep the eaglet as your own. First off, we fed it some chopped-up rabbit meat, then we anointed it, a messy job, with cornmeal and clay. After that, we named it, like a baby. Spider Coming Down, we called it. On the roof, attached to its frame, it watched the village doings, and to keep it happy and amused we gave it toys: a kachina doll cut from a flat piece of board (but not by my uncle), a bow and arrow, and some *piiki* bread. I am glad I was never an eagle, captured and kidnapped, then stuck on a roof for several months, only to be smothered to death in cornmeal after the kachinas had gone back to the San Francisco Peaks. The idea was that the eagle grew up among us, took a message back to those we stole it from, and so bound all of life more firmly together. I wonder. Imagine being out in that wind all the time, with no nest. What, I wondered, would we do if eagles came and stole our babies, lashed them to the side of the canyon for a few months, gave them eagle toys to play with, and then suffocated them in the cause of life bound more closely together? Would *we* stand for it? "The eagles have never thought of it," my uncle said. "We have done it so many times you'd think they would have copied the idea by now. But no. They don't come for us. They have no cable, no toys, no roofs. Their needs are different." I didn't believe him, they needed to live too. How would I have liked to be chained on the roof, up there among the wires and the reddish upper walls? Always in the wind when all I wanted was to nestle? The nest was their indoors. I learned about the birds, not because I wanted to capture them, but because they sang a tongue I'd never learn. Down on the desert floor you'd hear them by the thousand, not quite so many high up, where we lived. "Smother a young eagle in cornmeal, and strip its feathers off? Then bury it?" I kept asking Uncle George to let the eagles go. It was one thing to make them come and watch over us in June and July. It was quite another to kill them and send them packing, back to their ancestors, telling them what wonderful folk we were. "No," he said.

"It needs to be done. The eagles would be lost without us." I asked him about human babies, being smothered in cornmeal and then having their skin pulled off. He liked the idea. He said it had given him an idea for a new kachina, but the tribe wouldn't go for it, he said. *"Things happen only one way around. They do not happen the other."* I gave up, but all my life I have wanted to free the young eagles while their heads are downy white. Then, according to Uncle George, I went and tethered myself to a roof in Palookaville, waiting to be smothered to death in dollar bills. My toys: a gross of condoms, feathered; a vibrator; some lubricant; and a bunch of Quaaludes. I wanted to be taken back up to the canyon and thrown down for having been involved in the death by choking of a porno actress to whom, in the dignified sense, I had become attached. Silly word. Would I ever, I wonder, if we had ever been married, or just living together, have done something like that to her in the ordinary course of sexual—what's the word?—not intercourse, but congress? Has it ever happened? Or is it pure Palookaville? "What must you remember?" He'd asked me before that day. "Where do we go? What do we have to do?" I was almost word-perfect. "We head for Black Mesa, Uncle, and the coal mine. We say a prayer to the eaglet's mother at a cairn of stones, a small shrine. We take with us our field glasses and the six-hundred-millimeter glass on the tripod. We scan the red cliffs for white droppings and we try to take the eaglet when it is old enough to be taken away but not old enough to fly across the canyon. Wrap it in a shirt to keep the sun off it during the trip home. Touch it with a perfect ear of white corn. For the mother, in the empty nest, leave a piece of turquoise or a shined-up shell." "Lord, Uncle," I said to him years later, "I can still feel that rope harness around me when you lowered me into the canyon." "Once was enough," he quipped. "Some go again and again." I nodded, but my mind was on how we took the bird, put it in the house alongside an alarm clock, plastic dolls from the trading post, basins and radios and mail-order catalogs and paraffin lamps and family photographs and candlesticks, and soon after suffocated it to make of it a carrier pigeon to take a message from the gods. "It doesn't wash, Uncle." "The eagles," he said quietly, "don't seem to mind. Untether them and they come back as if they knew why they are here. Leave them be." While I, no eagle, am longing to tell him something passably important, about how her skin had a bluish tinge. She was underweight, sometimes almost bony, and one of her buttocks was round, the other a pear shape. I had never seen that combination before, nor had I done to anyone what I had done to her. What had happened was now so deep beneath my skin that there was no bringing it out into the light. Uncle, I'd say. Uncle, I'd say. *Nuncle.* That was all.

George

I am lost in a sound like that you make by placing paper over a comb and humming against it. If it is music, it is hard to tap a foot to. If it is talk, it comes from mouths underground, choked with mud. "If it is the voice of Sotuqnangu, then the god has a cold." "That is jamming," he says. "When the Russians want to block a station from reaching them." "So," I begin, "they have radios, but they do not like to bring in what radios bring in. Why do they have radios? By the way, I tell him"—my strength seems to be coming back just now—"when I switch my blood pressure machine on or off, the radio clicks." *"It picks you up,"* he says. "Yes, it will. But not my voice," I say. "Not your voice," he says. "It just picks up the charge in the immediate neighborhood, Uncle." I click things back and forth for a while to show him, but he isn't listening, he has grown bored with it all. Radios are not that new. *"Havana,"* he says, to prove they are not new to him, *"is to the southeast of us, and Moscow to the west."* But I am hardly listening to him. The more I hug the radio, the stronger the stations get, but as soon as I set it down, even on my knee, they all begin to fade. It is just like having faith in some god or other. Those you embrace will talk you lifelong. Those you put on your knee, and not to dandle them, have nothing to say at all. So you have to be generous, warm, with the messages coming in, such as they are. It must be different in Palookaville, where everybody knows what to do to get good reception. "High up here, on the mesa," he says, "you get things you have almost no right to hear. Not on a radio this small. Make the most of it, Uncle." "You mean," I answer, "in the time left to me." No answer, but I know what he thinks. Wear out the batteries, he means. When you can't see, use your ears. I tune in an easy-to-find station of what I know is called country western, and leave it on, loud, pulling a crowd together around me as I sit, leaned against my wall. Then someone says, to whoever is listening, "Try to say *sagebrush breath.*" A tongue twister. A dozen voices around me get it wrong, and so do I, as I stumble into something like *Stagebush reth*, and we are all getting it wrong in a cackle of laughter. So a radio can be fun after all, and the tongue twister, he says, is not from Havana or Moscow, but from a home station on the FM band, loud as a tornado. It doesn't waver or crackle. It just marches down on us like it was tumbling out of the mountains ahead of the kachinas coming down to pay us a visit. "Up here," he says again, "you can tune in just about anything. It's one of the advantages." Are they dancing? Something is going on. The dirt is trembling. The air is on the move. Giggles, gurgles. Now they are tapping me on the head and shoulders as they spin by. What dance can it be? Round and round, there must be a good dozen of them, limping to the music as it pours out from under my thumb. They call this power. It is kachina-like. You could end it any time. Once, when we lived our evenings by the light of kerosene, I found that, by placing a sheet of white paper on the fringe of the lamplight, I could brighten the whole room. It reflected it. He means the radio to do that for me, at least as far as my ears go, and perhaps my mind. Sitting here is bound to have the peace of paradise and all the sit-down comfiness of what Anglos call the afterlife. That is what he wants from what he does. Whether he gets it is a different matter. Judge nephews, I tell myself even as I begin to feel stronger, by their good intentions. He is not his own man yet. No man is who works for a living for another man. I will never know all the things he puts himself through in order to buy me pills, a radio, a blood pressure machine. They do not grow on trees, although maybe something of what some pills are made from grew on a tree someplace. A bush. A shrub. Some of it, Sotuqnangu be praised, comes from a place

in flowers where pollen rests, and who am I to turn my back on that?
Now I feel better, if only for a day, I see I am harking back to the
time when I saw. It doesn't seem that long ago, not as long ago as
you'd think it took for a man to lose his sight. One day, as the sight
was beginning to go, I stood in the doctor's office in Keams Canyon,
right there on the weighing machine, and around my neck I had my
nephew's field glasses, which I aimed at the scale, reading the numbers big as crows. The nurse came in and caught me peering down
like a man who has seen a very distant, rather shapely bird between
his legs, or his feet, and is hell-bent on figuring out which one it is.
The pounds-and-ounces bird, that's all. I meant no harm, but they
thought I was doing something mighty crude and got me off their
weighing machine in a hurry lest I messed on it. *Do the numbers look
that far away already?* My nephew couldn't believe it. It wasn't true, of
course, but I said nothing. It was fun to keep him guessing. Now, if
I'd turned the field glasses around, he would have had good cause to
fuss, what with the numbers being far too close. Doctor Matlock that
was. What a name. I had heard of fetlock, but this was new. He had a
rosebud mouth, as they say, and some of his eyelashes grew real long,
more than a couple of inches. Come to think of it, the old eyes weren't
very bad then, they couldn't have been; but these were the only eyelashes of that doctor I ever saw. For all I could see, he had no others.
He called me an old poop and told me to take my medicine like a good
old poop. And he said *Indian* like it was *engine* and he said *engine* as
Injun. Which brought him back to where he set off. There was no way
a man who weighed you like that, called you an old poop engine,
could get a man like me to take those pills, or not foul the weigh
machine. Something between doctors and me was all along bound to
get out of hand. It was no use trying. They wanted me there stark
naked while they peered at me in suits, like I was a disease on legs or a
hunk of lamb going off. Something they had to look at but would
never have bought to eat. It was that look they gave. It made me feel
filthy. It made me feel sick. I never felt sick until they started talking
about how well I thought I was and how wrong I was about it. If I
had known the word *Negatorio* back then, I would have used it to
them nonstop, to air my knowledge. I always felt they wanted me to
be sicker than I was, just to make me more interesting, like a sheep
with a broken leg they wanted with pneumonia too, but on top of
that a wolf bite on its eye, as if that would satisfy them. No, they
wanted a sheep that had caught its nose in a trap and had been half-

way into a quicksand before somebody hauled it out with a rope. That bad they made me feel. That old. That blind. Here they are all dressed up and I want to say to them, "Why don't you strip off too, then we will both be butt naked, and you can show me what is wrong with you. What? You have never had anything wrong with you? And you are not going to have?" I was glad to get back to the mesa and continue dying with my old cheerful smile.

Oswald

They all think you are dumber than a slab of ice. "Now I will set a little towel here," he says, Matlock, "right down beside the tooth, and are you sitting comfortably. Look at what I have when big boys come here. Sniff this. Yair. Look at this. A toothbrush, yes, and it has a doll's house so we can take the roof off, can you believe it. Now I brush your teeth with the nice toothpaste, all around your mouth. Isn't that fun. Your mother can do that for you and then your teeth will be white and smooth all over. In my cupboard, I am going to show you, I have a mouth mirror so I can see right into your mouth. Look how nice and clean your teeth are. Now I have a ruler too, so I can measure things. Shall I measure your fingers first, just to see. Now my fingers are too big to put inside your mouth, so I have these little fingers and a teeny weeny sponge and these small fingers I call tweezers, just like fingers made of tin, and here is a brand new cuddly little towel, you are going to like it, I can tell. Now we have something that can blow the teeth quite dry again. Shall we try it on the hand first. That feels nice, doesn't it. Now we will dry the teeth with it, it is going to feel nice in a different way. That was just like a

shower, wasn't it, there is nothing to be afraid of. Now spit out into
the little basin. Pretend you're aiming at a lake. You must be very
careful to aim well. Now I will show you a little toy we have in here.
Can you feel the cord tickling your fingers. It hurts just once and it
never hurts again. This small soft thing I am putting in tickles a bit.
Round and round it goes, where it comes from no one knows. Maybe
the Nazis or the Japs. Up through the back of your mouth and up, up,
into the eyes and the bottom of your brain. Be good now and sit still.
Be a good Enjun now and sit still. It will suck the bottom of your
brain into this little cooking pan. Half an hour and you will feel light-
headed, son, don't you worry none, just git on out there and take it
like a man. I going to get a little slide of you soon, a few speckles to
show what you did your thinking with, and I'll project it on the
whitest wall in Arizona, blow it up like it was a signature. Then you
can go fill your head with any kind of crap you find in the wigwam,
yair, bit of asbestos here, bit of straw from there. Got to keep the cold
out, yes sir. It is very nice to have a tooth brushed by a machine, isn't
it, and the tooth next door to it says *Me too*. Yes, these teeth like to gab
even while we are on the job. They want to be nice and white. I have
something real nice and sticky in my pocket, would you like to feel it.
It comes from Texas. We can put a little bit of water on it to cool it
down, see, hear the whoosh, doesn't that feel cool. Can you feel it on
your teeth now? The red spear is deep inside it and will go so fast
through you it won't make so much as a mark. Through the spine and
into the wall behind. You keep still, son, or we'll end up making you
bleed a mite. Naughty us, we have forgotten to put the ointment on
the tooth. That was very careless of us, wasn't it. Just open your
mouth a little wider, it's only a rubber mask with a kind of clothes
peg you can put your teeth around for a better fit. Then we hook it up
to these little cords and you will soon have fizzy sparklers right inside
your mouth. You lucky you. Later on your mama can do this for you
too. It isn't every Engine. Here in my armpit I have some nice pink
toothpaste for you to chew on. Here comes my nurse Mrs. Kolb with
a little box to put your head in, it has a cute little cushion of wool on
the bottom. Now sit back and have a lovely sleep. The air comes in
here right past the toothpaste and the little cardboard wings. It smells
really nice when it reaches up your nose. Here it comes, up your
nose, and out your ears, like you had a stethoscope in your mouth. We
will get it to sit carefully. Now you are having a lovely time while
you fall asleep. If you close your mouth tight, you will hear the music

too. That's the style. Don't worry, you will never catch your death of cold in here. Good. Like that. Some Engines we just smother with porridge, to get them quiet, before we drill deep into the jaw. But you're special, an old customer, we'll treat you right." Some hot guy in a white mask leans over me, blotting out the light, his breath heavy on me like the stench of rotting cabbages. "You have to laugh, you'd cry else." Who says that? One of the ones leaning over me says it. He wants me to coo to him. I coo. He barks. Now they are slapping cold cement and wet bandages around my head, tighter and tighter. No light, no air. In an hour it will be hard when they set fire to the lower parts of me and they'll spin me in the chair around and around till my corpse is dizzy, throwing up downward into the flames, which will surely have some beneficial effect in this awful climate, you are never any place that you aren't shivering like a machine designed to do it.

George

When you all of a sudden stop dying, your *I* comes back. You are who you were again. They can't see this from the outside of you, but your heart knows it. Like a piece of bright tin polished up. Set by the evening lamp, like a radio that brings the noises of Havana, Cuba. Yes. The farther you drift outward from yourself, the less you tune in to. The more you come back to yourself, to the center of things, the more you hear, the more you find coming toward you. It is lovely to waft back from the edge, as if some mountain lion has just done all of your breathing for you, for at least an hour. Well, I have been doing this for a dozen years. Nephew says I am lying. A year or two then. In and out. Over and back. Nothing steady, mind you, but this constant kitelike thing. You never know if you will get back to earth. It is like some young women hovering between girlhood and womanhood, when they are like mature women hovering between coming and not coming. That is what it is like to be blind and at death's door, as Anglos say. Does the door have a keyhole to peek through? Is there a slit cut in it for mail? Is there a shiny brass knob to hold on to during thunderstorms, provided you are not afraid of being struck dead by lightning? What I want to know is this. Did I come back from the edge because of a radio, or did I get a radio for coming back from the area where all you can hear is shortwave stations being jammed? My nephew is no longer working, and the thought nags at me. "Oswald Beautiful Badger Going Over The Hill," I say, "does this mean we have to give back all we've bought? The pills, the blood pressure machine, the shortwave radio?" *"Nothing of the kind,"* he says. He is going to become a carver, he is going to carve dolls, just like me. No one carves dolls just like me. Who would want to anyway? Now I seem a little better, maybe I could teach him something basic, nothing much, but enough to carve for the tourist trade. "I thought you were a goner, Uncle," he confesses. "You were a feather on the breath of Sotuqnangu for quite a while there. We did not know from day to day." He sounds as if he has smiled. I no longer reach out with my big ugly hands to feel at what people's faces are doing. Let's say he smiled, no argument. He smiled because I am back among the living, although that's a poor place to be when all you can do is swoon and fade, feel more alive when you are asleep than when you are awake. I mean, looking at it afterward: you have a strong sense of having felt better during the night, whereas the day is hard work. People have no expectations of you when you sleep. They leave you to get on with it. Well, how I've felt lately amounts to this: They treat me during the day as if I am still asleep, which I don't mind that much. They feed the sleeper, they wash him, they try to get him sleepwalking from time to time. They even help him to the latrine so that he can move his bladder, his bowels, in a dream that belongs to childhood, with a spanking at the end of it for being messy. The spanking I miss, thank goodness, but I still have that sense of having done something mighty wrong. "Carve, then," I say to him, "go ahead and try your hand. Use cheap wood. Not cottonwood root. Practice until you're a half-decent worker. Don't copy anybody. Use a free hand. Listen to what's inside. It is a better living than Palookaville. You can stay home and get rich." He laughs. "Rich I'll never be, Uncle. I've saved a bit, but nothing lasts that long." "Do the big gaudy dolls, then," I tell him. "Like the Navajo ones. Paint them glossy and make sure they have lots of teeth. Tourists like teeth. They like their dolls to look like wolves, and they like to think they have bought something that's been shot. What they really want is a stuffed fox, or a wolf. Carve them out of anything. They won't know the difference. Why don't you do a wolf with a wolf on its back? Three feet high. And don't tell anybody

I said so. George and Oswald will never be in the same trade. I remember when you were a child. You had cold chills in the gut and
your insides were all messed up from the worms. We thought you
didn't have much future, but now it seems you almost have too much.
You been trying to please the market all along, but now you have to
please the tourists, the buyers. Some collect the dolls I make, but that
is a very special thing and not a market you could hope to tap. It's
easy, though, to make them gaudy, flashy, some kind of reverend's
nightmare. Eyes that seem ready to pop out, Nephew. All the teeth in
the world. You could even hire helpers to paint them for you. Ship
them by the dozen in a crate. I've often been tempted, like once when
I wanted to have a car. Just fancied the idea of sitting in it, not so
much going anywhere. I am lucky to have a wall to lean against, a cot
to lie down in at night. Don't try to be too good. Don't carve yourself
into a corner. Ask yourself what they want, and then give it to them.
Don't try to express yourself, as they say. Don't do it for you, do it for
them. Then you will be able to buy your old uncle a car with braille
on the dials. A blind man's joke, Nephew. I'd have to know what
speed I was going at into what I couldn't see. At least I have seen the
Grand Canyon, thanks to Oswald Beautiful Badger Going Over The
Hill. It was one of the best days in my life, like the time your aunt
swam Mormon Lake. It has not all been blindness by far. My head is
as full of sights as a cob is full of corn. Ask your Uncle George. It's
enough to have a life, to be alive. Being alive is a worthwhile thing in
and of itself. There is nothing else, Nephew. And it doesn't matter
how poor a life it is, it's better than what is often offered as the only
alternative, which isn't an alternative at all. It is just going to the
dump. Don't you go fretting about the quality of your life, you just
make sure it has the quality of life itself. The rest will take care of
itself, good or bad. So long as you are able to tell the time, you don't
need to know how a watch works. Or something like that." He looks.
No: how I would love to begin to say something like that. I can't say
looks, but I think it, based on the things I hear. Let's say it. He *looks*
upset. I meant to upset him. I needn't see him to know I've upset him.
I've been upsetting people all my life without, after thirty years or so,
ever needing to look at the effect I've had. You can smell upset off folk
like that vinegar stench of leaves in the fall. It's in your mouth before
you open it. "You'll soon get used to the harsh things I say," I tell
him. "Now you have turned into a carver of dolls, I have to level with

you. When you were a movie actor, I didn't need to truth it up so much right there to your face. Now you have become serious, George The Place In Flowers Where Pollen Rests is going to be serious with you. Try to please. Don't force yourself on folk."

Oswald

He fell silent, and so did I, though my mouth worked on, growing up in one second. Never mind about eagles. What about Oswald and Trudy Blue? I was alone on the very top of the mesa, next to a crumbling stone wall, surrounded by discarded oil drums, ashes, doors braced with three planks in a Z shape, and cast-iron pipes, some for smoke, one for runoff water. Over the edge, just past the rail, was the void, the sea, almost anything beyond human scale. It was like living in a fort, and those tall tapered poles that came up from the roofs beneath weren't the tops of ladders at all but light artillery to repel invaders with. Everything was rock or cement, as urban a landscape as you find anywhere. Every step of every foot you heard and wondered at. Were there people up here in the wind and just below the clouds? Indoors, on that day, there was a feast laid out on carefully arranged sections of newspaper, on the floor, with plastic Dixie cups and bowls and buns and basins of hominy stew. Everyone squatted on the floor around it, eating as slowly as possible, everyone but Emory, my official father, who had gone into the bedroom to sprawl on his back on the bed, with two pillows under his head, his feet sticking out over the edge. He was reading a magazine, not inclined just then to be sociable: a bit off his food, a bit off color. That image and one other recall him for me as he was before he kind of drifted away into Winslow to work. I too would go sprawl on the bed to read, I too would head for the city. Doing everything slowly so as to savor it was beyond me. I was just not mystical enough, I suppose, although you didn't have to be very mystical. Just enough. Daubing other folk with mud on ceremonial days didn't appeal to me that much, or games in which visiting aunts gave the men token haircuts, as if scalping them. It is all fun if you have nothing else, but it always seemed to me not fun enough. There were long spaces in which nothing happened, nothing got said. Life had come to a halt, just to prove it could. I took with me the image of my mother, not so tall, portly, standing on the flat rock, trying to smile at what numbed her, in a floral dress with a neat round collar and a square crammed pocket, a red sweater over her shoulders as she looked westward to California. On the very edge, as if getting ready to jump. Next to a rectangular trough cut into the rock for water, like a tiny wet grave. Then Uncle George appeared behind her, nodding and consoling. Neither knew I could see them, but they must have sensed something of me in the high thin air around them. First my father, then me. Maybe Uncle George, too, was thinking about leaving the village, inviting himself into the world of commerce. Or so I thought. He never budged, but although he was always with them he was rarely of them. There was always that space in between them and him, and hardly anyone dared cross it. Chubby, hopeful people, these, with plump cheeks, rather like the dolls he carved, but here I was, leaving the fount of goodwill and family support. Had I had a sister, would I have gone? Why did my own people, unlike most of the others, breed so poorly? Was there a flaw that produced oddballs every time, but only a few? Restless and sterile, that's what we were, and maybe the one led to the other. After his Bessie's death, Uncle George gave up and married himself to the cottonwood root. He took me on as a distant apprentice, whom he could abide only because I was mostly away, and befriended my mother, a woman much more sedate and conventional than his Bessie. It was painful to see him trying to live with a dead woman in her sister's image. After a while, he gave up, decided against all kinds of substitutes, and threw his heart, what was left of it, into his carving. He carved himself back to sanity, I think. He expressed *himself,* which the other carvers rarely did. Those days he was Uncle George the

Gentle, a touch sad, but most of all a powerhouse of energy. All you had to do was sit next to him and you felt it humming inside him, coming off his hands like St. Elmo's fire, like magnetism. If only it had worn off onto me, or even someone else. I remember him, feeling at my skull and pressing it as if selecting a lump of wood to carve, then reading my hands with that odd, troubled look of his, letting them fall as he looked away toward Antelope Mesa, knowing perhaps that I was to be better with words than with wood, better with organs than with tools. "How," he would ask me with his heavy-handed grin, "is your tool, Nephew? Mine is sharp and shiny with use. Do you put it away when you go to sleep? Mine I wrap in a bit of leather, against rust." There was no answering him except with a soft, dependent grin: nephew to uncle. He wanted me to grin. I did. If he had been a woman he would have been a siren, I think. He would have led men on to disaster. You could see it in his eyes. There was something in him that wanted a big disaster soon. An end to the world. He wanted the whole village to go crashing down the mesa. He wanted it buried in never-ending snow. He wanted an end to things because his own life had ended first. And I think he wanted, then, an end to carving too. It was not enough, not until he began to age, and then it was a daily marvel, for which he would have sacrificed anything and anyone. He was happy, then sad, then miserably defiant, after which he soared into his gift until the doctors (as he put it) began to interfere with him. It was never the heart disease that fouled him up; it was the doctors, who, he always claimed, hated anything creative. He would ask them questions about himself, very personal ones, such as how long he was or was not going to live; and all he got, he said, was general answers right from the textbook. They treated his illness, he said, without ever noticing him. How could they miss him? He was a handful. How could he miss them? They pleaded with him, but he turned curt on them and half-mystical (not that he couldn't have been altogether mystical with them if he'd wanted). He tried to pay them in wood. In dolls. He refused to take the small plane that ferried patients from the one-strip airfield west of Polacca to the PHS hospital in Tuba City. "Fix me up to stay put," he told them. "My people need me." They did not, but he kept the myth alive. Who knows, he has probably lived longer this way than he would have doing things the other. Our Uncle George, as they saw at last, did not belong to them even though he sometimes went to see them, led in by the local Judas goat. All the same, he sided with me, urging them to let the boy go, let him sample the fleshpots. Who knows? He might become a doctor and come back to cure us all. With his illness he thought the whole village was sick too, in sheer headlong sympathy, and he kept urging even the halest of them, my mother included, to go see the doctors to check on their hearts, their cancers, their lungs, their blood, their spit. Interesting logic, his: he was ill, therefore he would recover if the whole village had treatment on his behalf. His heart throbbed on, giving him less blood than he needed, yet enough to keep his hands in motion. I think he saw doctors, at least those in Keams Canyon and the distant unvisited Tuba City, as competitors. I shall never forget his look of knowing envy when he first saw a rubber hammer, a scalpel, his first tongue depressor. Had he been able, he would have helped himself to a handful and continued to carve with those; all he needed was an orthopedic mallet, a few silver saws, and a cautery to keep the warmth within his wood. When I caught him using the field glasses to stare at his weight on the machine below his feet, I knew we had lost. With these, I thought, you should be looking for the white of eagle droppings on a distant mesa, not at the number 209 or whatever it was that day. Once upon a time the medicine was free, and now he goes without, except for the moldering mess in his cookie jar, flecked with brown and green, smelling like niter. "Throw them out, down the canyon," I told him. No, it gave him confidence to have them by him. Even if they kill you? "*Nephew,*" he said as loud as he ever gets these days, "they are too weak for that. The goodness is all gone out of them. They wouldn't kill a mouse. How light I felt when the plane brought us back." I gave up. He gave up. Everyone gave up. He had made it public that his cure, if any, was going to come directly from Sotuqnangu, and not from combinations of quaintly tinted pills with funny little logos on them. Take, at least, I begged him, the one made from the foxglove, the natural one. "Better, then," he blustered, "to chew the foxglove itself. Does it grow, up here." Since it did not, he decided he didn't need it. What ailed him had grown up here. So too, then, should what would cure it. As for the blood-thinning rat poison, as he called the Coumadin, or the quinidine made from cinchona bark (which he wrongly called malaria medicine), let the doctors feed it to the kachinas when they came down from the San Francisco Mountains. If it killed kachinas, it was bad. If it cured them, then all right. But kachinas were never sick. On it went, like that, as he cantankerously sleepwalked his way through the drugs of a modern culture. Maybe his occasional aspirin

had saved him, thinning his blood just enough, though he affected to
know nothing of any such process. All blood, he claimed, was thin, or
it wouldn't ever flow. "Yes, Uncle," I'd begin, and then give up. It
was, you might say, in his blood to differ. To differ and clot. To clot
and disappear. I think he thought he was made of wood, and god-
given wood at that. No disease was going to get in his way, slur his
speech, stun his sight, numb his hands. Somehow, dying and undy-
ing, going to the brink and then coming back like someone who has
seen the sun for the first time, he has endured. For him, it is enough.
Secretly, he does not wish to live; he hasn't wished to live for many
years, but he has soldiered on, with each day gleaning a shred of
desire to see tomorrow, at least to have the chance of considering if he
will grace it with his living presence or not. Not that he would kill
himself, plunging through the canyon or slitting his veins, but he is
capable of starving himself to death or of poisoning himself with his
time bomb of rotten pills. He would like someone to kill him, maybe.
A nephew, doubtless, so that, after his death, the police could round
me up and use their vaunted SWAT squad, for once chasing someone
worthwhile as distinct from trophy hunters lurking by night in the
old ruins in search of a pot, a plaque, a discarded doll. "Trust me,
Uncle," I used to tell him. "You can live forever. A little care now and
—" "Sotuqnangu," he began, starting up his standard Sotuqnangu
speech about the god he doesn't even believe in. "Don't fuss." He
meant to say, Leave me alone. I should have drowned years ago in
Mormon Lake.

George

"Praise everything. Belittle yourself always. Be true to others, but never to yourself. Tell them how willing and eager you are. Cooperate. Give in. Bow. Agree. Never take offense. Don't be anybody. Be a tool. Don't aspire, not even to a useful strangeness, which will get you a lifetime of trouble. You're awful quiet, Nephew. Maybe we need some movie music to stir you up. It must be tough having no lines, no action. You got to think it all up yourself like a mouse burrowing through thick corn. My so-called drive, a better word is in-it-iative (thank you, Mrs. Judson and Mrs. Holmes), has always been in my hands, which go their own way. Always did, wet or dry. I never thought about what they were getting up to. They were always feeling at things and folks with the naturalness of animals. Anybody who wants to be that way—to get that way—is just asking for trouble. It will not make you popular. You go ahead and feel at what you're not supposed to feel at, and then you carve something different from what you're supposed to carve, and that amounts to a lifetime's trouble. Beware the curse of being different. It may get you sometime into the history books, but it will set you back to front with your own people. Oh, they go along, they put up with you, but you do not rate with them, they never trust you, they keep waiting for you to betray them, and then, all of a sudden, they see that you have been betraying them all along in chubby kachina dolls. Only yours look this way, they tell you. They're all wrong. They will not do. Not even a mother could love them. And you not even a Navajo, a Zuni. They lay it on you good and hard. The trouble is, Nephew, by the time you learn wisdom, the folks you want to impress with it are dead and gone. You were not wise enough to make them wait around while you were learning how. My side aches. My head aches. My throat is thick with something tasting like fungus. My finger ends are numb. I am too dizzy to stand up. I can never lean my head back, because that makes me seem to faint. My nose is blocked. One of my legs has been twitching for weeks. My eyes—well, we know about my eyes. They are as permanent as the San Francisco Mountains. Now, you have minus all this, so get to work while you can. Get wise early. Then, maybe, we could afford another flight through the Grand Canyon. I don't have to see. I just have to know that others are seeing for me. It's that simple. What else can I tell you? Not a deal. Flowers are big suckers-up of sunshine. Always heed them. Talk with a twang ripe as a peach. Then folk will remember you have spoken. A wise man looks at a mattress and sees the stain to come in its future, so he right away figures out a response to how his mattress is going to be when, so to speak, he has lost control of it. When the Navajos got the flush commodes, at first, it all came up in the yard when they flipped the lever. I heard that from a lady who had one, and she said, You folk are so wise, you never mess with anything that is supposed to work. They jug-soaked us for years for hundreds of dollars just to keep it all from swilling up around the yard against the tires of the cars and trucks. I remember that lady. She had rings on every finger. She even had a little spray to point into her mouth and kill all the germs. I guess we missed something by not going along in such matters, but that is not a world I need explain to you. That is where you came from, until just now. Maybe it will be hard to put the clock back on your style of life. You don't have the option anyway, Nephew. You have come home to be an Indian all over again. It might not be too late. Don't let them ride you after I'm gone. You know your way around. I recall your telling me, just before we flew through the Canyon, how you can always tell the rubes who have never flown before. They always fill out the blanks for name and address on the tags they give you for cabin baggage, neat as howdy-do, plain for all to see whose house might be standing empty at that very minute. I heard you too, telling about the gangsters at the airports who look at the address on the bags you check and then get right out to where you live. Then they just empty out the house. You come home to nothing. We don't exactly have that problem, Nephew. They are more likely, if you are away, to start moving things in, to greet you with on your return. So much for country cousins. What you picked up in Palookaville don't work here. You have to learn from scratch. I would like to nap now," I tell him. "Just lay a piece of wood across my lap, for me to hold on to. Any piece of wood will do. Ordinary wood. Then it is like riding something very light. You hold on, but it does not support you like the crossbar of something you might be wheeling. No, it kind of lifts off with you as you go, not a tree or a broom handle, but a little stick. The evil of two lessers. Well, I must be getting better. I made you laugh out loud, Nephew. This old poop isn't as far gone as they was hoping he'd be. It doesn't happen often, but when it comes it is pure gold. They laugh to your face and cuss you behind your back. Don't let that happen to you. Never say anything unexpected, son. I mean nephew. Only my Bessie laughed as if I did not have a disease. She could laugh while swimming. She had the biggest lungs in the world. She could swim for a mile without breathing much. She was like oil on water. She was always wet. Never mind, it was a private thing I blabbed. Now to nap. Head to one side against a cushion made from feathers. Hands almost at peace. Chest busy, but forget it. Feet twitching just a little. Nose cold, but it will soon be numb, like my hands. This would have been a good time to take my pills, but I am already too far gone, too near to sleep. Do I need a pill, Nephew? Not to sleep, but to make sure I wake up again. Old pills, you say, older than you can use them. Then a new pill or two, some time. Before the seasons change. I am almost willing. Hoist me now. A good high hoist. I am a child again and the Ogre Woman is coming after me, clacking the sharp white teeth of her beak together. On her back she has a basket to put me in, to keep me in before she eats me. Here she is at the door. Listen to the hoots and the chanting. Now she calls aloud for George The Place In Flowers Where Pollen Rests. Bring him out, she yells. No, Mama says, you can't have him, he's okay. Mama has seen that hideous red tongue before, the knives and saws and axes. He's been very good, my mother calls through the door, and he's done his homework every night. She opens the door and offers Soyoko, the Ogress, a mouse, but that only makes things worse, Nephew. Here we go. The monster woman tugs me away from the door and off into the plaza, to be eaten alive. She stoops, panting and growling, touching the top of my head with her beak, but at the last moment my mother runs up with a rabbit and hands it over. Saved! No, one of the other ogres gives the Ogress a saucepan full of water, which she dumps on my head to teach me a lesson. But what lesson, I have no idea. Oh yes, they have made me pure again, pure as a young eagle. That was only once. Other times I was told not to speak so much Anglo and I recall having been dragged to the edge of a canyon and made to throw my baby bottle over. It will make you a good boy, my mother told me. So did the teachers at school. All it did was scare me out of a year's growth just when I felt I had begun to grow up. So save me, Nephew, from those old bitches with the clack-clack jaws, who first eat your lips, the tastiest, and then your eyes, your toes, your balls, your tongue. Shit you out in a big mound and then sink their asses into it to show how little they care for cleanliness. Surely they would never come for me at my age. What do they need with a mess of old bones? Days, though, I wake with the sense of having been bitten by just those jaws. They rake the front of my throat, they sip the blood. Then they go clonking away, for some fresher meat. I used to dread when they came, February or March, I can't remember. All that howling and roaring. I could not wait for July, when the return kachina shows up, all in white, and you knew they were going to head back to the mountains and stay there for six months. Odd that I have made an entire life out of carving doll replicas of them. But never the Soyoko, though I was tempted at times. Carve her and then set her on fire. Shove her blazing up her own ass, if you can do that. I always liked the clowns. They talked Anglo bad and pretended to ride motor bikes. They made fools of themselves and mocked the serious kachinas. So they got whipped and drenched and threatened with snakes. If I have to go, let the clowns have me, I am not scared of their round muddy faces or their big ears. I belong with them, forever feeling up the girls, pretending to play stinkfinger and fall down dead from the stench between the prettiest girl's legs. For that smell I would come back to life, Nephew. Why, I used to think, if the sweet young girls smelled as bad as that, what did the Soyoko smell like? It could kill you from the top of a canyon even if you were down below on the floor among the snakes and scorpions. No, the mudheads aren't the clowns, the clowns beat up the mudheads. One clown I saw had PRESIDENT JFK painted on his bare back and another had FAT ALBERT. Another was MR. PORTO TICO. Not RICO, but TICO, they got it wrong, it was even funnier that way. Thrash me with feathers till I die. Take me out, Nephew, and send me down for eagles. I promise not to come back. I want to go now. I want to enter the jaws of the Soyoko woman. Roll me between her enormous teeth. I am light as a feather on the breath of Sotuqnangu. I wouldn't weigh more than a mouse. I'm just a morsel. More what you'd spit out than wolf down. Something from between your teeth. Pretend I am in one of your movies. Ease me out. Off. There. In any direction. Have some fun with me first if you want. Wet me. Thrash me. Have snakes bite me. Just so long as you lift me up toward the sky, where the vapor trails cross and thin out. Make me one of those while I am little and so weightless. Send me home with a whisper. If only you knew more of life and death than comes from movies. Here I am, a blind man in sunglasses. Make me a memory, with snake, knife, or just a push." I never used to talk this much.

Oswald

When I look at him I see again my mother weeping to herself on top of the mesa at another of her family gone wrong. She and I have nothing to talk about. My father has come back. I cleave, good word, to Uncle George as if he were my own doctor, witch- or otherwise. All I need is a skill to speak to him with. I mean, something from my hands to shove at him, exempting me from having to talk. Look at this, my hands would gesture: I carved this. Then he says, in his bitter, impersonal way, "Good for blocking Navajo assholes." The man who can say that has never heard my Polaroid camera click as my breath fumed in the frost on the winter mesa. Or he has. He does not want reverence, he wants his quietus, he says. He wants Sotuqnangu to come down and hand over the chain of office to one who, for all his handicaps, behaves in a more godlike fashion: haughtier, louder, more blatant, more afflicted, less giving, less cloudy. My mother tries to nag me into making him see yet another doctor. "He eats them for breakfast," I tell her, "he needs to be struck by lightning, that's all. Dead, but still very much into kicking. That's him. He has no idea of how posthumous he is. What? Well, he's worse off than

he thinks he is." When he looked at her, I could see it in his eyes
when he could see, he wanted her to have been the drowned one, yes.
He no longer speaks to her, not even when she approaches him with
bread or stew. Pretending not to know who she is, he binds me closer
to him because he makes her less real. You cannot feel sorry for someone who does not exist. I read somewhere that genius is the ability to
will yourself a child again. That is him. He is that kind of mountain
air genius, to whom after a while you become accustomed, regarding
him as a kind of weather. At this height, I tell myself in my prosaic
way, he probably is not getting enough oxygen anyway, not when it
is cold out, which it often is, and he insists on sitting out in it and
breathing deep. "Hold your breath, Uncle." "Hold your tongue,
Nephew." It goes like that for hours. He wants to puff on a pipe and
blow smoke into a shrine somewhere in the mountains, but nobody
will bring him the makings or the pipe. His heart goes rambling and
his hands roam too, as if somehow translating cardiac into manual.
Hard to read him as it is, I have watched for hours as he signals in his
blind way, seems to motion for things he does not want, simply fitting his thumbs and palms to some cavort of the auricle in there,
shaping the ideal bulge for his blood to occupy, the mechanism of a
more perfect pump. Is that it? Or is it semaphore for Sotuqnangu, the
god who as I see it does not believe in himself because George The
Place In Flowers Where Pollen Rests is an atheist. It is as daft as that.
He's cranky, obstinate, doomed, but I can still muster some love for
him, maybe because he's stuck it out, played the devil with them, and
never looked back. Is that what I wanted to do and found someone
twice my age doing it better? I feel so close to him sometimes, it's as if
we both have the same disease. What's he know about death anyway?
Uncle George has surely never been in the tangles I've been in.
Things don't always turn out according to the book, not when some
of them get ramming. Three-way it was, two of us deep into her
innards, a third into her mouth, and somebody out of that tangle
wrapped his hands around her throat, and then the twitching began,
a fume in a fury, except nobody noticed, it was not that kind of
action. She was going down in flames. She couldn't talk, she couldn't
gesture, she couldn't break loose, so plugged three ways she sank
lower than she'd ever sunk before. With a camera recording it. Minute by minute it got more and more valuable, although nobody knew
it at the time. "We will never use it," they said, and then they had
trouble convincing the buyer that the girl had really snuffed it. There

was no death certificate, you might say, to prove it one way or the other. They sold it, though, not that we got paid any extra. Fluke-snuff, they call it. Not like a good clean shooting, which you can see on camera is no fake. She did not cry or scream, she did not even weep. We finished and we were none the wiser for, oh, five minutes. *Tell him now.* She never answered or moved. Two of us almost started again, turned on by her act, but it was no use, you could see that something awful had happened. There was this reek of dead fish. An old harbor–type smell. No blood, but she was paler than flour. Her eyes had the scalded look you sometimes get from flash. Wide open to receive, but getting nothing. "It isn't," I said. "No," they said, "she's faking. She's good at it. She's done it before." That was the guy with big hands. Arms, legs, torsos. Who was that old sculptor who did it? With snakes as well. Never mind. It was as close as I'd been. Close enough. Accessory, they'd call it. We never saw her again; she took a last flight out over the ocean on a dark night. It would have been safer by day. What would Uncle make of that? Another drowning? I used not to be callous, but that kind of thing burns something out in you. It hovers over you while you live a life of wondering. I have lived a portion of my life in a slaughterhouse, where for all I know they hose down the bodies. It is almost more than you can stand, except up here in the clean air of the mesa, with a blind man for company, and the injured looks of your so-called family. No, Uncle, we did not break her neck. She ran out of air to breathe. Not one of us had any murder-ous tendency, it was like a slip of the chisel, see, a knife hitting a knot in the wood. Well I'll be damned, look at that. You say something such. You exclaim and reach for a rag, hold it up above your heart to quell the bleeding. So, when he says to hoist him up, I think he wants me to raise him above the level of all the bleeding, only I know better. Hoist me, he could say, above the level of strangulation. Not really: he'd like to be shoved down to it. Odd, this: he that wants to go can't go and she's that already gone had no such wanting. "It's the breaks," somebody said. Uncle'd say that too. Give me life or give me breath. That kind of thing. You ask and you do not usually receive. You get, and then it is too late to wonder if you've just gotten what you se-cretly wanted all along. By then too late, and there is never an early to match it. That early only comes into being after the fact of the other, like some wisp drummed up out of the dawn by the noonday sun. It's what had not happened before what did. My mind slithers away when I think of it. My head gets hot. I want to roar. I talk to

him instead, calming myself if possible. It was some time ago, anyway. It feels like at least five minutes, so they have not had time. He is
sitting with a time bomb. So am I. We will both go off at some unknown point, but not together, that's out of the question. I'd ask no
favors. I'd end up doing jail porno, much the same stuff as before,
except for the lack of cameras. A youngish man from a dreamy people
isn't supposed to get into this type scrape, not ever, not locally or far
away. It is not allowed for. The kachinas do the killing here. The real
kachinas kill off everybody, and the fake kachinas just give you a
tough time, some of them anyway. The ones he carves, kind of the
third order of them, do nothing. Girls play with them and tourists
buy. "You have gone silent, Nephew," he says. "Are you wishing you
were back in Palookaville? Is it dull for you up here?" That stops me.
I would like it duller. So dull that no one saw me, even, or knew my
name to call me by. If only they had smothered me in cornmeal and
sent me into some other world. We give the eagles names, but nobody
remembers the names after the eagles have gone. It is often the same
name anyway, so the same eagle is always on the roof, two months at
least. "No, Uncle," I tell him, "it is lovelier here than in January,
when the unmarried women wear their black eye masks and the men
try to make them laugh by doing tricky dance steps. Then comes the
rifle fire to kill the buffalo as they run away. I would not swap life on
the mesa for anything." He doesn't believe a word of it, but he's too
far gone to argue. He thinks I am trying to be polite when I am trying
to calm my head. No, Uncle. Yes, Uncle. "I am truly at home here,
truly, at home, yes." He wants to toil at his delight. All he really
wants is a quiet afternoon, with the untrapped eagles settling down to
a steady survey of what goes on underneath them, and the one or two
TV antennas picking up that steely light coming in westward. The
smell of smoke and *piiki* bread baking. I know him. That is what he
wanted back then, since when he has lived in a series of shrinking
circles, like some prisoner being tortured. "Donate me an eye,
Nephew," he says, with brutal mirth. I ask him who would take his.
He does not need a kidney or I would. He needs a brand new human
suit with all new stitches. They could open him up and use a truck-
load of brand new organs in there. Now I have gone back a dozen
years. He is yelling down the canyon to make me come up, with eagle
or without. Did I imagine it or did his voice really vibrate along the
winch's cable? Like some old telephone. "Leave it," he says. "Nobody
got to have an eagle." "So they do. They do so, Uncle. I called it up."

"Trash all eagles," he says. "They're not spiritual at all. It is one big hoax, Nephew. Kachinas, well they are a different piece of mesa." "Hello," I call, unable to see them. "Anybody down there?" They haul me up like a fish caught. No, not that smart. An old boot full of water, but at least with an eagle in my hands for them to choke. Brown hands. Old eyes. Plump cheeks. Weary sun-stained eyes. These men have begun to look as if they are living too long. Something pushed past limits comes off them like damp. If they hadn't this to do, they'd have no idea how to waste their time. They can't all run the gift shop on Second Mesa. Uncle is the standout. He has his mystery. It has him. They wrestle with each other in the dark. The grain talks to the chisel, the chisel sends a message through his cupped palm up his arm and into his shoulder, tells it not to heave water or pickups stuck in mud, but to stay pliable, a big muscle aloft, just in case. An extra burst of power might be needed. You never know. We have had good times. I'd weep if he could see me. Can you hear weeping? The body shakes. Oh yes. He could plant his hand on my chest and feel it heave. Under the heave, he'd feel the juicy young pump he'll never have again. When I was little, I'd say I had an uncle and so got to thinking of him as A Nuncle. Like A Napron. I never said napron, but I used to say Nuncle till he chided me for being fancy. "Talk proper, boy," he'd say. "Sotuqnangu is on the ladder, listening. If he thinks you don't talk right, he'll seal your mouth forever. Then you'll be like a ball that has no bounce. Say *Uncle.*" But I do not. "Well, Nuncle George The Place In Flowers Where Pollen Rests," I'd begin, but he'd slap me down for the first word. Behind his defenses, kind of. You mustn't call him Daddy either, that really vexes him, he spits his soup out and waves the nearest saw, like an old Soyoko. What he doesn't know, though, is that I'd jump into the bag on his back without being told. I'd love to ride him on the downward chute, whacking his shoulders as he skids along. And when I looked again he had the wooden doll down his pants and he was kneading it like his own flesh. It was his way of being intimate. "Getting a taint of musk into the grain," he said when I asked, ever so polite about it. He aspirates wrong. "Hit thinks it is in the swamp or something. Tries to grow all over again. *Cottonwood,*" he says. "Did you ever see the like of it?" Mostly he goes unanswered. He always did. They let him ramble, waiting for the knife to slip, him to lick the blood as if that's what he'd been aiming at all along. A blood licker. "Better than any half-et banana," he tells them. "That is Georgey juice." In all his years of

carving, though, he let it slip less than half a dozen times, grumbling
Mitits or *Am-eche,* any of those words he likes to pick up and use
against their original sense. What a sight. Humming, chamfering, a
blaze of flakes. Something appears in his lap, white and smooth, a
hard-on like a scalded tree. He likes this joke, he always did. Then he
would remove it from his lap and carve the rest of it against his left
thigh, having seemed to pull it from out his bowels. You'd watch it.
Who wouldn't? It was conjuring. It was magic. It was his only way off
the mesa, where he belonged as the wind belongs. He belongs so
much there, like the expert traveler who knows all the airports in the
world, exactly where to buy such and such a kind of pastille for his
throat, and which men's rooms have a little shelf up high to the side
of the urinal trough, so you can slot your bag in there while you
empty out. He never carries a cabin bag too big for the space in the
men's room at the airports he is going to visit. Sophisticated, in a
word. Not a word heard much on the mesa, but they have the idea
okay. Asked his name, he points to the wood and the sky as if there
are faces in both. What I did not know until he showed me was that
one book he had his finger in was full of spiders, running through the
gap in the spine, along the edges of the binding, down across the
pages. It had been lying in a loft someplace quiet and webby. And he
could not make up his mind whether to squash them or let them have
the run of his hand as well. "They live here now," he said. "This is
their mesa. Would you swat them? Say a prayer to their spider-ness
first if you do, then make a fast end of them." He slammed the book
without taking aim, and I never saw him look inside it again, or so
much as curl a finger to mark it. Something about that book was
separate from him, and he heeded it deep down. "My finger," I told
him, "is never going into that book." He smiled as if he knew. The
books had read his eyes by mind light. It must have been that way. It
was the Anglo Bible, he said, and they only ever had but the one
bearded well-behaved kachina from the beginning of time, a brave
enough one, he insisted, but too much on his own. What he meant
was something mammalian faint-heart attributed back to the spawn-
ing god, but he'd never say it. He was fearsome mild.

George

Were he to lie by my side holding my hand it would be harder. Every little tremor would get through. Who knows what he'd catch just from the touch. Blow his breath into my gasps, forcing them back down my gullet. "Help me breathe, Nephew. Blow a gust into me." He could hold me like a baby, fold my hands together on my chest, then force me against him as if to boost my heartbeat with his own. Thump my murmur with his young life. It would be like having my own locomotive to haul me. Now it's all flashes of the bare land I've spent my days in. Blue of Mormon Lake and the nimble river that peters out short of Flagstaff. If you want to be dry, come here. Ocher pillars, teeth from a dead red mouth. Grainy flanks as if a massive knife had sliced through. Lined with ice. Spires above the flooded floors of canyons. Little bushes there like hostages. Or else. All my life that adage. Never mind what they think, it's how they think it. There she is with two horses, four wheels with rubber tires, kerchief keeping her black hair neat. Trundle by. They have something wrapped in rags, maybe another eagle. The horses have done it before, they know the way. Alongside them the canyon walls like a sky of rock. In a floral white-and-red frock. Someone cut antelopes into the wall for us to gawp at. Blockhouse castles too, where once dwelled whoever was first here. Rafters. Props. Ladders. Domes. Runoff spouts and masts for the telephone line. All done with an ice serif. Stay sheltered in the overhang. Kivas full of sunlight are where the gods tell dirty stories. That low winter sun warms the sandstone, makes it an ember. No photographs, please, it is against our rules. See how the heatless sun gilds the tops and sides of the village. A little pyramid without a base. The peaks have frosted tops, where the gods hover. Never so many trees as there, gold because iced. "Behold, Nephew, lambs tumbling down a sandy slope, its wavelets made by wind anew each day." You don't see much of them up here, cotton balls against a landslide of chocolate like the falls of the Little Colorado. Brown water full of dust. Buttes. Layers. Cones. Once they were hot. Even the Grand Canyon, bigger than everywhere. On and on, down and down, as you feel your breath leave you and not come back. Who can breathe such air? It is full of thin-spun glass. The sun's bunk, I called it. I did not say tomb. Clinging together, neither of us can squat. Who needs it. Or talk much. Not even see. He is too close to my blindness. On the hide of the cottonwood trees, mist cakes as the wind blows it. Gnarly and ridged. It feels like imitation trunk. They get to look so naked. Travertine makes the water blue, green in the ponds. My ballpoint's ready. What do I sign? Where. I'll give it all away. Not anyone's to give. Then you can have my looking privileges lifelong. I have missed water like a sister. Pedestals. Rocks. Logs. These I have known. Up on top the mesa turns blue, bruised, shale and clay all exposed by tireless weather. Curl up in a gully. It will keep you warm and toasty. Any niche or the wind will search you out. Once these rocks were logs, now tinted slabs of jewelry. You can't have a mountain for a friend. It does not need you. It waits for you, though, so patient, so long-suffering. All this granite dumped by something or other. Most probably other. Toadstools, dragons, potatoes. Any shape you want to make the place more friendly. Pink shale my godchild. Don't get too sentimental up here. They let you go on raving until the very end. That's how it takes you. They all know. Let him get it out of his system and he'll get out of ours. Take him to that mission near Tucson, white-lipped, white-antlered, white-faced. Lodge him forever with the saint under the linen in the glass case. In that murmuring reverence, all hushed save the chirping flycatchers outside. Nephew has adored it. It spoke to him, as did the birds of the desert. Ship me out then. My slab is waiting. They have cooled it with mountain sluices. Who could rot on such obsidian. Day was, with the Mititses, I learned five new words a day without a single smack in the mouth. Well, then, if you must be picky, Missuses. Their herselves with a long pin through each hat against the wind. Heaven help us that we should see they have hair. Large herds. Of? Of? Clouds. Old beasts of burden. Bison. Buffalo. Then what was their burden? Herds of amassed spirits, then. You could see clean through their jawbones and their faces were like atlases opened up wide with all the veins on the surface and the hills jutting like moles. Than them who's more welcome? "You're taking your time, George," they say. "You must have inhaled heartily as a baby. Let it out then. Let it go free, to somebody else. You've sapped it of its strength. Those big herds are bales of straw. How come?" Being well up on such things I'd have said camels ahoy, or at least mountain lion. The shapes are never the same two minutes together. Come for me they have in their unhandy way. Like a procession. Going backward. Oops, almost lost my mind then. Crimson over scald yellow. Purple cloud. Shafts of ocher coming through the maroon beeves. It is all swirling. Who stirs it? Slops and curd. It is nothing but the air around me all churned up like Sonora poppies on fire. Yellow of old pus made delicate in a flower's wands. Nothing softer than that bloom when it sags. It has that sticky cling. Almost a fluid. Comes off on your hands like orange glue. Sotuqnangu made it, through impetuous copyright. I never was a dumbo. Now the lightning. Nothing more common. Electric version of the faint lines on a sheep's bladder. My nephew's haircut, the Grand Canyon of the part. Crazy stitching in yellow all across a sky red to putrid. Still, you can think what you want in a thunderstorm. It does not heed you. It fizzles and thumps oblivious. The words are coming back as they will if you give up a lifetime of hand labor. Horny heel of hand at rest for now. The white dove of the desert is waiting for me. Galoshes off now. Unwrap the brow and iron the creases out. Feet in the air to tame the smell. It's all right. Somebody's number is up. Quick, count the years, the months, the weeks, the days, the hours, the tiny spiderlings of time. I have missed my turn. They came and left without me. Not far enough gone, they say. You have a bad habit of slipping back to what you love. One last tup before sleeping, Bessie. Juice flows while we snore in each other's armfuls. Then that line forms like a lightning strike down the side of somebody's face. Zag. A zig. It is all over the place. I have been struck by lightning and I struck it back right across the flash, too late, of course, but it knew what I was on about, oh it went off about its business. You're not supposed to talk back, George. No lip allowed. Now we'll have to start again. Count your lucky stars we didn't have a tornado come. You weren't much help. You're supposed to push, you know, like a mother. On my own? Like this? Death comes in like a greased black block of petrified wood. Well I'll be.

Oswald

"Clean him up," I hear. "The butt end, yes, and change his jeans. What about his eyes, though?" How to uncrust them? He would not ask, any more than he asks for furniture, a stool or a footrest, any more than he asks to be fed. It is more a matter of holding him back from some limitless promise he's just begun to believe in: amputee with visions of breasting the tape. "Hold still, Uncle, they are mopping you up." As if he were a remnant of some enemy formation stranded behind the lines in a forgotten war between, who remembers?, the Greens and the Browns. The long versus the tall. He looks choked, his jaw tightened around clenched teeth. He is holding something down, but nothing comes up. So, be peaceful. He tries to smile. A billy goat in rapture. Oh those old eyes, into which et cetera. I am neither old enough nor young enough for this. He would like his end delivered to him at the door where's he set an old cardboard box. Into this, please, Mister Parcel Man, Santa of souls. "Is it really in there? Have they delivered already?" "Tied with cord," I tell him, "in a plain wrapper." "Good," he says, "you don't want them all to know your business." He is dusting imaginary crumbs off his front. "Did the delivery man toot his horn when he drove away? Like the old days." "No, Uncle," I tell him, "but he waved a proud sort of wave. I saw it." "Did someone *sign?*" he asks, murmuring it. "They don't always bother," I explain. "They don't always want the signature. Who else would want what they delivered? They drop it off and get away from the scene of the crime with all possible speed." "Not much pride in their work," he growls. "You'd think they'd, well, spruce it up a bit. It's not as if it was just some free sample of soap or an ointment." "A life depends on it," I say, agreeing. "*I* wouldn't have said it exactly like that," he says, hurt. "He did wave, though, Uncle, as if he knew. He cared that much." "A special wave, you say. One of his best." "Yes." "I won't fuss then. He always did seem to like driving up here, especially if it was snowing, imagine that, and then he liked to wheel something big right up to the door. He's a real bringer. Big tin truck that goes smash and slam when he slides the door shut." Where, I wonder, is this all coming from? He must have heard in Keams Canyon or Winslow. Must have seen the United Parcels man and yearned, maybe a dozen times, for something to be delivered to his door. And now he gets this final delivery, *the* one. He could even refuse delivery. Goods damaged. He'd have to peek inside. With the UPS man watching him. *Oops,* we say. Something's leaking. There's a rattle of broken glass. We can't accept it. Sorry, he won't accept his end as ordered. "I want a death in good condition, Nephew," he says mildly. "If it's had a nasty bump, we might have to ship it back." He adores the thunder of the big wheels, the clash of the gears, the rumble of the trolley. He likes things brought home to him. Toys, calendars, catalogs. The TV from the mail order book. Now I see that someone has zipped him up in too much of a hurry in his coat, putting it on backward, maybe to fool the fates. Seeming to go toward them, he recedes, and makes no bones about it. I leave him be, though; what's the use disturbing him? His arms aren't quite as free, but he won't be using them anyway. Two more years, he pleads. Just to get things in order. He wants not to die while the sun is shining, or the wind is blowing, or the air has a temperature of any kind. Not while there is weather, ground, or pain. He would like to pick his moment, lordy yes. Have those chirpy birds of the desert come and lift him away with them on the beat-flap of a hundred thousand wings. Cactus pygmy owls. Billy owls. Screech owls. Killdeer. Elf Owl, whose quaint bubbling lovesong he has never heard at this altitude. Vireos. Cowbirds. Lucy Warbler who sings korea, korea. *Ko-re-a.* Phainopepla

of the swift wing beats, the shiny white disks on its shoulders, the
glint of epaulets. Satiny. Shiny. Come to get him in jet black. He
always thought I knew nothing about the desert. Up here
he's more likely to have a funeral chorus of buff-breasted flycatchers
or the Coues one that sings "José Maria." "What, Uncle?" Wet his
lips. His eyes. We do. He wants his nose blown for him, so we poke
into it with dampened tissue to make two airways, although heaven
knows what roosts above in the bridge or the sinuses. That eases him.
One croak, then a word: "Time." What time did they deliver it? "Ear-
lyish," I say. "It's all in the box?" "Nothing missing, I think," I tell
him. Now he is going to ask if he has to assemble it, find the batteries,
and all that. "Comes complete, Uncle George The Place In Flowers
Where Pollen Rests," close to incessant tears. He enters his own cozy
myth of how death comes. "Undo it, then, Nephew. Unwrap it. Get
the outside paper off it anyway." One yellowed fang a foot high?
Filched from Doc Matlock's office? I dare not look. Pounds of maroon
liver, into which a face has been carved. I have seen death close up,
just now, and I yearn to move away. "Look," he says. "A shiny
knife." I see nothing at all, but his hand is on the knife anyway. He
does not budge, but he wields the blade, backward in his parka as he
is. He carves a kachina in midair, following its outline with his
tongue. "Nine lives," he says aloud, as if he has rehearsed it. "All
gone." A child's expression of dismay at table. He is an Oliver Twist
today. His lamps are going out. Something greased and streamlined
moves through him, a quake, an ague, a fit, then he calms down. It
made him feel solid. Now he rears up again, raving about a double
sunset. Then back, gasping from the exertion. He is going to go on
like this for a hundred years, long after they have strapped his
nephew in the chamber of avenging gas. *Did a girl in, a nephew of mine?*
He seems almost amused. That satanic side of him comes to the fore
now and then. "How many are you allowed," he asks, "before they
get you?" And then I dare not speak of her anymore. What's in front
of me blots it out. I'm glad. I had begun to quail and shiver. What
would *he* do? Clean breast or tight mouth? He'd never have done it, or
been near it. He has never mixed with that kind of people. One of the
mind murderers he is, but nothing for real. Compared with what goes
on in his mind, our blue movies were nursery tales. I think of her
rotting body down somewhere on the floor of the Pacific, being swum
through by eels and spiny worms, all of her once most secret places,

and I think of him, who doted on his Bessie's swims. Where is Bessie now? Or what? Does he know that by his bed sits one of the damned? Guilt by coincidence, he'd call it. Sympathetic no doubt. "Off into the Canyon with you," he says. "Hide out with eagles. Find a cave and we'll lower *piiki* bread and stew to you twice a day. The eagles will give you some of their toys to keep you calm. After ten years it might be safe to come out. We'll disguise you as a kachina and let you out six months a year. Whip you and drench you in scalding water. You'll have to *pay*." "It was a Jimsonweed girl, Uncle. Nothing more than that. With teeth. She bit herself to death." He waves her away as something trivial. He can see the sense of bumping certain women off. Men too. He'll never blab. Too late to tell him, though. What will the next world do about it? Do they know already? In the next world perhaps they let you off. Once you reach it, you are beyond the executioner's long lever. "I did it, Uncle," I try to say: "I was part of it." "Did it go well? Was there dignity? Had she style?" I tell him what he wants to hear. No one is going to talk him out of it now. My uncle is backing me at last. I admire his crust, his gall. Wild oats. Even at the last he sows. He takes my part. He goes through the motions with me. I am not going to have to go away, called to the colors, volunteering to walk the razor's edge. Uncle George will take the problem away with him like a parcel. He was half into it, half in sympathy, so when he goes it will vanish with him, and I do not have to drop out of sight like the bad son I am. I wish. His new trick. He listens without hearing. I can hardly breathe. Everything is gasps. No one else is with us. "She was wearing a wig," I tell him, "blond over brunette, and it came off sometime during her last struggle. In the throes. At the end. She was the one who always complained that the beds we worked on were cold. Or rather the mattresses were." I tell on, repeating myself, asking him if he really believed I was making other kinds of movies in which I rode bicycles or fetched water as the Musical Indian. "A handful of spun glass," I tell him, "always gave the impression of something wet and slimy." He doesn't care. No longer can he play with the radio, the blood pressure kit. He is drifting into some last vision of his Bessie, whose spring-steel walk was hers alone, as if she had a vacuum between her legs. Her walk was an agile lope, hasty and flashy, a convulsive amble like some of the whores on Sunset. Is that what turned him on? Is that what he misses most? She was something of a jock, long-limbed for one of us, and loved the mountain trails. Big block of thick hair too. She was some-

thing to treasure. He could never keep up, walking or swimming. He
never tried to. He let her do his walking and swimming for him. And
her voice, they often talk of how she spoke. A quiet, murmuring,
bottled-up tone, sometimes very fast, as if she were speaking into a
microphone you could not see. Her laugh was an abandoned giggle, a
contralto almost, and it went on for several minutes once started. It
was something to admire, a kind of defenseless joy. So now he readies
himself to rejoin her, as he thinks. In a year he lives only a moment,
in a moment as much as a year. During the act of carving, he has been
known to pause for as long as a week, with the chisel held back from
the wood. Oh, he went and ate or slept, but the chisel was always held
back in his mind, and when he resumed he'd hold the chisel where it
was when he was thinking about what to do next. He has had a lot of
practice pausing. He holds on. He marks time while it marks him. He
outwaits all his impetuosities. He knows everything will come to him
if only he hangs fire long enough. Like death, for some sudden and
sneaky. For him the wages of waiting. The longest pause he made in
my own presence was when he supported a horse with a broken leg
while I ran for help. It must have been an hour. He did not move, and
he had actually, they say, begun to blend into the horse by the time
help arrived. He could do things like that. Will he ever speak again.
Lord love us. He *answered.* "Well, Uncle? It is going to snow." "Put
me out in it." He opens his mouth to catch flakes. A sigh comes out
graced with frosted breath. He will not be long now. *"Kwa'kwai,"* he
says, thanking me for leaving him outside. He would like me to sniff
some soap; he craves for something fragrant. I fetch it, waft it in front
of his nose. It seems to enliven him. He has enough strength to seize
it and hold it against his nose, breathing heavily, pulling the scent
into his lungs. Will Palmolive bring him back to us? Oil of the palm
tree? Now he has it in cupped hands against his face. He seems to be
praying to it. Maybe on behalf of the man I am going to be, if I
survive, Oswald the Fat, with a bulbous belly out front and an even
more bulbous rear behind. Jowls like udders. A small rosebuddy
mouth and an almost sickening desire to please, my face all hesitant
tiny smiles and pretty fidgets. A pleaser born. Not a carver or a prayer, not a leader or a swimmer, but one of the called-upon. Calming
airline passengers after they have missed their connections. Being
therapeutic to people. Oswald Beautiful Assistant. Something as
humble as that, as far from material witness as possible. Hollywood
"crowd *artiste"* grown up. Yet I have depended on him, even at a

distance. With him gone, I will float off into the void, babbling for mercy. I would even go with him. Nephew dies with beloved uncle— a Mesa tragedy. Just like that. With a knife. Bleed all over him to tell him I am coming too, don't slam the door. Don't waltz off without me. Leave room for Oswald. Save him a seat. Keep it warm for him. Squeeze in an extra one. Hunch up. Make room. Just a small one. Graft him on to your goodbye. Where is Oswald going to go now? It's one of those only too familiar patterns: the husband's death kills the wife, and the daughter dies of grief, which kills off her husband, widower for a week only, and all the way along the line of neighborly mortality. It doesn't take much. The kicked bucket clangs into every living room. The whole world is a rubber band stretched tight, ready to snap at the merest reminder. How many times has he said it? "I'll take you along in my pocket, Nephew." We could save him by having him rally long enough to watch my execution. His hand, which mind-reads, comes toward me, feeling its way into unfamiliar territory. Is this preliminary to the last clasp? It gestures in midair as if pointing to something in an invisible album. Why is he not cold? Out here, in this beginning sleet? His hand is warm, it warms both of mine. Nor does he tug it back. It represents him while he turns his face away. He never wished to die in warm weather, *any* weather; but now he seems to have begun to go in earnest. Wheezing, he coughs. Is this the onset of the death rattle? I have never heard it. No, he opens his eyes as if he could see and says, "I smell burning." "You smell smoke, Uncle?" "I smell seared meat." He is not very far gone, then, if he can say that kind of thing. "Shred up some mutton," he says. "I can manage *that*." "In a stew?" "Yes." He wants it now. I fetch. He drinks it thick. Others out fussing around him are like petals drifting off a plant. Only he is real. Only he is alive. Not only does he rally. He also picks up where he left off five days ago. Or five hours. This is the yield of pausing, if only I could work it out. Nothing can happen to you during a pause. Can that be it? So, if you pause nonstop, you become immortal. Only he pauses professionally, like this. He makes death stammer. He makes it give up the ghost it thought it already had. He waits death to death. Now he wants cheese, a hunk of Anglo bread, with margarine again. He never changes. It is this kind of junk that's preserved him. He is not someone living in winter. He *is* winter. He is cold-bringing Uncle. There is no winter without him. Winter is his own, it always was. You don't say Uncle died last winter. You say Winter died last uncle. Uncle killed last winter off, with stew and hard margarine. It has to be something like that, as if he were an armadillo disarming fate. Not only does he know how people think, as distinct from what. He knows how death kills and fails to kill, as distinct from whom. There will be no holding him now. He will cuddle snakes in a ceremony of his own devising. He will dress up as Sotuqnangu, as no one dares, and dance in the plaza, hot-foot and light of heart. He has become quite godlike, to use his own expression. Maybe he died when no one was looking, and this is the uncle who is going to last forever. Uncle Sotuqnangu The Place In Flowers Where George Rests. We all bow. We grovel. We bring him an endless supply of stew, a burned offering. His heart has become a kitchen, his hands are mesas. Shrunken, we live aboard him as if he were some ragged spaceship seeming to pause while exceeding the speed of light. He will take us all with him, away from the talk show hosts, the brown lettuce, the stench of gasoline, the need to vote, the artificial hearts, the speed limit, the brilliantines, the burst pipes, the enemas, the nits, the banks. Away from clocks and taxes. Uncle George is a whole people going home to stay, evicting themselves through heart-felt longing. My rear is numb from sitting by him. The cold has risen through three thicknesses of folded blanket. To go inside must seem like death to him. So long as he almost freezes to death, he will never die. He perches on the blade's edge. Not to seem to need life, he has no fear of losing it. No. I mean that, if you can bring yourself not to hang on at all costs, you will have no fear at all. You will not go. You'll be hard as carbon but you'll *be*. "Meet Mister Invincible," I said as I walked indoors, meaning him not me, but I knew something had rubbed off. The eagles did not know they'd die, and what they taught us was the art of pause, between the knowing that hurt and the knowing that smothered itself in light.

George

Forever quoting something I haven't read, where do I get such ideas? I'm numb. I'm blind. I'm done for. I still have what they call a lease on life. It will not do your bidding. I've come this far, I tell it. I can make it the rest of the way without help. No more shove. Just a kind little come-on. "Come on, George, try a *bit* harder. Another touch will do it. We want you here. Join us. Come across." They are not there. I am alone. There is nowhere else to go. Hope springs infernal. Not bad. The Mititses would be proud. Off we go again. Whoa. Ahoy. How do you say hello to the nothing that is there in place of the something you didn't want anyway? If you ask me, they are helping me out. Up and down. I was worse ten years ago. It all depends on your lines. If you have something good to say, you last. If not, finito. That is how my nephew talks. I doubt he ever strangled girl. He's meek and mild. The purpose of my still being here is to be here a little longer. Like a long stem with no flower at the end of it. Ask me out. Ask me in. Death is like America. Which is worse, the do-nothing of having been born into it or the do-something of having chosen it? Nephew would know. Strong here, weak elsewhere, he has both sides of my blood. If blood has sides. I'm waiting. I'm on the threshold. Chop me off. Why don't you buck up your ideas and put paid to me? I must have riled Sotuqnangu a great deal. He refuses. Do it yourself, slowcoach. If I could swallow my tongue, I would. No one can swallow your tongue for you either. So it comes to this. Like the man who lived on the ferry between two ports. When he died they buried him on land. It should have been at sea. Lend me out of your unmeasured store a goodbye, an Abyssinia. Not for long, just enough to get me up this chimney in the rock. I'll have a monkey's chin when I'm done. Ready. Steady. Go. There is no starting pistol. Go, then. Steady on. Ready, ever-ready. That's about it. It has no shape, no taste, no feel. This in-between is your classic blank. You would pay long thousands to get out of it. You have been made to pause to no purpose. Not obliged to go on, yet not allowed to mosey off. It must be for uncles only. It is what you get for loving fresh air. They leave you out in the cold. To ripen. To freshen up. To serve as a warning. One day, you become so hard they have to straighten you out with a chainsaw. Dolls are only dolls, not gods. Brighten up your ideas. I'd love to. Shine my shoes. Brush my teeth. Oil my hair. Any little standard maneuver to get their attention. Failing which, with a chunk of cottonwood root in one hand, the other planted firmly on my crotch, I'll hover like a seed that knows its address but not its town, I George The Place In Flowers Where Pollen Rests, whose only way out is through the resting place of pollen. It is as pollen that I come or go. I am an altar. An altar does not die. I am twice the man I was. Call me by both names at once. George The Pollen. George The Place. Done.

Oswald

Watching him die makes you want to be there inside it all, behind the scenes, with him playing host, a death rattle in either hand, his feet wadded together in that big felt boot, his voice an owl hoot gone baritone. On the outside is where I've been all his life, getting and fetching for him, not in hopes of a handout, just anxious to be on hand in the presence of a human being who knew what he wanted to do lifelong and did it, no excuses, no shoptalk, no toss-it-away smarts. Just carved. Like his holding up that horse. He just held it up and, for that holdup time, holding up was all there was. I envy him his ability to shut his mind. All the world outside him, that's what he wanted, that's what he did. Just imagine him going stag on a mattress for three or four other layabouts with a camera going purr all the time. He'd no more eat sheep's wool than air his cock to a lens. What he's always done may have been dumb, but it sure as hell was never trivial, that's what bites home when you ponder him, what he was and what he did. In a way I would fault him for unimaginative magnificence, but, my, he could insist. Never was there a better insister. He did not flake away. He did not sidetrack. He did not goof off. I know that's like saying a stone won't dance a jig, and good for it, but there is something about him beyond all terms of evaluation. Not good or bad, it has to do with his being steady. Him a mesa, me a pain. I get silly when I try to pin it down, waiting for the cops, but I do believe he doted on me a bit, sometimes more than any uncle should even on a prize nephew selected for eagle gathering. Let him be. I'll dig him up again, though. In my mind he will not rest. Portrait of the dodo as genius. He was a modern man for all his ancient ways: he lived in a modern time and said his no to it. That's modernity for you. And he went after his death like someone carving his last doll in a hurry, feeling worst when he felt best, knowing he should not, and feeling best when he felt worst because he was supposed to feel exactly that way. There remains the language of his hands, to which nothing he said has any relationship. He talked to change the air in his mouth, and he carved to change the universe around him. I do not read him right. I ought to understand. "The objective, Nephew, is to carve the wood rather more than you carve your thigh. Who wants a carved-up thigh?" He, he just hammered away at one thing. How many hundred trees did he cut up and change the face of, into dolls? Try if you can to imagine doing that in an afternoon. I do. He made a hole in the forest. He had the guts to talk on and on, through his fingers for the most part. He never thought in sections, units, pieces, but like a volcano, sat and brooded the one act. He overflowed or he didn't. He was so natural. I'd like to believe it, but I don't think it's natural to carve, whereas three-way orgies on a dirty mattress come from the heart. I almost believe that sleazy truth; and, if somebody else said it, I would. "Don't take on so," he'd say. "You're all upset." "Worse than that, Uncle, I'm on the run." "Well, who isn't?" He is all wise recipience. Fist my knee in that intimate but manly gesture of his. "Fix your mind on something else. Rub my toes, Nephew. Make them crack. Press on the pads. Come home in your mind and leave the dead to their deaths over by the ocean that keeps on rolling. You bought the cow," he says, "and your mother a smart woman with a nearly uncontrollable ass. Good old Fermina. Never mind. How'd you get into all that stuff?" I'd tell, but it would sound less like a reason, a motive, than like a whole series of trodden-down excuses. "All that's for whores," he says. "Misuse of the mouth." "A whore is what I was, Uncle." "And yet you are not rich." "I was working my way up to it." "Does your mother know?" "Only you." "I should have taught you serious carving," he says, "and one night in your sleep cut it clean off, set a wooden one in its place, lovingly tooled. Like that Dillinger. Just to make sure you devoted yourself to carving ever afterward." "I'm attached to it," I bluster. "Only for a lifetime," he'd answer. "Why don't you walk out to the edge of a canyon and say a prayer to the spirit of the girl. Say her name." He'd shrug, then say, "Who makes love to the dead?" Not a real question at all, but I could see how he was thinking about the dead and gone of the tribe, those living a death in life, those only mythic or dreamed, those behind the words we used every day, those whose spirits had been burned out or numbed. Many, many. Those who are only cannon fodder. Those who, like BertandAnna, never get treated as living human beings. Death in life: you carry it around with you like a skunk stench when all you want is new prints for your fingers, a whole set of fresh ideas for your mind.

Sotuqnangu

When was it anyway that he first felt that almost sexual itch in his thumbs as if, at the most impressionable age possible since being a mere suckling, he'd grazed on the dank satin belly of some siren made of wood, her mouth purging amber love gruel, her tongue a scarlet jelly shot through with stained glass cathedral lights, her voice a conch call from the Islands of the Blessed, her feet the tenderest roots white from long planting in the manganese-black soil, her breasts soft as fungus in cream, her loins a primeval forest between steppe and tundra except for the implanted ravine as hot as he could bear to touch, both his hands scarred as a result from the love acid vatted up in there, a plague on all comers? From the outset he shaped his teeth with his tongue, sucking all the while, hoping to prevail over the long haul, not to sharpen them but to efface the grain, almost as if honing a set of teething ivories for another child to chomp on, but they were his own, of course, and he has never to this day nicked his tongue or cheek on something too sharp to be within a human mouth, not that he is even now inhibited about grab and plunder, it is all open to his fevered touch, he sucks the velvet sap of trees, each nodule of the bark a teat to him, he chews the leaves with rabbity finesse, he burrows deep for roots whose scream on reaching the light eggs him on to greater onslaughts, and before he truly butchers it, its length, its heft, its pith, he tries to apprehend the tree as a whole, yes sir, grappling it to him as some fifty-feet-high whore whose places he scuttles up and down squirrel-like to reach and batten on, knowing full well he cannot have them all at once, but timing himself right and making urgent side errands of affection to keep the whole organism stirring quietly under his gloating thumb, not so horny as it is horny, not so long as it is wide, he having his own length, heft, and pith, not that any of this happens on the cleansed plane of so-called deliberate thought, it is rather an exploding impulse drawn from the dankness of the pine needle floor, brewed up among the rotten droppings of a million beasts and birds, none of them attuned to him but involuntarily building him his woodland sty in which to wriggle and fondle, plumb things and lard them with prehensile genius, puffing hard at the hardest point, then easing back as the knife bit softly along the grain, soft as an owl's belly, even as he chanted happily to those around him, ogling his prowess, I like it this way and no holds barred, no sir, soft and juicy, like a frogspawn cooked in gruel, it has no resistance to what loves it, it all comes through the hands like a waterfall of ravening, it flows through the shoulders even where many a fast coupe has skidded to its death, into the arms, like little well-fed mice running pell-mell under the skin as the muscles flex and shove, all coming together as a god's lunge, the wood as malleable as wax but to him only, who had long ago formed the earthy habit of calling trees by names, from a Sylvia of course to a Dorothy, an Alice to a Beverley, those names whispered in the crisp black of the San Francisco Mountain night, and they all kept asking hasn't he gone too far, you can hear him down in Mexico, he uses the forest like a brothel, he fucks children into the trunks, he rapes the hollow trees plunging his member into the termite-rich dust within, he makes a meal of the striplings, forest devourer that he is, and all he ever did was nod at them, I'll bugger your trees ladies and gentlemen so keep your distance, folks, a serious artisan is at work here, and he was, even saving the twigs to pillow his head at night, from which he absorbed many a sylvan thought, not that he lacked for those, most of all the honeyed thought that he was doing rather well for a mesa man habituated to bare rock and anemic shrubs, it was out of this world to have the planet's hide to chop at while, from on high, showers of deer and mountain lion uprooted by his busyness, fell in a dead-legged swoon, breaking their backs as they landed, bang, and he'd carved their warm bones into something in a trice, a few quick nicks and some chamfering and here was your rudimentary doll warm yet from the beast alive, which they preferred if they had to choose, O George The Place In Flowers Where Pollen Rests, we'd rather a cooled-off chunk of tree than a backbone cut to the quick from life, that being too immediate for something over the fireplace, if you take our drift, which he did, never one to ignore the slightest drift from acrid innuendo to black-mouth curse, he took it all in his stride because there was the most room in that mixed-up place of his, part aviary, part zoo, another part a botanical garden with fish living in trees with dark brown leaves and mating with gophers and raccoons, and they kept asking doesn't it gall you to have so much going on right next to you, and yet almost always out of control, that being a question, just the sort of thing he never faced direct, or answered, his fetish being to leave folks alone until they absolutely had to be trafficked with, then being the time to hand them a rough-cut pole with which to beat their brains to pulp, it being beside the point to explain anything of what he did, only the end product being eligible for public consumption, the gaudy but winsome doll nothing like a devil doll, such not being his religious métier, there to do his talking for him, except that everyone complained these dolls don't talk, they don't squeak, they don't suck, they don't cry mama and they don't pee-shit-burp-throw up, so he had to calm them down by reciting what the dolls could do beyond compare, like the Jimsonweed maiden, who can make trouble and drive you bat shit, folks, good looker without being beautiful, she preys on males just like the Spiderwort maiden from Jeedito Valley, who also comes to you at night in your dreams and drives you crazy, the point being how would nice folks like you, under no pressure, ever go crazy without the help of Chimon Mana and Pasom Mana, not to mention old Hachokata, god of the gamblers, a shaggy old liar in a breech clout as foul as ancient eagle dung, and the icy old god of the north wind and Palolokon the plumed serpent made of hoops covered with cloth and worked by a man behind a screen and, oh you're keeping me from carving with all these questions, one-horned gods and two-horned gods and the goddess of hard substances, may she be praised ugly by day a hag by night believed to be an immigrant from the Pacific Ocean, and the minor god of armaments and wealth, the two little war gods in feathered skull caps, with bull roarers and lightning devices, plus the gods of the cardinal points, all four of them; the Poker Boy, the Cottonseed Boy, Patches who wears a coat of mouse skins, the Salt Woman, and the Outcast Woman; but they had already begun to do a rehearsed-sounding chant against him, all you talk about is gods, most of whom are neither impersonated in the dance nor carved, you do not have your mind on the things of this earth, may your penis drip tar and your breath catch fire, but he was already bellowing names at them, fox, dog, mustard, cloud, peacock, coal, thunder, fish, rabbit, corn, and they were already saying that's better, George, urging him into snipe and turkey and bluebird and road runner and rattlesnake and hail and stone and Mormon Tea and cholla catus, chili pepper, bean, sand, horse, and rain, but he got fed up, told them to get out of his way or he'd call up Kwitanonoa the Dung Carrier to come and smear their faces with shit, and if that didn't work he'd enlist Tuhavi the Paralyzed Kachina, never imper- sonated out of gut-thick superstition, to come with his blind compan- ion and touch them off into fits, strokes, and other bodily maladies you would not think could come from someone in a pair of red moc- casins, a fox skin, a breech clout, and a rectangular mouth with a beard, his side horns turned downward away from the green bird- track on his forehead, and that was enough to drive them away, mut- tering he only deals with gods, he's just a big goddamned self-pro- moter hooked on the divine and the obscene, not that he cared so long as they insulted him at a distance, he was a high-class personage all right, already supposed to be involved in the smuggling out of illegal kachinas to places as far away as Wyoming and New Mexico, where he exchanged them for live white slaves to be introduced into the forests for the lumbering of trees all to be felled and carved of course to swell the traffic in white slaves as before to be introduced into the forests et cetera, where, after being deflowered by George The Place always with a long thin carved Sotuqnangu, thought by some to be the Anglo God of Holy Smoke, they became part of his personal entourage, except that the prettiest one he had drowned in springs or smothered in cornmeal, he wanted no competition with his kachinas, natch, and when he taxed them with the lies they told about him they answered, George, no sir, we wouldn't risk any of that, we just go about our business boot-faced, all we ever wanted from you was a little attention to our needs, we who spit and shit and never once looked a down-home god in the eye, come off it, beloved, it is time to deal with the living and the dying, why don't you come true for each and every one of us, take your godlike kachinas and burn them in the plaza, then we will mix a tea with the ashes and drink it laced with eagle blood, to which he responded in ripest Anglo, fuck that mess, he said, split my timbers, do you take me for a carved-out asshole, I'm the one who decides all that stuff, as to carving and who most inter-feres with the activities of people on earth, I have a pretty solid idea what matters and what doesn't, said so loud he seemed to be floating in a cloud of his own anger, so they went away, huddled, and then seized his wife, crammed her mouth with bubblegum, tied her hands and ankles with sheepgut, and drowned her in Mormon Lake to teach him a lesson about what matters in this world as distinct from the next, which is only a part of what we live among, beloved George our master carver, don't go off the rails again or we will have that sexy nephew of yours and mail his balls to Tucumcari to be ground into fertilizer for midget gardens and mouse ranches where the rich from Neiman-Marcus have tiny golden branding irons to put their markers on their herds of mice, as if you could do any such thing, he yelled, but they said she is drowned already, you proud hell-raiser, you had better go fish her out of the water, she is befouling it with her long legs and the crannies where you used to spend yourself, not that you can bring her back, uppity bitch everlastingly walking or swimming faster than anyone human, outstripping (your word, sir) good solid folk by minutes and miles, not that a stop hasn't been put to it, go carve the effigy of your wife's corpse, empty her out, hang her up to dry where the mosquitoes and birds won't make a meal of her, mainly the two toadstools of her famous gash, about which too much has already come to these ears, oh yes we haven't been asleep all these years, we have been listening to the ground, the bed springs, the soft illicit tree houses built for fornication in the highest branches, and all George could get out was you wouldn't dare, you mongrel shitlickers, I am the boss here, I decide everything, but they catcalled him from a distance, waving old underwear and yucca whips, calling *you fucked the forest instead of her*, and now, when it is too late, you will go and fuck the wrong woman, George, you have no idea what is whose, you do not heed taboos as old as time, you blunder through the cobwebs of our ignorance like a drunken mountain lion, you do not fit, and because you do not fit you want to cut us all to size, why don't you go carve hardened beaver turds instead, do something useful before you die of grief, she was never so clean as the night we dunked her, her flesh was never so white as after she floated around a day or two, the husband in question not even having noticed his bed was empty, and now she is like shelled eggs afloat in that spermy Anglo thing called isinglass, cold clammy slimy something or other they keep in big brown jars in their cellars, not that our information on the planet's other tribes is up to date, but all we need to do is ask old George, the widower, the one bereaved, with a wooden plug in his mouth, another up his ass, and an Anglo golf tee implanted in his glans to guarantee his good behavior, to come to his senses before they leave him for good and he spends the remainder of his unlovely days fishing tadpoles from out his wife's mouth, building a raft of kachina dolls to float her away to everlasting bliss, whose trumpets are made of cereal not brass, and he says goddamn, I do survive just about anything, I get by, whatever they do to me, they wouldn't go to that trouble if they only knew that everlastingly, because of all the heartbreak and mind wound I've had to swallow, all the soft carvable wood in Arizona belongs to me, yes sir, and I am not going to surrender it until every tree has yielded up a thousand dolls, mainly of gods, and if that is not a sop to the electorate, then I don't know what is, you don't traffic with gods like you was dealing with folks. Oh no. I feel it now just as much as when he carved me out. He tweaks me and curses as he works. How rough he is going over the armpit and groin for the first time. Imagine being human like him and having the same. It hardly bears thinking about. He is so strong that he does not need to carve, he could squeeze the wood into any shape he wants. Like dough. Better that than his none-too-sharp knife. Oh to strangle him as he carves. Oh to plug his nostrils and mouth, watch him puff. We are never big enough. Not even gods. He rubs his spit into me as he goes. He picks his nose and wipes his finger on me. Sometimes it falls away, but other times it gets chafed into my grain. How willful he is, and heavy-handed. Hates us until we're painted, and then he can just about bear to look. Those eyes looking down are harsh as files. The blade makes us howl, but he hears nothing. The wood I was complains nonstop about being cut into untreelike shapes. It never grows again. It cannot lengthen. Swell. He goes on, scattering it afar as shavings and ends, almost as if he was making a meal of it. When he gets to us he speeds up, quick to shape the thing he learns to hate before it has even come to life. Has he a name? Is he anybody or just a force? Who told him to begin? We wanted to be left in the wood, peas in the pod. Now he starts all this uproar and we end up in the hands of a little girl or a collector, always being caressed without being fathomed, always on the market without ever being put back where we belong, in the trunk. All this as if we were very junior to him. Given the chance, a top divinity such as I am would have a lot to say to him. How I would like to carve him from a trunk of flesh and blood, then smear him with cornsmut and colored spots. Into the Coalsack with him and never come out except aflame. Let some other put paid to him until he swears never to make anything like us again. He never carves us into the beings we want to be. He never gives us the things we want to wear. Oh for a white handprint dead central on my chest. Oh for a tableta of clouds and feathers to frame my head and make it vast as the dawn. I would like to bear a dish or a shell in front of me, brandish a butcher knife, hold a crook, or a slice of melon. When I see how the others are clad, I fret at being so naked a god. I could befriend him, did he but need a friend. Fetch and carry. Cook for him. Tuck him in at night. Wipe his son's backside. Kill the Jimsonweed girls who haunt his dreams, wear down their teeth. But the only need he has of me, of us, is that we remain dead, at everyone's beck and call. We see the full-sized version of ourselves in ceremonies and we boil with rage. It is one thing for a human to dress up as a spirit and then wash off before having stew and *piiki* bread. It is quite another to slash and file us into being and then leave us stranded in our greasepaint for the whole of time. Kill us, we whisper, burn us. Set us loose even if you cannot get us back into the tree. Only twice a year does he burn his failures, and, at hands like his, what chance have you of coming out wrong even if you pray and pray? He hears the prayer as a wisp of woodflake fluttering in the wind and trims it off short with a final flourish. O chiselmaster, I say to the departed mortal, you shall be master of the sinewed, eagle-patroled heights of airless thunder. *I* can make anything happen. Just so long as nobody hands an unfinished model of me to the nephew to finish off, to the hands that do not know. To keep whom from carving, and in order to make the plant of his guilt bear fruit, I'll bend every effort. Let him be involuntary for a while, made over into a volunteer, taking his skills to where they might fit in, far over the ocean. If he can't live here, let him live elsewhere: put through it on the way to God alone knows what. Was it because of him and his like, the effigy makers, that I at some point in the history of the universe unloaded from my multiple being the remnant later on identified as the corpse of God? For ages they thought they were finding stars, planets, moons, all of them brand new, but over the eons they pieced the dreadful relic together as one arm flopped through the tail of a galaxy, rending it apart, and my big toe bored a hole in an otherwise pristine blue sun, burning virgin blue? I am nothing if not creaturelike. Just as the Georges model me, so do I sometimes ape myself, carving a chip off the old block and allowing it to float through space like a rotting shark suspended in the fly-buzzed reek of a butcher's shop. *It's too big to be the model of anything else,* they said when they discovered the raw lump hovering between 7320 and Pavo (just a gob of godly phlegm). *This is the edge of the corpse of God.* But they were not Earthly beings, those. More advanced, they knew how to measure the debris of space, even though they had not reached the far reach of sophistication that lets the mind entertain an appearance without wondering what it is an appearance of. They did not know that, one day, they would be saying to themselves: *These were its fireworks.* The universe was not empty or heartless. The words came later, fudged up in the usual way, as if naming anything gave them power over it. I, we, all of us godly ones, too rarely put in an appearance in the flesh, but it goes without saying that our power includes the ability to make other universes, not just run them. Like Spider Woman. It is simply a matter of wanting to branch out: just as mortals always tend to think of making models of us, thinking ever smaller, so do we tend to think of ourselves as ever larger, and even such a yearning nipped in the bud becomes another galaxy, a nova, yet another object identified by nongods as The Biggest Object in the Universe. We weary of such blurbs, wondering why the Georges, they with such a strong impulsion to godhead, never think of a miniature's opposite. Even the word for it sounds uncouth and trumped-up: *Mastabbaturtur,* if such a word is even sayable. Yet who will make them if not we ourselves? *We* are not recognizable. That's the snag. That's what lets the Georges in, to travesty and maim, and sets the Oswalds copycatting them. It is as if they said, who have no right to say, *the verb to be is understood,* as it says in their books of grammar. All other verbs as bitable as mushrooms, but that one not: that verb forever and ever ours, every bit as misunderstood as we our awesome selves. And he? There being no verb for *being he,* he goes on being himself, shocked first of all by what he did, then by having gotten away with it, next by repeated cotton-in-the-mouth failures to tell his uncle, and last of all by Uncle's blithe acceptance of the deed. *Oh, you did? Well, son, nobody's perfect. You have to get out and mix with other dangerous young men. There's a place for you someplace, but I doubt it will be with a chisel in one hand, a lump of cottonwood in the other.* Oswald blanches, swallows another death (his father dies, his uncle lives on in legend), and, at long last, hears that hacking-slop sound of broadswords, as if from above, looking down on scenes of battle ripped from the middle ages, his eyes on the thousand-bladed airscrew as it whirls the blood away. A volunteer, he tells himself, is one who does a thing of his own free will: no accidents, no flukes. Recruiters line his future with carbon paper, glad to rent all that he weighs, all he can lift, and what they divine none too carefully as his wholly Indian sense of grievance now carving outward against a regime as foreign to him as white tie and tails. A leper goes forth to kill the rainbow and, as he enplanes, says "If Mister Dlöng could see me now."

Third World

Sotuqnangu

Again he saw the map, a page torn from who knew what book and thrust into his hand aboard the jet after having been passed along the aisle: first glimpse of the promised land. This is it now. It was a big leaf, green except for a central zone of yellow, a piece of cabbage going moldy, and with little sharp nodules he knew were the hills of the coastal plain. The brown vein running from top to bottom, well away from the edge, was the boundary between the promised land and Cambodia, Laos, but the wide red river that ran almost parallel to it, with violent scarlet arrows plunging south and east, was the Ho Chi Minh Trail, running through eastern Laos, in fact, while the parallel river offshore, in fainter red almost pink, showed where French paratroopers had come ashore in a war so long ago as to seem irrelevant. Another red line with four arrows ran in from the coast to join the Ho Chi Minh Trail as it swung through Cambodia to the Gulf of Thailand. Already it looked hopeless. He could smell the malaria, like the stench of overcooked greens and digging his finger-nails into his wrist he felt the leeches that lay in wait. He told himself that the slits and channels which crisscrossed the Mekong Delta had been made by caterpillars, borers, worms; touch that end of the moldy leaf and it would fall away into shreds in the searing heat. But even if it fell, just like that, while he was murmuring *cut it away, throw it out,* he knew he would have to be in there, land on the makeshift strip, and fight for the coastal plain and the mountain plateaux, crisp from the bottom compartment where those with refrigerators kept salad. Briefly powerful, moving toward Saigon at five hundred miles an hour, he crumpled up the map with one hand, squeezing it tight when it bulged bigger, wondering where to toss it, but then he uncrumpled it and tried to lay it flat on his knee, newly unruly terrain scored with new and random folds as if the whole area had suffered an earthquake. All he could do was accept the cheese and ham sandwich offered him by the high-buttocked hostess, whose hip grazed his face as she went by, leaving him an aroma of mingled disinfectant and warm rubber, and neatly fold the map into the shape of a half slice cut along the diagonal. Then he took a bite, through bread and cheese and ham and map, and spat it into the airsickness bag, and went on doing so until he had chewed up all of Vietnam and sealed it away in oblivion by folding the top of the bag over, as required, but wishing he could throw up too into the bag to bury the evidence. Those red Navajo arrows bothered him, like arteries with scorpion points, all of them aimed into the heart of his future. When he looked out, he was flying over a drabber, grayer version of what he'd just devoured, with only the scratched Plexiglas of the window between it and him. That piece of rotten leaf spread out wide beneath him and now it tilted sharply away, sucking him aside while all he could think of was being a good Indian boy being taught English by a Mitits Judson, his mind intent on clambering down canyons in search of eagles, his uncle on the lip of the sheer drop, holding the cable as if it supported him too. Minutes later the jet bumped on to the map, and he walked into the humid afternoon with the vomit bag in his hand, tipped it upside down, and showered the arrivals ramp with little wads of bread, vaguely remembering some Anglo story about Jesus feeding the five thousand on loaves and fishes, and grinning timidly as a sergeant struck the empty bag from his hand, asked him what the hell, and, without knowing what he did it for, kicked the bits of bread a couple of yards away. The bag blew off on the saturated breeze, and the big ripe-corn sun, like a pendulum minus its rod, trembled through the haze. Gulls he did not see squawked as they seized his droppings and bore them out over the ocean. His map was gone, but he knew where he was; the only trouble was that, from moment to moment, although he knew where he was, he could remember nothing at all, and all he wanted, from moment to moment, remembering this amid the hubbub of being marched into a so-called wonder shelter, was to lie in a hammock with a Keams Canyon popsicle on his exposed pubic hair, letting it melt and seep and shrivel up his pouch. Only when taut would he feel safe.

Bessie

It was all right, but afterward George liked to lie there cuddling and murmuring, not exactly sweet talk but that sort of thing, after when it was over, when I felt just full of get-up-and-go. He'd lie there, droning away, while I got up and out and about. He came from lazy folks to begin with, so you could hardly blame him. He said I was lustful but not so loving. His family used to lie in bed all hours, breathing the smell of themselves while the rest of the world was out planting, getting salt and water. He was always a dreamer. You talked to him, but he did not listen good. It was only by accident he heard anything. He liked to watch me swim, oh yes, but he would never try it himself. And he didn't much like to walk the trails. He liked to sit on his rear and carve wood, which is not much to say for a life, is it. He liked all that stuff. The china shepherd boy with the bushy-tailed animal, it could not have been a fox. The little spoons with crests from Phoenix and Flag. Never used. What would we be doing with such things? He liked mementoes. A bowl for nuts and a barrel-like thing for cookies. What is that, I more than once said. This, he said, was a marmalade jar or a jelly jar, with a tiny shovel in it to scoop it up with. Junk from the gift shop. He was always a sucker for gift shops. I was always a sucker for heroines, like Nancy Rogers, a widow from Keams Canyon who found she had cancer in eighteen-seventy-something, but she did not have the doctor's fee of twenty-five dollars. She was a nurse, so she knew how. Twenty-five dollars, Dr. Henry Matlock told her, or forget it, Nancy. She drove home in her wagon, packed a big basket with muslin rags, food, and a butcher knife, then she cooked her sons enough food to last them a week. She was ready. The boys thought she was going to visit a friend, but she rented a room for a dollar and a half and locked herself in. She prayed first. Then she sat on the edge of that squeaking soft infested bed and sawed away at her own breast until it came free in her hand. She survived to say, Dr. Matlock, here's a little something for you, this is your less-than-twenty-five-dollar tit cut off. It is all yours now. Put it on my account as a credit. Say fifteen bucks. She went on nursing everybody else. She was some lady. You got to get out in the world and help yourself. Is things much better now? You have to keep on top of yourself. You have to keep fit. I wanted to start a Nancy Rogers Club, but nobody cared enough. I was the club. She had no fans. They thought she was Roy Rogers's wife, the cowboy in the movies. I sometimes wondered about the people I came from, always dressing up and playing with dolls. I was not that religious. I said to hell with both Hopi and Navajo. To hell with Indians. Let's be Americans instead, I always said, and quit this old-fashioned stuff. He once went visiting where they had a flush toilet with a seat and a lid. While he was emptying his bladder, the seat and the lid fell on his penis, and he yelled that it was clear no man lived in this house. He had asked first how to do it and he was mad they fell on him right after he lifted them back and got going. Well, have you been anywhere else since you were last there? When I asked him this, I had to say *been* real hard and then he'd understand. One day he nailed some ribbons to the top of the doorway to keep the flies out, and it worked, but it was just like him, to have the lid drop on him and some ribbons handy to nail along the frame. They say he went his own way, but I think he did pretty much as he was told. He never left the mesa much, he carved the sort of thing they liked to see. He pleased himself, but he wasn't no Nancy Rogers. I know how they pay you out for being the least bit different. I have this perfect body, this bush of brown hair, I stand in the shallows, and then I am gone, into the glitter of the sun on the ripples I make. I was never fat. I guess I supped a lot of mountain water. I was like a wolf. I was best in the dark, when you sometimes can't even see the water. What was I doing with a George? He slobbered and could last forever and once he came to me with that thing of wood and I told him about Nancy Rogers. Carve a tit for her, I told him, and mail it to Keams Canyon. I don't need your *thing*. I know what is sick and what isn't. The man with the wooden horn had best not charge. Nor did he need to, with that wooden thing. He was quite adequate with his real one even if he did get sore in no time at all.

Sotuqnangu

Far from dying, he nonetheless felt he was already dying out, like a chant. Only just arrived, only there a couple of weeks, he felt removed from history. And, looking back on the eating of the map, or at least his chewing of it along with the sandwich, he also felt cut off from his own kind, the good-natured dreamy ones up on the mesas, walking miles for water, living in no present, no past, no time. When no one was home upstairs, so to speak, whatever happened didn't count. There was no one for things to happen to. Maybe everyone felt the same way, wanned or diluted, which was death's way of getting you ready, so that when the worst thing happened there wasn't enough of you to resent it. He could hardly believe it. Shoving bits of the map into his mouth on board the jet had been bravado. Imagining himself hemmed in with bloody-faced Cong torturers who burped into his face had been the result of fatigue and fright. He wondered when he would stop woolgathering, if ever, and tried to fix his mind on something permanent that would have no meaning beyond itself. Then he could write:

*Dear, dead Uncle George The Place
In Flowers Where Pollen Rests:
Military life has a flavor the
sheltered never know — I saw that
tacked to a notice board.*

No, that was no use, it would only draw attention to the very thing
he wanted to play down. Instead, his restless head, circling like a dog
that wanted to sit down, steadied itself with the so-called wonder
shelter, which was nothing more than a semicircular length of corrugated iron, an enormous cylinder cut lengthwise exactly in half. It
was the sort of thing he'd seen on construction sites back home, but
here there were dozens of them at the airport, with planes or crates
sheltered under them. No front, no back, nothing holding them
down, although he could see sandbags piled up to provide a measure
of safety and privacy. No one lived in them, however, or even
lingered. The heat under the metal was fierce and caustic, and they
were always arranged side by side in such a way that whatever breeze
there was never blew through them, but against their flanks. Tin
mesas, Uncle. Row on row of them, and very temporary looking. I
guess you could house us Indians in them, but they would have to
move us around a lot to get the wind blowing through. Almost a
touch of home, and the one thing you can say is they aren't made of
jungle. You could fry an egg on the metal if you had an egg. Not that
we aren't getting regular chow, I just thought of the egg at that moment. Big red tanker trucks drive up and they fuel the jets, but they
look just like fire engines to me. That was enough to tell him. What
reassured him was the way he could go bang his fist on the tin, or iron
(all metals bore the same heat here), and then the whole thing would
echo like a submarine. What you doing, son? My hand was numb, sir,
I was trying to get the use back into it. He walked away, told that was
a mighty good way to break a bone, and then what use would he be?
In those early days he still had time to muse, to wander off the reservation, to do things that appealed to him for their utter uselessness.
Not far from the dying, as he told himself, he had become an in-
between person. Nothing appealed to him anymore. They had been

flown all this way for nothing. Into the jungle for two days, and nothing happened, so he had wandered off, thus encountering the enemy, he was convinced of that. Then choppered out again as the line changed. From airport to jungle, then back to next to the airport, like a canceled move in chess. All he found to do, with his boots and socks off, was to study how the soles of his feet fit together as they must have in the womb, the ball of one foot into the other's arch. The contours matched exactly, so they were like two land masses that had broken apart millions of years ago. Or he would go look at a burned-out Super Saber demolished by a rocket right there in one of the wonder shelters, which proved that something happened here once in a while. The plane had slumped sideways, its skin frail and powdery like aluminum foil after long years beneath the burner on a kitchen stove. Touch it, it just broke. He clambered into the cockpit, his teeth on edge from fingernail contact with the roughed-up metal, less hot than the iron of the shelter, and pretended he was a god coming down from the San Francisco Mountains, but the stench of cordite and burned plastic sickened him, so out he got, convinced of only one thing. When this so-called war was over, he would look for something obviously trivial to do and he would do just that, some low-grade activity that entailed no grades and no drill, no chain of command and no highfalutin hogwash about how life has a different flavor for those who fight for it. A life more or less without flavor would suit him fine. He would change his name, grow wolflike teeth, and switch the TV on and off all day, preferably one that did not work, and he could watch his image reflected on the empty screen, reading the news, announcing the Miss Hemisphere Contest, selling a toothpaste, fixing a hernia in a big blast of operating theater light. Yes, he said, I have always been interested in eagles, sir, only to be told that the military were interested only in soldiers who got on with their job. Then they found things to make him busy, but too late: he had already discovered his talent for the wasting of time. He had seen the light emanating from a religion of gentle, daily paralysis. He would not have to try and his life would be as easy as perspiring; he'd sell old comic books in a wonder shelter, making a slight profit. Or, if there were no takers, he'd sit and read them all the same, over and over again, lost in thunderland, maybe on some crate or other writing *Osmald*, an elaborately serifed copy of his name, making it real pretty to stare at until the day, through having stared at it too much, he found

it alien, not his own at all, and then he would know the war had been
fought not in vain. A hero would be home to fit the soles of his feet
together until they refused to come apart. And then the numbness
would set in.

Bessie

Up from among the weeds with a mouth full of sludge, a gash full of slime, I'll sprawl out over them like a plague, bring them up in boils all over their glistening inner skins. That, and more. Like a monstress. I'll teach them the facts of drowning and of being drowned. When I had no wheels, I'd walk thirty miles to get to that water, every bit as far as Nancy Rogers walked to get away from her cancer, and it was worth it every inch. Not for him, though. I dragged him only once. They dragged the lake. He dragged me down. If I'd been less eager to teach, I'd be coming to life in some other man's bed by now instead of remembering the soft bottom of the lake. They say there are no lakes within walking, or even trekking, distance of our people, but it depends what kind of a walker you are. I was my own unicorn. I never cared whether the steak sauce in the smeared bottle ought to stand in the sun on the inside windowsill or go behind whichever photo frame. I was not a dainty lady. I was a burper. Cleaned up after me he always did, cursing about the time taken from carving. If they'd had the guts, they'd have forced my face into my bowl of soup and drowned me in that, or into soft wet sawdust,

which is how we kill foxes and eagles. I am a bit of each. I was. All of
me is festering now, but it gives me something ripe to slide into their
bed, ohyes, between their legs, I am like an enormous rotting green
bean loaded with maggoty egg yolk and slithery ferns. I choke and
disgust them, coiling myself around them as they writhe, bringing
them my own special dead young woman's stench, sour as bobcat,
razor-sharp as lowland bog in summer heat. All of my syrups are
rotten, all my skins have holes in them like doyleys. There is no
kissing me now. I'd crumble. Come on, George, plant your horn in
my yellow moss. Come on, Fermina, you hard-boiled slut, lick a dead
girl's pubic bone, suck her pelvis clean. I'm game, let's do something
no three humans have ever before even thought about, except in the
Pyramids, among the dead, one dead one to two live ones. The only
pretty sandwich is the one that has dead meat in the middle and no
shreds dangling. Live meat be my bread.

Sotuqnangu

The bugs, he knew, were already inside his shirt and pants, moving easily past the frontier of his belt, the lower ones heading for his armpits and his face, the upper ones for his groin. Dry scratching ones, moist and delicate ones, they all moved; and try as he did to tell himself that it was only tiny globes of sweat, he worried and fussed. They slid in the faint invisible sheen of that sweat. They fed on it and savored it even as he remained in the position demanded, belly-flopped in the darkness, as close to mother earth as the accumulated debris of the forest floor allowed. It only took one bullet, one rocket splinter to do it, he'd been told, so he tried to burrow under the spongelike hunks of rotting foliage, heedless of the chemistry that had brought the leaves down like leaflets, and with a gasp of disgust shoved his face down into it too. Had it been daylight, he would have been unable to resist easing up into a sitting position to scour his waist for evidence, whether or not his head got blasted away in the act. As it was, he began to wonder if what tickled him and brought bile into his mouth had mandibles, antennae, pincers, or just a sucking snout. Did the crawlers leave snail tracks behind them or little nick marks where they had paused and fed on him? In the act of moving about on him, were they fighting one another, in their slimy or scuttling way? In a word, he dwelt on them much as they were dwelling on him, and he kept himself from screaming and running amok, on to the nearest mine or punji stick, only by fixing on things that had no name and no identity and envisioning them in detail as things that walked the moon, snails and slugs that cruised the magma of a distant unwelcoming planet, pink and mauve things mingling their glisten with his. And, through this second-by-second version of remote control, he almost made himself into an area to be occupied, tested, and then retreated from. He was no longer a human, but the most recent layer of the ground, hot and sodden, and as unoffended as the compost itself on which he lay and tried not to squirm. Unable to fix his mind on something distant and wholesome, he stood his ground, as it were, and hit on a way of getting through the next minute, and then the one after that, nonetheless flinching and shivering as if he had the jungle sickness. If he could manage to keep on doing this, among all the other safety tactics, he knew he would out-live the year and never have to belly down again. When something was too much to bear, but he was obliged to bear it, he wiped out all notion of an "I" as fast as he could and took things from there. His core went blank. Then, after he was free to move around again, he felt an urge to leap and strut, like a dog shaking itself dry, but all he could do was wriggle about inside the outline of his body, shivering himself back to usual. In a way, and this amazed him, he missed the bugs; those that flew through the cloying night air were of a different order, damnable but not intimate. Having schooled or steeled himself, medium young as he was, to undergo being crawled upon, or at least the sensation of that, he minded no longer having to do so. There were no bugs at all. There was just a puddle of sweat. A paddy of sweat. Nothing crawled on him, but his skin had crawled, as folks back home liked to say when they weren't in the jungle at all. Here he sweated all the time, like some experiment set up in a chemistry lab to go all night and day, unsupervised, just to see what the result would be. He perspired in much the way the jungle glommed on to whatever sunlight filtered through the clouds, venting pure oxygen in return, so that all manner of creatures might live. As fast as the salt formed around his waist, under his eyes, in his crotch, it dissolved again, but its tide marks showed on his shirt and pants: a white that showed against an older more faded white in a process that could go on forever, although for him it would only take a year. He pictured himself, at the end of that time, wholly encrusted in salt, like some freak out of the Anglo Bible, and told himself he'd last if only he kept licking himself, another dog comparison. So close had he been to the jungle floor and the clotted undergrowth, he felt almost as if he were walking on himself when finally, although never quite upright, he walked on it. He trod on his own tremors, wishing his clothing did not stick to him like adhesive bandage, and then tear free, only to stick again. Birds and animals he'd become accustomed to, but not the insects and the snakes, the first full of blood like blisters on his tongue, the second too clever and nonhuman by far. They all *lived here.* That was what sickened him; they had not asked him to come, and to them he was only the enemy or food, which was bad enough. Worse, though, was that other enemy he never saw, but always aiming and shooting, triggering and releasing, from not far away and, after they had gone, leaving reminders that impaled or just went bang. In a place so hostile, he felt, there was no sufficient way of striking back, other than to set it afire, and almost all of it was too wet to burn. He felt immersed and wished he could go home for a snake dance, or just to watch his uncle carve a doll. *What's that, Uncle George?* A Cloud Maiden. *And that big flat wing behind her head?* The tableta. Now hush up. Or Uncle George The Place In Flowers Where Pollen Rests is going to lose his place and cut his hand.

Emory

When he was small, then bigger, almost grown up, George was a busy walker, his limbs were always in motion like he was spraying things with them. There was too much energy for one. His rear end twitched, he couldn't sit still, he fidgeted the hides off toads. Mama held him down a lot, but I, as I recall, tried to get him moving again, somebody to play with at last. That did it. He got fired up real soon and Mama gave up on him, at least until fourteen or thereabouts, when he slowed down some. Calmed down. A commotion turned into a rest. I showed him mine and he showed me his, the thicker, mine the longer, why there must be a hundred billion shapes for it, every man is different. "How you going to know that?" he asked. "Who has time to look? They'd never let you do it, give your life to such a thing." "No, I told him, that's not it. It's easy. You have to be a university. Then they let you." We went on to other things, but I remember how, one day, we stretched the skin on each of us so that the other's would tuck inside it along with the other's thing: two cocks in one foreskin. Talk about stretching power. More than a condom, I used to think. Nothing would ever break, I told him, it was designed to last. And his inside my skin was hotter than mine, it had some furnace inside it somewhere, and I should have known, I just thought he was my little brother and would follow my lead. He did. But he had a mind, no, not a mind so much as an energy all his own. It shoved him and drove him, he kept linking his hands and thumping the fist of one into the palm of the other like a boxer who couldn't get fights. On the mesa nobody took much notice of anything you did. Their heads were full of rituals, pieces of time nobody ever remembered happening. Their heads were full of ancient spaces. You could do this or that and it was only ever like a ripple of wind among the corn. Things went away as soon as they happened. Maybe it was this that drove him crazy. Most of them liked to carry water, fuss with a plant in the ground, or just wait around to warm up as the sun got high. George, though, he was feisty, not to fight, but to mess things up, to argue and disagree, to go opposite like he was born to it. He was different, but very likable with it, talking to himself a lot, stubbing his toe into the soil and kind of standing all of him on that one toe, or swinging on a door from its knob because, he said, all the land under him was flooded. He was smart, you have to say that, he could think like a bird could sing, but he didn't like thinking, he wanted something tougher, which is why he turned to carving with our father, who wasn't half bad at it. George, though, he took to it like a baby to the breast. He had control, strength, and he didn't need to look. His hands knew their way from the first, turning the wood and testing it, but he didn't get to carve cottonwood root until he was older. We were close for a while. He was bright in school, but I was the one who went away from the mesa, even if just to work in a store. He was the one who went away all famous to community college or wherever they go. To me he was always the little brother with his dickybird inside his big brother's skin, like a plum, facing each other, him wrapped in mine. The trouble, I thought, was that I couldn't be wrapped up in his while he was wrapped up in mine. Nature didn't allow for it, there was no way. They make no special allowance for brothers. I should have known better, though. George would always find a way. If you stretch your thumb out wide as far as you can, it makes a right angle with the side of your forefinger, and that is what we did, ramming the angle up against our noses, palm over the mouth, as if to say *My* at what we'd done lower down. You popped your eyes and made a hushing noise. It was forbidden, but who by? We were mated. We were mates. We jerked off together in dark rooms full of spiders and floating sunlight and the spiders couldn't figure out what kept landing on their webs and weighing them down. *"Something,"* George said once, "that for a short time actually flew. Don't you wish you was a spider, just to watch it land?" It was then we began to understand that children, babies, are made in a different way from what we'd thought, the man peeing up into the behind of the mother. *"Not pee,"* said George, "but something clever like this. See how pretty."

Sotuqnangu

Another thing that sickened him was the obligation to shoot into the darkness, aiming as best he could at a flash gone so fast it was more something on his retinas than still out there, steady as a lighthouse or a buoy. He felt he was firing at his own memory, and his sense of the distance in between was vague. If the flash was bright, then it was close and big. If dim, it was maybe out of range. He fired anyway, but with an increasing sense of futility. If he hit anyone, he never knew; nobody screamed, so he was either missing all the time or shooting them humanely through the head, and the brain didn't have a chance to tell the mouth to howl. Not that he wanted to hit anyone at all. He had learned that being shot at didn't necessarily make him want to shoot back. It was boring, inefficient, and dangerous. It showed them where he really was, and his main instinct was to play possum and wait them out; to hell with body counts that depended on a lucky dip of death, bullets that skidded off trees into human heads, livers, and throats. When he had to shoot, he did so in private rhythms, such as *one*—pause—*one, two, three,* or *one, two*—pause—*three, four.* Sometimes, to these rhythms he found words to say, sipping a tribal hallucination

that went *tab—let—a. Tab—let—a.* Or *Pa—look—a—ville, Pa—look—a
—ville.* His brain was too numb to do more than note the rhythm of
what he did, as if between his hands the M16 were a pulse that he
controlled. The sheer chanciness of things wore its way into his unmilitary skull and refused to go. He tried to calculate the odds of
being hit by a stray round, and of hitting someone else the same way,
but all such attempts faded out when he summed up all the factors:
the dark, the uncertain human eye, the quiver in the wrist, the humidity, the rain, the presence of creepers and trees and birds actually
in night-bound flight. He'd rather shoot fish in a barrel so long as he
didn't have to carry away the fish. More and more, as he became
inured to the garbage smell of the vegetation, wondering where the
hell the oxygen had gone, he fired high into the sky, puncturing the
roof of fronds and interwoven branches, popping his rounds clean off
the rim of the planet where they dawdled and, subconsciously, promising himself to do better by daylight. He couldn't see the so-called
enemy even then, but at least there were trees to aim at, and the
enemy was an anonymous propaganda-ridden peasant who meant
him no harm at all on the personal level. The two of them were lethal
only as representatives of something they never quite understood or
cared about, yet for which they had to put their lives on the line. He'd
even thought of surrendering, but he didn't know how to go about it,
and, deep down, what he was most afraid of was the chance that they
might send him back to his own platoon. The first time he really fired
at anything by night, and tried to hit it, was when he opened fire on a
scream. The sound had begun as an impeded wail, almost that of a
trapped and tortured rabbit, but a minute later it had swollen into a
long, wavering voluntary in response to erratic blurts along the
nerves of whoever it was out there in the jungle, ripped apart beyond
control. At first he tried to numb his ears, telling himself that all the
screech and warble of the jungle night were as much as his ears could
take. When that failed, he moaned inside his throat, trying to blot out
the noise from within. He hummed, he swallowed with his breath
held, he made a grinding noise; but none of this worked. So he stuffed
his ears with leaves softened and balled up between finger and thumb,
heedless of tiny insects still alive within the ball, but that was no use
either. If only he could scream himself, but that would be crazy. Why
did no one gag the wounded man? Or put him out with shot or
needle? Now the scream seemed to split, as if the lower pitch were
coming from the mouth, the other—the high, reedy, tingling whine—

through the nose, but both registers pleading and abusing, asking and cursing. Jungle fowl joined in, uttering private panic calls, animals he'd never heard joined in the din, and then there was a colossal exchange of small arms fire followed by a shower of incoming rockets. The scream went away, but then picked up again, weaker and intermittent, and he realized he was still firing at that only too human sound, damning the one in agony and hating him for his pain. Perhaps one of the bullets found its mark. The screaming ceased, and all he could hear was a dry lapping sound of some nearby bird, and the straight-from-the-street abuse of his sergeant telling him to quit firing at random and keep his eyes open. Okay, he mouthed, so long as I don't hear him. Days later, when he fired, day or night, he was still shooting into the pink mouthful of that scream, trying to make the rawhide-taut muscles give up the ghost and let him be inhuman again.

Emory

He never said anything outright brotherly, though he may have tried to put it into one of those long stares of his. He was the younger, so different from me as summer from winter. As boys we played tag, games with a ball, treasure hidden on the mesa, but he was always at a distance, not so much brooding as going away behind that stare. He stared to make you think he was looking at you, but his mind was never there. He hardly ever answered, and then he became skillful with a knife, a rasp. The rest is tribal history, and my own poor efforts with pottery fell into the trough of his fame. He was very good, don't get me wrong, but he never talked to me about what I was doing. It didn't matter to him. It was a hobby, whereas what he did was the big league. It was his sex life, at least it was that until he clapped eyes on the girl I'd seen when she was a child, chubby cheeks, a strong jaw with a mole just beneath the left-hand corner of her mouth, a bold curved forehead, and usually smiling. One eyebrow, the right, didn't run all the way but halted halfway across the space above her eye. As if she hadn't come out right and needed to be sent back for fixing. Pigtails, then, in tight yellow ribbons, her expression one of trusting valiance. She looked valiant, I mean. She was eager, spry, and she chirped nonstop, more bird than girl. He never saw her at that age, he being younger. He first laid hands on her when she was twelve or thirteen and beginning to sprout as a woman, and then he married her, Bessie Butterfly, wiping the smile off her face from the first, he was always laying down the law and she was always racing off to swim in that accursed lake where she drowned. He drove her to it, he drove them all to the brink sooner or later with that kindly inhuman way of his. He saw us all as cuspidors for him, things to use and then leave well alone. On he went, heedless of the pain and the ill will. It is a wonder they did not drown him instead of her. I see the yellow ribbons and the braids going under for the last time, though of course she wasn't wearing them then. He never needed the guidance that only an elder brother can give. He needed other men's wives, that was all, something hot and slick to shove into, and then he was off again, frisky as a dog, ready to carve wood into funny shapes. He came up after me and then he passed me, like a runner, and I was forever calling after him to wait a bit, to hold on, George, while he ran ahead. I never had that time of need and respect. You expect certain things in life, and you have a right to them. A lot of people admired him, but not so many liked him. He needed only to be him-self, with hands so warm you actually jumped when he touched you. It was as if he had been keeping them hot in the bowels of a friend. That's the sort of thing he'd do. Anything to help him carve. He never bothered with corn or animals. And, his dolls apart, he wasn't a holy man. If he believed in any supernatural being, it was only be-cause he couldn't think of anything else to do. He took advantage of the gods as he did of people. I never forgave him after he carved Tuhavi and Koyemsi, the paralyzed kachina and the mudhead who were left alone in their village after a disaster, so the blind man car-ried the paralyzed one on his back. "You," he told me, "are the para-lyzed one." He meant it to hurt, but, when it did, he said I'd upset him by being hurt. It is the only kachina whose horns turn down. Soon after, he was using my wife for his filthy practices. I don't care that he was blind, that he went blind; he was blind to others long before he went blind, and that's the truth. He used people and then kicked them away like dogs. Now it is too late to go back and I have another life. It was he who sent me away to trade and whoring and I wonder which blind man's back I will be riding on next, all the way to the grave. With the younger brother gone, the elder's bound to be next, but I would like all those wasted years back, the time with Thomas and Abbott, even if I had to live them out in a month while burning at the stake in the snow.

Sotuqnangu

Amid the stink of the jungle, never mind what time of day, there was one human smell he always managed to pick out, and it was from this he recoiled most of all. Not excrement, which caked him. Not vomit, whose aroma came wafting through the vegetation like something being filtered out. But what he told himself, with sadistic distaste, was the smell of blood, not only sweet like a beetle-infested rose, but somehow *dusty*. He could not explain how blood reminded his nose of summer highways, attics full of unopened cabin trunks and parcels marooned in brown paper anchored for ever by dried-out knots; but it was not unpleasant, he found, and he actually began to inhale that dustiness to clear his head. When a breeze delivered it, or higher humidity than usual penned it up in a clearing, he wrinkled his nostrils, put all thought of bloodshed out of his mind, and told himself that nothing stayed hideous forever, not even the high-pitched stench of baby slop they took along with them wherever they went, and not even the bad-fish taint of vomit. He had resolved to tutor his nose, and whenever he nicked a finger on his rifle, or rubbed against a thorn, and saw the bright crimson bead swelling in the perpetual dusk of life among and under the trees, he inhaled it lovingly, telling himself sawdust, brick dust, window dust was decent and would save him. He took out his penis and rubbed it raw until it bled, and it was as if this cast a spell on those who'd hurt him, aiming at his groin. His dust was good. One big thing he did not like about eating in the jungle was having to perspire into his food; sweat rolled off his nose and chin and, in spite of the elastic bandage he wore as a sweatband, trickled all the time into his eyes. As a result, he saw everything blurred, even his food, which tasted like heavily salted processed liver. It was almost a crime, anyway, to be eating in that green oven of the maimed and dead, and the only consolation he knew was the big waft of wind from the choppers when they came in to pick up the wounded. If he slept, even for only an hour, he dreamed of air-conditioning, leaning over the grille and inhaling Anglo air while his neck dried and cooled. Or it was a dream about gigantic mats of jute imported from India and rigged so as to create a billowing wind when the punkah-wallah tugged the cord. He lived and dreamed in slime, awaking in a headsweat that made him scratch his barbered scalp until he scraped it raw, which is when the flies really came after him, making him flail as if giving signals. After a while he wore his helmet as much as he could bear it, because it made him sweat all the more, and the scratches on his scalp would never heal. His nails were rimmed with blood. His entire body itched, and he could feel the tiniest vermin stirring in the angles of his body, quietly taking him over from head to toe while he waited for the year to go by, distantly hoping he'd be wounded enough to be shipped out, but not badly enough to get him zipped up in a plastic body bag. A claustrophobia of trees became a claustrophobia of bare trunks, which offered less cover, and he began to shrink even from the nearness of so much air. He'd thought he'd like to see the sky, and even the smoke that filled it, but now he longed for the close womb of the green jungle, wanting not to be seen while he bellied or hunched across a light and airy mattress of twigs and branches which had replaced the old soft floor of moss, leaves, mud, and what smelled like used tea leaves. It was like crawling over a beaver dam, with always a twig's end to punch him in the eye. Inhaling dust and flies, he shot when told, but his mind had long since parted company with his body, which ran and ducked through a horizontal butcher's shop strewn at random among the trees. Two kinds of trunks were all he knew, and he tried to numb himself to awful sights: faces like huge squashed raisins, silky intestines drying in the sun amid a devil's commotion of outsize flies. Such, he kept telling himself, was the net result. It was bound to happen, just as an egg dropped into a hot pan fried. And now there were dead zones, deader than on any map, where only insects thrived, all other forms of life having been abolished. Burned stumps and charcoal bracken were all that remained, and he found himself longing for just one flower to touch, to pluck, to roll up into a tube shape and gently chew when there was nothing to smoke. A child again when he could run across an open area, he dreaded stumbling. Once he had got up speed and misjudged a leap in open daylight, going his full length into a bush whose embers were still hot and singed his face. Inside was the cadaver of a Vietcong, but so far deteriorated by fire as to be merely a bundle, a human doughnut swathed in blackened rags, and where his face had landed was something soft and rippling, a slimy pillow the outer layers of which clung to him like the rubber of an exploded balloon. Right there on his cheeks he smelled the stench of a newly raked barnyard. Yelling as if wounded, he then blundered his way back from the bush and the corpse, at which he fired to make them keep their distance. Rebuked for acting without orders, for doing something not only nonsensical but reckless too, he babbled insults at his lieutenant who, in the end, shrugged and gave him an extra duty: shooting payroll masters of the Vietcong, from ambush of course. The first time, he put a shot through the canvas bag the soldier carried. He shot the money first, then the shoulder, the thigh, the chest, the eye, like a novice three hundred yards from a range target, soothing his unruly head by thinking of the payroll master as Digit One, on whom he'd scored no bull, but an inner and several outers. Killing was better than butting headfirst into the bowels of the dead. It was cleaner, or clinical, as everybody said, though his flesh crawled for hours afterward, and he itched furiously along the top of his feet: a new place that had never bothered him before. From this point on, he began to think abstractly of his war experience, arguing dizzily that, if he lasted long enough, there was nothing he would not discover, and he would come out with a beautifully rounded memory of Vietnam, not an object of joy to be sure, but complete in its way and thus abominably perfect. Anything that happened filled a blank in the diagram of what he had to undergo. Then he began to volunteer, wondering how much longer it would be before he stepped on his first and last mine. So what was sequential had now a shape of sorts, and it was as if he were some expert-in-the-making, who'd come away with a total knowledge of Vietnamese birds: the Audubon of Chu Lai. With such thoughts constantly in mind, he found it easier to fool himself that what he did wasn't what he did. It was something else. It was almost fun to spray a paddy field with lead and see how Charlie ran, scurried, and slithered until the shattered upfling of the arms, the melting of the legs, the scarecrow topple. All this he did as if by remote control, waiting for some heavenly vengeance to batter his own head to bits; but the way to counter that was to have enough speed and, later, more than enough grass. He went abroad with a bubbling, zesty heart, and at night he giggled among the giggling, amazed at an erection brought on by the pornography of blood, power, and merely nominal, temporary hatred. He was less a soldier than an energetic pawn, less a killer than a lethal extension of his own indifference, less himself than he was the familiar of those who lived alongside him. Each felt the others, both the live and the dead but especially the dead, enter into him, diminishing responsibility to an affair of style. Once the premise of the body count was clear, the rest followed as easily as the rules for place settings at a formal dinner. A blind man could find the right cutlery, in the right order, just by feel. And so he began to heed some dim tradition of his own, doing this time what he did last time, then doing it again as if it were second nature, which it was, and uniquely his, not anyone else's, although all of it was killing, with or without scruple. Not that he quite got to like it, but it was what he was there to do: his own slice of the everydayness of death. All he had to do was bring to the act a quirk, a mannerism, and it was no one else's; he was not anonymous when picking his nose while firing one-handed, or whispering *This for Uncle* while finishing off a wounded Vietcong straggler, pleading in his agony for help. A tinge omnipotent, he shied away from the very thought and fixed his mind on whatever couldn't shoot back: the mucus in his nose, the fluid in his knee, the pain like an eaglet lodged behind his liver. And he never reported sick.

Fermina

Who knows how long he'd gone without. Nobody was counting. It was as if he had become quiet as a tree. Who ever had thought of him in that way wasn't doing it anymore. He had that deep look that went right through you as if you were smoke. Now, who ever was smoke? In time, though, he came calling, saying nice things rather more than howdydo. He kept on touching, his hand on my elbow, my waist, the top and back of my shoulder. He's getting close, I told myself. Another week of this and he is going to try it, not something to try with a married woman. But it was better to try it with a married woman whose husband was more or less away a lot of the time. There was something right and proper in that, if nowhere else. The big hands on me, they were frightening. One grab and you were done for. No, not so big, but burly, and aggressive. They were never still even when they had a hold on what they wanted. Fidgety hands that could hurt. They could hurt even when they were wide open. A slap from him was the equal of being hit by somebody else's fist. Not that he struck me much, it was really his way of saying something and making it firm. If you were in the way, you got swatted. Then he said his sorry.

Said sorry, mam, as if I were somebody he had hardly met. Rough dry skin on him, but mine was like oiled, he said. I slithered about, he told me. I was all smoothed out, and he kept saying how great it was that I would lie still and let him do his things to me. He had had his share of busy women forever moving around while he was trying to fix his mind on something to do with his fucking. He did not just do it and have done, he had to wonder about it in the doing. Not that he said anything right then, but he told me afterward, how it had all gone through his mind like fire or scalding water. The first time, even though we both knew what was going to happen next, he was weeping his widower's tears onto my bush, right there into the hairs to soften them up, I guess, to open up to him. I felt more sorry for him than desirous, but who says you are supposed to feel anything. They come along and slip their hands up your clothes and then they pump it into you as fast as wind. It is never much, but he lasted longer than some I could mention. And while he wept he was sniffing, not that he needed any excuse to sniff at me. He smelled at whatever he wanted and then he drew it deep down into his big lungs. It made him harder, which was good, but he said I smelled like ferns, which made no sense, I never having smelled that smell. If I did, though, I know it would never be like ferns, but more like some flower, some bird's plumage. I don't know how it starts, but you can tell from how people look at you. You know they must have only a vague idea of you, they stare at you but only as if you were a deer or a fox. An *a*. Like in the games we played as kids. You stood there and you were the south. You were not allowed to move until the next game began. It was boring. They already knew where south was, they just wanted to keep me from playing. It was spiteful of them always to have me stand for south or north. It was unnecessary. "Do you know my name," I would ask him, but he would never say, calling me Woman or You, as if I were the pox or some saucepan of greens cooking. Not that he ever treated me that badly, but he treated me with aloofness, I guess you would call it, as if he had already decided that, in becoming what he wanted me to be, I had turned into a fallen woman. Fallen from what? A man would have to have a very long thing to fuck his wife from Winslow and he could not even send it along on the bus like a length of hose. He must have been using it on the whores in that town, shoving it up among the maggots and the awful sores they are supposed to have. At least you can say this much for me. Fancy woman, I was clean. George was wider than what I was used to, if as

little as I ever got was being used to anything at all. How little can be
said to be a lot? He was wider and thicker and so he caught me on the
right places and rubbed me sore. He did not have to make me a
mother as well. She goes to his one-room shanty, they say, so she is
going to swell and even her own children will spurn her, which they
did not, they were too sorry for me. Fatherless kids have this funny
homing quality. They latch on to somebody and they do not let go,
like they were drowning and had a hold of their mother's hair. Funny
that I should think of water when thinking of him, but it's natural,
she being such a swimmer and all, a hiker, a truly busy body who did
everything faster than everybody and better according to her. Her
mind, he said, was always on the next thing she was doing to do. The
thing she was doing was as good as over. Made him feel
like a mourner, he said. There was no serenity in her, no peace. She
was a fidget, scared of moss gathering on the soles of her feet or
between her legs. I think she just drowned, but some think she was
put paid to, her being a bit unpopular. Held her under, they say, then
left her to float in the lake. George would never think such a thing or
have anything to do with such goings-on, even if it did fit into his life
better. His grief was real, it landed right there on the hair down
below. People don't weep there for effect, they mean it. Then there
was baby Oswald and all the talk. If only my Emory hadn't showed
up once or twice, they'd have had me for sure, but the issue was
cloudy because of that, and he was not a man to say anything to or
about anybody. He left it all blank and from time to time came back
to see his new son. It was hard to think that Emory and George were
brothers. It was easier to pretend that George and I were brother and
sister, which would have been disgraceful, but we both knew that his
brother had left because George was so good at what he did, the
carving and such, whereas Emory was better at selling things, so he
was away in Winslow with the Sigafoose Toy Company. It was better. He was not fitted for life with me or any of us. It was hard on
Thomas and Abbott, but Oswald was a fine third son who kind of
cheered him up from a distance. Now he had all the more reason to
go away to make extra money for the extra mouth he had to feed. And
George helped too. He was making more money from kachina dolls
than he liked to admit, even with his head on the pillow afterward.
You would call it an untidy relationship, but in a way it worked since
those who ought to be away from it were, and those who needed to be
near without being too close were that. It was like looking at the sky.

In the white dawn, white is arising. Then comes the yellow dawn, as
it should. After that the sun paints us with light, the sun is up, as we
say. Then there is sunshine all about. Soon after, the sun is midway,
soon descending, getting nearer his house, entering it, gone home.
Gray, evening, midnight. I used to tell myself that we had that kind
of thing. Order. Calm. Something dependable. It was the same as the
difference between Oswald and Emory when they made a wall. Oswald's would have a rough surface to catch the light even after the
light had begun to wane, as it were, recovering it or stealing it away
from itself, whereas Emory's would be smooth, just like they told him
in school. That was George in Oswald, Emory was like glass. Anyway, who am I to throw stones? I did something unmentionable and
to date have not paid the price. "Fermina," they used to say, "there is
something in you and we know what it is." But that was a long time
ago. Old news. Old gossip. They no longer care about whose Oswald
is, he is more Oswald than he is anybody's, and that's how it should
be. In the end you don't care who was whose as long as they are
somebody. Unless, I suppose, you happen to be the husband in question whose wife's been shot full of somebody else's coming. That
could offend, I guess. It is not exactly the same as putting butter into
a dish. This means that long ago I got used to being thought a hussy
and simply got on with my life, even after George lost interest. His
lustful grief lasted only a couple of years and then he went back to his
real love, wood. To him, women were only incidentals, to be used or
not, according to his mood. I always used to think that he would
really like to build a life-sized kachina doll and spend the rest of his
life bludgeoning it into good behavior. You can't have everything,
though, and to the best of my knowledge he never carved anything of
the kind. If he had, though, he would never have had to tell it to lie
still, it wouldn't have gone off swimming without him. Would it have
had a naughty slit? Would he have cared that much about it? With an
imagination like his, it would have been enough if it looked like a
canoe, it would not have to have looked like a woman at all. I often
wonder that anyone that inhuman should have spawned a son. Not
that he was cruel, ohno, he was just kind of away from us all, happy
to make something nobody else thought of making. I used to think he
he was talking to the gods when he said he was talking to himself. No,
he said, they will only listen to you when you are talking to yourself.
Addressed direct, they turn a deaf ear. He could hardly, at least in the
early years, help to bring up his son, but he soon grasped the role of

uncle and began to make the right noises when others were watching. It would have been better if George the father had been less like an uncle, or Emory the father only in name had behaved less like a father, but that is the way things turned out in the early years. It is the woman who bears the burden anyway, who wipes their little rumps. Those others, full of seed, are more like plants we trip over and then we get a nettle burn for life.

Sotuqnangu

Now he pretended he was the enemy, clad in black pajamas, his feet in thongs, at his hip a green pouch made in a jungle workshop. He had no weapon, his duty being to shove along an old-fashioned bicycle modified for a payload of a hundred pounds. Two bamboos connected him to the handlebar and the seat column, each the length of his arm, and with these he steered, juggling the handlebar and pushing with his right hand. A People's Porter, with two massive sacks roped to the bicycle's frame, he blinked to clear the perspiration from his eyes, but down it rolled, along his cheeks to his lips. Honor-bound to make fifteen miles a day on the flat, nine in hilly country, at least within his impersonation, he wobbled into it and out of it as the mood took him, yearning only to go to sleep amid the blurred, puzzling daylight, putting the pajamas to right use. Now the bicycle was steering him, shoving and heaving his arms back and forth. He was an erect cripple, walked along by his crutches. He was the big sack corded to the frame and camouflaged with a couple of small branches. Having no food tube containing enough rice and dry rations to last him a week, as was usual, he would have to eat the leaves, and then they—the others—would shoot him out of hand unless the leaves poisoned him first. It would be no worse, eating the leaves, than eating flowers, which he had once tried. His sandals had been cut from an old truck tire. The pajamas had once been a tarpaulin or a rectangle of blackout material. Nothing he had was new or fresh. All of it had been formerly something else, and exhausted in that use: secondhand or third, a clumsy improvisation. Now, cursing, he unlashed the two bamboos, let the bicycle fall over onto its side in the undergrowth, and made an elementary stick music, wondering what had possessed him. In grade school had he heard a rhythm like that? Hollow, eerie, louder even than the mutilated-sounding squawk of all the jungle life around him. After a rest, he got up and walked on without the bicycle (it had no pedals anyway), slashing two-handed at the brush, trying to talk himself into an exhilaration he could not feel, as if he were out for a summer walk to the Little Colorado River with his uncle, looking for cottonwood root, or catching turtles for shells to make knee ornaments from. Two bamboos were too much, so he slung one away from him in what was meant to be a high parabola, but all it did was crash invisibly into the foliage. Tooting through the other, something between a march and a makeshift solo on clarinet, he advanced at a fast-diminishing pace, dreaming he could walk so slow that an observer would see no motion at all, as in some movie he recalled when time had frozen, but not quite: everyone was still moving, but at only a millimeter a day. Heedless of mines, whose position he was supposed to know anyway, he inched forward, heedless too of twine strung between two trees at shin level. All he had to do was shove one foot forward and the twine (sometimes it was wire) would pull hand grenades out of tin cans nailed to the trees. Since the safety pins had been removed, the grenades would explode. He half smiled at the thought of all the armed grenades lurking in cans throughout the jungle, nestling, getting hot and rusty, waiting, waiting, mindlessly ready to do the only thing they could. But grenades were modern, whereas spiked balls were not, they were big balls of heavy mud studded with punji spikes. When you released the trip wire, the ball swung hard into the track and half impaled you. In shallow pits there were bows with their ends embedded in the sides, and arrows under tension against the string, aimed at the track. This was how the Indian-like tribes in the highlands killed game, but the Cong had taken it over. The arrow rested on the lip of the pit and would shoot somewhat upward, groin height, say. The bamboo of the punji sticks had been hardened in fire, and the most fearsome stake traps not only had spikes pointing upward, to go through the sole of a boot as you crashed down on them with all your weight, but also stakes in the walls, pointing down, so that you reimpaled your foot when you tried to drag it out. He paused, halting his leg a fraction of a millimeter in front of a trip wire. He stood between two grenades. To his right was a bow and arrow in a hand-deep pit. Left of him the spiked ball awaited his belly. All he could do was go back, but he knew it, someone had crept up behind him and strung another line that released a gigantic battering ram which would not just mash him but loft him high and away into the jungle. Only the shrike impales its victim, he thought; there was no time for thought. Oh but there was, there was all the time in the world; he was not going to move ever again, but would stand here until he rotted, and even his skeleton would not trip the booby traps, so well he had schooled it. There he stood in an enclosure made of wire and cord, surrounded by the lethal contraptions of a primitive people: the most cost-effective weapons of the entire war. *Thorn in my side,* he miserably told himself. *Thorn up my ass.* Time did not stop, but it dilated, and from the other end of the track, which was not far, something was coming toward him. Salt in his eyes blurred everything, even the ogre advancing on him on its hind legs, a travesty of the erect human, and he remembered another gait, surely not his own, of someone who walked on the balls of his feet, springy, as if to suggest perfect adaptability, arms crooked a bit, moving in a jaunty mild rocking strut as if to music from afar. From home? Nothing like that was coming toward him. Why did his mind incessantly recoil into opposites? A hair below his elbow touched one of the trip wires to his side, and he shivered, yearning to lift the slimy roundness from his eyes, but afraid even to blink. Then came the enforced blinks of waiting too long between blinks. Nothing exploded. No bangs. Not even a rustle. The apparition kept coming toward him, taller than any animal could be even on its rear legs. Not at the strut, not jaunty, not even cautious, but evenly coming on with no attempt at stealth. Hemmed in by the trip wires, he trembled and held his breath, a dedicated oscilloscope who would never rush things again, never bolt his food, gulp his beer, read books by skipping from chapter beginnings to chapter ends. Now all of him was numb. What swayed in front of him, he knew it, was only the shadow of someone advancing under cover, a yard or two off the track; but that made no sense, there wasn't enough sun to cast a shadow. How could it be real, walking more slowly than he stood? Was the distance between them shortening? The figure seemed to move, but was not visibly nearer, yet not walking backward either. Maybe it was. He had heard of jungle ghosts, tropical trolls who smudged you like a fly. All they were was tremendous zones of energy at rest, who all of a sudden blazed into action for an entire day, then fell still again for a month or two. One eye cleared after one of his crescendo blinks and he saw the wristwatch, a true hallucination this, and it kept coming nearer, a small spot of renegade light, swung on an arm that grew from a loose black sleeve. And this was not, as he had thought, some silhouette from the San Francisco Mountains, a god-ghost, but a floppy broad-brimmed khaki hat atop a plump-cheeked female face, the expression of which hovered between amusement and slightly doctored surprise. Round her neck she had a salmon-colored silk scarf tied in one knot at the throat, and she was close to being buxom. The mouth made no motion and he knew how tight the teeth were behind it. She had an M16 slung in front of her but made no move to use it. Instead, with the fastidious ease of a connoisseur, she looked behind him, then to either side, nodded at so complete an arrangement, and remained there, the other side of the trip wire to the two grenades. She might have been appraising a roast of beef, a newly ironed table cloth. No, he urgently told himself, they didn't have roasts or table cloths. Her cheeks were ruddy, almost a separate structure, inflatable surely. Like those at home. Her black pajamas were caked with oil and mud, but the scarf was clean. She gave off an aroma of ferns, at once acrid and heavy, both vinegary and sweet like a chocolate malted that has sat too long. His head was telling him things he didn't want or need to know. Now she drew herself up straight, motioned with the M16, not urging him to move but, as it were, confirming him in his place, ticking him like an item on some inventory, and he had begun to wonder if she saw him as one of her own, ludicrously caught in his own traps, or one of the enemy come to quadruple death. Had it been she who had crept up behind him and boxed him in with the fourth booby trap? Had she then circled her way round to look him in the face? She seemed unsurprised to see him, so maybe he was something she herself had dreamed up, whereas he had had no part in the making of her. No, I am not one of them, he told himself angrily; I am not a spy either. Clothes do not the man make. Nor a uniform. She knows nothing about me. What if I were naked, would she prod my scrotum with the rifle's tip? I am obviously not an American, I am going nowhere, she is going to release me, gently removing the grenades without letting the arming lever strike home, and then using a couple of hairpins to make them harmless. She has no hairpins anyway. The hair is too short. Somebody's been feeding her good. Can she be a camp follower? One of those jungle nymphos we've heard about, who cook and sew as well? What shook him was that she belonged in a Phoenix restaurant, plunking down the teapot and the fried noodles to nibble on as he ordered, as always, the seafood Go Ba, the sizzling Go Ba, never mind how it ought to be said. Elegantly scripting his order on her pad in cursive Chinese characters as if he really had ordered in another language than his own. What she did next was mildly relevant, although utterly uncalled for. Jutting her face at his, without the faintest expression, she let out a long burp and actually vocalized something during it, two or three syllables, then walked briskly back the way she had come, laughing in a mellow, erratic voice as at some choicest morsel of gossip. Soon after, he unfroze, made sure there was nothing after all behind him, or on either side, and did a sluggish about-face, determined to find the bicycle, rummage through the outsize sack for something to eat, something to use, to smash, to give away, all of a sudden eager to rejoin the human race, theirs or his own, it didn't matter which. Here in the jungle he was landlord to the tenant called his mind, and all its aberrations convinced him to give it better housing. The woman could have shot him where he stood, so she too had become one of his keepers, all of whom, one day, he would have to hunt down and kill, simply to reassert his freedom. Bite the hand that feeds, he told himself, but do not bite it off. There was a limit to the kindness in the world, and he was prepared to cut down on the share he got, the share he gave.

Fermina

The living and the dead, they all have faces. It would help if some of their faces would go away. As for Emory, not living and not dead, but alive, he has that sensitive look to his eyes. He can be hurt. His lips are thick and rather straight, but they show a lot of him to the world. That's the way in if you want to do him harm. The eyes could weep, easily I think, they always look just dried up after some commotion or other. And his cheeks are sucked in around two up-and-down creases made not by smiling but by disappointment. It's a face of patiently putting up with folks, me included, and it has settled into a kind of handsomeness I never thought would be his. As faces go, it is gentle and sensitive, willing to listen, willing to share whatever ails you. This is the face I wanted by me when his brother began to move away from me, having had from me over several months all he wanted in this lifetime. Oh, Emory, what have we done to each other? What has George done to us in his pushy way? *That* face, dead or alive, had none of these creases and hollows, none of his willingness to hear you out. No, it was all George, steaming ahead, always knowing what you were going to say, which meant he never listened to you half the time. Same hair, though, same as Velma, their mother—long, straight, lank, and white by forty. More like a skullcap than like hair. A wig, maybe. You could go lift it off, you almost think. Three wigs on one shelf, and they could pick up one of the three at random, wear it, and nobody would know the difference. Mother and two sons with one hairstyle among them. Oswald makes a fourth, of course, not that I noticed it when he was a child, but, as he grew, the hair began to turn into that neat little skullcap and no barber in the city could make anything of it. So Oswald started with a crew cut, just to look different from the three of them. Now, what I want to know is where did I get to in that boy? Nothing of Fermina at all. I was just a delivery girl. They made him up between them, all three, and his mother was just a bystander. My boy had two fathers and two mothers. Maybe more. And Bessie was his true mother, if you can have children after death. It was all a thing of theirs, I was the one left out, lugging the baby bundle in front of me for nine months and Emory, when he looked at all, looking harsh and hurt, but saying not a word. If that is what I wanted, I could have it, but he didn't have to watch me having it. Life has been like that. One dies, another goes away, then another goes away, and you are left with other people's memories. Is that why I look down so much, as they say? Not out of shame, it's too late for that, but more out of knowing if I look up I won't see anything to cheer me up. I am going to be a very old woman, I can tell. A creaking gate. I get these flashes of light and then a headache like granite splitting, which lasts for days, and then I am all right until the next time, but my head stays sore to the touch for days. It must be Sotuqnangu tapping me with his lightning stick. Teach me a lesson. Keep my old legs together. Why, at my age, if I went and laid on the plaza stark naked with my legs wide apart, they would only stand a cardboard box in between and ask how much it cost to rent the space. A woman is some kind of magic box, full of all the right chemicals. She has a few brief moments of pleasure and turns into a small natural oven in which things bake for much too long. Out they come, howling, and that's the sum total of what you came into this world for. It isn't much to spend fifteen years growing up for. Some kind of pan is what I am, deep with solid sides, but not so easily scrubbed and put to use again. A woman grows old just by being serviceable. Then, one fine day, they throw her out. The Georges do it, the Oswalds do it, the Emorys do it, even the mothers do it. This, they say with one of those squeezed-boil smiles, was what your life was like, Fermina, you

won't get another for a while. Just like that. I am supposed to smile
when I am spoken to, otherwise behave and keep quiet. Be there for
them. I am not even here for myself. I filled a space, but I don't know
much. I know how to cry, how to bleed, and how to stay awake.
These are things there is no need to pass on to the next generation.
These are for me. What did Oswald say? You're always here, it's wonderful to come home. What I said was It will be truer still when I'm
dead and gone. I am beginning to believe it now, how he took her to
the lake and held her under, he only a bit stronger than she, but
enough. Did he then swim out with her to the middle of the lake? He
couldn't have gone to the middle of the lake on his own. He just
floated her away with a shove from the edge, all he needed was a
foot's deep. All past, it doesn't matter to the living and the dead will
never be heard from, not in my house at any rate. Why don't I care?
Am I just a savage? I read books, I read at least one a year, not every
year. I ought to be telling somebody, Oswald or Emory, but who are
they to worry about such things? It once was cozy and now it's bleak.
He was a man who had sudden whims. Amounting to wildness. It's
an ill wind anyway, even up here on the mesa. He was a cuddle, when
in a cuddly mood. Just like Oswald. They could be real spiky too.
Cactus in my arms. Between my legs. A rough, coarse breed of men
whose gentleness they keep for wood and rock and eagles and little
private poems they say to themselves up on a crag somewhere. Actually, I think he stumbled, once, George, and he somehow snagged a
cord that had fallen around her neck and gone under some outcrop of
rock, dragging her underneath, to where he couldn't get in time
while she thrashed about and he howled with all his mouth to wait
and hold her breath. Too late. That was it. She skidded, he tripped,
she fell and rolled over and under, and he dove and dove, but he could
never swim more than a couple of yards. What was the cord doing
around her neck then? Not a cord, but the belt of her dress, that was
it, a fancy one she had slung over her neck while she adjusted something, and it snagged, it caught on an eagle's claw, then she went over
sideways, some of those pools have no out, they're all top, and between the bottom of the lid and the top of the water there isn't air
enough to lift a feather. All of a sudden he was in love with a dead
woman, high-handed, prancy, as she was, and he was looking for an
ordinary woman just to like. He found one all right, he went home
like a shot arrow, straight into the heart of the target. Don't you
forget I loved you, he was shouting at the water as she slid away, most

of her already under, just a faint bulge now and then showing where
she was. He kicked the water, he smacked it, he yelled for help as loud
as a wind. And then, I think, he calmed down and wondered about
what would happen next. Stems caught on her mouth. Fish came to
say hello. Then like a plane landing she tilted down real slow, at just
that little tilt they have, and glided all the way to the bottom so as not
to bump too hard. What did she do down there before she came up
again? They could drag till doomsday, but they'd never have found
her if she hadn't come up of her own accord. The lake let go of her
once it had made sure. They actually had to rope him down, to an old
pickup, to keep him from leaping into the lake to join her. It was
quite a do. You could never tell him he was overdoing it, though, he
wanted her to hear him, I don't doubt. He was sorry it had come to
this, having to be rid of her somehow, water, fire, soil. She was an
eagle he sent off as a messenger to the gods. Something like that. He
never lusted for me before that. He did what he did to be rid of her,
not to get at me. I could have been had whatever the circumstances. I
was there. Like an empty cabin with the stove turned off. He never
planned anything, he just waited to wake up each day and then made
up whatever he could to pass the time. Did they say glided or glid?
Glode? You never know it all alters when it gets into folks's mouths. If
I was where they invent how to talk, I'd burn half the words we have,
I'd burn all the Anglo words, I'd make us go back again to grunts and
howls. They fit the wilderness better. In my opinion. They say he had
an eagle's head in his mouth for days after that. An actual head. No,
they said, it was a chicken's head, beak outward. Others said it was a
claw that dangled, and while it did he mumbled claw talk as if his
tongue had been torn. Some grieve and some show off. Then he took
to carving like he was killing the wood he worked between his hands,
as if the trees had all of them bent over and stooped down to shove
her under the surface. He hated his hating. He didn't know what to
do, legally, with chisel and knife, but you could see him eyeing necks
and tongues. He was going to get somebody sooner or later, it was
obvious, but all he got was me, a woman common as water whereas
she, well she'd been his waterfall, his thunder, his gale, and that was
all she ever wanted to be. She should have lived in the trees from the
very first, like her life depended on it, and wiped her rump with
leaves, poor nothing that she is.

Sotuqnangu

When he did have chance to try fitting the soles of his feet together, he felt how cracked they were; the heels were two big calluses, split deep like earth in a dry summer. Trying to file them smooth with a piece of rock (in itself a rare find in a country that seemed to have no geology), he managed only to make them bleed. So he tried to distract himself while rubbing the splits beneath the patina of fresh blood, developing his idea of how best to go to waste. Everyone cared, especially those who told Indians what to do. They knew how things ought to be and then they made the dumbos go and fix them. What he wanted was a society in which no one knew what the hell to do about anything. Nobody had any ideas and nobody had any authority. Life would no longer be taken seriously, but trivially, as the mortar shells took it, the grenades, the bombs. If all this dough went on shredding the very thing that made the planet different from the moon, then life wasn't worth bothering about in the first place. It was always replaceable, there was always plenty of it around. Once again he was goofing off along a jungle path, heedless of booby traps, orders, rain, with the little vomit bag from the plane in his hand, like somebody walking down the road to mail a letter. But this time he had company, a German shepherd, having been assigned to a scout dog team, and the dog's name was Jook, a Vietnamese word meaning "sworn friend," more particularly someone with whom you have exchanged buffalo sacrifices. Only a dog could detect trip wires, mines, tunnels, and of course people, unless it was thoroughly exhausted or the rain was too heavy or the vegetation too thick. Once again he paused at the trip wire with the grenades in cans on either side, between two trees, and waited for Go Ba of the plump cheeks to come sidling down the trail in black pajamas and salmon-colored scarf. Jook would do his talking for him. It was almost dark, though, and in black she would hardly be visible, so it was as well he had the dog along. What happened next was that he saw her coming before the dog sniffed her, before the dog saw her even, and she advanced just as before, same scarf, same rifle, same fat-thighed sway, and the watch on her wrist. He was going to hand her the vomit bag with the map of her country inside it, magically restored by his teeming imagination. Pretending he was the dog, he tried to summon up at a distance the stale aroma of her body in the pajamas, of matted body hair, clotted discharge of blood, excrement ill wiped away with leaves, but all this did was to excite him while Jook looked sideways as if no one was approaching them. See, he told the dog, there she comes—Go Ba of the Salmon Scarf. Right to the trip wire he edged while the dog hung back as if aloof, and then she was right upon them, not even checking her pace as she swaggered through the trip wire and on down the trail. No explosion, not even the firing levers clicking as the wire released two duds. And still the dog looked away, as if she had never been. The only difference was that she left behind her a pungent, and for him nostalgic, smell of American toilet soap, not medicinal or harsh, but lavender, cedarwood, or mountain raspberry, he couldn't be sure, but it brought back a world of beauty parlors, his mother shampooing either him or herself, heads swathed in towels with frayed, stringy nap and tiny soaps from the Hopi Motel nested lovingly in the drawer that held her best. Go Ba had gone, but her perfume filled the jungle, leaving it a booby-trap heaven in which desire, bewilderment, and nostalgia almost made him cry. So: the booby trap had not gone off, but such things happened. So: she had taken an overdue bath, but why was she always walking alone, encountering him either with a burp or wordlessly, and why did she take him so much for granted, where he had no right to be, certainly not on his own, even with a scout dog called Jook, a sworn friend? The dog had failed. Go Ba had gone. The map in the bag he put away. Not that he had been hoping for conversation, just maybe a hug or a smile, a fast flash of her thighs as she dropped her pajama pants in one sudden down and up motion. He wasn't sure, but he had little chance of seeing her again, and the dog would be no earthly use in locating her for a third chance. What he did not know until later was that, in order to fool the scout dogs, the Cong washed with American soap and so could not be sniffed out of hiding. The thought persisted, though, that going into the jungle to that particular trail would always bring her out for him. Something automatic came into play. She would appear for no one else. She was his alone to conjure up, and all the dog could find were mines. He slipped the leash and Jook stood awaiting the next thing, which became a slap on the rump, at which the dog sauntered off the trail in pursuit of something more smellable than Go Ba. Now, in his mind, at least, she came waltzing back and gave him a can full of cooked rice. *Jook*, he said to her, which made her laugh that mellow cascade of tones again. And this time she didn't smell of toilet soap at all. He gave up, he gave up on the daydream, the hope, the sequestered hunger for something civilian to happen, for someone just as out of place as himself to come out of the jungle, natural as a tiger or a water buffalo. The dream was around his shoulders, bigger and heavier with each day. But a dream doesn't weigh, he said, a dream is like a cobweb. You owe it nothing. It does not say on it, in sloppy lettering, Front Toward Enemy, like the Claymore mine does. Dream is like putty. He realized that, if he had to choose between a dream that flopped and an actuality that gave him nothing, he would have to find a safe place in between, not so much a wonder shelter of the mind as a technique for quiet self-disposal. It helped, he absently decided, if you thought of space in terms of time, and vice versa. Denature the whole damned thing until it no longer reaches you. Then he decided to learn about forgetting, reasoning in his erratic way that what the mind omits the body does away with. He had read, in some gossip rag, a serious article about how in the hospital the circulating nurse hands sponges in packages of five to the scrub nurse, who opens each package and counts the sponges while the other watches. As sponges are used, the circulating nurse fastens them together in bunches of five, and before the incision is closed both nurses check the tally of sponges used against that of sponges accounted for. In some such way, he was hoping to neutralize his life with congenial ritual, being where he did not want to be, which in the most refined sense meant also not wanting to be anybody at all in that slum of endless chlorophyll. And certainly not as an Indian from the most other-worldly tribe of all, whether or not he had the schooling smarts. He had, somehow, to live through it all and go back to brooding, unchanged, Oswald Beautiful Badger Going Over The Hill once again.

BertandAnna

We not dumbies all year round. We know what folks like when they
telling the truth. We got the wood shavings in our pockets, keep our
hands cozy all winter long. No room in there for the hands of other
folk, not that we mean about it, just isn't room for two or three hands,
one pocket. You can tell they'd like to, though. They all do. They
would like to walk around in close blanket all day BertandAnna-ing
everybody with warm little Hi's, they know how, though they don't
always say it. Too cold up here for folks, so they wrap themselves up.
All kinds of ways to keep the wolf out. Foot behind the back of the
knee, then change feet. You got to keep the feets warm up here.
Hands in your armpits, same kind of thing. Tongue well you curl it
around back into the top of your mouth. Some little spitsoft plug of
cloth in your backside too, it keep a draft away. We walk around all
day, you got to be warm for that. No good giving folks a cold Hi, they
likely to say BertandAnna doesn't BertandAnna us none too friendly
today, it must be the cold. When it is not July we tell them it is not
July, they seems to like that made certain when we pass by, and when
it is January we tell them it isn't something else. Folks like to dream

away from what things is. We bring them back to earth. It's cold
because it isn't warm. That is a great shock to them as was thinking
otherwise. Hi, BertandAnna, they shiver, and we nod at them, tell
them the truth and the time and the season. There is so much to
know, so much to forget, especially if you're dummies, just mumbling
around to pass the time of day, collecting up old toothpaste tubes or
the silver paper, this going for the blind appeal down-mesa somewhere, maybe in Keams. That nephew of his, now, or whatever he be
under the sheet, he maybe the kindest of folks when you run across
him, him fresh back from the big city, the movies. He always look like
he going to tell you something real soft and gentle, like something he
found back there he really have to tell everybody about, but he too
shy, he too timid, maybe, he never quite get it out of his system, it like
a bird trapped in his chimney. He seen something, though, long before his uncle did. He have it on his mind the whole time, he not able
to smile quite that open smile of his early, since then he sort of fussy
spoken, look behind him a lot, he have no idea how often he doing
some of these things. He give us his Hi like he was a dummie too, but
we know better, he one of the smartest heads of corn on this mesa, he
going one day to build a big bridge link it to Flag, then the big churns
of milk they arrive every day. They gonna let us clean the churns
with little mops and silver polish, you can see it in their eyes, lordy
yes, they have plans for BertandAnna, got us blowing and wiping our
noses now, walk around with the wad of tissue in place right where it
count if you taken by surprise, it happen mostly in the cold, they got
us trained like two dogs. Well, what you got for us today,
BertandAnna, they say, and we time them and Hi them like they was
real close friends, there is no body we do not speak to. Sometimes get
an old coffee can full of soup, stew, whatever it's called, and we do
this silly talk about it, you hold it Bert, my hands is hot, no you hold
it, Anna, you got thicker gloves. We snow it, usually. Two, three,
handfuls tames it fast. Roll it around your mouth, then spit it back to
thicken it up, make it hold the inside of the can better, not come
spilling up against your face when you tilt. You don't want a noseful
or an eye. Got to get just the right amount, like that day Oswald, he
the nephew, hold the can for us in the streaming storm, he never
mind, he got a big spoon from somewhere, kind of a ladle for it. Of all
folks, he give us the most messages to take. You go to my uncle
George The Place In Flowers Where Pollen Rests, and you tell him,

okay, Uncle George, and that be all. Off we go. Uncle George, he send one back, even if nephew standing only three or four foot away, it far to shout, him old. Okay back, we tell him, with that funny little walk of ours stiff-legged like we born stretched.

Sotuqnangu

Throughout history, men and women have succumbed to infestations of themselves, when something not essentially them took them over and fed itself on them, regardless and inhuman. So with Oswald, aching to be where he was not, yet not knowing where else to go, and making within his head the mental equivalent of the mid-Atlantic trench or the dead zones of outer space in which no star shines, no haze of multicolored gas trembles and bloats. Things passing through his head left traces that did not belong to him. Not that he felt possessed, it wasn't that personal. There were thistles in the garden of his mind, and all he did was let them be, half suspecting they were the beginnings of the nullity he craved, the ballast that might save him from being blown away. Haunted, he thought, it's like being haunted by a ghost that has no attitude to you yourself. This is what it's like to grow up, when your being lengthens out. He learned not to cling, to the crazy fact of the map, the abortive escapades with the bicycle, Go Ba, and the dog called Jook, but occasionally with no help from him these things grouped themselves at random and then he, as if looking wrong way through a telescope, heard them out, saw them through, wondering why nothing essential came to him, that he could take a pride in having and embellishing. The dog bit Go Ba. The dog became adept and trotted through the jungle, disarming every booby trap for miles, and Go Ba followed behind, reconnecting the wires, the cords, adjusting the arrows back into tension in the bows. Both dog and woman used the map, but they came nowhere near him, even though he tried to invade his own head and accost them like creatures of his own making. Now and then the voluptuous woman stripped naked in heavy rains and just stood there, being sluiced down, and the dog stood by her pajamas. He even saw her produce from a pocket the lump of toilet soap that made her unsmellable to the dog. And all the time he went through the motions, did as he was told (to some extent anyway) without quite abandoning his originality of mind. He had a fleeting sense that Fermina, his mother, was monitoring him from afar, checking his performance for—well, he didn't altogether know, but he felt observed, mentally fingered, not by God or his mother, but maybe the patron saint of bunglers who at the last moment in each fiasco would leap in to save him. Those around him had no idea of what coursed through his mind, his reasonably well developed mind that lacked credentials only, but he just knew someone was keeping tabs on him, for better or worse, even if only a superior version of himself—the Oswald he could have been but never would be, *because of circumstances.* Yes, he decided, he was a mediocrity being watched over by a cleverer man who thought his thoughts for him while he got on with the business of pounding the Cong. It was all right with him, it didn't make him nervous to be spied upon or overheard, but he just wished the entity that oversaw him would really take the initiative and work the super-miracle of getting him home again. Through an error in the paperwork, one day he would be rolling in blood, mud, and leeches, and only a day later he'd be buying hamburgers in Keams Canyon, on his way to take his mother to Doc Matlock. It wasn't that kind of being, however, it was a long way from being that practical, or helpful; it was rather some force that he thought invented him, linked him up from moment to moment, and it alone knew the blueprint, the potential Oswald that could never be. So then, he was haunted by these slivers, ricochets, echoes, trembles, these flashes in the pan of himself, without ever knowing what they amounted to, and sometimes having no idea if he was imagining them out of sheer defiance. He lived, though, gradually learning the trade of war. By night he watched over and through a visual detector mounted on a tripod, reveling in the stealth of it as he snooped on the enemy almost a mile away, almost doting on the tube that intensified the image as many as forty thousand times, half hoping no one out there had aimed a similar tube at him. Trip flares were one thing, blazing in different colors and revealing the enemy's direction of travel, but this scrunched-up telescope was an object of intense fascination as he turned it on creatures other than men, spotting (he thought) tigers and buffaloes, snakes and small scuttlers whose name he did not know. The night life of the jungle became his exclusive property: an infrared circus, a ballet of slither and scamper, pounce and dodge. That was the friendly side of it, whereas when they schooled him in the use of the so-called starlight scope, attached to a rifle, he was less enthralled, being obliged to shoot the enemy revealed as much as four hundred yards away. Sometimes he fired, sometimes not; no one knew exactly what he saw, or what he aimed at only to miss, on purpose. He much preferred the fat, squat scope whose beam fanned out magenta from the rods and cones within his eyes. The night belongs to Charlie, everyone said, because Charlie marched, trucked supplies, and laid ambushes under cover of darkness, but he himself had lifted the lid off the darkness, and he longed to have such an instrument on a balcony in Los Angeles or San Francisco, to observe the nightlife of his fellow Americans. The biggest scope of all, the AN/PPS-5 radar one that picked up vehicles six miles away and personnel at three, he never used, but he had heard about it, that voyeur's Rolls Royce. He asked, but they said no, not now, not in this area, we don't need it. Something from boyhood stirred again as he aimed his raygun far and wide, quietly and with cumulative relish populating the night, going without sleep to do it, even volunteering for extra duty, convinced he'd never see Go Ba through *this*, or the unleashed phantasmal dog trotting uselessly around in a maze of soap trails. They were paying him, not much admittedly, to be a naughty boy again, and sometimes he reported things that were not there, just for effect, and now he knew how the astronomers felt out at Palomar, sucking the universe down onto their enormous mirrors, watching it purr and laze, erupt in fire and smother itself with dust. Looking is my occupation, Marco Polo had said, but he never had an AN/PPS-5 or a NOD (Night Observation Device). If he had, Oswald said, Marco Polo would never have come back from his travels, he would have been at his window watching all the hairless quim in China. He tried this on the guys, but it fell flat, and instead they made jokes about

him, about how he liked to look instead of getting shut-eye he was
entitled to. Yeah, he said on more than one occasion, I am a real good
looker, ain't that so? Rarely had they seen anyone so gently impas-
sioned with a piece of equipment, so ready to let it become his entire
life, little realizing that what he saw down the tube was mostly of his
own devising; rosy shades he saw, and embalmed-looking oblong sil-
houettes, the blurred checkerboard pattern of warmth and cool
sensed in contrasting colors, but most of all Charlie transfigured from
the enemy into figures thrown on a wall by hands combining in front
of a light. He "threw" people as a potter throws jugs, making them
pliable to his needs, twisting the tools of his trade to make an under-
cover poetry that saw him through. His cussed streak, still there, had
quieted down; he rebelled in secret through his eyes, actually seeing
dozens of the female enemy but never confusing them with Go Ba,
even spotting large animals that might have been dogs on the loose
without once exclaiming *Jook.* The Vietnamese ate dog anyway, or
just killed them out of hand in incest rituals, and he decided Go Ba
had been fat with dog; whenever a brother and sister had gotten it on
together, there she'd be to savor the exorcism feast while the offending pair stood in the nearest river to munch the penalty of animal
excrement offered to them on the tips of sticks. That was not his
world, but he heard about it, he imagined it going on, even in the
nights when jinns walked the forest. He saw himself in slightly in-
flated terms that felt like a military promotion: the lighthouse keeper
of Vietnam, the Magellan of the Mekong Delta, an essentially civiliz-
ing influence among the brawny boys of war. Where astronomers
talked in light-years, he amiably invented the light-hour, the light-
minute; the exact distance didn't matter so long as he had some means
of making himself remote from what he and the others did during the
day. And this he happily wrote about to his mother, saying it was
rather like being a tourist who went out only at night, who saw
everything by moonlight, to whom Charlie had become something
more complex then just the formal enemy—rather like the daubs or
the handprints of nostalgic monkeys equipped with paints. His was
the war of peering, and all day, with prickly eyes, he entertained
mentally the images gathered from the night, coppery reds and iron
sulfate greens, heads in the shape of cakes or tureens, trunks of tiger
grafted onto men, legs that multiplied through a quirk of light, trucks
that became loaves of bread, bicycles that uncoiled themselves like
snakes, animals that fused with one another on the run. He saw ap-

ples with mustaches, penises with wings, stethoscopes made of leaves and creepers, tigers that lined themselves up with the bars of cages and vanished forever. Come morning, they'd ask him, "You been getting good shit, man?" and he'd answer the best eye shit this side Flagstaff, Arizona, man. "What happens in the night, not even a priest, a whore, and a ghost would believe. It's incredible." But when the others took their turn, they saw nothing unusual, reported it and artillery blasted it to bits. The more his nightly duty fattened into his private peep show, the more he fudged, the more imaginative his reports became until the day, inevitable but in its anticlimax delicious too, they took him from the NODs for keeps, and something in him wanted to quote a painter in his own defense: the one who worried that what he painted wasn't "there" at all, but only in his eyes. He couldn't remember who, so he said Marco Polo instead, which made them laugh, and convinced him that, one day, he would find an occupation utterly worthless and do it supremely well, or one that was utterly magnificent, and at this he would become so bad that nobody would recognize it. Mousetrap cleaning, he vowed, raised to the status of restoring old masters, or—he couldn't think of it, but, finally offering himself reading the mind of a god at a speed of one letter per year, he fell asleep for his first free night in two and a half weeks. His military future was in doubt, but his head was full of images, neither of heaven nor of hell, but from the intermediate zone where the sun began to stammer, the earth to jactitate in sleep, and the mind of humankind gratefully to err.

Fermina

cept among the dead who dont hear music at all even if if they lucky
they pick up this kind of right down inside of you wondering when
you talk to yourself tight as a needle and without any of the trimmings it amounts to soulwhisper thats what I call it and you got to be
careful not to get it right you got to be careful not to offend those of
yours as has already passed over otherwise they wake up to all the
other worse things you done wrong they got memories like wallpaper
to call you up with flog your back make you drink your own blood in
your own water it must sting that and when your done they really
start in on you about the honeyjuice where your legs meet as if your
legs was two perfect strangers never introduced feeling each other up
under cover of a thunderstorm in the outhouse and your saying anything to stop him as if you wanted to no george its too big it is not
human size it was meant for something else building homes with or
dams or airports it isnt decent to be so big it will split me wide open
it is no good in the mouth you need a tent not a woman a canyon not
a me just you take it where it belongs go shove it into the lake full of
dead swimmers I have no idea what happened then but what happens

now I have to take charge of it is rotten it is like a great big tumor it is full of something that scalds and then cuts you open leave it in the snow some winter to shrink it even a chisel would not scar it or a knife make it bleed there are saws that could not cut through it george it ought to be rested on sawhorses in between uses it is not yours or ours it belongs to the mesa in fact a mesa is what it is it was I am all of a sudden full of peach preserves thick like motor oil all rippling around in a big swamp in there as if no not some god but some wind some rain some ocean had done this to me a plain ordinary woman who wanted no trouble and here I am already bulging with slithery stuff that can not have just come from a man with a name more like a landslide an avalanche as full as if you had shot me full of a five course dinner packing even the gaps between my ribs and putting meat on every bone it must have already bit home it wont run down even if I jumped up and down all might out here in the cold where emory might have drowned in it waiting for that iceberg up me to melt and give up its big white ghost so george can carve it into something useful for the mesa folk when they look at the stars all that high and out of reach they never need refueling but george does he can only do this once a week like the river in spring it cracks open and starts to flow you ever heard a river clatter past you all white lumps and crags now i am in love with a tree it has to be that side of it i have no way down or off it isnt right it isnt decent but it is all i have i am nobody now i have the smallest inside voice of all my kin a little chirrup of sighs and coughs it is like saying howdo to a polar bear slamming at you two feet away as if youre his breakfast that is not love or lust or whatever it is its one big thump into the silent center of you and then the afterglow that is like being blinded in your tenderloin i am grateful for a week away from it there must have been bleeding like a dead husky in there i dont have time to swab it mop up he comes again and again over the weeks his pants were never up but now he does it through the fly the whole thing open ready to start before we even begin and i believe it doesn't ever go down on him anymore it must be the week long wait that does it to him a cream pelt an ore white hot an eye bleeding white paint uphill like no river no lake no falls no human shudder thy will be done he sure free with his hands as well wherever he go

Sotuqnangu

The war, inasmuch as it was a war at all, undeclared like something
smuggled through customs, was a big raucous commercial for a product Oswald had forgotten. Thousands upon thousands were ready to
lay down their lives for politicians, who only came into being because
otherwise there would be an intolerable void in a nation's boredom.
Unless it was all coercion and they had all been forced into it; but the
idea of that force, the holy consuming spell that swept people barely
above the age of consent into anonymous conflict with other people
barely above the age of consent, nagged away at him night and day.
In the old days the plains Indians, in order to create a eunuch for
tribal purposes he found obscure, had thonged a youth naked to a
pony, which then galloped about, castrating the youth as it went. His
own predicament was similar, but he couldn't just walk away one
night with his NOD in hand and join the vast army of the disen-
franchised. There was no such army. There were loners who stayed
loners if they lasted. By definition, loners didn't join, they did not
cluster or merge. And he would no more join the Cong than volunteer to enter a cage in the Hanoi zoo. What it came down to, in the

end, was faces and bodies, and the bodies he found he could be callous about, just as mother nature was; but mother nature never saw your face, he was sure of that, and at night, with a meticulous relish approaching that of a naturalist, he had seen scores of faces, maybe a hundred, blooming busily out there. He had watched peerers peering, guards and sentries yawning, mouths opening around food, and heads drooping in sleep. They were all capable of friendship, they were all equipped with lethal weapons, they all had numbers, but he knew them by their faces, not that different from the daytime faces of the Vietnamese in the hamlets and paddies, and he found himself adding features from the day to the faces seen at night through the lens—vexation here, stupefied exhaustion there. The faces of the night came from an old, scratchy movie, maybe a composite assembled from incomplete copies, so there were gaps and jerks, and the magenta or green faces swam into and out of focus. But he knew them as well as a pack of playing cards: the ruefully dutiful face next to that of the downcast automaton, that of the eager conformist next to that of the fidgety stoic. He saw convinced people most of all, faces that did not relax even when locally unseen, as if some ideological novocaine had settled in for the duration. Feeling the tension of his own jaw and mouth as he stared into the darkness at the untidy album half a mile away, he had wondered how he looked to them, to an observer poring over *his* face at a comparable distance. The face was the dignity. It was where the mercuriality of being was. And it was never merely a matter of faces that smiled, scowled, looked happy or proud; it was much more complex than that, with untold and interminable shadings that sometimes registered an emotion, an attitude, lasting only a few seconds, and then gone forever. That combination, say, of irate relief shading over into exhilarated willingness, tinctured this time with slyness or naiveté, was rare in the history of that face. There might be close repeats, but they would never be exactly the same as this particular one. And that was something vital, missing so far as he knew from the individual intercourse of earthworms, ants, and hens, but he wasn't so sure about tigers, buffaloes, and dogs. In some creatures, the face was in the sense of smell. All he knew for certain was that he had picked up some abiding principle which, if even half attended to, meant that no one would ever kill anyone at all except in reasonless rage. Yet they did, all the time, conned into undervaluing the other's face. He no longer had access, though, to the tube that brought the night to life; he had had his share of faces, and all he could do now was linger on the memory of them. Stranded as shells on the uneven beach of his mind, they were there for the picking, and he suddenly realized what a handsome people the Vietnamese were, and tried to decide what it was they had that Koreans or Japanese lacked. Filling sandbags, or manhandling triple dannert barbed wire (three coils in a pyramid structure), he hit on neat sociability. No. Well, neat mobility, then: their features rippled gently. No. Proportionate grace. What the hell did that mean? Smooth and vibrant was better. Their faces were never quite at rest. Then he tried for negatives, and that was easier. Nothing blockish, square; nothing stony or drab. Perhaps they were the Latinos of the Oriental world. They were its Brazilians. It would take him the remainder of his days to figure out what made them unique, even in their sadsack black pajamas, pith helmets, or floppy Boy Scout hats. Go Ba's face, for instance, whether she was figment or real, or mostly figment plastered on to a forgotten glimpse, had something of this quality: a contained but accessible geniality that said, look, we live in a fertile country, life down here on the plains isn't too bad. He wished it were that simple. All he was doing, he recognized with a sour smile, was trying to pin down charm. But usually you shot it before you pinned it down. You blew it up in the dismal mental circuit of I, who don't want to kill you, will kill you, who don't want to kill me, before you lose confidence in my peaceable nature and jump in first. It was ghastly. Thousands of little deals and pacts went begging for lack of a word, and all those truant little armistices, between one face looking at the other face looking back at him, or her, never happened, in the Delta, on the Plateaux, the Coastal Plain, or away up on the trails made by stags and porters. Instead, they dug in behind barbed wire, claymores, and trip flares. At each bunker stake, helicopters dropped the standard pack of empty sandbags, two sheets of pierced-steel planking, and one shaped demolition charge. Then they built the bunker, but they absolutely had to complete the outer defenses by last light, yearning for the perfect circle of 131-feet radius but never finding the right terrain. He could never get over the juvenile thrill of watching grown men take a rope of that exact length and mark out the circle of the bunker line, as if preparing for baseball, and he often imagined his uncle's shack at the dead center of it: the low wall he liked to sit on or prop his back against while carving; the door that would never close properly, which George The Place In Flowers Where Pollen Rests refused to fix, in spite of winter's drafts; the sagging single bed inside, the brick sink at its foot, an honor guard of foot-high kachina dolls in the niche at its head—the spirits of nature copied from dances in which his people dressed up and became bigger, mightier, than themselves. No comfort, no style, no touch of a woman's hand; Uncle George lived out of doors as much as he could, and cared not where he laid his head. (Or in whose lap, said some.) He lived to carve, and an old box to him was a throne, a lump of wood was a mystical command. This was the place Oswald remembered better than his mother's, in which "Uncle" Emory was rarely to be seen, not that much at ease (as he said) among his kin; he was most often to be found in Keams Canyon. To keep sane, he was drawing on his childhood like mad, on the childhood of just about everybody back home. Once again he learned how to make a candy last by careful, tentative sucking. He heard the noise of children crying, younger than he, and was glad he was almost ten, certainly beyond tears and whines. Like Fermina, out in the sun to have a nibble, he gently covered his cookie with a fresh but unlaundered handkerchief to keep the flies off. He heard himself at school, murmuring angrily in the toilet, "I know I don't know, but *why* don't I know? Am I unteachable?" And then, in a flash, he was thinking how young Uncle George had died. No, of how Uncle George had died as a comparatively young man, who could surely have gone on for almost a quarter of a century more. He'd paid his dues, Oswald decides, just as I'm paying mine here. If I get out of this, I'll have paid for what I did, at least in my own eyes. Now he saw his uncle again doing one of his favorite things, Uncle's that is: putting a book outside to weather for at least a year, to turn to rot and swollen pith, and even all the way back to wood, if that was possible, which is when Uncle George would begin to carve it into something else. Now his mother's face displaced that of Uncle George, and she was telling him he was full of rattle for one so little, that she was getting the wind up because Uncle George was getting his mad up, and Emory his. They were going to come to blows about her. "I feel quite over-faced," she'd say, meaning the prospect of it was almost too much, like a heaping plateful. "Why don't you," he said, "do with them, Mama, what you do with me? Touch their hands with a hot spoon fresh from water on the boil?" No, she told him. The job of an Oswald was to make sure of the Dick Walmsley prize for woodwork, not kachinas but book ends, or if not that then the Edna Bowman prize for public singing, although he knew in his heart that no matter how much he O'ed for them he would never have the wings of a dove.

Later on, though, between twelve and fifteen, he did that other impossible thing: he saw his mother's sturdy back and scratched it for her on command. Her skin was like oiled silk, above it her own long hair and not the neat-cropped pageboy of his uncle, which in even later years he came to associate with the image of the pianist Franz Liszt. But he was here now, although "there" had somehow come more alive and would have to be put firmly out of mind if he wasn't going to get careless, wandering about with his mind not on his job. Death was like a canyon on the prowl, unsatisfied with those who fell into it or were thrown and actively looking for prey. I do not, he tried to say to himself, want everything to blow away. I want—things to stay put. I do not like change. Out here everybody is like a weight lifter and what he has to lift is his own life, past and future. It is no place to weather a book.

Fermina

Always getting ready to sneeze, he puckers on a poison. I rock him, he throws up. I stroke him, he howls. This is not a baby, it's a devil. Suck and spew he goes as if he is full of lamb chop. It goes into him like milk and comes out of him like meat. He does not like the touch of human hands, but if you breathe on him he quietens down. He wants the air rolling past him, he might have been an eagle. Even into his mouth and up his nose he likes it, much harsher than just breathing it in. He was born on a calm sunny day so maybe he misses the wind usual up here. I wish I was a cloud to handle him more gently, though, a cloud without rain, impossible I know, but special babies have special needs, have to have messengers sent out on their behalf for feathers, pollen, mouse fluff, anything soft. A fine name he has anyway, brought to mind by how tender he is, so unready, so flinching. What I would like for him is a place where even the pollen is safe from bees or breeze, the securest of little indoor worlds, a fleecy eardrum to lay him on, a navel of moss, a nest of earlobes. Nothing has to grate on him until he is at least a hundred years old. My last baby, this, he has one brother to show him how. When as much of a woman's insides comes out as there is baby, it is time. Weigh them in pans, side by side, and there is as much innards as baby. George stops now and then or would be nothing left inside to spoil. This is no baby for the fields, for carrying water, driving pickup trucks. I can tell, but I don't know how I know. I am both ways. He is so delicate, so touchy, but he also likes that fierce breath blown up his nostrils and into his mouth. He wants to be babied while the strong wind blows. He wants the wind to howl while he twitches in every other part of him. He is no heavier than a glance, a sigh. He sometimes weighs a ton as well. He is an all-sorts baby, a tough little shrinker who will not fit into this world any too well. He chortles when I'm rough with him, he screams when I'm too gentle, he smiles when I blow hard on him, he screams when I don't blow on him at all. A mother is supposed to understand, but as soon as I think I know exactly what he's like he turns different, he goes another way. He looks as if he already understands everything I say to him, I coo it or I hum, and he looks impatient as if I'm talking all wrong, not how he likes it, not what he wants said, it is all puzzling, but you can tell in some ways he's a delicate one, in other ways a moose. Oswald Beautiful Badger Going Over The Hill. He can live up to that with a bit of luck, a sweet and loving name for a boy. If he had only been a girl, I would have had a pair to show off, one of each, but the gods are good. He comes from where eagles die, from the soft muck we smother them in. We have been given an eagle back to fuss over. He will grow at his own speed, a youth until eighty, a young man until a hundred and fifty, old as the sun. Naming him is unwise, he will be many boys in one, each calling after the other to leave him alone in future. His bowels blasting like a little river beast. His lungs like rafts. His eyes full of an unseen wonder I know is no reflection of anything I have seen or am to, wherever, whenever, as I turn to the source of the dawn and say thank you for this breezy baby. It is nice now we can name our own babies instead of having Mrs. Judson and Mrs. Holmes do it. How far back we go, to the day he killed a rabbit with his boomerang and we all ran, I got to the rabbit first and gave him cornmeal cakes. A rabbit made my future for me. A carver made this baby, but he had an eagle's help. I am the goddess of hard substances, ugly by day, a beauty by night, I come all the way from the Pacific Ocean. I am gentle and kind. I do not mingle with people. I am never impersonated. I take part in no ceremony. My picture is in none of the books. I am a faultless liquid saying please.

Sotuqnangu

People existed, Oswald was sure, who saw others in much the same way as they saw flowers, which bloomed and dried within an accepted pattern of time. You kept replacing them, just as his uncle kept some grasses—sometimes even a few straws—in a jelly jar on the ground in front of the never-used makeshift fireplace. Every three or four days he took the dried-up ones to the trashcan and slid the replacements in with a fond murmur. He gave them no water, as if his mind was mainly on the cottonwood root he carved and his thinking told him that wood needed no water, not after the root had been unearthed. So he gave his grasses and straws no water, almost as if clamming some dumb animal for slaughter. Oswald himself had an almost innocent, lifelong yearning for things at the halt. He was just about the last man you would want to send to a war anywhere, not if you wanted something finished with, the war decided. Only too well had he learned from his tribe, his uncle especially, the sovereign slowness of things, the way in which ongoingness was better than any outcome. Whatever life was, it was a blur fit to worship. He was surprised to be still alive, seeing how sensitive he was to commonplace changes, to rust and verdigris and woodrot and crow's feet, varicose veins, grasses and straws. Now, though, he had begun to feel like a young embalmer. Death was just another of life's meaningless halts, a little flurry in the dignified process, and here he was wrapped in it. So he was rather proud, in his surreptitious way, that he did not think of the Cong as amalgamated gook because all Orientals looked alike. The Night Observation Device had clinched that for him, whereas it might well have persuaded him otherwise. Night ogres, those transient blurred faces in the eyepiece, could have made him lump them all together, but his view was different because, in the act of spotting, he brought more of his imagination into play than during daylight hours. At night a certain ambiguous magic came into its own, but by day he saw specific faces or nothing at all, merely vegeta- tion or rock formation from which unfriendly fire arrived. He still toyed with the notion that, by popular consent, the war must be given up as a bad job, and everyone go home to a quieter, more fitting destiny; but that was naive. If any such thing came about, it would be done in a political way; the politicians who had started the carnage wanted the right to end it too, in their own stilted fashion, on their own gobblydegook terms. He winced at the gook in that word, but left it alone fast; it was a word he used or didn't use, it wasn't the words that mattered, it was the frieze of faces in the thinned-out light coming down the tube of the NOD. Humanity in the round, he thought with a smile, as his mind impulsively shifted to something else, the one aircraft carrier he had seen, like a big gray arrowhead plonked on the water, with what looked like a big-city street running along it, on either side of which sat the overgrown toys of war, white- painted jets lined up at forty-five degrees to the center line as if by some compulsive child. Two ramps grew from the take-off end. Was that the stern or the bow? There was another runway too, at a slight angle to the other, back by the superstructure. And everyone lived underneath in the gross block of the hull, enclosed and conjecturally safe, with a bunk to lie in, a table to eat at, flush toilets, a place to buy toothpaste. They even had movies. His yearning grew, to be aboard a *carrier*, or, failing that, to have a wonder shelter of his own, and not to be twenty-four hours a day confined to what did not confine him half enough: bunkers or the open fields, the paddies, the banks of the rivers. When you're in the open too much, he decided, you lose the sharp outline of yourself, and it's not that you're always exposed, it's more the prevalence of things; humans do not live in landscapes, they live in deliberately manufactured settings, in which contrarily, they long for the natural landscape, whatever that is. Nature is suffocating, always ready to show you what the scene would be like if you weren't in it. And the difference between a towel rail and a tree—he stopped, unable to take the thought further, although he knew there must be a vital difference. Neither heeded the human presence, and both could comfort, but nature was alive, that was it; it swarmed and churned around you, it could mop you up, it was a giant engine not much different from when there were no humans on the planet at all. But the carrier was a giant engine too, an engine from within the human community: not just a roof over the head, but a manageable vehicle. He wanted very much to be *carried*, that was it, not briefly in the choppers he hated because they had no wings and could not glide, but in a system attuned to human control. Standing up for one dangerous moment, merely to fling a grenade into the brush, at somebody he had no knowledge of and no opinion about, struck him as not merely foolish, but beside the point. There was no better reason for doing it than for not doing it. And this was true for both sides. He could not find any essential link between the so-called strategists, the pros who doted on war, and the suckers who fought it for them. The only link was power, of which they had enough to compel you while you didn't have enough to refuse—a travesty of the natural law which made buds bloom because they didn't know how to refuse, and puppies grow into dogs, lambs into sheep. He wanted to commit what he'd heard about, thinking a double life got only a single death. He'd pretend to go along, but would rebel and refuse. He knew how to do it, but he wondered what it amounted to. Toss the grenade, but mentally will it back. No: toss it, then mentally part yourself from it. Yet it exploded anyway. How toss it and still do no harm? His mind was as much hemmed in as a fire support base, and there wasn't even a heavily guarded exit/entry point. Fatuously, he wondered if the generals and colonels would go and fight a private war of his, against somebody who vandalized his pickup or the draft lottery that made you cannon fodder even though your grades were good. How farfetched and presumptuous that those generals and colonels had already assumed this Oriental war *was* his, and that they were helping him to fight it. They genuinely believed they were implementing the popular will. Yes, he said with almost malevolent finality, when somebody's hobby gets out of hand he turns it into a cult. As if the whole nation were suddenly forced to become stamp collectors, tight-rope walkers, dealers in used cars. In a truant sense, his war was with the generals, not with the Cong at all, and the only way to win it was to die.

George

Fathers ought not to watch sons too closely, but it was strange to see him there in the darkness as by moon I did, first hugging the damned thing, then smashing it with an ax, along the grain until he had enough strips of wood to smash it crosswise. And then the fire, from newspapers and kindling until it was all aflame and he just stood there cursing and spitting, weeping and moaning. That he had at first seemed to stand it upright and shove himself into it is something I do not claim to understand. He was always a little off, a bit touched. There was the glory of the gods in him, but also something like wood-worm. He is very secret, he is nobody's but his own. He sees us all in some magic family only he knows about. He never tells even when you ask. "What was that on fire the other night," you ask him, and all he says is something about a fresh start and wooden teeth. I am not going to think about him again. I would not know how. He is not turning out like a man at all. Something silly in him has taken root. He will never plant corn. Always hauling something white like pus from out his eye like he was crying beforehand, but thick, you could tell he wasn't regular, never content to toss a snot away but forever shaping it, earwax, this stuff he hauls out of his eyes, bits of soil or straw, it was all that same to him, he didn't care for the shape it came in. He could improve on things like he was taught by Sotuqnangu himself. Up in the San Francisco Mountains. I sometimes weary of folks and all their messy holes. I have done a lifetime's kachina carving up here among the wind with all the thankless chores. I am content to stroke my mouth and feel its old man's trembling. Something Anglo to him I don't fancy. He liked the schoolwork, pity he did not invent some kind of patent razor for them to make a fortune with, put me and mine for the rest of our days easy under some vines with a water fountain not too far, safe out of the eternal wind like a son should instead of forever having his hand up somebody's underwear to see what sex they were. "Hands off," I tell him. "What are hands for, Uncle?" "Don't anyway," I say, "be *quiet.*" "How do you talk to hands," he says. "They have a mind of their own. How do you send *them* to school?" You would think, if you didn't see his feet on the ground, he was riding a horse through life, and his ass on fire.

Sotuqnangu

If it weren't for the coolie hats, their black shirts and black shorts, he could have thought himself on a construction site in Arizona, one of some twenty convicts belaboring the earth with a hoe in the torrid afternoon. Then there was the apparent vow of silence, the only sounds being those of hoe clanking on rock, the shuffle of rubble, the sleek whisper of moved soil. Nobody grunted as he strolled to and fro, motioning for one of them to straighten the line or clear a small area left rough. At once they complied, eager to do anything to protect their village, Hoai My. They had already built a rampart seven feet high and pounded stakes into its top, two rows of stakes a yard apart, and strung barbed wire between them, with loose strands of it curling back and forth like some unruly crop gone to seed. Behind this flew the flag as if daring the Cong to come and get it. Now they were clearing a walkway at the bottom of the parapet, slapping the soil down hard, which was not easy because there was water, and some of them were ankle deep in it, nonetheless slapping and splashing as if they enjoyed the exercise. Behind the barbed wire he could see a range of mountains, almost like earth dumped on the area be-

hind the wire, but the mountains were far away, and they had no
snow on them. It was not the San Franciscos. There was also a crude
structure made from half a dozen poles almost like the high chair of a
lifeguard, but he had no idea what it was for, it was the wrong side of
the wire for a sentry post, and his lazing mind improvised it into an
object from some devil cult, awaiting an airplane built from bamboo
and straw, aimed skyward at an angle of forty-five degrees. To get a
better view, he climbed up the ramp and stood on the narrow strip of
earth between the edge and the first line of wire. The sky looked full
of sulfur. He thought he heard parrots not far away, certainly nearer
than the muted gunfire that erupted from time to time, making the
workers look up, stare at one another in serene exasperation, and then
resume just a little faster without so much as a look at him. No, there
were no parrots, it was the noise of machinery unoiled and out of
sight. Half of those digging might be Cong anyway, and the paradox
appealed to his double nature, to Oswald also Roy. The so-called secure hamlet program worked well, provided it kept the Cong within
from the Cong without, and it looked mighty neat, it was neater than
the outside of most stockades, and it would outlast the war and end
up disguised with ribbons and streamers. Laundry would dry on it
and animals be penned inside it. Then the bird arrived, perched on
top of the outer wire, made a small jump, collided with a strand that
wobbled about in the wind, and then fell into a ragged coil on the
ground between the twin lines. Out, he told it, you got all that sky,
but the bird, a hand-sized thing, had snagged its wings. Reaching
through, he scored his wrist, then his arm, the bird pecked at him, he
recoiled, and this time gouged himself on a spray of spikes. So he
stripped off his shirt, wound it around his hand, and tried again,
happy to have something to do, something small and unmilitary. But
it was no use. The bird remained caught until, cooing gently at the
pain, he managed to smooth its wings back, bending them more than
he thought possible, and then he tried to guide it through the maze
one-handedly, lifting and twisting, then rotating his arm as if drawing something from a hot oven. The bird was bleeding too, but it was
out, and it made no attempt to fly away, it sat squat on his palm, not
so much looking at him as entranced, waiting for him to make the
next move. Set it down? Toss it aloft? He had handled live eagles, of
course, and he had removed one or two canaries from cages, dead and
stiff. This was a pale gray bird, slight and isolated, and he wondered
where it had come from. Did it think they were building an aviary?

Did it think? It squirted onto his palm. He put the bird on the ground, wagged his finger at it, and wiped his hand on the soil. He could hear the flag buffeting about behind him and the continuous hoes. The bird began to flutter, testing its wings like a fledgling, then it flew up and perched on his shoulder, remaining there even as he straightened up again, dizzy as his blood drained down. He felt as if he'd been promoted. Back to human being. And he was content to stand there, his shirt still around his bleeding hand, he and the bird presiding over a scene of rural peace, watching others work. Life could go on forever like this, but instead he moved cautiously down the rampart and scooped up a handful of mud and clay, which he began one-handedly to fashion into a small nest, a crude saucer with vertical sides. How fast the sun dried it as he watched and the bird went on ignoring him, though its strut feet on his naked shoulder were as intimate a piece of attention as he had known in months. All of a sudden he realized the majesty of standing still, being a post or a rock. He was a perfect target of course, there on top again, with the nest at his feet and the wire at his back, almost as if asking for it, daring them to shoot the bird first just to prove their marksmanship. He felt oddly heraldic, part of some pattern or emblem: not peace, or modified peace, or even village doldrum, but more like time frozen into a crystal lattice. The bird's feet were replicas of the sprigs of wire. The bird's eyes were the most neutral things he had ever seen. The wings lay still, apparently unharmed, but he could not be sure, and now the villagers had paused in their work and were staring at him as he stood, almost at attention, leaving the bird on his shoulder. One villager raised his coolie hat and gestured at him, and all he did was nod, point at the bird with his swathed hand, and motion them all to resume. Jook the dog was gone, but this bird was more loyal, and he wondered if it would fly after him when he went back to camp bare-chested. Now he inspected his hand, licked the blood away, and slowly unfurled the shirt, spread it on the wire in the correct silhouette of a target. Next he enclosed rather than held the bird in his torn hand and set it inside the makeshift nest, making the sound of a puff-whistle with his dried-out lips. The bird stayed put, shuffled a bit as if to settle in, and he scrambled down the slope, forgetting his shirt, and not even remembering it when something whistled through the air above him, but not the bird's mate, or any bird at all. He hit the dirt. The villagers were flat in the mud and slop, a long line of black cloth dotted with fallen coolie hats as if mushrooms had sprung up unseen.

No more shots, but his shirt was still on the wire, and all he had to do was scramble up there and retrieve it. He took several deep breaths, but he did not move. He tried to work out in numbers, murmuring one second, two seconds, how long it would take him to leap up there, tug it off the wire, and then collapse back to ground level. More deep breaths, but still he did not go, and when he did, his knees were jelly, his face felt hot and bloated, the shirt would not come free until the third or fourth yank, at which he toppled backward. One of the shots had smashed clean through a button. The other was a millimeter away. Someone who was supreme with a telescopic rifle had spared him. Had whoever it was seen his antics with the bird, marveling at an Indian playing naturalist, making himself a target? He had piqued somebody's prowess, that was all. Any fool could hit a man, but who could hit a button on a given shirt? He decided the bird had saved him, but he did not want to keep it, good-luck creature that it was. It made no move; indeed, it seemed asleep, its beak up-pointed as if monitoring a daytime star. He waved at the foreman to halt the work, grabbed his M16, which he should have had with him up there beside the wire, and showed them his shirt before putting it on. Smiles, derisive and incredulous and sly, hovered in front of him, but no one said anything to him, though the villagers muttered among themselves. He said goodbye and thank you to the bird and trudged away, turning back once, when he saw all of them motionless and watching him out of sight, then a second time, puzzled as one of the men walked gently away with what resembled a flying saucer cradled against his chest, but it was only one coolie hat on top of another, with the bird inside, ignorant of its destiny, its luck, its effect on the young amateur soldier walking away in the other direction, unable to tell anyone he'd been spared, maybe for the first time in his life, with two fingers against his chest, where the holes might have been. Because he was alive, he wanted more, right then and there aching to walk off with his uncle to hunt for cottonwood roots, or to go long distances with him for the same reason in the pickup truck.

Fermina

At other times George was musical, leastways he talked about it, the Slest, he called this thing, it made the sounds of ice bells. He had heard it played on a tape or the radio. No, that was later. It was this Apperknowle told him about it, played some for him, when he came to buy dolls. Then there was this other guy Apperknowle knew about who had written a song, no it was longer than a song, it must have been a serenade. Called the Raw and the Cooked. "I can see that," George shocked them all by saying, after he had heard the sounds of it that Apperknowle had with him. "I got the point now." "The point," the other said. "What point?" George laughed and said it's easy. "All the raw music is played on hunting tools, see, like bow and arrows, knives, slingshots, spears, traps, nets, shotguns, and the cooked part is played on tin trays, and basins, and spoons, and mixmasters, and oven doors, and you get the sound of blazing open fires in there and the fat crackling off the meat into the fire and then that sudden spurt as it catches." George thought it was all very ingenious, to have divided the world of food up like that, and he said to tell the guy to do another now, this about the frozen and the thawed-out. "One would rattle like tongs," he said, "the other would squish and make a slap-slap sound. Ask him for me," George said. "Ask him to do me one of those suites about the raw wood and the wood made into dolls. That's just like raw and cooked. I have some good ideas on that, too, but the problem is you can't tell a raw doll from a cooked one, so to speak, on the level of sound. Only a very fine ear could pick that up. If, say, you were to rub either one with a chamois leather close to the microphone." Now I think of it, though, it wasn't until lately that he knew what a microphone was, or pretended to know. So there can't have been much time between him hearing the music and Oswald getting him a radio and some other gadgets. Here I was thinking it was many years back, and it was no doubt only one or two. Time has a sled. Its dogs do snarl. Everything goes back in a fast flurry of ordinary snow which was a big piece of your life. I'd die if he came back now from the dead or wherever it was he grumbled off to. I'd be smaller than when I talk to myself in the marrow of my bones a snowflake would be too big an umbrella for the likes of me under *that* hurt and I would no longer know my name I'd be a *her* just that and let the fire go out that keeps my heart from giving up the ghost as if I had been gagged with feathers by some old cold-bringing woman whose name no i darent say even that theyd push me under the ice of some frozen lake unnamed where even in midsummer they dont have seasons when they really hate you and what you did as if folks could be in control of their bodies all the time like bodies was dogs why some folks cant control even their dogs all day least of all their silky wets. Good old Uncle George The Place didn't know what he was talking about anyway, according to this Apperknowle, but he let him down light, he could see how old he was and he was trying to buy as many dolls as he could before the price went up.

Sotuqnangu

He also knew that what Dennison and Schulz, like mind degenerating into matter, would say over the next ten minutes was as predictable as continuation of the war. Something else moved into his mind and clothed his ears, not the memory of the bird accepting whatever he did with it, or the dry pluck of its claws on his bare shoulder, but the sense that he had walked today in the valley of the shadow of choice, where someone for reasons of symmetry, pride, humor, or perversity had done the undone thing, making reflex murder into a diagram, a didactic sample of behavior, in part a card and six-gun trick out of the old West, in part a benign warning to keep off the grass outside the ville, and most of all an act of racial semaphore, done with lens and mirror, connecting him to another human by means of his offcast shirt. Just conceivably, this marksman took the war as trivially as he himself, was going through the motions with the same mutinous vacillation, the same finding that this carnage was not, as everyone wanted to think, experience, but merely irrelevant, a waste of time, a thundersheet brandished and thumped by a well-heeled fraternity of cavemen hopelessly trying to match the commotion of the stars as they cooked and spewed and blew themselves to bits. Not quite, though. A sharpshooter that good would be at least a hard-stripe sergeant, a real NCO, and what had happened was that he, a professional, had seen an amateur lolling around in full view, something no pro would dream of doing, and had slapped his knuckles. He could have regaled him with even more prowess by shooting the beak off the bird, or the bird off his shoulder, but not as good as the shirt, his husk, his wrapper, his effigy, snagged on the wire as if he were in the backyard, back home, having a rest while watching his uncle. Yes, he said, with self-conscious young grandeur, fully aware that, for the next week or two, he was not going to feel afraid, although the logic of that was skewed. The warning, if that, had been to take care, not to do it again. He'd obey, but he could not rid himself of the zany delusion that, instead of walking into the jaws of death, he had sunned himself without his shirt on a windy mesa, visible to none but him.

Fermina

even if when only one of your three boys your four men your five I got to stop counting it will never begin and if not that it will never end well fermina when one of your boys is a black sheep *the* black sheep he gone rotten he let down the dignity of the family the tribe then you got to you are bound to love him more its not playing favorites its more like a law of heaven look after the busted the broken the gored the godforsaken all of them so i sometimes dream he is coming home already on the greyhound not a dog but fast of course between the rows of lamps from here to los angeles it cant be far if a poor indian made it to and fro to where his bank was all the money from his making movies i wonder if he is a star and too modest to tell us all about it it wouldnt matter here on the mesa except to george and we are coming home together in secret with our heads next door to each other on the pillows they hand out or is that on the planes anyway we are like two kachinas that have come home from the san francisco mountains disguised as clouds no they are clouds already sometimes they do not have to change it is within their natures to be both ways although not at the same time and we get him free of all that heartless concrete home to the heartless rock of the mesa he wont care once hes used to it again the fumes the smoke the din all gone he hear the eagle squeal again and the children fetching uncle george his fleece-lined boot for whatever cold is in the air a real snap he says

Sotuqnangu

Still the sharpshooter's perfection haunted him, evoking a summer image of the almost elastic clunk when ball hit bat, bat hit ball. That was when the hardness of wood yielded just a little, slewing a few million atoms aside to make a cushioning cavity for the ball, although the bat's contour varied not a jot. That was when the ball flattened slightly during an instant of miraculous timing, and all the other hits were mere percussion, battery, mayhem. For no more than one second, bat and ball were fluid in their contact, each yielding to the other, a banana and a balloon in slow motion. Mellow, right on the meat, the once-in-a-lifetime hit. No, he told himself, I will hear that sound again, next summer, once, maybe twice, but never again will a sharpshooter let me off; next time, whoever it is, he will drill me like a pudding. So it haunted all the more, an impossible event not provided for in the customary rigmarole of night and day, life and death, hit and miss. I have used up all my luck in one throw, he decided, and some guys have no luck in one throw, he decided, and some guys have no luck at all. Now I owe the bank. There is nowhere to be safe, I will die of a cold in the head, my heart will stop beating when a cloud goes over, my brain will quit next time I hiccup. Nothing in life was ever going to treat him half as well as that marksman, the finesse of whose charity left a stain behind it on the front of his chest, which no longer belonged to him, not to his country, but to a monk who set himself on fire in downtown Saigon, not that he had seen him in the act, he had heard about it, then seen a page from an illustrated magazine, passed around like a state-of-the-art pornographic picture. The burning monk sat at attention, eyes closed, facing the blaze in front of him as if it were not there, just a miasma, even the flames along his thighs, mounting up his chest, much higher than his shaven scalp. That kind of stillness, of the mind as well as of the body, was what the master marksman had, like a being independent of time and space, of breath and blood, pain and death, and he wondered how anyone began to become that exact in self-control, asking no advice, heeding no opinion, and so utterly within himself that nothing he did failed to represent exactly what he was. That, he said, was excellence in life, either as sniper or as human bonfire, and you did not have to go that far, into affairs of life and death, you could achieve it within a brace of shakes, discarding what of you did not belong, picking up or developing what you lacked, until the red-letter day when you put yourself together and the pieces never came apart again. Every bit of you was behind everything you did, like the panther making its kill, the butterfly coming out of its chrysalis, the shrapnel leaping away from the grenade as it exploded. This sense of things intact and intricately meshed made him uneasy. It was something he expected not only in others, but in himself, yet he could not find the technique, he felt untidy and scrambled and somehow improvised, dreamed up by men flawlessly on target who abstained from shooting. There were men so close to the afterlife that the pain of being burned alive was merely a passport stamped, a ticket punched. There were men who arrived at this stage, this pass, unthinking. And then there were the likes of him, stumbling about under the moon, hiding from the sun, entranced by the holy grail of perfect discipline, in itself a military concept, but broader, richer, more inspired, the gist of which was blunt. Either you had it and pliantly took charge of every second as it came, or you just were not yet ready to be alive and a third of your life had passed you by.

BertandAnna

Him of the stiff face look through you into your other day. What his name. Him holy. Not a like, not a nasty. He be unharming us. We walk, he sit, nobody say. By we go, him not look, him cut. He somebody's sooner or later. We not so dumb, is we. If others want to call you dumb, okay no need to call it that yourselves. I got a Hi from him one sunny day, it more than most folk get. Anna too. Him hearty as young deer. He BertandAnnas us when him in a good mood. Other days he cut your innards out with his knife, fry you in front of your face, offal and all. One day somebody have tied her hand to mine with rawhide and wet it, we in the snow tramping around, but he see, with his doll knife he slash it in two, make us together again. Now or then one or other of us two we do it in our pants walking around, and he the only one who laugh, nod, say he done it himself more times than that. He says you go sit on it till it dry, then you that much closer to yourself, *Bertanna.* He no wash any more than us. Did they ever have to hose him down. It would be when they lowered him into the ravine, then they poured buckets of it over him from on top, they made him cleaner than a wolfprint. Most times you Hi him he does a

Hi back, it's his way. You don't make him lift his eye from the blade or he have no fingers left. Not as ugly as us, but he no cloud maiden in the face. Big, worn, rocky chops, all the bits of how he looks hate being next to each other tied with rawhide, anything they could hand themselves when he was born. This a fearsome baby, one say, he come to no good. Well, he come to a rich good, he a man of stuff. Hi, George The Place In Flowers Where Pollen Rests always get him answering Hi, *Bertanna*, The Place In Clothes Where Shit Go Bad. Give you the time of day, he go to heaven, open a goodwill drugstore where all the dumbies get free breakfast. Him wide and woody, his heart out on the blanket for you to lift and feel, it beat away like some trapped animal. We slap it hard, bring the blood to its cheeks, we tickle it where it lie there wobbling, and all he do is laugh, yell, It is a big fat waste of time, *Bertanna*, it not strong enough to drive a toy train from the catalog. Gave it him back into his chest where he hold it in place with wood shavings and some handfuls of new snow. We all three not have long to go, but he have much to lose while his Bertanna have much to gain by just lying down on the snow as comfy as we can and leave it at that. Our pockets pocketfuls of fresh.

Sotuqnangu

At this point, feeling wholly inadequate, he began to fit in as perhaps only those who feel inadequate can. The life-style of the grunt became his own, an oblivion fed by uppers and downers, Jimi Hendrix tapes, grass, and porn. He found some wire and made himself an outsize earring for which he pierced his ear with a bayonet doused in scotch. Pigs, chickens, cows, became his targets just as much as the peasants who did the laundry by day and put on black Vietcong pajamas at night. Grass tar darkened his face long before he took to overloading the skin of his entire body with the camouflage paint used for night operations. Each night, before he tried to sleep, a *Playboy* bunny sat on his face, half choking him while he yearned not for her but for something removed from the war, this being the tiny swathed fists of a gloxinia's buds. *Never happen*, he said to almost everything, or *That's a load.* If the world he lived in was stunted and small, he adjusted to it, actually mouthing its landmarks: treeline, perimeter, firebase. The only magic was that of medevac choppers and as many joints as he needed. Only with his M16 on full automatic did he feel secure, and when murmuring the uncouth-sounding monosyllables that designated equipment: *Loach* and *Rome plow*, though he sometimes said *Chinook* as well when he was really up. If he had to make do in a dismal round of ponchos, leeches, dump fires, satchel charges, moldy canvas webbing, swamp water, C rations, milk snakes, monkeys, sandbags, and pliable candy bars, then that was okay. He went to great pains to keep his flak jacket closed, cupped his hands around every match he lit, and went without sleep to keep his rifle clean. The noise overhead of a Psyops soundship testing its tapes of a baby crying and a mother screaming lulled him, and he knew that he could keep mosquitoes from filling his mouth by clamping it shut around a smoke. After a while, he realized that nearly everyone else had slogans or Batman fetishes on their helmets, or graffiti filched from the raunchiest washrooms in the world, mostly crudely drawn slits or polyps, hard to distinguish from the aces of clubs and hearts. One guy carried a small apple his wife had kept in her armpit for a month after they'd ritually peeled it. Another had a very old bagel sealed in a plastic sandwich bag. Others had one cup of a bra, G-strings, photos of their women, their dogs, their cars, their favorite football players; but these they carried in the helmet, not on it, or in their most secret pockets. He had nothing, though, except his plastic-coated Soldier's Prayer, which seemed as distant and useless to him as the flicker of an unnamed star. Nor did he want Che, JFK, Hendrix, Lyndon Johnson, Martin Luther King: no effigies, and certainly no Bible. Nor did he crave such things as walnuts, cherries, champagne corks, monkey's paws, or Saint Christophers. He wanted the baby buds of the gloxinia plant, and that he couldn't get. In the end, he couldn't remember when the idea first came, he found a way out, wiggier than anything anyone had thought of yet, inspired no doubt by talk of ferocious montagnards with plastic pouches full of ears and other bits of the Vietcong anatomy. It required a bigger bag, of course, so he stole a poncho equipped with plastic straps, and then, while others traded Salems for grass, began collecting, the rule being that nothing paired —hands or feet—could come from the same cadaver (or live Charlie). He was going to build his own gook, if only he could stay in the same place for long enough; otherwise he'd be dragging his construct after him all over Vietnam. It was almost too easy to find the pieces, less easy to begin fastening them together, but he found cord and wire, rags and strips of camouflage chutes. Each night he hunkered down and arranged the parts on the flattened-out poncho while others watched as best they could, peering in the dimness at what he was assembling. They could never tell, and often he did it by feel. After only a month, he had an almost complete gook, who would soon need a name. Already he, or it, was too near completion to be disassembled each night for carrying round, so he lugged it behind him, towing it like a plastic sleigh from place to place: a homemade corpse, minus only a head. He became a looter of the dead and wounded, but always finishing off such of the wounded as he felt obliged to dispossess of body parts. And another home-made rule said that the eyes had to come from separate places, like the penis and the scrotum. Having at last improvised a needle from the metal of a ration can, he began to sew with medic's cat gut, and now the whole thing took form. Nuncle George, he decided to call the exhibit, and grunts actually got killed trying to belly over from other positions to have a look at how unlike a man his monster looked. The stench, though, of tannery and brewing hops and Japanese fields, had become unbearable, so they staged a mock execution, but only after a mock trial, in the course of which Nuncle Gee was sentenced to be dipped in shit, circumcised with a firecracker, suffer his tongue cut out and his eyes, then to be burned at the stake to the sounds of Hendrix's *Foxy Lady*. Even the lieutenant joined in, for he knew what was coming, where they had to go next, and he knew that most of them would not be coming back. Dipped in 'palm, Nuncle G for George filled the noon air with the same kind of smoke as came up from landing zones, though less purple, and they left him there, fresh-noosed, dangling from a tree like a Cartesian diver that had floated up from the bowels of hell and found equipoise in between there and the bottom of the pall of smoke. For weeks afterward, guys offered him bits of gooks to repair his effigy with, even arguing that the monster should have two heads, genitals sewn across his mouth, an alien penis in either eye, and so on. He refused, heeding some vestigial rule of propriety, unwilling to make a parody of his creation, and it was only a week or two later that he found his talisman, abstracted from the pocket of a newly dead grunt: a fishing lure with whiskers, double hook, in the shape of a fish's head amputated just behind the wide-open dot of the eye. Silvery white with a few longitudinal red stripes. The back of the head was filled with plastic, but concave enough to accommodate a finger's cushion, so he could hold it facing him, forefinger in the cavity, the line-loop against the nail, and the hook pointed backward, the whiskers toward his face. It was all he had ever wanted, and its silver sheen expressed better than Uncle Gee ever had the tortured delicacy of being, as he himself expressed it, out of time. But he found it acceptable only because the making of Uncle Gee had preceded it. Before then, it wouldn't have worked for him at all: an echo without a sound preceding it. He had given the gloxinia buds their teeth, and each hook tooth had its barb.

Sotuqnangu

Back he dreamed, to some time between when Spider Woman mixed earth with spit and when Uncle Gee came to life like a sculptured stench, and he began to remember what others remembered, his mind quivering with relief. The police, having failed to get anything precise as distinct from vivid from BertandAnna, had tried to construct a case against Uncle George the widower and nonswimmer who in his time had pretended to swim a stroke or two, with an elongated clawing motion after he lofted himself onto the surface, a depth of ten feet only, accomplished in a trice, and then he was easy meat for lifesavers: When she got into trouble with the other two, who clung to each other even in the water, he was unable to bring help, he had to watch and he had already blotted out that awful scene by the time they began to interrogate him. "Now," says one, "if he'd gone and drownded them dumbies cause he was mad, that might have made sense, only he didn't. She saved em and lost her life in doing it. He was nowhere near as an able-bodied man should have been. He wasn't even close." "*He* doesn't swim, *he* carves dolls with a little knife. From wood. All the time." "Sure makes you wonder what he really wanted to be cutting at." To prove it, they drove him there in their official van and threw him in the deep, where he would have drowned had they not fished him out none the worse. They could tell he had no idea how to swim and so could not have been out where Bessie drowned unless he had a boat, and he had not. He'd gone to watch, out of a lifelong passion for the grotesque, whereas (the police said) it was a foolish idea in the first place and he should have put his foot down. "She was found in thirty feet depth." Fermina sighed. "Lakes don't sit still, whatever folk think. Everything on the planet moves a little. I could hardly swim," George said with a sublime shrug, "out there to bring her back. I was never much of a life saver." "You just watched." "I did and I didn't. I never thought for a minute she would have trouble with water. It was *her* element. Like wood is mine. You don't get your own element wrong." "Maybe you did it without thinking, George." "Think away," he said. "She didn't down in wood, did she?" "And then," Fermina persisted, "you invented a story." "The trees are full of birds, Fer'." "And there was no proof one way or the other." "When these hands get itchy," he told her, "I get cravings. I am going to carve. Goodbye." He shambled to his feet and kicked the door shut on his way out. "You'll never convince me," she called after him, heedless of overhearers. "Your mouth is in between your legs," he yelled. "Give it something to eat. Or drown it. Go drown it." She eased the door open again and went to sit, her head pulsing fiercely as if she had just heard vital evidence without recognizing it. All of a sudden she knew what Oswald meant when he told her about watching the Friday-night fights on TV in Palookaville. "They whack one another to pulp," he said. "That's how I feel after a week's hard work. That's what brings me back to life. All the guys I can't whack for myself, they whack them for me. Every time somebody hits the canvas, it's somebody who called me an Ethiopian asshole. After all, Palookaville's a boxing word. Like showboat." Vaguely she wants to whack somebody herself, but isn't certain who or why. She wants to shed the worry of it, the steady guesswork that leads her only to the next question session with Uncle George. If nobody knows, she thinks, then why do we have to worry ourselves with it? What is it in us that always bites off what it can't chew? Why can't my mind *be said?* If it was a genuine accident, I'm a moral woman, helping out. If it wasn't, I'm an accomplice and a whore. I'm a whore anyway. But there's a dignity to that Fer'. All through Oswald's childhood she wondered, even as the topic like a receding sunset appealed to her less and less. Were she wrong, the gods would have brought Oswald from her womb hare-lipped and blind, gimpy and just like BertandAnna. Somehow she believes in divine justice and asks herself what ghastly crime made BertandAnna the way they are. Why did they do it? Even through his adolescence she never quite left the guess alone, gradually over the years persuading herself that George was one of those people who, even while telling the truth, get uneasy and look shifty. They are so unused to telling it, they begin to giggle, it seems so inadequate to them, whereas lies come better dressed, promise to please, and change overnight into something even handsomer. Yet who was handsomer than him? Once again the injustice of things gnaws home to her. Truth has no right to be the handsome, overbearing brother-in-law who moves into her bed as if, all her life, she's hung a sign out, after drowning her sister-in-law, unloved and unadmired, let's face it, but kin all the same. Who was *he* that he could change his mind about lives like some people change an ordered sandwich. It was all too simple. Too athletic, the girl outdid herself, and that was that. No cramp. No period. Unless she killed herself with George along to witness. Except she was never the self-killing sort: quick-tongued and restless, always helping folk along with a heavy shove of her hand or her mouth. A bossyboots, as BertandAnna had said. Now she begins to think George wasn't there at all on that day. He only went there when she didn't come back. Could BertandAnna, maybe walking their goat (a good hike, to say the least, but distance meant no more to them than logic), have done the thing? With their mindless strength, pretending to hug her to death, simply shoving her down and sitting on her in the shallows with the milk churn between them empty. Dumb clucks drown athlete. What a shock. The idea dies an instant natural death; Bessie could have knocked them cold with one punch, both of them. Fermina, as ever, chokes her mind to keep her body sane, little knowing how well in some quarters she is understood.

Sotuqnangu

Something of a character to his fellow grunts, therefore, he wished he weren't, preferring to be just one of the guys, and invisible. Having made an adjustment through ghoulish hobby and unmilitary high spirits, he now went to the other extreme; having soaked himself in what he had to live in, he wanted to rid himself of his own recent past. Walking, bathed in sweat, to a firefight that unearthed and killed only two VC of undecidable rank, he wished he were a hundred feet up instead, opening the flexie of a gunship and plastering dozens of VCs to the walls of the hooches. Having messed with their corpses, he felt his bows to death had been made, and now he wanted it at a distance, killing through understatements such as probe and discreet burst. As it was, the heavier they fired, the less they heard the incoming mail, and a theory began to go the rounds that, if you all fired hard enough, fire coming the other way never got through. He was holding his breath more than usual. He felt empty, light, fragile, twitching violently at even a breeze or a click of grass, and he felt angry at the ground for not receiving him more easily when he flung himself down in a burping panic and tried to blur into it. About now,

his ears began to hear only themselves, not the incessant *tfteet* of
bullets and the rattle of shrapnel, but a soughing of trees behind his
eardrums, interrupted only by the twing of a fine wire snapping
again and again. Tracer whipping through the elephant grass into a
group of bodies in green plastic body bags on the lz seemed only a
means of making the overall stench worse as the corpsegas spilled
away from the mess that nobody wanted to clean up. What he blinked
away from the gritty surface of his eyes felt thick and caustic: stuff
that had never been in eyes before, and when, during lulls, he heard
about the VC another platoon had greased and then skinned, he felt
his head make a nod that no one saw. It was too late to feel disgusted,
and that was true even when, not far away, he saw civilians being
shoved or tossed out of choppers he registered the fact only as
something that looked almost normal: something else happening, as if
supplies were being roughly unloaded from a chopper in a hurry to
get away. He had defused atrocity before he came to it, which might
have made him a more useful soldier, but he went ordinary and
numb, as if, all around him, someone had staged a mythic revel for
young princes of no rank, in which he took no interest, not even
reading what he saw on their helmets and flak jackets. Deliberately
blurring his eyes until the letters became a smear, he disdained what
others read and flashed: I AM THE RED REVENGE, DRACULA NOW, DIG ME
GOD, not even noticing names and slogans that kids were dying for.
Instead, he soldiered on in a private, pliable sentry box of his own,
where everything smelled yellow, the visible broke up into refracted
colors as if he were crying all the time, and nothing could reach him.
It was a circus. Clowns ran it. Slop wasn't wet. Stench wasn't solid.
CS gas, broken glass, the bleached-slate color of the dying, belonged
to a performance behind glass, and what was real was the scab of
impetigo along the top of his ear, ever scratched and ever wet, and the
longer his nails got the worse he clawed. Early, he too might have
held his water until he ran across a dead VC with open mouth, but
now the abominable did not even include wetting himself where he
lay prone. Babies did this in the first flush of eagerness to be at ease,
and he longed to be one of those Indians who live on the beach in a
hut that was one gigantic leaf and spent their days spearing fish. War
to him, apart from the chance that it might erase him altogether, was
negligible, telling him that love alone makes life bearable, but it also
makes death an unbearable terminus to which, alone, you're willing
to go. He was as alone as the dead, yet living within a reputation for

wiggy bloodthirstiness. He quivered and writhed. He rubbed his face in the mix his own saliva made with mud, and yearned to be wounded soon, but never in the throat. That was the wound they feared the most. Those who got it in the neck never got past the triaging stage. Down went his chin to cover the heartspoon, as if he were ready to dive, whereas in fact he became an ace at spotting mines or booby traps slipped in behind them after they advanced. That his neck made a good target from behind didn't worry him at all. Hell was in front of him, and he nibbled his way through it a day at a time, except he no longer knew what a day was, any more than the others, who, during a few so-called days' R and R free-slept themselves into a twenty-five-hour day that had no clock. Someone he could not name grew from a germ in his head, not so much ex-girl-friends fusing together as some endearing outline toward which he slithered over the mud, and not necessarily female, just tender and his own, whereas the letters from his mother he no longer read or opened, but carried in a wad against his butt. Now who would shoot him there? Of course he needed the Dexedrines more than ever and actually began to talk again, although for the most part only about *contact*, jargon for a brush with the Cong, and such euphemisms as *response-to-impact*, which meant someone blown to bits. Savoring these words and phrases, he seemed to be tuning in to some almost available serenity. What happened did not exist for him so long as he spoke of it in a certain way, not uttering the syllables as the others did, with holy deadpan, but as if he were quoting a war ballad he rattled his banana clips to a private rhythm, fondled the nightpaint on his chin and cheeks, and began to talk about some tiger lady awaiting him on a mountaintop, in an *ao dai* and snakeskin shoes, and a come-home-to-me chone layered with Jell-O, custard, whipped cream, and peeled almonds. "Sawf an' crunchy," he said. "Guess I'll get me some." Yet nothing he said, in his mild outrageous way, compared to the myth that had grown around him, especially the lie that he used to say to other grunts, "Cut me a piece when you can, I'm short a hand." Too many had seen him licking his bayonet clean for the story to be true, but he milked it, all right, pretending to lick his clean bayonet while at rest, and making sure eyes were on him before he even slid it out. Usually, with half a dozen in a circle round him, he'd sing:

> Once there was a Vietcong
> who had a schlong so fucking long

he trimmed it with his bayonet
but a whole platoon could kneel and pray on it.

That got them. They went champing to kill with his rhymes on their lips, and the last line usually became a marching or shuffling song which developed an existence of its own, and they made up rhymes of their own, linking it to *pee-on-it, do-on-it, frig-on-it,* et cetera, little realizing how tenderly low he'd brought them, and what they were really mouthing was a psalm for the dead done with outrageous levity. Nor did they quite know who he was, what he had been, a young man torn between the acute otherworldliness of his people and, at least in Palookaville, a life-style in which he murmured thank God the penis is blind and cannot smell.

Mitits Norah Holmes

He would like to be spontaneous, you can see that, but something
tribal holds him back. He wants to pass muster. He wants to be free
of them while remaining one of them. It is no way for a boy to grow
up. He can think and count, but something doesn't come through. He
holds back, he won't show that piece of him, whatever color it is. The
half smile turns into a sneer or a scowl, mainly because he does not
know what to do with his face. He seems not to know if he has
brothers or sisters, but he says yes, it has nothing to do with their
names. According to the roll, it does, and he has a younger, no, an
elder brother, with whom, however, he does not play. They are in the
same school, but the elder doesn't look after the younger, they seem at
odds about something you have to guess at. Oh well, there are other
children and other problems, but when you notice how intense he is,
how ready to flinch, you want to reach toward him with, I don't
know, a stuffed bird, an unknown flower, and say now, George, what
do you make of this, go fly it or plant it where you think it goes. I
never do, of course, I check his numbers and his letters, and he tends
to write without much punctuation and to add without ever trying to

make the total at the bottom. He likes to add, but he does not want the sum. It may not ever matter. He will spend his life digging, peeking up girls' dresses, breeding, being awed by what awes these people. They really belong in the Amazon somewhere. I still think we ought to show them how to use a telephone or plug in an appliance. You never know. Some of them will have to go out into the world one day and make ends meet. What is it in all of their faces that seems otherworldly? Something chubby, lumpish. They have too much jaw, cheekbone, mouth. They eat wrong, they eat too much. Lively and quarrelsome, they have something stolid in them that says, It doesn't matter what you say, we know what's really going on behind things. It isn't the way you think it is. The world is very different. You don't belong to it. That's what their giggles mean to me. To think I gave up a solid marriage with a Boulder lawyer to stay here and teach rudiments. I could go back, he would still have me. He never did marry, nor did he ever show the faintest inclination to feel inside my blouse, and away with propriety. *"Afterwards,"* he'd say, but there are some cuddles allowed, it isn't all pig-in-a-poke. "Arnold, dear," I'd say, "either we do something now or I have to go on trying to be a school teacher. I am qualified." He wanted me not to work. I wanted to do something. You do not win diplomas to save a rectangle of wall from severe sunlight. So now I am married, so to speak, to Isabel Judson, that bigot. Never asked for her hand in anything. I have the brains, she has the hands. I do the hard subjects mainly, like English and geography and math, whereas she does handwork and crafts, painting, and so forth. She also shows them dances they have things far superior to, done, I tell her, with snakes and no clothes on, in the streaming rain, when it streams. I am my mother's heir and Isabel is hers.

Sotuqnangu

He now found the contrasts of a trooper's life too much to bear, as if he'd never noticed them before. Trying to flesh out the endearing image of the nameless being (who could have been a god), he groped for a face, but it was the wrong one: narrow-nosed, taut, and petulant, as if not enough flesh and skin had gone into its making. He wanted it good-humored, with features generously heavy clad in the soft luminous skin he'd seen on Mexican women he could not remember when; but he remembered the skin, supple as cream and ageless. He tried again, but the overstretched face came back, and there was no body at all. That was the fault of all the bangs around him, the different flashes of different kinds of abrupt light, from little coronas of white sparks to flood lightning when a shell exploded, or a rocket. Some he heard coming, some not, and he cursed his mind for tying to fit the sound of arrival to a bang whose flash he'd already flinched at. It was hard to cook up and polish an image of loveliness when, like everyone else, he was taking pills that actually made his diarrhea worse so as to expose him to less risk of being hit while in the squatting posture. His mouth was always dry from red laterite dust. His

ears had begun to work again, though his nose was blocked, which
was why his mouth was so dry. I'll soon have it knocked, he told
himself. How much more time? There were eight more months, and
he knew, he just knew, that if he didn't get lightly wounded soon he'd
get fatally wounded long before the end of his tour. He found omens
in everything: the sigh of a cow amid the thunder of night bombardment while he crouched in a makeshift bunker whose sandbags were
spilling in all directions. Fumbling open a pack of cheddar cheese
with crackers, he wondered how many times he'd done just this, and
if the last one he'd ever open would taste different while the flies
buzzed him and the guard dogs yawned their disciplined yelps. I'll
soon have it knocked, I'm wrapped real tight. This is 1969, or it was.
He had never yet thrown a boot at a rat, but he was working up to it,
and he'd toyed with the idea of making a blindfold from parachute
material so as to shut out the flashes that killed his sleep. Thin eyelids,
that's what hurt him most; but, with a fold thick enough, he'd get a
good night's sleep, like a condemned man who had fallen asleep during his own execution. The cigarette burned his lip. Some gook,
trapped on the German razor wire out there, was beginning to howl
in earnest, at least until the familiar dry rigid noise nearby of large-
bore ammunition going off. That blew the noise off the wire. A fat
thud of rotors invaded his sleep, their gust blew his hair away as if it
were a toupé, and then the survivors of a night patrol came blundering in and turned on the radio to shut out the memory. He was glad,
because the first of the countervailing horrors had just begun to gnaw
at him: the bodies he had plundered for his Uncle Gee had started
coming back, seizing from him what he'd stolen from them. One
hand plucked at his groin, tugging, wrenching. Another spanned his
wrist between thumb and middle finger like a bracelet that would
tighten and tear his hand off. Another pair of hands found their way
to his throat and began to remove his head. He was being teased
apart, tickled and then seriously wrung. The dead stayed dead, but
the mutilated dead had a passion for being intact, and there was no
way he could fend them off, neither shouting nor convulsively shrug-
ging. Nor did he get any help from the lovely image he was trying to
dream up. It only looked away while the zombies put themselves back
together at his expense, then grouped themselves as a motley squad in
front of him, leering and hideously pointing at the gaps in his anatomy, the ragged ends of his arms and legs, the snipped stem of his
neck. Blue and yellow fabric from a chute, roughly folded and twisted

tight, kept the flashes out, but not the parade of the dismembered, and when he woke, or at least ripped the bandage from his eyes, everything was out of focus as if the air were full of pollen. And those who saw his eyes of startled pale aluminum etched with bloodshot tracery thought he was beginning to freak out. He looked crazy, eyes wide open as if he could not gather enough light. He did not blink. No tears came. There was only that twin middle-distance fix, of eye muscles that had ceased to work, although he couldn't cure himself of the simple habit of looking. He shoved his foot against the berm as if he could not see it there in front of him, and when he looked someone in the eye, it was as if he was examining them, ranging from the detail of the nose to the detail of the mouth, in the eyepiece of a telescopic rifle a thousand yards away. The tint had almost gone from the pupils and there were only two ovals full of all-purpose school glue just beginning to dry and form a shiny crust. Haunted eyes, bleached eyes, eyes full of space and blaze, eyes through which another, not he, saw things much as he saw them when he was asleep. Only he had not scrawled some kind of calendar on the back of his flak jacket, but it was fixed in his head like a football season schedule. It didn't matter what he did. *That* he knew. He had only to get through each day by doing something, never mind how abominable, and, even in the act of killing or shooting a corpse to make it flutter, he repeated I am alive, doing this, I couldn't do this if I weren't alive. That made things easier, but he couldn't do it while asleep, when he dreamed he was dead, surrounded by the rapacious dead, nipping his skin, plucking at his organs, lifting pieces of him wholesale for approximate prosthetic fit. Then the sergeant said there was a big bad bastard of a push into Laos ahead of them. Some asshole with a fancy map had ordered it, to end the war. The sergeant rarely evaluated anything in such terms as those. At the news, one guy shot off his big toe, another began jerking off whenever he could, and another went and sat on the parapet, offering himself as sniper bait except that nothing happened, so maybe it was the sniper's birthday or there was toe jam in his backsight or for once there was nobody watching. Then the guy stood with legs apart, hands above his head with palms mated, and the sniper got him within seconds, as if having made him a deliberate gift of life: You get back down, Injun, or else. Now Laos loomed over them like an abstract stench: not somewhere they were going to, but a somewhere which had come to them.

Mitits Isabel Judson

Noun or verb I ask him, but there he is, a mere boy, mounting himself in the schoolroom behind his desk, which he has already carved the living life out of. Out of which he has already carved the living life. And the thing is there behind it, for which no word is right. Playing with himself while he carves holes through the one-inch thickness in front of him. To have one of those things that grows and to have to bear all that uncontrolled flesh before one all life long. No. We stand here talking to those whose minds are on what can swell and what can be entered. Noun or verb matters little to them. Conjugate, did they only have the brains to figure the etymology, would please them more. I always wiped the slime away, I thought it was a disease, and it is hard now to think such a discharge was natural: a gland named for Cowper or Bartholin, I cannot recall, but you can be sure they both did unspeakable peering before they made that part of our anatomy famous. Look at something else. His handwork, from paperchains to little cardboard farms, is talented. These things are more real to him than we are. He gets lost in it, he watches his hand do for him something he never had in mind, then takes the credit as men do. He can be really happy when he is not in this world, which is mostly. A boy of ability who does not concentrate or work hard enough. "You don't understand," I tell her. "These are savages and primitives, not eccentrics. They don't just have a difference in taste, they think differently from you and me. All they want is to get away, back to what they prefer. They were shanghaied into this school of ours. They are here by government, not through choice. They should be teaching us, not the other way around. This is their country, not ours. The system is ours, but not the way these children really want to speak. Their grammar is altogether different. They do not look at things in the same handy categories as we do. Honest, Norah." She laughs and says they still can dance. As if that were the point. What a combination: an artistic prude, her, and a clever would-be trollop, me. I often wonder what they do to one another in the bus on the way back. Nothing, maybe. They have taboos, they do nothing that isn't in their tribal code. (Nor do we Anglos.) Anyway, him, the aloof boy, he's only one of several I wonder about, not including his brother, but one girl who seems always to be having her monthlies, you can smell it, and so can they. She sits in a perpetual island of silence. And another one who seems to stammer worse each week. Nothing to do, he ought to be away in a special school, not babbling here. Maybe they will make her a shepherd when she goes home to stay, and he can talk to the sheep. One more trip to Boulder, and I'll be done, altogether committed to a career that formed itself like a dream on the rock of refusal. One more year and then I'll be schoolmarm for life, with whole areas of my body unexplored, rotting and wasting away for lack of a straightforward yes. He could electrify me, I know, would he only make the first move. I think of all the gross things we all do every day of our lives, and we haven't a voice in that, so why pretend the other gross and rather nicer things don't exist at all? We are gross, let's face it, and get on with it, Arnold. He cannot bring himself to be lustful. Or desirous. Or even to long. He wants me as an archway, a flowerbed, a trellis. He uses silly words like *bidden* and *overture*, as if he were a priest or a conductor, but he's just a company lawyer. Maybe I need one who's in another area altogether, like Criminal. When Arnold's mother goes, he will leave here for good. I find it hard to believe that his mother was never a school teacher; I thought everyone's mother was a schoolteacher and the daughter followed in her footsteps. Arnold is our knight paladin and we are two old medieval spinsters howling silently in our mutual tower. We have done some good, they all say so, but it's the undone that's undone us. Now, what does *paladin* mean? Any of the twelve peers at the court of Charlemagne the Great. I wonder what became of the other eleven. Only once did I venture up there to the mesa to watch them at their wild diversions. The dance was too percussive for the likes of me, oh yes, and the snakes looked tame enough, or tamed, but there was one man whose face seemed all forward bulge, as if all the stuff in the back of his head and the sides had been shoved into the front, he was concentrating so hard. And so would I have been: between his bare chest and a handful of snakes there was only a fancy necklace. He had an armful of them like a store clerk with ribbons, and they kept coiling around and peering, unwinding and reaching forward, but they let him stroke them and nothing went wrong. I wondered if he had hypnotized them or calmed them with the laying on of hands. Never had I seen snakes carried around like a shawl over an arm, and I am convinced we have something to learn from Indians, not about the dance, never that, but about being hospitable to our fellow creatures however loathsome. It would have done Arnold good to see them, but he would not go, he had seen all the savages he wanted to in one lifetime. This other man, though, all he had to defend himself with was a few split yucca sticks; they weren't for self-defense though, they were for something quite different, maybe thurifer or shepherd's crook. If only they could milk them, just as ants raise aphids to be their cows.

Sotuqnangu

Such a preparation, indeed such a hazing, surely entitled him to membership in something special, in which he could take pride for the rest of his life; but there was no reward, no signal exemption, beyond not getting killed or wounded in the neck, the balls. He lived as if the real he hovered at arm's length just outside his body, like some deployment of wires and terminals, fizzing and crackling, and that he knew was his soul. Had the others ever felt the same? No one talked about such things. There were taboos against it. Luck, he'd learned, was something that came your way only if you never thought about it. Maybe it was like malaria. You hunched over a radio, if you had one, and tuned out your worry. Or, like one of the guys there, you memorized something holy and resonant, then said it aloud to blot out everything else, even during rocket and mortar attacks. "A thousand shall fall at thy side, and ten thousand at thy right hand; but it shall not come nigh thee." He too knew it by heart, and he felt it was good enough to settle for. Murmuring anything like that was almost enough, provided you had the sense of joy in your own life: not in its richness, et cetera, but in the mere facts of breath, blood, and peristalsis, which those wounded in the neck could never do, able to make only the noise of squirrels fucking in the trees, with the sounds of high-pitched breathless panic in which, somehow, a saw got hot on metal. You are good to me, he told his anus, his heart, his lungs. Don't quit now. We have been through a lot together. You are going to Laos, where you've never been before, but the motions are the same, there is no difference in what counts. Uncle, he said, my liver is still filtering, I can still make saliva (although less than usual), and the fluid in my kneecaps hasn't drained away. What more can you want when guys are getting shredded all around you? There are few lucky wounds. Tempted to write It Shall Not Come Near Thee on his flak jacket, he decided no: it would anger the others and it might egg fate on. But he did, after much thought that included the mute observation that he was a clever bastard with one year of college (mostly A's for smarts, D's for inertia), scrawl on his helmet with white lead paint a couple of names: Scylla on one side, Charybdis on the other. "Two old whores," he told them. "It was always a threesome for me. Man, if you ever want to sharpen and sustain your appetites, get the extra broad aboard." Boxers had done it, he knew, right before an important fight, to purge their systems of irrelevant violence. Something like that. Asked how to say their names, he offered Sill and Dibdis, two Greek lice who reeked of goat cheese and olive oil. His head was in between as, sexually speaking, it always was. He seemed to them wiggier than ever, but he was at least alive, and they respected anyone who managed to get through a month, or two. No one copied the names from him; but before they took off for Laos, after being newly equipped by air drops from black and yellow chutes, they all daubed fresh mottoes on their own helmets, the back of their flak jackets, the insides of their wrists: *Fuck the Corps, Eat the Apple, Time on My Side.* Something unalterably pathetic struck him when he remembered such words rather than read them. What flummery, what drab and dismal formulas guys took with them when they were up against it, as if death could read, or sheer bloody blindfolded lousy luck knew English. Noise was the lingo of death, but what was the lingo of luck? *Math,* he decided, and at once cast around for the mathematical symbol for what was random. Had he ever known it? Only X, which he dared not inscribe on the flak jacket because it looked like a reminder to the executioner. He wanted a map of Laos, but the sergeant told him to can it, the map was wrong, the map references would always be wrong and nobody could say half the sucking names these bastards

called their places. Farther you went, the harder the names were. Or
they all sounded alike and, although you marched, you only got from
a Binh Long to a Binh Dinh, from Binh Thuan to a Nin Thuan.
Second Mesa to Red Lake was easier. They should call every place
Quim Phuck, the sergeant told him, and leave it at that. *Yair*. Everyone said that. Everyone liked to *yair*. They liked a group truth, and
that his mind was off like some firefly on the fringe of their stand-
down yammering meant nothing to them. He was alone among the
shrapnel, the rockets, the mists, the crude monosyllables of the place
names, and there was nothing he could do about it except keep living
in order to get stoned. His tear ducts were blocked, which was why
both his eyes had been running nonstop for a week, and his head felt
like his feet did when, back home, he got up and stuffed them into
shoes but left the laces untied, on which he then trod while blundering about, unable to budge the foot he lifted. We're going to cut the
Ho Chi Minh Trail, the scuttlebutt told him. Like a vasectomy. He'd
never been invited to a vasectomy, but to this one he'd go with a bit of
a giggle, his head held high in his ancient Greek helmet, and on his
lips the constant plea to X, god of chance, for it not to be in the neck
or the balls. Out of his own depths had come an upside-down exhilaration, a Saint Christopher made of excrement and tar. Two Dexes
later he told them, "Damn straight, I feel omni. Fuck all grave special-
ists. Guess I'm going to get some soon." But he never said what and
they were too much in agreement with him to ask.

Sotuqnangu

"You keep looking down," she says. "What's wrong?" Young Oswald knows but can't word it, not this jazzy white scumble that soars up at him from under his chin where the front of his brand new T-shirt catches the sun and the white logo of a city's spires seems a snow animal caught and flattened against him, nowhere near out of sight but scrambling up toward him to bite his chin. Or it is just appealing to him, doing only that, but still a scramble that nags at the fringe of his vision, making his chest look too big, too close, too much a chest certainly for someone twelve years old. He wants to wipe it off like flour, press it into the texture like spilled milk, he wants it to flap its starchy wings and take flight, then return to him, hovering, a white bird of the high peaks, unknown and unnamed, an alleluia bird born of a gull and a snow fox, right out of his book of *Birds from Elsewhere*, which he's retitled because not a bird in it looks familiar. It is in fact *Birds of the Northeast*, bought for him at the Variety Store in Keams Canyon by an overcaring uncle full of paternal shyness. George has always bought people the wrong presents, mainly because he never knows how other people think or what. His only clue is how they talk, which he assumes is always a cover-up, so he ends buying them the opposite of what they want. He's cussed he is, yet predictable, at least in variety and department stores. To him, only a kachina doll is worth having, to cuddle, to worship, to stir with, to hide under the bed, to hammer spiders with, to scratch the back. "Never enough," he says. "I'm flat out as it is." "That," somebody says, "is why people have nephews." "The gods decide," he says. At his most sullen. "Emory—" someone begins. "Emory," says George The Place In Flowers Where Pollen Rests, "is an *imitator.* Bird calls is more like it." Cruel, they tell him. He doesn't hear, and assumes he is being complimented, urged back to work. He pats Oswald's chest, flat-handing half of that city in a fulsome gesture of ownership. "One day, Oswald," he says, "one day soon." "And the Grand Canyon, Uncle George?" "Eagles," he answers. "Icebergs, caves, glaciers, domes of coal, mountains of salt, people cut from wax." It never happened, though, and it was Oswald who took him the few places they ever went: the Canyon, yes, then Matlock's office, the gift shop on the mesa, the rebuilt variety store in Keams Canyon. It was as if the apprentice had to become the uncle-father almost before he had grown up. "*Wowy, wow-ee,*" said Oswald, and his uncle picked up the habit, although never in front of something, always in front of its idea, its repute, its possibility as a place to go to and unload a hundred dollars, along with Fermina and the boy. A family outing that, over time, blurred and became woefully majestic. "Know what, Uncle? We have family innings, all the time." That damned boy, not only gifted (a bit), but smart-mouthed too. Words aren't wood, however. Nothing tempts George from carving, neither Australia nor Phoenix, neither Manhattan nor a subscription to the most famous news magazine. As the boy's voice gets lower, George's gets higher, scratchier, and he begins to speak huskily from the back of his throat, as if parodying the sound of what used to be called quinsy (dog in the tonsils). But, as soon as Uncle George learns he sounds funny, he shuts up, turns into a creature of nods and beckons, waves and scowls. He should be talking Italian in that high, strained Mafia voice: *Ay, Giuseppe, che fa? Va bene?* This is Oswald talking, doing his uncle after the fashion of movies he's seen, taken by *Emory* when Emory remembers to go through with the façade of a child bearing his name. At least this goes on until George hears Oswald "doing" him, and he at once lowers his voice to where it used to be, an octave lower. Uncle George, they say, at last spit up the puppy that was choking him. "Hey, Giorgio?" Slap right across this other kid's face, who was only imitating Oswald. George in retreat, scowling and lumbering like a scalded bear, harangued by the mother who does not, ever, like having anyone hit her children but herself. George, they begin to understand, has to be left alone a lot, not meddled with, asked, invited, egged on, cared for, like he is a glacier, a stack of firewood. He did not come from this world and he is not responsible for it, but waits out his busy, high-strung days in rapt taciturnity, an uncle with an overendowed head. All he needs is a drum, a blanket to make smoke signals with, a gong to bang for food (two bongs mean fried). "When I am quiet, I am thinking," he tells them. "When I am thinking, I am quiet. I am almost always quiet or thinking." He is twice a stone, then. Only once did he lift, because a nephew caught him napping, the veil. "Something like a golden tent flap," he said, "floating across the part of your mind that sees without needing eyes, with faces like woodknots. Eyeshit. Headsoup. The wood red-hot between your hands. Don't ask. I don't tell. You better pray for a quiet life, son, don't you go asking for this load. All you got in the end's what you think you got. Go to school. Find oil. Learn Russian. Leave me alone to rot. You get something you can kill, not something that kills you. I do not sleep. I never remember what I ate. Half the time I genuinely do not know my name or yours or whose mother your mother is. This is a lather to live in. Stay away from it. It is one of the meanest ways of staying poor I know. It's as if"—he bunches up his hands and rams them against his belly with blunt and awful force—"these hands had been sunk into my innards red-hot and clawed, and all my life trying to get out of there and fasten themselves to the right place on the wrist. Like that. Leave me alone, boy. Don't ever be thunderstruck." George was always modestly superb. It took years before Oswald felt bold enough to go and coo inside that charmed, barbed circle around him, but go he did, inching his way, careful of the hands as if they were celebrated beasts in the act of mating, their cries of hurt ecstasy unheard, their movements fast and perverse, with, now and then, skin thin-draping after them like the top lifting off of boiling milk. One day, for sure, he was going to carve out a marvelous place for himself alone, no uncles and no brothers: somewhere he could go that others couldn't: Moscow, The North Pole, Rio, and saying their names was half as good as already being there.

Sotuqnangu

And nothing happened. They did not go to Laos. The Vietnamese troops had to be made ready, put on invasion alert. But a captain showed up, asking for him, and came right to the point, although seemingly the worse for liquor. "Been hearing about you," the captain said. "The brass has been hearing about you. All the way to the top. Which is a waste of the brass's time. We do not want to hear about you. You're a college Injun, you got some smarts, they say. Made yourself a gook. Right? You eyefucking me, soldier? Don't. You are not one of these dumb-minded social undesirables. Don't behave like one. You want to make yourself a monster? You wait until this here war is concluded, then you go marry one. Joke. Your boots are red with mud. That does not make you one of them. So far you have not shot up the radio so you can go off doing what you damn well please. But you have done bad. Don't you quote the pisscutting *Iliad* to me. These hooches here have hollow walls, where they keep their weapons. But that is also where some of you keep the ears, noses, penises, breasts you have cut off in your finest frenzies. Mutilated corpses are clogging the rivers. The Navy has complained. Never mind. We got a job for you guys. You will go and clear the rivers of corpses, and then you will sew back on whatever you have removed. There will be an inspection, and if you don't come up with some inspection-worthy bodies in chop-chop time, your ass will not be worth a roach's tit. You got that? I don't give a shit what you kill, but you do not mutilate and you do not choke the rivers. Burning is beside the point. I do not want to know that you burned it. That is a fact for you, it is not a fact for brass. You did what you did. Now you will undo it. Where you get them jungles? You are one unmilitary mess. Personally I do not approve of the living in the dead's duds. It jinxes the whole operation. Worse than rat bites and no salt, dear johns and well-trained men beating off under the nearest banana tree, which is how you get your head blown off and your cock frozen fast into your hand. Now. This is to tell you what you will personally go do. You are going to be hell of unpopular with your fellow grunts. It's the smartass ones that foul things up. Like you. You come here for some kind of scalping practice, is that it? You have what we refer to as deviant ideas. Make a clean war dirty. What I am saying is not ethical, it's a matter of drill, like cold beans and motherfuckers for breakfast. You did? Why, there are some outfits with creases in their pants to this day. They have gloves with which to save their hands from the elephant grass. Otherwise the hands are a mess of festering pus, and then they have to be wrung into action. Tidy's what I mean. That is my direction, you little slumball mortician. You missed your trade. You need a dose of walking point for a month or two. I'll arrange that too. You got everybody upset. You thought you would fit the war to your own hang-ups. We are going to fit you to the war, son. I personally am going to *bust* you to the rank of boot lieutenant, which is as low as anyone can get. I don't hold with no college boys running around giving orders like this was some summer camp. White bars with hooch girls fetching and carrying for them is too damned much. Getting blow-jobs in lean-tos, with six packs and spiked grass. While some of us been doing our damndest to run this mother of a war. You get this. You do not belong. There is your pariah, you got that big fat college word? There is your outcast. There is your leper. You, you jumped-up sonofabitch, are all three. You want to cut an ear, a tit, here and there, that is okay, it might even make a man of you. But you do not tamper, you do not sit around in the stoked-up middle of hell and build yourself a Frankenstein like some kid building a plane from a kit. Don't you correct me about the classics, you smug little soapcock. I suppose you tried to arrange some air-conditioning for your gook? Who would believe it? Nice and fresh for you to fuck? That is how syphilis began in the Pyramids. It was called necrophilia and don't you interrupt. Can you recite the eleven general orders? Right, I might even ask for that later on. We'll see what you know. Then some knuckle push-ups and side straddle hops. We heard about your super-gook and your far-out vocabulary. I happen to have been one shallow point short of Phi Beta Kappa, so don't you academ-e *me*. We are going to help you become a soldier again, before we send you any place, just as if you had stepped out of the enlistment bus and you put your feet into the yellow footprints a considerate service has had painted on the pavement. So's you will not put a foot wrong, from the very first. I am Captain Bartram. Learn that name, buddy boy, and get your little asshole puckering. I am worse than any rocket blast. You think about this and your ass will come up into the back of your throat. Your first sergeant will instruct your platoon sergeant what to do with you. You think you are some kind of revel, some kind of agitator? You are going to sabotage what we seriously call the war effort? I am talking honcho, son. You need a haircut fast." And then the captain offered him a Hav-a-Tampa cigar with a wooden mouth-piece, an echo of Florida, which he took and accepted the light for, only to have to tell the captain how the first version effigy had smelled and looked, if he had added female parts to the male trunk (he had not), and whatever else he'd done to it. "You like to see?" Oswald said. "You got the stomach. Sir. *You.*" As if, he thought, we had a peephole and were eyeballing the eagle pecking away at the liver of that other old Greek. The captain puffed away in loud-mouthed clouds, almost fussing him up while bawling him out, as if in the preliminary to some reluctantly awarded medal for original and constructive service. And what he still, in his greenhorn way, did not know about the war, the captain told him about nurses whose flak jackets were so crammed with Tampax you couldn't get your arms around them, whores in Hong Kong with fresh-fried British breakfasts (liver, onions, bacon, eggs, tomatoes, and toast) in their vulvas, rich for eating, and how strong men had blubbered when their captain denied them an ear for their collection, which browned on the necklace rope and stank and withered up. He heard him out, as rank required, although not the decorum of intellectual equals. And then the captain had gone, with a string of well-rehearsed grandiose curses, and they marched to the nearest river and began hauling out and burning the ballooned bod-

ies, none of which they had thrown there in the first place, so that the
presidential yacht could sail upstream to a divine rendezvous. It was
the Saigon River. The VC bodies were slate blue by then. Some of the
biting fish held on even after the body on the hawser came out of the
water on to the embankment. You only just started, the squad sergeant told him. You and them others, you gonna burn some other
stuff, so they poured diesel fuel on the barrels of human excrement
and set fire to those as well, polluting, as he thought, most of Asia,
and that was the stench he remembered after they landed, the air-
conditioning of the Braniff jet went off, and the door opened to over
one-hundred-degree heat, and a stewardess in routine uniform an-
nounced that they had arrived. "Welcome to Vietnam, boys. See you
in a year's time. Don't you take any wooden nickels now." And, he'd
mentally added, keep your pockets clean. It was as long ago as all of
his life rammed into a sleepless night, and he was waking to a new
dream in which the whole world smelled like half a million men's
insides. "Ohno," Captain Bartram told him, "I don't want to look.
You put it all together. I want to keep it blown apart." It was then
that Oswald decided to put Uncle Gee into a better state of repair,
not out of defiance, but opportunely reminded. When something you
have made begins to come apart at the seams, he decided, you owe
something to your original labor; between you and it there's a bond, a
blemish of honor. So long as I want to haul it after me, I'd better keep
it in hauling order. It reminded him of an old thought he'd had in
LA, deep in the heart of Palookaville: a human being isn't really alone
with his/her/its own sex organs in an uncaring universe, but
swamped with other people all in the same state. No, he had told
himself back then: you really are alone: balls and pecker in the bosom
of mother nature, and all the other people are just window dressing
through which you can see the horizon, the stars, and the big green
sludge coming to get you because it runs the whole show, mindless
monster that it is. It uses bodies like a plant does flowers. Back to
work he went, when he could, with needle and gut.

BertandAnna

Our favorite though is come in out of the cold, which is the most used
message on the mesa. We sometimes go tell somebody that without
having been told to tell them, then they see what is going on, and give
us a message to take back, as if a message had been sent by Bertand-
Anna in the first place, and we go, they send another message back.
To and fro, out of puff, it high up here, and we got a whole season of
being friendly to them all. We never wear out. What they do when we
gone? They send a message for BertandAnna, they want to be told
things. It snowing. You cold. It not July, now. They want you home.
Out of the cold. What other folks is going to talk like that to other
folks? They too busy to say these things. Their minds too busy, too
full. We the empty heads, the best of all the emptiest. We got time and
the willingness. It don't matter how little, it worth telling somebody
hello. Even those who stare don't hello you back, maybe because we
smell or burp a bit, maybe because we don't walk quite straight
withouting our sticks, wobbly on the ice, a bit stoopy in the July
sunshine, you can't be right all the time, but you got to look a better
happy among all these folks who say, Where *these* from? They wasn't

sent for. They just come. One day. They never gone away. It be like
that a lifetime for two. Shove us, they don't do that anymore, but the
children sometimes run right into us, and we say, *"Whoa, horse,* you
gotta look where you going." Children bounce off you, we sort of
lumpy and heavy. Folks like to lay their heads on us, even the nephew
when he on the point we declare of going to cry, him wanting to be a
good carver as his uncle, something like that, he homesick for Hollywood, all them miles of whitewashed streets, streets we do not have of
any kind up here. We walk the paths each day to keep them down and
easy to see. Some folks won't walk a path until it be just about gone in
the overgrown. Put the mess in the bins. We help a lot. Gather up bits
of newspaper, Uncle George's shavings day after day, he cut some
special soft for us without being asked, but he cross we take it, he save
that for a Mister Apple from Tucson. "You just thrown away all the
packing." He not know we lined our pants legs with it, little plastic
bags of it stitched to the inside, we walk around, they never know,
with little see through sausages of shavings hung around our legs to
keep the cold away. Uncle George he been carving all the time, it like
a harvest of wheat or something, he make the chips fly like the wind
the snow, and we the top-notch collectors. Sacks and sacks of it, we
burn or we stuff pillows with it, we must be the cosiest couple on the
mesa, we like got a goose for us with fluff it come each day and we
line the shack, up, down, all along, in there it like being in god's
pocket. With the mice who find it long ago, they all come back, nestle
down and keep us perky. "Come in to warm," we say, but they never,
they know maybe we let it flow in winter, when it hard to move, and
then it all bind together you can hardly disturb it ever after. We heard
tell of some ig-loo up north someplace, and it the same thing, but they
got shavings of ice to cuddle with, the same part being they water it
to make it hold together. All winter long. Summer they do not get.
We better, we get summer a long time, and then air out the shack, get
ready to walk around with summer messages, Get out of the sun, Do
not drink all the water, and folks soon be in better shape, they know
from one another what is going on. It's nice. Yair, but not as nice as
what Oswald say he do one day, ride us in a Rolls Royce through
Hollywood. We mess it up good, we tell him, if it one of they bad days
when. Oh no, he going to put each of us in a big plastic supermarket
bag to keep us decent, we be at the open roll down windows on each
side Hi'ing everybody we pass. TV in there, big bottle of hooch. You
get bacon and eggs if you ask. Music from those big speakeasies. The

man in front with a peak cap, he never once look back to say what kinda folks we driving about these days. Oh no, he do his duty, tour us best he can. It not easy with all the other cars. Nothing smash into nothing only one hair breadth away. Oswald, he got the map and he show the big star homes. Who they, we ask, we never heard of these folks. They got big names for living in big homes. Wipe hands on little hot wet rags. That good. Nice on the face too. It breezy in there from the cold that blows at you. Catch your death. Now, Oswald he glad hand us all through it, us nestled up good in them pear-green market bags, no they garbage bags you put Bert and Anna in, you going to dump us someplace? Take out the dummies in the Rolls and drop them at the garbage dump. They never know we was people, they grind us up with knives and pump us away like sludge. Then we get past the Hi, we do not say just Hi, we start to squeal and yell with liking it so much, and the folks not hear a word of it, they outside in the sun, and we like in a grave, got our toys along with us and one of the whistles you blow. It like having everything you hope for all your life all at the once and the nephew he not even made a list of what he gave. Like he forgot it as soon as he handed it over. This for you, Bert, and that for you, Anna. The spinny plane. The doll. Now we got enough to travel through space, which is easy cause there is nothing in the way, not like Rodeo. Rented the sucker, he say, it not his. But who care? It never happen, but one day soon, he say, just to show it can be done. Man like that could head the tribe. He know what folks is suffering about. But how he choose who to go with? He pick them that have been the least places, like he say, fill up their eyes with all that they never knew about before, then bring them back home to dream of it like it never was. Keep the toys. Bert he never let on but he throw up from the swaying of that car. Into his bag, but he brave, never complain. It make the air in there a bit furious. Anna, she never tell, but she got the belly ache all through, it double her up good, but she still peek at the dudes going by. No, Anna say, we going by them, not the other way, there be only one person in motion at one time. Now we fill the bags with shavings for the winters to come. Like lots of sheep got into there and got stuck against it, their wool all come away, so now they got to climb into the bags with us. We got a flock to tend and some of them's folks. When you been half as good as dead since before you was even born, you never worry much about what going to happen next. You there for folks to lean on, tie their mules to, stand in the snow to fix a certain point. Never mind so long as they stand us together, back to back, from to front, side by side, it all the same wonderful. We got a here to be there in. We got a who to be. Through and through. Two folk, one ghost. Only thing is, we do not know how to BertandAnna ourselves. It kind of bounce away from us, a rabbit running from a fox. All we do is head for a pool, look in there, see who be present, and say a nonstop Hi. You guys look great. You never go away. Last as long as light so long as you got Hi's a plenty. Hi to mices everywhere. One day soon we going to meet them olive oil Greek tycoons who drive their Rolls Royce cars on boats. Mister Ee-pam-in-on-das and Mister Con-stand-ur-os.

Sotuqnangu

Burning corpses by the Saigon River, he felt like a renegade Hindu, at least until somebody, trying to wipe out stench with sound (it worked the other way), or being grossly cute, began playing Mary Hopkins's version of "Goodbye," which was mostly fugal variations on that one word. But nobody played any music at all when they set fire to the oil drums of excrement, as if no one could have heard anything through the clotted-feeling smoke. This was what he had let himself in for instead of writing blue books, term papers, and answering dead-head little quizzes, and in a way it was heftier, more grown-up, more like what he'd always imagined Experience ought to be. His mind lied. Distantly he yearned to be the self-conscious owner of what they called a short-timer's stick, which a soldier made when he had about two months to go in his tour. The knob of wood between each pair of notches was a day to serve, and at the end of it the soldier cut it off the stick, until on rotation day all he had in his hand was a tiny stub. The unpracticed reverse of this was a stick that kept getting longer, knobbly as a windpipe and unwieldy, and that was how he felt today. Yelled at by the drunken captain, who secretly admired

him for his depravity, and now doing chores that made KP a South
Seas paradise, he dreamed sullenly, even when someone yelled,
"Chow down!" He had no appetite for food, cold or warmed up, and
he knew that a month of duties such as these would make him light
enough to blow away. Why, he wondered, do they burn shit near the
LZ? Surely the smoke disturbed the pilots. Or was it a deliberate
attempt to camouflage? He had had enough of such wonderings, and
the inane distinctions he felt obliged to draw. He longed for Laos, for
its mountains and ravines, which was all he knew about the place.
And a place was what it was, rather than a country; another zone in
hell. Would it be cooler? When did the dry season end? How wet was
the wet one? The dry season was full of rancid steam. Only a klick
from the river, he and half a dozen like him were merely filling up
time. That was it. For all he cared, the shit could remain in a stinking
heap, when it smelled worse than during burning. Barbaric housekeeping, he thought, his mind on housekeeping cottages on a Florida
Key, or in Marina del Rey, as if such places still existed. He knew that
a slab of existence had become his. He had survived something unspeakable, and again he groped for the face of his imaginary being, its
name. But no, Uncle, the words don't matter. Again he saw the petulant, thin-nosed face, the top lip too close to the septum,
the tiny mouth unclosable, the jawline frail, the whole combination
exuding bad temper and just maybe nymphomania as well. But no
physique came through, not even a bird body, a four-legged body, a
sea creature's taper in sheathed meat. One day, she or it would speak
to him and see him through. He had heard of such things, from the
Angels of Mons who had floated above the trenches in World War
One to—he lost the thought because someone had said *Chow down*
again, and this time he forced himself to accept a can of lukewarm
sludge, wishing the whole emphasis of the place weren't on what it
would soon have to be, when deliberately accelerated peristalsis
fought the pucker of fear as the anus dove upward into the tube away
from what made the muscles in the back convulse and, if you were
lying down, lifted you an inch into the air. There were big guns in
Laos, he had heard, with which they bombarded Khe Sanh. Were they
what the brass was after? Maybe the ground in the mountain area
would not be as soft and mossy; walking would not be like wading
anymore. A recon patrol had just come in, with little to report, but
out of the gray sky rockets began to rain down, and he ran for shelter
under the canvas-and-two-by-four lean-to, laughed hysterically, and

tried to cover the distance between it and the nearest bunker without touching the ground. His boot got somebody in the face, who cursed him with face in the dirt, and then there were no more rockets, but the *put-cap* of small-arms fire began from somewhere inside the tree-line, a mild unlethal sound, during which he saw white phosphorus go up and land, followed by another white from distant but friendly mortars which aimed at the white and then fired for effect. Abruptly the small-arms fire stopped and the rockets did not begin again. Some-thing that killed you should not be that banal, he thought. Rockets were terrific, but the tick-tack—or however others heard it—of the machine gun was too slight, too mild. Only if it hit you did you really know its caliber. It was an awful joke, but he had managed to come up with it, even while several fellow grunts, ripped away from life like grass cut from a lawn, had earned the right to a Conex container which had a small generator on it to refrigerate the body with. He tried to call it unreal, but what had happened resisted the word, so he cast around for anything to call it—unspeakable, grotesque, mind-blowing—but there was nothing appropriate except perhaps *cheap*. What had happened was cheap. It wasn't worth having. Maybe, then, where nothing was worth having, your own life was nothing to hold on to. Then he hit on *priceless:* the lives that went the way of all flesh went cheaply as could be, whereas the lives that remained were price-less. You could not invest in your own survival. There was no way of buying it. You followed routine, as you did when on patrol in the darkness, holding the hands nearest you, or the back of somebody's shirt and watching for the glow of phosphorus from the smear of wood pulp on the back of the helmet just in front of you. That way, no one got lost, though some did die. Sometimes, during heavy rain, it was impossible to breathe, and he'd learned how to furl his poncho round his shirt to make a cache of air. Maybe those who lived had learned to breathe from a little private cache of luck formed in mo-ments of panic: squatting to dump into an oil drum already aswill with monsoon rain and others' leavings as free to float away as bottles on a tide, or, after the leeches had affixed themselves during a river crossing, deciding to let them drink their fill and then fall off rather than burning them off with a smoldering cigarette. There were ways, all right. He looked at the jungle and told it he had gotten this far without any advice from it, as it from him, and neither could teach the other. Almost as many of those who knew everything died as of those who stayed greenhorn through and through. It was all in the breaks. So he volunteered to become a LURP, doing long-range reconnaissance work with a mail-order hunting knife, a little portable stove for making hot chocolate and meatball spaghetti, freeze-dried. He could just hear himself, crawling through the brush by night, impaling and disemboweling, not because he wished the VC any harm, but for something to do, something that made him take up a deliberate attitude to the destructive element he was immersed in anyway. *No way*, they told him. It would take months to build up his visual purple, months of what they laughingly termed nightlife, sitting without lights and shunning daylight like the plague, not even allowed to watch the match he lit when he had a smoke, and not even allowed the dim red light of the visual astronomer. Blindfolds, dark glasses, eyes scrunched up. He'd have to become a raccoon. Yet they respected him for asking. The captain did at least, drunk or sober, joshing him about having compiled his own gook, and regaling him with the story of an outfit up-country where big brass had insisted the ears be sewn on again for decency's sake. Spiteful or careless, whoever did the job had sewn the ears on upside down, whereas penises, they were easier, and noses, well, and who cared about tongues? He would learn to find the gooks by smell, he told them, his dogtags in his boots and laced around his ankles. He'd tape the moving parts of his M16 and remove the trigger guard. He'd hardly breathe, he'd lose weight, and he would wear his hair in a Mohican cut just to make himself feel more fearsome to himself. Reptilian, like a human Bangalore torpedo, he'd slither through the night, silent as a plague, and learn the lingo too. Hell, he would accomplish one, two, three tours before resentfully going home, his chest full of medals, his night-afflicted face aged like a prize walnut. "It is not that easy," they told him. "You want it easy. You cannot be anonymous. You will have to live and die as you. Only special persons can carry the card that says this is nobody that we know: *Working for military intelligence. If dead, do not touch or remove. Report the location of the body.* He smiled and gulped a mouthful of the peanut butter that stanched his diarrhea, at least until the next swig of grape juice. If he played the C rations right, they kept him sweet; but he could never quite figure out the exact finesse required in balancing the least amount of vulnerable time against always being taken short. He who ran, ran dry. No, not until the peanut butter. He who blocked himself lived long. No, because he was due for a long squat. He who kept himself regular, then, was best off. No, because regular guys got shot all the time. So he

tried all ways and fixed his diet accordingly. No long-range reconnaissance patrols for him, but the captain, still wowed by his Frankenstein impersonation, promised him a few days at the rear, before
Laos, but after their next operation, a search and destroy: us looking
for him while he is looking for us, they told him, but they were
teasing him, whereas he already saw himself being flown to the map
location aboard a chopper labeled *Brutal Cannon*, his mind ever ahead
of the misinformation he wrung out of them, and thinking, oh casu-
ally toying with the internal fact, that during a firefight you could
shoot just about anyone at all, even one of your own officers if he had
not watched his mouth too well.

Fermina

He has this little card saying the times of airplanes going to Hawaii. He does not need it, he is not going to Hawaii, not ever, but he fusses if he can't find it on him. "Why," I ask. "It is something to hold on to," he says. "Like Uncle George with his dolls." "No," I tell him, "you and your Uncle George have nothing in common." "Oh no we don't, do we," he says, and he is laughing a bit. I think he has poisoned himself with funny food. What he eats in the city is not normal. He puts marmalade in his coffee, he says. Ice cream on his eggs. He smears his bread with orange juice frozen solid but just beginning to soften. He does nothing right. On his meat he has whipped cream from a can. It is all part of a plan, he says, to get him ready for all the things in life that go wrong. One day he walked around with thumbtacks in his shoes. He combed his hair with a pencil and left it as it fell. Some days he wets his underwear, soaks it through, before he puts it on, and then he goes out in it. "Life is going to be better to you than that," I say. "Fat chance," says he. "I won't count on it." "It won't," I say, "if you don't, if you don't hope." "He told me hoping has nothing to do with it." "He has gone far from us, never to come back." "Don't cry, Mama," he says, being brave. "It will be all right in a few years." I couldn't see how. I still don't. Only his uncle can manage him. Holds a honed blade to his throat and pretends to cut. Oswald likes that, it brings him back to life. Uncle George is going to cut my throat. Then Uncle George says no, his throat is open to the air already, he was going to cut a mouth in the face, but the gods have provided him with one. It will be all right. No cut today. Ah that George. One day he said nothing but the word *fuck* nonstop, morning to night, as fast as he could, as if his mouth had been struck by lightning. Even Oswald was shocked. He was like a machine. He was asking the gods to interrupt him, he said. Strike him dead. "They don't care what kind of language you use," I told him. "They care how you behave." "I'm pushing," he said. "I push like a borning baby." "*You* push like a sex-mad ram," I told him. "Fuckfuckfuck—" "You used to be quite the sobersides," I told him. "Till this." On he went, dry-mouthed, it was hard work and a ring had formed around him, laughing like mad. He acted up. You can see them alike, the two. Forever trying to get into trouble, trying to do the impossible. I'd be better with Emory back than this. Two wild men trying to make the gods thirsty for blood. They want attention, not affection. They want to be stared at. They want a landslide to have their name on it. They want Sotuqnangu to slam them in the skull with his thunder stick. They want what goes unwanted. They sit in the cold and Oswald takes out a box of matches he's stolen from some hotel and he lights a little fire that George cups his hands around. They play naturally together. They both like to be burned, cut, bruised, splashed, scalded, stung. Who else would want such things? These two see themselves as targets. Two bad boys ripe for whipping by the kachinas with yucca. There is no stopping them. They ask for it. At least they're not the drowning kind, like some they have around here. They are milder than murderers. They laugh the same. Hand movements almost identical. Voices on the same plateau. Jabbering out of the same quick mouths as if talking didn't have to be thought up first. Cruel, squinty eyes that they tighten up when they laugh. There is always something tickling them. They have a secret. Do they know they have another secret? My secret? Does Oswald? Oswald would believe only what his uncle told him. Anything else is women's clatter. Burly-faced Oswald doesn't have George's steel. You can see just how his face will crumble under challenge, which is when George's will get sharper like a weapon. Oswald dithers and

looks for what to do. Tell me, Mama. Tell me, Uncle, He's like that.
He depends. Oh that his brother and my husband would come back.
A change of loudmouths on this mesa would go down well. But only
Oswald goes, to whatever dark thing he says he does. One day he will
not come back except in chains, I can feel it now with a mother's
mind.

Sotuqnangu

Having survived that last rocket attack, he found himself wondering if he weren't invulnerable, and then wondering why his mind allowed such foolishness. Four or five months at most was all he'd seen of Vietnam, and he wasn't sure because he hadn't, like many of the others, daubed his calendar on the back of his flak jacket. He could no longer count, but he knew the rainy season was coming up. A mere beginner, he knew that only those who'd lasted through a couple of tours had the right to meddle with the notion of being invulnerable. He knew too that those who took their R & R early, for one reason or another, died soon after they came back, as if gentleness and cleanliness had sapped them of luck. And here he was, with one more search and destroy to get through, on the edge of that very pattern: a few days of toilets with doors, toilets that flushed, steaks eaten in the air-conditioned mess hall, an actual bed with sheets . . . followed by the coup de grace. So, instead of telling him the opposite, his mind ought to be saying *vulnerable*, you will soon be easy meat, you will soon be gone, blown away. A foolish intuition had come upon him out of nowhere, into which he would soon be blasted. It was a sign, then, an augury, a harbinger, a back-handed warning, and he marveled at how easily things went into words. It should have been more difficult. It should have been painful, but it never was. Everyone around him kept saying, "There it fucking is," as if that were the perfect summary, much as his mother said, "It all depends" (which gave him the image of everything hanging by a noose from a girder). He himself thought in different words, too many of them, and his mind had begun to freewheel, entertaining on the level of language just about anything at all. His mind was kvetching, weary of mud and violence and of having to sort out, nonstop, the true risks from the imaginary ones, the superstitions from the lethal odds. At last, while a lungfish trapped in a puddle made the noise of someone wounded in the throat, he told himself that, vulnerable or not, he'd take the chance to get away to where, in order to sleep, he wouldn't have to go through the fantastic, complex ritual of tuck the quilt back under your feet, then pull it tightly up under your chin, then tuck the sides under using alternate hands, which was when you set your M16 like an axle across your chest and, deftly if you could, swung the top of the quilt all the way over your face and head. Next you jammed your elbows to your sides and reached behind you to pull the quilt tightly behind your head, like a self-serving mummy already in the casket. Thus wrapped, he could sleep awhile, get out fast if he had to, and nothing from a rat to a snake could get to him. You might get claustrophobia, he'd learned, but at least a rat wouldn't bite a hunk out of your face while you dozed. All they did was rummage about over you, and on you. The joy of sleeping with his face in the open got him through the search and destroy mission, which was to clean out certain spider holes near an abandoned graveyard. What caught his eye most, though, was a water buffalo dragging a crude wooden plow through a paddy field, an old woman shifting water from one field to the next by hauling a bucket back and forth over the dike. Up came the lid of the first hole, down went the first few fragmentation grenades followed by a few clips of ammo. The only sound was that of miscellaneous explosions. After repeating the dose, somebody lifted the lid and shimmied in, passed out the mutilated people, arms and legs first, then the bodies proper. The water buffalo and the old woman had not even paused, but then the troopers who'd whipped out their cameras and flashbars, flipping them into the open as naturally as they would packs of bubblegum, wandered over to the paddy for some local color. Now the buffalo actually paused, as if it knew, and the old woman

instead of looking into the cameras turned her back, and none of their
boisterous shouts could make her budge. So one of them took a shot at
her, aiming to miss, which made her turn, but with a face of indifferent nonexpression, almost as if she'd made the bullet loop back
around her and enter the shooter's brain. Next thing, she babbled
something fast and low, no doubt her own version of There it fucking
is, and went on dragging the bucket through the slop. He knew then
that he would survive, would go have his hair cut, see Miss America
(who was over on a visit), pay for a whore, and come back with the
same dry, poised adjustment as the old woman. Nothing fugazi about
her, or him, and the awful dream in which all the hazards came together to kill him in his first week back was just a bad bubble his
mind had blown. Full of hot pizza delivered by chopper, he really
would not lose his M16 and, in a panic, snatch up a Russian rifle
booby-trapped with plastic explosive and so blow his face away. Nor
would he, because somebody only spitting distance away trod on a
spring, lose his upper half to a Bouncing Betty landmine exploding at
a height of four or five feet. No, he would die of boredom in a store
room full of Brasso, rubbers, fruit cocktail, Tampax, shoe polish, camera film, and shower shoes, while the Shirelles in a stuck groove sang
"Tonight's the Night." His luck was bound to repeat in the same way
as the song. It was all going to come true. It did. "Ok, you got your
jive job," the captain told him, "you and your pet zombie." He ate a
couple of mouthfuls of peanut butter, then with shotgun in hand
slithered half a klick rearward to where a village barber sat him on an
upright dining-room chair mounted on a C-ration cardboard box
squashed flat on the mud and cut his hair for twenty piasters, right
there in the open while Uncle Gee sagged and waited in the rain.
With all that coming down, it was hard to tell if the barber had cut
the hair or the wet had flattened it, but he didn't care; his scalp felt
bare and cool, his brain calmed down while he rested the shotgun
across his lap under the moth-holed tablecloth which, every now and
then, the barber removed and wrung out. "*Him* now," he said, flash-
ing money. Skin pulled off with the hair. The barber cursed as Oswald looked away tenderly at some huge French villas fringing a
rubber plantation. He laughed and imagined he saw condoms dangling full from every branch (these trees had branches still), and he
actually saw laundry hung out to dry in the rain and servants polish-
ing the windows from inside, their arms and heads thrust out amid
the little mopping, rotary motions. Now, who lived there? To whom

did they belong? When he took Uncle Gee to look, a Vietnamese brandished a broom at him in the doorway and a small dog ran out and collided with his legs, yap-scolding him. Already he was in the outside world, the paradise behind the lines, if lines there were, where the laundry girl with two front teeth missing asked him, "Suck?" and he was sucked, once, twice, thrice, while one of her hands held the block of soap, a priceless possession, and the other the tuber of his resurrected blood. He saw none of the sperm, but lounged against a garden wall smoking opium-spiked dope while she washed his duds, a house servant moonlighting while the owners sat out the war in Paris. Why was there no damage here? Why did the windows have glass? When she came back with his clothes still hot from the iron, and heavy with a seared-damp smell, she sucked him again with a cigarette in her mouth, glued to her lip cornerward, and the ash fell on his glans and he didn't care. She even held it for him when he peed, and that was free, a bonus to a good customer while he remembered the phrase *a double veteran*, which meant a guy who killed the whore he'd used. No way, he thought: not this one, any-way. Not with a shotgun. I'd take her back, just the head, to show the guys. They must think Nuncle Gee's a filthy-drunk Indian; he's floppy. His woozy head stung. The laundress had gone away in her black sneakers, almost certainly VC, but who the hell cared? His duds were clean, his wad was well and truly shot, he had just a fourth of a klick to go now, and it was raining only lightly. When, finally, he sat in a room thinking about shaving himself, after playing like a child with the toilet's flush, he looked up and saw a monk face looking at him: black-ringed eyes, face black-streaked from camouflage paint, eyes heartbroken ebony and lusterless, and a rusty earring in one ear. Then he not so much recognized himself as admitted the possibility, but didn't believe it until he had tested it out by moving his eyelids, his mouth, his shoulders, as if the parts of him no longer belonged together, and the mouth, say, might not be his whereas the eyelids and the shoulders were. That swoon was sleep. He had not tried to recognize himself by his own smile. But in his sleep he smiled and only sudden death would wake him. Now he held Nuncle Gee up to the mirror too, in his new duds, and he looked almost human, like Oswald. With the slowness of a lifer he shaved, savoring the water, the hot, the cold, the radiant chrome of the faucets and the toilet's wobbly lever. The mirror made him cringe or duck at first, but his shotgun was too far away. Now he bathed Nuncle Gee, marveling as blood turned the water rose, and trying not to smell the smell, he dried him on one of those big fluffy white hotel-type towels, then laid him on the cool clean bottom sheet of the other bed in the room, and drew the top sheet all the way up, under the chin, so the head in all its wistful green ferocity aimed a silent bark at the room, the skull red from the attempted haircut. Now Oswald knew that he was going to leave Nuncle Gee here for them all to minister to, including the bit of himself the multiple corpse contained. They had the time, the facilities, and they sure as hell had an obligation of some kind. He would spend a last night with him here, in pleasant circumstances, then go his way, adding his sunglasses to the face, capping the skull with a fresh facecloth as if putting muslin on meat. Actually, with the air-conditioning, the smell was not as bad as usual. On the way to the messhall Oswald saw hoochgirls and mama-sans galore, guys on the ground playing cribbage while stoned, the relics of yesterday's barbecue, dogs of all kinds waiting poised at the frozen alert. Shivering at an air-conditioning even fiercer than the room's, he took coffee, a steak with fries, and a beer so cold it made his throat sore. He began to cough from the crisp sharp cleanness of it all, amazed how uncomfortable he felt. It was worth it, though. Oswald's mind was far away, or rather his mind was not a mind, no longer an instrument of sorts but an area. He was saying goodbye to Uncle Gee, to that wordless effigy of rags and collops assembled from a dozen or a score of unknown, unknowable, men, all of them relegated now to the level of fertilizer, farther than far from the dainty hands of loved ones. How could he ever have called it Nuncle Gee? What insensate longing had driven him to do that, as if to fuse a holy memory with rank abomination? What was the link between pieces of dead Asian strangers and his beloved father? Was he trying to make himself believe that this was what Uncle George too had become, unshot by soldiers, true, uncarved by night-crawling fiends such as Oswald, yet just as much undone as Nuncle Gee. Goodbye, he said, to the one uncle or the other, uncertain who was in the room under the dim light that leaked in from the compound, mouthing goodbye to chops and slices, fly-blown bloat and sodden veil of skin. He needed to say goodbye, to one, to a dozen or a score, to thousands, because goodbye was the prelude to going away. Forever. Back to the ordinary mayhem of Palookaville. Then he began to murmur to it, to the patchwork human, this time with no thoughts of Uncle George at all, confiding to it about Trudy Blue, Clu and Stu, the half-baked depravities of those few years when he worked as a stud and could not even find work as an extra as an Indian. Out it poured. Oswald might have said as much to the corpse of Trudy Blue, but he knew that corpses sometimes arose and walked and talked. They blabbed. This miscellaneous collection of a human, though, was hardly likely to get under way, so Oswald told it even things he did not know he knew until now, and it lay there festering in the antiseptic half-light, its face agleam as if a genuine live human were just recovering from a fit of sudden tears. Oswald confessed and swept out the slaughterhouse of his mind, at the last apologizing to the now unreachable man behind each stranded part, half arguing that it was a poor effort yet his own: where so many had been blown to bits, at least this shattered-looking one could seem a whole. He did not look too hard and he kept his gestures to furtive hand taps, aiming at the top of the thigh, the round corner of the shoulder, all of this under the sheet, of course, while seeping into it. At last, for lack of anything else to do, he switched on the light, came to attention, saluted the thing in the bed, switched off the light, and went and lay there alongside it, only the spoiled sheet between them. The stench was back, so he blundered across to his own bed and tried to sleep, haunted and stertorous, wishing he were some beast of prey, able to move on to the next kill with not a qualm. Oh how hard he had tried. No more guilt. All the peace and privacy in the world were his, and his life trembled then like a meniscus on a full glass of water, bulging slightly up. It did not matter that he was alone. Each time you were alone, and kind of drenched in it, you were usefully rehearsing the bottom line of life and death, whereas companionship prepared you for nothing. This chunk of time today was his, but next evening he'd return to the mud and the rockets, the oilcan toilet, the drenched grunts and their chronic jungle rot, their fingering of their tattoos, their busting caps at anything that moved out there, their pathetic cleanup with a wash-and-dry napkin smelling of lemon, peeled from a foil sachet like an outsize condom. Again the cold beer bit his soft palate and his throat, and again he warmed himself with coffee. After another steak, he picked up his helmet and went back to shower, which he did for half an hour in oblivious, yawning, wasteful ecstasy. Miss America had come and gone, insulted by the nurses, ogled by the men, who said to her whatever came into their minds, which made her ask if she was going to have to talk to them all day like this. She swung her hair at the wounded, the apple-firm meat of her thighs and rear in the red, white, and blue miniskirt, and was driven away, to politer areas. The hoochgirls were all that was needed here, except they had the wrong-shape eyes, and the nurses were lieutenants who would not even look at lieutenants, never mind Indians. A Red Cross parcel was all he got: a mouth organ, some bubblegum, and a toothbrush that folded up. He was happier with the cement floor of the shower, the door that swung on the john and the sliding bar that sealed him in. He listened to Hanoi Hanna on the radio, doodled with pinochle in a quonset hut, went into the kitchens and set his hands on a block of ice that had a gigantic hole through it, big enough for an arm, and troughed on pizza and ice cream in alternate mouthfuls, then watched some guys playing poker outside a tent, got his boots buffed by a Vietnamese kid with a box. That night's movie was going to be *Flying Down to Rio,* in black and white, but he would miss it, he would not think of it, Rio could break his heart. Rockets landed off target, but everybody dived into trenches and bunkers. Then a mama-san was trying to sell him fish-heads and hot peppers, but he wadded up some bills and gave them to her anyway. Wondering if he could do such things, he went and got himself a new D-handle shovel for filling his sandbags with, of which he had begun with two dozen, but was now down to maybe ten, so he got some new ones, then a fresh supply of halazone tablets, replaced his P-38, the ration-can opener that sounded like a pursuit ship, and at last went for the mail, the gin for the officers, the five-dollar party packs of smokes, the ten-dollar joints that had soaked in opium. He would ride back, if he was lucky, in the chopper that brought hot food. No one had written to him, but his mother had sent an almond cake, which he ate sitting on the bed with the pitifully small stack of mail beside him. Oh. He was doing it in the wrong order, he knew, but he went and had another steak topped with bacon and baked beans, passed up the beer, then reclaimed his shotgun from the arms room, and went to ask how to get back, still gnawing on the tongue depressor he'd picked up in the dispensary. A Cobra gunship would deliver him. Nuncle Gee, after the screaming stopped, would get a decent burial. It was as simple as that. Shangri-Laos, he joked to himself. That was next, and he just hoped he wouldn't be flank man on some patrol, having to hack his way through the elephant grass while the patrol itself took the valleys or the made paths. He was tired of having to warm up his food with plastique explosive, a bit of which burned just like Sterno when you put a light to it. He wanted to be on a firm beach, just about anywhere within toe touch of the South

China Sea. He wanted to loll in the rack with a straw hat on and live in a private hovel made of tin, cardboard, and cast-off ponchos, with a plug of mucus in his throat killing him while the nurses slept through their lunch hour, and dreaming about the canary yellow of the Braniff jets that brought them in and took them out. If there was a slot machine in the enlisted men's club, he'd play and practice his Vietnamese, murmuring *didi, didi mao*, how to say fuck off in another language, best mouthed from under the straggly brim-fringe of a field hat. Or he'd keep saying "Die High," which was written on some helmets, and then go nowhere at all. He was thin enough now to escape the draft, thinner than guys who'd starved themselves before their physicals. It was still better to be that thin than have the green-pus drainage from your dressings, like some of the wounded in the wards. If he had to be wounded, let it be in a grown-up attack, and not one of those crazy charges with gook teenagers in the front to absorb the fiercest fire, and let it be not in the head or the arm, because anyone wounded in those parts was not outlifted. You stayed in the jungle to bleed. No medevac for you. Now it was time to leave Nuncle Gee, those on longer R and R's, the nurses and the hoochgirls and the mama-sans and the pogues, those rear-echelon goldbricks who tapped typewriters and shuffled paper. Almost an armadillo, he juggled his shoulderblades to adjust the metal plates in his flak jacket and climbed aboard with his gear, trying to save his face from the rotor gust. He should have walked, shotgun at the ready; he was back too soon, without transition or tapering off, where it was still raining, as if the rain knew an underprivileged area when it saw one. The M16 was his again. The rest of the cake was theirs. *"Would you just look at this dude,"* they exclaimed before wandering away secret with their mail, almost, he thought, like wild beasts with a hunk of the kill. The chopper's corkscrew landing had thrown his stomach loose, but the tongue depressor was still between his teeth, beginning to fray and soften. Had the shoeshine boy's box exploded yet? They often did, soon after the kid had gone. The lieutenant was explaining that, in steep terrain, it was easier to go up than down, and the boots right above your head weighed less when they fell going up than when they fell already going down. They rehearsed putting on the rucksacks the chopper had dropped off, each at least half the weight of a man. The only way was to face a tree or anything else to grab, otherwise you couldn't get up with half your own weight humped on your back. "One hill to the next," the lieutenant said, "and the stragglers will have to catch up in the cool of the day." But there was no such thing, although in the mountains there was bound to be some kind of cool someplace. The captain grinned and asked if he had gotten himself some. "More than some, sir," he said. "A real workout." But he was still on the straight chair in the rain having his hair cut, still in the pounding shower with his feet on the concrete floor, his eyes open to watch Nuncle Gee. "Look at this dude," someone said, and the nickname stuck. One day away and he had a name. "He done left his friend behind back there." Oswald nodded. "The last leave," he said. "He bought the farm." They giggled. "Would you just *look* at this dude. Just look at him. He look so clean."

Apperknowle

They say that his mother once had to stay a night in a motel and she was entranced by it, scarcely daring to breathe in the presence of so majestic a bed with the coverlet all sharp angles and the rug so soft and thick from wall to wall, she did not believe there could be a floor beneath it. The whole room was overpoweringly tidy, the vinyl polished, the toilet made new by its arrester ribbon of low-grade paper. She stood for a whole hour admiring it and then had to be cajoled into using the thing at all: denting the bed, lifting the paper strip off the toilet, actually opening the shiny drawers, and she loved one chair, not an easy but one with a curved back and sides that she could pull up to the writing desk and so close herself off from the world, fenced in by an almost complete hoop. The softness of even that common-grade toilet paper made tears come to her eyes. The blanched facecloths and towels, all laid out for her to spoil, moved her more than most of the echoes from her tribe's religion. The hot bathwater gushed out without end, so she just let it run and run, waiting for the end of it, which never came. Premature paradise, this, which she wished for her George when his time came. He would go to some fluffy, white, sanitized, right-angled place with a goodnight mint on the pillow and an unused cake of soap sitting in a shallow porcelain dish. She wished none of this paradise for herself, having already had it without warning. Whoever had cleaned it was a demon of rectitude. But she was not used to seeing her droppings swirled around beneath her in the wide mouth of the toilet, spun as if in some whirligig farewell until they scurried down the hole to the place somehow connected with home mesa. That, she thought, and said, was going too far. Encyclopedias were cleaner, she said, but to whom? With lips bitten back? With both eyes closed. With her hands frozen to her flanks? She told George and warned him not to fall for Anglo ways in everything. She need not have worried. To George in his mature years a commode was a place for washing binoculars and to hell with encrustations. There she stood in his mind's eye, forever, at what Marines call the fourth position of attention, in the presence of what it sometimes says on maps, northeast of the compass rose printed on the Arctic Ocean, *Unexplored,* for which one map misprints the word *Unexploded.* Rightly since the Arctic of fiercely tamed linen she stood among was every bit a bomb.

Sotuqnangu

Then his life fragmented like a grenade. They were in Laos, lifted in to set up fire bases on the ridges while the ARVN marched through the valleys. There was less climbing than he had expected, but there was enough. The Vietcong were all around them, but merely observing; or so the lieutenant said, and nobody lower in rank had the slightest idea what was going on. It was almost a phoney war now, up there in the purring cool of the ridges, with occasional bouts of what was called probing by fire. He got used to the different sound of choppers; heard from higher up and sometimes seen from above, they seemed less intrusive, oddly integrated into the landscape down there and no longer the rowdy boxcars they had been at the jungle LZs. He saw human beings falling from them or being thrown, but all that belonged to another order of experience. If anyone was in for trouble, it was the ARVN columns in the long, steep valleys. He yearned not to have to go down again. One sniper harassed them, at regular intervals, from so far away he had no effect. Or he was a lousy shot, and the lieutenant said not to take him out because they might put a real marksman in his place. Dumbo, they began to call the sniper, then

Zorro, and Zorro he remained, neither killing nor improving. They had arrived, dug in titty deep, as they called it, after treading down the vegetation; but the soil was so hard that their shovels broke, as did their machetes when they chopped the trees. Down went the first wall of sandbags, filled with stony soil, then they laid the logs on top for an overhead, on top of which they set more bags against possible mortar attack. Lazy up there in the spacious-feeling heat, he hoped they would never leave, which would mean emptying the sandbags and filling them again a day's march away, with full rucksacks, uphill or down, it made no difference. It was donkey work. Now he knew that the superstition about everyone's getting killed soon after an early R and R, such as he'd had for one day, was wiggy hogwash. He was alive, in fair spirits, and he could feel the rest of his life up along there in the future, tugging him toward it, beckoning, inviting, hushing his quibbles and strewn out there in the space between the mountaintops like sun-streaked wispy cloud, through which you fell if you grasped for it too soon. He had a profound sense that his warranty had not expired, that no shaped charge—with all its explosive force going one way—was aimed at him, or ever would be. No idiot with infrared telescopic sight was going to blow him away. No rocket was going to land on him because some cherry had broken squelch, just itching to play with that radio. He would not be left disemboweled for the wild pigs to chew up. It would just go on raining on the straw huts and the colossal Buddhas in the temples with the back-to-front swastikas. Another cake would come, and another Christmas, by which time he would be gone, his dues paid, his other life rebegun. Gnawing away at the tongue depressor, which somehow gave him an outlet for his excess energy, he began to enjoy the mountains, the hint of the bleak among the intact lushness. Maybe he would grow ripely mad, make a pet of some wandering scout dog, and at last think of something pithy and magical to scrawl on his helmet. Then they moved the firebase twice as the columns in the valley advanced in the trap laid for them, and still nothing happened, nothing major. There was one day of intense blue sky, which lifted their spirits and made him daydream of Phoenix in winter, but then the clouds came back and, soon after dawn one day, there began a whole series of slams and thuds in the valley below them. Tanks and heavy artillery bombarded the troops in the ravines and friendly aircraft bombed the VC close in. It was a multiple disaster that went on and on. There was cannon fodder galore down there and no military way out. As fast as aircraft bombed the guns and tanks, other guns and tanks in other places took over the bombardment. The air was full of radios telling the bombers what to bomb, but when they bombed it they realized they should have bombed some other place as well in an aerial imitation of H and I fire, harassment and interdiction, which denied the enemy useful terrain. As far as he could see or fathom the carnage in the valley, they should have bombed the whole damned thing end to end, actually wiping out the ARVN battalions by coming too close. He prayed that they would not have to go down into the fire zone. Could they be of use? The war down there was a matter of maps and force majeure, a battle of the juggernauts, and there was nothing a platoon might do. Yet they would have to get out sooner or later, he could see that, and then they would have to go down, into the bloodbath. He didn't need book smarts to know that. But no one retreated. The ARVN battalions held fast in spite of, as the rumor went, fifty percent casualties, marooned in their own landscape by their fellow countrymen. He tried to picture the White House, where all of this was understood and figured out, but all he could see were talc-white mesas in ruins as if heavy rockets had landed there too. They rebombed the bombed-out areas and the noise, heard from so high up, was akin to that of a TV movie heard a couple of rooms away, with the volume turned up full. No people screaming, no meat flying through the air, but a constant drone of planes that swept back and forth along the line. Then rockets began, invisible, soaring up the valley sides, launched from halfway down, where the VC had camouflaged roadways, which the bombers could hit only by accident, and he was down in the sandbagged ditch with someone's boot in his face. The ground quivered, the air filled with a smoke that smelled like scorched buttermilk, and hail or gravel thrashed through the trees. The radio went, blasted into the now denuded trees along with its operator. He knew because the lieutenant, arriving in a ragged dive, told them so; the other sandbagged ditches had already blown away, and all the survivors tried to claw and butt their way into a space intended for three or four at most. Roofed over with bodies alive or dead, for which he distantly felt grateful, he tasted the musk in the soil and felt an electrical discharge run through the bodies on top of him with each bang and, high over him, like suddenly torn thin metal, shrieks and pleas. Somebody was yelling For God's sake stop, but, if anything, the rocket avalanche intensified, with an extra rocket now between each pair, and then rockets in those two extra spaces, as if some demonic thun-

derbolt thrower were proving the infinite divisibility of time, or of
anything else. By now the mass on top of him moved as one: no more
uncoordinated flinches and jerks, and he knew that something hideous was ripening up there, squeezing the wind out of him, and all he
wanted was something heavier than sand, something really solid. His
ears were numb, but his head was streaming wet with something not
sweat, and some outpost of his mind began to hope they would not
rush the ridge now the perimeter was smashed. There was no need.
The rockets had zeroed in, and now they were doing the upward
version of what the planes had done: pulverizing the previous target
until there was nothing, absolutely nothing, to clean up, only hen-
sized pieces of people smoking in the highland bracken. He
called out, muffled by the knee against his mouth, asking pointlessly if
they were there, if everything was okay now, and when he tried to
move, not to get out but to pull all of himself together in an effort to
get even lower, he could not move the dead weight above him of half
a thousand pounds. The taste of panic was coppery, wire in his
mouth. His pants were full of sludge. Something, perhaps liquid, was
burning his eyes. He threw up into his mouth, but his teeth were
jammed shut against the ground with his lips hauled out of shape
sideways. Again and again he heaved, longing to pass out and let
history have its way with him, but he didn't, he didn't even have one
of those low-blood-sugar swoons he'd had before, in Vietnam. The
wump-wump of the rockets he now heard through his stomach. He
was licking the verdigris off a moat, quaking and shaking. All his
adrenaline had gone into the slight bulge between his eyes, where it
hummed and brewed. He tried to run vertically, down to where the
earth was hot. He heard a score of radios listing coordinates, then
pleading, bleating, in a crescendo of giant atmospherics, and then
they fizzled out as he began to float with pulped head and hollowed
bones, down slowly to where the rocket launchers and the mortars
were still being fed by Vietcong like busy bakers loading loaves.
There came a sharp pain in the core of his gut, as if a knitting needle
had pushed in, and he flooded with relief that it was not his throat, his
groin, and he remembered—or someone identical with him remembered it for him—that those wounded in the arm and head stayed in
the bush. A wound in the gut could get him home. The tongue depressor was all the way down his throat and he choked to bring it up,
which he could do only because he was being lifted, and so he
shammed dead until a voice asked him if he knew what shit this was.

He'd known, hadn't he? He'd know again. The so-called mission had a name. "Welcome," said the captain, whom he could not see for blood and mucous grit, "to Dewey Canyon Two, son. The name is all there's left of this here mission. What's that in your mouth? Howdja like to go collect the mail? Far as I can tell, there's only you and me to read it. Not even a corpsman. Now, why don't you get up slow-like, out of all that shit?"

Henry Matlock IV

You never know. At first I thought he was coming right at me in some kind of charge. He hated doctors that much. Big shaggy brow on him, big hands, but the arms short like the legs. A look fit to kill, to scalp. Like some Apache from a Western. Only the tomahawk was missing. He must have been in a bad mood. Really ticked off. The two of them, him and the fancy nephew, put up at the motel while he wore the monitor for twenty-four hours. After you say yes to the Minotaur, you say yes to the monitor. It cuts us all down to size. They rambled about some in the spring mud, which was good as we got some exercise and stress readings on his heart. The result was a mixed bag all right. The nephew kept the time and wrote down things in the little diary. He got atrial flutter as high as 280, fibrillation up to 130, and some sinus as low as 52, with variable multifocal PVCs seen rarely in nonsustained runs of bigeminal. This had gone on a long time. He said he'd felt it, but he never thought it amounted to much. I was against cardioversion. It had to be done with the anti-arrhythmic. I heard them talking out in the yard. It was like a scene out of . . . "It is beating like shit all over the place," the nephew told him. "Doing

you no good at all." "Maybe a good bump on the chest, Nephew?"
"That's for something different, Uncle. You're not a heart attack, it's
the way it beats." "Could we cut it out and fix it up?" "No. You will
have to take medication." "How long for?" "For life. All of it, your
medication." "I will never remember," he said, the brawny Indian
with the glaucoma stare. "I'll head for the canyon. Catch eagles."
They were an argumentative pair, the young one eager to please,
more at ease in a doctor's office, but his uncle interested only in the
tools of another trade: scalpels, hammer, stethoscope, the usual
things. He said nothing, but he kept his eyes on them as if wondering
how best to slip a couple of them into his pocket. His look was dark
and sly, but querulous. Then I found him right after the eye exam in
the other room, standing on the weigh machine with binoculars, a
pair somebody had left on the john cistern. He was looking at his
weight through them reversed, which must have made the numbers
hard for him to read. Maybe, though, he was just trying to make
himself dizzy, feel a long way off the ground. No hospital for him, he
said, he didn't have long to go anyway, he'd sooner wait up on the
mesa. In any case, he had worked out a special relationship with the
Almighty. Something about a bribe. I guess he prayed a lot. And he
was naked, silver hammer in his hand, half into the beginning of a
war dance, actually hopping in place on the scale, though without a
sound. Instead of getting off when told to, he waves the hammer,
looks me far into the distance with those back-to-front binoculars,
and shouts for his nephew. We wrestle him off the scale, into at least
some of his clothes, then yank the hammer and binoculars from him.
Now he starts a yowl until the nephew with the delicatest touch
imaginable cuffs him gently across the cheek and whispers something
about misbehaving in other people's kivas. He meant those underground ceremonial chambers, and I was kind of taken by that view of
my back room. Ceremonies of the blood test, the dusty new diaphragm. The uncle came to heel at once, although he fondled that
part of his face until he left. You might have thought he'd been
beamed with a two by four. I wrote out the slips and handed them
over to the nephew, who shook his head. "I'll get them," he said, "but
he'll give them to children as candies." Then, I told him, he would
have a lot of dead kids up on the mesa, their perfect hearts fouled up.
"I'll keep them," the nephew said. "You'd better," I said. "He's dangerous." After they had gone, I was congratulating myself on getting
them off and away without serious pilferage when I found the binoc-

ulars in the toilet bowl, the hammer in the cistern, and a pad of
prescription forms gone. I guess he was going to write down the sum
total of all the ideas in his mind. Up there, they get to thinking precious little. The wind unsettles them until they go stir-crazy. Their
minds are not on this world. They look through you with that
chubby-faced stare as if the angel Gabriel was standing right behind
you. You are transparent to them, I think. They left ocher mud all
over the floor and one of them, right where the sign said *we aim to
please, will you please aim,* had wet the floor like he had a watering can
with one of those tin roses fastened to it so as not to bump the petals
off. Not only that. As they walked across to the nephew's truck, one
he'd borrowed, I saw the uncle take aim and slap him right across the
face, quite hard, to pay him back, and then they walked on together
like bride and bridesmaid, happy as can be, the one senile as a loon,
the other I would think one of those very well-preserved gays, who
works out with weights a lot and watches his diet. Slim in black jeans,
whereas his uncle had a stevedore's build. A slap in the face from him
might end up being final. I don't know. He was failing from lack of
help and self-control. He could only manage another five years,
maybe more. Their faces looked alike. They both reached their hands
without any warning for things that weren't there, cupped as it were
for water from a faucet or a spring, wide apart to capture a bird or
rabbit. They both flinched at things. Every bump from outside, every
creak of the wood in the building, and they were both flinching,
craning around to see what it was. They could have been two cons on
the run, two burglars casing the house. Anyhow, I said as they were
going, You've had your matutinals good and proper, I have other
patients waiting. "Yes," says the uncle with a laugh, "but not as dead
as he is. He's from Hollywood, if you don't mind." "Mind?" I said. "I
was an autopsy man." Spelled it out to them too: *au-top-sy.* "I've seen
it all." "You've seen nothing like him," said the nephew. "He happens
to be a genius." "No kidding," I said. "Yair," the nephew said, "he's
better than that. He never gives autographs, but when he does he
carves them with a chisel right into their hands." "He doesn't sign
paper," I said, but they had gone already, bickering at a slow march
and moving their hands high through the air. I wonder who dumped
my things in the toilet as if to render them harmless while they, out
in the mud again with charcoal clouds over them, looked like two
survivors from the botching of Eden, their consanguinity the only
civil barrier left to them as they squooshed away, two undertakers

trying to undertake themselves until hellfire bared its breath and
made Indian coal of them. *De moribundibus.* . . . Those glasses have
never worked right since, but what can you do to a hammer? Some of
our tools outlast even what we do to Indians and the Latin language,
and aren't they a real pair, the Indian and the Latin, I mean, not the
other two.

Sotuqnangu

He could not get up, but the captain was pulling him without actually standing in the trench, and then he hauled a body clear, which made things easier. It was like being born cesarean fashion, he thought, being dragged into the world through innards, bones, and raw meat. There was blood all over him. He could taste it and feel its different modes, from caked to clotting and fresh flow, but what shocked him was that he could hear what the captain said, whereas he'd concluded that he was deaf, with the echo of the incessant bombardment crisp yet foamy inside his cheeks somewhere. He felt the captain checking him out, exposing him to the light like a prize plant, murmuring and prodding, and then that voice of the compassionate assessor telling him the blood was not his own at all, "You been shielded, son." He heard the rattle of a canteen and then felt water against his glued-up eyelids, seeping into his eye with a purgative sting, but, when he could see he did not look down at the mess he'd emerged from, he stared down the ravine at the sticks and the smoldering trunks of the trees. A pain through his back, he said, it must have been a splinter, it came all the way through, but the captain told him otherwise, "Boy, you are not even concussed, you are intact as on the day you were born. Now, would you like to build *me* one good intact American trooper from what is under these sandbags?" He had seen purple sponges by the sea, big khaki polyps of seaweed, that looked more human than what remained of the others. Nothing moved in that maroon and charcoal combination, and already there were flies faint-footing on what, only minutes ago, had been intimate, glistening, withheld. He tried to find the anger within him somewhere, but it was lost, and all he felt was an impersonal sickened defeatedness at the bodies' ruin, which neither heaved nor cracked a smile, neither Dennison nor Schultz, one black, the other white, but Dennison eviscerated beyond help as if his bond with Schultz, the Teuton blond, had been made blatant. Their innards looked the same, all jumbled up in the paste, the sauce, of war. He looked the captain in the eye, but the captain looked away, blinking tears, then left him to make another check, dismally calling names and questions through the windless smoky midday air. No answer came, not even a scream or a whimper, and then he saw the captain crouched over some body, beating its chest with the flat of his hand while he looked uphill to the crown, his helmet off upside down on the incinerated bracken, as if he expected help from somewhere, or the breath of life to blow down from the very top, quickening the dead man under his hand, and his hand the first to feel that movement as the rib cage lifted, the diaphragm stirred. No birds. No scurry in the blackened brush. Not even the sound of caps being busted as somebody somewhere still fought on. No squawk from the radio, no smack-flap of chopper rotors. Then he heard the tinkle of dog tags' being removed and tied together: a last reunion, but he still had the image of the captain hunched over the corpse, his face an extreme of indignant appeal, his crewcut sopping wet, his mouth frozen open, his gaze up the mountain one of total antagonistic disbelief that the lieutenant's body had been blown away during what had been essentially an observation exercise. Then the captain put his whistle in his mouth as if to call time, but he did not blow or he was sending out a signal only dogs could hear, a mute decipherable Lights Out aimed up at the Pole Star, wherever that was. There was nothing to be done, but he knew the captain, who had sent him to fetch the mail with a shotgun, had almost got him killed, that was the proof of the superstition. The others should have survived as well. *He* had brought their mail to them. He had been away, to eat steak and be sucked and flush the toilet time after time. Had he been away for a couple of days, instead of one, he would have been dead for sure. All he saw now, as with transcendent tact he overlooked the bodies, was smashed cameras, jungle boots like canvas sneakers built up to cover the ankle joint, the military knives called K-bars, unused M16s, cans of lima beans and ham otherwise known as motherfucker breakfasts, all of it wrenched from its owners and users by RPG rockets, the cut-rate shoddy clutter of combat severed more or less intact from the Dennisons and the Schultzes, who could never make a tree. "Number Ten," he said, meaning The Worst. "Dewey Canyon," he said, mouthing the expedition's name as if it held the key to bringing them all back to life, guys whose names he'd never even known. "This here," the captain told him, "was Dewey Canyon *Two*, don't you forget it," and then he walked away, not even trying to walk straight, not even seeming to aim his feet at anything in particular, almost as if trying to walk horizontally off the mountain into cleaner air. Obviously it was the name of someone, or it was so close to sounding like a name that it conjured up an autograph in some long-forgotten album: a friendly, national, comprehensive-sounding name, as American as blueberry pie. It gave the expedition class, and without exactly wondering where the name had come from, he began to murmur it, caught between aversion and doting, his mind on the one unmodifiable fact: *It was where I did not die*, although there must be hundreds of other survivors. He stood, flooded with a perverse exhilaration, spared to savor the novelty of having been spared, and all of a sudden on that blasted hillside as beautifully balanced as an eland, potent as a grizzly, as alive as the mist-swathed sun. Dewey Canyon lived on in him, and in the captain, and he knew he would never again mess about with the hands and feet, the ears and noses, of the maimed. His buddies, pulped together while they made an overhead for him, had taken him beyond such games, and this he told the captain, "Sir, Captain Bartram, I am ready to go home to the mesa." "We sure as hell are," the captain told him, casting a hand at those beeves in rags, with the body hair somehow combed or blown straight and fixed with a brilliantine of blood. "If all these maimed were brought together," he began, but paused to hawk and spit. Well, when someone is split wide open from chin to fart, there isn't much for anyone to do. Now they were supposed to head down the mountain, to link up. "Ohno," he heard, "we have to wait in this exact position." They washed their faces. One canteen, which rattled, was full of blood, they had no idea how, and there was a boyish head trapped above head height in a blackened tree, looking down the valley past them, as if tuned in to the first medevac chopper, and dangling beside it like a catkin was one of those lengths of rubber tube which hung from helmets and kept their matches dry. "What a guy needs now," the captain told him, "is something to soothe him. It's okay." They sat and smoked opiated grass right there among the carnage, waiting for some sniper to take them out, heedless of weather and rank and protocol, as if they were among the first men on the planet, obliged to give thanks to no one and no thing, two willing idiots amid the dank swill of the atmosphere, from time to time exchanging a few key words—"chone, schnitz, greased, on-a-loop, getting some"—and then like village elders whispering quiet asseverative *yairs* and *sures* before they began to giggle, red-eyed with grass and grief, slapping their thighs and the churned-up ground as if they did not know where it ended and they began. Then the captain told the story about how a tiger in the Saigon Zoo back in '63 had pissed on Henry Cabot Lodge, right through the bars of its cage, and he had said, Lodge not the tiger, "He who wears the pee of the tiger is assured of success"—they wheezed helplessly—"in the coming year." When found by the medics from the first chopper, quiet alert men with useless drugs and tourniquets, they were fast asleep and at first taken for dead, as if exploded together back-to-back, one gazing through his eyelids north, the other likewise south, but with their eyelids alive in the agitated shiver of REM sleep. They woke only when the graves registration people began trudging about with green body bags, dropping two here, five there, and everyone stared at them as if they were a couple of crazies, *isolatos*, outriders, inexplicably fallen asleep at the feast of life. Then his mind made itself the gift of believing the so-called ordeal, not so much an ordeal by fire as by insolent and unfathomable chance, was over. Fate or whatever else you called the algebra in the sky had made its choice; it had lunged at him and the captain and missed, and it would not swat them on the recoil just for completeness' sake. His legs came to life and they ran him into what, before the bombardment, would have been tree cover, but there was no foliage left, and he tried to tell his wobbling feet to send him back. No, he was not crying, no he was not mad. It was just a lot of accumulated energy that needed an outlet, and then he could be quiet and think, with his hands in his lap and his gut finally unknotted. Perhaps he and the captain would set up a small tent in what remained of the forest, trapping and cooking small game over a bit of ignited plastique explosive, with straws in their mouths to denote their retired nonchalant status, two veterans amiably reminiscing all through the dry season, which he imagined into being that very instant, mauling the calendar as it was a survivor's right to do. He was hungry and what gnawed him inside, not a hunger but a slow visceral thudding from a rubber nozzle, had to be smothered in beef and steak sauce, just to keep it from touching the wall of whichever pipe it was making hurt. By now his innocence should have gone, buffeted out of him by high explosive and low morale, but he felt he knew less than ever, it was all new and dumbfoundingly gross. The force that killed was too damned much by far; it did not merely sap the victim of his life, it butchered him up and shredded him into something like human terminal moraine, while the force that preserved kept the mind as well as the body going, which was more than the average survivor wanted, content instead to marvel at the wrists that still connected hands to arms in some miracle of lunatic exemption. *"One's coming,"* the captain said, having followed him to where he crouched in the abstract lean-to made by a couple of fallen charred tree trunks blurred by what looked like outsize tinder flung through the inverted vee. *"One what?"* he heard himself inquire, but the chopper noise was louder than his voice, it was louder than any bombardment, louder even than the white and yellow flashes that now began to puff and widen right there on the canted shelf the chopper was aiming for. *Incoming,* his mind registered, hoping it was not. But the chopper landed, they scrambled aboard onto what felt like a waterbed made of full-up body bags, and up they went only, as it seemed to him, to collide with something, not a tree but a rocket curling up and hitting the chopper sideways, and he and the door gunner briefly flew, then hit the wrecked undergrowth stiff and breakable while the chopper, backfiring like an old tractor, swung unwieldy and blazing away from the hill, hovering and threshing in the free air of the ravine until with one big and one small explosion it drifted away and down like a twirling outsize seed, and no one jumped, and neither he nor the door gunner saw any of it, the gunner knocked senseless by his fall, and the one who with a delirious doped giggle thought his name was well and truly Injun landed on his back, all breath knocked out of him, but still able to think, and obliged to believe it, *This is where I did not die.* Had it not been for the smoke he and Captain Bartram had shared, he would not have had the bravado to go on thinking that, if you kept

faith with what you lived through, you would live through it indeed.
It was not over, but he knew it was not going to end with him. It was
going to end some others like Dennison and Schultz, men of all colors
and weights and shapes. I am a piece of it, he insisted to himself, and
soon its pressure, its raggedness, its wound-up heedlessness, will even
out, and then there will be an aftermath. Another chopper is bound
to come. The rockets had done their job, the chopper was nowhere to
be seen, and he slowly got up, felt himself as if he were poultry, and
began to drag the insensible gunner toward the shallow trench still
cluttered with bodies and slashed, blood-soaked sandbags, where he
shoved and rummaged, not even wincing as he laid ahold of something soft and slippery, until he'd made a space for them. Three burst
sandbags covered the gunner, who was still out cold, and under another he put his head, bringing his arms out and over to hold it down,
like a gigantic compress for the back of his neck. He tried to think of
home, but all that came was a spray of half-relevant images that refused to mesh together: a broken gutter beneath which they had
rigged an old door to drain the flood away from the foundation of the
house; the drawer whose underside he'd lined with pencil lead, making it so smooth and slick the drawer came right out at you as if
propelled from within, showering your feet with cutlery and plastic
scoops; the motel's old toilets whose water pressure made a slight
narrow-gauge whistle, a warning about all the gallons of water that
had backed up behind the valve and wanted to get through. Home
Sweet. But the home he finally settled for, to calm his head, was one
of those French villas that fringed the rubber plantations, and what
he had to do was build one from the ground up, first excavating the
site with a shovel, in slow lump after lump, tying two earthworms
together if he found them in the same shovelful, and savoring each
load of soil, its humid mystery, its tang of sulfur mixed with lime, its
crumbly mucous clay, its lack of mind, its indestructibility. Then in
his overheated mind's eye, as the marijuana wore off, but not the
opium it had been soaked in, he brought the bulldozers in, calculating
the exact volume of the foundation, deepening it here for an un-
Vietnamese den, there for an indoor swimming pool, until the foundation had become a miscellany of shafts and wells, graves and quar-
ries, as if the villa were going to be underground, or mainly so, out of
deference to rocket attacks. Then he laid the pipes, figuring the exact
cost of pipe brought overland from Saigon, or Vientiane since this
was Laos. No, where *was* it? The villa was in the lowland, so it must

be Vietnam where he was constructing it. Conduits for air-conditioning and heat he lined with glazed earthenware lined with fine mesh to
keep rodents out, and then he pondered the problem of the floor,
quite oblivious of the fact that he had just confused a villa with no
basement with one that sat on a gigantic cellar, from whose depths
hot or cool air would rise through galvanized iron ducts, square in
cross section and wide enough for a man to crawl through, at least
until he reached the grilles in the room above. When the next chopper arrived, he was figuring the cost of hollow doors versus solid, but
he croaked at them and was lifted up and in and out. "Hide me good,"
he told them. "Hide me down deep."

Apperknowle

Whenever I come to the mesa, I wonder at the nephew, living spit of the uncle, but hewn from coarser fiber. Thicker, mighty handsome face, but too eager to please, of which you could never accuse his uncle. Testy old stick, he loves to bargain. Half the time he just refuses to sell. Lets me come all the way up here from Tucson, then decides he can't bear to part with it, offers me a Flute Player when I want a god. Carve more gods, I tell him. Oh no, he is not open to that kind of suggestion. He goes his way like an old baroque slug with his nephew licking up the drool, and him silver-lipped from all that profitable employment. I have to pay cash, he prefers silver dollars, but I finally talked him out of it after the bank ran out and refused to go along. If you paid him enough, you could use the nephew in any way you desired. He looks so—exploitable. You'd think he'd have girlie magazines around him, but instead he reads textbooks of biology. Krafft-Ebbing on the mesa. The guy is a researcher, I guess. He'll never be a carver. Something about him makes me uneasy, he has this blithe amenable open look like he could sell you anything, even the shit from your own rear end. Yes, a turd carver, that's what he'd be. I much prefer the old goat, blind and mad, but every half-inch of him a craftsman, an artist. Even his senility seems sculptural. How they stare up here, unaccustomed to the sight of an American male, white, urban, well-to-do, wearing a black cape with scarlet satin lining. It's the lining that gets them, but I have seen them pointing at my ascots too, the lime green one especially, which never happens in other places I frequent, from the rare books store on Campbell to the classical music store on Speedway. It all makes Tucson seem the core of a sophisticated civilization flung here on directed sperm from another galaxy. What would they do if they knew the furniture in my townhouse is bolted to the floor with flange and screw? When I own something I do not like it to move, least of all a human one, but that brings problems. I buy his dolls, I keep him in the black, he damned nearly keeps me in the red. It isn't every connoisseur who translates dividends into kachina dolls, just like tnat, without so much as a thought about cruises, Alfa-Romeos, a life by the sea. I am as hooked as ever I will be. The trick is to run down all the dolls he's forgotten he's carved. One of these bright days I would like to have a museum of my own, full to the rafters with his dolls, *all of them*. Nary a one missing. The Apperknowle collection of the works of Uncle George, et cetera. He's a Picasso if he's anyone, but you could always talk Picasso into doing things he'd never done before, whereas this George is wholly unbribable, lord of all he carves. "Look, there are huge gaps," I tell him, but he takes no heed of gaps, not that kind anyway. What does he want? Neither money nor fame. He wants to be left alone, like a god. He wants to be revered. He is. He wants to be immortal. He virtually is. There is this something else, though, this kind of silent begging, like the chicks of the golden plover, who dare not raise their voices for fear of predators. What he wants he is too humble to ask for, since what he wants isn't humble at all. I'll do anything for him, read the whole of *The Death of Virgil* to him in case he spots a family resemblance somewhere, or talk to him in Tagalong, the language of parasites. Anything. Tell him how, in the days before blindness, if he had looked down at himself in the act of making water, he'd have seen the fluid coming out of the meatus like a thin yellow blade tapering and then actually twisting into something wider, a lovely mutation if you study it, one of nature's incidental felicities. No, he just rattles his bag of doubloons at me (it also hold a headband, glasses, pills, cold cream, earplugs, an eagle's claw, even an old and no doubt useless condom from way back in his youth) and blathers his usual thing about an impulse from the San Francisco Mountains. What's he say? That thing? *No man decides his carving. The kachina talks to you, or not. You have to wait for the spirit to move the hands.* I personally would call that a fever of unknown origin. He's crisp about what he will not do, but mushy about the things he does. You never know. You can never quite pin him down. Even when he isn't lying, he looks as if he is. I ask him to carve for me a Cold-Bringing Woman kachina, but he doesn't even answer, he just stares away in the rough direction of the Pacific like a homing seabird, and that is that. He's boss. He is just the sort of guy who will not link how I looked when he could see to how I might look now he can't see me at all. He doesn't make connections. He just doesn't need the same kind of information as other human beings. He draws me back to him, like an old crag you expect one day to talk, or a polar bear who'll quote Edith Wharton. You never know. You, as he says in his bizarre Anglo, *gotta wait.* So I wait, with the corrupt nephew, who might perhaps be recruited or toppled into gayness, if only I had the time. See him in LA? Only when I'm desperate, and that I never am. He reminds me, daftly enough, of the young Hamlet parading around with the medal that has his father's profile on it. He dotes, he craves, he yearns to emulate, but he doesn't have the brains, the gift, the go. Verily, as they used to say in Shakespeare's time, he's one of nature's journeymen, servitors, half-malleable apes, something fuzzy between hair scorpion and tumbleweed, between pariah and pimp. Usable, no doubt, but unpoised in his differentness. If only . . . no. Keep him in reserve, for later on, for after later, with Uncle gone, the nephew in the saddle. Call me Melvyn, do. Melvyn Apperknowle: 602-524-6558. Doctor to many but Doc to none.

Sotuqnangu

There was not really a pause. The threat, or the promise of one, did not hover there in slewed futurity for imaginative hearers to fill in while the speechless threatener held his fire. It was nothing like that. His mind was full of hiatuses amid which a complete utterance figured as a long dash, a dam against the flux of broken couplings. *Interrupted* was a word he liked. It spoke his life for him. What he said aloud was rarely what he thought. Causes had strayed a long way from their effects. The statements he resumed, either aloud or within himself, were not those he began with. Two twinks held his jaw to keep him from crying out and so giving their position away. His temperature was 104.7, but he stayed on line, grating his front teeth against one another sideways, telling himself that dengue fever was just another something else. Soldier through it, it would go away. The reek of gunpowder and rotten fruit hung around him like gauze, but it was only his wholly mythic reputation as a baby killer, none of which would have come about if only his father had not strewn seed in his mother, or if Oswald had been killed and his photograph would lie forever on a rectangle of maroon velvet enclosed in a gilt-and-oak frame, fourteen inches by twelve, from the variety store, alongside his ribbons, as if in some holy concentration camp of the face. We were the blurred, he told himself, the generation put away to dry. We have no faces, fewer names. We need the mythmaker, not the man of history, the TV interview. We sublimed from vapor into frost. We were not water. We were the blurred, he began again, homing in on an echo that ridiculed fox hunting, helping the rabid to do the bloody for the blasé. No, the bloody for the biased. One day, he was sure, an utterance would come along that summed it up so well it would never need to be thought about again, as in *all hell broke loose.* Nobody ever said it that well again. What, then, of those who'd chickened out and, as if agreeing through a bull horn, had turned their backs on the tree line and the villes and the bulldozed paddies and the elephant grass, and had re-enlisted for three years so as to get a reassignment off the line, while the non coms sneered, picked their noses with their pencils, and took the cowards to their bosoms like an infestation of lice? Was anybody making history, as they were told? Not just history but world history. They would go down in history. Well, everybody born went down in history, there was nothing else to go down in. History was a piggy bank full of diesel fumes and the peculiar molasses reek of shattered rubber trees, for which, after the fighting, receipts were signed and handed over as if to maintain the continuity of property, and world history be buggered. In that denuded world, all extra syllables fell away. An ambush was a bush and the dreadful fake whiskey was 45. All of a sudden he realized that what he had needed all along was someone, such as Bartram, to whom he could *not* tell all this, giving him reverse indulgence from a stance of heedless understanding. Bartram already assumed what he wanted not to tell, and this was why he held on, hung around, neutering himself for a pittance. The wailing wall did not need to hear, it had been wailed against so much, and it had done its own share of wailing too. Bartram and he had merely taken up related positions in the same landscape, like two inmates in the LBJ, the Longh Bin Jail, one a lifer, the other a lifer in training. Given a few years in which to establish their different ways of serving time (which meant obeying it too), they would approach a unique zone together, say a forest clearing with picnic table and benches, upon which sunlight beat with scalding intensity, making the tabletop white. They would approach from different directions, Bartram coming past the ornamental iron chair incongruous in the forest, he past the just as incongruous potted plant hanging from one of the lower boughs. Artificial forest or not, it would be better than a pier, a pinball parlor, a dreamed-up lighthouse off Glen Canyon Dam. He sighed a complete, almost many-syllabled sigh. There, among those widening shafts of light, with candy wrappers and banana skins under their feet, they might sit at the big lid of light the table was and actually begin to talk. They might make history yet.

Abbott

In the light, such as it was, I could see how the mice had eaten
through the outside velvet, coming and going both ways. You'd think
they would take the easy way in through the main entrance, like feet,
but they don't, they like to chew. Caked silver slime, not theirs,
caught what was left of the light and sparkled. The mold did not. Nor
did those damp-looking patches that could have been blood. They say
this is what they suffocated his wife with underwater, forcing her
head into it, then pushing it down along her neck. They will say
anything out of boredom, especially those who have forgotten or
never knew the old stories. It would not have been on her feet or she
would have saved herself by swimming with her arms and using her
feet as a fluke. No, it must have been over her head, and the stains
were froth and spit. If so, how set his feet in it now? It was she who
ordered it from the catalog. Part of their life together, instead of
having a fire to shove their stockinged feet toward. Hers would have
been in those yellow and red striped football socks she liked to wear
not so much to keep the cold out as to prove how different she was,
how much of a man. She was laughing at the joke when they shoved it

on her, but after a while you hardly heard the laugh at all, it being by
then less of a joke. It took half a dozen of us to wrestle her down, but
the rest was easy, once the head was under. The legs flailed then
stopped. The arms we held anyway. Can this ever have been
true? From so long ago, it too has webs and mousedirt in it. They say
she was part Navajo anyway, more Navajo than anything. She could
never settle, she was like a fox among shrubs. He got over it so fast,
squirting into our father's wife. He would probably have done it in
any case, whether he had a wife or not. Of course he won't smell her
on the boot. It is his feet that are going to warm it. I carried the boot.
I am still drawn to it. I carry it now, having fetched it. "Now the
other foot, Uncle." His nephew helps, eager as ever, though what
reward he expects I have no idea. Knowing Uncle is its own reward,
and he would be the first to say.

Sotuqnangu

When he was really down, he felt like one uninvited to the feast of life, but when he was up he had the strange feeling that he was a test specimen being experimented on. That was when he sensed purpose in the awful mutation of his days from boredom to horror, from boredom with horror to ecstasy in front of something commonplace. The main thing was to find, in everything that happened, a use, a design, a means to an end. He did not want to think of the war as an end in itself, a mad machine that ate him raw. But to persuade himself the war was transitory, and that he would outlast it, called for day-to-day persuasion way beyond him. There was always the day on which he couldn't swallow what he'd made himself believe the day before, and the feeling he kept coming back to was that he was lost in a process, a growth of fungus or the decomposition of a carcass, in which he was expendable, something over which he had no control. Things looked controlled, but they were not. True, colonels had maps and radios, they planned and schemed, they took compass bearings and issued orders of the day, but this was only the most pretentious form of the jitters. It was something to do while waiting for things to go wrong. An overriding force was there to get them killed, many of them anyway, or maimed, as part of some big sacrificial offering not to the gods of war, but to perishability itself, which needed no homage. Why, he wondered, play into the hands of the very thing that wipes us all out anyway? War was a superfluous extra helping, an attempt to side with death because death always won. He was on the winning side. So were they all. Because the high-ups were not sure what would happen—some live but some die—they made the worst happen, just to soothe their minds. He had heard about the loneliness of command, the agony of having to send soldiers to their deaths, but he never believed it. Professional soldiers rejoiced in their proximity to death, the fingering of it and the provision of it; death was what they had instead of god, or art. Yes, he said, if you do it to yourself you are not a pawn, not a lamb to the slaughter. It was a faint distinction, but it explained not only war but hunting, big game fishing, and the noose, the garrote, the guillotine. Although the bonze who burned himself alive had risen to a new level of passivity, he had taken the initiative too. Maybe that was better than living the kind of double life he himself had had. Up to now. As of now. He felt his mind spin and wilt; a double life should give him double value, especially if lived under an alias, but that had not happened. Instead, his points of contact with humanity were dwindling. No, not points, *they* could not dwindle; but contacts, collisions, kisses. No one kissed him, shook his hand, patted him on the back, or placed an arm around his shoulders as if to say, "Oswald, my friend, it's not *that* bad." Well, it wasn't that bad, but it felt like an afterlife lived in preparation for something else, though what it would be he had no idea. Maybe another war, utterly silent, and with no casualties, no weapons, no enemy, but easily a million soldiers milling around in a steamy landscape, brush and jungle, wondering if there was an enemy and how to identify him since they all wore the same uniform, spoke the same language, wanted the same thing: not to be there at all. In that case, why were they there? It was as if a folk memory had persisted long past its usefulness, and they patrolled the jungle tracks, the highlands, only because they had an indefinable hangover from mere enmity, mere belligerence, nestled still in the snake brain, the horse brain, the human creature could not shed. This vision almost cheered him up, akin to the leave he refused after 365 days of war, a leave so anticlimactic and deathlike, he had actually not wanted to go back, by then unable to adjust to the world of drive-ins, milkshakes, corner drug-

stores, newspapers, dates, not to mention the ceremonious, dawdling
life up on the mesa where nothing happened that was new. He'd
listen to the daily news compulsively, with fierce unremitting nostalgia, no longer a college casualty, not yet a veteran or a patriot, but a
member of an exotic sect who had used up ten years in one, had
literally spent themselves, tuned in to something so implacable that
memory was not big enough to hold it, and the truest recall was in a
quiver of the wrist, in suddenly seeing a streetful of Americans as
cannon fodder. He was always imagining what a rocket, a grenade,
could do to them. Back in the lap of the wholesome, he would dream
atrocities; the dog Jook scuttled through the streets, and Go Ba in
black pajamas sat on the foot of his bed. What people did to occupy
themselves he would hardly see. Forever his mind saw the blood, the
bone, the muscle, beneath and behind, as if all he knew was structure,
intact or spoiled. And he had stayed where he was, a homebody, in
the spirit of someone who having had a nightmare resumes it as a
dream, better than being awake. Even the sadness of the hostesses in
the bars quickened the sense of life in him; he knew how to live
through *that*, and, like some knot of pain at last coming to the surface,
the things he knew spread out again, gruesomely unfurled, and he
smiled the sick smile of the outcast coming home when he again saw
the wonder shelters, the arrow-shaped aircraft carriers, the ranks of
wire enclosing the secure hamlets and their birds, the door of the
enlisted men's club emblazoned with a big fat number, a black unicorn, and a *Playboy* bunny. It was here that cold Cokes, ice cream,
Carling Black Label, and el-primo no-seed, no-stalk marijuana gave
their true value. Crazy, but he did not want to be reassigned off the
line, not now, to work with South Vietnamese troops because he'd
had a year or two of college; he needed to see the people of the night
again, flickering in the infrared, half-naked grunts standing up out of
their bunkers with their hands clasped behind their heads, yawning
and stretching while they watched the smoke of a B-52 bombardment
a long way from the outer wire. Through the NOD one night, he saw
an ox towing a heavy machine gun swathed in rags. He was a twink—
a recruit—no longer, but a sophomore at least, and, since this was
war's campus, accelerating you no end, maybe a junior already.
Whenever leave came he would spend it in Japan or Hong Kong, *in
the rough vicinity*, where he might fit in, and not have his mother
calling him a delinquent, and store owners, gas station attendants,
eyeing him as if he had a disease from which he should have died:

what was he doing still walking round, doing what others folks did? Not that he had evolved any philosophy of life; he just had certain reflexes he was comfortable with. Some parts of him no longer worked, but what was left was enough. He was a high-rig worker with no fear of heights, a pearl diver who could hold his breath for over two minutes, and it was beside the point that he could no longer write letters, or even read them; his mother's letters were examples of cursive script, and they fell into that category when they arrived, acknowledged as signs of her presence over there, but unread. He opened them and then just put them away. She was alive. And so was he, an empty stapler who only needed staples in order to function again. There were thousands like him, he was sure, and they were the unkilled who'd learned to cut their coats according to their cloth. Staples? Cloth? He shrugged at these civilian images; he was getting wiggier every day. Standing on top of a bunker, almost a squat steeple of sandbags, he was a target once again, almost as high as the top of the flag behind him, but this was safer terrain, and his shirt had already been shot. Clambering down, he bumped his knee, but instead of cursing he merely registered that this was what had happened to someone who no longer craved to be home in California. Seated in a folding chair almost all structure and no fabric, he glanced sideways at a stack of ammunition boxes, idly noting the words MI DUALGRAM, FUZE FOR HOWITZER, staring through the language. Nothing had ever seemed so foreign, so drab. And even the nearest word, MIST, or was it MI37?, said nothing to him. Words had come away from what they represented, and that was a blessing. That was how the deity, if any, saw him, not as a mind or a feeling heart, but as a replaceable quantum on the loose, a unit in transit until rotated out. He fell into a sit-up sleep, and then the chair fell sideways just as a dream began.

Thomas

It was dark in there and we could smell the mice. I knew by feel. One hand into it found some wads of fluff, mice wadding to be sure, and I left it in place as likely to be of extra warmth to him. Two hands in and I didn't want to go back out into the cold and put the thing over his feet, put his feet deep into it among the mouse wads, the webs, the mold. Where had it come from? Ordered from which catalog? The smell of it was something between wet buckskin and old molasses. You would not shove your face into it, but it was all right for feet. No one had used it in a dozen years, it was too fancy, it was too clever. It drew too much attention to you. Someone had walked around with it in the plaza, but with only one foot inside, which made for a lopsided walk and much laughter. Humor's the leaven, I say. This time, out came a mouse, along my hand and up my wrist onto my arm, as if it had been waiting for years in there, leaving behind its babies, its whole family. "Hello, you," I told it, but it was not much for talking. It scampered away, like a soul. Had it looked at me? Had it already gone to find him? Had I mashed the baby mice down there, shoving my fist in like that as if I had expected some enemy in hiding. George

The Place In Flowers Where Pollen Rests would shove both feet into a paste of squashed mouse. The blood would already be cold. But the boot would warm, the best part being that the heat from one foot met that of the other head-on. He could rub his feet together in it as if they were mating.

Sotuqnangu

After the second medevac chopper bundled him away at a crazy tilt, and medics looked in vain for the cause of the pain in his back and his insides, he told them he wanted to change his name. So far, he insisted, he had been an anonymous phenomenon; but no one took him seriously, and everyone began to interrupt him, which is when he developed the habit of saying "Hold the phone" to shut *them* up, after which he filled them in again on how he felt about things, with an impatient caustic anger he had never known before. They kept transferring him while what they called his psychosomatic pain kept "referring" itself to different parts of his anatomy: shoulder thigh, liver, some place behind the eyes. In the confusion he got paid several times over, then wound up giggling in a psychiatric ward, issued a lock-in razor each morning with which he shaved under supervision. Group therapy merely bewildered him as he had nothing to say, and when he at last consented to speak he spoke with such rhetorical and obscure fervor that no one understood him, least of all when he quoted. The highbrow fuckup, they called him, the fancy fraud, omnier than wigged-out. Just *listen* to him. Then they shipped him home to a temperate March whose curt sunlight made him flinch when it landed like dust on his face. He had swallowed a fishing lure, he said. Once and for all. Months passed while he blamed it all on herbicides and they told him it was all in his mind, he would get over this falling into a crouch at every firecracker, every jackhammer that snorted in the street. His discharge, when it came, was a piece of computer printout on which his Social Security number had place of honor, so he tore it up small, mixed it breakfast cereal and thick milk, and sent it through his system as if he had drafted it for arduous duty. "All I got," he told them, "was a purple fart and six ways to Sunday." But that was not how he talked on the mesa, where he was a nephew only, bound to fail, as he explained to himself in stultified midnight reveries, using up the energy allocated him to live the rest of his life with. And, because half the world sneered when he told them where he'd been, he stole a phrase from somewhere and used that to explain everything, his phantom ulcer, the choked tear duct of one eye, his sudden flinches into the crouch position, his forever looking behind him. It had been perhaps the most successful regimental-sized action of the war. I'm home, he told himself repeatedly, as if the phrase had exorcistic power, I'm home from the land of the Jimsonweed.

Sotuqnangu

That dream not a dream still felt like one. It stung. He had been where, in a much more severe and restricted way than in the life called civilian, people suddenly were just not there, all their mannerisms had vanished, there was nothing of them moving about in front of him. He kept trying to pull into the light the thing that nagged at him about it: there was some resemblance between the gaps left by those killed and the space ignored by those who went everyplace by car. What was it that made the one blank tug at the other in his mind? Maybe it was this: those who never noticed the spaces in between starting point and destination had already achieved the serenity he wanted to achieve regarding the dead. The dead left a blank it was hard to get used to, and he noticed each blank more than he noticed the living. And here he was, back in the country that devoured space and threw it aside, eager to get where it was going, whereas to ponder as he did the blanks left by the dead was really an attempt to get where they the dead had gone. He felt he would fare better up on the mesa, where most folk walked, or trudged was the better word; they had never arrived at that cross-country oblivion of the modern Amer-

ican, to whom neither intervening space nor death itself was part of
any given journey. He wanted to get it clearer, as if in readiness for
spelling it out to somebody, but only Uncle George would have listened. Not-thereness, he called it, he had never met with it before, not
even at the lowest pitch of depravity in Palookaville, where Trudy
Blue, the first of those killed in action (as he put it to himself, not
without a wince of shame), had just been there and seconds later not
been anywhere at all, and he had had this experience dozens of times
since then without having found the answer to it other than grief and
indignation. No, it was something else, not so much personal as the
sublime version of an everyday minus sign. Life, war, love, lust, all
had this subtractive quality he found unnerving, and there was always enough room for the dead to be disposed of into, just as there
were always replacements enough to keep things moving. For the
time being he formulated it like this: a people impatient with space is
adjusting to death, but he knew there was more to it than that, and he
groped after another, more complex thought having to do with, yes,
death again. The dead come back to life as soon as you have forgotten
they died or lived. Where that happened, he could not say, but he
knew you had to forget them to set them free. The more you grieved
for them, as he did for Uncle George, for Dennison and Schultz, the
more dead you made them, because the blank of their not-thereness
kept hitting you in the teeth, rather than the other blank of their
never having been, and therefore their never having died. He sighed
in the sun, having squeezed an ice cream cone to pulp. His first.
States-side anyway. A man more rational than he would never have
gone to Mr. Dlöng's motel, urged there like a madman with a tooth-
ache, eager to plant his tongue among the shuddering nerves of the
cavity. You don't want to go see the one Asiatic, do you? He did, and
Mr. Dlöng's handshake was like a handful of wet dishcloth. The man
had no conversation whatever about Indochina. Nothing to say of Stu
and Clu. Oswald did not mention them. It was not as if he had never
been away, as the old saying went; it was as if he had never been there
in the first place. He was a new-made stranger. Dlöng still had the
same perspective. "It was rough." He finally got it out. "So," the other
says. "Lots of guys not coming back." "Twentieth century," says
Dlöng. "Glate waste." "You can say that again." Dlöng does not.
This, Oswald told himself, is only the halfway house between back
there and the mesa, where your future will be at. Will the handshakes
up there be as cold and soggy as his? Already Emory was touching

palm to palm with minimum expression, Fermina was holding his hand and drawing him toward her with it, her hand scampering up his arm like a small impetuous clumsy animal, and BertandAnna were bumping untidily into him as was their way. Yes, he told himself, *we* change verb forms according to the object not the doer. You can hardly be surprised when you discover, all over again, that what matters to them is not where you've been but where you went to it from: not Treasure Island, Timbuctoo, or Shangri-La, but the three mesas under the same weather like some climatic BertandAnna. Would it seem the same old collection of ritual gestures amounting to nothing? He knew what the mesa would be like without Uncle George, he'd seen and felt that before enlisting; but he himself was different, farther along some spectrum, not of growing up (he doubted if he'd ever grow up that far), rather of being unable to take anything human anymore. An empty mesa, now that might match his needs, with just some eagles, rabbits, mice. He had heard about vets who went off into the trees and became mountain men, wild men, unpardoned outcasts and unpardonable because the only pardon could come from them, and they were no longer in a giving mood, the givingness had been shucked out of them. He braced himself, took a deep breath, saw Dlöng the Oriental grin at him with all the fatalistic condescension of the ages, and booked a flight back to Flagstaff, plunging back up to altitude, he told himself, north of which town were the San Francisco Mountains, northeast of which was the tourist gawp across the Painted Desert to the three mesas, right over the lake in which Aunt Bessie drowned, and the names did a sudden geological change from such words as Walnut Canyon and Sunset Crater, Two Guns and O'Leary Park, to Moenkopi, Hotevilla, Oraibi, Shongopevi. He felt like a truant astronaut, finding Jovians on Mars, not Anglo at all but primitive, drenched in time, unworldly, as likely to fly off the rind of the planet as to burrow deep into it. *Going home.* No, that was not it. Going away from being at home nowhere. That was more like it. Still not right, though. What, then? Getting some, as he'd said however many times back in the jungle, and he realized now that it never mattered what the *some* meant. What mattered was being alive enough to get and say get. Get anything. In a mood of sentimental completion he felt everyday welcomes would disrupt once he set foot on the mesa once again, he began murmuring the names and their Anglo equivalent, to him by now as lyrical as anything in any language he had ever heard: George The Place In Flowers Where

Pollen Rests, Bessie Butterfly Disappearing Over Flowers, Fermina
Corn That Has Been Rooted, and even Oswald Beautiful Badger Going Over The Hill, fixing his heart on what in them there was of
transient and elegiac motion, of luscious fixity, knowing that, to
them, he had long ago come to stand for Mister Facing Both Ways,
more Anglo than mesa, more ambitious than rapt. This was spring,
with the cold gone, the snow melted, the wind lashing the mud until
the mud turned to dust and the dust to clouds that needed only rain
to make mud again, and the rain came. He smiled as he sipped orange
juice and vodka, checking to see that the flight coupon and boarding
pass were tucked into the inside pocket of his—he didn't know what
it was called, flight or ticket envelope. Up on the mesa, they would
soon be planting, setting up windbreaks, plowing, and poetically
sweetening the desperado weather by calling it such things as Whispering Noises Of Breezes, whereas down in Phoenix and Tucson it
was gorgeous: dry and chastely mellow, cool at night, cool enough for
a log fire in the suites of the fanciest hotels. He knew that, during
spring, there would be no ceremonies as such, but many, many
dances. He had come home in a time of no ritual, but of much work,
and he might pass unnoticed, curtly told not to amble around like
that but to get out in the field and do the one thing he could never see
himself doing. Burning drums of excrement by the Saigon River, yes;
or making an Uncle George from Cong corpses, of course. To farming he still said his homeless no, even though most of the Palookaville
had been knocked out of him, one way or another, and he literally had
no trade or calling save that of retired exhibitionist. He could hear
the voices already. Fermina: *You don't carve, your hands are going to get
mighty bored.* Emory: *Blood is thicker, son.* Thomas: *Plant it like this.*
Abbott: *He's right. Like that.* BertandAnna: *You got any use for a cupful of
stars?* They would not know that, in his pocket, he had the cashier's
check for the wages of sin, such as it had been, he naturally having
never been paid off for the manslaughter of Trudy Blue. Then there
was his back pay. Together the two would enable him to start up a
small business in Keams Canyon, maybe the vulgarest of pseudo-
kachina dolls, or, if not that, then something more secret, a factory for
making the same, as secret as the underworld rituals in September
that match the February rituals in the upper one. He was going to
make his way in this world at last, feeling, at least in his own heart,
that he had paid his dues, made his amends, and come up with a clean
sheet. Death of all kinds he had faced down, natural, accidental, and

military, and he had begun to think he was invulnerable, not to slight things, but to the massive lunges of fatality—the kind of thing that Uncle George had become such an expert on, figuring that anything he could not understand wasn't worth understanding in the first place, mainly because the gods, excepting only Sotuqnangu, were dumb and desolate beings locked in bad-tempered shortsightedness. Oswald had no gods, but he was full of the relentlessness that grows from repeated and flukey survival; not that he in any way believed he had a charmed life, and could get away with anything. He didn't, but he did think the odds were in his favor more and more the later it got, as if he had left his good luck to compound while he was away at the wars, making the mesa a place safe for heroes and mystics to live on. He was just a touch smug about this, and he knew that he would not go blind before he had made his little into a lot.

Fermina

After so many homecomings that did not take, he has come back. This
one will work. I'll make it work. Sometimes a woman feels the world
has gone right and she feels so small, so kind of come through it all,
that she wants nothing more, content to spend the rest of her days
lowered, at last in her place with all her sweetness around her, no
more your uppity missus, breathing real gentle and shallow because it
is all right now and the line around her is complete, it is all she asked
for all she ever wanted a bit of trim here and there but at heart she
wanted to sit by the fire and say the same things over and over again
out of elated gratitude then touch a hand to each just like this their
shoulder or their hair their hands than which nothing is closer and I
was always one for hands whether I think of myself as a big or a little
woman neat or untidy it has been either way these years cleaning a
wire hairbrush with a pencil I have only to push the eraser against
the rubber bulge and the bristles all come back like something new-
grown back to their old length Oswald Emory Abbott Thomas my
kin and kin has a smell to you they don't need to be looked at only

touched or sniffed it comes natural and at heart I hear some very far off piano music about all folks being together under a roof of flowers though tiles would do where it is warm and I only live through them I live no other way.

Fourth World

Sotuqnangu

He talked to Emory about all kinds of things, but couldn't bring himself to talk about Vietnam except in casual, terse references that omitted so much they might have been allusions to quite a different war, the Boer, the Crimean, the battle of Dien Bien Phu. Least of all could he voice the extraordinary sensation of having begun in orthodox terror, which told him he was human, only to graduate into reflex acts of sick relish, after which he had turned to the war as his natural ethos. Not only had he volunteered to walk the plank, he had gone on walking with the plank far behind, strolling on the air of carnage and alienation, a being exempt, whose life decided itself in the simplest way: if you gave up enough, then what remained was safe. Or so he thought. Folly, of course, and a secret part of him knew that; but more often than not he mustered a smile, and the smile lifted into his mind, from where he could not remember and did not care, Buddhist clergy in gold and yellow robes, crouching in front of a barricade of concertina wire while one of their number, in a pale blue smock, addressed them through a microphone linked to a battery in a shoulder bag. He liked their faces, their look of powerful introversion, their downcast gaze, and how many of them wore horn-rimmed spectacles. There were even times he would imagine himself in just such a golden or yellow robe, and he would crouch, gaze unanalytically at the ground through thick lenses, and leave all the talking to someone else. His head would be shorn, of course, like theirs, to cool his brain, and at his shoulder there was the short pole that bore the yellow flag with three horizontal red stripes, a flag long enough to drape the face of the bonze behind him after the fashion of a hooded mantle worn by an Arab. *Burn us,* he whispered, they have a word for it. When one of the bonzes shifted position, supporting himself with a hand flat upon the soil, he was careful not to let it stray into the space of those seated beside him. The line was invisible but it was there, magnetic and keen, a border between contemplations. "You see," he'd tried to tell Emory, "it was their way in that part of the world, but nothing came out." There was no getting this abstruse and almost illicit self-promotion into the rough and ready of everyday talk; it had to remain a private dimension, fatuous no doubt and even smug, but he would have it (he reasoned) so long as he never expressed it. He had gone away a boy and he had come back a man, as some wiseacre slack-mouthed it. The truth was much different. He had gone as a youth and come back a child, he almost said a child of God, but he held back from that, saying only a child of nature who had killed as nature killed, with the same out-of-the-body abstractness as allowed his hair to grow, postwar, into a pony tail, beneath which there crinkled always the shaven skull of the bonze. Not for him the quick nibble of the electric typewriter; what had happened had congealed deep within him like a lodestone, and the world was wide open for him to turn carpenter or mailman, horse trainer or mud engineer on an oil rig, millwright or welder, except that he had turned to none of these things. He had gone out there like a compass registering magnetic north, and now his north was true, a zero that existed only in the minds of aspiring humans. There was no need to try, he was already immersed in the livingness of life, he was a piece of the planet's fabric being used, even while asleep or inert. His cells paid his dues, and he was at last secure in some postwar limbo in which the only sound was that of radios being clicked on and off, the old signal that things were so bad you dared not even whisper a warning, although now it meant nothing about danger, it said only that he was present at the switch, and that there was nothing to say except danger, don't hardly breathe. That swift, clattery click was coming from the battery in a bonze's bag as he stood erect in his blue shift, with not one of his words coming out, but only the click-click of acute danger, about which the seated priests in gold and yellow knew everything since it was their stock in trade, long ago minified into a token presence to be reckoned with and then, over the course of successive ages, relegated into a humdrum norm, like the existence of flies.

"Come with me," Emory said, and Oswald went along like someone in a trance. "Feel at this," Emory whispered, and Oswald took from him something light and grey, shiny-soft like graphite dust, in the rough shape of a French loaf. "It's a piece of moon rock, smuggled down," Emory told him. "You mean like the seven-foot petrified man made from beef and blood and egg whites and iron filings, the one they found in upstate New York last century? I keep track of these things," Oswald said. "I know something about them." Emory half smiled: "Well, what an outburst. I could sometimes really think you were my own son. Actually," he said, "they made a big cake, with sugar and molasses and salt and phosphorus as well, and then they carved it into the figure." Oswald's mind was on the Nuncle George he had pieced together in a distant jungle, but Emory wanted to pursue the seven-foot man. "All right," Oswald said, "you mean the one with its hands clasped on the front of its right thigh, covering its privates. I've seen pictures. I saw them long ago. I saw them only the other day. They finally tossed it into some lake." "Well, Oswald," Emory said, "this is nothing like that. Not what I have here. It's for a client, who requested it. I supply things of all kinds." "Yes," Oswald told him. "It was you who flooded the market with all those Mickey Mouse kachina dolls. And Minnies. And Donald Duck and Goofy." "We did them on demand," Emory told him. "Well," Oswald said gently, "Uncle George would kill you on sight with his bare hands. If he could come back." "*Uncle* George," Emory said with a bitter twist of his full-lipped mouth, "my brother, nearly killed me and several women with his bare penis. There should have been some way of stopping him, but he got away with all kinds of things. You happen to be one of the results if that pleases you any. Now, this moon rock." "No," Oswald told him. "I don't care to." "The real thing," Emory was murmuring. "Feel how sleek and cool it is, how light." "Like Mickey Mouse," Oswald said. "Thousands must want one. You're made again, Emory." Emory attempted a growl which didn't quite come off: too fast, too high-pitched. "I," he said, "fought pain with money. I was *made* years ago." "You never," Oswald began, but Emory was taking the thing off him, positioning it with dainty care within a blue velvet bag. "If you could fit wings to it," he said, "it'd fly." "What's the point," Oswald said. "To fondle it," he said, "to stroke it, to know you have it." "Then when," Oswald asked him with outrageous solemnity, "are you going to show me the Martian's hand, the slice of rainbow, the unknown animal from the heart of a comet? Uncle George's wonders were in his head." Nothing fazed Emory, however. "That brings me to what you're here for. You're invited, don't forget." Already guiding him through an archway, then past a small lake, to a rear door, he commanded Oswald to tread gently and use his eyes. Oswald saw only a field full of buttercups, pale yellow, and was going to turn away to face the stately hunting lodge–type home when Emory said, "No, watch." Nothing happened. Why wasn't some goat munching the grass in between the buttercups? There was no in between. "I don't need a pastoral scene," Oswald said, "from Winslow to take back to the mesa. I can go hug Mama a hundred times a day. Somebody has to." "You're still not looking," Emory said. "Don't you see? Only once a year and I waste it on you," he said. "It's all a matter of timing." Now the lemony hue in the yellow fluttered in the breeze, although without seeming to bend back the stems. Then the whole thing seemed to lift as if the buttercups were growing at enormous speed. Oswald heard an engine pounding somewhere and coming close, some plane no doubt. The bed of yellow quivered, became an untidy magic carpet and lifted up of its own accord, the heads of the flowers wafting up from the stems as if sucked by an updraft. The whole field of flowers was on the move, had risen several feet above the ground, the grass, and was moving away from the two of them as well as upward, and Oswald could see that it was a mass of yellow monarch butterflies, ruffled, jerky, windblown, but there were so many of them that their erratic moves just linked them all the more together, and off they went, now at roof height, like a big pale yellow comforter heading for another field, for other eyes. Or, Oswald wondered, was this one of those times when, instead of things lifting with him, he began to sink away from them, tugged by some vengeance of gravity, down into a shaft of his own making that began cool but got hotter the closer he came to the center of the Earth. He had had this sinking, swooning feeling

before and ascribed it to his ulcer, but never with something so lovely
in view. He willed them back, even if they were Emory's, but how
should he plead with a host of butterflies, with an Emory watching,
looking at him down the shaft. He tried to hold on, but the distance
increased and he knew he would never have such a chance again.
Burn it into your brain, he told himself: you could have gone and
walked gingerly among them, barefoot and tiptoe. You might even
have flicked a few hundred aside and made a place to lie down among
them, your head at the level of their conjoint wings, listening, rubbing noses. Oswald would at last have vanished under a tapestry of
moonshot yellow, unseeable except for the faint stir now and then of
the butterflies over his nose and chest. He would have died from
inhaling wing dust, that airy mustard seed of the lower air. He would
have died of delicacy. "You really laid it on," he told Emory, gasping.
"You can't lay things on," Emory said. "It happens, almost to the day
each year, like the swallows coming back to Capistrano. It's what I
have. It's what I have because, in other ways, I have so much I don't
want." Oswald was not ready for what Emory did next, but knew he
was supposed to feel shocked or won over. Emory's fly was open and
his organ lolled against it. "Nothing wrong with it, is there? Here,
feel." He forced its fatness against Oswald's thigh. "Fermina, your
mother, didn't like it any." His face was red with heat and rage. Was
he going to slit it all the way down its length, as in the old Arab
custom? Oswald dismissed the thought, tried to fix on the helicopter
he thought had disturbed the butterflies, or they might have stayed
and foraged for days. "Look," Emory said, "how clean it is, how
average. Not one of your monster ones. It was never in no horse or
sheep, no loaf of bread, no man. It fills a woman up, so why would she
want George instead of me? I have learned lately that a man comes to
a certain point. He begins to look back at things, the life he's actually
had. No more room for dreams. As if the clouds had blocked the sun
for a while. He says, Oh this was when, and on he goes, at last seeing
that accidental things have become final ones. He doesn't like it. An
Emory says, Oh, this was when a George The Place In Flowers
Where Pollen Rests must have sprayed sperm into my wife and so
given me a so-called son. I get to be the father in name. Then we tune
up all the finer shades of uncledom until I feel close to being your
natural father. Let it pass. As I say, I look back and I suddenly feel
about life like somebody who's been long years in a wonderful balmy
climate and one evening it gets cold and starts to rain, Oswald, and he

says Oh, good, I'd almost forgotten how wonderful a brisk crackling fire can be, the pleasures of having the doors and windows closed, the warmth of the comforter on the bed, the closeness of other bodies while we sleep. He doesn't mind if things have gotten chilly. Secretly he's rather glad. I ought to kill you, but I'm not the killing kind. Have you ever been castrated? If you had a knife you'd maybe want to cut it off at the root, wouldn't you? Tell me, though. You're the son, the *offspring*. What was *wrong* with me?" Oswald groped. "Mama was looking for novelty, man. Uncle George, he was mighty forceful. He could be." "Especially if there was a woman at the other end of it," Emory said with a manicured snarl. "Look, Uncle," Oswald said, "leave it alone. You made it in spite of everything." "I made shit," he said. "It is too damned late." Emory quietened, adjusted his fly, then got a second wind. "Even if you was going to be shot by firing squad," he said, "and the last thing that happened to you was to have Cleopatra come and kiss you, then your life'd be richer, wouldn't it, even if they shot you just the same?" I want to go, Oswald thought, I don't care. I don't want to visit his bigshot's house, see his rock, his cock, his dough, or anything else. The butterflies were good. Let's leave it at that. I would like to go after them, never mind where they headed. Uncle George's wife was Bessie Object Disappearing Over Flowers, and that is pretty much what the butterflies have done, vanishing by flying above themselves. Sometimes they called her Bessie Butterfly. She too flew off, was in the habit of flying away, to swim or whatever else. You have to leave the mesa sooner or later. Unless you're Fermina or Uncle George. Emory was at last sealing his groin away, although not without, Oswald's keen eye noted, a faint pretense of difficulty, as if what was being stowed away was too big for its allotted room. No man is his penis, Oswald tells himself; he has no need to be, though some of us have come mighty close. He let out an Indian cry, realizing all of a sudden how he sounded like someone trying to talk through a yawn. He wanted to sign something, the guest book or a travel voucher, and have done with Emory. When I write *Oswald*, he wondered, and people see that little curlicue on the top of the *O*, do they expect my head to have a little hair quiff to match, pointing forward with the same eager lift? The day he arrived back in the States, amazed anyone could do anything so prosaic as arrive back from what he'd seen, he'd seen a sign saying COMBAT ILLITERACY and for a moment thought it was a disease that soldiers picked up while Over There. Now he was walking toward Emory's house after all, in a series of shuffling lunges, as if walking had at last been denied him along with almost everything else. "Good night," Emory had said to him as he walked away, dismissing Oswald's view of life rather than Oswald himself. *"Gnite."* It was the transcendent goodbye invalidating all subsequent greetings. From this place, this house, this lodge, this home, Emory was going to have Oswald driven home by a man in chauffeur's uniform who had to be paid double to go up to the mesas at all, certainly in this season when dust was mud. But Oswald knew that once he was home Fermina would mop his brow and wash his feet. Or something like that. For once, he thought, he was getting maudlin, with help from a vengeful memory.

Now, in a present so doomed-feeling he thinks the recent past enclosed it like a flower in a paperweight, his eyeballs have begun to pain him, the sockets for some reason are squeezing them. A slight drying and crinkling of the skin on his hands has begun too, brought on by nerves. One of the toes on his right foot will no longer bear his weight when all of a sudden he turns and changes direction. Who, he wonders, is affecting him. I do not let him know. These and other bits of ache and pain he has brought again and again to Fermina, who dismisses them as Anglo maladies curable by some thousand deep breaths of mesa air, by the scores of spiders who will soft-gait over him during the next few months. He has not brought Emory back with him, nor will he. There is no bringing Emory back; he has moved on to another stage in life, along with his profits. Emory has always been astounded by how much money you can make by giving the market what it wants, even in the realm of fancy goods rather below soap, suitcases, and oils to bathe in. His dolls have made him rich although more and more eccentric, and the Sigafoose factory goes on making them fifteen hours a day. He is a man not often heard from who will be heard from less and less as he leaves his money to work for him while he tans, lazes, and dreams, wondering what the big deal about fatherhood really is, and pampered by Ellen the former nurse and army technician who never learned to draw blood without leaving a bruise. Oswald has come home again, a gratuitous ghost, thinner and feebler, a weird sight with his ponytail and earring, the way he hunches over where he thinks his ulcer is, like a whole planetary system of a body crowding in around its sun, ever closer. No more than his Uncle George does he have much faith in doctors, in

Keams Canyon or anywhere else, having decided to bear it without
grinning, to pay himself back for being what he likes to call less than
loyal. He is not so much a veteran, in his own eyes, as a leftover, a
trace, a ranting eyewitness, determined now to embrace his heritage
or die in the attempt. Stu and Clu traipse through his mind daily,
although that was years ago. He has not returned at all to
Palookaville. His money is with him, wrapped in plastic bags and
hidden in Uncle George's old shack together with the remaining
kachinas, which he'd kept all along in the tough silver-colored plastic
garbage bag. Two dozen kachina dolls, cushioned in torn newspaper,
occupy little space, not much more than a newborn lamb, so his portable world is a discreet thing, neither heavy nor cumbersome. He
has come home in the spirit of someone who has been operated on
and waits to see how well things have gone. A month or six, it matters
little to him; he has no intention of ever going away again. Surely the
mesa has enough manna to help him resume his life with dignity and
gladness. Thinking so, he seems an optimist, giving in still to some
assumption about the goodness of the Sotuqnangu whom Uncle
George, but almost no one else, carved. There is a tidal wave of comment, though, on which he tries to thrive, say what they may. "The
whipped dog returns to his vomit," for which Fermina slapped Abbott. "The pride of Los Angeles is lickin his wounds," for which she
did not slap Thomas, who never goes quite as far as his testy brother.
"Him come a-begging, he got to be given to," say BertandAnna.
"Him fought de war for all of livin human folk, Engines as well, and
he gotta get back inside his skin, fur and all fore he freeze up like
some car. One day them Japs will try again." BertandAnna will never
get beyond the first two world wars, their vision of the enemy being a
German doctor in a Japanese helmet with leer and mustachios, right
out of four or five propaganda movies from the second war, seen in
Keams Canyon on birthday treats, for convenience their birthdays
having been made one, Bert's, March 16. No one quite knows the
year. Flagstaff is as far away for them as Borneo, but they have in
their time made expeditions, mostly with Bessie Butterfly Disappearing Over Flowers to watch her swim, and mostly by pickup truck.
They no longer remember the time she failed to come back to the
surface of the lake, and they did not know how to help or even drive
the truck, so they just hugged each other tight, in their wet clothes, in
the cab and waited for the next thing to happen. Ever suspected, yet
never thought capable, they have blotted out what they cannot under-

stand, but the scene endures for them. They know they did something bad in the lake, actually overwhelming Bessie without meaning to, ever reluctant to part their hands and so achieving four hundred pounds that still weighed heavy in water. At the back of their minds, they wonder sometimes why things didn't go wrong the first time out, but it took them several dips to overcome their fear, after which they became grandly sure. They remember Bessie as kind but chiding, one who remembered everything and wanted others to do the same, whereas mostly they have made a career of letting memory drift like ink diluting in a glass of water, the only thing that matters being to *Hi* anyone who comes near, which is their version of living for the moment. The police will long remember their vivid, useless testimony, full of *she deep down and all froth* and *her up again once a yellin out* and *them little brown ducks tryin to lift her up us underneath her her like the root of some water flower.* When in doubt, they said the name of a color or a time of day, or patted some part of the body. Their mummery accompanied an unnecessary accidental death, but their joint mind lifted away at once to other matters, such as, in the tribe, the house belonging to the wife, the covering of windows at someone's birth, the unsatisfactory taste of batter without egg. Several times, in the old days, at Matlock's prompting, some sort of move was made to have them put away, but in the eyes of civilized folk they were already put away just by being where they were on the mesa among all them Engines. So they have mostly been left alone, to greet and beg, to hang around and mumble, harmless harbingers of some terrible day when everyone will be born like them, as Matlock said, *dumb, numb, and then some.* They like Oswald, though, and in their cloudy, shoving way have welcomed him back, almost as if deputed to represent to him the low status he will have, the kind of folk he belongs to, as distinct from other folk who belong to themselves and those like them. What ails them he will catch. It will rub off. "It'll soon," says Abbott, "be BertandAnnaandOz. We'll have to run a rope around them to keep them together lessen they stray into the main herd." Slap-slap from Fermina. Why does he say these things to her? Could he not murmur them to himself or to the squeamish, gentler Thomas? "You, Abbott," she says, "you are going to get a mouseful of cleanser one day soon, you older than him, you oughta know diffrant. I'll break your back for you before you scare him off. Oswald has been away to war and he not the boy he was. He better." When really pushed, she uses Oswald's words to scold them, as if to invoke horrors they need never know, but worth threatening them with: *PalOOKaville, NegatOrio, the Ameche,* any one of which will kill at a thousand yards. They cling to her, snidely fawning, two prudes she doesn't know are prudes, but dismisses as grown-up jailbait, cannon fodder, good experimental material for hospitals. The son she wanted by her was too long away. Now he is back, he himself has become the criterion to be judged by. He can do no wrong, no right, his thereness sufficient like an Anglo angel made of dawn-colored ribbon. Uncle George's shack has no electric light, not even a kerosene lamp, but only candles, which Oswald is glad to have. They make him feel he is living by Uncle George's unused ration of earthly light. He has the old haversack too, with the moldy pills, the ancient condoms, the cold cream, the earplugs, the headband, the glasses, the eagle claw, and the wad of twenty-dollar bills rolled up in place of the batteries in Uncle George's blood pressure machine, which no longer squeaks or churrs. Could Oswald but carve, he would. The atmosphere is right. There is enough wood lying around for three or four dolls. There are the paints. The tools. The dust and shavings. Fermina kept it as a shrine, vaguely hoping that one day a small plaque would go on the door saying who George was and what he did (some of it, anyway). After all, his work would be gone from the mesa by then, scattered among stores and museums and collections and private homes. By candle-light Oswald counts with the door barred, the window blocked with Uncle George's old plaid scarf. Now he thrusts the bills into the fleece-lined two-feet boot that Abbott and Thomas used to go fetch for Uncle George's chilblains, and there he sits, knees drawn up under his chin, pining for a movie, a pinball parlor, a war, and above all someone to love to whom he is unrelated: some stranger whose neck will not break too easily, whose breath will not fail like a newborn bird's. He hears the wind of early autumn, smells snow on the air like shredded smoke, hears ghosts thumping in the ground under him, senses the spiders plying their trade in corners, and wonders why he told Fermina almost nothing about Emory. She did not ask. She would hardly believe it. A man of many faces, Emory, he thinks, is going to die in a head-on collision between his Mercedes and a Rolls Royce driven by a banker. Fermina's face is like an open wound with the bleeding stopped, but only by some invisible tourniquet wrung tight within the skin of her neck. She chokes on absence: George's, Emory's, Oswald's (that part of his absence he will never be able to remedy), and maybe Bessie's too, without which George would almost certainly have left Fermina alone, not having enough energy even in his prime for both carving and the hot demanding flesh of Bessie Butterfly. So: absences over and done with grieve her still, as if a divine pattern has been broken up, and its slew will deform their lives for ever, as she thinks it must if she is ever to rid herself of guilt. She has paid, yes. She has to go on paying, though only she knows why, she should have drowned, or died in childbirth, or gone to work at Sigafoose and gotten rich on what was made with lathes. She hugs Oswald tight as if he were only thirteen years old with a high fever.

Maybe to make his mouth water, Fermina tells him what she is going to cook for him, and his mouth goes on watering although she never quite gets to the actual meal. It isn't so much a planned repast as a loose, excited jumble of treats, to be cooked and served in any order, not necessarily served in the order cooked and not even cooked in the order served—some of it is going to reach him raw. "Rabbit corn bread," she tells him, "what the older folk prefer, special when they recall how hard times were, but you have to get the bowels from a freshly killed rabbit." "I don't deserve it," Oswald says, "I haven't done that well or been away that long." "In that case," Fermina says, "a fat prairie dog, I say fat because fat ones are milder to the taste, you got to singe the fur right off to budge the fleas." Oswald falls into a prudent silence, hoping she will forget all about it, his mind on how prairie dogs will stand on their hind legs to kiss and nuzzle, paws in front of them like boxers or humans eating corn. Whatever she cooks from her garden has come from her own mother, since daughters inherit their plots from their mothers, making an unbroken chain of chilies, especially where plentiful spring waters flow beneath the earth's surface where the terraces gardens are. Now she is on about muskmelon and how hard it is to save it from the cats, who love to get among the melon strips left out on the rack to dry. "In the old days," she tells him, "we women used to go out in working parties when the peaches were ripe. We had to sweep the dirt off the rocks, then split the new fruit and put it on the rocks to dry. Trouble is, the weather changed and did not change back, so now we have poor fruit crops because of late freezes, so you'll have to do without." "It's all right, Mama," he tells her, "I'd just as soon have some piñon nuts, roasted with a touch of salt, I've been away too long, I'd just as soon have cornmeal sauce." "That's only for folk who's ailing," she says, "or very old." "Well," he says, "just *look* at me," and she does that mellow, slightly confidential laugh of hers, as if she's laughing at something different from what everyone else is laughing at. "I'll go get you some water," he says, "I can drive. While you plant the food. I'll head out to the windmills." "In the bad days," she tells him, "children weren't allowed to play with water, not to splash or paddle, not even to put a bit in a thimble for our dolls to drink when we played house. And when you went visiting, and you felt thirsty, you had to come home, Oswald, so as not to waste their water." "Bad old times," he says. "At least we knew what we was doing," she says, her mind on sun chokes rubbed with oil or enfolded in silver foil and baked like potatoes. Cushaw squash she offers him, the green-striped, but he is remembering something from his childhood about wolfberry jam and potato clay, the fine clay found at the mesa's foot. "Make a thick cream of it," he says, "and you use it as a dip against the acid in the wild potatoes." "You got a memory," Fermina murmurs, moving on to corn smut, with which Oswald too has smeared his face to look frightful. "Dandelion greens," she says, and he is quick off the mark, telling her that they eat these in Palookaville too, with oil and vinegar, and they are a great delicacy if picked when young. She has been asking around for lamb, but there is none to be had, the last lamb being killed and eaten when Thomas's ewe had twins. One they butchered and one they kept, to make the ewe's life easier. "Beef jerky," she says. "Long thin strips?" She is trying him. "So long as it is oven dried," he says. "That's better, always." He knows he has been away, for various reasons, but he still marvels that things go on much as before, the women still preferring to mash their chili paste by hand. Only the youngest use blenders. If your sauce tastes too hot, you stir in an egg. He knows the old routines, the wearing of rubber gloves when you handle hot chilies, or, if you have no gloves, the whole business of not touching your face, lips, or eyes, then washing your hands as soon as you can, then rubbing them with a gentle oil. It comes back, like a fountain springing up from the soil through the tracery of blood vessels in his arms and legs. She is giving him back to the earth, his birthright, through his belly, or she would if only she would cook instead of talking about it. All her days, she has thrown cooking ash into the pan in which her corn is boiling. Always an enamel pot because the ashes do something funny to metal ones and the metal ones to the hominy. Who first discovered this? Did they have names back then? Before thumbprint bread, fingerbread, before greasewood stirring sticks and peach-twig *piiki* trays? He has never gone to mine salt in the Grand Canyon, or in the Zuni lands, but he knows how his grandfather did it, always fancying a touch of rock salt on his blue marbles, doughballs made of blue cornmeal, blue being the most religious color, as in the Catholic religion of the Anglos, though for different reasons. "Well, Mama, what will I get?" "String beans," she says. It will have to do. He knows how to do it, too, holding on to the end of the pod and pulling the bean forward between his teeth to take out the string. The string he then puts on the rim of his plate. "I'm better at fasts, really," she says, giggling. "I mean after fasts." "When," he says, like someone reciting under hypnosis, "you have to drop a bean into the sand to see if it's hot enough and if it is the bean browns or you drop some water in and if it sputters the sand is hot enough as well." "Parched beans after a fast," she says. It was always like that, best done with older beans from the year before. "After four days," he tells her, "it ought to be refried beans at least," and she knows what he means, the essence of the fast being food without fat or salt, coffee and Kool-Aid permitted. An empty belly, he was taught, brings you closer to the Creator, in which case, most of all in Winslow although sometimes in Palookaville, he has been close, almost perched on the deity's cloud-capped shoulder. Whenever Oswald looks up from whatever he is reading, there is Fermina with a powder of flour on her nose and cheeks, her hands and wrists clotted with dough as she heaves and shoves the mixing basin, getting it right, not too sloppy, not too stiff, and then the bits of dough end up on her face as she wipes it with the back of her hand, or even on her hair, once combed outward into two sharply angled cones like buffalo horns. All she does now is wear it short, much shorter than his, but she has not complained, nor has she asked what book he is reading, if reading rather than dipping is the word. She is making him something, that much is clear, and it looks like fingerbread, all he wants is for her not to ask about money or kachina dolls. Her mind seems wholly on cooking these days anyway, and he wonders what he is going to do, alone in Uncle George's ill-furnished shanty, in a place where he cannot weigh himself, play pinball, or find himself a girl friend who knows where Vietnam is. Back to college, he thinks, but college is no realer to him now than beheading is a severe form of hairdressing. Every now and then his world shunts, quivers, goes all wrong, upside down and out of focus, as if he has swallowed wrong, and, he knows it, he just knows it, Stu and Clu have been dumped into the Hanoi River in two oil drums filled to the rim with dung. *It's all over, Oswald. They are not there anymore. They have moved over so that the living can spread themselves again.* He is sleeping later and later now, getting up at noon, and staying up half the night either reading by candlelight or just musing, sniffing the cool air outside, the cooler air indoors, wondering if the soul or spirit can leave kinds of thumbprints, on the sill or the wood or the walls, and waiting for himself to change, maybe like the bisexual slug which, in the act of mating suspended from a strand of slime while intertwined with another slug, sprouts from the side of its head glossy and fragile sexual organs of startling white, a mix of fungus and jelly, with frills and teats for the asking. That kind of change, after which both slugs retract their organs; one falls to the ground, the other climbs its tree. Except that, for Oswald, the organs would remain forever outside his head, the side of it, like an erupted sousaphone announcing his difference from humankind and even slugness, blatantly in the market for something or other, but unlikely to find it on his home planet without getting into trouble again, even while nibbling a piece of fingerbread broken off between finger and thumb. It is eating blue cornmeal ground medium fine, and two cups of water, but also like eating his mother's hands, their dipping and stirring motions, their flex, their pauses and lunges. He is masticating her movements, the motion she put into the bread in welcome on his return, drawn to do so not by the residua of ritual (she more homespun than formal), but by some long-resented resentment of him as a child when, just perhaps, she fed him badly out of rage, denying him seconds, hurrying him up, refusing his thanks or praise, because he by coming into this world unsigned had lost her a husband, the true peace that aloneness has a right to bring, and the unquestioning adoration of Abbott and Thomas. That is how it was, she thinks, and he doesn't really know, he has lived too much in other places to know any more what went wrong in this. And, of course, in the end she had lost him to George, that ultrapaternal uncle, to whom a woman was merely a vessel, a dam, a mixing bowl, a bowl for boiling corn in, a place for his grease-wood stirring rod to plunge and squirt. The fingers in the fingerbread are hers, but they keep on growing back and whole, and Oswald is eating her out of hands and home, a result, she's sure, of living alone and staying up all hours looking at the sky, he says, wondering if Uncle George will beam down on him for a holy instant. He sees the meadow in which the stars seem to stammer, and he wonders *why so much of it*, why such a colossal spread having nothing to do with us at all? If they have a message, it's in code, you have to make the best of it, like leftover fingerbread crumbled up in hot water to make a tasty and, unless you add dripping or chopped meat, not very sustaining breakfast drink. Now he talks the language of Fermina after all, whose idiom to herself in her communings has been spastic and uncouth as if, under the dainty cooking apron, she is only blood and glands and syrup, like something improperly cooked and served up before the world half-ripe. Could she, he wonders, make a nourishing dish by cooking a pair of entwined slugs with their sex organs at the ready and out, like they were on the Ameche or something, big white fins at their ears to pull in the message from Sotuqnangu? He has sickened even himself with this, though it is no worse than rabbit intestines. Cut off the forelegs at the first joint, then cut the skin off the back legs, this is not exactly like berthing an ocean liner, after which tie the back legs firmly together, when you hang the rabbit upside down from a hook to haul the skin down off its thighs, then off the trunk, the head, the front legs. You then throw it away unless a trophy hunter. Now cut the back feet off at the heel joint and, this is the part that separates the greenhorns from the pros, with a keen knife slit the carcass down the front, careful not to cut too deep, and pull out the tripes. What is left can be cooked although with the constant promise of disease, and this is why Fermina buys from the market, a nice change from the parched desolation of the land on which she lives, mirror of her life as mandated by one husband, one brother-in-law, and three ill-assorted sons. Now grind the intestines well and fine so long as they come from a freshly killed rabbit. Waste not, want never. Where has he brought that from? Where has he *brung* them from? He too likes the past form of the verb to be the past participle, putting the pastness of things beyond doubt. He likes to say *I have ate*, just like Fermina, whose *He has went* has always struck him as the most final thing he's ever heard. She herself has yet to learn the difference between the so-called strong verbs, that change their vowel, and the weaker ones that don't and simply add *-ed*. *Uncle George died* sounds to him too weak and temporary, as if it really ought to be *dieded* or even *dode*, which he has never heard a human say, though he thinks there will soon be a first time, so harsh is life up on the mesa, as in Palookaville, as in Keams Canyon, as in Winslow, as in Vietnam. The language we talk, he decides by moonlight, hasn't caught up with how bad things are. I don't blame Fermina for burying herself in cooking. Hands deep in the dough is just like body deep in the earth. It comes to the same thing in the end. Whatever you lose yourself in, as we say, amounts to a rehearsal for when you're really lost to yourself, if that makes sense. I wish I could have told that to Uncle George. If I whisper it loud enough, though, either Abbott or Thomas lurking at the window will pick it up. Who do they think I've stashed in here? Miss America? They watch to see the dough and the kachinas, but all they see is books by candlelight. "Now we got you all fixed up," Fermina says, as if she has fed him on the fat of the land instead of an outsize portion of fingerbread, "I got to ask you a question why you kept goin and goin away, off mesa all the time." He wonders where to begin, if at all, trying to fix in his mind the point at which he knew he could not stay around Uncle George anymore, when he knew adoration had its limit, not to mention embarrassment, and shame honed down to a fine pencil point. Uncle George had his grandeur, to be sure, but of a narrow sort, and in truth he never needed anybody but himself, he needed Fermina, sum total, maybe about an hour and a half, which is what his climaxes and passages of insensate, unwilled need amounted to. Oswald tries to begin to start to intimate this to Fermina, but something clamps him down. It is not something he can say to his mama, the used, the defiled, the betrayed, who these past decades has kept body and soul together mainly by not thinking about anything, but making of her mind an empty apron pocket, cleansed even of its fluff. "No," he tells her. "It wasn't any one thing." "Which things, then?" He knows, all right, but he isn't going to lay it all out for her, he the apple of her eye. I left Uncle George, he tells himself almost in rebuke, because I was his *audience*, and it is the role of the audience sooner or later to go away just as it came. An audience is not permanent, any more than a parasite is, a brown-noser, a bumsucker. You ask for trouble in spades, don't you, if you go on treating your real father as your uncle, once you know who's who. That's why I swung to his side the whole time until, natural as a newborn foal, I left him, left her, left them, full of an itch to do somewhere else what I couldn't do on the mesa. Be me. A me of any stripe. Bastards, not to put too fine a point on it, don't have that many choices. They walk a slippery way with many a snigger befouling the air around them, and how's that for a fancy Palookaville way of talking. It was just as natural to go there as it was to beat the draft to the punch and volunteer, with life or the gas chamber facing me, Stu and Clu with rights of life and death over me whenever the whim took them. I should have killed them as well, but I wasn't your experienced hit man back then, and even later on I had to have orders. I had to be told. "No, Mama," he murmurs. "You don't appreciate the mesa right until you've been off it awhile. More than awhile. Other folks, they count." Like movie stars. Like apartment folk, who do not go out to capture eagles in canyons, who walk their dogs on leashes, who drive cars to visit with a neighbor a hundred yards away, who shower several times a day, take their meals in fine restaurants with waiters you have to pay just because they do their jobs. You have to pay them extra. A percentage. "No wages," she blurts. "They don't get wages?" "They do, but what you give them at the table gets figured in." She can see why he came back from all that, but she says nothing and tries to track his worried, creasing face, track the mind behind it as it unravels the skein of cause and effect, spurious cause and unassignable effect. Icicle Boy she sometimes calls him in the privacy of her own head, for his being, well, so remote and cold, so far from the warm center of a family that, if she could only admit it to herself, hardly exists except as one of adultery's keener tropes: the illicit sire gone to his rest, the revulsed and ingenious cuckold, the bitter siblings alert to every flick of the bastard self-hounded into oblivion among the plastics and the carhorns, the automats and the awnings. Such *stuff*, she comments as the edge of the unspeakable swims into view, and she has to remind herself in a hurry that it was all done to her, she was passive, the raped, the spoiled, the one badly done by. If it hadn't been for the drowning. If it hadn't been for BertandAnna, whom she suspects without knowing what to do next if she should be right. Whatever happened over at the lake was accidental. She has lived a life of insulting accidents, as if a violent wind had taken a dislike to her personally and vowed to whisk her away, ripping out the blood line along with her, including the one big blood vessel unrecognized by the medical profession: the one that ties you to the soil, the rock, the underground water. "Noise," she tells him. "City noise." "You get used to it," he says. "Like being by the ocean. Jungle noises are louder, and the racket in a pinball parlor is something, when all the machines are going." She takes all this on trust, unable to figure why he went, unable to construe the yearning for other pastures, unable to see the likeness between her craving for another man between her legs and Oswald's furtive wanderlust. It wasn't like that at all, Fermina, she encourages herself, as always. He came from a spot on the sheet, it was never from no act of lust. There was no pleasure in the begetting, that goes without being said. He sort of crept to life. Yet he became every bit as big as they are, and how they hate him for it. Now why, because George was the gifted one and Emory the smart, didn't Oswald come out gifted and not smart, if you go by who the real father was. You can't have one child from two squirts, can you? Two fathers gifting the baby equally? Maybe it can happen, but who can she ask? Matlock would laugh, most of all now he has become, just like his father, a guffawing imminent retiree, delighted to let the Engines drop off their perch and fall rotten to the ground. He would tell her anything to sicken and upset. Ask who then? It was the kind of thing that George The Place In Flowers Where Pollen Rests would know, or at least have a confident guess about, blaming everything on Jimsonweed. "Oswald," she says, eager to firm up the future when she cannot fathom the past, "you not are you going to go away again." How can he say? The concept he has learned from a people who live on concrete and say Negatorio, scent themselves with Canoe, and screw all the time like animals with no season, is called *playing it by ear*, which he has no intention or chance of explaining to her. "Only for a day trip," he says. "Where to?" His mind flies up the Grand Canyon again with Uncle George, leaves the line of battle to go fetch the mail for his fellow twinks and get himself some, abandons her parlor, and goes hunting in the foothills for Emory the absconded owner. These things afflict his memory more than mere events should, seeming to nibble and haunt, always offering more as some dreadful pattern heaves into view and the Canyon (the Grand not the Dewey) becomes a chasm into the hell of the flesh, the laundry girl who sucked him with a butt in her mouth becomes a hag of fate with halitosis of the nostrils even, and the parlor itself becomes the battleground on which life degenerates into the mere bang-bang of ballistics, the automatic flicker of a cheap light, the rattle of a meaningless score leading only to yet another number that will never remember who the scorer was. What's worthwhile is in the chinks between all these things, he tells himself as if in some strident prayer. You have to work a way through it or your whole life, the juicy little entity you are, becomes a scumbag nine-to-five. I have never worked nine to five, it must be worse than two to four. "It's the quiet time of the Women's Society Dances," she is telling him. "Until November." The sound of this reaches him in some Sunset Boulevard of the jungle, a canyon full of clashing balls. "One or two nice and quiet girls," she says. How are their necks, he thinks. Can they abide the work under the lights with the cameras aimed at their slimy pleats for hours on end while they fake it and try to think about nicer things like a new TV or an outfit to walk out in? I have gone ahead into the age of lasers and she is still trying to sell me on steam, the wheel. He grins and she misconstrues the grin. "For a minute you looked happy," she says, warm with relief. "I never know," he tells her, "when it isn't going to steal up on me and catch me off guard. Really, I enjoy the candlelight, the memories of Uncle George my father, and the peace of the nights when I look up and see all of that floating past us, knowing nothing about us or needing to." "Then it doesn't know," she says, "that Apperknowle's back again. You got a caller. You got a friend. One of your own kind I suppose you would say, not one of us savages with no running water, but somebody from the outside world you spent so much time in when all we was hoping was that you would come and see your mother, your brothers, most of all with your father being away so much at the Sigafoose. You have no idea of the hurt you cause. It isn't just a matter of doing anything particular, it's just sitting around to be together in case anything happens, as it mostly never does. It's a quiet life here, leastways until they say they will evict us and put us on the Navajo land, and evict the Navajo and put them on ours, or evict us all and put us someplace else where we don't belong, or evict us, throw us right out, and forget to put us anywhere at all. We'll be just like wanderers, that's all, from place to place with no idea of the seasons. It could happen. It happens to thousands and they don't care when the highway goes right through their yard, but it would matter here. Do they want to run a highway right through our village? I don't think so, but they could do it out of spite. Look here, Fermina, they would say, one of your sons is making trouble down in Palookaville. That's nothing, I'd say, he was always making trouble here. There seems to be no place for him to fit into except maybe the Anglo army. It has always been a problem, I'd say. And then they would tell me that you are going to have to live up here all alone while they move the rest of us away. How would you like that? Looking after an empty mesa?" She runs out of breath and ideas, and Oswald realizes how often she tends to talk not about specific things but about the vague reputations of things, always at one remove from what happened or what might. Her tirades are speculative at best, mainly exercises in rhythm and self-venting, aimed at no one in particular, intended to ease the pressure behind the steam whistle of her

brain, she being aware of herself not only as a woman betrayed and
defiled, made forever after to walk out of step, but also as a woman
doomed from the outset, not that she behaved badly as a child, it was
quite different. She somehow got unlucky, as anyone would with
George The Place In Flowers Where Pollen Rests being too close,
willing to use and exploit anybody within reach just so's he felt better
and he could then, having made use of them, ignore them for weeks.
Sometimes she felt like a post office or a laundry, and her facial expression had mutated from the courtly exasperation of the young
bride to the puckered-in mouth of the woman who, having discovered
her capacity for sexual abandon, sought to camouflage it in testy temper, the very thing she can't sustain with Oswald, for whom some
quite impulsive tenderness breaks through, as if his presence dispos-
sessed her of all other natures. At least until tenderness, twisting
against itself, begins to blame him for being so different, so much of
an outsider as to provoke in her extreme emotions that drain her and
leave her gasping in a proper emotional muddle, trapped in a voluptuous aversion she feels ashamed of, as if she were two women in one.
Oswald has too many faces to be doted on, yet not enough to quite
escape her wrath. When she chides him she is chiding Uncle George,
Emory, Thomas, and Abbott, the whole tribe, for somehow being
fibers in something woven in hell against her enduring happpiness,
when all she expected was a quiet life, a gentle going on, not everything erupting in her face from murder or suicide to adultery and
bastardy, not to mention a son in trouble here and there and then off
to the war, from which he returns looking somehow criminal. Some
folk, she knows, just don't have their minds on being human, they
always want to be something else, different and somehow better, as if
the laws no longer apply, and they can be a dozen folk at different
times, like eagles with wool instead of feathers and lambs with claws
and mice that roar like cougars and prairie dogs that bound about like
rabbits. Somewhere in the midst of all this she knows there was a
starting point at which she told Oswald a visitor had come to see him,
not when the man, Apperknowle, had arrived, or where he actually
was, it being enough to set her going that he was a man from the
outside, whose sloven entity she did not want coming up to the mesa
in Oswald's wake like a disease or a wind, to upset and distract him
from what she supposed his main effort was going to be: assimilation
back into his birthright, entailing the death of memory, the birth of a
snowman in baby form, not this time from egg and sperm, but from

the mixing of hope with hate. "At least," she says, coming up for air, "he hasn't been here a week twiddling his thumbs." At the Center, he muses. "At the Center?" he asks. "Where *you* live," she answers, "or whatever goes on in that shack that Uncle George couldn't bear to be inside of." Nosing around, Oswald thinks, and at once leaves her at a lissom trot, his mind on the remaining kachina dolls and to a lesser extent on the money, not that he doesn't trust Apperknowle, who seems well enough heeled to begin with, it's just that he doesn't like his few possessions to be within anyone else's reach. What? As if the luster might rub off or their aura wane? Not quite. Once open and rather defiant about it, Oswald has become secretive, rather like a genius about his working habits. "You just came," he says after the handshake, the other's hand limper and damper than ever before. "An hour or so," says Apperknowle. "I didn't just come, though, I came for something, I came to talk about the rest of the dolls and what you'd like for them. Two dozen, you once said?" "I hate to part," Oswald says. "They're my folks, really: the dolls. They are my Uncle George. When I want to lay hand on Uncle George, I reach in and find me a doll to touch and it is almost as good as having him pat me on the back of my hand. I'm not in a selling mood."

"Ninety dollars apiece," Apperknowle says. "At least for the real kachinas. Flute players are fine. People like them. But this is for me, just me. My own collection." "Your own collection," Oswald says slowly. "What about *my* own collection? What's your collection going to do to mine? Tell me that." "We can forget about it," Apperknowle says. "I've had a fine time sitting here in the sun. It's cooling down up here already." "I don't have to," Oswald says. "I really don't." "Then don't. Know how you feel." "Half a year of college," says Oswald. "Do you have any vacancies down there in Tucson? You need a man to look after things? Your garden, your car, your dolls." "It isn't a matter of education," Apperknowle says. "There isn't a need, I'm sorry. You want off the mesa again." "I sometimes," Oswald whispers, "feel I have to run off it downhill all the way like somebody out of a mental asylum. I don't know how Uncle George, I can't imagine —" "Your uncle was locked in. He could hardly carve down there on Speedway in a little storefront window. A problem of veracity arises, simplistic as it seems. It's the kind of thing that does matter." "Like Emory at the Sigafoose company," Oswald mutters. "It was never for real." "Well," says Apperknowle, all of a sudden brisk and impatient, "what about it? I didn't exactly come up here to go over your future, pertinent as it may be. The remaining dolls by him—you are their keeper, whether you like it or not, and in effect you are keeping them from everybody. Not even the light shines on them." "How you know that," says Oswald. "You been at my window?" "Yair, by tele-scope from Tucson on Mount Lemmon, looking at you over the Mogollon Plateau." "I reckon," Oswald tells him, "I'll hold on to the rest. Just in case." "In case of what? You have the weirdest sense of the future, Oswald." "I have no sense of future at all. If I part with these dolls, I'm cut off from the past as well. Uncle George may not have been a saint, but he was my father, and I want to have something of him by me. I've too much of my mother already. I sometimes think I'm beginning to grow downward back into boyhood. It's her way." "We could always put on an exhibition," Apperknowle says. "I don't have to own these things. I have my own. You have yours. Your uncle was a wonderful craftsman, artist. I may not have done right in this life, or seen well, but I know that much. I want to see him get his due. You could be there. Have your picture taken with them. As the *son*. How's about it? I know you don't need the money. How about the fame?" "I'm thinking," Oswald says. "It's a good habit," Apperknowle says. "Out of fashion, but every now and then we have a recrudescence." "A what?" "I brought you something anyway, just the kind of thing for a thinking man marooned on a mesa after serv-ing his country in the jungle and facing down the latest eruption of the yellow peril." "You brought a doll back?" "I brought you this." Oswald perks up and looks, hand already out to receive the gift before it is even proffered. A rustling plastic bag encloses it. *"Neckties,"* Os-wald exclaims, off guard. "Feel again. Or rather feel if you want to guess. Don't just guess. Feel and guess. It's more fun than being shot at by gooks and abused by mothers. Isn't it?" "Two books," Oswald sighs. He had really been hoping for neckties or a shirt. *Two* books. "Yair. One about kachina dolls in case you ever wanted to carry coals to Newcastle. Never mind. The other, you can see, is newer. One is pageantry, so's the other. Dolls and stars." He takes them, strokes the spines, and hands them over at last. Oswald scans the book on kachinas, nodding in faint appreciation at the gaudy costumes, the garish masks, the feathers and the tabletas, those castle-shaped head-dresses of wood that surround the doll's head. The other is a book on stars, Kleinsobel's updated for the fourth time. Oswald glows. Not for long, though. He smells something against him in all this, and vaguely suspects that someone is ready to adopt him all over again. He does not want to be wanted in this way. He does not want to want it. He does not want to be anybody's, dangling from their apron strings, their hands, their bankbooks. People must sense the craving in him, he knows, but then they overdo the favor, although he realizes he is blaming Emory mainly and, in a distant way, Uncle George, both of whom had ample cause to wish him close, even if only for appearances (Emory), and most of all for the blood bond (Uncle George). Even the Army mothered and fathered him in its inept, graceless fashion, even the abusive captains, sensing that vacancy, that wound, that incompleteness. Apperknowle is saying, *"I do have your attention,"* and Oswald answering, *"That's all you got,"* but that is the merest sideshow while his head churns on about belongingness. Does he even belong to the soil in that classic way everyone takes for granted? Or is he just a feather on the breath of God? Where had he heard that phrase? Whose was it? Was there always a phrase for what ailed you? Had it all happened before? Was there nothing new in the slipshod realm of disease and yearning? Tempted to use Apperknowle, he wants to do so without becoming involved with his life. He studies Apperknowle, the graying wavy hair, the long thin nose, the touch of plump all over his medium-height body, the length of his fingers, the smallness of his feet and ears, and tries to begin to figure him out: curator, but able to get away a lot; sexually perhaps ambivalent; financially without a care. He comes in a Firebird, but not from Phoenix, Oswald thinks with a grin, momentarily cheering up. Come on, the guy means you no harm. Five minutes later, after some empty palaver about the upcoming women's dances, Oswald and Apperknowle are examining the last kachina dolls as Oswald with exaggerated care lifts them from the plastic sack and stands them on the rickety table in the quite sufficient indoor light of early afternoon. Oswald hardly touches them, but Apperknowle holds them firmly, palping them and relishing their bulginess, at which Oswald shakes his head. Don't rub the paint off, he says needlessly, fancying himself all of a sudden in the role of a Chinese emperor unearthing his penis collection. *"These,"* Apperknowle tells him heavily, *"are not the first kachina dolls I have laid my hands on."* What they have in front of them happens, quite by accident, to be George The Place In Flowers Where Pollen Rests's maturest work, done when he could still tell olive green from emerald green. Oswald doesn't know the difference, but Apperknowle does, restraining his delight and instead muttering as if to pawnbroke the dolls, murmuring an occasional "Not bad, *not bad,* " as Oswald more with the air of a conjuror than of an owner reveals them and sets the gaudy ones alongside the drabber ones, the little by the big, aloof in his way from the miniature pageant in front of them, a tiny population of masked Indians with nowhere to go except back into the bag or down to the museum in Tucson. Apperknowle sighs with genuine envy, wondering at the hands of the man gone and the spoor their toil has left behind them. A spaceship might be awaiting this little population of formal-faced indigenes, none of them stamping a foot or getting ready to dance as in the latest vogue, but firmly planted on their softwood bases in a vital trance, their faces set in this or that expression but, as always in Uncle George's work, tinged with affability as if the face were settling down again after a good-humored, rather spiky exchange, the lip line not yet quite straight. And these are masks, except for the one Fluteplayer, who does not qualify as a true kachina. Now they are all out on show, and Oswald can find nothing for his hands to do other than hold the blood pressure machine so tight it might even register his pressure, but it would spin out the numbers only on a roll of twenty- or fifty-dollar bills. Apperknowle is sitting in the presence of hard cash he has paid Oswald already, not that he can tell, and Oswald is dreaming about how his uncle made these pieces with his son and nephew close by him, hovering dangerously between puberty and adolescence, and fussed as only a growing boy can be fussed, but never a teenager. Uncle George carved while telling obscene tales and often enough Oswald had to imagine the affection Uncle George felt for him, although that made it nonetheless real. He wished it so. It is as if Oswald's childhood toys have erupted from dead time, in their center the cat-faced god Sotuqnangu with the clouds on his pale blue shoulders, in front of him a tiny Return kachina, only five inches high, yet oddly crisp and svelte in almost total white with just a short green-maroon-black-and-white kilt, a red steeple coming from its head. He could never have carved this during his blindness: too small and fiddly, whereas a big Sotuqnangu is a different matter, ideal for hands going partially numb. Apperknowle suddenly realizes that he himself owns most of the dolls from Uncle George's blind period, and he knows much more about all the dolls than Oswald does, for whom they have enormous sentimental value, not as tribal artifacts but as nephew-uncle things. The Return kachina, he knows (he knows so well from study and talk that he doesn't think of it as knowing), signals the time for the visiting kachinas to head back to the San Francisco Mountains in the middle of July. Their absence coincides with the period he does not have to be on campus to teach, and he always returns to his chores there with an excited sense that the kachinas are returning with him, for, more or less, the winter semester. Oswald is saying, No, he would not like to have them all taken off his hands, whereas for a fee he would let Apperknowle exhibit them in Tucson, but not one of those traveling exhibits. One trip only, to Tucson and back. "This isn't just my nest egg," Oswald says, *"this is my heart."* Apperknowle fusses with them, touches and rearranges them, not enough of a savage or a primitive for some quick current to flood from them into his nerves, yet awed in a fashion more abstract appropriate to an atavistic sample of Renaissance man. He dotes on them, he knows what they stand for, and he knows what they cannot do for him, so he envies the whole tribe their capacity for enchantment, for believing not only in the dolls but in the human-sized real kachinas, dressed-up humans with superhuman impact. For him the engine does not roar, the god does not come down from the machinery, impatient, imperious, bad-breathed, aching to swat and chide. Nor for Oswald either, who sometimes feels that he has himself been filched from a museum display, in glass-enclosed formaldehyde or not, on which the card read *Nephew Sapiens?*, and everybody passed it by with a giggle, not knowing the species or not wishing to. Someone, one day, he thinks will sell him too, out of the plastic bag into the frying pan, as a slave, a pet, an ulcerated curiosity, and then Apperknowle will have to come and pay his bail. "Well, that was out of this world. How do you feel about shipping them to Tucson?" Apperknowle has an enthralled look. They bargain. Oswald starts putting the dolls away, halts, bargains again, then brings a couple back into view to sway the man. "Done," Apperknowle says. "You shall be there the whole time. They'll be safe and you'll be comfortable. The best of hotels, the best of care. You'll never regret it, we'll make a movie record of the whole display." It is out before Oswald knows what he is doing. "I once did a few, low-budget things. Way back when. Before the military." "Then," says Apperknowle, "you won't be camera-shy. We will be able to interview you about your uncle. I collect movies." Now Oswald realizes that the last thing he needs in this life is his face plastered all over the TV screen; you never know, maybe Stu and Clu, if alive, will be watching. Perhaps they are nonstop watchers, have been watching him all the time, biding theirs. "Only in a kachina mask," he says, and without any identification by name. "I'm just the nephew." "We'd film this house of yours." "Without me in it," Oswald says. "Without you in it. Granted." Stu and Clu are realer to him than Sotuqnangu is. "Yair. Without me in it or out. No me anywhere. I'm camera-shy about my face." With the money, he is going to give Fermina some appliances as a substitute for having her third son close to her. Or he will buy some cheapo car. But who needs a car on the mesa? A truck, then, to fetch water in. "One of those interviews off camera," Oswald is saying. "Like when they talk to criminals. My voice over, see. I wouldn't have to be seen at all. And you could distort my voice like they do." He is getting carried away. "How soon?" he asks. He will need another blood pressure machine in which to keep the extra bills. "Fifties," he says. "That's right." Apperknowle calculates. "Three months," he says. "When the kachina season starts. It'll be a neat counterpoint, obbligato, to the real thing up the road. End of January, I guess." Oswald cannot think this far ahead. "Five hundred down," he says. "And a guarantee. A contract." "Yes," says Apperknowle, "I wasn't trying to cheat you anyway. It'll all be on the up and up." Oswald is already tying up the sack with cord, reapplying the belt. He has not packed them so well this time and he knows that, later on, he will have to open the bag up and do it all over again. For now he wants them out of sight of all curators and brothers and mothers and orphans and hermits and lepers and police and hobos, fire-eaters, candy merchants, census takers, moviemakers, spies, private eyes, and uncle-fathers. Part of the dolls' essential existence, he believes, is that they not be seen, but repose in sacrosanct darkness as if Uncle George had carved them blind and his chisel, his knife, his rasp, his saw, had cut darkness into them on his behalf, deeper than the bottoms of all vees, down into the soul of the wood, so that the doll if exposed to too much light will babble or wobble a bit. "Got to get their beauty sleep," he says. "You keep them close by you?" Apperknowle knows the answer. "Uncle George's last request," he lies. "Then," Apperknowle tells him, "you have by you a sackful of untempered human magnificence. You should be proud."

It is a relief when Apperknowle goes, promising a contract within a couple of weeks; Oswald likes money enough, but not having to talk about it with those who know more about it than he does. He examines the two books. He would have preferred magazines, which he thinks make fewer demands, letting you dip and hunt, whereas a book requires something over and beyond even the call of duty. So he riffles and scans, soon setting the book on kachinas aside as too close to the bone. In any case, those dolls depicted in it do not resemble Uncle George's work: they look sharper, thinner, classier, not as vulgar as the stuff churned out by Emory's Mickey Mouse factory, but they do not sing to him on the level of nostalgia, hero worship, love, on which he feels at ease. Uncle George's work is too much part of Oswald's private life for it ever to seem a subject for debate in the public domain. There is nothing sentimental in what he reads about kachinas, never. The star book, on the other hand, does offer tables and charts, which he can peer at with his usual mix of innocence and drive. In the past, back in Palookaville, he has looked at a few issues of astronomy magazines, bemused that so much is being said about what is so far away and so heedless, relentlessly personalizing the night sky as if the writers, the stargazers, knew from the start that their enterprise was doomed. They were just whistling cheerfully behind Sotuqnangu's back. He liked the computer-assisted blowups, though, of stars and nebulae, and the immaculate calm of the drawings. So many readers sent photographs in, made on their own telescopes with special cameras, and Oswald had always wondered how many hours it took, how many thousands of dollars, to get things rigged up right in the first place. Such patience he had seen before only in Uncle George, whose steady lean over a hunk of wood had something of the same stonelike persistence, as if all you had to do was go as slowly as a star seems to, and then all would come out well. At least he knows that the sun is a star and that planets, which do not flicker, are not stars. A beginning. Yet the prospect of reading the small print for over three hundred consecutive pages daunts him, even though he has little else to do with his days since essentially he is a graft up here, unneeded and undesired, almost as if he were some Anglo photographer muscling in to get pictures of what the tribe wanted to keep to itself. Perhaps he should strike out and befriend the alien stars as Uncle George befriended the unspeaking god Sotuqnangu: a feat of sheer, shameless imagination for which he would receive credit only from himself, a feat far harder than the reading of books on kachina dolls, magazines printed on glossy paper that seems more intended to catch and disperse light than to be a place for print. One thing he notices, and rather likes, although he looks at the pages in question with unwilling interest, afraid to be trapped into any kind of system that demands things of him. He has a passion, fiercer since Vietnam, to keep his mind empty, so that when anything really worthwhile comes along it can fill his mind to the brim, with nothing in the way. So far, nothing has, but he expects it from almost any quarter, from one of the sudden apparitions BertandAnna make, from something cooked (as distinct from described at length) by Fermina, even from Thomas and Abbott, whose combined sarcasms invoke a whole realm of orthodox experience denied him: marriage, fatherhood, planting, reaping, talking to girls while they mix dough. He looks idly at the pages headed "The Names of the Stars and Their Meanings," amazed they have names, especially such weird ones as Acubens, Al Bali, Alcor, Aldebaran, Algeiba, and Algol, already making the strange even stranger, and making him wonder almost aloud in murmuring interrogatives who the people were who first dreamed up such names. Yet which was the first animal to dream of another animal? It is like trying to put a name on fire, he thinks, going from one furnace to another in the steel mills, say, or the blacksmith's forges, and trying to call one lump of flames, oh, Alcor and another Algol. Why not the other way around? Surely all fires have more in common with one another than they don't. So all the names ought really to seem alike. Well, they do. He looks back over the alphabetized list and thinks for a moment that they are. The nature of starry fire has dictated the names. Then he realizes he is wrong, that the names tend to seem alike because they are all from the same language, not that he knows it is Arabic. He turns to the end of the list and finds a half page of Z's: Zaniah, Zaurach, Zavijava, Zosma, and so on, thinking once again that what they share is the element of fire, but soon again discerning the feel of the same language: something bony and concise, unsayable and barklike. He has not seen any Latin names so far, so his bewilderment is less confused than it might have been. Now he turns back to the beginning of the list and finds that the stars not only have names but *speeds* and colors. Colors maybe, but *speeds?* They must be traveling, then. Not every star named has a given speed, at least in the list, so he wonders if some stars are wholly stationary, whereas Aldebaran, say, is pale rose and is receding from Earth at thirty miles a second. He likes the thought of that onrush, from nowhere to nowhere with, presumably, nothing in the way. The heavens must be as

empty as my mind, he thinks. Could actual stars be soaring through
my head, getting from here to the Dinnebito Trading Post in a second? Amazed as he is, he enjoys the calmness with which he is taking
all this. You don't fall apart when you say thirty miles a second,
which is what? He figures it with laborious awe. One hundred and
eight thousand miles an hour. What a speed. It doesn't sound bad, at
least until he compares it with the speed of light, and then it sounds
lead-footed. All the same it's a decent speed to be leaving the mesa at
even if it is only one six thousand two hundredth of the speed of light.
His head bulges. Somehow he sees himself from behind, seeing the
back of his head, that impersonal tod, and suddenly has a sharp sense
of what it is like to be a skull around a pair of eyes, creaking and
aching as the eyes widen and weep, squeeze and purge, and all around
him there are stars like arrows going very fast although seeming
never to move at all, sometimes colliding (they must, he thinks), but
for the most part lofting and cruising independent of one another
with no mind thinking them and no heart feeling for them save his.
Under his chin and behind his neck and above his weird hair parting
and in front of his face, all of them fizzing about in a nearby farness at
least as far as the eyes have it, they stick to the speeds they happen to
have survived at for who knows how many million years, etched,
etching their presence, in the big bowl of night the Persian poet
Omar Khayam wrote about. Oswald's head fills with rosy stars going
away from him and (he shudders that they turn their backs on him)
lilac ones, like one of the two Algenibs, coming toward him at only
one and a half miles a second. Some stars, he finds, do not have their
color or their speed listed, as if some stars are transparent and do not
move toward you or away. He prefers the active ones, the gaudy,
wishing he could link what he sees overhead nightly in total mesmerized incomprehension to the charts in the book, to the uncouth-
sounding names and the preposterous speeds at which, he dreams, he
would love to fetch water from the windmill for Fermina, or have a
quick weekend in Palookaville, a return visit to Laos. If you traveled
as fast as that, Stu and Clu would never see you, no sharpshooter
would be able to draw a bead on you and plug you through the skull.
He sees the names have meanings, though names and meanings far
from what he can make sense of: claws and virgins and the good
fortune of the swallower, the beak of the hen, the tent, the cavalier,
the follower, the right arm, the stars of the flock, the mane, the wing,

the elbow, the head of the lion, the ghoul. Some highly inventive and unstrung person has been letting his imagination run away with him, Oswald decides. Not all that is up there. He has not yet fathomed the notion of a constellation that supposedly matches a human shape, as Indus an Indian, but his head is agog with words to say and tints, speeds, motion toward and motion from, as if some obscure celestial code has sprung to life where, before, there was only a dotted blank he peered at in uninitiated scorn. Now it is packed with goodies just for him, out of nowhere, as if the Anglo Santa Claus has landed by helicopter on top of the mesa, the whole sky in his sack. How, Oswald wonders, can he relate the chart to the heavens. What will be above him when he looks up tonight, if it happens to be clear? Claws and virgins? The beak of the hen or a tent? It is almost too exciting to contemplate, but he thinks he is the only believer. Even Uncle George, the delver into mysteries, would find it hard to credit this, although he seemed willing to believe the preposterous yarns Apperknowle had spun him about blind men in history, blind men in the Amazon, the autopilots in the rest of the world beyond the wide water that keeps on rolling. Oswald contents himself with the thought that for him the entire business need have no bearing on the sky at all, but will remain an arsenal of ideas, hues, and speeds, something unutterably private, something between him and the devisers of this arbitrary scheme. Then he finds the star maps, with some of the stars' names imprinted on it, and sees the lines that link up this and that star into Rorschach outlines. In an hour's fast, breath-held reading, he has got the hang of it, and sees for the first time that the stars are always there, by day as by night, and that his head is not on something flat but set centrally like a seed in a gourd full of stars. It is all going on around him, whizzing and zooming, rolling and curving, as if someone much vaster than Sotuqnangu has invented four-dimensional pinball and plays it all the time, heedless of people living or dying. He lights two new candles, making a note to himself to get more from Fermina, and reads away, in a more analytical mood. After a while, something seems to strike him: the stars rushing away are reddish and those coming closer and closer tend to be bluish. He wonders why. Why do they have different colors? For the same reason as Anglos are white and Gringos have blue eyes and Indians are browner. Whoever is playing four-dimensional pinball enjoys variety. All of a sudden, Oswald exclaims, goes to the window, whips the

drape aside and looks out at nobody at all. Amazed, he realizes what
he likes about his discovery: there is nothing, no one, between him
and whatever it is that does not care about the people on the planet.
Once you have come to terms with that, as he thinks he almost did in
Laos, all the consolations begin to arrive, but by then it is too late. Is
it really that simple, he wonders. Make your peace with the stars and
then you need nothing else except out of boredom. All the good and
all the bad that happen to you belong in the same category; to the
uncaring cause up there, Sotuqnangu or some other, all that humans
feel is decoration, not even that. The consolation of company, he tells
himself, mean nothing to him who looks up at the wasted stars, so
many with nothing to do, and does not mind. Yes, Oswald, when you
know the big pinball in the sky doesn't care about us, you tend to love
them all, yourself included. They have no idea. They warm themselves up with visions of goodness, and all the while the scope of
heavenly interest has moved on to some other place, some other creatures. No more mad guesswork for me. No more piety. I'll be indifferent to what's indifferent to me. I might have had a better life, given
half a chance. I feel somehow shredded, left to molder in the sun, like
something on the rim of a plate: a string from an eaten bean. It should
have been better, fatter, more colorful, but I know how to deal with it
now. I'll make the best of what's at hand, oh yes, Mama, then I'll
bring the bacon home to you. My nights are going to be wonderful.
Most folks think of night as only a good night's sleep, had or missed,
but night is when the greyhounds race up there, and watching them,
studying them, growing to worship them, you're not fooling yourself,
or them, you're learning to recognize a certain style of talking. These
are the ways of the universe. This is how they run. They don't
change *that*. Once you get used to the fact, you're home. When he
eventually calls the number on Apperknowle's card, a voice answers
"Petrified Forest. Holbrook Chamber of Commerce. May I help
you?" He hangs up as if electrified, his mind full of wooden kachina
dolls turning to stone. Apperknowle, he sees, is the mocking sexton of
live dolls, his father's death all over again.

His eyes water from the strain of candlelight, but Fermina gives him
a six-pack rolled in stout white paper, fresh from the store courtesy of
Thomas and Abbott, who would rebel if they knew they were bringing candles for their little brother. Now Oswald resents the days,

although he knows the stars are still there, haring along their appointed courses with the huge slowness of nature, stars easily bigger than the entire solar system. Facts fall into a head he now thinks went previously unused, but he is whimsical about it, never organizing his bits and pieces. His idea is that if the universe itself is organized then its inhabitants don't need to organize it for themselves. Yet some itch persists, some yearning to impose himself on the unthinkable, massive flow of it all, even if he tells no one about it. Not quite like scoring his initials in wet concrete or plaster of Paris, it's an urge to sign what is going on, not as the author, not even as a witness, but more as a fellow conspirator, one who has tuned in readily with infatuated disgust. No, too strong: with infatuated pique. Something like that. You know how fluid human metaphors can be. He also finds batteries for his flashlight and, a souvenir from a motel in Palookaville, a luminous tiny flashlight for reading menus by (it says it on the side on a piece of paper shaped and printed like a fortune from a fortune cookie and slid inside the sheath of plastic). He has noticed a great deal in the astronomy book and so, he reasons, has a plank to stand on. The more he learns, the more he'll find he doesn't know, and then he'll go after it, no holds barred. Now he has a sheaf of the old pinball parlor leaflets, mostly shiny paper, but with an occasional one matte, almost a thin cardboard, and these are the oldest. His pen is an old fading fiber-point, thick pointed and not as black as it once was, but it serves him. He needn't write much, he just wants to get some basic information down, and then begin to draw conclusions, wholly untroubled by any thought of skimpiness, being careless, or taking everything on trust. He ignores the names for the numbers now, first of all noting down all the stars traveling away from him, but only if their speed is given. So he readily assembles these, beginning with the A's all over again, in a roughly written table on the back of the first *Big Game* leaflet, the legend of the lost calling up all the mystery and adventure of the African jungle, the distant beat of tom-toms, and the eerie, right-on-top-of-you cries of wild beasts:

Aldebaran—pale rose, 30 miles per second
Alnilam—bright white, 15.5 mps
Alnitak—topaz yellow, 11 mps
Bellatrix—pale yellow, 11 mps
Betelgeuse—orange, 6.5 mps

    Capella—white, 18 mps
    Enif—yellow, 3 mps
    Gemma—brilliant white, 1/2 mps
    Kochab—reddish, 10 mps
    Pollux—orange, 2 mps

He chokes briefly, having swallowed wrong in his overwrought condition, knowing this is what everything comes down to, although he sees he is well past the halfway mark and doesn't seem to have many stars to play with. Maybe those coming toward him will be more numerous. No, the list is short, just a sample. He feels relieved and continues copying. There are only five more. Pollux, he writes, oran— no, got that already. He scores out the second Pollux and resumes:

    Regulus—flushed white, 1.2 mps
    Rigel—bluish-white, 15 mps

He turns the page in a fever.

    Scheat (it sounds bad, he grins)—deep yellow, 5 mps
    Spica—brilliant flushed white—1 mps
    Unuk Al Hay (he loves the sound of it)—pale yellow, 2 mps

"Done," he sighs, wishing for a million more. Well, several dozen anyway, and he realizes he's forgotten to find out how far away each one is, but he waits on that, even if it might be useful, thrilled with the sense of himself as the midnight scientist by his lamp, figuring out how everything works. Now he figures it, adding up the speeds, and the answer comes: 132, which he divides by the number of stars, 15, to get the average speed of the stars moving away from him: 8.8 mps. He wonders who ever knew that before, or cared about it. What he really wants to know, though, is the most favored speeds of stars. There are two 2s and two 11s, but there is a 15 with a 15.5 by it, and—he counts up —between 1/2 and 3 there are actually 6 out of 15. So, he decides, the favorite speed of stars going away from him is low, between .5 and 5 miles per second, which looks very neat and almost makes him weep. He never knew before. Almost half of them are slow. Now he wonders if the slow ones all have the same color, so he pores again over his rough-hewn chart, joining a yellow to a white to an orange to another yellow and another white and yet another yellow. The yellows have it. The range of color, he decides, runs white through yellow. *"Of York,"* he murmurs, running through a familiar mnemonic for the spectrum, which he recalls from the time he wanted to be a night reconnaissance man, but his visual purple would have taken too long to build up. *"Richard of York Gave Battle in Vain,"* he says. The pale ones are going away from me slowest, whereas—well, that's obvious. Now he wants to know if the slowest ones, meaning the palest ones (orange Betelgeuse he quietly forgets for the moment), are the biggest ones or what. The chart in Kleinsobel does not tell him, so he switches his attention to the stars that interest him more anyway because they are coming toward him, even if heedless of his presence. Is there, he wanly wonders, any such thing as a boomerang star? It starts by going away from you and then it comes back, or it starts by coming toward you, then buggers off. Now who are these aliens showing such an interest in us and our planet? He has soon compiled his second list, all the way from Algeiba, approaching at 24, but with no color given, which irritates him, to Zuben Eschamali, pale emerald, otherwise known as the Northern Claw, coming in at 22. Now he figures them out, surprised at first that 23 are coming toward him whereas only 15 are going away, but it does make sense, he thinks, there's bound to be some favoritism among the astronomers. They don't like being snubbed any more than other folks. He divides 23 into the total and obtains an average speed for stars coming toward him: 8.68. Amazing. Almost the same as those going away, which was 8.8. Has he just discovered the favorite average speed of stars? No, just the average; the favorite speed is different, whereas one really fast one can change the average a lot. He mentally damns Algeiba, the fastest comer with its 24, then pores over the numbers once again, as even the most gifted humans must. The result dismays him. Between 1.5 and 2 there are four, between 3.5 and 5 there are also four, and between 6.5 and 7 there are five. There are also two 10s. He hands the palm to the 6.5–7 group, consoling himself he has also discovered that a good half of the stars coming toward him on the mesa, or wherever else he happens to be while on the planet, prefer to do so at a speed somewhere between 1.25 and 7, and more than half of them in the range from 1.25 through 11. In the range between 14 and 24 there are only four stars. He knows he has discovered something, then takes a separate sheet, to keep his head clear, and writes:

Average: *Going* 8.8,   *Coming* 8.68 (close)
Favored: "   .5–5,   "   6.5–7 (different)

It almost looks as if the comers pick up where the leavers leave off, with only one mile per second in between, but he knows it doesn't work like that. He remembers to investigate the colors, and checks the colors of the comers whose speeds are closest together, obtaining a blank (Alioth), a white, a greenish white, a brilliant white, and a topaz yellow. All a *bit whitish*, he tells himself, except for that first one. How can I find out? There is lots of information for the picking. Just in one small book. It's like taking charge of things for once. I must say I like finding one star I have heard about before. He means Polaris, another topaz yellow, traveling at 10, neither slow coach nor greyhound. Navigators rely on it because it never seems to move, but Oswald knows better, and he knows it is getting nearer all the time. Anew he wants to know how far away they all are, and how near. The distances can't be all alike as if the stars had been fixed on the inside of an open umbrella. He falls asleep, his calculations on his lap, in the old rocking chair that will not rock, his Uncle George long ago having nailed wedges to the rockers to keep them still. Oswald sleeps for several hours, awakens with a jump at three in the morning, and at once looks out the window, sees nobody, goes outside to see if the sky is clear, which it is, and thinks he sees Polaris, twirling or stirring. Mice and spiders walk over the scrawl on his leaflets while he is outside. As if he knows, he dusts the paper with his hand when he returns, lights a new candle, anchoring it on a blob of hot wax on the metal plate, and begins to look through his night's work. He cannot recognize it, he must have lost something. No, he counts, checks the signature with its quiff. There is one sheet too many signed with his name, written in his own hand, but none of his doing, unless he wrote it in his sleep. It is an old ad for topless bars, familiar enough, but what is done by his hand on the other side is not. His hand shakes as he reads what looks like a complicated query, addressed by himself to himself, but written in his sleep, so did he walk as well?

> **What about these?**
> **Kapteyn's Star: radial velocity 150 m.p.s.**
> **Barnard's Star:** "   "   73   "
> **Groombridge:**   "   "   60   "
> **61 Cygni:**   "   "   40   "
>
>   Yours, *Oswald*

There is even a line drawn around it as if it is an invitation of some
kind, but from whom? From himself? Maybe the book itself has written him a message, from the interior, so to speak. Did *he* scribble it,
this neatly, in his sleep? Perhaps it fell out of the book and had been
addressed to some other reader by yet another reader. This is a new
book, though, bang up to date, with all the latest on the upcoming
missions to Mars and the outer planets. Perhaps, then, someone in a
bookstore in Phoenix or Tucson happened to be riffling through, saw
a passage he disagreed with, and asked for a piece of paper to leave a
message on for the next reader. Or someone, having already written
the message, found a suitable book to enclose it in after looking
around bookstores for days. Preposterous. Something has happened
for which there seems no rational explanation. Oswald is more dis-
mayed to find the thing cached among his made-over leaflets than to
find there are stars going so fast, though he vaguely wonders, with a
piece of his mind not engaged in present dumbfoundedment, whether
they are coming toward him. He hopes so. Most of his mind worries
about the message, at last decides it was a piece of paper already in the
book, then retracts: his own handwriting? His own signature? He
lights an extra candle, this time a long fluted one of pink wax, a
dinner or party candle, not one of the basic practical kind usually to
be found on the mesa. He tries to think of his eyes, which must surely
be betraying him. He tries to think of an eye not as an e-y-e. but as
👁. It does not work, the message remains, there to ruin his neat
tabulation of what is whizzing through the back of beyond. *"Imagine,"* he murmurs, meaning: *fancy that.* But the last thing he wants is

to imagine his mind abruptly losing control and unfitting him for further studies in the speed of stars. Never before has he had this steady a solace from a puzzle. Never has he wondered about the numbers tied in to the things that twinkle and the things that don't, the great balls of fire and the great balls that reflect it. Now it has all gone wrong the instant it begins. Not only will there always be more information than he will ever get, there will be forces, agents, interlopers, messing around with his head, his self-reliance, his confidence. He sees a lifetime ahead of weird messages left on his table, in his books, on his lap while he sleeps, even tucked into the plastic bag of money and kachina dolls. Frozen into his rocking chair by shock, he fails at first to notice the presence who edges through the doorway: *Uncle George,* he gasps, but this is an uncle rigged out in a double-breasted blue suit and a black tie, his hair like dead grass seen through a blizzard, his eyes mere sockets in which inexplicably there gleam little flashlight bulbs, one in each. His own eyes heat up. All he can see in there is the red glow of the tiny wire, as if the battery is running out, but the eyes gleam across the dim-lit room, aimed at him as if to compel or complain. In one hand Uncle George has an irregular white stick of some heft here and there, which Oswald at last recognizes as a human backbone with its bottom tip on the ground. His uncle leans on it as if it were still part of his own body, now external. There file through the doorway several other figures with flashlight eyes, each with his hands on the shoulders of the one in front of him, each with a backbone shillelagh, each like barefoot Uncle George. The first comer, however, has no eyes at all, Oswald now sees not even flashlight bulbs but only sockets that appear to have been filled with cream or gauze; his head is a bust of marble or stone, and when he opens his mouth, as now, there comes a roaring of ocean, not the manual surf of applause, but the real thumping foamy thing, as if a gruesome dyspepsia labors beneath his throat. Uncle George says nothing, motions with his bone cane to Oswald asking him to rise, but Oswald cannot move, his mind still stunned by them in the order of their arrival, from the white-socketed bust to the one behind him, wearing a blouse with a deep scalloped collar, almost a woman's garment, incongruous with the double-breasted suit. The man behind him is taller, has the same red-ember eyes as Uncle George, but these behind the thick lenses of spectacles made from brass or gold, and he has a toothbrush-type mustache, while the third comer has his head canted somewhat upward as if to declare that he is dreaming: no mustache, no eyeglasses, but he sports within the lapels of his double-breasted suit a shirt broadly striped in white and pale blue, collarless so that the luscious silk necktie goes around his naked neck and the floppy knot has only his Adam's apple behind it. Oswald knows not where to look, or why, but he goes on looking, eye-locked with Uncle George, who nods, then from behind him produces a battered suitcase with a strap dangling loose from its top, the kind of strap that porters sometimes use over one shoulder. Oswald has to open it. Thump it goes on the linoleum, flap goes the lid, on which someone has affixed an airline address label, but not filled out. At first Oswald can see only newspaper and corn silk, but his hand rummages as he stares up at the ghostly four and feels what might be skittles or table legs, but too small, and then he knows. Four new kachina dolls catch the candlelight, made in heaven he is sure, and he tries to identify them, wishing he had Apperknowle's guide by him. All he sees are ruffs, feathers, kilts, bits of wool, and face masks of primitive simplicity. On the table he stands them, awed and horrified as they begin to glow and shimmer, emitting a light far brighter than the flashlight-bulb eyes of the three ghosts with eyes. Something begins to dawn on him, but Uncle George, in a wholly unfamiliar voice, begins to speak, introducing the ghosts in an almost robot, pinball tone. "Barnard," he says, indicating the man with curdled eyes. "He comes from close at hand and travels fast." Oswald turns his gaze to the next arrival, the one in the scallop-collared blouse, and this is Kapteyn while the man with golden-rimmed glasses over his rosy glowing eyes is called 61 Cygni and he of the blue-and-white soccer shirt is Groombridge. "I," Uncle George tells him with mastered disgust, "have been allowed off the reservation of the dead. I asked Sotuqnangu. He said yes. So now you have the full complement of four kachinas on the table, one for each ghost, more luminous than any candle. Gape at them, adore them, love them, but do not ever attempt to sell or show them. These are for your eyes only. Should you attempt anything vulgar with them, they will disappear, first having blinded all who have looked on them. Be a good nephew now, and get on with your studies. We do not stay anywhere for long. Good night." Only Uncle George speaks. The others do not even make a sign, but file outside again, with an odd whistling sound, not of surf, coming off them, and Oswald can no longer hear even Uncle George although the lips are moving over the toothless hole of his mouth. Oswald closes the suitcase for him, stands it in front of his uncle, and steps back as if to save his life from the zone of death and ghostliness. The shillelaghs scrape on the rock and grit outside, then cease abruptly. All five have gone, winging or fizzing or wafting. For lack of anything else to do by way of response, Oswald looks at the shining kachina dolls on the table, and opens his book. The dolls vanish. He closes the book and the dolls return. It works every time. Now he peers into the index, but by candlelight only, of course, and the table of contents, at last finding a table entitled "A Few Stars of Large Proper Motion," and he wonders what "Proper" means even as he finds his four ghost guests and two others called Cordoba and Lacaille. He is astounded to discover that they do not come from far away. Blue-and-white Groombridge comes from farthest away, natty in his blue serge suit, then Kapteyn of the scalloped blouse, with in line behind him, murmuring something non-stop, the gold-bespectacled 61 Cygni, and Barnard of the curdled eyes. He wonders who these men used to be, no doubt some of the blind allies Uncle George used to talk about, or about whom others talked to him, especially in the days when blindness began to dominate his thoughts. "Yes," Oswald whispers with quivering lips even as the phantom kachinas on the table vanish because the book has slipped from his grasp and opens up again on the floor, *These are the autopilots as he used to call them, each man once upon a time the autopilot of his tribe, each blinded so as to have to fly on instruments forever.* Now he realizes that all he has to do to know is want to know. Some energy enlightens the more than willing. He thinks of the autopilots in the order of their arrival through the door, in single file, then of them according to their speeds. It was their distance away that kept them from arriving in the order of their speeds. Of course. That was common sense, but Oswald and common sense are more light-years apart than the farthest of *them*, soccer-stripe Groombridge, was moments ago from his roost. For a while there, logic lapsed, and Oswald was on his own, but without the customary resources of beleaguered humans, shifting as best he could with a mind untrained for the outrageous, and even his war experiences have not geared him for outlandish cosmic intervention, least of all one (little that he knows it) that allows his Uncle George, not so long gone, to walk aboard as one of the living dead, in the ether, in men's minds, among the discoverers of stars after whom the stars got named. Uncle George is the only Hopi among them, maybe the very first, and Oswald marvels at his reappearance, little knowing that doodles with the afterlife are a god's way of writing sonnets; but he prides himself on having known all along that Uncle

George was special, one of a kind. Yet Oswald still has a prosaic side
to him: except for George, the dead are the dead, the living the living.
So he clings to stolid categories, and the day has not yet come when
after hearing certain chords of Ravel he will think a hitherto unknown color now exists, a glint from the ear to the eye. *Rengigo*,
maybe. But tonight he has gained an insight of sorts, an intimation
not so much holy as overwhelming, its main say-so having to do with
the human imagination's need to make something because nothing
else can. It is Uncle George's credo, this, handed down obliquely and
unpalatably as a hunk of raw pterodactyl flesh. A wink from the
autopilot and Oswald has something on which to build before he too
turns into a star. Do some, he wonders, never *star*, but just go out
forever?

"You not livin right," Fermina scolds him. "You got night for day like
you was ashamed to be seen out, like you dassent set foot on the mesa.
You askin for something." "They came to get me," he says, "and they
let me be. I was scared out of my wits. I've no wits left." "You need
your mama then." "My mama needs me, that's more like it. I don't
blame you, but I'm not much to be with right now. Stargazing." "You
burnin up more candles than them Anglo churches." "Getting used
to candlelight. It's soft and gentle." She shakes her head indignantly.
"No job, Oswald, no feed. You got money? You got a bit from someplace?" "No, Mama," he lies. "I have to work out some deal with this
here Apperknowle." "They do say he has a lot of mighty curious livin
behind him. Come here from some other country long years ago."
"He's here now," Oswald adds redundantly, but making sure of the
fact. "To stay." "You not eating right," she says. "More stew." "More
stew," he says. "I enjoy it all." "You eatin like your Uncle George:
bread and margarine. One of these days I am goin to make you a
special—" "Make me a special, then. See what I do with it." She
knows what he'll do, but he has no idea when she will get around to
it. Special means rabbit meat roast. He lives in a tense world in which
birds seem to be answering the kettle's whistle and his shadow arrives
on the ground a second or two before he appears. His life has become
one of hermitic dependency. He sleeps by day if he can, prodded
from time to time by Thomas and Abbott or Fermina when she has
the energy to go on the warpath with a bowl of hot soup or new
bread for his tin box of a larder. He feels he is crouched on the edge of

something tremendous, but at the the back of his mind he realizes how the four incandescent kachinas named for men and sired by stars are going to keep him on the mesa forever. He has become as much a keeper of the flame as Apperknowle himself. Certainly the book seems to control their comings and goings, but he is hoping that there will be other things that control them too, such as willpower and dreams. What if he loses the book? No, the book is arbitrary, they could just as easily have fixed on some other means. Who then were the four apart from Uncle George? Pharaohs, he says, they were genies, phantoms, knights, beings as commonplace as *piiki* bread but somehow promoted to a higher level on which they broke the rules, made exceptions to the rules, and did their best to make you not afraid. They were also just as much part of him as they were themselves. They knew no limits save that of the speed of light. They knew other mesas, other solar systems, and other galaxies, of course, but they retained the local touch. They spanned ages and countries, languages and climes. They were all that was left of their living, but at least there was something left, whereas, say, Emory's pinball parlors will slip from his hands as readily as rain, like Uncle George's blood pressure machine, much as the military assault named Dewey Canyon lost its terrible and bloody link with the men it killed, the landscape it ploughed up and neutered. Oswald can see he is going to be kept on the mesa, made into a homebody, by something having little to do with the mesa at all, just when he was ready to leave. Or? He wonders if it would make any difference, so long as no one laid hands on the book. Phantoms live forever and do not ever have to wait, having no sense of time. He sighs, wishing he were eight or nine years old and could apprehend the event with full innocent gusto as if it had walked right into him from the corner cupboard of his dreams. He can still bleed, perspire, move his bowels, but he has become extra-human as well, and with a degree of skepticism he'd not have felt as a boy. He is reassured to find that Uncle George's touch of genius is bearing fruit in the afterlife or the other life. With all that energy unexpended he has been recruited to a big-league team. Cordoba is probably not the half of it. He will have other names as well. He will groom Oswald for something wonderful, as Oswald has always hoped, and successfully, whereas Oswald knows he has no future as a carver of kachina dolls and never had. What am I, then, he wonders. A go-between? A visionary? I come from a people with a less than highly developed sense of the everyday. Now I am in my

element, I have come into my inheritance via the back door, through
bastardy, hero worship, depravity, bloodshed, and funk. I have pre-
vailed and now I not only know the favorite speeds of stars coming
toward us and going away but I am in touch with the stars themselves, their white-hot knitting, their blast-furnace hiccups, their incessant successful mindless fire. Now he wishes, just as he wished he
were younger, that he were older, old enough to die and join forces
with Uncle George in space travel or tele-porting: whatever it is he
does to get around from core to arm, from tail to coalsack. Surely
Uncle George's ghost has not had any dealings with Fermina herself,
he muses. The shock would kill her. She would blow up and the
pieces of her never be found. No, he has made contact with the right
one, one who met him halfway. On he goes, half-congratulating himself, half of him worried that the whole thing has been an hallucination; but the Fastest Star kachinas continue to do the book's bidding,
even by day, so he no longer eats off the table but holds a saucepan in
his lap, spilling and showering himself with crumbs. If only Uncle
George Cordoba had left the suitcase, specially adapted as it must
have been for the portage of volatile kachina dolls. Does he intend to
bring some more, maybe kachinas of the slowest stars this time? This
uncle is really being an uncle, bearing gifts at last, tuning his nephew
in to a world unknown to the uncle himself on the radio that used to
bring in Havana, London, and Moscow. This is much better than
listening to static in the mesa wind. That he has few friends and no
lover worries Oswald not a bit. With things accomplished on this
level, all else will come; he is sure of that. Once you have made your
peace with the worst that can happen to you, everything else is
plums. He smiles at the thought of showing the star kachinas to BertandAnna, to Fermina, his two brothers, even opening his stone shack
up to the whole mesa. What gets him going full tilt is not the San
Francisco Mountains but an affinity with autopilots from other eras.
Uncle George knew all along, Oswald decides, that he was an autopilot, unrecognized as such except among the highest conclaves of ga-
lactic sway. How could something so complex come from so simple
an act as receiving a book and trying to figure out from it something
as straightforward as the speeds of stars? Millions have done this before with no obvious result; why should I be different? Answering
himself, he makes it firm: it will happen only to those who believe it
can happen and this is a frame of mind for which his people have
prepared him well. They have little else, but they have this readiness

for spells. As fast as he opens and closes his astronomy book, the autopilot star kachinas come and go like twirls of silver fog, and he has no need of a witness, only of a name, which he soon finds, calling them, after some elated pondering, the suitcase stars, easily exceeding the permitted weight.

Keeping the astronomy book open for his own peace of mind and eye because having the suitcase stars ever before him is wearing, he studies his living quarters with a critical eye, deciding, Yes, this is the kind of place a man could die in, be sick in, could never invite anybody to. So long as he lives in this, he need never worry about folks barging in to talk or to look at his kachinas. Apperknowle, the savvy collector, stays in the sunlight as much as he can. Abbott and Thomas hover at the window, thwarted by Uncle George's old plaid scarf which Oswald has smoothed out to maximum area. If only Uncle George had not stopped the rocker from rocking, Oswald might have rocked into view as his brothers peered in, making their habitual cursory comments on his character and his ways, but once he is out of view he is out of it, he does not rock back into it, and by the same token once he is in view he remains thus unless he shifts his chair. The other kachinas are still there, safe in their sack, but now Oswald's interest is divided, the category of kachina has split in two, and the disappearing act has ousted the mere simplicity of always being there. It is stone, he says of where he lives, so what do you call it? Hovel, shack, shanty, cabin? Is it a hut? What did Uncle George call it? He never spoke of it any more than he made direct references to his armpit. The place was part of him, and the only unusual item in it was the big fur-lined double boot in which he kept both feet warm by enclosing them with each other. Trying to sleep with his own feet in it, Oswald has had trouble, sensing that one foot is like a graft, bound hard to the other so that their natures might mingle. *Here I am*, he tells himself. It might be any day of the week, almost any time, I am light-years from the country in which the big insurance companies have odes sung to themselves on the TV screen, I am out on the edge of the invisible riviera of the visible world. At this point, even as he begins to succumb to the pageant of himself, BertandAnna walk in, not having knocked, and at once come close to him where he sits in the rocker, touching him and shoving him in fun as if to provoke him into standing, which he does not do, pushing away at them instead, at the mighty collops on their hips and arms. They have come to romp, to cavort, in their slow-motion way, in between times apprising him in an idiom he can only just fathom that Abbott has the last of his six colds a year, Fermina isn't sleeping too well because she has an ache in her back, and some Navajo have been walking house to house with a petition BertandAnna cannot understand but have signed anyway. Today they smell of mothballs and fried grease, as if they have just cooked an ancient bathrobe unearthed from its drawer, but their faces have a glow, an unusual perkiness, he tries to attribute to its cause. "You got an extra supply of candles," he hears. "You got lectric light in dem candles like you was come from heaven with a fistful of light. Thomas he seen your table full of near a dozen candles blazin away like there was nivver goin to be darkness again, but he dassent come in see fo hisself, no he off and tole Abbott, who say he musta stole them from some place, there was never yet no body needed a dozen candles on his one and only table, so Fermina she say he been long time in the darkness in the jungle, jungle a soft squelchy place fulla snake an slug, so he need an extra ration of light to keep his head straight lessen some slimy worm come up from under his chair and bite him where he was never bit afore. Hit could hurt him a lot iffen he was dozing in his chair and he have no stick to thrash it with, put paid to its noozance like the Sunday School teacher used to thrash them as would not say Lord Jesus, hear dis prair. Abbott been looking in again," they say to him. "No. *Thomas.* Well, they both alike they peers an awful lot for two." Why there must be folks all over this here mesa done only one millionth the peering them two asscuddlers done this past week alone. Would Uncle let me show the suitcase stars, just once, to keep them goggling and spraying explanatory spit for the rest of their days? Oswald sees at once how close he is to grandiosity with self-importance creeping up on him real fast, but he wants an audience and BertandAnna garble things so that his secret will be safe with them. Up he gets and closes the book with a snap that makes them jump a bit. They wheel around and see, terrified. On their knees, they begin some groveling apology for their lives this far, fisting their eyes and sobbing into their laps as they kneel forward and almost overbalance into the table the suitcase stars are shining from. "*Kachinas,*" he says, to quieten them a little, but they are too far gone in their combined bout of the shakes. It is as if all their lives they have dreamed about and dreaded this self-contained energy come to get them, stuff them into a sack and hurl them down into a canyon as bait for eagles or coyotes. *Kachinas* is the word they dare not say, and all they can muster, confronted with this live-wire prodigy from the most bleached-out of dawns, is *Hi, Hi*. Oswald almost laughs. You do not say Hi to stars or even to kachinas, though it is better than saying nothing at all, especially when a star has waited an eon and a kachina at least six months. "You shoo got some stuff fixed up dere, Mistoswald. Like the end of the world." Did they really speak in unplanned unison? He studies their faces, the pockmarks, the blotches, the scars they bear from being beaten or having several joint nasty falls, the wild oratorical eyes, their remaining teeth the color of corn, and decides they are worth talking to about it, so he regales them with his tale of wise men turning into stars who leave their fiery signatures behind them in the forms of dolls who dance so fast they cannot truly be seen but only guessed at as they cavort and pirouette on station, sliding upward and downward like pistons of flame, come all that way to brighten up the lives of the two most misunderstood people on the mesa. Three with me, he thinks as, like candles appearing to melt and then reform in a twinkling, the suitcase stars do and redo their monotonous voiceless, otherworldly, automatic act, and Oswald finds himself all of sudden craving for the real thing in doll or human form, weary of the mere mystery of unquenchable light, wanting corn smut and warm flesh, a ruff of Douglas fir and a wooden steeple like an inverted golf tee painted red and growing from the top of the return kachina's head. "We want the fake," he murmurs. "The real thing isn't friendly enough." I crave something crude, not mud or murk but something that has more need of me. I don't want to have to worry, I want to be able to open the book and not worry about accidentally closing it, which lets all the furies out like they were some molten saints a-fidgeting to dance themselves to death. Leave to the dead the dead's own toys. Why, if I was a god or some other fancy apparatus in the sky, I'd want my own kind of pinball for sure, just like Uncle George he gets his kicks from stuff like this, I am still in the world of rabbit stew and *piiki* bread and I want something more in line with the tastes of the living. What do I do? Close the book and let them wear themselves out? Open the book and worry myself into a caniption fit about how much fizz they'll store up while I'm reading? Even a black sheep of a veteran deserves a choice. I am ever so little a bit pissed off with miracles for the next few years or so. Right, I am going to brighten up BertandAnna's lives or is it life, I am going to show them how and then they will never be seen again like the family with its first TV. Mystery will flow like water while they gape and yell.

In its column of light, each revenant star grows a creamy tadpole tail, then a progeria head blazing pale blue, as it tours up and down like a Cartesian diver trapped in elements only to be guessed at. How can something made of light, trapped in light, be so easily visible? Whatever the answer, he decides, it has more to do with the willpower of each wizened head than with the visual properties of sapphires melting among diamonds. He stares so hard at each suitcase star in turn, then at them all together, that his vision blurs. Even as one or two ascend while others sink, he begins to see retina images around the columns themselves, no longer tubular but fringed with skirts and valances as if some force were flattening them out, denying them a dimension. Then they round out again and the trimmings vanish. He is back to what he started with, stunned by the apparition of a star as an aging boy; indeed, these stars seem to age before his eyes, as if his eyes are causing the changes as the shimmer becomes a white smut of motes. He is glad that by opening his book he can slow their decay, and he wonders how, if stars live as long as he thinks they do, a boy star aging can ever look older than these: Groombridge and the rest, as if there had to be wrinkles within wrinkles, and, behind every frail bone, one even frailer. He has heard about snowmen in the Sahara, or read about them, and understands the paradox. They die so fast, even if landed in the desert intact by refrigerator cargo planes. But these nursling stars, named for men who age impossibly fast even as the star heats up and turns into a red giant, defy his mind. He cannot fathom how the faces achieve this doomed and paper-thin angularity, as if hope fretting had bitten its lips to shreds. No, he thinks, that isn't the way at all: it happens through some terrible suction from within, some sapping of the face's marrow, until all that's left are heartbreaking diagrams for features. No lips, no eyes, not even a sharp and flange-like nose, but only slits or dots amid the ages-old parchment. These were men, fathers, who had given their all to become like the stars, and he was, just maybe, the only human ever to have seen them plain, without the finery of their blaze. The Man in the Moon was nothing to this parade of broken misters whom Uncle George, as loving as ever, had co-opted to shock him, to bring him back to life, and introduce him to a time span vaster than anything he'd known, against which all that is human is colossally trivial. Oswald melts with them, ages in his heart, feels his skull shrink and twist, his hair fall out, his teeth, his swollen eyes, and wishes he could go with them back to where they go when he once again opens up his book. Uncle George, bless him, he tells himself, has come back to show me the insignificance of death against the spectrum of the stars themselves. If stars can do it, so can we. Now he can hear voices exclaiming mildly, "Grayshuss, *Mistoswald,*" Bert or Anna is saying, it is certainly not their combined voice, but Oswald's eyes are firmly shut against the unquenchable miracle of the suitcase stars. "Somethin wrong, Mistoswald," they both tell him. "She gone out. They's bust." He keeps his eyes closed, hoping more than wondering. Again they tell him, now beginning to tug at his jeans, his plaid shirt, even his ear, almost as if engaged in some furtive exploration of his body, getting deeper and deeper the longer his eyes remain closed. *"They gone,"* he hears, but he doesn't believe it; he partly hopes the visitation is over, he partly wants to see the fireworks just once more. He looks, at nothing. There is no husk, nothing charred, no tube of extragalactic glass through which the charges poured. No sign of the suitcase stars. Kapteyn, Barnard, Groombridge, and 61 Cygni have taken their leave. Uncle George was not kidding when he said not to show or vulgarize. He opens and shuts the book like someone trying to shake a defective appliance back to life, but nothing happens. The book is the only link he has to the life they had. He looks out the window half expecting to see Uncle George with his finger raised in I-told-you-so, but all he can see is one solitary crow seeming to diagnose something on the ground in front of it. "Yair," he murmurs to BertandAnna, "that was it, all right. That was it." All they had to do to make him want them fiercely was to go away. It is too late, at least according to Uncle George's warning, and again he feels like someone fresh-home from Vietnam, wondering why the people in the streets aren't shooting at each other more often. Or just back on the mesa after two months in Palookaville, or a year in Winslow being nightman and daydream specialist. A dimension has moved away from him or he has moved back. It is not clear, but all of a sudden the magic and the mystery have backed away from him as an unlikely keeper. He goes on talking to BertandAnna, makes a movement toward the kettle on the stove but fails to finish it, rises from his rocking chair, and takes the book out into the early fall sunlight to cure or mend as if it were made of leather or broken. "Sure was bright some," say Bertand-

Anna, jaws in unison. He says nothing. "Like light on a rope was one of them fancy soaps." "Soap?" he says. "You could read yo little book, Mistoswald, by the light you done well git them for as long as you did. We best be movin along now." "Don't you tell," he says uselessly. "We seen nuthin, Mistoswald. Nobody listen to us anyhow. These days we Hi's somebody nice and they runs away like we has the plague or sumthin. You gotta be very polite even to git around from one day to the nixt." "More than polite," he tells them. "You got to be careful too. You got to say what's expected of you, and not a peck more. Then you might get away with whatever you do. If you don't, they'll sew your mouth up and pitch you into the canyon." "Sow us moufs up. Sow us moufs up?" "Yair." My uncle should have sowed mine up while he was alive, and pumped me full of Paris plaster to keep me stiff and safe. They nod eagerly as if they understand and are volunteering for whatever it is he is talking about. How *do* they time their utterances to get this weird Siamese-twins effect of the mouth? They are talking again, well wound. "Mistoswald, you bin good to us. We'll get you sumfin good real soon." Echoes of I'll go get me some. I got enough. "This an extra you gotta have. We's plannin a birthday party for the two of us. There's a gonna be cake and fizz an rabbit meat." "Can't hardly wait," he says. "Hi," one of them says, echoed by the other. "You gonna get a great big Hi that day for sure, Mistoswald. Hi, we's born again, we'll say. We's new. We's come around again just like the kachinas from the San Friscos." "See you then," he says, wondering if Uncle George will have further punishments for him: bolts of light through the brain, stardust up his nose to scald and scar. BertandAnna have gone in their four-legged waddle, and now Thomas and Abbott unstick themselves from his window, knowing they have not seen what they have seen, too late for the suitcase stars, but they have seen Oswald feeling up the voluminous underwear of BertandAnna, butting his nose up her frock, into his fly, and Uncle George has not installed these visions in their heads. Thomas and Abbott see what they want and then they tell their wives, a simple and effective bush telegraph requiring no help from tape recorders, Polaroid cameras, or blood samples in plastic bags. When Oswald is in view, Oswald is in the wrong, and no amount of yelling by Fermina changes their basic full-grown loathing. And when Oswald is invisible he must be doing something shameful or it would be right in front of them. It is no use Oswald's ever accosting them in his burly, friendly way and saying to them Groombridge, Kapteyn, Barnard, Sixty-One Cygni (said *Sig-nigh*), or the same names in a different order, as if calling up old high school friends, or even telling the suitcase stars the names of Thomas and Abbott to get them into trouble higher up. Oswald knows he has been fencing with opponents of his own making, shadow boxing too, living on a plane that Thomas and Abbott have no conception of. Only suave Sotuqnangu. Hell, he thinks, they don't let you get away with anything. I showed them to BertandAnna, which some would say isn't like showing them to real folks at all, them being first of all Engines, and then dumb ones at that. Somebody has to like them and I do. They hardly count to other folks, who must be so scared of being that way themselves they won't come near. They know how bad it would be to be them, but they never let knowing it affect the way they treat the BertandAnnas. Well, whoever holds things against you held that against me. I am hardly to blame for anyone who peeped. He murmurs self-vindications into his bread and cheese, his first food in seven hours or so. Boy, did we ever have some times together when they flashed and rippled on the tabletop. I'm back to normal now. The only thing wrong with me is that me and my mama we don't know why we have always been looking for something that's never there. It isn't in life for anybody. It's just a witch's brew, too much wanting in an overheated head. Take it from me, you Groombridge guys, it's slumming whenever you come here. They want things down to earth, not upsky. All over again, my book is just a book, but for a while there it was beginning to come on strong like a good book should. It really opened up. I really opened up to it with both legs. Unlike you I wasn't in full regalia. When he looks out again, as he now compulsively does, convinced that his brothers have made a lifetime commitment to spy on him, he sees BertandAnna stalled. They have not advanced at all but remain a dozen yards away, not talking to anybody he can see, but oddly stranded-looking as if celebrating the wonders of air to breathe or ground to tread on. They seem to be looking into each other's eyes and their arms are interlaced as in the old game he himself used to play: *Belthorses*, in which two children can move side by side like two ponies belted together. Leave them be, he tells himself, they're just practicing their Hi. They are, rapt and attuned, greeting each other with the minimal pregnant monosyllable of America too much in a hurry to say hello. It reminds him of something Apperknowle said about some prof at Phoenix or somewhere who said of another prof who lived out in the desert: too busy being Thoreau to even say hello.

Oswald knows who Thoreau was, having written an essay about him in his final year at school, groomed by Mititses. He feels so relieved that he goes out onto the sunlight to where BertandAnna are still standing thunderstruck. What they saw has just exploded within them and they are trying to pin it down, assign the event to some order of experience. "You sure got good ghosts," they tell him in their halting babble. "Not anymore," he says. "You're on your own for ghosts now, folks." "They gone," BertandAnna ask him, "back to the San Frisco Mountains? Where they lives?" "For all I know," Oswald says, "they have gone back to hell. Only you, just you saw them. It doesn't matter because I'm not going to tell anybody." Nobody would believe it. They nod, first Bert, then Anna. "You gonna bring them back, Mistoswald?" He wonders if, peculiarly gifted as they must be, they see things like this all the time. Their heads and eyes are full of weird apparitions, dumb presences at which they smile covetously, wanting to head off up into the corners of the room right beneath the ceiling and play with the creatures up there, or down under the linoleum where flat folk live. All I have given them, he decides, is a novelty, one among dozens. Then why are they standing stock-still out here, marveling at what they saw? "Once there was one," they tell him, "it kind of straddled us, its wings was spiderwebs, it touched us with a horny tail, it was whispering to us about eagles and where these eagles lived they had trees made of what you cough up, they was trees of spit. Then he come to our feet with his tongue like broken glass and then he in our clothes feeling all our places with a spit hand and he sure liked us he pulled and rubbed till we was all wet with it. Then he gone away." Oh, Oswald concludes, they thought what they saw today was this thing come back. I sure pick 'em. One of his own apparitions comes back, a recent one this, seen at Emory's country place: a human, presumably, mowing the grass, not in the usual fashion but in gas mask and yellow oilcloth cape, a big sombrero on its head, and seated on one of those motor mowers you can ride, except there were two smaller mowing machines attached with cables, so they trundled along behind the main one. It was like some devil engine from World War Two as if the mower were seeding the lawns with death and it might have been Emory himself in disguise, so to speak, having one of the crazy fits he always had when the non-Emory taint of his third son boiled up within him and no amount of self-absorption in trade or toil could blunt the edge of that bedroom melodrama, he could hear the wet sperms dripping like rain on gutters, lolling right there on the nether lips of his wife, on the slicked petals, ready to infest his homegrown idyll as if all his life so far he had done things wrong, so this was the comeuppance arranged in heaven: a simple squirting of slops where they did not belong, to be followed by growth of the incubus, the maturation here and elsewhere of the pest, the graft, the surplus one, Uncle George's lonely-man by-blow. Emory had an untidy heart, as Oswald knew, but there were insensate lengths he would go to that Oswald had no idea of, and when he saw the triple mower he was kind of new to Emory in that incarnation, unable to figure the man. No wonder BertandAnna were amazed. Now he knows what sort of stuff haunts their heads because he's seen what surprises them. He sighs: I know them better than I know Uncle Emory. They are accustomed to horny scaly creatures with harsh tongues that straddle them, and feel them up, whereas this was like four candles of maneuvering light, easily rigged as a conjuring trick if I wanted to fool them and they would never have known the difference. Why bother? Who has to try, with miracles all around us? He begins to peel from his face the little flesh-colored patches he applied in his cabin, and BertandAnna coo with delight, thinking he's removing scabs or scales they had not noticed when he came outside. Glory be, says Oswald, I must have been out of my wits wasting ghosts like this. It goes to show: when you can waste half an hour of your life, even under the intense pressure of some goddamned vision or other, doing stuff like this, then you have sunk kind of low. I belong with these two, they have it all figured out to where they believe there is nothing worth doing beyond saying Hi nonstop. They munch time like it was bread, primed for the marvelous, which leaves them mostly alone, but when it shows up they sure are ready to give it their sole and undivided. "Groombridge, Kapteyn," he says to them with the easy intonation of someone saying *franks and fries tonight folks,* "Barnard and Sixty-One Sig-nigh." Now they smile at him, they nod, they have received it in its full complexity. He wonders what on earth they think he said. They are making no attempt to repeat it, the magic formula of star travel, star portation, star removal, even though he himself is thrilled to have been so close, so right on top of, a thing so alien to human encounter. It was worth being alive for, never mind how lousy everything else to date had been, from the sleazy auspices of his arrival on Earth through the disaffection he felt about an uncle-father who could teach him nothing (he was so ungifted at porn flick and jungle war, with homicide somewhere in there and then the finale of bookish nightwork as if it had to be the last sacrament). "Something shiny," he says. That is all I ever needed. I was going to find a cardboard sword and charge jumbo jets as they took off, right at them while their big noses rolled toward me. Anything reckless, mad, off the wall. That was me. Looking outside of human contact for a human answer, that was me, and that was me fouling it up only days later. I stared at them with so much delight it wore my reverence out. That's it. I got careless. Oswald, you were always careless with magic, thinking you could always imagine such stuff into being anyway, but when the real thing shows up you behave all wrong. Reason: you were never trained to behave right. Folk have founded enduring religions on a less-firm basis than those autopilot suitcase stars. I am beginning to think of them as Groombridges, grouping them, which is the beginning of familiarity, which breeds familiarity, not contempt. He still has his arms around BertandAnna, long arms around that double unwashed girth, and out of nowhere comes another answer: they went to the lake that day with Bessie Butterfly Disappearing Over Flowers to bathe, to get clean after months of having nothing to bathe in, water being like uranium on the mesa except to Navajos. Bertand-Anna have stuck the tiny nose pads on their own faces now, are still peeling them off his and with monotonous giggles putting them on each other's nose and cheeks. Disease transfer by consent, he thinks. We got something in common. They somehow pushed Bessie under, I somehow strangled Trudy Blue whose real name was, I just don't know anymore. I never heard it but twice.

"You ever," he is asking Fermina, "got the feeling that you just somehow muddle on from day to day, making the most of just about any damn thing that comes along, doesn't matter what so long as it's there to be done something with? Like that." "Some question from a son," she says. "Youse lucky. I was always wanting a day to come along that didn't have something in it I was spose to make something out of it. I don't honestly recollect more than four or five days my entire life when nothing happened and then there was that bliss. Yes it was blissful, that's a word. When you get very old maybe it happens then, somewhere between you last gasp and you last drink of water." "Like in the old movies we watched and when we talked about it after. Nothing connected to nothing," Oswald says. "All we had in mind was kind of reliving it afterward. We'd say, Yair, what about when he said stick it and the other guy plugged him and when the plugged guy plugged him back and he said gee I hadn't counted on that. Everything you said began with When or Yair when. We lived in stuff that had already been lived through on the screen. It was always when and we didn't say said, we said when he goes, and then we'd say what he'd said." "Plug your mouf with food, that's best," she sighs. "I wouldn't be a mother again for all the desert in Arizona. I would like to be born unable and let other folks do it all." He tells her his theory about Bessie Butterfly and how she had taken Bertand-Anna to bathe in the lake, it was like her wasn't it. The light wanes abruptly as if something has just taken a big swig of it and sucked the sunset dry. She has no intention of talking about Bessie Butterfly, but she doesn't exactly refuse, she just lays her worn hands on Oswald's front and begins to push him gently away from her as if she were removing a beam crushing her leg, then as soon as he starts to bulge into overbalancing she pulls him back toward her, hand up to feed or strike him, but it only pats his cheeks and puts him vertically to bed. He knows now about the person in sombrero and gas mask mowing the grass at Emory's place; the person working thus was somehow charging the lawn on the horizontal plane, dominating it, making it lie down and be good. Now one of her hands rests upon the other as she sits in the small armchair she has always sat in, deep cushioned but with one arm glued back together. She will not use a cushion under her elbow, she will not let him pad it for her, she likes the nongiving quality of the wood underneath her, she says. "Lessen I slip right through to whatever horrors is underneath. Just waiting to get me. You sure," she says angrily, "she didn't get them all the way out there to watch them do it." "Do it, Mama?" "Yair, she was a watcher, I reckon. She would have had some awful Anglo disease between her legs too. She drowned herself out of spite. She knowed what was a-comin." "Naw," Oswald says, relapsing into what he thinks is the vernacular, "it was accidental all of it. She had just about everything to live for." "Don't lie to me, boy." "Mama, I said nothing." "Hers was a miserable life with *him*, she wanted some other body to have it, she didn't want his children you could tell that a mile away. They do say she paid BertandAnna to hold her under, to sit on her like she was a sack." Oswald realizes now that whenever he talks homewise to her it charges her up with accusation, so he tries to make his speech formal again to curb her. "Who said this about a sack?"

"Paid them," Fermina insists, "imagine that, she wanted it that much." Her glasses slide into the shoe-cleaner glove. "None of us will ever know, Mama," he says, "it's crazy to go on about it." "I'm not crazy not yet, though there's some as is working hard on it." She seems about to break into song, some old heartbroken elegant refrain addressed to the powers that let women lead miserable lives and never never take them out of them with a wand or a storm or a check or a piece of the divine floating down like a slice from one of those hunks of soft greenish plastic foam they stick the stems of flowers into to make them stand. "When," she says, "a woman's crazy, then that's all she got. Her crazies is all she ever have put past a certain age." "Huh?" He watches her prod the little log fire, make his bowl of thin clear soup, pat her forehead with her handkerchief as if she can see the exact effect of each motion in some mirror, and then roll up the sleeves of her blouse to stroke her arms with rapid, coercive movements borrowed from first aid. "What you fixin to do, Oswald, now you's left school?" Solid, jagged sarcasm, and he knows it is time to get out, head back for his unheated cabin, whatever ghosts await him there in the cuttable silence Uncle George left behind him like a pall around his knives and rasps, and the shelf of cans. *Them few cans*, he hears inside himself as if some innate vernacular said the words for him, *is paradise*. "There going to be an exhibit, a show, in Tucson and Phoenix of Uncle George's work, what's left of it, of him. Mister Apperknowle is going to put it on in a month or two." "You call him Doctor." "He doesn't cut nobody, Mama. He's no sawbones." "Him a doctor still. Abbott said so." He pauses at the door, looks back at her churning face, heavily veers back to kiss her on the bridge of the nose, a place both intimate and bony so not committing him too much or offending her either. "Gnite," he says, echoing Emory, as if his entire life has been echo, shadow, looking up and standing back. Except for the war, when he was a somebody, a somebody nobody ought to have to be. Her loud old-fashioned alarm clock gives out a creak then develops a shudder in its spring somewhere, failing to attract her attention which is on the grayness of the window, her face half dropsical, her hands all in a fast infolded bother as if wringing grief's or anger's neck. "Ten o'clock," she announces as his foot touches the rim of the rug, and the clock rings its alarm as if it is time for her to get up. She does it so she will not fall asleep in her chair instead of going to bed. She wakes herself up, often enough, to go to sleep. *Gnite.* He is gone, as away from her as one dead and laid out for eagles. His cabin is cold.

He pounds his arms against his sides, chuffing his breath. His eyes
tear. He checks. Nothing is missing. He opens and shuts the astronomy book without result of any kind. Near his face the candle feels
warm, but warmth with a disappearing and inaccessible point that
flutters about in the drafts. He hears his feet. He sees his breath full of
shadows and crevasses as if a skier were trapped in there somehow
and had flailed its volume to get out. Into the big double boot go his
nephew's feet. He cannot sleep for being too cold, so he empties all
the drawers, makes a heap of sweaters and shirts and underwear on
the floor in the corner, tosses the blanket on top and himself on top of
the heap at the sprawl, somehow hoping to sink in deep. From above
and behind, his feet in the red fleecy boot seem to have been trapped
in some prosthetic appliance shoved on him by a sadistic Santa Claus.
Fermina trembles with fatigue, she cannot keep her feet calm under
the covers, but she does not sleep. She remembers something so
strange she no longer believes it, the woman was not herself, yet how
did she Fermina know about it then when she saw how cold baby
Oswald was and, unable to find anything textile at hand, took down a
jar of jelly from the shelf and opened it up, then began to lard him
with it, scarlet by kerosene light, until he was the stockiest baby in
America. Then she wrapped him in brown packing paper and rolled
him in corrugated cardboard, amazed at herself at how eccentric she
had become. If she did it at all. Doing it ranks among the staged
pamperings in her head; she knows she doused him or smothered him
in something gooey and then tenderly wrapped him as a parcel, after
which, for days, she took her time licking him clean, and he took to
the sensation from the first, half convinced at some intimate fragile
level of his being that he was a foal or a kitten. It is what she opposes
to her memory of Bessie Butterfly brought back dead from the lake,
off her coming an aroma of camphor and stale chrysanthemum, her
body all flopped out, her eyes fishlike in their glazed open availability
as if now the whole world could pour into her head through them,
meaning for once she was standing still. When George The Place In
Flowers Where Pollen Rests saw her, he doubled over forward upon
her and threw up, racked and heaving, but he soon recovered enough
to cradle her head in his arms and coo birdlike into her unhearing
ears, his hands deeply thrust into her bushy hair as if he too were
drowning, floating away, and he had to hold on to something. She
seemed to have shrunk inside her skin, but there was on her face no
look of offense taken, no response at all except the stunned peace of

the gone. Whatever she had been doing with her life was over now. Of course Fermina was grieved, but even at this point, as she remembers it, she felt the tiny Oswald begin to come into being, creeping from the dead woman's pores across the ground in between and taking Fermina by mellow, seedling storm, long before George laid hands on her. Next day George moved out of their quite well-appointed stone house with its cushions and antimacassars and hectic zigzag blankets and as if to declare his new profession of solitary lived on in the shack, which Fermina like one going to voluptuous execution cleaned out for him and tried to make cozy, but he would have none of that, the coziness, he wanted it to be a kind of crypt. Stone-cold. Earth-dank. Rodent-busy. Sackcloth he had never heard of, but they said he collected rough twigs and made his bed upon them on the bare earth, thereupon dreaming, Fermina says, of enormous thrustings into something soft and juicy, hers by grace of Sotuqnangu, his by importunity. That was later, though, whereas the immediate babble surrounding the event had to do with a sheep Bessie Butterfly had rescued, so some said, and with the role in this and other things of BertandAnna, who when inquired of by mesa police talked only of the things they understood. Asked what happened first, BertandAnna said *brown, muddy,* and when asked about being in the water clapped their hands and mimed the splash, their last word being *black*. It was no use asking them, sopping wet as they were, expecting her to come back to life and cheeriness after her post-swim sleep, unable to construe the long pale green strand of snot coming from her nostril, the quiet look of broken pulp she assumed there on the table in the cultural center, the faint but poignantly precise whiff of baby caca coming off her as she went through all the easings up of death. Days after they were saying Hi to her body, lying in state in its bridal gown. To them a long sleep befitting one so energetic on land and in water, her death brought enigmas to the mesa, but unsolved unlike those other enigmas poverty and hardship. There had been no sheep, no foul play, no suicide, but only a thunderbolt of bad luck, so the police said, Bessie Butterfly having for reasons unknown tried to bathe BertandAnna, which act turned naturally into an attempt at a swimming lesson, which ended as tragedy in water neither deep nor murky. She drowned beneath them while, no doubt, they giggled at the weird sensation, never having before in chilly lake water having ridden on a semibuoyant drowning first-class swimmer. George's vigils grew longer as he guessed at the brutal operetta that must have gone on above the tumult under the torn surface. He touched her putty face, he patted her dislocated-seeming shoulders, he made the moans of a cow in labor, he let his hands grow soft from lack of sawing and chiseling, until he could stand it no longer, he by now half hugging the table on which they had laid her in the secondhand one-piece bathing suit of black, thick rayon, in itself almost funereal. "Eh," he whispered to the wood, "you trod upon your shadow, you knew you were more solid than any effect of light and water. You who could lay upon water let it lay on you. You fell through the top and your stars fell with you down to where little worms play with what meat arrives, inches only from where you were happier than you were with me, and the dummies trod you down the more you wriggled. A young face unfit for olive tints. Were you wood, I would recarve you now, I would make you float forever and ever," but he could not voice the rest of it, the certainty that if only he could ob-serve it he would like to go drown himself on her behalf, choking on his bloated heart and slack affinity, wanting like hell to be shut of it all forever, telling himself that he was willing to lose anything if only he could lose grief. "*Kill*," he said. He already had BertandAnna by the throat, a chisel in his other hand, but he knew it was a dream because he could not grasp their burly throats two in one hand, it would lose him the chisel. He did nothing about it, not ever speaking to them, because his head was full of Bessie Butterfly's teasing, slightly crackling voice that halted and recovered with an invisible smile behind it as if she were somehow broadcasting, talking to every-one and no one with genial wry correctness amounting to no more than a nighttime whisper as she closed the show, reciting the wave lengths and the local translators. Tune in tomorrow as if tomorrow were a show. "*I'll* bathe them," he said to Emory. "*I'll* scrub them." "Hush." "Shove their noses," he said through his tears, "into the warm sand until they stop heaving about. I seen their dirty under-wear enough. I'll squeeze the bubbles out of em." "You'll hush," Fermina told him, "or you'll have nobody to hush up for." George has seen Matlock's annotations in his elastic-bound black book and he cannot see how a death and a life can be reduced to a shorthand so crude as *F. Ind. 28. Acc'l d. Drwnd.* "She had awful loving hands," George sobbed, "not for pastry, bread, but for touching you like they sunk through to your backbone and softened it up." "*Then don't hush,*" Fermina said then. "*Let it out.*" And that, she tells herself as she rubs her feet together violently as if hoping for a spark as she tries to quieten down for sleep, is how it all began. If I'd of hushed him he'd of hushed all right. I drownded in his upset. Son of a bitch found out how crying made his cock go hard. She banishes the live and dead George, the satiated and uncondoned, the cocksman and the ghost, and closes her eyes, squeezing them tight with her brow.

Again he looks out from where he lives, wryly noting that all his looks are afternoon looks now. He sees mountains and stone, a whole range of ochers and browns, a fine rock walkway with a sturdy wall on the dangerous side. He can almost imagine it otherwise, with soft green grass cushioning the eyes, sheep nibbling it, and over there in the declivity a small lake reflecting heaven and houses painted red and yellow: a gussied-up version of the moderately austere mesascape he's used to. "With one wand," he murmurs, yearning for the suitcase stars to pay him a return visit. He does believe in magic. He has to after what happened, almost as magical as the time he saw his mother run out into the plaza in a loose-fitting nightgown, her hair tumbling around her ears, chamber pot in hand, the white of the combs in her hair (she slept in them), crying out for Uncle George the dead, yelling, *"Let me touch him once again,"* in full view of everybody, hunting for the blue jellied sturgeon lips, wanting to make of her entire body a warm plaster, but boisterous death had wrung him from her, and all she could manage to do was leap, no more than a few inches off the ground, but for her a massive trajectory beyond gravity and compasses, beyond direction itself, a hopeless upward shunt such as she had never imagined eloquent. Tiptoes. Bend at the knees. Up she went, on her way to him as if obliged through some local decorum to keep her leap tiny, but she leapt with all the breath in her even as they murmured and pointed, scoffed and told evil stories, and when she came down again it was as a different woman, formally widowed by that jolt, never again able after such a demonstration in daylight to mourn Uncle George again in public. Had he wanted her, she crazily reasoned, he would have drawn her up after him from the mesa so that they could see how tender and close their misbehavior had been. She became unnaturally calm after that, fixing on Oswald when she could the twisted feelings from her loss of George and asking for nothing else, neither sexual nor affectional, just a woman saved from the pickle she'd been in and determined to brave it out among the tittle-tattle. The wind drying her face, curing it like leather, was the present re-seizing her as if it cared, not to make anything fresh of her, just to enlist her in the travailing hordes who unable to reckon with death worked hard for a living in mute mechanicality, knowing there was nothing else and that only a dumbfounded response kept them sane; the deepest canyon of all was there, red-fanged and alert, ready for them all, and more, it had all been seen to since the beginning of time, since before Spider Woman, and only their ornate costumes in the dance kept at bay the awful successful continuum of disease and rot and the ultimate depravity of people turned manure. The faithful set all this aside, but the morbid questioning ones among them could see through the lush fabric of their beliefs, it was not camouflage, it was not a defense, and they knew the kachinas came from the mesa itself, close at hand, from the house next door, and not from the San Francisco Mountains, not ever from there, not that different from Santa Claus, the only Anglo kachina they had heard about. This was true for Oswald long ago, sometimes for Uncle George (who, however, retained a proprietary interest in faith as in wood; it was what he carved, after all), and now and then for Fermina mildly afflicted with the same doubts as Bessie Butterfly herself, the woman who had transferred her faith into athleticism and dared to show her naked body to the dormant kachinas if ever they were looking toward the lake, if they had eyes to see. Not that the four of them disliked pageantry, they needed it all the more as a distraction from their lack of cosmic trust. They needed a pageant that actually changed things, made the dead come back and the unborn go away, exercising its power over everything and not just a few privileged items. What good were masks and gourds, ruffs and kilts, if all they did was give the people something to do? They could not lull themselves, these freethinkers, with mere lively leaping and chants, they wanted something from the back of beyond, something a wooden kachina doll was as likely to provide as any dressed-up neighbor braying and cavorting. The cottonwood was no farther from the source of what decided things than the dances were. *"Jollification,"* Fermina would say to George at her boldest in the old days, meaning that was all there was to these exquisite homegrown dramas, whereas all she wanted, for her or for them both together, was an abrupt change in life, not on the level of pretend, and she would give out one deliquescent murmur and know that it had happened, it had happened all right, and there was no turning back. "Look," she'd say, and show him her extravagant walk, maybe a parody of what was danced in the plazas, as she swung her left hand high and vertical up past her head while flinging her right one upward and across her collarbone to touch her shoulder. In private she would walk about like that, demonstrating as best she could her own way of summoning presences from the fabled San Franciscos. All George would do was nod, knowing she would find any halo heavy; she was as an insect, surely a desirable and pretty one, but an insect all the same wing-trapped in the sludge of his doubt, through which he managed to force himself, of course, day after day into the heart of the cottonwood root, whereas she were she not trapped would blow away deep into the maw of what ailed her, and he was glad as far as that went that his doubts were thick and sticky. All Fermina wanted in her mellow prosaic way was a life that made no sense to anyone, but with everyone admitting how baffling it was, or a life that made complete sense with everyone suited down to the ground. "*Ah,*" George would tell her, "that's a lot." "Oh," she would answer him, "it ought to be one of the guarantees of coming into the world at all, like little Oswald, it ought to come with the skin." "Only certain death does that, Fermina." "You tell that to a woman with her third baby." "I do. No way around it, woman, you got to swallow the nails in the cream." "That's diffrant," she said, "*you* can't tell me that. I don't want you to tell me that." "Tell yourself then," George answered. "It doesn't matter s'long as you know." That was how they left it, George always knowing when a thing was impossible the way the sky could not be hauled down and used as a scarf. What the hell is it, he thought, that she's dying to have? Nothing human. She wants to be a woman apart from all of humanity, exempted. There was never anybody yet in that category save these dolls of mine, but then, they don't have any of the advantages either. Born dead, they do not die, that's kind of what I relish in them. His relish, he knew it, was all-consuming; like death itself he would accept anyone that came along, anything, he had some unbiased omnivorousness that kept him sweet, adept for all occasions, at least as he saw it. Who could get irascible when he was so special as that, and why? George never quite figured that out, much as he tried, regarding his whims and moods as flickers in a personal weather he was not responsible for, it was what came with his gift, he left it at that. His yearning, however, to know the heart of Sotuqnangu nagged at him. Why not dismiss the god once and for all and leave it at that? Why bother ever again when a flake of doubt had told him it would abide; he didn't have to have a doubt as big as a mesa, a flake was more than ample, sinking the ship of his happiness inexorably, never mind how slow. On he pushed, eager to implant himself in wood, worried by how he'd managed to sink a ship with a flake rather than a leak, a typhoon. He persisted with what, in later years, Oswald would come to call Uncle George's St. Francis delusion, which was when George held out his hands to the birds and flies, lower down to rabbits and foxes, and they never came to him, but George said they were going to, he could feel that tingle in the tips of his fingers, it might take twenty years, but come they would, once they got things straight, he was just another creator after all, subordinate but related. *Don't you worry none,* George told him, *Oswald Beautiful Badger Going Over The Hill, you might think I'm on the earth, I am, but I'm huddled by a star. Crouch by that wall of mine and it's all there for the asking. Distance don't make no diffrunce. You got to tune your mind in keen, then it will all come to you, streaming down like something poured toward you from a pitcher, nothing fancy but a sense that you're a part of something bigger'n you can ever say. That's me. Not us. Just a few have it, but if they have it, it drives them crazy happy. It isn't any god's, it's just there, part of what landed here without being asked for.* Oswald never understood this, but he virtually memorized it as something to pore over in the vast tedium of sleepless nights to come, as an anodyne to suck on while honoring the memory of his uncle, that baffling, tetchy, indomitable man of peace and pique, of pills and margarine. It was no use trying to copy him, but he was willing to be influenced by some seepage from father to son (real), uncle to nephew (fake), of honor and shame mixed, unwilling to lodge in the weird theological halfway house invented by Uncle George, but willing to use his figures of speech from time to time, to esteem his dolls as George's dolls, not the mesa's, not his mother's, not Sotuqnangu's and not the wood's, durably severed from any force in the San Francisco Mountains. If Uncle George had a gangrene of the mind, untreated, then Oswald saw himself as an amputee, a vivid turn as images go, but not my best by far (when knowledge is complete, what arrogance tries to prove it?). It was always the same, with George The Place In Flowers Where Pollen Lies saying the same things to Oswald, such as, Be Quiet, Be Still, Shut Up, Calm Down, Hold On, all said gently but implying the thrash of a whip, and only once did George say to Oswald, *"You have laid violent hands on a holy thing, give the doll to me, its life is still between the tree and me."* Oswald gave it up, half hoping George would use the chisel to cut his Oswald's fist, just so long as he would leave a mark or say a thing his son could understand. He was sixteen before he really believed he was the son rather than the nephew, and in a way he warmed to the usages of uncle to nephew, and vice versa, as a formal and distant banter a father and son could not arrive at, conjuring something courtly and rhetorical out of what had come to be a scandal on mesa and off, reaching to Keams Canyon and even Winslow. Time and again they would indulge in valiant little exchanges whose gentle almost forced propriety thrilled them both; the asperities were not those of a father to his son, for as such they would have hurt, and the gaucheries from Oswald were different too: born of leniency, destined for praise, they had two roles, then, and soon learned to deal with awkward matters as uncle and nephew, as father and son only with trivialities, so that when Oswald complained that all he could hear on the mesa was the bleating of sheep his *uncle* told him the wings of butterflies were audible too but that the sheep bleated so as not to hear them. They bleated to make a darkness, a deafness, amid which Oswald only too often thought he was alone, asking his father-uncle, depending on the occasion, all sorts of things about the abounding crush of summer heat, the pinchy snare of winter cold, but also what seemed to Oswald queries uncombinable with anything: *Uncle, is it all right to scratch my crotch? Uncle, is it all right to pick my nose? Uncle, is it all right* (he always called him Uncle, but Father under his breath from the day that he knew) *to let the candy from my dooie spill into my pants?* With a broad hand, he seems now to recall Uncle George's saying, "Flog it into the open, boy. Don't be shy about it. Show it who is boss and it will never betray you except at night, which is really its time to roam, it likes to leak and seep then, it gets everywhere, it grows legs and tentacles, it loves to roost in a cranny when, by rights, it should be floating all over the mesa like dandelion seed. Emory and I, well, we used to play games to see if there was a limited amount of it, see, but he could always fetch another drop up, I think it came direct from his brain. He was a ready and fast comer, Emory was, whereas your uncle, he hardly ever did at all, only when under a lot of pressure. My advice is always mop up afterward and treat it as sweat." Perhaps, Oswald thought, he had never heard any such thing, but his father's, his uncle's, ways of handling rasp or knife had something of the moves attributed by the Mititses to what they spoke of as self-defilement, as if they had seen and known, hooked obscenely up to a rubber one mailed plainwrapper from Culver City, coaxing it and slamming it about but able only to make it squirt warm water whose colorless effusion could hardly meet their needs. Yes, Oswald had told himself, stack up all the appliances people have bought and used to egg on that vital part of us and you could fill the Grand Canyon to the very brim. Things that buzz and bore, flick and smack, suck and goad, needle and throttle, make swell up and itch, all those gadgets of satisfaction, I've seen them all, I've been there, as in a very distant corrupted childhood where the madam meets the strange metallurgists of space flight and their lightweight wares, where the whore with her whip and selection of rubber bands meets the mystic who withholds his sperm. I have been there, a traveler in a terrible land of rubber bladders, seethrough tubing, talcum powder, and fetchily named lubricants. It's a wonder I survived. I could hardly introduce my trade to the mesa, naughty-handed as my people are. It feels even longer ago than it really is, done by a sibling whose memory makes no more sense now than radio atmospherics. Three Oswalds have died. He has changed like that knife he once read about, whose handle they replaced and then the blade, so was it the same knife? He isn't sure, but he thinks he is no longer who he was. He wants less, at least of things mundane and named. He wants more of things he cannot quite pin down, such as the suitcase stars, and he suddenly wonders why he never wondered what became of people, they were more than ships passing in the night, weren't they? Emory himself, the quaintly canny eccentric long lost to the mesa and his kinfolk, was more than that, surely. And his Ellen, practical, earthy, a book-keeping sweetheart? What of Captain Bartram, Dennison, and Schultz? Two of them dead, maybe three, but to Oswald they are alive until he forgets them, when they will become doubly dead. Yes, he says, you are not really dead until you aren't worth remembering. Do we remember people as being dead or, since they died, only as being alive? There is a parade of mouths that jabber at us, hands that hold ours, eyes that plead for contact, and all of a sudden it has gone and you are going through the same motions with different people. Now you've learned how, it's okay. People are dreadfully interchangeable. If Stu and Clu are as dead as Trudy Blue, there will be an Al (he cannot think of a rhyming name) and a Mac to replace them, and a Marci Tint for her. "It does not matter, Mama," he says, he who talks to Fermina much more in her absence than when she's there. He thinks of all the people he is never going to know, all the years he is never going to see: the faces, the seasons, the wars and sports and pastimes, the inventions and the prices, and has a momentary mournful fit, whispering an elegy in advance for the guessable life to come, and wonders just how much tenderness there is in the human race for all its forbears, those who have slaved and cried, guzzled and fornicated, invented and whispered, loved and killed, carved and sung. He does not think of himself as having actually lived a life, only one made of in-betweens, leftovers, to which he has applied himself more than such things deserved, as if he has been Napoleon, George Washington, Albert Einstein, all in one, taking himself seriously as would one who has *applied* to be born, and adduced convincing arguments to that end, and then has agreed to make as good a job of things as he can: the earning of lucre, the curious career goals, the search for a satisfactory orthodox private life and a solid hamstrung reputation. All these are mysteries to him, he does not know the way toward them, he improvises his living somewhat in the manner of a kit delivered but left unassembled and obliged to put itself together without, unless very lucky, batteries and glue. Over the next few months he is going to ponder all these things, telling himself he has come to the mesa to take stock, as if there were some mercantile inventory of himself to be done, and then declared, so that they will say, "You heard about Oswald Beautiful Badger Going Over The Hill? He came out in the black." "Oh, what's his trade then?" "Carrier of hot embers. Icicle Boy. Coyote Man. Aligner of stars. One who makes thrones from branches of spruce." Actually, he thinks, the record should go something like this: heroworshiper, extra, GI, nightman, which doesn't sound like him at all, and the record should show instead hanger-on, porno stud, cannon fodder, pawn. He recoils from that too, reassuring himself that since he returned to the mesa he has become something else, much more than the son of his uncle, the nephew of his father, in short a keeper of kachina dolls, a custodian of suitcase stars, from which it is only a hop to something altogether more august and dreamy, could he but twig how to reach it. It is like trying to cut through the congested acid smell of all those porno rooms in godforsaken motels to a plateau on which there shines, tonic and unrestricted, the sun of Acapulco and Bermuda, New Guinea and Brisbane, where he has never been and no doubt never will be. Oh the silent scream within him as his jissom rose for the umpteenth time and because of that he could go eat steak again. Here, though, could he but tap the vein, life is going to be newer and brighter, despite the Thomases and the Abbotts, the loss of magic, the ever-growing need to deal with the Apperknowles, whoever they are. Fermina is on his side, never mind how tricky she can get. Those who don't hate his guts might help him from time to time. All he has to do is carve, plant, or mingle well. He recalls Uncle Emory in the mountain woods, and knows that his own future is not going to consist of watching game shows in which dollar amounts flash on to a screen and a hyperactive audience applauds the amounts like a horde of the bravo shouters who go to concerts to hear themselves. He hears what is not going to happen: 100,000 dollars—the audience goes mad and screams; 250,000—they hurl themselves at the screen and lick the number; 750,000—they tear each other to bits in a frenzy of vicarious greed. It is like the old game shows, without the prizes; in days to come, he knows, he just knows, people are going to say *Dollarday* when they meet in the street and *Dollarbye* when they go. He himself is like one heading into the funnel of mysticism, entering the outer lip of the wide cone splayed out like a perfectly symmetrical glass woman's labials, then despite some slips heading for the narrower portion until he reaches the end of the main tube which conducts him to an Oswald in his prime, clear of vengeance threats or someone sent to rub him out, a mesa notable whose vocation is to toe the line. Although it will take him several months to develop it, he has a plan of sorts, nothing to do with Apperknowle, who is going to pester him by mail for quite a while with questions about Uncle George, but reentry into the fold without his having to go too far toward life as lived by all the others. He is not going to carve (he could pass muster, at least knowing how to use the saw and knife) or open a pinball parlor on the mesa (the elders would vote it down) or bring them up to date on recent wars (he has one or two lectures within him) or head back to college (he could, he thinks, after oiling his smarts). He is going to read and study, staying on in the stone shanty and looking into tribal lore to see if there isn't some kind of niche for him. Surely in so varied and ingenious a set of tribal myths there is a vacancy for him, some slot natural for his somewhat twisted maturation. He would like to tell them what it is like to be several times over a survivor, but without any of the stock formulas survivors use. He would even like a date or two, but going through the motions of that up here would be like—is there anything like it, he wonders, anything enough like it to be useful. Like asking a suitcase star, Groombridge or one of the others, to be a firefly. No, he isn't that good or that desirous. Fermina would love to fix him up, muttering vaguely about men on the shelf, wallflower sons, and so forth, none of it aimed directly at him but at the world, amorphous author of all woes, the world she would like to give a good scrubbing and hiding to quite soon.

Living quietly on the mesa he has come to think of as his, Oswald begins to discern the merits of the pensive life, to which he would never have come at all if someone had recommended it. The days are so much alike (as, he grants, they might also be if he worked in an L.A. body shop), they begin to merge, and he finds this snowlike pileup ravishing, as if days are being poured out at him from the time factory over there in the east. The women's ceremonies are going ahead, but he takes no part in that, his mind on something else, his books, his stargazing done with boyish impetus since the arrival of Uncle George's ghost and his once daily stroll through the village just to be friendly, to implant himself in their sight even if only to an- nounce that he is here today, as he was here yesterday, as he will be here tomorrow, home-come in humility if not glory, and willing to hold his ground even if he can't figure out how to uncivilize himself. Palookaville will never let him him go, of course, but he has let go of it, mainly by selecting a vignette from here or there—the Ossa Negra, the sex shops, Stu and Clu—and trying to install them next to stars, to shove them into the middle of constellations, thus setting them in a context that makes them ridiculous and impertinent, but minifying them too. It is his Cro-Magnon comparison, as fatal to anything ephemeral as to anything evolved. It destroys not only the princelings of porn but also the automobile, the telephone, paternity, Death Row, blood pressure machines, money, and shame. Nights he peers at the unchanging pageant above his head and tries to make himself accept its arbitrary shape, its utter indifference to him, at least as something to be looked at, whereas the suitcase stars have told him something different. He has intimate knowledge, he thinks, a special icing on the familiar notion of stars. Unlike everyone else, he is involved with them too in a way that no one in his or her so-called right mind would credit, even though the canny savvy side of him knows that no one lives on stars; the ghosts who came to see him were not from planets, not in that sense *beings* at all, but resurrections of prowess turned into scalding furnaces with handy names. Yes, he tells himself, stars are friendly after all, stars are where the dead ones go; it figures because the planets are full of those living aboard them. Belatedly, he wants to grow up right, become one of the team, knowing he is wholly special for the unique vision vouchsafed him, as perhaps it is to all serious astronomers. There he sits, indoors reading with the crickets that saunter out at night frisking and bouncing around his naked feet, sometimes giving him the sense that he is fidgeting his toes about among a heap of delicate basketwork, or out in the spiky cold of mid-fall, heedless of mice and birds, his eyes glued to the brooches above him, an infatuated pragmatist slowly pondering his way across the eons and the spaces, somehow trying to pass through his head all the expirable that has been since the year dot of the big bang, a god, an observer, a traveling star all rolled into one. He is a transparent sea creature only one sixty-fourth of an inch long, but he is also someone holding a garage sale to dispose of inexplicably acquired shoemaker's lasts, tie selection racks, and tables with taxidermy legs. He is Groombridge (mainly because he likes the name better than the other ones), but he is Uncle George as well, Thomas and Abbott restrained at least as far as their surliness to him goes, and he is all those others, those shrunken faces lodged at intervals along the curve of time: Velma, Alf, Bessie Butterfly, as the first of whom he nurses Uncle George the baby, shoving the rough ruddy nipple into his unsearching mouth, with the next of whom he bewails his uncle's lack of interest in corn, with the last of whom in a fit of masochistic horror he drowns. He relives his babyhood, from which or was it later he recalls three silver spoons given to Fermina to say he doesn't know exactly what, but each has a little decorated shield at the top of its handle, one saying Flagstaff, another saying Phoenix, the last saying Tucson. Spoons for marmalade, sugar, or, if there happens to be an open vessel for it, salt. She still has them, but he has their souls, willing them back to the source of metals. Whatever it is that he's doing, it is becoming easy; everything passes through him now that his defenses are down, not belonging to him, but grazing him with its command performance of a passage and making him feel part of things. It is not so much a tribal reentry as one into matter itself, as if all along he had bothered only with matter's reputation, its cleverest feat being to have evolved itself into mind, except that he thinks the other way is cleverer, mind into matter, mind turning itself into silk or magnesium, whereas the man Groombridge turning into a star, that didn't count, whereas *a star coming to see him under the name Groombridge*, that was different, even if the mind converted into flame and ghost were not Groombridge's at all. Who had Groombridge been anyway? From which mesa, city, college? Oswald gapes at his ignorance, knowing he becomes the more ignorant the more he finds out, wishing he could only be swept up past the grand march of intellect into combustion, fusion, fission, so that his motes would come fluttering back like the burned paper from a Pope's election. If there were a vacancy for a witch doctor, he would apply for it, eager for on-the-job training, but his people do not have witch doctors, they are too advanced for that. Instead he tries to create a private niche in which his meal of life so far might not be irrelevant, though the mesa needs neither studstar, warrior, nor nightman. He feels so far from them, to whom he has come home. There is not even a need for a nephew anymore, or for a son. He is almost grateful for the spying interruptions of Thomas and Abbott: "You looki pale," says Thomas, to whom endings don't matter or even sound. "You bin jerkin off nights," says Abbott. "I have been reading," Oswald tells them. "Book after book. There's a lot to find out." "About who then," says Abbott. "We know who. Look," he says, "look at them two, would you look at them." BertandAnna come strolling toward them with a look of radiant hilarity. Abbott and Thomas are already laughing and Oswald asks why, only to be told to look. "They been for their checkup," Abbott says. "They been doctored. They gonna piss straight now." What, Oswald thinks, *neutered*? What's the need. Ignoring his brothers, BertandAnna come toward him, her mouth especially wide with her grin, indeed forced wide as if, Oswald decides, she were one of those Bantus with a ring in their lips, forcing the whole structure outward until they have a kind of shelf coming out at you from the level of the lower teeth. No, she has the buff matt disk of a diaphragm in her mouth intended, if intended at all, to preclude some impossible miracle of fellatio. The sun catches its surface, bleaching it, and then she has gone by, only to return in her armlock embrace with Bert whispering something that might be *We gone all modern* or *We gone and got us one,* and Oswald thinks yes they are acting just as if they have a baby to show off, not the opposite. To them it's a miracle, a gadget to make them breed, they can't imagine anything so crazy as the other way around. They should be wheeling it around in a little baby cart, cooing and braying, its possibly having only one eye and a cleft lip, as if they would care. He, Oswald, would accept them in, enamored as he is of matter, even its vagaries. Have they just got it wrong, he wonders, or has somebody been playing games. He asks, but they wave him aside: when he's asking he isn't looking, and they want him to look, they want everybody to look, and they themselves don't want to listen. He makes as if to tug the diaphragm from where it does not belong, but she closes her mouth around it with only a small gap left through which she might whistle, so he tries gesturing, obscenely perhaps, indicating the groin, the region of bladder and ovary, but they bypass him, circling slowly within the circle of jeering admirers around them, her mouth slacker now, back to its buff plastic O offered to the sun to gild, and he waves Oswald off. *"We been seen to, Oz,* he says. *"We won't be in no trouble again, not ever, see."* His mouth is open too, but empty, but in his hand Oswald sees the tube of magic goop, which he now squeezes and begins to massage in his hands, spreading the yield thin and then applying it to his face, then hers, which gives BertandAnna an unholy gleam as if something truly preternatural has shone on them, and Oswald marvels at the contradictions of circumstance, the limp in human nature, the bungling of the dumb, the malice of the wise. Given a contraceptive device to play with, are they worse than he was making blue movies in which, to be sure, he misused parts supposed to be saved for the beloved only, whose discovery of them matches his discovery of hers, with all breath held and mind agape. BertandAnna are already walking away, almost as if their inside legs have been tied together, but that is an optical illusion, they are not tripodding away, but walking so as to time the inside legs with superhuman perfection. They have arrived in the twentieth century only to make fun of it. He is glad, but alone in that. He hears the guffaws, the rough embroidery of carnal scorn, and wishes he too could go around with in his mouth, if not a diaphragm, a rubber blown up like a party favor, then a badge of some sort, a flower, an owl's head, a star. Nothing, he decides. I am through with pranks. He vows to spend more time with BertandAnna, mildly amused that of all the folk on the mesa he is best qualified to coach them in erotics, control, and protection. Did she, he wonders, fill her mouth with goop? Now Abbott, in what at first seems a friendly fashion, goes after BertandAnna, putting an arm around them, but his hand goes to her mouth and tries to fish the diaphragm out while he abuses her in a crescendo voice, saying words such as filth and dummy, until Oswald, ever reluctant to intervene in mesa spats, goes after them, seizes Abbott's hand at the wrist and jerks it away from behind, then applies to it a little exotic and almost forgotten judo which spins Abbott all the way around and then to the dirt. "You leave him be," says Thomas, "he only doin what's right." "What's right," Oswald tells him, *"is* leaving folks be." "You," Abbott says from ground level, "you couldn't piss into a cowboy boot if the instructions was printed on the heel." "He's a vet, Abb." Thomas in his pale blue shirt is an awkward peacemaker. Oswald does a brief trill on his discordant Palookaville whistle, the noise that irritates Fermina and doesn't quite gratify Oswald himself. He whistles it all the same, though, for something unfriendly to do. "Yair," he says. "A vet." "You don't got your machine gun," Abbott says, making no attempt to rise. BertandAnna have sailed on, their minds on something grander and sillier, attentive only to those things on the planet that work well with how they feel, shunting off discordance with an eyelid flick as something not real, a conundrum as much part of the weather as of any bit of human behavior. On they trudge in their mutual waddle as Oswald, out of nowhere, finds the thought: these guys have wives, I never see them, they never show, they leave all the insulting and name-calling to Abbott and Thomas, they are never witness to anything their husbands do, as if they have their men's reputations at home on some mantel shelf, dusted and shiny, beyond the taint of those who'd bad-mouth a pair of paragons. *"Negatorio,"* Oswald says after some pondering. It is the word that fits. "Don't you do that again, Abbott, or a certain vet will lift you by the short hairs and dump you down that canyon. Leave folks alone." Astounded at his outburst, Oswald remembers how he once backed away from two goons who wrecked a pinball parlor; he, the trained and accidental killer, has shied away from fisticuffs for ages, as it feels, and now the change in him, maybe Groombridge-inspired, George-dedicated, gives him a lift, back into the world of muscularity, though clearly he is out of shape, in which he will always be ready for Stu and Clu and whoever else they enlist to come and get him. Why, he muses, I could beat these two to pulp and still have steam enough remaining to catch an eagle, plant corn, go swim with Bessie Butterfly. Now he sees what makes him laugh as he looks at Abbott on the ground; Abbott's hairpiece has come off and the oblate-looking bird's nest of hair lies beside him as if Abbott is hoping it will reattach itself and he will not have to go through the humiliation of retrieving it and smacking or patting it back into place. "Hell," Oswald says, "some itchy camel must have come by a-scratching hisself like crazy and he left a hairball behind him, lessen it was something he threw up when he saw the low general standard of beating up the poor and defenseless get on this here mesa. You can't bash them better than that, Abbott, you should go get yourself some of that old Vietnam training, boy.

What're you? Ninety-four? You ain't got long to wait afore they starts
to beat you up yourself. You already got no hair. Day will soon be
here you have no muscle, no bone to speak of. You'll be like some
overgrown jelly fish in a wheelchair waiting for some kind soul to
wheel you fast toward the canyon and let you go full speed into it.
Whoo." He makes the sounds of a crash dive and tapers them off into a
silence broken only by the gentle sough of the breeze, a few squab-
bling small birds, and the faint sound of hammering from a hundred
yards away. Oswald resumes his banter, amazed to be doing something he has not done since Vietnam, elated to have mobile command
of his mouth again, to be able to expel the frothing abuse his mind
dreams up. Abbott has made an occasion for him, Abbott has brought
back into play an Oswald who when the mood seizes him will play
with words as if, behind all the façades and palavers and rigmaroles of
everyday, he were basically a happy man always able to tilt his mood
in a trice into conformity with some private inarticulate ovation
chanted by his cells and his fluids, as if to say simply we're glad we're
here, we're glad we're yours, we've seen a lot of folks who really *were*
for a while, then just as fast *weren't.* Deep inside himself he knows it is
all right between him and the world and whatever destiny he has is
bound to be a balm he is not going to carp about, he is going to let it
have him, swallow him, turn him into corn manure, but until then he
is going to manage that thing—spontaneity—that always seemed beyond him unless he rehearsed it like a dog a trick, which was strange
since everybody else had it and made no bones about showing it in
the intemperate weep, the overcome laugh, the hairtrigger sneer. Oswald has always, he thinks, been lacking in this, as capable of it as of
sneezing, but slow to erupt as if his mama or Mititses had schooled
him to be calm as a landscape like nurses, like officers, surgeons. He
has this cooled quality, he thinks, not endearing but in the long run
the badge of somebody who somebody can trust. Now he has manhandled Abbott and Abbott is too shocked to put his hair back on.
Thomas has gone away in disgust, seeing one brother on the wrong
side altogether, the bastard backing the half-wits, the other brother
cowed by a simple shove and airing his baldness prematurely. As
shouting begins, Oswald looks up, severs himself from his self-es-
teeming reverie, and sees BertandAnna a long way off waving to him
from the top of a four-foot wall (his eyes measure the range, the
height, with a sharpshooter's rehearsed finesse). Then they begin to
call, but only a series of Hi's interspersed with his name in full, "*Os-*

wald" that is, as if they are outbound for some superlative destination, have tickets and trunks, are waving to him from the top deck of an ocean liner. He knows how much their little says, though, waves back and, going over to Abbott, strengthens his point by making Abbott wave back too, offering to belt him in the teeth toute suite if he doesn't get that arm up. "Yes buddy, just like this, and you shout now, you got lungs you air them out," and all of a sudden he realizes he is using the idiom of Captain Bartram, those very cadences that implanted an order in the twink's resistant brain. *"Yair, you go get you some,"* Oswald yells across the mesa, *"you get yourselves some good.* Whatever it is," he says under his breath, I gotta make this bastard wave again. He picks up and replaces the hairpiece, then snatches it back and stuffs it into Abbott's mouth, telling him a long pent-up truth to a percussive rhythm that matches the lunges and tugs. "Call me bastard again, brother Abbott, and I'm gonna nail your balls to the floor and pour gasoline all around you, then we gonna light it up and hear you call to BertandAnna. *Bub,*" he calls him too, he has no idea why, it not being one of Oswald's words like negatorio, Palookaville, ameche, and so forth. Oswald has never shoved Abbott around before and he is staggered by how easy it is as if the man is made of fluff and moss, he who lurks at the window (he may never do so again), he who feels scrawny and not muscular but whose mouth bleeds with snide asseverations coming from the sour hopes of a wronged brother to whom Uncle George was never an uncle, any more than to Thomas; it was always Oswald, in the way as a baby, fondled more than the other two accustomed to having Fermina all to themselves, then somehow more conspicuous as a youth, forever with George The Place In Flowers Where Pollen Rests, then making the enormous leap away to the city, after which it was almost predictable that he would get himself embroiled in a war and survive it, coming home to haunt them with his earring and his desolate whistle like someone created specifically as an anti-Abbott, an anti-Thomas, two men who had grown, wed, and bred. They have done all that is expected of them and now they are spent whereas Oswald has done nothing expected of him and rules the roost with Fermina cooking him favorites and dainties, taking them over to his shanty where he sleeps all hours, friendless, wifeless, jobless, and no doubt mighty well-to-do. "You done with me?" Abbott has his hair back on. Oswald says "Brother Abbott, I haven't even begun." "Then you kill me," Abbott mumbles. "You do it." But Oswald has a smile for him, saying, "Home to your mama, now, Abbott, you got lots to tell about." "I didn't mean no harm," he says, and Oswald says "You got no right." "You saw what she was doin," Abbott says and Oswald says "I saw what she was doin, it was one of the few things that woman at her age and in her condition I mean state is able to do and that isn't much compared with all the terrific things you see coming from an able-bodied pisscutter like yourself with a hairpiece and a strong arm for them as don't rightly know how to defend themselves against unprovoked attack in the middle of the day-lit day with another brother to help and she no doubt having gone through all kinds of stuff at the hands of the doctor to get that thing, which I am sure she don't need, she was wearing as a favor. You get me." "What you mean," says Abbott and Oswald strikes right back. "Don't you worry what I mean slong as you know what I will do, I got the nails I got the hammer I got the gasoline and somebody sure as hell will supply the match." "Okay," Abbott says and Oswald he says "Okay then." So Abbott gets up, groaning as if his shoulder is dislocated. "You musta killed a lot of gook," and Oswald says "They ain't gooks, they ain't anything anymore. We killed them all. That nation is all babies now, just kids. They ain't nothing else left. You never suspicioned that, did you now? You don't read the newspapers, Abbott. There they all are, on sale every day, and it don't mean any more to you than that hunk of coconut mat on your soft head. Fi was you I'd shave it all off. I'd go bald next time I lit out after some old woman with a new toy. You got me?" "We all got you, Oswald," he says and Oswald answers. "You say you're sorry then," and Abbott says it, but Oswald says: "Not to me, to her." "I don't know." "Come with me then." "I don't know." They go and Abbott mumbles to both BertandAnna and she takes one deep, uncomprehending, valiant, sly look at him and says, "Ah kin smell him. He been hung to sweeten up." "Yair," Oswald says, "I can smell him too. He don't smell too good." "Was he saying Hi," she says. "What was you saying, Abb? He won't say Anna, he won't say Bert. You damn well say it to them both." Then it happens. Oswald feeling on top of the world feels the dear familiar terrain upend itself like an umbrella of earth and rock blowing inside out and going away from him fast as if tugged and he is on his belly looking down at it as it falls away from him leaving him high and dry and heavy with them looking at him as if he has turned to gold right in front of their eyes. BertandAnna urge him home, shuffle him along, with Abbott perplexedly in train. "You passed out," he hears Fermina saying, "you need your food. You light-headed." "Not me," he says. "Well, I did forget my cheese." *"Cheese,"* BertandAnna exclaim and Fermina, she says "Yair, he likes it," and Oswald says "I'm weaker than I thought," and Fermina says "We oughta strap him in bed till he well. His Uncle George, he'd go without food for days like he was blaming himself and we'd have to pick him up and full his mouth." All Oswald knows is that this has nothing to do with suitcase stars but something from resonantly way back to do with a schoolboy forced to sing *O for the wings of a dove* standing on a chair because he was short and had a callow baritone voice worthy of training except he would never get that kind of schooling there so they stood him on that chair, the Mititses did, and he sang with tears boiling down his cheeks because he thought he was going to fall, away from the azure and the white arms and the chiming spoons and the soft linen cloths, all the way to where the eagles piled up their dung as if with a pyramid in mind, and he did fall, the chair wobbled, he went with it, he cracked his head open, they had his head stitched back together, it held for years, but maybe it was now open again, which is why BertandAnna are smiling. No, they heard the word *cheese* and think they are going to be photographed while Oswald recovers from his faint. "Like," he says, "my mind trod on a banana." But no such bright improvisation deters Fermina, who shoos away Abbott and the returned Thomas and BertandAnna and takes him in to nurse. It is her face he sees but behind it generations of plump-faced creasy-skinned women with dark eyes whose very spine marrow was black as molasses like the dank secrets hoarded between shawls in the bottom drawer of the chest while they put up with their men, abided with them like the soft hymn said that they were trained to sing to please some Anglo god shaped like a triangle. *That* he sees, but he sees too one general face masklike and less human than cursed with punitive geology, the whole epidermis cut up with crevasses and trenches, weals and scorings, as if some racial glacier had shouldered its way over them. They were faces not pretty for long but best cherished in movement over an agitated torso moving to the dance handed down from people who were spiders and snakes, fudged up by superior beings from a handful of spit and dust: faces lit by wavering flame and seasoned by ungenerous weather and therefore faces that huddled together even in the act of mothering, when all mothers mothered as one, and then when they went away and said hush go to sleep it was all of them going their separate ways wounding him with too many goodnights like knife slashes just when he wanted to get up

and play with them all, his eyes prickly with fatigue, his mind trembling fast with the recondite grievous knowledge that once you said
good night you had said good night to them all and they would go off
to mother animals in some Anglo zoo, nurse the dead in Flag, and
suckle weakling puppies. "Oswald," his mother says, "you been
throwin up."

He would remember this. It was as if mother nature had asked of him
only that he allow himself to get sick, in this case to let his ulcer have
its way with him, in order to lavish upon him all the processes of
renewal and healing. Some erosion of his will had to happen and then
he was on the mend like a disjointed rainbow coming back together
from all parts of the sky. He has never felt so good, not merely from
the plain food but food nonetheless that Fermina has cooked and
punctually brought, from a breakfast at noon to midday meal about
three and dinner just before she goes to sleep about nine, a skewed
day for her but ideal for him, who bones up on stars and kachinas in
about equal measure, knowing that the winter solstice is coming and
that once the women's society dances are done with, imaginative
things will begin to happen. Most of all he studies the Pleiades, the
seven stars representing seven universes, and the stars in Orion's belt.
Soon someone who keeps the same hours as himself but without
sleeping into the day will view these stars through the ladder opening
in the top of an underground ceremonial chamber and sing the seven
songs celebrating the building of the human house on Earth in a kind
of archaic bricklayer's hymn to his craft, from foundation laying to
the building of walls, then the sealing off in which a roof goes upon
beams and the plastering on of the final coat. It is also the creation of
the body to house the spirit, something Oswald up to now has always
felt giggly and queasy about, wondering why his people take things
with such elaborate solemnity as if life could not look after itself in its
infernally random permanent way. Why should humans have to fuss
to buttress it, to keep it safe and sound? The other songs impress him
less although he can sense their unmediated holiness: song of the
niche or the place for the heart, song of the wood sticks upon which
things are hung, song of the fireplace. He likes the building songs
rather than the cozy-making ones, his mind accustomed (he thinks) to
the vast interstellar spaces where no rocking chair, no bed, no table,

spoils the purity of emptiness. He does not like to think of himself as one who having gone to the ends of the earth has come home to toe the line for good reasons; no, he is doing it, if doing it he is, mainly because he can't think of anything else to do, and his newly found interest in astronomy gibes with what his tribe is sometimes doing. All he knows is that the seven songs must be done with by the time the Pleiades sit halfway between the western horizon and the midnight sky and the three stars in Orion's belt rest across the hole through which the ladder peeps. Such as that is, he tells himself, wondering if he should knock a hole in the little roof of his shanty to view the heavens through, then shaking his head because his image of the heavens includes such things as suitcase stars and such names as Groombridge and Kapteyn, unknown to his people. He has at least the stars and the kachinas in common with them, which is no small helping, he thinks, of their mystery, but he has no desire to officiate or to be asked to officiate or to be asked to train to be one of those who officiate. He wants to do something of his own in the spirit of Uncle George and even, paternity be damned, Emory too, who struck out in the good sense and made an independent life in the shadow of nobody at all. A model of his awe is what Oswald wants to make, but he is no carver and certainly no priest, no chief of a given clan, so he tries to cook up some way of doing for himself what the tribal ceremonies cannot do for him, he being mystical-minded without being superstitious, what egregious popularists have called the chauvinism of the heart, little knowing that such an unselective catch of earth ecstatics includes an Oswald too. He needs to be, he needs to know, he needs to exult, he needs this third more than almost anything else, reasoning in his cumbersome way that, since only those alive can think it up, then those who are alive should try to do it, it being one of the abiding human options honored more in the breach than in the observance as they used to say in Palookaville, Vietnam, and Tempe, where he went to college for that brief grade-stricken year. He will not hack a hole in his roof, he will not sing the seven songs not even as if standing on a chair and a good many years younger, he will work out something of his own having to do with his stars and their stars, his apparitions and theirs, his heart set on something so calm as the pink underground room in which Apperknowle claims he goes to read and think and listen to music, or on something even more remote such as the Coudé room in observatories where, he has read, astronomers sit at ease and watch the light bend winsomely down toward them ensconced in a little house separate from the telescope itself as if the murmuring rays of light have been chopped off from the universe that made them and made manageable for those who do not actually ride the telescope itself as if it were a spaceship but lounge among heavy machinery in a separate housing, a kind of projectionist's booth in reverse, he guesses. He has read so much or rather has dipped too much, so that his head swarms with names way past Groombridge— Tempel-Swift, Oterma, Schwassmann-Wachmann, Pitiscus, Messier, Tycho, Kepler—and he wants to bed down for an eon with them in his own version of the Coudé room which in his frayed mind assumes some of the qualities associated not only with the projectionist's booth aforesaid but the opera box, the prompter lair, the parking attendant's booth, just so long as it is small and comes equipped with all he needs to make his preliminary obeisances to the stars that made him while he dreams ever so tenderly about how light in coming together all the time from reds and greens and violets so far apart is a bit like the kung fu zealot whose delirious leaps and adroit recoveries exhibit the same flawless instinct for perfection. Thus his mind moves, savage and savvy in one, too tainted with book smarts for him to be at ease among his tribe but too primitive for him to soar among the smart. He gets by, he gets by increasingly, marveling at the names of all those who have preceded him in a quest popular and complex yet not more popular or more complex than the legends (the *leg ends*, he laughs to himself) made up by his people. When his mind soars most, his ulcer pains him least. Even Abbott newly brought to heel brings his tray of steaming soup, sliced cheese, *piiki* bread, and margarine left in the silver paper like an ingot. "You gettin good service in this hotel," Abbott tells him, and Oswald says "Well I won't always will. It's new," and Abbott says "That day'll come none too soon for me," and Oswald says "You got nothing else to do." Abbott goes away grumbling, waving his arms full out as if to fend attackers off and BertandAnna come shuffling in, their conjoint breathing heavy as if they have come uphill, but no they have not been downmesa, they have brought him a handful of feathers in case he needs them. They want to thank him, but all they say is *Hi*, predictably enough, followed by *MistOz* or something like it, their greased faces gleaming, their eyes up on the corners of the room as if secret presences like interior gargoyles are sticking their tongues out at the trio of humans below. They would like to be humans, at least in the normal way, he thinks, and I would like to dance like a kachina, but the folks up here save that for the venerable, the mighty, the pious. How do I get in, how do I get by, how do I get picked? He well knows that it will have to be illicit, they will hardly behead him for a transgression, but they would stop him and whip him for going too far. He does not want to profane the local arcana but to latch on to them for his own purposes, like someone dieting on Communion wafers and holy wine. For some reason he knows BertandAnna will help, so long as he keeps the uttered word to a minimum; it is their sign language, their semaphoring, that is so taboo, so outrageous. A woman with a diaphragm in her mouth is likely also to have, stashed away somewhere, a baby carriage full of obituaries. On the verge of thinking this, he in the end does not, the pieces hover at the fringe of his mind's and ear's eyes, but do not come together, so he is fortunate to have presiding over him the team he thinks he himself has chosen: Sotuqnangu, though in some disrepute since Uncle George, Groombridge, and the rest, and at a farther distance nameless others with an acute interest in his fate: several of the watchful in fact, hands rubbing, eyes gleaming, mouths open for speech, almost as if fusion itself were to begin to take credit for making a star. He asks BertandAnna for some old rags and they seem to understand. He shows them a picture in the book Apperknowle brought him, then a second, at both of which, not quite in unison, they exclaim, Bert coming out with an *Ah*, Anna with something more like *Ho*. They point at him and nod and to an extent he has become their child, a rabbit reared by grass.

BertandAnna know it, but Oswald has forgotten that in December and January you have to walk about in the quietest manner possible with soft, subdued reverence as if a mighty presence is lurking ready to turn on you, as it is. Harm no animal. Kill nothing. Never knock on the door you are about to enter. After dark it is wisest to remain indoors, but if you should have to go outside best smear some ashes on the face or the moon will anoint you with droplets of blood. Cut no hair or Kyaamuya will end up making a nest with it. And do no digging. It is a dangerous time, finely balanced, and the slightest shift will bring down upon the shifter all manner of linked-up mayhem, but there is another side to all this and it has to do with the telling of stories: the cold season is the time for storytelling whereas anyone who tells a story during summer will end up being bitten by a rattler. Ideally everyone should stay close to home, curled up in the kinds of small spaces that intrigue Oswald, like sentries in their sentry boxes. If BertandAnna, by now his regular visitors although at hours other than Fermina's, could explain things better they would spell all this out to Oswald, but Fermina takes over, cautioning him in explicit words while BertandAnna make intimidated gestures at the doorway, the window, at the sky which will eventually go dark as if it's cursed. After a while he knows what has stirred them up so much and now his mother is chiding him for his ignorance. "Yes," he tells her, "I have been a far piece away and I am more used to a TV screen than to any mesa taboo." "You could join in. Tell a story." She explains the need, reminding him of the old ways, when everyone took a turn in coming up with a story—"the story goes around the circle, Oswald. Or it used to." Now he knows he has been to Palookaville; until this very moment he has forgotten the stories Uncle George told him, or told to whoever gathered around him as he carved, his hands busier than his mouth, his voice wavering with this or that dramatic emphasis, with long pauses while his hands seemed to narrate instead, so that everyone who heard him made some ineradicable connection between wood and story and then between trees and fiction and then between the way the world was before there were people in it and the idea of tribal guesswork. To hear story was to witness the world in the act of being populated; people were improvised by a busy god plying his whims until this or that confected shape pleased him and he let it abide, a sample, a promise, a seed, from which all the storytellers who have ever been would spring. He knew what he was doing. As he weakened, Uncle George told stories less and less, just as he hardly bothered to carve, delegating things to Oswald as much as possible, but as Oswald knew, Uncle George's head still combed through the ancient narratives, most of them bawdy or filthy, that being his preference, groping for something pliable or flexible, not the story itself but the emphases it could take, like a table welcoming the ephemeral commentary of light upon it, this way or that. What he wanted but could not invent for himself were stories about the span of his own life, whereas all the stories he knew were set in the past, well not so much the past as any one of the three earlier worlds, and they all had this final, finished feel to them, they were all cut and dried not so much because they used the past tense as because everyone knew what was coming, there were few variations of a major kind. And George had always wanted the stories to go the other way, to have the outcome contrary to the time-honored one, but no one ever rose to that, and when he himself did it they cackled, clacked, walked away, as if he had broken the taboos about gentle walking, having his hair cut, or not putting ash on his chops when he ventured abroad at night. Heaven help me, Oswald thinks, is that what he wanted me to be all along? He told me the old tales in the hope that I'd take them over and alter them beyond recognition. I had no gift for that, though I recall having invented for him and him alone yarns about Palookaville, mothered by shame, fathered by frustration. He had no idea how fictional the whole thing was. *"Once upon a time,"* he begins, fixing upon his mother the stare of exasperated filial piety, "there was a young man from the tribe. All his life he had wanted—" "You *begin,*" she scolds him, "by saying *Aliksa'i.* Then people know a story is coming. They almost always begin with the statement: People were living on the mesa, or in this or that village." "Right." Oswald sighs. *"Aliksa'i.* They were living on the mesa. This young man was living on the mesa and it was December and it was warm, the ground was soft. It being night he wished to go out and look at the stars, the seven Pleiades and the stars in a line in Orion's belt, so he went out, heavy footed as was his way, and knocked loudly on his mother's door. She came to the door and hushed him with the palm of her hand, then pointed at his face, which was clean and not covered with ash, although there was blood dripping from his eyebrows down to his nose and cheeks. *Look* at you, she whispered." "She wouldn't do that," Fermina says. "Don't interrupt, Mama. I'm doing the telling." "We always do. We say *oh* and *oh* all the time, just about at the end of every sentence, at every sentence end." "Anyway, she did this," he resumes, "and he explained to her that he had just interrupted his digging to go have his hair cut. I brought you a rabbit, freshly killed, he said." "Oh no," Fermina says. "You're mocking me. You are mocking all of us. You don't care. A rattler will bite you even in cold weather if you tell stories like that. Hush up." "Would you like the story about the carver of kachina dolls who died and then came back as a star with some other stars he had with him in an old suitcase and he set them on a table just like kachina dolls and they began to shine, but only whenever he closed a certain book? They would not shine while he was reading, they didn't wish to disturb him. Then one night they went away, but for a while there it was like having the whole universe in his backyard, the stars had names and the names were those of famous people who had passed on but had in their time been mighty gentle and understanding with stars, always hoping to

be one later although they were not allowed to state any preference
for color unless it was the first one, yes, they could have one choice,
but they didn't always get it, there were sometimes more blue stars
than red, so then it would be a big red star that they turned into, it
went like that, although some of them if they were lucky would be
double stars a bit like BertandAnna, separate beings but close together and hardly to be parted. Mother? You didn't say a single *ob.*"
Fermina says nothing, both aghast and mesmerized. He isn't doing
too badly although, she is sure, down to the bottom of her primed
atavistic being, he is wasting his time. Story is not to invent, story is
to repeat, to make sure of things, to give folks something to depend on
so that they always know what is coming and can exclaim on cue
while the teller waits for them. "There's stories, Oswald," she tells
him. "And there's lies." "Not lies, Mama. It's from real life." "From
whose real life?" "Somebody I know," Oswald says, backing away
fast from himself, unable to conjure himself forth as eyewitness to an
act of magic nowhere to be found in the canon of wonders. "Some
guy I knew back in . . . L.A." BertandAnna are nodding as if they
know, having in between times Palookavilled themselves half to death
with drugs, depravity, and dice. "Somebody real," he insists. "Yair.
Somebody real that sees stars dancing on a tabletop. Just like that. It's
hard to believe but it happened." "Who was this carver then?"
"Somebody like Uncle George. Uncle George The Place In Flowers
Where Pollen Rests in L.A. Getting himself some," he says in the best
impromptu terminology available to him, "whatever it was that he
had to have at—that moment in time." (The shade of Captain Bartram hovers before him, not like a star at all, but his military bars of
rank are shining on his dress uniform and his chest is a dappled
spectrum of ribbons.) She gives up. "That is no story, Oswald. You
got to try again. Don't you remember nothing? Try saying *Once upon a
time* and see what comes. *Once upon a time they were living on the mesa.*
See what comes. Like that." Nothing comes. He tells her so. She
prods him again, saying his *Aliksa'i* for him, then *"They were living on
the mesa,* Oswald. *People were living on the mesa.* I began it for you."
With an ear wrongly attuned he keeps thinking she is talking about
the elixir of life, her repeated *Aliksa'i*s having tapped another word-
hoard than the one his forebears used. Maybe it all works out for the
best, he decides. The beginning of any story is a kind of elixir in itself
before the thing gets old and worn, although maybe the beginnings
always feel like new as if the teller beginning is always fresh since the

Aliksa'i bit isn't part of any one given story. No, it is what the teller brings to the work of the moment right after having filled up on somiviki and therefore being all ready to go because flooded with the goodies like calcium, manganese, magnesium, iron, all from the ashes of saltbush giving the meal its bluish tinge, we're a healthy people and no mistake. So that part is new each time even though thousands have mouthed it, saying, "Come and get it, folks, this is an old tale new told." So elixir isn't far off, it is story that keeps you young or creates that open willing attitude that people have, the little sharp shiver they get, just before a movie or a story begins. I mean the flush of anticipation, *yair*, which if the baby only knew about this stuff would be how the mesa babies ought to feel after being cooped up in a dark room for three weeks but with a sudden blast of sunlight to come when the mother holds the babe up to the local star daring it to burn. It is as coldly wonderfully original as that and I am awed, Mama. My Mama does not know, does not believe, that I not long ago had a second exposure to the stars, much less orthodox I guess but exciting as ever being born, and there was no mother holding me tight I was holding myself I was holding myself in and my breath too it was so wonderfully ridiculous all of it almost sexual in a way except that part of me just drained anemic with delight a lot better than coming. You get a soft-on, that is it, from Groombridge and his boys, Uncle G. and the rest, all maneuvering their bodies in a blaze. I wish I'd had a Polaroid to make it permanent what with folks' being so skeptical about retina images of marvels, even here where marvels are ten a penny provided they're of the old school. Some of these old traditions, folkways, are so solid it's like bumping into a person, a windmill, a snowman, one of those recliner chairs oiled till it flicks out its landing pad with hardly a squeak and out your legs go, like Mama's, in front of you as if you have just grown them. "Start again," she is saying and he says "*Elixir*, Mama," and she says "That's better, now get the rest of it right" and he says "Once upon a time they were living on the mesa and the ground was hard as iron, it was hard as titanium, because the weather was cold as Antarctic metal, your skin would stick to it, it was so frigid," and she says "Oswald, you will never be told, I thought you had it," and he says without the faintest interrogative intonation "Mama, why don't you give me up, I'm a hopeless case."

"No," she tells him, "you're new to it. What you need to do is try another day. Think about it first. You can't get into it just trying." Now he remembers that Fermina, a woman who has always hovered between being well spoken and uncouth has for many years been trying to catch up with things by reading the encyclopedia all the way through except that she long ago bogged down among the A's, somewhere between Andorra and angora, even if only to gain a sense of context, of a world she knows too little about, her main problem being that she has tended to focus on pictures at the expense of text, which means that her sense of the A-world is incuriously visual. She has been roving to and fro in an almost circular fashion in a palace of somebody else's delights. The book, solidly bound with a headband at the top of its spine and lavishly illustrated ("*for the likes of me,*" she murmured on first seeing it), does not mention Oswald under O and she knows she was being unrealistic to look. What stuns him is that she was reading it in the same circular way when he first went off to Palookaville and that she has been doing the same with it during his time in Vietnam and Winslow, yet not exactly repeating herself either, each time over the years finding something new about Albatross or Argonaut (the marine animal) that is not in the book at all but in the uncertain area where her mind meets the facts. Some of what she thinks she has read she has imagined, dreaming as she dozes off each night about this bird or that fish, embroidering them like an inspired zoologist usurping the role of a god given to endless afterthoughts. So she leaves nothing untouched, as it was, nor does she leave last week's or last year's affectionate improvisation untouched either, her privilege being to cancel anything she no longer quite fancies. Not that she talks it up, she lets it lie, as it were keeping revised nature in her lap against emergencies, when she can retreat into flora and fauna of her own devising whose fishes have dragonfly or biplane wings and whose birds have snakelike tongues. Once upon a time she angrily told Oswald, who had been airily theorizing about how much better off she would have been if childless, that he had no idea what he was talking about. "Before you talk about it, you should do it. Anyway, a marriage without children is like a wound without salt." "Did you just make that up" he said. "No," she told him, "but it's the first time I said it, I was waiting for the right occasion. I'm deep." He has noticed that, never mind how deep she is, she tends to favor natural things over man-made and among those things with simple names she can say, so when she wrote to him in Vietnam and Winslow she wrote out the long names with slavish care, these being the names she would never say, whereas something like Ant she could both say and write with ease, so he heard a lot both ways about ants. What he will never know is how closely the world pictured in the book seems to hem her in, not the close-knit hierarchy and myth-headedness of the mesa, which seems to her rather remote and spacious, but this book-ish thing with animals she otherwise never sees or hears about though she would like to. Animals first, always, because that is her way and the most natural part to cleave to, then countries, all the rest being somewhat abstract and smoky, *not for her* as she puts it to herself, so that even when submitting back in 1944 to Uncle George's lovesick thrusts, she had before her mind's eye the spiny back of the alder-fly larva without quite knowing what it was, or a baby alligator hatching from its egg with the squirming upward twist of a young dolphin, or the black-and-yellow front face of an angelfish, to her a compressed butterfly waiting to stretch its wings. By the same token George her lover who charged into her even as she advanced with a sedate shove of her loins became a marine creature or a bird, which metamorpho-sis made it easier for her to think she was being assaulted by an animal that knew no better and could not be schooled. Where these creatures roamed she was a free woman needing no alibi or excuse. She was just being natural, said *natchrel*, and she was Fermina no longer, Fermina was down among the distant F's as far away as the moon itself, where she was certain she would not find herself any-way, listed neither for beauty nor for shame. In other words she had got away with it and always would, and she had got away with having an Oswald too, who was not listed either. Year after year the unread unconsulted volumes with the odd barklike sounds imprinted on their spines (*Aar–Azt* on the first) gathered corn dust and windswept sand, their compiler having had little sense of the urgent unlettered woman who would shunt them into oblivion because the first volume was enough in all the condensed glory of its heavy cream-laid pages: to be savored and plumbed only through magic, though, never to be read straight through as if it were a book, or consulted as if it were a tome of reference, or merely stroked as if unread it were some kind of keepsake evoking a face, a hand, a certain way of saying goodbye for ever. No, she dreamed her way back and forth in it, a prophetess of her own making at large among uncomprehended forms but un-cowed by their strangeness as if, on some unlucky day, she might give birth to one of them by mistake, maybe as a punishment, but it was only Oswald on top of Abbott and Thomas, punishment enough she has often said, and that has to be that. Easy, because no man molests her anymore, she has withdrawn into some chaste continuity not of her own making but willed upon her by sky and sand, by the San Francisco Mountains, her role in life at least on the mesa being to be wanted no longer, but put up with, although in different ways her three sons fuss and nourish her, scarlet woman turned a slight embarrassed pink, and ready to bleach into the white outline of one who has sinned and paid. "This book," she tells Oswald, "could do with a good scrub." It is one of her lines and she sees the thing mired in suds, the heavy bristles abrading the sheen of the photogravure, colors and black-and-white alike as if the brush had claws. "Dip it in some lake," she says. To tease, knowing she can get away with such things now. "It isn't a *story* book anyhow, it isn't one of those *and then he* books that make you wonder a lot about what's coming next because in this case you don't have any idea, but in the other kind you have some glimmering like the smell of cooking, and you can say Oh the next thing that happens will be that the woman fetches hot *piiki* bread to the table." I am only ever five years old, Oswald tells himself, I have never been older to her, all those years coming afterward being some kind of mirage to her, a camouflage netting to hide a child behind, but she busts through and finds me all over again. Maybe she does it for them as well, but I have a hunch that she does it just with me, actually urging them on to get older and older as fast as they can go. He decides to call his memory into view and flog it for a story told him by Uncle George, not to get himself popular on the mesa, but to please Fermina, to whom reading is a kind of visual hang gliding only, the truth being that she expects stories to come out of the air and out of mouths; in print they are as trapped as the aardwolf in her encyclopedia, as Oswald himself in her notion of him as a permanent child. Well, wasn't there one about a girl killed so she could be raped, at least by the clan leader? Not invented by Uncle George, but told anew in his scatterbrained rough-handed way as if he were looking at the reverse side of some famous tapestry and you could just make out the design from what he told, amid the embellishments and willful emphases. Oswald tries to suck all of his mind into a small core at the center of his head, there to sort it through and come up with only what matters. Things come, mixed in with a forlorn, almost strident song of *Ayo-o* repeated endlessly as if the singer were a clock or a metronome determined to wear the mesa away. Even as he tries to gather his wits, he sees faces at his stark little window, hears voices at the doorway, the local bush telegraph having worked its miracle once again at a speed quite different and separate from the one he thinks and recollects at. Unrehearsed he readies himself for a public display of talents he doesn't really possess, counting on the ghost of Uncle George, on Groombridge and Co., on sheer good luck, to get him through, now vaguely recalling that if his uncle cut himself while carving he did not waste time mopping or dabbing the wound, he just picked up a hammer and hit it hard to numb the nerves or, if not that, then to give the affected area something worse to feel. All I need now, Oswald tells himself, is a hammer in the head, and after that one a bigger one followed by an even bigger one until the zone of pain is too big for the head to know where the hurt is. "To work," he says in a voice louder than usual. "I'm ready to try. Let's go outside, it's brisker there, it'll wake me up." "It used to be called How The Old Wizard Plotted To Seduce The Beautiful Girl," he begins, "but I call it The Old Goat and the Gorgeous One. I don't like long titles." Abbott and Thomas and their wives and their miscellaneous children and BertandAnna and a whole slew of unknown others form an untidy ring as he sits against Uncle George's wall and almost without noticing accepts a hunk of wood, a knife, mainly for him to whittle with as he tells, but also to engender the right atmospheric associations. Fermina taps him with a limber switch as if he is five years old. "Okay," he begins, but she taps him again, harder, and he recovers, says the magic word *elixir* followed by those others: *"They were living on the mesa at this time."* Here we go, his mind tells him, this is it, over the dizzying edge into the wind on a little float of eagle feathers, from where there is no coming back. If this doesn't bring back the suitcase ghosts, then nothing will. As the world shrinks to that intent little group, he hears life's elastic creak and senses the San Francisco peaks drawing in closer, clocks beginning to slow down, birds above them starting to beat their wings less, even small rodents and snakes pausing about their chores to give him a wide berth, to which he responds that no berth can be wider, oh that it were on an ocean liner taking him to Hawaii where nothing like this will be asked of him. "Elixir," he says again and, taking a deep breath of cool afternoon air, begins, at first hewing chunks from the old story and abbreviating them out of sheer incompetent impatience, but then he starts to move the knife over the wood with delicate slight motions as if threatening a throat held between his hands. He scrapes a bit harder as he says the next bit. "She had one brother, this beautiful girl who everybody wanted to make love to, and they kept on coming to the house at night to talk through the hole in the wall while she was grinding corn, but she took no notice of any of them, so all the boys talked about was how to get her for what they wanted, and just talking about her got them all excited, as their chief saw. Look, he said to them, each day this girl goes off to the Excrement Place to relieve herself. She goes about mid-evening. Now what I want you to do is gather up some things to make corncob darts from and a cornhusk wheel. You know what I mean, the kind that people throw feathered darts at. Make this and then you can roll the wheel past her when she comes by and then one of the darts can hit her in the foot. This will be a special dart." Startled by the outbursts of *oh* and *yes*, Oswald pauses, for rather too long; they already motion him to get on with it as if he is woolgathering and they want him and his little frail skiff of story among the rapids and the white water, perched on the brink of catastrophe, so he begins to cut into the wood, deciding to make the story more mysterious than he has planned; he is giving too much away in too few words, he thinks, he wants to make them beg for it, so he rebegins, this time installing as it were parenthesis within parenthesis and that within a mystery and the mystery within his private unutterable memory of the suitcase stars come to fuel him for precisely this even though he remembers it wrong and omits the standard formulas of tease. "What he wanted to do, you see," he resumes, "was something bad, which you could never guess at, even if you had the wren feathers in your own hands, the wren being a crackpot bird. And of course he smeared something on the point that you would never know about and are not allowed to know about since it would kill an elephant even, only just a little touch, and there is no knowing where he got it from, several of his family having died already from handling it for him without the gloves used for handling peppers. Yes, it was deadly, but not to him. He was careful. Now, what happened next you would never be able to tell from what has happened already. It was awful. It was so awful that I can hardly bring myself to tell you about it. I have to stop now, folks." He makes as if to rise, toss the scarred hunk of wood away, and head for an Excrement Place of his own, but they tug him back as he wants and urge him to continue, crying "It can't be that bad, Oswald. We have heard it before." "Not this way you haven't," he says. "Let us be the judges of that." Even BertandAnna wave hectically at him, so he speeds to the place at which the girl bursts into tears because the dart has hit her heel and she at once feels faint though she pulls it out herself. "Her parents quieten her as she swells even under the ministrations of the medicine man and the next day toward evening she dies without having gone near the Excrement Place, which is some way from where they bury her: the southeastern edge of the mesa, where her brother goes to lie beside her on his stomach by clear moonlight." He wonders why she died so suddenly. At midnight he wakes and, in Oswald's own words, "looks over at the grave," even as Oswald begins to shower the area with wood shavings as if talking while in the main carving rather than the other way around. "Some creature was crying," he says, and they all stiffen. "East of the butte, you see. At the foot of the mesa. They keep moving about, these sounds do and you will never guess what was making them. I can't bear to say. You will never guess. It was something so— it was really something, they should never allow such things to happen. The hair was standing up on the brother's neck by now and he kept imagining all kinds of terrible things that might be making the noise. Do you want me to go on? Could you stand it? He looked high and low but he saw nothing until he saw this terrible-looking creature coming out of the north, throwing things right and left, and making this dreadful sound as if it was trying to throw up while strangling itself with a spare paw and all the blood was beginning to hum and spurt out of its ears. It was AHHHHH GRAAAAAY WOOOOO LF with teeth as long as my arm and bowels dangling from its jaw while it made that awful sound. What was behind it you could never guess, but it was three men in a line, coming like this: one man, the second man, the third man, coming in that order so that you could count them up from either end getting the same answer and they showed no sign of wanting to change and walk behind the wolf in line abreast. Next they began to do something so horrible it is hard to tell you about it, I wish we could omit this altogether, it is unfit for human ears it is so unbelievable, who would want to be so cruel as to tell decent people about it. Shall I stop here? Do I have to say it?" "You do," they tell him, "and hurry up. We know what's coming. Get to the wolf again and the grave and the girl." Oswald flashes his knife vaguely toward the west and goes right to it. "The brother decides not to kill the wolf, that slavering bloody-jawed horror, and watches the men lifting his sister out of the grave then wrapping her up in something, like the carcass of a butchered sheep. A lamb. Now the wolf walked behind them away, the third man to arrive now leading and he was the one who carried the girl due north past the eastern side of the village along the base of the mesa. They always knew which direction they were supposed to go in, and their faces were hot with shame and hurry as if an extra sun was blazing down upon them by the light of the moon, which you can't have without the sun being there, which means there were two moonlights. When they got to the north base of the mesa, up they went to the top where they headed east as if they had a map which they did not and then they vanished into an underground chamber where all kinds of boys and men were shouting and jumping around. In he peeked as they put his sister, I can hardly bear to tell you what came next, to the north of the fireplace, what a place to put anyone's sister, and covered her with a wedding robe. That done, they smoked over her body so finely clad and began to sing. The next thing is too awful to say. She began to stir as they sang to her. Either they were singing about her but not to her, or they were singing to her but not about her, or they were singing about her and also to her, or they were singing some other way I forget, the main thing being that she stirred but without being able to see although at this time she began to uncover herself as she burst into tears." At this point he has to pause for all the exclamations and cries of indignation to vent themselves and for Bert to coax Anna into buttoning up her blouse again. "Now a woman said I will comb your hair, beautiful one, and this was the girl's aunt who took her over to a stone bench to do it. Yes. She did. Now the boy decided that they were all going to do something to his sister. They were getting her ready for something unmentionable so he ran home and told his grandmother, who said Right, this is something that requires lightning sticks. She sprinkled water all over her body and rolled a dab of dirt against her skin until it was a round ball the size of a thumb and then she cut a small piece off and put it in a bag. It was like one pellet of sheep's droppings. When they went back to the girl there were four of them and she was still lying there north of the fireplace, but as soon as they arrived, the chief from the Excrement Place made a move toward the girl, actually setting his hand on her belly, so you could see he wanted the girl for himself and had just been using the boys to get her. Everybody there was a witch or a sorcerer, which is funny, like overkill, couldn't the one guy have done it himself? Without all that help." "That would make less of a story," they tell him with impatient smiles. "Hurry up. Your hand is bleeding." He hammers a big rock against the cut and resumes, his voice just that bit

higher now from strain and concentration. "Now the old chief was
climbing on top of her, but the grandmother let something loose
among them all and it was a fly she had fashioned out of her own dirt,
but they killed the fly shouting Look, something has come in, kill it
fast. Now the old chief shouted *I am going to break her in* just as the
grandmother released something else and this was a fast-flying bat
with nasty teeth. As the old chief shoved forward to get into the girl,
the girl went backward pulled by the fast-flying bat, who had done
this kind of service before and wore silver wings on its breast just like
an airline captain. An amazing thing. The bat itself was the plane it
was captain of. The old chief shoved away into where he thought the
girl would be with her love pleat wide open to receive him and instead rammed it deep into the ground actually cutting it on a piece of
buried glass which would give him a painful disease in later years but
that was much later. What happened now was past all believing because those who had come to rescue the girl used their lightning
sticks on the whole place and there were lightning bolts everywhere,
bangs like distant thunder and flashes like the sun coming up in a
split second. It was dazzling. Everyone started to yell and some of
them were yelling because the lightning had ripped them apart and
soon they were all crawling around minus this or that part of themselves, hacked up as if for a big feast. Some had no arms and some had
no legs, so they were groping around and none too particular about
what they grabbed and tried to stick back on to them, pressing an arm
where a leg should be and even a head where a buttock should be and,
what is even more extreme, a belly where a head should be, all that
shiny gashed intestine from the inside where an outside bit was better. It was a mess. Some men had women's legs on them by now and
some women had penises where before they had had nothing at all
except a kind of purse to put money in. They all came out ugly of
course, but they had ugly spirits to begin with, so that was only just.
Now the brother and sister as well as those who had rescued them
decided to go home, where they at once began to plan a celebration
dance with long hair kachinas. Are they the ones you want to have us
be? the girl asked. Of course, the boy said, we'd be less likely to get it
wrong. Four days went by and no one suspected what was going on,
but they knew something strange was in the air when they heard
peculiar calls coming from the underground chambers, and then out
the kachinas came and began to dance. They danced as if the end of
the world had only just gone by. It had. After the dancing, the boy

went up to each kachina and handed over a prayer feather, but of course he did not give one to his sister. Now folk began to say, *Oh she only pretended to be dead and all that so she could have them dance, it was an excuse. She never really died.* That same evening the boy made a shinny ball for those who had helped him. He made one of the old-fashioned kind out of deerskin and wool, not cloth or canvas, and handed it over to the two young demigod brothers who had helped him to rescue his sister, whose name we still do not know. It was a long time ago, so long ago in fact that the two brothers or twins could be grandchildren of Spider Woman, so you can see how long ago that was." "You're missing things out," Fermina whispers with a grimace, her hands rending something in midair. "I've nearly done, Mama. Leave me be."

"Whenever after that any of the witches and sorcerers who had interfered with the girl got outside the underground chamber and tripped over some little thing on the ground, well, they died right there, and in the end not one of them was left, but it is unlikely that this would have happened if the brother had not made the demigod twin brothers the gift of the shinny ball. Life went on as before as it always should after wonderful events. Here the story ends." Pouring sweat, he feels as if he has climbed a mountain with no help from the demigod twins. As far as he's concerned he has told the story with fastidious austerity and enormous dramatic flair. "Who could have told it better?" "Hundreds," his mother informs him. "You missed too many things out and you rushed. They talk much more than you let them do. And you didn't get the names right." "I never did know the names. Uncle George, he never used the names. He just told the story." "Uncle George was a carver. What's this?" She is looking at the lump of wood he has hacked and scraped during his performance. A sorry-looking thing, it is no more a rudimentary kachina than someone's arm is, but Oswald runs his fingers along it with an appraising, tuneless whistle. He can see where he might deepen a cut, creating a neck or a pair of hands. Not that the mystery has invaded his mind; he now realizes that, for him perhaps as never for his uncle, telling and carving go together, not that he is ever likely to be good at either, he the host of the suitcase stars, the gazer at unplumbed heavens, the graft who recently recovered the power of a strong arm over the Abbotts of his world. Abbott has slunk away with a sideways curse tossed out and backward as if handing him a final cankerous F. Thomas vouchsafed a feeble smile before following him, and their wives and their brood just wandered off like tumbleweed blown in and out again, seed turned back from human into thistledown as if commanded to by the omnipotent demigod twins. It is BertandAnna who have enjoyed this tale most, as brother and sister might. They applaud him with clenched fists so as not to make a noise, their faces working in little humble flurries of agitation somewhere between dumbshow and grimace. "You tole it, MistOz," says Bert. "You sure the best in all Ahzona." Anna says nothing, just nods, her plump face an acre of approbation, her uncared-for teeth showing, her eyes looking in different directions, or so it looks to Oswald, her hands prodding and shoving Bert to say some more in praise. Oswald notices the price tags still attached to their garments, the givaway a red line through the previous three prices, so that BertandAnna seem to be wearing them as badges of mercy and heroism, or survivors' dogtags not their own. Where are their parents, he wonders. Long gone, no doubt, if not one way then the other. These two are brother and sister, man and wife, to each other, I guess; they never have to go away for anything, outside of each other. It's kind of like having a tribe of two. I have *two* fans anyway. You never know. In small beginnings you find the germ of enormous improvements in human tastes. Or something like that. What the hell am I talking about, to myself? He watches BertandAnna out of sight, which always take a while, and then walks rather unsteadily (one of his legs has gone to sleep) back into his shanty. No one offered him an evening meal, not even Fermina, who seems miffed by the whole thing, so he yanks his bread and cheese out of the tin cookie box and settles down in the nonrocking rocker, wishing there were margarine too and then he would feel even more like Uncle George, who of course would have stayed on outside with his knife flying through helices of disciplined inventive motion. Oswald, however, likes to preside over the table on which the suitcase stars once danced like fluorescent tubes on limber limbs: his altar, his place, his holy of holies, his own underground ceremonial chamber, kind of, ant-ridden and spidery, mouse-trotted and cricket-fluttery, bee- and wasp-buzzed and fly-specked, all of that, with several pieces of rock coming loose in the walls as the concrete crumbles into a less than useful powder that is not cement. His own place all the same, though, it smells of him, that semidamp burnished fried emanation. He has not bathed for some time and he longs to head for the lake to spend the day sluicing his body where Bessie Butterfly sluiced hers, again getting that headstrong feeling: No, she wasn't my real mama, of course, but I can see what he saw in her and how he'd have liked a touch of that to go through to his child if they'd had a chance. That springsteel walk of hers I've heard so much about and the way she swung her arms around, sometimes catching people in midswing. I bet she swam a ton. If I went there to swim would I disturb her ghost, any more than Uncle George would when he went to her grave? He never went near her grave. To him, she was buried in sky and wind, not in water or earth, and never in fire. I could go with BertandAnna and hope they wouldn't pull me down as their next victim. Here they are. I think of them and they appear. They are indeed at the door waving at him something small but shiny on one side. He sees the colors flash, then the colors go as they tilt the other side toward him. You would never think two people could comfortably carry a postcard between them, but they do, all four hands in contact with it as if it were the source of all their energy. *"Mail,* they tell him. Fresh from Amehca. Oncet we got one too." "Mail up here never is," he says. The postcard from Fermina has been to Vietnam and back, depicting fall, and he tenderly recalls the letters she used to send him, all numbered, tracking bit by bit her advance through the first volume of the encyclopedia, then forgetting what she'd said, and in her next letter going backward toward the first entry of all.

Since that day Oswald has begun to walk faster like someone in the act of learning how and doing well, even though as Fermina points out his grasp of his native language is none too firm. "You'll come to it," she says, "like I came to the first B in the encyclopedia. B for Babel, a lot of noise, right after the last A, for Aztec. You can't stand still." He tells her he won't, but he'll never master the lingo: "I don't hardly ever need it, Mama, not to talk in. I—I can tell stories in it better than I can talk it." She cups his forehead in her right hand and presses tight as if to contain all the devils and the steam within, maybe to squash him into sleep as if it were soft loam, and he will repose there until his next tale's told. When he walks away she marvels at his gait, a slow sprint with his feet close together almost on point and his hands far out from his body as if to ward something off or partly to achieve flight with his wings at severe anhedral. It is the gait of some impatient sleepwalker who hurries on to a destination that merely discharges him to another, and so on, there being no reason to stop, though he has smiled at one girl called Freda, with a rough voice and a perfect skin, another called Dextra, with a mellow voice and a skin blemished by something hormonal. Smiles is all because his head fixes on something more urgent he wants to witness and enjoy, having set his heart on Soyal, the second phase of Creation at the daybreak of life. The very word is magical, not that any vivid dance heralds its use, the time's arrival; all Oswald can do is what the others do, fasting in a withdrawn and frenzied reverie as life-the-much-beloved creaks back among them from out of an eroded darkness in the figure of the sun, come back to them on a certain day, come back for another year as well. Now everyone feels warmer even on the mesa where the winds have only just got into their stride. He is not allowed to look at the stealthy measurement going on in that house high up where they watch Sun House Mesa and the shadow coming closer and closer to a mark on the west wall. He bides his time, knowing the sun watchers allow for a day or two this way or that: he is heedless of the rabbit hunt to come, the feast and the ritual blessings. He wants to see the most dramatic thing of all, which he only vaguely remembers from his boyhood, when during the afternoon, today, a white figure comes from the east staggering and wobbling like an infant learning to walk, clad in a turquoise helmet with a red gourd on top, a red, green, and black kilt, a white ruff and red-ringed moccasins, with long feathers in its hand. "You might almost think," he tells Fermina, ill at ease being alongside him among so many watchers that she almost wishes he wouldn't speak at all. He persists, though. "You might almost think it was an old man who can hardly walk from cramp or rheumatism, who's been away too long in the underworld, and he's trying to get his legs to move as they should, but they're too stiff." "No, Oswald," she says, "it is the child of the year, it is the year in its first childhood, not its second." Its legs are soft and sluggish, the muscles are as feeble as soft new bread. They watch the mysterious chaste figure waddle its way through the village, following humbly behind as it as it makes four stops, one to daub four lines on a wall with cornmeal, at the door to the Flute Kiva where it sings a halting yet sturdy song, then in the plaza where the song seems mellower and more confident, and last of all at the entrance to the main ceremonial chamber where it plants the four feathers it has been carrying. "Who is it," Oswald asks, but Fermina slaps his hand with unobtrusive hardness. "You can't ask *that*. You don't ask that. *Behave.* It is someone being supernatural." He does, but his mind has lit up as if the suitcase stars have come back to him. He nearly expects eagles to sprout from where the return kachina has planted the four feathers. He would like to address the wintry whitened figure and ask him who it is (it is always a male) and how it feels to be got up that way, wandering and faltering through the village with all eyes on him like, Oswald thinks, the last runner to arrive in some big-city marathon, and the spectators haven't made any motion to go away because they know the last one is coming although in a bad way and they want to see if he will make it to the tape if the tape is still there. It is almost more interesting than watching the winner, who does not often come homeward with rubber legs and little sense of direction, the truth being that they identify with the worst loser making his colossal effort, little realizing that what they see is the hard-up year stumbling back among them, badly in need of meat, glucose, a slice of bread. Dimly recalling another life he has had, Oswald tells himself that, if he could only film this kind of thing for the art theaters, he would make a killing, but to film it is taboo, it has never been made into a motion picture, yet a motion picture it truly is, amazing not least for its silence broken only by whispers and the songs, as if the year were stealing in among them currying favor without asking for help, the two black bars of its eyes and the black base-up triangle of its mouth asking nothing, offering less, as if some celestial snowman has at long last managed to lift himself and however painstakingly reach their very doors, to him a light-year of pain and reeling, to them a miracle homegrown, planned in an underground chamber yet austerely evocative of the white Arctic wastes where wind is the only music and life is the least popular thing of all, a freak in a zone in love with its own homogeneousness, as willing as not to be a planet of landscape only, uncluttered with folk whose hearts long for fire, whose bellies long for flesh. Oswald knows that he is looking at no footrace or its lone survivor, but at a denuded pageant whose burden is *There might have been no one here at all, ever,* and this is enough to stun him into a silence his mother can stand, attuned in her random careless way to the beginnings of awe in her black sheep son, little knowing however that he sees things as follows: as if the Earth, unable to look at itself through any but the eyes of living beings, all the same got a look at itself in the act of being only a bit more populated than it is not, vouchsafed thus an image of possible and awesome death which only this white trained klutz can quash. He tries to envision spring without any human any sheep any mouse to witness it, and he begins a long inward shuddering at the thought, pondering the sexless appeal of a merely visitable planet open to visitors from far away but dead as a doornail once they've left. He can see it now, the sheer destitution of land whose white vapors and busy volcanoes go unwatched for centuries, oh much longer than that, and the vapors and the volcanoes do not even know what they are, that they are there for no one at all, destined to follow a curve of gaseous mineral obeisance forever and ever as the winds wax and wane, the ice thickens and thins, the light muddies or clears, uninterrogably unseen. It is not Fermina's homespun view of things, but he and Fermina have the same sense of what desolation really is, and that is something beyond kachina shrines and blessings performed by chiefs: something let loose by Oswald's visions of the suitcase stars, cooped up by Fermina's one-volume encyclopedia, and revived in his case only by his belated awareness of the homely among the vast, in hers by a sudden new sense that even a black sheep must find his own way both out of tradition and into it. True Palookaville, he now knows, is whatever there is of the eternal without a human heart, either the cold or the cold's emptiness or the intractable fires that blaze amid the empty cold quite unmitigated by a Groombridge here, a Stephan there. We do not deal with it in its own terms, he says, up there and out, we deal with it in things as homemade as cornhusk dolls, and that is what my father saw, and the rest of his life however good or bad it was was only ever what he somehow pushed into his kachinas. Maybe, he begins to wonder, it doesn't matter what you think so long as you think of something. Any activity will do. It is not the anthem of *keep busy* he means so much as that of *be aware of needing to do*, to meddle, to mess, to fret, to sport, to hum (he adds them all and a score more), vainly trying to fix on what quality it is in a mindless star that makes it make a human mindful, not the skin of a Freda that seems to have a thousand mellow amber lights gleaming stably beneath it, and not the willowy slither that is a Dextra's walk, and not what made an uncle carve (that uncle carve a father out of his very own bone), and not motherliness, not spite, not manslaughter, not perversion, not pain. It is coming to him slowly as an almost spastic Return Kachina aims at the village from light-years away, eyes on that nodding yellow light, where it belongs year after year. He sees what he has to do if only he can manage it, arrange it, whether or not he breaks the local rules. Once he has done it, no force can undo it, can undo his doing of it.

One gesture and he is at least free as the sun to which the locked-in Earth turns and tilts for reasons only its passengers can know. "You'll be proud, Mama," he says as they stroll back to her house, there to muse and reminisce, yet with a sense that all they do and all they say is as nothing compared to what the Return Kachina's arrival has renewed. "I feel small," he says. "You are," she says. "Not a single one of us is big today, neither the living nor the dead. Nobody is anybody today," she says, "we are all together: we are those who have been visited, that's all." "There's a lot to come," he says. "It never seems to stop, once it's begun. It isn't ordinary life at all. Like always being at the movies," he says. "I don't know," she says. "I never did it." "I did," he tells her, "and after a while you feel as if there is nothing outside the theater and you just dare not go back into the light again. You sink down in your seat and try to forget you're even there." Fermina dozes, Oswald holds her hand, waving Abbott and Thomas and their brood away, beckoning BertandAnna in, wishing for Uncle George, George's parents Velma and Alf, a lieutenant and a captain, Emory, Dennison, and Schultz, Bessie Butterfly, the Mititses, just so long as his world holds together, patched and cobbled as it is. He remembers something Fermina told him about the one time she went into Keams Canyon to work as a maid: no, he corrects himself, a cleaning woman, and she got carried away, not only cleaning out the refrigerator with breath held at the novelty and the grandeur of it but combining all the unfinished tubs of margarine into one and doing the same with the marmalades and jellies, then lining up everything else according to height with the tallest things toward the rear like soldiers on parade. The family couldn't find anything for weeks. By Fermina's standards her own world, impromptu as it was on that occasion, had held together even under stress, whereas she had mangled theirs; she had gone away feeling soothed by the whole thing with everything left in order, but she never again got anything so newfangled, so lovely, to mess with, which was a waste of what she always called herself: a good tidier, aching to tidy up Oswald's appearance, get the ring out of his ear, the uncouth whistle out of his mouth (she doesn't like the way it forces his upper lip up over his teeth toward his nose), and the longer and longer ponytail sleek and tight as a leather whip.

"You never know," she says, "they hardly ever do it anymore. You grow up as a little girl and they give you the doll, saying who and what it is, and you learn how to look for it in real life, in the dances and the ceremonies, but the one you just saw is very rare. They must have decided to do it whether they were entitled to or not. I must say I was glad to see it. Old friend sort of feeling." "Like seeing a movie star after you've kept their picture, their photograph," he says, "forever." "Not like that," she says and he says, "I didn't mean that, mother, it isn't the same, I know. So that was the Return Kachina. That's its name." "The Return Kachina. It used to be different in the odd-numbered years from the even ones, but I can't remember how. I am older than I look. Older than old." "And more beautiful than you will admit, Mama." "Watch your mouth," she says. "Wash it out. What I am saying is there's something wrong when folks have to go to some Anglo guidebook to find out how to do their own customs. That is what they did. They looked it up and then they went ahead, going through the motions like . . ." "You were going to say something." Fermina does not answer, but changes the subject to his story and how badly he told it, telling him he needs to work on the language, learn to tell how the people in the stories talk for the sake of talking. And stop embellishing. He blames the movies, Palookaville, the war, anything he can think of, then tells her that he would like to work on the story again. "In this version the girl does not stay dead, but comes back to life as a zombie, sleeping all day and working all night. I'm out of practice." "You never were in practice." "Uncle George and I told stories all the time." "Never told them right. He didn't care. You could never pick it up from him. He pleased himself. All that fuss they made of him, but he was never carving for them, he was always doing it for himself although he pretended diffrunt. Your uncle was a big pretender." He gives up and goes out in search of BertandAnna, whom he brings back to his shanty to see his book and tell them what he has in mind. They shake their heads, Bert in a long slow fluttering motion, she with a decisive twist, left-right, right-front. So he works on them and soon has them laughing the laugh of guiltless play. They adjourn to where the two of them live and for the first time he sees the bed up against the wall as if they sleep standing up. He asks and they explain that they lie on the floor, they do not use the bed at all, they kept falling out of it. Their saucepans are jammed together, the smallest in the next largest and so on, and they never unjam them but cook in the smallest one with water in the others to conduct the heat. He cannot decide if they are inspired or crazy. On the floor they have in no particular order the rags and cast-off clothing of thirty or forty adult years, a big flat nest of fabrics easily two feet deep, fit for burrowing in, and when he rummages around his hand finds a plate or two, some shoes, at least one bottle, and several other things so deep down he can't identify them: either soap tidies or bottles of glue. He knows what he wants, though, and finds it, asking them if he may and they just wave at him, laughing because they are going to help him even if they have to stay up all night to get him ready. He hates the mothball reek, not that they have made it; the reek comes from things cast off by others who put the balls into their drawers in a last desperate attempt to keep things whole when the clothes were only imminent castoffs and then found the smell so bad they had to get the stuff out of the house as soon as they could. It all ends up at BertandAnna's wrapped around full or empty or opened cans, and Oswald wonders how two people never mind how far gone they are can go to sleep on a smear of baked beans a month old, wetting themselves into the blankets, and washing only when someone like Bessie Butterfly takes them to the lake. They survive, he says to himself, and that is more than some do who're right as rain in the head. They are my welcome here on the mesa. They have absolutely no bias at all. They take what comes. If Fermina saw this she'd cut their throats. He spends the next few hours with them, until dark, and marvels at how they have a bit of everything, a shabby cornucopia tucked untidily into their bed linens, never called upon before. He finds an old dress, a dead and topless can that once held a year's supply of shortening, and something from who knew what missionary exploit into the land of the savages but maybe Mrs. Matilda Coxe Stevenson's foray with an umbrella in 1886: a can of black boot polish with a flightless Australian bird on the lid. Could the white heroine really have tried to bribe her way into the kivas with this after her umbrella charge on the assassin red-devils failed? He has the devastating sense that he has just switched centuries and that BertandAnna are like ageless magma into which he has tumbled. The diaphragm is nowhere to be found, of course, and he wonders if she has found out where to put it and if she will leave it there for keeps. The pretty mottled case she hands to him with a leer and he somehow knows it's his to play with for a day at least, and that is all he wants. Off with his bundle he goes as BertandAnna watch him out of sight, past a couple of ladders, then a short walk on rock, followed by a right-angled turn toward his shanty a hundred yards away. By candlelight he sets up a piece of broken mirror and plans his work. With the spike in his knife he punctures the can with two eyeholes after first testing it around his face. First, working from inside, he makes a small hole, then widens it from outside, then widens that from inside to force the spiky shreds of metal back out again and away from his eyes. Then he daubs black polish all over the outside of the can, lets it dry matt, but does not shine it up. For something illicit this is going too fast; he has all night to tinker in unless the suitcase stars decide to visit him again. He does not like that flatness of the can's bottom, which for him is now the top, so he rummages around and finds an old woolen cap infinitely stretchable that he pulls wide open and jams on top of the can, creating a kind of dome. On he toils, checking his appearance now and then in the book from Apperknowle, now tying off the wrists of the dress's long sleeves with cord, now opening the sack of Uncle George's kachina dolls to see what's really there. Is there a model of what he's going to be? There is not, although for a moment, clasping the bulbous heft of Uncle George's carving, he feels a father's hand on him again. He is going back to Laos by way of Palookaville and Win Slow (a name he cannot think of now in any other form for the signatories of his battered postcard to still be living in). He snacks from the tin box with Uncle George's kachinas watching him and sips the breakfast drink his mother made for him, all the time inhaling some aroma of unabashed accomplishment, telling himself over and over that he now knows what to do, no longer a child or a youth or a twink, no longer a nightman or a black sheep. No: the aroma said all that was over, he was calling on the witchcraft of the Groombridge group and the handcraft of his Uncle George, adrift now from all those faces jeering and taunting, mocking and making raspberries just because he fell pell-mell out of his father's loins into his mother's for a fate blacker than corn soot and harder than obsidian, not of his making but formatively his even as much as all the know-how the various legions of Mititses all over Arizona had pounded into the unwilling heads of Indians, some of whom were bright after all and went on to distinguish themselves without the *de rigueur* tomahawk and deafening warcry, about all of which he had heard in the mossy dulcet nest of his infant days, wondering if he too were going to grow up into a redman despite his mother's hatred of bloodshed and wild whooping Navajo-like cries, with here a pin, there a pin, here a rag breech clout, there a powder for killing nits. Or

he would grow up into a cissy instead and have to eke out a living
doing pretty nothings once in a while while they all sniggered behind
their hands divided into the thumb on the nose's left, the fingers on
the right (always done left-handed), and here he was now like some
extinct bird rising from the mesa that bore him, sending up no smoke
signal, emitting no whoop, hardly an Indian at all by some melodra-
matic standards, not standing on a chair to sing *O for the wings of a
dove*, which he still could if only the chair wouldn't rock, but awaiting
his own majesty, up from the soles of his much-traveled feet to the
frown on his brow, heedless now of venerable carvers and drowned
wives and tender lustful mothers and siblings full of bile, not to mention the casual Camel-smoking fellationists of Asia, the pinball virtuo-
sos of Win Slow, the girls whose necks broke in sexual extremis. All
that has gone, even his recent fillip to his own good cheer in the guise
of the suitcase stars, with whom he has a treaty of nonaggression. As
he rushes past them, the hue of their red shifts or their blue shifts is
no more than a faint gleam from a fiery hearth, irrelevant to one
whose eyes are rolling who thinks his heart has at last become a red
velvet chamber in which molten gold pours while a voice from no
movie he has seen says he has really lived in spite of everything. He
has been somewhere, has been someone among the folk of Earth, even
if all he can remember right now is how, in the hospital, the clank-
clank of the ventilators for those veterans choking on their own mucus or unable to breathe at all had the same sound and rhythm as a
French or at any rate European locomotive waiting in a siding: that
severed hollow *clonk clonk clonk* was the same whether it shoved the
steam out or the air in.

"I'm ready," he whispers to the nocturnal mouse at his feet. He is
ready in mind although he still has work to do by candlelit looking
glass. He feels like an entire civilization trying to get a glimpse of
itself before dying, whether in a shard of pottery, a busted rearview
mirror, a sheet of water combed by prickly sun and coated with lar-
vae.

Once, in Vietnam, he had looked at himself in a mirror and had not
known who he was. Who he could be. Now he sees one who is the
complete adversary of all things familiar. He recoils and holds his
breath to calm his thudding heart. He has done it this time. The
feather ripped from an old 1930s hat of Anna's lolls sideways from the

top of the woolen ski cap. In moth-holed black gloves his bootblacked hands do not show but rather rest on his hips, invisible. He has no red moccasins, so he has wrapped his feet in old rags meant to simulate wildcat skins. Will they unravel when he moves and bring him flat on his face? He will soon find out. His breath makes a fog in the below-freezing pre-dawn of his one and only room. The birds have begun and amid that uncoiling ovation he thinks he hears the rattle of a cactus wren, the flutelike note of a gambel quail, a pyrrhuloxia going *cheek-cheek* in forlorn friendliness, the garrulous drum roll of the Gila woodpecker, the high-pitched piercing soprano of a lucy warbler, the unmusical chatter of the Richmond becard that cries *ko-re-a* as if emitting steam. All night in this existence or in another he has heard, as well as the put-put-put of a cactus pigmy owl, the yipping and yapping of a coyote, the hooded skunk scratching away, the squeals and coughs of foxes. He looks at himself and wants to use an old word: he is affrighted at how he looks: inhuman, yes, but not even inhuman in a human way. He has gone and a ghoulish troll has taken his place, by name Mastop, the death fly kachina unseen on the mesa in several generations, yet permanently eligible if only those folk who run things could make up their minds. Oswald smiles with grim self-righteousness having chosen to remind his people of their stamp. Is it time to go? The sun is up, the local sunwatcher must already have noted it and drawn it, numbered it, on his calendar. As Oswald reasons, if the rarely seen solstice kachina could show up yesterday, and quite officially too, then why should not a Mastop show up today, never mind how unofficially? It brings out the adventurer in him, the rebel, the inventor, the thwarted scholar who learned the names and calls of the birds to such an extent he now hears birds that aren't really there at all and live lower down, in the desert; but he has at least studied them, and the stars, the kachinas' suits. He is not without information, never mind how primitive it is. Now the pink vague dome of day opens above him, inviting him to spring up and be swallowed by the washed-looking infinities, by the blue that is all volume and no time, by the air that does not sustain at the farthest reach and would inhospitably fling him back again on to the lid of an undug grave. All he has to do to begin is budge himself from where he stands like one marooned in an old splendiferous painting of cardinals and clerics all aswill in lavish robes, peering into the eye of God, leaving their green-velvet cushioned chairs forever behind them. Where did he see that? No one is going to come and tug him out into the arena.

He can stay here forever, out of his eyes' corners catching a glimpse of himself in the splinter of mirror: not as himself or as a human, but as this thing, honored and revered and indulged, and it is not like being in military uniform, to which you are allowed to bring your face whereas a kachina is not. He wishes he had a gas mask now, the better to mimic the face and nose of the death fly at its work. He closes his books, checks the two bags behind the chest of drawers, flings the scarf back from his window, pops an old and fluff-coated candy into his mouth, the better to keep silent with, and cracks the door, glad of the freshet of new cold that moves in at once in a six-foot-high slice. One hundred yards to go and then he will turn left into the thick of them. How long he survives to get away with it is up to them. He makes his move. Coming toward them they see something familiar from a hundred years ago, from before they were born, but part of dolldom certainly. It is more or less right as far as costume goes although the walk is hesitant as if picked up from the solstice kachina of yesterday. The woman's dress is black with faded reddish-brownish designs and the legs are naked but black as well. The black recedes, though, with the white commanding their attention in the shape of two big white handprints on the chest, one on one leg, two on the other, two on one of the inert arms, one on the other. The true hands are not moving, black in their gloves, but the hands on the chest seem to be in constant motion, beckoning, receding, advancing palm outward, coming on and off lighthouse-like above the blurred shuffle of his obscure feet. All this black conveys to them the interstellar vastness he has traveled through to be here this dawn, and the roughly triangular patterns of dots on either cheek stand for stars: on his right the Pleiades, on his left the Dipper, not an accurate rendition to be sure, but evocative enough although some think he has the belt stars of Orion on them both. There are different versions, but the holy gist remains. He has come an unthinkable way and that fact has reinforced itself historically since the Mastop kachina has been so scarce. He has been journeying all this time. Yes, the grass ruff is in place around his neck and this is the vegetable world; this is right and good. Others, however, who have now begun remembering, ask why there are not two of this kachina, who used to come in twos, but that is only the result of the white hands all over him. The hands limn the touch upon everything of humankind, the imprint, the scar, the ruination, the healing hands of the medicine man upon belly, heart, and head. At least he carries the black staff ringed with white to make a ladder up which all human beings can climb to the next Emergence if that is not too grand a word for it. "Don't you know," one says aloud, "that stick is the same as the one we put on graves to help the dead on their journey? It's correct, but the head is crude, it's just a can." No one cares, they want to lap up the spectacle, hear the weird symmetrical shuffle of the money in the tin that is his rattle. "No," someone is saying, "you have it wrong: the black stands for the soil, not the sky. The black is ground." On Oswald goes, managing to convert his nervous totter into a steadier march, still seepage-slow but in more of a straight line as he recalls he ought to be visiting certain specified sites, but he forgets which they are, he wants to air the apparition he is and that is all. Until the priests lay hands on him for blasphemy. He has something else to do, though, and as the crowd begins to form, making itself into something definite to pass by, he grabs one buxom woman of middle age and spins her around, then forcefully as required begins to tup her hard, doing little hops as he pushes, an almost ludicrous feat, but for those who remember one that fits. Now they see this, other women push forward, the married, the barren, those who have lost a child, aching for Mastop to bump against them, aching for the gray fly to make them ripe, he who stands for the germ cells of all humanity, with his triangular white mouth, his wide popping just as white eyes. His touch is keen. It burns. It makes the people as fertile as the soil. He can hardly see through the holes in his tin can now, it has slid about during his contortions, so he adjusts it even as various members of the Bear Clan begin to object that, whoever it is, he has some of it defiantly wrong: no bows tied at his wrists and knees, no white earmuffs (how could he with his ears inside the can?), no beard of fur, and worst of all the head's mask is the wrong shape, he has not even taken to beating the dogs that yap around him, and he did not even approach from the northwest as required. No one cares. Mastop is back, to ripen the seeds they bear within their carbohydrate-fattened bodies, whether he comes from another mesa altogether, from Anglo hell, or is simply so magical that, instead of being a supernatural being impersonated by a man wearing a mask, this is the supernatural kachina itself, weary of approximations, models, dolls, come all the way from the San Francisco peaks to perk them up and make sure they get to bed and breed. Enthralled and undismayed by those who have begun to carp and shout, they nod benignly at the muddled apparition who ought to be leaping around and cavorting wildly, hammering the dogs and sometimes the watchers with his stick. After a while, wholly unawed as it seems to Oswald, they tell him not to hang around but to head back where he belongs, west of here, at the foot of the cliffs. They both revere him and shove him around, so he is not a real kachina after all but a human impersonating a human in the act of impersonating a kachina, which is quite different. They do not know, they do not care to know. He has come into this wasteland, he tells himself, and, half-blind in his tin-can mask, has livened it up, stirred their primitive side for them, and done them no harm. He has indeed come a vast distance, dealt at first hand with the stars, and hunted the wildcat for its pelt. Looking back, he thrills as he sees them looking at him, front view, knowing that he has green frogs painted on the back of his tin head, painted like all the white hands on him with acrylic from Uncle George's jars. Seeing him front-on is better, though. He is still an apparition to them, they who had no Mastop planned and got one all the same, but no longer quite so shocking, whereas Oswald is still awed by himself, by his daring, by his outrageous look, and he still feels that primeval shiver, that impersonator's high, as he hovers there in full view unwilling to head for where a Mastop belongs after his act is done. He has skipped certain observances, to be sure, but the something to look at was better than nothing at all. He feels he has proved something whether or not he still tingles, gasps, feels as if some outlandish energy has lunged through him without quite yet leaving him. *Was this how Groombridge felt when first he turned into a star?* What does he look like? I look like a charcoal statue spattered with white, he tells himself. I look the part. I played it. I came home as something they wanted to see. Something better and bigger than me flashed through me, I'm sure of that, and not just adrenaline, not just the syrup of homemade delight; work the frenzy high enough, you scare yourself and them more than halfway to death, and something comes in, something takes over. You become a suitcase star. You are never the same again. He can almost sense the discrete posthumousness within him of father who begot him in a high hailing wind of lust in a very distant century, unbuttoned his own carver's dusty pants and made him right there and then with Fermina urging him to hurry and finish, either because she could hear the cavalry of doom already thundering toward them or because she wanted that much sooner to be choosing a name like Oswald Beautiful Badger Going Over The Hill: *Kuwányamtiwa*. He mouths his name as Bert, apologizing for sick Anna, receives him at the foot of the cliff, removes his tin head, and gently begins to undress him as if ministering to a corpse, pokes fun at him for going out with the price tag still on the ancient dress ($1.75) and the diaphragm case opened up like an oyster and lashed to the side of his knee. He sees Fermina coming toward him with a smile of disturbed entreaty such as he has never seen before on any human face. He has broken all the rules to stun her with pleasure, and it was high time; he has ravished himself too, has never felt so electrified, so inherently in trim. Will he ever do it again? He has a year to think about it in. Mastop the death fly has vanished into thin mountain air and all that remains is the naked pretender at ease under the gaze of his mother, the weeping Bert, and whoever else may have been watching over him as, poised between incommensurate powers, between fleshpots and pariahdom, he made his bid. The stars and the corn go on and ripen. The mesa does not blow away on its own cold breath. The stone shanty that has held him will go on holding him. He tugs on his jeans, he buttons his plaid shirt, he rubs at the black on his hands. And then, as if heeding the first mesmeric hint of a direction given, he walks back alone, unsteady but tranquil, toward the bed he was conceived in, waiting, if not for doom to crack, at least for the undernourished scurry of its tiny bell.